Johann Wolfgang von Goethe, Frederic Henry Hedge

Goethe's popular Works

FAUST

Johann Wolfgang von Goethe, Frederic Henry Hedge

Goethe's popular Works
FAUST

ISBN/EAN: 9783741124464

Manufactured in Europe, USA, Canada, Australia, Japa

Cover: Foto ©Andreas Hilbeck / pixelio.de

Manufactured and distributed by brebook publishing software
(www.brebook.com)

Johann Wolfgang von Goethe, Frederic Henry Hedge

Goethe's popular Works

GOETHE'S POPULAR WORKS.

THE PEOPLE'S EDITION.

EDITED AND REVISED BY DR. F. H. HEDGE AND PROF. L. NOA.

FAUST: A TRAGEDY.

BY GOETHE

PART I.

EDITED AND ANNOTATED BY F. H. HEDGE, D.D.

METRICAL VERSION, BY MISS SWANWICK.

ALSO,

A PROSE TRANSLATION OF THE SAME,
BY A. HAYWARD.

PART II.

TRANSLATED BY MISS SWANWICK.

TO WHICH IS APPENDED

CLAVIGO, EGMONT, AND THE WAYWARD LOVER.

BOSTON:

ESTES AND LAURIAT,

301-305 WASHINGTON STREET.

1883.

CONTENTS.

FAUST.

INTRODUCTION BY THE AMERICAN EDITOR.

THE notion of a formal compact with a personal fiend, once so prevalent, had in the Middle Ages a special application to such as were versed beyond the mark of their time in the mysteries of physical science, like Friar Bacon, Albert the Great, and Cornelius Agrippa. Dr. Faustus, of German tradition, was one of those to whom this suspicion attached. Johann Faust, not to be confounded with his namesake, the reputed inventor of the art of printing, was a veritable historical personage. Born at Knittlingen, in Würtemberg, he studied medicine, and also magic, then a recognized branch of learning, at the University of Cracow, visited various parts of Europe, and afterward led a wandering life in Germany, professing supernatural power, and styling himself *philosophus philosophorum*. Melancthon, as reported by his pupil Manlius, speaks of him as having visited Wittenberg some time after the battle of Pavia, 1525, and as boasting that by his magic arts he had procured the victory in that battle for Charles V.

He is also mentioned by Philip Begardi, a physician of repute in his day, in a work entitled "Index Sanitatum," published in 1539.

Around this slight nucleus of historic fact there clustered, in the sixteenth century, portentous accretions of fabulous matter. A supposed league with the enemy of mankind was precisely the soil for such growths. Gast, a theologian of the time, who dined with Faust at Basel, as he says in his *Sermones Conviviales*, represents him accompanied by two devils, one in the shape of a dog, the other in that of a horse.

His death, of which nothing certain is known, was depicted with great horror of circumstance as a warning against commerce with Satan. By some he is said to have been torn in pieces by the Adversary when the term of his service — twenty-four years — had expired; by others to have been turned on his face in the coffin as often as he was laid in the right position.

The earliest printed narrative of Faust's adventures is that of Spiess, published in Frankfort, in 1587. An English translation of this in 1590 furnished Marlowe with the subject matter of his "Dr. Faustus, a Tragedy," which enjoyed a brief popularity on the English stage, but was not published until ten years after the author's death.

Goethe appears to have derived his knowledge of the Faust legend partly from the work of Widmann, published in 1599, and another more modern in its form, which appeared in 1728, and partly from the puppet plays exhibited in Frankfort and other cities of Germany, of which that legend was then a favorite theme. He was not the only writer of his day who made use of it. Some thirty of his contemporaries had produced their Fausts during the interval which elapsed between the conception and completion of his great work. Oblivion seems to have overtaken them all, with the exception of Lessing's, of which, unfortunately, we have only a few fragments. The MS. of the complete work was unaccountably lost on its way to the publisher, between Dresden and Leipzig.

It is known to all who are familiar with Goethe's life and writings, that the composition of Faust proceeded spasmodically, with many and long interruptions between the inception and conclusion. Projected in 1769, at the age of twenty, it was not completed till the year 1831, at the age of eighty-two. The reasons for so long a delay in the case of a writer who often composed so rapidly, have been widely discussed by recent critics. The true explanation I think is to be found in the fact of the author's removal to Weimar when only a small portion of the work had been written, when only the general conception and one or two leading ideas were present to his thought, and before the plan of the whole was matured. That change of residence, with the new interests, the official duties, the multiplicity of engagements attending it, made a thorough break in Goethe's literary life. Several works begun or planned were left unfinished, and Faust among the rest. Some of these were never resumed, and the same fate would apparently have befallen Faust but for the urgent solicitation of friends. He took the MS. with him to Rome, and from there he wrote, in 1788, to friends at home, that he was going to work upon his Faust again, and that he thought that he had recovered the thread of the piece. For " thought," Bayard Taylor says " felt sure;" but Goethe's language was not so decided.* The thread of an unfinished work after the lapse of fifteen years is not easily recovered; my own opinion is, that Goethe never did recover it; and hence the long delay in the completion of the work. We know, at any rate, that the only addition made to it then was the scene in the Witch's Kitchen. That, as we learn from Eckermann, was written in the villa Borghese — the most unlikely place in the world for such a composition. In the midst of southern and classic associations, this extravaganza of northern diablerie! In 1790 a fragment of the First Part was published, wanting several of the best scenes in the work, as we now have it. Then again there is a long gap. Meanwhile he had become acquainted and intimate with Schiller, and at his instigation he made several unsuccessful attempts to finish Faust. Grief for Schiller's death, which occurred in 1805, caused new delay; but at last, in 1808, the First Part was published entire as we now have it in a uniform edition of the author's works. Meanwhile a portion of the Second Part, comprising the whole of the third act, had been already composed. This was published separately, in 1827, with the title, "Helena, a Classic-Romantic Phantasmagoria." With the exception of parts of the first act in 1828, nothing more of the second part

* "*Ich glaube*" is his expression.

of Faust appeared in print during the author's lifetime. But the octogenarian had rigorously bound himself to finish it if possible before, as he said, the great night should come, "in which no man can work." Fortunately the closing scenes were already written. Slowly and painfully the work proceeded at intervals during the three remaining years, and was not completed until within seven months of his death.

Had ever a poet's masterpiece such a genesis? Birth-pangs extending over sixty years!

The history of its composition reveals itself here and there in the finished work, especially in the second part. The first half of the fifth act gives one the impression of an outline not filled up, indications instead of representations; a design imperfectly executed. Single passages, striking in themselves, are loosely connected, and this first half bears no proportion to the last. The fourth act is rich in suggestion, but labors in the structure. The third act, an exquisite poem in itself, is an interlude, and does not further the development of the plot. The same may be said of the Classical Walpurgis Night in the second. In short, although one grand design may be supposed in the poet's mind to have comprehended and clinched the whole, the want of unity in the execution of the Second Part is painfully apparent to all in whose estimation the interest of single portions does not compensate for the halting of the plot. Even the First Part, with all its grandeur and its fire, its pathos and its sweetness, bears marks of interruption in its composition. A single prose scene contrasts with strange though not unpleasant effect the metrical movement of the rest. Gaps and seams and joints and splicings are here and there apparent. The work is too great to be injured by them, but they bear witness of arrested and fitful composition. The scene with Valentine, one of the most spirited, is introduced with some violence by Mephistopheles' serenade before Gretchen's door. The Walpurgisnachtstraum, or "Oberon and Titania's Golden Wedding" is lugged in with no motive in the drama, whose action it only serves to interrupt. In old English poems the divisions are sometimes called

"Fyttes" (fits). It has seemed to me that the term would be an apt designation of the scenes in Faust. They were thrown off by the author as the fit took him.

But the effect of the long arrest which, after Goethe's removal to Weimar, delayed the completion of the Faust, is most apparent in the wide gulf which separates, as to character and style, the Second Part from the First. So great indeed is the distance between the two, that without external historical proofs of identity, it would seem from internal evidence altogether improbable, in spite of the slender thread of the fable which connects them, that both poems were the work of one and the same author. And really they were not the same. The change which had come over Goethe when returned from Italy had gone down to the very springs of his intellectual life. The fervor and the rush, the sparkle and foam of his early productions had been replaced by the stately calm and the luminous breadth of view that is born of experience. The torrent of the mountains had become the river of the plain. Romantic impetuosity had changed to classic repose. He could still, by occasional efforts of the will, cast himself back into old moods, resume the old thread, and so complete the first Faust. But we may confidently assert that he could not, after the age of forty, have originated the poem, any more than, before his Italian tour, he could have written the second Faust, purporting to be a continuation of the first. The difference in spirit and style is enormous.

As to the question which of the two is the greater production, it seems to me a very preposterous one. They are incommensurable. It is like asking which is greater, Dante's Commedia or Shakespeare's Macbeth. As to which is the more generally interesting, no question can arise. There are thousands who enjoy and admire the First Part to one who even reads the Second. The interest of the former is poetic and thoroughly human; the interest of the other is partly poetic, but mostly philosophical and scientific. The one bears you irresistibly on; you forget the writer and his genius in the theme. The other draws your attention to the manner, and leaves you cold and careless of the theme. The transition from the first to the second is like the change from a hill country to a richly-cultured champaign; from the wild picturesqueness of nature to the smooth perfection of art.

In one respect, at least, the Second Part is nowise inferior to the First, namely, in rhythmical beauty. It abounds in metrical prodigies, proof at once of the marvellous plasticity of the language, and the technical skill of the poet, whose versification, at the age of fourscore, exhibits all the ease and dexterity of youth, and to whom it seems to have been as natural to utter himself in verse as in prose.

The symbolical character of Faust is assumed by all the critics, and in part confessed by the author himself. Besides the general symbolism pervading and motiving the whole, a symbolism of human destiny, and here and there a shadowing forth of the poet's private experience, there are special allusions, local, personal, enigmatic conceits, which have furnished topics of learned discussion, and taxed the ingenuity of numerous commentators. We need not trouble ourselves with these subtleties. But little exegesis is needed for a right comprehension of the true and substantial import of the work.

The key to the plot is given in the "Prologue in Heaven." The Devil, in the character of Mephistopheles, asks permission to tempt Faust; he boasts his ability to get entire possession of his soul, and drag him down to hell. The Lord grants the permission, and prophesies the failure of the attempt. "Well, then, be it allowed! Draw this spirit from its Source, and if you can lay hold of him, drag him with you on your downward path; and stand ashamed when you are forced to confess that a good man in his dark strivings has a consciousness of the right way."

Here we have a hint of the author's design. He does not intend that the Devil shall succeed; he does not mean to follow the conclusion of the legend, and send Faust to hell. He had the penetration to see, and he meant to show, that the notion implied in the old popular superstition of selling one's soul to the Devil; the notion that evil can obtain the entire and final possession of the soul, is a fallacy; that the soul is not man's to dispose of, and cannot be so traded away. We are the soul's, not the soul ours. Evil is self-limited; the good in man must finally prevail. So long as he strives, he is not lost; Heaven will come to the aid of his better nature. This is the doctrine, the philosophy of Faust. In the First Part, stung by disappointment in his search of knowledge, by failure to lay hold of the superhuman, and urged on by his baser propensities, personified in Mephistopheles, he abandons himself to sensual pleasure, seduces innocence, burdens his soul with heavy guilt, and seems to be entirely given over to evil. This Part ends with Mephistopheles' imperious call, " Her zu mir," as if secure of his victim. Before the appearance of the Second Part, the reader was at liberty to accept that conclusion. But in the Second Part, Faust gradually wakes from the intoxication of passion, outgrows the dominion of appetite, plans great and useful works, whereby Mephistopheles loses more and more his hold of him, and after his death is baffled in his attempt to appropriate Faust's immortal part, to which the heavenly Powers assert their right.

Such is a brief outline of the fable, and this is the issue prefigured in the Prologue in Heaven. But whether this was Goethe's original plan is somewhat doubtful. The Prologue in Heaven was not written until the larger portion of the First Part had been published. It seems not unlikely that Faust's salvation was an afterthought, and that Goethe's original design was to follow the legend, and consign his hero to the Devil at the end of his career. We may suppose that riper thought rejected such an ending, and occasioned the temporary arrest of the whole undertaking, until the idea of the Prologue in Heaven occurred to him as offering a way of escape from the sorry finale of the legendary Faust, and a better treatment of the theme.

But the Prelude on the Stage " proposes to traverse the entire circle of creation, and to pass with considerate rapidity from heaven through the world to hell." This seems to imply the intention, after all, to make hell the terminus of Faust's career. And yet the Prelude on the Stage we know to have been written after the publication of the first instalment of the play, probably at the same time with the Prologue in Heaven. Here, then, is a contradiction, — the Prelude pointing downward to the Pit as the woful consummation of the plot, the Prologue in Heaven directing to the skies. The contradiction can only be solved by supposing that the author forgot himself for the moment, and wrote in the sense of his original design.

Another discrepancy has been noticed by the critics. Chr. Herm. Weisse was the first to call attention to certain passages, from which it is evident that Goethe's first intention was to represent Mephistopheles as the emissary of the Earth-Spirit whom Faust invokes in the first scene of the First Part. The Prologue in Heaven, which, as I have said, was an afterthought, provided another and better way of introducing this leading character, but the passages referring to the former method were suffered to remain, either from inadvertence or want of time and will to rewrite them. And so we have in the First Part of Faust these croppings out of an earlier formation of the poet's mind, like the upheavals of a lower stratum of the earth's crust. It is a proof of the author's genius that, with all these irregularities, the play has won for itself the suffrage of two generations, and maintains its place as the literary masterpiece of modern time.

The Prologue in Heaven was at first an offence to English readers, on account of its seeming irreverence. The earlier translators omitted it, or all that portion which follows the Song of the Angels. Anster thinks to evade the difficulty by using the German "der Herr," instead of The Lord. But the Prologue, as I said, suggests the motive of the piece, and foreshows the conclusion. To omit it is to prejudice the right understanding of the whole. And as to irreverence, it is not necessary to adopt Mr. Lewes' apology drawn from mediæval use in the Miracle Plays, whose representations of Deity are accompanied with familiarities of speech quite shocking to modern sentiment. The Faust-legend was not a mediæval production, and the puppet-plays founded upon it are not to be classed with the old miracle-plays. Nor had these puppet-plays, any more than the legend itself, a prologue in heaven; rather, some of them, a prologue in hell. The Prologue is Goethe's own conception, suggested, as he tells us, by the book of Job. But nothing could be further from the poet's intention than to travesty or degrade that venerable poem. The alleged irreverence of Mephistopheles' conference with "The Lord" requires no other excuse than that Goethe's devil was bound to speak in character. He is the spirit that denies, the mocking spirit. His whole being is a mockery of the Holy; he can speak only as he is. Madame de Stael would have had him spiteful and defiant; it was Goethe's choice to make him skeptical and scoffing, a kind of exaggerated, infernal likeness of Voltaire, of whom Goethe says that in his youth he could have strangled him for his irreverent treatment of the Bible. In reality, there is no more irreverence in Mephistopheles' talk than in that of Satan in Job. What differences them is the humor so foreign to the Hebrew, so characteristic of the modern mind.

In the old Faust legend, the compact with the devil specifies a term of years, during which Faust was to have all that he desired of earthly good, and at the expiration of which Mephistopheles was to have possession of his soul. In Goethe's play, no date is agreed on; the hero stipulates for only one draught of full satisfaction. "If ever I shall lie down satisfied, if ever you can flatter me into thinking that I am happy, if ever you can cheat me with enjoyment, if ever I shall say to the passing moment, 'Stay! thou art so fair,' then you may lay me in fetters; then may the death-bell sound, and time for me be no more."

The intrigue with Margaret, which follows the scene in the Witch's Kitchen, and occupies, with the exception of the Walpurgisnacht, the remainder of the First Part, constitutes no portion of the original story. It is an episode of Goethe's own creation. But the interest of this episode is so intense, its pathos so overpowering, that the interpolation has become the real bearer of the drama. It is this that Faust first suggests, and stands for with the mass of readers.

The character of Margaret is unique; its duplicate is not to be found in all the picture galleries of fiction. Shakespeare, in the wide range of his feminine *personnel*, has no portrait like this. A girl of low birth and vulgar circumstance, imbued with the ideas and habits of her class, speaking the language of that class, from which she never for a moment deviates into finer phrase, takes on, through the magic handling of the poet, an ideal beauty. Externally common and prosaic in all her ways, she is yet thoroughly poetic, transfigured in our conception by her perfect love. To that love, unreasoning, unsuspecting, to the excess of that which in itself is no fault, but beautiful and good, her fall and ruin are due. Her story is the tragedy of her sex in all time. As Schlegel said of the "Prometheus Bound," "It is not a single tragedy, but tragedy itself." When Mephistopheles, with a sneer, suggests that she is not the first who incurs the doom that befalls her, Faust, in his transport of penitent passion, bursts forth with the reply, "Woe! woe! by no human soul to be comprehended; that more than one being has sunk into the depths of this wretchedness; that the first did not atone for all the rest with her writhing death-agony in the sight of the ever-pardoning."

It is important to note, as throwing light on the author's design, that, surrendered as he is to the reckless pursuit of pleasure, Faust's better nature is not utterly extinguished, but asserts itself from time to time in strong rebellion against the dominion of his baser appetites. The potion administered to him in the Witch's Kitchen has inflamed his animal passions, and after his first encounter with Margaret, he bids Mephistopheles to deliver her at once into his arms. Mephistopheles declares this to be impossible, but engages, when Margaret is absent, to conduct him to her chamber. While there, overcome, it would seem, by the spirit of the place, the abode of purity and innocence, he repents his purpose, upbraids himself, and vows never to return. He will not pursue the game. The box of jewels, which Mephistopheles has brought as a lure, he does not care to leave. Mephistopheles ridicules his scruples, and himself deposits the jewels in the girl's wardrobe.

Again after making her acquaintance and winning her affection, he still resists the temptation to abuse the power he has over her. He seeks to escape by leaving the city and betaking himself to the wilderness. But Mephistopheles discovers his retreat, and works on his compassion by representing how Margaret pines for him. Faust replies, "Thou monster, begone! Do not speak to me of that beautiful creature. Urge not the desire for her on my already half-crazed senses." But finally, as if feeling himself impelled by irresistible fate, exclaims, "Hell, thou wilt have this victim. Help, devil; what must be, let it be done quickly. Let her doom fall upon me, that we may both go to perdition together."

And at last, obliged to flee the city on account of the death of Valentine, whom he has killed in a duel, after plunging into a vortex of mad dissipation, indicated by the revels of the Walpurgisnacht, when he hears of the arrest of Margaret, he does not leave her to her fate, but returns to rescue her at the risk of his life.

As the First Part deals with individual character and destiny, so the Second spreads before us the great wide world of public life. We have the imperial court, with its gaieties, its jealousies, its intrigues and financial embarrassments, which Mephistopheles relieves by the device of a paper currency; we have war, we have industrial enterprise. And in the midst of these we have two interludes, in the second act the classical Walpurgis Night, which commentators interpret as symbolizing a mediation between the classic and romantic in literature and art; and for the whole of the third act we have the Helena, supposed to symbolize moral education through the influence of the beautiful.

By the discipline of these varied experiences, Faust is led on through the hundred years of his earthly life, to the supreme moment when, contemplating in imagination the benefit which must accrue to coming generations from his labors, — a free people on a free soil, — he exclaims, "Might I see that consummation, I could say to the moment, 'Tarry, thou art so fair;' the trace of my earthly days will endure for æons." "In anticipation of that exalted happiness, I already enjoy the highest moment." Then, in accordance with his own stipulation in the compact with Mephistopheles, he sinks back and expires. The Lemures seize him and lay him in the grave. Mephistopheles claims his soul, and summons his spirits, the lean devils with long, crooked horns, and the stout devils with short, straight horns, to aid him in securing his prey. Angels come to the rescue; they scatter roses, which purify the air, and charm the sleeper with dreams of paradise, singing, as they scatter, —

> "Roses with tender ray,
> Incense that render aye,
> Hovering, fluttering,
> Secret life uttering,
> Leaf-winged, reposing here,
> Blossoms unclosing here,
> Hasten to bloom!
>
> To FAUST.
> Spring round thee beaming
> Purple and green, —
> Paradise dreaming,
> Slumber serene!"

But the breath of the demons blasts and wilts the falling roses; they shrivel and at last take fire, and fall flaming and scorching on the hellish crew until they are forced to retreat; all but Mephistopheles, who stands his ground; but, entranced by the beauty of the angels, neglects his purpose, and fails to secure the immortal part of Faust, which the angels appropriate and bear aloft.

> "This member of the upper spheres,
> We rescue from the Devil,
> For whoso strives and perseveres
> May be redeemed from evil."

The last two lines may be supposed to contain the author's justification of Mephistopheles' defeat and Faust's salvation. Though a man surrender himself to evil, if there is that in him which evil cannot satisfy, an impulse by which he outgrows the gratifications of vice, extends his horizon, and lifts his desires; pursues an onward course until he learns to place his aims outside of himself, and to seek satisfaction in works of public utility, he is beyond the power of Satan; he may be redeemed from evil.

One could wish, indeed, that more decisive marks of moral development had been exhibited in the latter stages of Faust's career. But here comes in the Christian doctrine of grace, which Goethe applies to the problem of man's destiny. Faust is represented as saved by no merit of his own, but by the interest which Heaven has in every soul in which there is the possibility of a heavenly life.

And so the new-born, ascending spirit is committed by the Mater gloriosa to the tutelage of Gretchen, "una poenitentium," now purified from all the stains of earth, to whom is given the injunction, —

> "Lift thyself up to higher spheres!
> When he divines he'll follow thee."

And the Mystic Choir chants the epilogue which embodies the moral of the play.

> "Mortal that perishes
>   Types the ideal,
> All that faith cherishes
>   Thus becomes real.
> Wrought superhumanly,
>   Here it is done;
> The ever womanly
>   Draweth us on."

In editing Miss Swanwick's Faust, which seems to me, on the whole, the best of the English metrical translations, I have added notes to Part I., where explanation or comment seemed to be needed, and have made a few verbal alterations in the text. The second Part I have left unaltered.

F. H. HEDGE.

DEDICATION.[1]

Dim forms, ye hover near, a shadowy train,
As erst upon my troubled sight ye stole.
Say, shall I strive to hold you once again ?
Still for the fond illusion yearns my soul?
Ye press around!   Come then, resume your reign,   5
As upwards from the vapory mist ye roll;
Within my breast youth's throbbing pulses bound,
Fanned by the magic air that breathes your march
    around.

Shades fondly loved appear, your train attending,
And visions fair of many a blissful day;   10
First-love and friendship their fond accents blending,
Like to some ancient, half expiring lay;
Sorrow revives, her wail of anguish sending
Back o'er life's devious labyrinthine way,
The dear ones naming who, in life's fair morn,[2]   15
By Fate beguiled, from my embrace were torn.

They hearken not unto my later song,
The souls to whom my earlier lays I sang;
Dispersed forever is the friendly throng,
Mute are the voices that responsive rang.   20
My song resoundeth stranger crowds among,
E'en their applause is to my heart a pang;
And those who heard me once with joyful heart,
If yet they live, now wander far apart.

A strange unwonted yearning doth my soul,   25
To yon calm solemn spirit-land, upraise;
In faltering cadence now my numbers roll,
As when on harp Æolian, Zephyr plays;
My pulses thrill, tears flow without control,
A tender mood my steadfast heart o'ersways;   30
What I possess as from afar I see;
Those I have lost become realities to me.

PRELUDE ON THE STAGE.

MANAGER. DRAMATIC POET. MERRYMAN.

MANAGER.

Ye twain, whom I so oft have found
True friends in trouble and distress,
Say, in our scheme on German ground,   35
What prospect have we of success?
Fain would I please the public, win their thanks;
Because they live and let live, as is meet.
The posts are now erected and the planks,[3]
And all look forward to a festal treat.   40
Their places taken, they, with eyebrows raised,
Sit patiently, and fain would be amazed.
I know the art to hit the public taste,
Yet so perplexed I ne'er have been before;
'Tis true, they're not accustomed to the best,   45
But then they read immensely, that's the bore.
How make our entertainment striking, new,
And yet significant and pleasing too?
For to be plain, I love to see the throng,
As to our booth the living tide progresses;   50
As wave on wave successive rolls along, [4]
And through heaven's narrow portal forceful presses;
Still in broad daylight, ere the clock strikes four,
With blows their way towards the box they take;
And, as for bread in famine, at the baker's door,   55
For tickets are content their necks to break.
Such various minds the bard alone can sway,
My friend, oh, work this miracle to-day!

POET.

Oh, speak not of the motley multitude,
At whose aspect the spirit wings its flight;   60
Shut out the noisy·crowd, whose vortex rude
Still draws us downward with resistless might.
Lead to some nook, where silence loves to brood,
Where only for the bard blooms pure delight,

20

Where love and friendship, gracious heavenly pair, 65
Our hearts true bliss create, and tend with fostering
    care.

What there up-welleth deep within the breast,
What there the timid lip shaped forth in sound,
A failure now, now haply well expressed,
In the wild tumult of the hour is drowned;   70
Oft doth the perfect form then first invest
The poet's thought, when years have sped their round;
What dazzles satisfies the present hour,
The genuine lives, of coming years the dower.

MERRYMAN.

This cant about posterity I hate;   75
About posterity were I to prate,
Who then the living would amuse?   For they
Will have diversion, ay, and 'tis their due.
A sprightly fellow's presence at your play,
Methinks, should always go for something too;   80
Whose genial. wit the audience still inspires,
Is not embittered by its changeful mood;
A wider circle he desires,
To move with greater power, the multitude.
To work, then!   Prove a master in your art!   85
Let phantasy with all her choral train,
Sense, reason, feeling, passion, bear their part,
But mark! let folly also mingle in the strain!

MANAGER.

And, chief, let incidents enough arise!
A show they want, they come to feast their eyes.   90
When stirring scenes before them are displayed,
At which the gaping crowd may wondering gaze,
Your reputation is already made,
The man you are all love to praise.
The masses you alone through masses can subdue,   95
Each then selects in time what suits his bent.
Bring much, you somewhat bring to not a few,
And from the house goes every one content.
You give a piece, in pieces give it, friend!
Such a ragout, success must needs attend;   100
'Tis easy to serve up, as easy to invent.

A finished whole what boots it to present!
'Twill be in pieces by the public rent.

POET.

How mean such handicraft as this you cannot feel!
How it revolts the genuine artist's mind!   105
The sorry trash in which these coxcombs deal,
Is here approved on principle, I find.

MANAGER.

Such a reproof disturbs me not a whit!
Who on efficient work is bent,
Must choose the fittest instrument.   110
Consider! 'tis soft wood you have to split;
Think too for whom you write, I pray!
One comes to while an hour away;
One from the festive board, a sated guest;
Others, more dreaded than the rest,   115
From journal-reading hurry to the play.
As to a masquerade, with absent minds, they press,
Sheer curiosity their footsteps winging;
Ladies display their persons and their dress,
Actors unpaid their service bringing.   120
What dreams beguile you on your poet's height?
What puts a full house in a merry mood?
More closely view your patrons of the night!
The half are cold, the other half are rude.
One, the play over, craves a game of cards;   125
Another a wild night in wanton joy would spend.
Poor fool, the muses' fair regards
Why court for such a paltry end?
I tell you, give them more, still more, 'tis all I ask,
Thus you will ne'er stray widely from the goal;   130
Your audience seek to mystify, cajole; —
To satisfy them — that's a harder task.
What ails thee? art enraptured or distressed?

POET.

Depart! elsewhere another servant choose!
What! shall the bard his godlike power abuse?   135
Man's loftiest right, kind nature's high bequest,
For your mean purpose basely sport away?

Whence comes his mastery o'er the human breast,
Whence o'er the elements his sway,
But from the harmony that, gushing from his soul, 140
Draws back into his heart the wondrous whole?
When round her spindle, with unceasing drone,
Nature still whirls th' unending thread of life;
When Being's jarring crowds, together thrown,
Mingle in harsh inextricable strife;   145
Who deals their course unvaried till it falls,
In rhythmic flow to music's measured tone?
Each solitary note whose genius calls,
To swell the mighty choir in unison?
Who in the raging storm sees passion lour,   150
Or flush of earnest thought in evening's glow,
Who, in the springtide, every fairest flower
Along the loved one's path would strow?
From green and common leaves whose hand doth
          twine,
The wreath of glory, won in every field?   155
Makes sure Olympos, blends the power divine?—
Man's mighty spirit, in the bard revealed!

MERRYMAN.

Come then, employ your lofty inspiration,
And carry on the poet's avocation,
Just as we carry on a love affair.   160
Two meet by chance, are pleased, they linger there,
Insensibly are linked they scarce know how;
Fortune seems now propitious, adverse now,
Then comes alternate rapture and despair;
And 'tis a true romance ere one's aware.   165
Just such a drama let us now compose.
Plunge boldly into life — its depths disclose!
Each lives it, not to many is it known,
'Twill interest wheresoever seized and shown;
Bright pictures, but obscure their meaning: 170
A ray of truth through error gleaming,
Thus you the best elixir brew,
To charm mankind and edify them too.
Then youth's fair blossoms crowd to view your play,
And wait as on an oracle; while they,   175
The tender souls, who love the melting mood,

Suck from your work their melancholy food;
Now this one, and now that, you deeply stir,
Each sees the working of his heart laid bare;
Their tears, their laughter, you command with ease. 180
The lofty still they honor, the illusive love,
Your finished gentlemen you ne'er can please;
A growing mind alone will grateful prove.

POET.

Then give me back youth's golden prime,
When my own spirit too was growing,   185
When from my heart th' unbidden rhyme
Gushed forth, a fount forever flowing;
Then shadowy mist the world concealed,
And every bud sweet promise made,
Of wonders yet to be revealed,   190
As through the vales, with bloom inlaid,
Culling a thousand flowers I strayed.
Naught had I, yet a rich profusion;
The thirst for truth, joy in each fond illusion.   195
Give me unquelled those impulses to prove; —
Rapture so deep, its ecstasy was pain,
The power of hate, the energy of love,
Give me, oh, give me back my youth again!

MERRYMAN.

Youth, my good friend, you certainly require
When foes in battle round you press,   200
When a fair maid, her heart on fire,
Hangs on your neck with fond caress,
When from afar, the victor's crown,
Allures you in the race to run;
Or when in revelry you drown   205
Your sense, the whirling dance being done.
But the familiar chords among
Boldly to sweep, with graceful cunning,
While to its goal, the verse along
Its winding path is sweetly running;   210
This task is yours, old gentleman, to-day;
Nor are you therefore in less reverence held;
Age does not make us childish, as folk say,
It finds us genuine children e'en in eld.

MANAGER.

A truce to words, mere empty sound,   215
Let deeds at length appear, my friends
While idle compliments you round,
You might achieve some useful ends.
Why talk of the poetic vein?
Who hesitates will never know it;   220
If bards ye are, as ye maintain,
Now let your inspiration show it.
To you is known what we require,
Strong drink to sip is our desire ;
Come, brew me such without delay!   225
To-morrow sees undone, what happens not to-day ;
Still forward press, nor ever tire !
The possible, with steadfast trust,
Resolve should by the forelock grasp ;
Then she will ne'er let go her clasp,   230
And labors on, because she must.

On German boards, you're well aware,
· The taste of each may have full sway ;
Therefore in bringing out your play,
Nor scenes nor mechanism spare !   235
Heaven's lamps employ, the greatest and the least,
Be lavish of the stellar lights,
Water, and fire, and rocky heights,
Spare not at all, nor birds nor beast. ·
Thus let creation's ample sphere   240
Forthwith in this our narrow booth appear,
And with considerate speed, through fancy's spell,
Journey from heaven, thence through the world, to hell!

PROLOGUE IN HEAVEN.

The Lord. The Heavenly Hosts. *Afterwards*
Mephistopheles.

The three Archangels come forward. [5]

RAPHAEL.

Still quiring as in ancient time
With brother spheres in rival song,
The sun with thunder-march sublime
Moves his predestined course along.
Angels are strengthened by his sight,   5
Though fathom him no angel may;
Resplendent are the orbs of light,
As on creation's primal day.

GABRIEL.

And lightly spins earth's gorgeous sphere,
Swifter than thought its rapid flight;   10
Alternates Eden-brightness clear,
With solemn, dread-inspiring night;
The foaming waves, with murmur hoarse,
Against the rocks' deep base, are hurled;
And in the sphere's eternal course   15
Are rocks and ocean swiftly whirled.

MICHAEL.

And rival tempests rush amain
From sea to land, from land to sea,
And raging form a wondrous chain
Of deep mysterious agency;   20
Full in the thunder's fierce career,
Flaming the swift destructions play;
But, Lord, thy messengers revere
The mild procession of thy day.

THE THREE.

Angels are strengthened by thy sight,   25
Though fathom thee no angel may;
Thy works still shine with splendor bright,
As on creation's primal day.

26

MEPHISTOPHELES.

Since thou, O Lord, approachest us once more,
And how it fares with us, to ask art fain,　　　30
Since thou hast kindly welcomed me of yore,
Thou see'st me also now among thy train.
Excuse me, fine harangues I cannot make,
Though all the circle look on me with scorn;
My pathos soon thy laughter would awake,　　　35
Hadst thou the laughing mood not long forsworn.
Of suns and worlds I nothing have to say,
I see alone mankind's self-torturing pains.
The little world-gold still the self-same stamp retains,
And is as wondrous now as on the primal day.　　　40
Better he might have fared, poor wight,
Hadst thou not given him a gleam of heavenly light;
Reason he names it and doth so
Use it than brutes more brutish still to grow.
With deference to your grace, he seems to me　　　45
Like any like long-legged grasshopper to be,
Which ever flies, and flying springs,
And in the grass its ancient ditty sings.
Would he but always in the grass repose!
In every heap of dung he thrusts his nose.　　　50

THE LORD.

Hast thou naught else to say? Is blame
In coming here, as ever, thy sole aim?
Does nothing on the earth to thee seem right?

MEPHISTOPHELES.

No, Lord! I find things there in miserable plight.
Men's wretchedness in sooth I so deplore,　　　55
Not even I would plague the sorry creatures more.

THE LORD.

Know'st thou my servant, Faust?

MEPHISTOPHELES.

　　　　　　The doctor?

THE LORD.

　　　　　　　Right.

MEPHISTOPHELES.

He serves thee in strange fashion, as I think.
Poor fool! Not earthly is his food or drink.
An inward impulse hurries him afar,   60
Himself half conscious of his frenzied mood;
From heaven claimeth he its brightest star,
And from the earth craves every highest good,
And all that's near, and all that's far,.
Fails to allay the tumult in his blood.   65

THE LORD.

Though now he serves me with imperfect sight,
I will ere long conduct him to the light.
The gardener knoweth, when the green appears,
That flowers and fruit will crown the coming years.

MEPHISTOPHELES.

What wilt thou wager? Him thou yet shall lose,   70
If leave to me thou wilt but give,
Gently to lead him as I choose!

THE LORD.

So long as he on earth doth live,
So long 'tis not forbidden thee.
Man still must err, while he doth strive.   75

MEPHISTOPHELES.

I thank you; for not willingly
I traffic with the dead, and still aver
That youth's plump blooming cheek I very much pre-
          fer.
I'm not at home to corpses; 'tis my way,
Like cats with captive mice to toy and play.   80

THE LORD.

Enough! 'tis granted thee! Divert
This mortal spirit from his primal source;
Him canst thou seize, thy power exert
And lead him on thy downward course,
Then stand abashed, when thou perforce must own, 85
A good man, in the direful grasp of ill,
His consciousness of right retaineth still.

MEPHISTOPHELES.

Agreed!—the wager will be quickly won.
For my success no fears I entertain;
And if my end I finally should gain, 90
Excuse my triumphing with all my soul.
Dust he shall eat, ay, and with relish take,
As did my cousin, the renownèd snake.

THE LORD.

Here too thou'rt free to act without control;
I ne'er have cherished hate for such as thee. 95
Of all the spirits who deny,
The scoffer is least wearisome to me.
Ever too prone is man activity to shirk,
In unconditioned rest he fain would live;
Hence this companion purposely I give, 100
Who stirs, excites, and must, as devil, work.
But ye, the genuine sons of heaven, rejoice!
In the full living beauty still rejoice!
May that which works and lives, the ever-growing,
In bonds of love enfold you, mercy-fraught, 105
And Seeming's changeful forms, around ye flowing,
Do ye arrest, in ever-during thought!
(Heaven closes, the Archangels disperse.)

MEPHISTOPHELES (*alone*).

The ancient one I like sometimes to see,
And not to break with him am always civil;
'Tis courteous in so great a lord as he, 110
To speak so kindly even to the devil.

THE FIRST PART

OF

THE TRAGEDY OF FAUST.

DRAMATIS PERSONÆ.

Characters in the Prologue for the Theatre.

THE MANAGER.
THE DRAMATIC POET.
MERRYMAN.

Characters in the Prologue in Heaven.

THE LORD.
RAPHAEL
GABRIEL } The Heavenly Host.
MICHAEL
MEPHISTOPHELES.

Characters in the Tragedy.

FAUST.
MEPHISTOPHELES.
WAGNER, a Student.
MARGARET.
MARTHA, Margaret's Neighbor.
VALENTINE, Margaret's Brother.
OLD PEASANT.
A STUDENT.
ELIZABETH, an Acquaintance of Margaret's.
FROSCH
BRANDER } Guests in Auerbach's Wine Cellar.
SIEBEL
ALTMAYER

Witches, old and young ; Wizards, Will-o'-the-wisp, Witch Peddler, Protophantasmist. Servibilis, Monkeys, Spirits, Journeymen, Country-folk, Citizens, Beggar, Old Fortune-teller, Shepherd, Soldier, Students, etc.

In the Intermezzo.

OBERON.		ARIEL.
TITANIA.		PUCK, etc., etc.

THE TRAGEDY OF FAUST.

Night. — A high vaulted narrow Gothic chamber. —
FAUST, *restless, seated at his desk.*

FAUST.

I HAVE, alas! Philosophy,
Medicine, Jurisprudence too,
And to my cost Theology,
With ardent labor, studied through.
And here I stand, with all my lore,   **5**
Poor fool, no wiser than before.
Magister, doctor styled, indeed,
Already these ten years I lead,
Up, down, across, and to and fro,
My pupils by the nose, — and learn   **10**
That we in truth can nothing know!
This in my heart like fire doth burn.
'Tis true, I've more cunning than all your dull tribe,
Magistrate and doctor, priest, parson, and scribe;
Scruple or doubt comes not to enthrall me,   **15**
Neither can devil nor hell now appall me —
Hence, also, my heart must all pleasure forego !
I may not pretend, [7] aught rightly to know,
I may not pretend, through teaching, to find
A means to improve or convert mankind.   **20**
Then I have neither goods nor treasure,
No worldly honor, rank, or pleasure :
No dog in such a fashion would longer live !
Therefore myself to magic I give,
In hope, through spirit-voice and might,   **25**
Secrets now veiled to bring to light,
That I no more, with aching brow,
Need speak of what I nothing know ;
That I the force may recognize
That binds creation's inmost energies ;   **30**
Her vital powers, her embryo seeds survey,
And fling the trade in empty words away.

33

O full-orbed moon, did but thy rays
Their last upon mine anguish gaze!
Beside this desk, at dead of night,   35
Oft have I watched to hail thy light:
Then, pensive friend! o'er book and scroll,
With soothing power, thy radiance stole!
In thy dear light, ah, might I climb,
Freely, some mountain height sublime,   40
Round mountain caves with spirits ride,
In thy mild haze o'er meadows glide,
And, purged from knowledge-fumes, renew
My spirit, in thy healing dew!

Woe's me! still prisoned in the gloom   45
Of this abhorred and musty room,
Where heaven's dear light itself doth pass,
But dimly through the painted glass!
Hemmed in by volumes thick with dust,
A prey to worms and mouldering rust,   50
And to the high vault's topmost bound,
With smoky paper compassed round;
With boxes round thee piled, and glass,
And many a useless instrument,
With old ancestral lumber blent —   55
This is thy world! a world! alas!
And dost thou ask why heaves thy heart,
With tightened pressure in thy breast?
Why the dull ache will not depart,
By which thy life-pulse is oppressed?   60
Instead of nature's living sphere,
Created for mankind of old,
Brute skeletons surround thee here,
And dead men's bones in smoke and mould.

Up! Forth into the distant land!   65
Is not this book of mystery
By Nostradamus' proper hand, [8]
An all-sufficient guide? Thou'lt see
The courses of the stars unrolled;
When nature doth her thoughts unfold   70
To thee, thy soul shall rise and seek
Communion high with her to hold,

As spirit doth with spirit speak!
Vain by dull poring to divine
The meaning of each hallowed sign.   75
Spirits!   I feel you hovering near;
Make answer if my voice you hear!
      (*He opens the book and perceives the sign of the
        Macrocosmos.*)

Ah! at this spectacle through every sense,
What sudden ecstasy of joy is flowing!
I feel new rapture, hallowed and intense,   80
Through every nerve and vein with ardor glowing.
Was it a god who charactered this scroll,
Which doth the inward tumult still,
The troubled heart with rapture fill,
And by a mystic impulse, to my soul,   85
Unveils the working of the wondrous whole?
Am I a God?   What light intense!
In these pure symbols do I see,
Nature exert her vital energy.
Now of the wise man's words I learn the sense;   90
    " Unlocked the spirit-world doth lie;
     Thy sense is shut, thy heart is dead!
     Up, scholar, lave, with courage high,
     Thine earthly breast in the morning-red!"
          (*He contemplates the sign.*)

How all things live and work, and ever blending,   95
Weave one vast whole from Being's ample range!
How powers celestial, rising and descending,
Their golden buckets ceaseless interchange!
Their flight on rapture-breathing pinions winging,
From heaven to earth their genial influence bringing. 100
Through the wide sphere their chimes melodious ring-
    ing!

A wondrous show! but ah! a show alone!
Where shall I grasp thee, infinite nature, where?
Ye breasts, ye fountains of all life, whereon
Hang heaven and earth, from which the withered
    heart
For solace yearns, ye still impart   .   106

Your sweet and fostering tides — where are ye —
    where ?
Ye gush, and must I languish in despair ?
    (*He turns over the leaves of the book impatiently, and
        perceives the sign of the Earth-spirit.*)

How all unlike the influence of this sign !
Earth-spirit, thou to me art nigher,   110
E'en now my strength is rising higher,
E'en now I glow as with new wine ;
Courage I feel, abroad the world to dare,
The woe of earth, the bliss of earth to bear,
To mingle with the lightnings' glare,   115
And mid the crashing shipwreck not despair.

Clouds gather over me —
The moon conceals her light —
The lamp is quenched —
Vapors are rising — Quivering round my head   120
Flash the red beams — Down from the vaulted roof
A shuddering horror floats,
And seizes me !
I feel it, spirit, prayer-compelled, 'tis thou
Art hovering near !   125
Unveil thyself !
Ha ! How my heart is riven now !
Each sense, with eager palpitation,
Is strained to catch some new sensation !
I feel my heart surrendered unto thee !   130
Thou must ! Thou must ! Though life should be the fee !
    (*He seizes the book, and pronounces mysteriously the
        sign of the spirit. A ruddy flame flashes up ; the
        spirit appears in the flame.*)

SPIRIT.

Who calls me ?

FAUST (*turning aside*).

    Dreadful shape !

SPIRIT.

                 With might
Thou hast compelled me to appear,
Long hast been sucking at my sphere,
And now —

FAUST.

Woe's me! I cannot bear thy sight.   135

SPIRIT.

To know me thou didst breathe thy prayer,
My voice to hear, to gaze upon my brow;
Me doth thy strong entreaty bow —
Lo! I am here! — what pitiful despair
Grasps thee, the demigod!   Where's now the soul's
      deep cry?   140
Where is the breast, which in its depths a world con-
      ceived,
And bore and cherished; which, with ecstasy,
To rank itself with us, the spirits, heaved?
Where art thou, Faust? whose voice I heard resound,
Who toward me pressed with energy profound?   145
Art thou he?   Thou,— whom thus my breath can blight,
Whose inmost being with affright
Trembles, a crushed and blighted worm?

FAUST.

Shall I yield, thing of flame, to thee?
Faust, and thine equal, I am he!   150

SPIRIT.

In the currents of life, in action's storm,
      I float and I wave [9]
      With billowy motion!
      Birth and the grave,
      A limitless ocean,   155
      A constant weaving
      With change still rife,
      A restless heaving,
      A glowing life —
Thus time's whirring loom unceasing I ply,   160
And weave the life-garment of deity.

FAUST.

Thou, restless spirit, dost from end to end
O'ersweep the world; how near I feel to thee!

SPIRIT.

Thou'rt like the spirit, thou dost comprehend,
Not me!   (*Vanishes*) 165

FAUST (*deeply moved*).

Not thee?
Whom then?
I, God's own image.!
And not rank with thee!   (*A knock*).
Oh death! I know it — 'tis my famulus — [10]   170
My fairest fortune now escapes!
That all these visionary shapes
A soulless groveller should banish thus!   ·
   (WAGNER *in his dressing-gown and night-cap, a lamp
     in his hand.* FAUST *turns round reluctantly*).

WAGNER.

Pardon! I heard you here declaim;
A Grecian tragedy you doubtless read?   175
Improvement in this art is now my aim,
For nowadays it much avails. Indeed
An actor, oft I've heard it said at least,
May give instruction even to a priest.

FAUST

Ay, if your priest should be an actor too,   180
As not improbably may come to pass,

WAGNER.

When in his study pent the whole year through,
Man views the world as through an optic glass,
On a chance holiday, and scarcely then,
How by persuasion can he govern men?   185

FAUST.

If feeling prompt not, if it doth not flow
Fresh from the spirit's depths, with strong control
Swaying to rapture every listener's soul,
Idle your toil; the chase you may forego!
Brood o'er your task! Together glue,   190
Cook from another's feast your own ragout,
Still prosecute your paltry game,
And fan your ash-heaps into flame!
Thus children's wonder you'll excite,
And apes', if such your appetite: 195
But that which issues from the heart alone,
Will bend the hearts of others to your own.

WAGNER.

The speaker in delivery will find
Success alone; I still am far behind.

FAUST.

A worthy object still pursue!   200
Be not a hollow tinkling fool!
Sound understanding, judgment true,
Find utterance without art or rule;
And when with earnestness you speak,
Then is it needful cunning words to seek?   205
Your fine harangues, so polished in their kind,
Wherein the shreds of human thought ye twist,
Are unrefreshing as the empty wind,
Whistling through withered leaves and autumn mist!

WAGNER.

Oh, Heavens! art is long and life is short!   210
Still as I prosecute with earnest zeal
The critic's toil, I'm haunted by this thought,
And vague misgivings o'er my spirit steal.
The very means how hardly are they won,
By which we to the fountains rise!   215
And, haply, ere one half the course is run,
Checked in his progress, the poor devil dies.

FAUST.

Parchment, is that the sacred fount whence roll
Waters, he thirsteth not who once hath quaffed?
Oh, if it gush not from thine inmost soul,   220
Thou hast not won the life-restoring draught.

WAGNER.

Your pardon! 'tis delightful to transport
Oneself into the spirit of the past,
To see in times before us how a wise man thought,
And what a glorious height we have achieved at last. 225

FAUST.

Ay, truly! even to the loftiest star!
To us, my friend, the ages that are passed
A book with seven seals, close-fastened, are;
And what the spirit of the times men call,

Is merely their own spirit after all,   230
Wherein, distorted oft, the times are glass'd.
Then truly, 'tis a sight to grieve the soul!
At the first glance we fly it in dismay;
A very lumber-room, a rubbish-hole;
At best a sort of mock-heroic play,   235
With saws pragmatical and maxims sage,
To suit the puppets and their mimic stage.

WAGNER.

But then the world and man, his heart and brain!
Touching these things all men would something know.

FAUST.

Ay! what 'mong men as knowledge doth obtain! 240
Who on the child its true name dares bestow?
The few who somewhat of these things have known,
Who their full hearts unguardedly revealed,
Nor thoughts, nor feelings, from the mob concealed,
Have died on crosses, or in flames been thrown.   245
Excuse me, friend, far now the night is spent,
For this time we must say adieu.

WAGNER.

Still to watch on I had been well content,
Thus to converse so learnedly with you.
But as to-morrow will be Easter-day,   250
Some further questions grant, I pray;
With diligence to study still I fondly cling;
Already I know much, but would know everything.
                                                  (*Exit.*)

FAUST (*alone*).

How he alone is ne'er bereft of hope,
Who clings to tasteless trash with zeal untired   255
Who doth, with greedy hand, for treasure grope,
And finding earthworms, is with joy inspired!

And dare a voice of merely human birth,
E'en here, where shapes immortal thronged, intrude?
Yet, ah! thou poorest of the sons of earth,   260
For once, I e'en to thee feel gratitude.
Despair the power of sense did well-nigh blast,

And thou didst save me ere I sank dismayed ;
So giant-like the vision seemed, so vast,
I felt myself shrink dwarfed as I surveyed !　　265

I, God's own image, from this toil of clay
Already freed, with eager joy who hailed
The mirror of eternal truth unveiled,
Mid light effulgent and celestial day : —
I, more than cherub, whose unfettered soul　　270
With penetrative glance aspired to flow
Through nature's veins, and, still creating, know
The life of gods, — how am I punished now !
One thunder-word hath hurled me from the goal !

　Spirit ! I dare not lift me to thy sphere.　　275
　What though my power compelled thee to appear,
　My art was powerless to detain thee here.
　In that great moment, rapture-fraught,
　I felt myself so small, so great ;
　Fiercely didst thrust me from the realm of thought
　Back on humanity's uncertain fate !　　281
　Who'll teach me now ?   What ought I to forego ?
　Ought I that impulse to obey ?
　Alas ! our every deed, as well as every woe,
　Impedes the tenor of life's onward way !　　285

E'en to the noblest by the soul conceived,
Some feelings cling of baser quality ;
And when the goods of this world are achieved,
Each nobler aim is termed a cheat, a lie.
Our aspirations, our soul's genuine life,　　290
Grow torpid in the din of earthly strife.

　Though youthful phantasy, while hope inspires,
　Stretch o'er the infinite her wing sublime,
　A narrow compass limits her desires,
　When wrecked our fortunes in the gulf of time. 295
　In the deep heart of man care builds her nest,
　O'er secret woes she broodeth there,
　Sleepless she rocks herself and scareth joy and rest ;
　Still is she wont some new disguise to wear,
　She may as house and court, as wife and child appear,
　As dagger, poison, fire and flood ;　　301

Imagined evils chill thy blood,
And what thou ne'er shalt lose, o'er that dost shed
    the tear.

I am not like the gods!   Feel it I must;
I'm like the earth-worm, writhing in the dust,   305
Which, as on dust it feeds, its native fare,
Crushed 'neath the passer's tread, lies buried there.

Is it not dust, wherewith this lofty wall,
With hundred shelves, confines me round,
Rubbish, in thousand shapes, may I not call   310
What in this moth-world doth my being bound?
Here, what doth fail me, shall I find?
Read in a thousand tomes that, everywhere,
Self-torture is the lot of human-kind,
With but one mortal happy, here and there?   315
Thou hollow skull, that grin, what should it say,
But that thy brain, like mine, of old perplexed,
Still yearning for the truth, hath sought the light of day,
And in the twilight wandered, sorely vexed?
Ye instruments, forsooth, ye mock at me, —   320
With wheel, and cog, and ring, and cylinder;
To nature's portals ye should be the key;
Cunning your wards, and yet the bolts ye fail to stir.
Inscrutable in broadest light,
To be unveiled by force she doth refuse,   325
What she reveals not to thy mental sight,
Thou wilt not wrest from her with levers and with
    screws.
Old useless furnitures, yet stand ye here,
Because my sire ye served, now dead and gone,
Old scroll, the smoke of years dost wear,   330
So long as o'er this desk the sorry lamp hath shone.
Better my little means have squandered quite away,
Than burdened by that little here to sweat and groan!
Wouldst thou possess thy heritage, essay,
By use to render it thine own!   335
What we employ not, but impedes our way,
That which the hour creates, that can it use alone!

But wherefore to yon spot is riveted my gaze?
Is yonder flasket there a magnet to my sight?

Whence this mild radiance that around me plays, 340
As when, 'mid forest gloom, reigneth the moon's soft
    light?

Hail, precious phial! Thee, with reverent awe,
Down from thine own receptacle I draw!
Science in thee I hail and human art.
Essence of deadliest powers, refined and sure, 345
Of soothing anodynes abstraction pure,
Now in thy master's need thy grace impart!
I gaze on thee, my pain is lulled to rest;
I grasp thee, calmed the tumult in my breast;
The flood-tide of my spirit ebbs away; 350
Onward I'm summoned o'er a boundless main,
Calm at my feet expands the glassy plain,
To shores unknown allures a brighter day.

Lo, where a car of fire, on airy pinion,
Comes floating towards me! I'm prepared to fly 355
By a new track through ether's wide dominion,
To distant spheres of pure activity.
This life intense, this godlike ecstasy —
Worm that thou art such rapture canst thou earn?
Only resolve with courage stern and high, 360
Thy visage from the radiant sun to turn;
Dare with determined will to burst the portals
Past which in terror others fain would steal!
Now is the time, through deeds, to show that mortals
The calm sublimity of gods can feel; 365
To shudder not at yonder dark abyss,
Where phantasy creates her own self-torturing brood,
Right onward to the yawning gulf to press,
Around whose narrow jaws rolleth hell's fiery flood;
With glad resolve to take the fatal leap, 370
Though danger threaten thee, to sink in endless sleep!

Pure crystal goblet, forth I draw thee now,
From out thine antiquated case, where thou
Forgotten hast reposed for many a year!
Oft at my father's revels thou didst shine, 375
To glad the earnest guests was thine,
As each to other passed the generous cheer.
The gorgeous brede [11] of figures, quaintly wrought,

Which he who quaffed must first in rhyme expound,
Then drain the goblet at one draught profound,   380
Hath nights of boyhood to fond memory brought.
I to my neighbor shall not reach thee now,
Nor on thy rich device shall I my cunning show.
Here is a juice, makes drunk without delay;
Its dark brown flood thy crystal round doth fill;   385
Let this last draught, the product of my skill,
My own free choice, be quaffed with resolute will,
A solemn festive greeting, to the coming day!

(He places the goblet to his mouth.)
(The ringing of bells, and choral voices.)

CHORUS OF ANGELS. [12]

Christ is arisen!
Mortal, all hail to thee,   390
Thou whom mortality,
Earth's sad reality,
Held as in prison.

FAUST.

What hum melodious, what clear silvery chime,
Thus draws the goblet from my lips away?   395
Ye deep-toned bells, do ye with voice sublime,
Announce the solemn dawn of Easter-day?
Sweet choir! are ye the hymn of comfort singing,
Which once around the darkness of the grave,
From seraph-voices, in glad triumph ringing,   400
Of a new covenant assurance gave?

CHORUS OF WOMEN.

We, his true-hearted,
With spices and myrrh,
Embalmed the departed,
And swathed him with care;   405
Here we conveyed Him,
Our Master, so dear;
Alas! Where we laid Him,
The Christ is not here.

CHORUS OF ANGELS.

Christ is arisen!   410
Perfect through earthly ruth,

Radiant with love and truth,
He to eternal youth
Soars from earth's prison.

FAUST.

Wherefore, ye tones celestial, sweet and strong,   415
Come ye a dweller in the dusk to seek?
Ring out your chimes believing crowds among,
The message well I hear, my faith alone is weak;
From faith her darling, miracle, hath sprung.
Aloft to yonder spheres I dare not soar,   420
Whence sound the tidings of great joy;
And yet, with this sweet strain familiar when a boy,
Back it recalleth me to life once more.
Then would celestial love, with holy kiss,
Come o'er me in the Sabbath's stilly hour,   425
While, fraught with solemn meaning and mysterious
      power,
Chimed the deep-sounding bell, and prayer was bliss;
A yearning impulse, undefined yet dear,
Drove me to wander on through wood and field:
With heaving breast and many a burning tear,   430
I felt with holy joy a world reveal'd.
Gay sports and festive hours proclaimed with joyous
      pealing,
This Easter hymn in days of old;
And fond remembrance now, doth me, with childlike
      feeling,
Back from the last, the solemn step, withhold.   435
O still sound on, thou sweet celestial strain!
The tear-drop flows, — earth, I am thine again!

CHORUS OF DISCIPLES.

He whom we mourned as dead,
Living and glorious,
From the dark grave hath fled,   440
O'er death victorious;
Almost creative bliss
Waits on his growing powers;
Ah! Him on earth we miss;
Sorrow and grief are ours.   445
Yearning he left his own,

Mid sore annoy;
Ah! we must needs bemoan,
Master, thy joy!

CHORUS OF ANGELS.

Christ is arisen,   450
Redeemed from decay.
The bonds which imprison
Your souls, rend away!
Praising the Lord with zeal,
By deeds that love reveal,   455
Like brethren true and leal
Sharing the daily meal,
To all that sorrow feel
Whispering of heaven's weal,
Still is the master near,   460
Still is he here!

BEFORE THE GATE.

Promenaders of all sorts pass out.

SEVERAL MECHANICS' APPRENTICES.

Why choose ye that direction, pray?

OTHERS.

To the hunting-lodge we're on our way.

THE FIRST.

We towards the mill are strolling on.

A MECHANIC.

A walk to the Wasserhof were best.   465

A SECOND.

The road is not a pleasant one.

THE OTHERS.

What will you do?

A THIRD.

I'll join the rest.

A FOURTH.

Let's up to Burghof, there you'll find good cheer,
The prettiest maidens and the best of beer,
And brawls of a prime sort.

A FIFTH.

You scapegrace!   How! 470
Your skin still itching for a row?
Thither I will not go, I loathe the place.

SERVANT GIRL.

No, no!   I to the town my steps retrace.

ANOTHER.

Near yonder poplars he is sure to be.

THE FIRST.

And if he is, what matters it to me! 475
With you he'll walk, he'll dance with none but you,
And with your pleasures what have I to do?

THE SECOND.

To-day he will not be alone, he said
His friend would be with him, the curly-head.

STUDENT.

My! how those buxom girls step on! 480
Come, brother, we will follow them anon.
Strong beer, a damsel smartly dressed,
Pungent tobacco — are what I like best.

BURGHER'S DAUGHTER.

Look at those handsome fellows there!
'Tis really shameful, I declare, 485
The very best society they shun,
After those servant-girls forsooth, to run.

SECOND STUDENT. (*to the first*).

Not quite so fast! for in our rear,
Two girls, well-dressed, are drawing near;
Not far from us the one doth dwell, 490
And sooth to say, I like her well.
They walk demurely, yet you'll see,
That they will let us join them presently.

THE FIRST.

Not I! restraints of all kinds I detest.
Quick! let us catch the wild-game ere it flies, 495
The hand on Saturday the mop that plies,
Will of a Sunday fondle you the best.

BURGHER.

No, this new Burgomaster, I like him not; each hour
He grows more arrogant, now that he's raised to power;
And for the town, what doth he do for it?   500
Are not things worse from day to day?
To more restraints we must submit;
And taxes more than ever pay.

BEGGAR. (*sings*).

Kind gentlemen and ladies fair,
So rosy-cheeked and trimly dressed,   505
Be pleased to listen to my prayer,
Relieve and pity the distressed.
Let me not vainly sing my lay!
His heart's most glad whose hand is free.
Now when all men keep holiday,   510
Should be a harvest-day to me.

ANOTHER BURGHER.

I know naught better on a holiday,
Than chatting about war, and war's alarms,
When folk in Turkey are all up in arms,
Fighting their deadly battles far away,   515
We at the window stand, our glasses drain,
And watch adown the stream the painted vessels glide,
Then, blessing peace, and peaceful times again
Homeward we turn our steps at eventide.

THIRD BURGHER.

Ay, neighbor! So let matters stand for me!   520
There they may scatter one another's brains,
And wild confusion round them see —
So here at home in quiet all remains!

OLD WOMAN (*to the* BURGHERS' DAUGHTERS).

Heyday! How smart! The fresh young blood!
Who would not fall in love with you?   525
Not quite so proud! 'Tis well and good!
And what you wish that I could help you to.

BURGHER'S DAUGHTER.

Come, Agatha! I care not to be seen
Walking in public with these witches. True,

My future lover, last St. Andrew's E'en,   530
In flesh and blood she brought before my view.[13]

ANOTHER.

And mine she showed me also in the glass,
A soldier's figure, with companions bold;
I look around, I seek him as I pass,
In vain, his form I nowhere can behold.   535

SOLDIERS.

> Fortress with turrets
> Rising in air,
> Damsel disdainful,
> Haughty and fair,
> These be my prey!   540
> Bold is the venture,
> Costly the pay!

> Hark, how the trumpet
> Thither doth call us,
> Where either pleasure   545
> Or death may befall us.
> Hail to the tumult!
> Life's in the field!
> Damsel and fortress
> To us must yield.   550
> Bold is the venture,
> Costly the pay!
> Gaily the soldier
> Marches away.

FAUST and WAGNER.

FAUST.

Loosed from their fetters are streams and rills   555
Through the gracious spring-tide's all-quickening glow;
Hope's budding joy in the vale doth blow;
Old Winter back to the savage hills
Withdraweth his force, decrepid now.
Thence only impotent icy grains   560
Scatters he as he wings his flight,
Striping with sleet the verdant plains;
But the sun endureth no trace of white;

Everywhere growth and movement are rife,
All things investing with hues of life : [14]   565
Though flowers are lacking, varied of dye,
Their colors the motley throng supply.
Turn thee around, and from this height,
Back to the town direct thy sight.
Forth from the hollow, gloomy gate,   570
Stream forth the masses, in bright array.
Gladly seek they the sun to-day ;
The Resurrection they celebrate :
For they themselves have risen, with joy,
From tenement sordid, from cheerless room,   575
From bonds of toil, from care and annoy,
From gable and roof's o'er-hanging gloom,
From crowded alley and narrow street,
And from the churches' awe-breathing night,
All now have issued into the light.   580
But look ! how spreadeth on nimble feet
Through garden and field the joyous throng,
How o'er the river's ample sheet,
Many a gay wherry glides along ;
And see, deep sinking in the tide,   585
Pushes the last boat now away.
E'en from yon far hill's path-worn side,
Flash the bright hues of garments gay,
Hark ! Sounds of village mirth arise ;
This is the people's paradise.   590
Both great and small send up a cheer ;
Here am I man, I may be one here,

WAGNER.

Sir doctor, in a walk with you
There's honor and instruction too ;
Yet here alone I care not to resort,   595
Because I coarseness hate of every sort.
This fiddling, shouting, skittling, I detest ;
I hate the tumult of the vulgar throng ;
They roar as by the evil one possessed,
And call it pleasure, call it song.   600

PEASANTS (*under the linden-tree*)
Dance and Song.

The shepherd for the dance was dressed,
With ribbon, wreath, and colored vest,
A gallant show displaying.
And round about the linden-tree,
They footed it right merrily.   605
　　Juchhe! Juchhe!
　　Juchheisa! Heisa! He!
So fiddle-bow was braying.

Our swain amidst the circle pressed,
He pushed a maiden trimly dressed,   610
And jogged her with his elbow;
The buxom damsel turned her head,
"Now that's a stupid trick!" she said,
　　Juchhe! Juchhe!
　　Juchheisa! Heisa! He!   615
Don't be so rude, good fellow!

Swift in the circle they advance,
They dance to right, to left they dance,
The skirts abroad are swinging.
And they grow red, and they grow warm,   620
Elbow on hip, they arm in arm,
　　Juchhe! Juchhe!
　　Juchheisa! Heisa! He!
Rest, talking now or singing.

Don't make so free! How many a maid   625
Has been betrothed and then betrayed;
And has repented after!
Yet still he flattered her aside,
And from the linden, far and wide,
　　Juchhe! Juchhe!   630
　　Juchheisa! Heisa! He!
Sound fiddle-bow and laughter.

OLD PEASANT.

Doctor, 'tis really kind of you,
To condescend to come this way,
A highly learned man like you,   635
To join our mirthful throng to-day.

Our fairest cup I offer you,
Which we with sparkling drink have crowned,
And pledging you, I pray aloud,
That every drop within its round,   640
While it your present thirst allays,
May swell the number of your days.

FAUST.

I take the cup you kindly reach,
Thanks and prosperity to each!
(*The crowd gather round in a circle.*)

OLD PEASANT.

Ay, truly! 'tis well done, that you   645
Our festive meeting thus attend;
You, who in evil days of yore,
So often showed yourself our friend!
Full many a one stands living here,
Who from the fever's deadly blast,   650
Your father rescued, when his skill
The fatal sickness stay'd at last.
A young man then, each house you sought,
Where reigned the mortal pestilence.
Corpse after corpse was carried forth,   655
But still unscathed you issued thence.
Sore then your trials and severe;
The Helper yonder aids the helper here.

ALL.

Heaven bless the trusty friend, and long
To help the poor his life prolong!   660

FAUST.

To Him above in homage bend,
Who prompts the helper and Who help doth send.
(*He proceeds with* WAGNER.)

WAGNER.

With what emotions must your heart o'erflow,
Receiving thus the reverence of the crowd!
Great man! How happy, who like you doth know 665
Such use for gifts by heaven bestow'd!
You to the son the father shows;
They press around, inquire, advance,

Hushed is the fiddle, checked the dance.
Still where you pass they stand in rows,   670
And each aloft his bonnet throws,
They fall upon their knees, almost
As when there passeth by the Host.

FAUST.

A few steps further, up to yonder stone!
Here rest we from our walk.   In times long past, 675
Absorbed in thought, here oft I sat alone,
And disciplined myself with prayer and fast.
Then rich in hope, with faith sincere,
With sighs, and hands in anguish pressed,
The end of that sore plague, with many a tear,   680
From heaven's dread Lord, I sought to wrest,
These praises have to me a scornful tone.[15]
Oh, could'st thou in my inner being read,
How little either sire or son,
Of such renown deserve the meed!   685
My sire, of good repute, and sombre mood,
O'er nature's powers and every mystic zone,
With honest zeal, but methods of his own,
With toil fantastic loved to brood;
His time in dark alchemic cell,   690
With brother adepts he would spend,
And there things contrary compel
Through numberless receipts to blend.
A ruddy lion there, a suitor bold,[16]
In tepid bath was with the lily wed.   695
Thence both, while open flames around them rolled,
Were tortured to another bridal bed.
Was then the youthful queen descried
With many a hue, to crown the task; —
This was our medicine; the patients died,   700
"Who were restored?" none cared to ask.
With our infernal mixture thus, ere long,
These hills and peaceful vales among,
We raged more fiercely than the pest;
Myself the deadly poison did to thousands give;   705
They pined away, I yet must live,
To hear the reckless murderers blest.

WAGNER.

Why let this thought your soul o'ercast?
Can man do more than with nice skill,
With firm and conscientious will,   710
Practise the art transmitted from the past?
If duly you revere your sire in youth,
His lore you gladly will receive;
In manhood, if you spread the bonds of truth,
Then may your son a higher goal achieve.   715

FAUST.

O blest, whom still the hope inspires,
To lift himself from error's turbid flood!
What man knows not, is just what he requires,
And what he knows he cannot use for good.
But let not moody thoughts their shadow throw   720
O'er the calm beauty of this hour serene!
In the rich sunset see how brightly glow
Yon cottage homes, girt round with verdant green!
Slow sinks the orb, the day is now no more;
Yonder he hastens to diffuse new life.   725
Oh, for a pinion from the earth to soar,
And after, ever after him to strive !
Then should I see the world below,
Bathed in the deathless evening beams,   .
The vales reposing, every height aglow,   730
The silver brooklets meeting golden streams.
The savage mountain, with its caverned side,
Bars not my godlike progress. Lo, the ocean,
Its warm bays heaving with a tranquil motion,
To my rapt vision opes its ample tide!   735
But now at length the god appears to sink;
A new-born impulse wings my flight,
Onward I press, his quenchless light to drink,
The day before me, and behind the night,
The pathless waves beneath, and over me the skies. 740
Fair dream, it vanished with the parting day!
Alas! that when on spirit-wing we rise,
No wing material lifts our mortal clay.
But 'tis our inborn impulse, deep and strong,
Upward and onward still to urge our flight,   745

When far above us pours its thrilling song
The sky-lark, lost in azure light,
When on extended wing amain
O'er pine-crowned height the eagle soars,
And over moor and lake, the crane   750
Still striveth towards its native shores.

WAGNER.

To strange conceits oft I myself must own,
But impulse such as this I ne'er have known:
Nor woods, nor fields, can long our thoughts engage,
Their wings I envy not the feathered kind;   755
Far otherwise the measures of the mind,
Bear us from book to book, from page to page!
Then winter nights grow cheerful; keen delight
Warms every limb; and ah! when we unroll
Some old and precious parchment, at the sight   760
All heaven itself descends upon the soul.

FAUST.

Your heart by one sole impulse is possessed;
Unconscious of the other still remain!
Two souls, alas! are lodged within my breast,
Which struggle there for undivided reign: 765
One to the world, with obstinate desire,
And closely-cleaving organs, still adheres;
Above the mist, the other doth aspire,
Which sacred vehemence, to purer spheres.
Oh, are there spirits in the air,   770
Who float 'twixt heaven and earth dominion wielding,
Stoop hither from your golden atmosphere,
Lead me to scenes, new life and fuller yielding!
A magic mantle did I but possess,
Abroad to waft me as on viewless wings,   775
I'd prize it far beyond the costliest dress,
Nor would I change it for the robe of kings.

WAGNER.

Call not the spirits who on mischief wait!
Their troop familiar, streaming through the air,
From every quarter threaten man's estate,   780
And danger in a thousand forms prepare!

They drive impetuous from the frozen north,
With fangs sharp-piercing, and keen arrowy tongues;
From the ungenial east they issue forth,
And prey, with parching breath, upon your lungs; 785
If, wafted on the desert's flaming wing,
They from the south heap fire upon the brain,
Refreshment from the west at first they bring,
Anon to drown thyself and field and plain.
In wait for mischief, they are prompt to hear;   790
With guileful purpose our behest obey;
Like ministers of grace they oft appear,
And lisp like angels, to betray.
But let us hence!   Gray eve doth all things blend,
The air grows chill, the mists descend!   795
'Tis in the evening first our home we prize —
Why stand you thus, and gaze with wandering eyes?
What in the gloom thus moves you?

FAUST.

                              Yon black hound[17]
See'st thou, through corn and stubble circling round?

WAGNER.

I've marked him long, naught strange in him I see! 800

FAUST.

Note him !   What takest thou the brute to be?

WAGNER.

But for a poodle, whom his instinct serves
His master's track to find once more.

FAUST.

Dost mark how round us, with wide spiral curves,
He wheels, each circle closer than before?   805
And, if I err not, he appears to me
A fiery whirlpool in his track to leave.

WAGNER.

Naught but a poodle black of hue I see;
'Tis some illusion doth your sight deceive.

FAUST.

Methinks a magic coil our feet around,   810
He for a future snare doth lightly spread.

WAGNER.

Around us as in doubt I see him shyly bound,
Since he two strangers seeth in his master's stead.

FAUST.

The circle narrows, he's already near!

WAGNER.

A dog dost see, no spectre have we here;   815
He growls, doubts, lays him on his belly too,
And wags his tail — as dogs are wont to do.

FAUST.

Come hither, sirrah! join our company!

WAGNER.

A simple poodle, he appears to be!
Thou standest still, for thee he'll wait;   820
Thou speak'st to him, he fawns upon thee straight;
Aught you may lose, again he'll bring,
And for your stick will into water spring.

FAUST.

Thou'rt right indeed; no traces now I see
Whatever of a spirit's agency.   825
'Tis training — nothing more.

WAGNER.

              A dog well taught
E'en by the wisest of us may be sought.
Ay, to your favor he's entitled too,
Apt scholar of the students, 'tis his due!
          (*They enter the gate of the town.*)

Study.

FAUST (*entering with the poodle*).
Behind me now lie field and plain   830
As night her veil doth o'er them draw,
Our better soul resumes her reign
With feelings of foreboding awe.
Lulled is each stormy deed to rest,
And tranquillized each wild desire;   835
Pure charity doth warm the breast,
And love to God the soul inspire.

Be quiet, poodle! Rush not round thus! Stay thee!
Why at the threshold snuffest thou so?
Behind the stove now quietly lay thee,   840
My softened cushion to thee I'll throw.
As thou, without, didst please and amuse me,
Running and frisking about on the hill,
So my shelter I'll not refuse thee;
A welcome guest, if thou'lt be still.   845

    Ah! when within our narrow room,
The friendly lamp again doth glow,
An inward light dispels the gloom
In hearts that strive themselves to know.
Reason begins again to speak,   850
Again the bloom of hope returns,
The streams of life we fain would seek,
Ah, for life's source our spirit yearns.

Cease, poodle, cease! with the tone that arises,
Hallowed and peaceful, my soul within,   855
Accords not thy growl, thy bestial din.
We find it not strange, that man despises
What he conceives not;
The good and the fair he misprizes;
What lies beyond him he doth contemn;   860
Snarleth the poodle at it, like men?

But ah! E'en now I feel, howe'er I yearn for rest,
Contentment welleth up no longer in my breast.
Yet wherefore must the stream, alas, so soon be dry,
That we once more athirst should lie?   865
This sad experience oft I've proved!
The want admitteth of compensation;
We learn to prize what from sense is removed,
Our spirits yearn for revelation,
Which nowhere burneth with beauty blent,   870
More pure than in the New Testament.

To the ancient text an impulse strong
Moves me the volume to explore,
And to translate its sacred lore,
Into the tones beloved of the German tongue.   875
    (*He opens a volume, and applies himself to it.*)

'Tis writ, "In the beginning was the word!"
I pause, perplexed!   Who now will help afford?
I cannot the mere word so highly prize;
I must translate it otherwise,
If by the spirit guided as I read.   880
"In the beginning was the Sense!"   Take heed,
The import of this primal sentence weigh,
Lest thy too hasty pen be led astray!
Is force creative then of Sense the dower?
"In the beginning was the Power!"   885
Thus should it stand: yet, while the line I trace,
A something warns me, once more to efface.
The spirit aids! from anxious scruples freed,
I write, "In the beginning was the deed!"

Am I with thee my room to share,[18]   890
Poodle, thy barking now forbear,
Forbear thy howling!
Comrade so noisy, ever growling,
I cannot suffer here to dwell.
One or the other, mark me well,   895
Forthwith must leave the cell.
I'm loath the guest-right to withhold;
The door's ajar, the passage clear;
But what must now mine eyes behold!
Are nature's laws suspended here?   900
Real is it, or a phantom show?
In length and breadth how doth my poodle grow!
He lifts himself with threatening mien,
In likeness of a dog no longer seen!
What spectre have I harbored thus!   905
Huge as a hippopotamus,
With fiery eye, terrific tooth!
Ah! now I know thee, sure enough!
For such a base, half-hellish brood,
The key of Solomon is good.[19]   910

SPIRITS (without).

Captured there within is one!
Stay without and follow none!
Like a fox in iron snare,
Hell's old lynx is quaking there,

But take heed!　　　　　　　915
Hover round above, below,
To and fro,
Then from durance is he freed!
Can ye aid him, spirits all,
Leave him not in mortal thrall!　　　920
Many a time and oft hath he
Served us, when at liberty.

FAUST.

The monster to confront at first,
The spell of four must be rehearsed;

Salamander shall kindle,　　　　925
Writhe, nymph of the wave,
In air sylph shall dwindle,
And Kobold shall slave,

Who doth ignore
The primal four,　　　　　　　930
Nor knows aright
Their use and might,
O'er spirits will he
Ne'er master be!

Vanish in the fiery glow,　　　　935
Salamander!
Rushingly together flow,
Undine!
Shimmer in the meteor's gleam,
Sylphide!　　　　　　　　　940
Hither bring thine homely aid,
Incubus!　Incubus!
Step forth!　The spell concludeth thus!

None of the four
Lurks in the beast:　　　　　945
He grins at me, untroubled as before;
I have not hurt him in the least.
A spell of fear
Thou now shalt hear.

Art thou, comrade fell,　　　　950
Fugitive from hell?
See then this sign,

Before which incline
The murky troops of Hell!
With bristling hair now doth the creature swell.			955

Canst thou, reprobate,
Read the uncreate,
Unspeakable, diffused
Throughout the heavenly sphere,
Shamefully abused,								960
Transpierced with nail and spear!

Behind the stove, tamed by my spells,
Like an elephant he swells;
Wholly now he fills the room,
He into mist will melt away.						965
Ascend not to the ceiling! Come,
Thyself at the master's feet now lay!
Thou seest that mine is no idle threat.
With holy fire I will scorch thee yet!
Wait not the might								970
That lies in the triple-glowing light!
Wait not the might
Of all my arts in fullest measure!

MEPHISTOPHELES

*(As the mist sinks, comes forward from behind the
stove, in the dress of a travelling scholar).*

Why all this uproar? What's the master's pleasure?

FAUST.

This then the kernel of the brute!						975
A travelling scholar? Why I needs must smile.

MEPHISTOPHELES.

Your learned reverence humbly I salute!
You've made me swelter in a pretty style.

FAUST.

Thy name?

MEPHISTOPHELES.

The question trifling seems from one,
Who it appears the Word doth rate so low;				980
Who, undeluded by mere outward show,
To Being's depth would penetrate alone.

FAUST.

With gentlemen like you indeed
The inward essence from the name we read,
As all too plainly it doth appear,   985
When Beelzebub, Destroyer, Liar, meets the ear.
Who then art thou?

MEPHISTOPHELES.

     Part of that power which still
Produceth good, whilst ever scheming ill.

FAUST.

What hidden mystery in this riddle lies?

MEPHISTOPHELES.

I am the spirit who evermore denies!   990
And justly; for whate'er to light is brought
Deserves again to be reduced to naught;
Then better 'twere that naught should be.
Thus all the elements which ye
Destruction, Sin, or briefly, Evil, name,   995
As my peculiar element I claim.

FAUST.

Thou nam'st thyself a part, and yet a whole I see.

MEPHISTOPHELES.

The modest truth I speak to thee.
Though folly's microcosm, man, it seems,
Himself to be a perfect whole esteems,   1000
Part of the part am I, which at the first was all.

A part of darkness, which gave birth to light.
Proud light, who now his mother would enthrall,
Contesting space and ancient rank with night.
Yet he succeedeth not, for struggle as he will,   1005
To forms material he adhereth still;
From them he streameth, them he maketh fair,
And still the progress of his beams they check;
And so, I trust, when comes the final wreck,
Light will, ere long, the doom of matter share.   1010

FAUST.

Thy worthy avocation now I guess!

Wholesale annihilation won't prevail,
So thou'rt beginning on a smaller scale.

MEPHISTOPHELES.

And, to say truth, as yet with small success.
Opposed to nothingness, the world,   1015
This clumsy mass, subsisteth still ;
Not yet is it to ruin hurled,
Despite the efforts of my will.
Tempests and earthquakes, fire and flood, I've tried ;
Yet land and ocean still unchanged abide ! 1020
And then of humankind and beasts, the accursed brood,
Neither o'er them can I extend my sway.
What countless myriads have I swept away !
Yet ever circulates the fresh young blood.
It is enough to drive me to despair !   1025
As in the earth, in water, and in air,
In moisture and in drought, in heat and cold,
Thousands of germs their energies unfold !
If fire I had not for myself retained,
No sphere whatever had for me remained. 1030

FAUST.

So thou with thy cold devil's fist,
Still clenched in malice impotent,
Dost the creative power resist,
The active, the beneficent !
Henceforth some other task essay,   1035
Of Chaos thou the wondrous son !

MEPHISTOPHELES.

We will consider what you say,
And talk about it more anon !
For this time have I leave to go ?

FAUST.

Why thou shouldst ask, I cannot see.   1040
Since one another now we know,
At thy good pleasure, visit me.
Here is the window, here the door,
The chimney, too, may serve thy need.

MEPHISTOPHELES.

I must confess, my stepping o'er   1045

Thy threshold a slight hindrance doth impede ;
The wizard-foot doth me retain.

FAUST.

The pentagram thy peace doth mar?[20]
To me, thou son of hell, explain,
How camest thou in, if this thine exit bar?   1050
Could such a spirit aught ensnare ?

MEPHISTOPHELES.

Observe it well, it is not drawn with care,
One of the angles, that which points without,
Is, as thou seest, not quite closed.

FAUST.

Chance hath the matter happily disposed !   1055
So thou my captive art ?   No doubt !
By accident thou thus are caught !

MEPHISTOPHELES.

In sprang the dog, indeed, observing naught ;
Things now assume another shape,
The devil's in the house and can't escape.   1060

FAUST.

Why through the window not withdraw?

MEPHISTOPHELES.

For ghosts and for the devil 'tis a law,
Where they stole in, there they must forth.   We're free
The first to choose ; as to the second, slaves are we.

FAUST.

E'en hell hath its peculiar laws, I see !   1065
I'm glad of that ! a pact may then be made,
The which, you gentlemen, will surely keep ?

MEPHISTOPHELES.

Whate'er therein is promised thou shalt reap,
No tittle shall remain unpaid.
But such arrangements time require ;   1070
We'll speak of them when next we meet ;
Most earnestly I now entreat,
This once permission to retire.

FAUST.

Another moment prithee here remain,
Me with some happy word to pleasure.   1075

MEPHISTOPHELES.

Now let me go! ere long I'll come again,
Then thou may'st question at thy leisure.

FAUST.

To capture thee was not my will.
Thyself hast freely entered in the snare:
Let him who holds the devil, hold him still!   1080
A second time so soon he will not catch him there.

MEPHISTOPHELES.

If it so please thee, I'm at thy command;
Only on this condition, understand;
That worthily thy leisure to beguile,
I here may exercise my arts awhile,   1085

FAUST.

Thou'rt free to do so!   Gladly I'll attend;
But be thine art a pleasant one!

MEPHISTOPHELES.

                    My friend,
This hour enjoyment more intense,
Shall captivate each ravish'd sense,
Than thou could'st compass in the bound   1090
Of the whole year's unvarying round;
And what the dainty spirits sing,
The lovely images they bring,
Are no fantastic sorcery.
Rich odors shall regale your smell,   1095
On choicest sweets your palate dwell,
Your feelings thrill with ecstasy.
No preparation do we need,
Here we together are.   Proceed.

SPIRITS.

Hence, overshadowing gloom [21]   1100
Vanish from sight!
O'er us thine azure dome,
Bend, beauteous light!

Dark clouds that o'er us spread,
Melt in thin air!   1105
Stars, your soft radiance shed,
Tender and fair.
Girt with celestial might,
Winging their airy flight,
Spirits are thronging.   1110
Follows their forms of light
Infinite longing!
Flutter their vestures bright
O'er field and grove!
Where in their leafy bower   1115
Lovers the livelong hour
Vow deathless love.
Soft bloometh bud and bower!
Bloometh the grove!
Grapes and spreading vine   1120
Crown the full measure;
Fountains of foaming wine
Gush from the pressure.
Still where the currents wind,
Gems brightly gleam.   1125
Leaving the hills behind
On rolls the stream;
Now into ample seas,
Spreadeth the flood;
Laving the sunny leas,   1130
Mantled with wood.
Rapture the feathered throng,
Gaily careering,
Sip as they float along;
Sunward they're steering;   1135
On towards the isles of light
Winging their way,
That on the waters bright
Dancingly play.
Hark to the choral strain,   1140
Joyfully ringing!
While on the grassy plain
Dancers are springing;
Climbing the steep hill's side,
Skimming the glassy tide,   1145

Wander they there;
Others on pinions wide
Wing the blue air;
On towards the living stream,
Towards yonder stars that gleam,   1150
Far, far away;
Seeking their tender beam
Wing they their way.

MEPHISTOPHELES.

Well done, my dainty spirits! now he slumbers;
Ye have entranced him fairly with your numbers; 1155
This minstrelsy of yours I must repay. —
Thou art not yet the man to hold the devil fast! —
With fairest shapes your spells around him cast,
And plunge him in a sea of dreams!
But that this charm be rent, the threshold passed, 1160
Tooth of rat the way must clear.
I need not conjure long it seems,
One rustles hitherward, and soon my voice will hear.

The master of the rats and mice,
Of flies and frogs, of bugs and lice,   1165
Commands thy presence; without fear
Come forth and gnaw the threshold here,
Where he with oil has smeared it.   Thou
Com'st hopping forth already!   Now
To work!   The point that holds me bound   1170
Is in the outer angle found.
Another bite — so — now 'tis done —
Now, Faustus, till we meet again, dream on.

FAUST (*awaking*).

Am I once more deluded! must I deem
This troop of thronging spirits all ideal?   1175
The devil's presence, was it nothing real?
The poodle's disappearance, but a dream?

Study.

FAUST.   MEPHISTOPHELES.

FAUST.

A knock? Come in! who now would break my rest?

MEPHISTOPHELES.

'Tis I !

FAUST.

Come in !

MEPHISTOPHELES.

Thrice be the words expressed.

FAUST.

Then I repeat, Come in !

MEPHISTOPHELES.

'Tis well,   1180
I hope that we shall soon agree !
For now your humors to dispel,
Here, as a youth of high degree,
I come in gold-laced scarlet vest,
And stiff silk mantle richly dressed,   1185
A cock's gay feather for a plume,
A long and pointed rapier, too ;
And briefly I would counsel you
To don at once the same costume,
And free from trammels, speed away,   1190
That what life is you may essay.

FAUST.

In every garb I needs must feel oppressed,
My heart to earth's low cares a prey.
Too old the trifler's part to play,
Too young to live by no desire possess'd.   1195
What can the world to me afford ?
Renounce ! renounce ! is still the word ;
This is the everlasting song
In every ear that ceaseless rings,
And which, alas, our whole life long   1200
Hoarsely each passing moment sings.
But to new horror I awake each morn,
And I could weep hot tears, to see the sun
Dawn on another day, whose round forlorn
Will satisfy no wish of mine — not one.   1205
Which still, with froward captiousness, impairs
E'en the presentiment of every joy,
While low realities and paltry cares

The spirit's fond imaginings destroy.
And even I then, when falls the veil of night,   1210
Stretched on my bed, I languish in despair;
Appalling dreams my soul affright;
No rest vouchsafed me even there.
The god, who throned within my breast resides,
Deep in my soul can stir the springs;   1215
With sovereign sway my energies he guides,
He cannot move external things;
And so existence is to me a weight,
Death fondly I desire and life I hate.

MEPHISTOPHELES.

And yet, methinks, by most 'twill be confessed   1220
That Death is never quite a welcome guest.

FAUST.

Happy the man around whose brow he binds
The blood-stained wreath in conquest's dazzling hour;
Or whom, excited by the dance, he finds
Dissolved in bliss in love's delicious bower!   1225
O that before the lofty spirit's might,
Enraptured, I had rendered up my soul!

MEPHISTOPHELES.

Yet did a certain man refrain one night,
Of its brown juice to drain the crystal bowl.

FAUST.

To play the spy diverts you then?

MEPHISTOPHELES.

                  I own,   1230
Though not omniscient, much to me is known.

FAUST.

If o'er my soul the tone familiar, stealing, [22]
Drew me from harrowing thought's bewildering maze,
Touching the lingering chords of childlike feeling,
With the sweet harmonies of happier days: 1235
So curse I all around the soul that windeth
Its magic and alluring spell,
And with delusive flattery bindeth
Its victim to the dreary cell!

Cursed before all things be the high opinion,   1240
Wherewith the spirit girds itself around!
Of shows delusive cursed be the dominion,
Within whose mocking sphere our sense is bound!
Accursed of dreams the treacherous wiles,
The cheat of glory, deathless fame!   1245
Accursed what each as property beguiles,
Wife, child, slave, plough, whate'er its name!
Accursed be mammon, when with treasure
He doth to daring deeds incite:
Or when to steep the soul in pleasure,   1250
He spreads the couch of soft delight!
Cursed be the grape's balsamic juice!
Accursed love's dream, of joys the first!
Accursed be hope! accursed be faith!
And more than all, be patience cursed!   1255

CHORUS OF SPIRITS (invisible).

Woe! woe!
Thou hast destroyed
The beautiful world
With violent blow;
'Tis shivered! 'tis shattered   1260
The fragments abroad by a demigod scattered!
Now we sweep
The wrecks into nothingness!
Fondly we weep
The beauty that's gone!   1265
Thou 'mongst the sons of earth,
Lofty and mighty one,
Build it once more!
In thine own bosom the lost world restore!
Now with unclouded sense   1270
Enter a new career;
Songs shall salute thine ear,
Ne'er heard before!

MEPHISTOPHELES.

23 My little ones these spirits be.
Hark! with shrewd intelligence,   1275
How they recommend to thee
Action, and the joys of sense!

In the busy world to dwell,
Fain they would allure thee hence :
For within this lonely cell,   1280
Stagnate sap of life and sense.

Forbear to trifle longer with thy grief,
Which, vulture-like, consumes thee in this den.
The worst society is some relief,
Making thee feel thyself as man with men.   1285
Nathless it is not meant, I trow,
To thrust thee 'mid the vulgar throng.
I to the upper ranks do not belong ;
Yet if, by me companioned, thou
Thy steps through life forthwith wilt take,   1290
Upon the spot myself I'll make
Thy comrade ; —
Should it suit thy need,
I am thy servant, am thy slave indeed !

FAUST.

And how must I thy services repay ?   1295

MEPHISTOPHELES.

Thereto thou lengthened respite hast !

FAUST.

                       No ! no !
The devil is an egotist, I know :
And, for Heaven's sake, 'tis not his way
Kindness to any one to show.
Let the condition plainly be exprest ;   1300
Such a domestic is a dangerous guest.

MEPHISTOPHELES.

I'll pledge myself to be thy servant *here*,
Still at thy back alert and prompt to be ;
But when together *yonder* we appear,
Then shalt thou do the same for me.   1305

FAUST.

But small concern I feel for yonder world ;
Hast thou this system into ruin hurled,
Another may arise the void to fill.
This earth the fountain whence my pleasures flow,

This sun doth daily shine upon my woe,   1310
And if this world I must forego,
Let happen then, — what can and will.
I to this theme will close mine ears,
If men hereafter hate and love,
And if there be in yonder spheres   1315
A depth below or height above.

MEPHISTOPHELES.

In this mood thou mayst venture it.   But make
The compact, and at once I'll undertake
To charm thee with mine arts.   I'll give thee more
Than mortal eye hath e'er beheld before.   1320

FAUST.

What, sorry devil, hast thou to bestow?
Was ever mortal spirit, in its high endeavor,
Fathomed by Being such as thou?
Yet food thou hast which satisfieth never,
Hast ruddy gold, that still doth flow   1325
Like restless quicksilver away,
A game thou hast, at which none win who play,
A girl who would, with amorous eyen,
E'en from my breast, a neighbor snare,
Lofty ambition's joy divine,   1330
That, meteor-like, dissolves in air.
Show me the fruit that, ere 'tis plucked, doth rot,
And trees, whose verdure daily buds anew.

MEPHISTOPHELES.

Such a commission scares me not,
I can provide such treasures, it is true;   1335
But, my good friend, a season will come round,
When on what's good we may regale in peace.

FAUST.

If e'er upon my couch, stretched at my ease, I'm found,
Then may my life that instant cease;
Me canst thou cheat with glozing wile
That I be pleased with the repast,   1340
Me with joy's lure canst thou beguile —
Let that day be for me the last!
Be this our wager!

MEPHISTOPHELES.
  Be it!

FAUST.
      Sure and fast!
When to the moment I shall say,   1345
"Linger awhile, so fair thou art!"
Then mayst thou fetter me straightway,
Then to the abyss will I depart;
Then may the solemn death-bell sound,
Then from thy service thou art free,   1350
The index then may cease its round,
And time be never more for me!

MEPHISTOPHELES.
I shall remember; pause, ere 'tis too late.

FAUST.
Thereto a perfect right hast thou.
My strength I do not rashly overrate.   1355
Slave am I here, at any rate,
If thine, or whose, it matters not, I trow.

MEPHISTOPHELES.
At doctors' feast I will this day
Attend, my duties to commence. —
But one thing!—Accidents may happen, hence   1360
A line or two in writing grant, I pray.

FAUST.
A writing, pedant! dost demand from me?
Man, and man's plighted word, are these unknown
      to thee?
Is't not enough, that by the word I gave,
My doom for evermore is cast?   1365
Doth not the world in all its currents rave,
And must a promise hold me fast?
Yet fixed is this delusion in our heart;
Who, of his own free will, therefrom would part?
How blest within whose breast truth reigneth pure!
No sacrifice will he repent when made!   1370
A formal deed, with seal and signature,
A spectre this from which all shrink afraid.
The word its life renounces in the pen,

Leather and wax usurp the mastery then.   1375
Spirit of evil! what dost thou require?
Brass, marble, parchment, paper, dost desire?
Shall I with chisel, pen, or graver write?
Thy choice is free; to me 'tis all the same.

MEPHISTOPHELES.

Wherefore thy passion so excite,   1380
And thus thine eloquence inflame?
A scrap is for our compact good.
Thou under-signest merely with a drop of blood.

FAUST.

If this will satisfy thy mind,
Thy whim I'll gratify, howe'er absurd.   1385

MEPHISTOPHELES.

Blood is a juice of very special kind.

FAUST.

Be not afraid that I shall break my word!
The scope of all my energy
Is in exact accordance with my vow.
Vainly I have aspired too high;   1390
I'm on a level with but such as thou;
Me the great spirit scorned, defied;
Nature from me herself doth hide;
Rent is the web of thought; my mind
Doth knowledge loathe of every kind.   1395
In depths of sensual pleasure drowned,
Let us our fiery passions still!
Enwrapped in magic's veil profound,
Let wondrous charms our senses thrill!
Plunge we in time's tempestuous flow,   1400
Stem we the rolling surge of chance!
There may alternate weal and woe,
Success and failure, as they can,
Mingle and shift in changeful dance!
Excitement is the sphere for man.   1405

MEPHISTOPHELES.

Nor goal, nor measure is prescribed to you.
If you desire to taste of everything,

To snatch at joy while on the wing,
May your career amuse and profit too!
Only fall to and don't be over coy!   1410

FAUST.

Hearken!   The end I aim at is not joy;
I crave excitement, agonizing bliss,
Enamored hatred, quickening vexation.
Purged from the love of knowledge, my vocation,
The scope of all my powers henceforth be this,   1415
To bare my breast to every pang, — to know
In my heart's core all human weal and woe,
To grasp in thought the lofty and the deep,
Men's various fortunes on my breast to heap,
And thus to theirs dilate my individual mind,   1420
And share at length with them the shipwreck of man-
    kind.

MEPHISTOPHELES.

Oh, credit me, who still as ages roll,
Have chewed this bitter fare from year to year,
No mortal, from the cradle to the bier,
Digests the ancient leaven!   Know, this whole   1425
Doth for the Deity alone subsist!
He in eternal brightness doth exist,
Us unto darkness he hath brought, and here
Where day and night alternate, is your sphere.

FAUST.

But 'tis my will!

MEPHISTOPHELES.

       Well spoken, I admit!   1430
But one thing puzzles me, my friend;
Time's short, art long; methinks 'twere fit
That you to friendly counsel should attend.
A poet choose as your ally!
Let him thought's wide dominion sweep,   1435
Each good and noble quality,
Upon your honored brow to heap;
The lion's magnanimity,
The fleetness of the hind,
The fiery blood of Italy,   1440
The North's more steadfast mind!

Let him to you the mystery show
To blend high aims and cunning low;
And while youth's passions are aflame
To fall in love by rule and plan!   1445
I fain would meet with such a man;
Would him Sir Microcosmus name.

FAUST.

What then am I, if I aspire in vain
The crown of our humanity to gain,
Towards which my every sense doth strain?   1450

MEPHISTOPHELES.

Thou'rt after all — just what thou art.
Put on thy head a wig with countless locks,
Raise to a cubit's height thy learned socks,
Still thou remainest ever, what thou art.

FAUST.

I feel it, I have heaped upon my brain   1455
The gathered treasure of man's thought in vain;
And when at length from studious toil I rest,
No power, new-born, springs up within my breast;
A hair's breadth is not added to my height,
I am no nearer to the infinite.   1460

MEPHISTOPHELES.

Good sir, these things you view indeed,
Just as by other men they're viewed;
We must more cleverly proceed,
Before life's joys our grasp elude.
The devil! thou hast hands and feet,   1465
And head and back are also thine;
What I enjoy with relish sweet,
Is it on that account less mine?
If for six stallions I can pay,
Do I not own their strength and speed?   1470
A proper man I dash away,
As their two dozen legs were mine indeed.
Up then, from idle pondering free,
And forth into the world with me!
I tell you what; — your speculative churl   1475
Is like a beast which some ill spirit leads,

On barren wilderness, in ceaseless whirl,
While all around lie fair and verdant meads.

FAUST.

But how shall we begin?

MEPHISTOPHELES.

    We will go hence with speed,
A place of torment this indeed!   1480
A precious life, thyself to bore,
And some few youngsters evermore!
Leave it to neighbor Paunch; — withdraw,
Why wilt thou plague thyself with thrashing straw?
The very best that thou dost know   1485
Thou dar'st not to the striplings show.
One in the passage now doth wait!

FAUST.

I'm in no mood to see him now.

MEPHISTOPHELES.

Poor lad! He must be tired, I trow;
He must not go disconsolate.   1490
Hand me thy cap and gown; the mask
Will set me off in glorious state.

       (He changes his dress.)
Now leave it to my wit! I ask
But quarter of an hour; meanwhile equip,
And make all ready for our pleasant trip! 1495
       (Exit FAUST.*)*

MEPHISTOPHELES (*in* FAUST'S *long gown*).

Mortal! the loftiest attributes of men,
Reason and Knowledge, only thus contemn,
Still let the Prince of lies, without control,
With shows and mocking charms delude thy soul,
I have thee unconditionally then! —   1500
Faith hath endowed him with an ardent mind,
Which unrestrained still presses on for ever,
And whose precipitate endeavor
Earth's joys o'erleaping, leaveth them behind.
Him will I drag through life's wild waste, 1505

Through scenes of vapid dullness, where at last
Bewildered, he shall falter, and stick fast;
And, still to mock his greedy haste,
Viands and drink shall float his craving lips beyond —
Vainly he'll seek refreshment, anguish-tost, 1510
And were he not the devil's by his bond,
Yet must his soul infallibly be lost!

A STUDENT enters.[24]

STUDENT.

But recently I've quitted home,
Full of devotion am I come
A man to know and hear, whose name 1515
With reverence is known to fame.

MEPHISTOPHELES.

Your courtesy much flatters me!
A man like other men you see;
Pray have you yet applied elsewhere?

STUDENT.

I would entreat your friendly care! 1520
I've youthful blood and courage high;
Of gold I bring a fair supply;
To let me go my mother was not fain;
But here I longed true knowledge to attain,

MEPHISTOPHELES.

You've hit upon the very place. 1525

STUDENT.

And yet my steps I would retrace.
These walls, this melancholy room,
O'erpower me with a sense of gloom;
The space is narrow, nothing green,
No friendly tree is to be seen: 1530
And in these halls, with benches lined,
Sight, hearing fail, fails too my mind.

MEPHISTOPHELES.

It all depends on habit. Thus at first
The infant takes not kindly to the breast,
But before long, its eager thirst 1535

Is fain to slake with hearty zest:
Thus at the breasts of wisdom day by day
With keener relish you'll your thirst allay.

STUDENT.

Upon her neck I fain would hang with joy;
To reach it, say, what means must I employ?　　　1540

MEPHISTOPHELES.

Explain ere further time we lose,
What special faculty you choose?

STUDENT.

Profoundly learned I would grow,
What heaven contains would comprehend,
O'er earth's wide realm my gaze extend,　　　1545
Nature and science I desire to know.

MEPHISTOPHELES.

You are upon the proper track, I find,
Take heed, let nothing dissipate your mind.

STUDENT.

My heart and soul are in the chase!
Though to be sure I fain would seize,　　　1550
On pleasant summer holidays,
A little liberty and careless ease.

MEPHISTOPHELES.

Use well your time, so rapidly it flies;
Method will teach you time to win;
Hence, my young friend, I would advise,　　　1555
With college logic to begin!
Then will your mind be so well braced,
In Spanish boots so tightly laced,
That on 'twill circumspectly creep,
Thought's beaten track securely keep,　　　1560
Nor will it ignis-fatuus like,
Into the path of error strike.
Then many a day they'll teach you how
The mind's spontaneous acts, till now
As eating and as drinking free,　　　1565
Require a process;—one! two! three!

In truth the subtle web of thought
Is like the weaver's fabric wrought:
One treadle moves a thousand lines,
Swift dart the shuttles to and fro,   1570
Unseen the threads together flow,
A thousand knots one stroke combines.
Then forward steps your sage to show,
And prove to you, it must be so;
The first being so, and so the second.   1575
The third and fourth deduced we see;
And if there were no first and second,
Nor third nor fourth would ever be.
This, scholars of all countries prize,—
Yet 'mong themselves no weavers rise.   1580
He who would know and treat of aught alive,
Seeks first the living spirit thence to drive:
Then are the lifeless fragments in his hand,
There only fails, alas! the spirit-band.
This process, chemists name, in learned thesis,   1585
Mocking themselves, *Naturæ encheiresis.*

STUDENT.

Your words I cannot fully comprehend.

MEPHISTOPHELES.

In a short time you will improve, my friend,
When of scholastic forms you learn the use;
And how by method all things to reduce.   1590

STUDENT.

All this my brain does so confound,
As if a mill-wheel there were turning round.

MEPHISTOPHELES.

And next, before aught else you learn,
You must with zeal to metaphysics turn!
There see that you profoundly comprehend,   1595
What doth the limit of man's brain transcend;
For that which is or is not in the head
A sounding phase will serve you in good stead.
But before all, strive this half year,

From one fixed order ne'er to swerve!   1600
Five lectures daily you must hear;
The hour still punctually observe!
Yourself with studious zeal prepare,
And closely in your manual look,
Hereby may you be quite aware   1605
That all he utters standeth in the book;
Yet write away without cessation,
As at the Holy Ghost's dictation!

STUDENT.

This, sir, a second time you need not say!
Your counsel I appreciate quite;   1610
What we possess in black and white,
We can in peace and comfort bear away.

MEPHISTOPHELES.

A faculty, I pray you, name.

STUDENT.

For jurisprudence some distaste I own.

MEPHISTOPHELES.

To me this branch of science is well known,   1615
And hence I cannot your repugnance blame.
Customs and laws in every place,
Like a disease, an heirloom dread,
Still trail their curse from race to race,
And furtively abroad they spread.   1620
To nonsense, reason's self they turn;
Beneficence becomes a pest;
Woe unto thee, that thou'rt a grandson born!
As for the law born with us, unexpressed; —
That law, alas, none careth to discern.   1625

STUDENT.

You deepen my dislike. The youth
Whom you instruct, is blest in sooth.
To try theology I feel inclined.

MEPHISTOPHELES.

I would not lead you willingly astray,
But as regards this science, you will find,   1630
So hard it is to shun the erring way,

And so much hidden poison lies therein,
Which scarce can you discern from medicine.
Here too it is the best to listen but to one,
And by the master's words to swear alone.   1635
To sum up all — To words hold fast !
Then the safe gate securely pass'd,
You'll reach the fane of certainty at last.

STUDENT.

But then some meaning must the words convey.

MEPHISTOPHELES.

Right ! but o'er-anxious thought, you'll find of no avail,
For there precisely where ideas fail,   1641
A word comes opportunely into play.
Most admirable weapons words are found,
On words a system we securely ground,
In words we can conveniently believe,
Nor of a single jot can we a word bereave.   1645

STUDENT.

Your pardon for my importunity ;
Yet once more must I trouble you :
On medicine, I'll thank you to supply
A pregnant utterance or two !   1650
Three years ! how brief the appointed tide !
The field, heaven knows, is all too wide !
If but a friendly hint be thrown,
'Tis easier then to feel one's way.

MEPHISTOPHELES (aside).

I'm weary of the dry pedantic tone,   1655
And must again the genuine devil play.

(Aloud).

Of medicine the spirit's caught with ease,
The great and little world you study through,
That things may then their course pursue,
As heaven may please.   1660
In vain abroad you range through science' ample space,
Each man learns only that which learn he can ;
Who knows the moment to embrace,
He is your proper man.

In person you are tolerably made,   1665
Nor in assurance will you be deficient:
Self-confidence acquire, be not afraid,
Others will then esteem you a proficient.
Learn chiefly with the sex to deal!
Their thousand ahs and ohs,   1670
These the sage doctor knows,
He only from one point can heal.
Assume a decent tone of courteous ease,
You have them then to humor as you please.
First a diploma must belief infuse,   1675
That you in your profession take the lead:
You then at once those easy freedoms use
For which another many a year must plead;
Learn how to feel with nice address
The dainty wrist; — and how to press,   1680
With ardent furtive glance, the slender waist, 25
To feel how tightly it is laced.

STUDENT.

There is some sense in that! one sees the how and why.

MEPHISTOPHELES.

Gray is, young friend, all theory:
And green of life the golden tree.   1685

STUDENT.

I swear it seemeth like a dream to me.
May I some future time repeat my visit,
To hear on what your wisdom grounds your views?

MEPHISTOPHELES.

Command my humble service when you choose.

STUDENT.

Ere I retire, one boon I must solicit: 1690
Here is my album, do not, Sir, deny
This token of your favor!

MEPHISTOPHELES.
Willingly!
(He writes and returns the book.)

STUDENT (*reads*).
ERITIS SICUT DEUS, SCIENTES BONUM ET MALUM.
(*He reverently closes the book and retires*).

MEPHISTOPHELES.
Let but this ancient proverb be your rule,
My cousin follow still, the wily snake,   1695
And with your likeness to the gods, poor fool,
Ere long be sure your poor sick heart will quake!

FAUST (*enters*).
Whither away?

MEPHISTOPHELES.
      'Tis thine our course to steer.
The little world, and then the great we'll view.
With what delight, what profit too.   1700
Thou'lt revel through thy gay career!

FAUST.
Despite my length of beard I need [26]
The easy manners that insure success;
Th' attempt I fear can ne'er succeed;
To mingle in the world I want address;   1705
I still have an embarrassed air, and then
I feel myself so small with other men.

MEPHISTOPHELES.
Time, my good friend, will all that's needful give;
Be only self-possessed, and thou hast learnt to live.

FAUST.
But how are we to start, I pray?
Steeds, servants, carriage, where are they?   1710

MEPHISTOPHELES.
We've but to spread this mantle wide,
'Twill serve whereon through air to ride,
No heavy baggage need you take,
When we our bold excursion make,   1715
A little gas, which I will soon prepare,
Lifts us from earth; aloft through air,
Light laden, we shall swiftly steer; —
I wish you joy of your new life-career.

Auerbach's Cellar in Leipzig.
(A DRINKING PARTY.)

FROSCH.

No drinking? Naught a laugh to raise ? 1720
None of your gloomy looks, I pray !
You, who so bright were wont to blaze,
Are dull as wetted straw to-day.

BRANDER.

'Tis all your fault ; your part ye do not bear,
No beastliness, no folly. 1725

FROSCH

(*pours a glass of wine over his head*).
There,
You have them both !

BRANDER.
You double beast !

FROSCH.
'Tis what you asked me for, at least !

SIEBEL.
Whoever quarrels, turn him out !
With open throat drink, roar, and shout.
Hollo ! Hollo ! Ho ! 1730

ALTMAYER.
Zounds, fellow, cease your deaf'ning cheers !
Bring cotton wool ! He splits my ears.

SIEBEL.
'Tis when the roof rings back the tone,
Then first the full power of the bass is known.

FROSCH.
Right ! out with him who takes offence ! 1735
A tara lara la !

ALTMAYER.
A tara lara la !

FROSCH.
Our throats are tuned. Come, let's commence.

(*Sings.*)
The holy Roman empire now,
How holds it still together?   1740

BRANDER.

An ugly song! a song political!
A song offensive! Thank God, every morn
To rule the Roman empire, that you were not born!
I bless my stars at least that mine is not
Either a kaiser's or a chancellor's lot.   1745
Yet 'mong ourselves should one still lord it o'er the rest;
That we elect a pope I now suggest.
Ye know, what quality ensures
A man's success, his rise secures.

FROSCH (*sings*).

Bear, lady nightingale above, [27]   1750
Ten thousand greetings to my love.

SIEBEL.

No greetings to a sweetheart! No love-songs shall
          there be!

FROSCH.

Love-greetings and love-kisses! Thou shalt not hinder
          me!

(*Sings.*)
Undo the bolt! in stilly night,
Undo the bolt! thy love's awake!   1755
Shut to the bolt! with morning light —

SIEBEL.

Ay, sing away, sing on, her praises sound ; — the snake!
My turn to laugh will come some day.
Me hath she jilted once, you the same trick she'll play.
Some gnome her lover be! where cross-roads meet,
With her to play the fool; or old he-goat,   1760
From Blocksberg coming in swift gallop, bleat
A good night to her, from his hairy throat!
A proper lad of genuine flesh and blood,
Is for the damsel far too good;   1765
The greeting she shall have from me,
To smash her window-panes will be!

BRANDER (*striking on the table*).

Silence!   Attend! to me give ear!
Confess, sirs, I know how to live:
Some love-sick folk are sitting here!   1770
Hence, 'tis but fit, their hearts to cheer,
That I a good-night strain to them should give.
Hark! of the newest fashion is my song!
Strike boldly in the chorus, clear and strong!

(*He sings.*)

Once in a cellar lived a rat,   1775
He feasted there on butter,
Until his paunch became as fat
As that of Doctor Luther.
The cook laid poison for the guest,
Then was his heart with pangs oppressed, 1780
As if his frame love wasted.[28]

CHORUS (*shouting*).

As if his frame love wasted.

BRANDER.

He ran around, he ran abroad,
Of every puddle drinking.
The house with rage he scratched and gnawed,
In vain, — he fast was sinking;   1786
Full many an anguished bound he gave,
Nothing the hapless brute could save,
As if his frame love wasted.

CHORUS.

As if his frame love wasted.   1790

BRANDER.

By torture driven, in open day,
The kitchen he invaded,
Convulsed upon the hearth he lay,
With anguish sorely jaded;
The poisoner laughed, Ha! ha! quoth she, 1795
His life is ebbing fast, I see,
As if his frame love wasted.

CHORUS.

As if his frame love wasted.

SIEBEL.

How the dull boors exulting shout!
Poison for the poor rats to strew   1800
A fine exploit it is, no doubt.

BRANDER.

They, as it seems, stand well with you!

ALTMAYER.

Old bald-pate! with the paunch profound!
The rat's mishap hath tamed his nature;
For he his counterpart hath found   1805
Depicted in the swollen creature.

FAUST AND MEPHISTOPHELES.

MEPHISTOPHELES.

I now must introduce to you
Before aught else, this jovial crew,
To show how lightly life may glide away;
With the folk here each day's a holiday.   1810
With little wit and much content,
Each on his own small round intent,
Like sportive kitten with its tail;
While no sick-headache they bewail,
And while their host will credit give,   1815
Joyous and free from care they live.

BRANDER.

They're off a journey, that is clear, —
They look so strange; they've scarce been here
An hour.

FROSCH.

      You're right!   Leipzig's the place for me!
'Tis quite a little Paris; people there   1820
Acquire a certain easy finished air.

SIEBEL.

What take you now these travellers to be?

FROSCH.

Let me alone!   O'er a full glass you'll see,
As easily I'll worm their secret out,
As draw an infant's tooth.   I've not a doubt   1825
That my two gentlemen are nobly born,
They look dissatisfied and full of scorn.

BRANDER.

They are but mountebanks, I'll lay a bet!

ALTMAYER.

Most like.

FROSCH.

Mark me, I'll screw it from them yet.

MEPHISTOPHELES (*to* FAUST).

These fellows would not scent the devil out,   1830
E'en though he had them by the very throat!

FAUST.

Good-morrow, gentlemen!

SIEBEL.

Thanks for your fair salute.
(*Aside, glancing at* MEPHISTOPHELES.)
How! goes the fellow on a halting foot?

MEPHISTOPHELES.

Is it permitted here with you to sit?
Then though good wine is not forthcoming here, 1835
Good company at least our hearts will cheer.

ALTMAYER.

A dainty gentleman, no doubt of it.

FROSCH.

You're doubtless recently from Rippach?   Pray,[29]
Did you with Master Hans there chance to sup?

MEPHISTOPHELES.

To-day we pass'd him, but we did not stop!   1840
When last we met him he had much to say
Touching his cousins, and to each he sent
Full many a greeting and kind compliment.
(*With an inclination towards* FROSCH.)

ALTMAYER (*aside to* FROSCH).

You have it there!

SIEBEL.

Faith! he's a knowing one!

FROSCH.

Have patience! I will show him up anon!　　1845

MEPHISTOPHELES.

Unless I err, as we drew near
We heard some practised voices pealing.
A song must admirably here
Re-echo from this vaulted ceiling!

FROSCH.

That you're an amateur one plainly sees!　　1850

MEPHISTOPHELES.

Oh no, though strong the love, I cannot boast much skill.

ALTMAYER.

Give us a song!

MEPHISTOPHELES.

As many as you will.

SIEBEL.

But be it a brand new one, if you please!

MEPHISTOPHELES.

But recently returned from Spain are we,
The pleasant land of wine and minstrelsy.　　1855

(*Sings.*)
A king there was once reigning,
Who had a goodly flea —

FROSCH.

Hark! did you rightly catch the words? a flea!
An odd sort of a guest he needs must be.

MEPHISTOPHELES (*sings*).
A king there was once reigning,　　1860
Who had a goodly flea,
Him loved he without feigning,
As his own son were he!

His tailor then he summoned,
The tailor to him goes:　　　　　　　1865
Now measure me the youngster
For jerkin and for hose!

BRANDER.

Take proper heed, the tailor strictly charge,
The nicest measurement to take,
And as he loves his head, to make　　　1870
The hose quite smooth and not too large!

MEPHISTOPHELES.

In satin and in velvet,
Behold the younker dressed;
Bedizened o'er with ribbons,
A cross upon his breast.　　　　　　　1875
Prime minister they made him,
He wore a star of state;
And all his poor relations
Were courtiers, rich and great.

The gentlemen and ladies　　　　　　1880
At court were sore distressed;
The queen and all her maidens
Were bitten by the pest,
And yet they dared not scratch them,
Or chase the fleas away.　　　　　　　1885
If we are bit, we catch them,
And crack without delay.

CHORUS (*shouting*).

If we are bit, etc.

FROSCH.

Bravo! That's the song for me.

SIEBEL.

Such be the fate of every flea!　　　　1890

BRANDER.

With clever finger catch and kill.

ALTMAYER.

Hurrah for wine and freedom still!

MEPHISTOPHELES.

Were but your wine a trifle better, friend,
A glass to freedom I would gladly drain.

SIEBEL.

You'd better not repeat those words again !   1895

MEPHISTOPHELES.

I am afraid the landlord to offend;
Else freely would I treat each worthy guest
From our own cellar to the very best.

SIEBEL.

Out with it then !   Your doings I'll defend.

FROSCH.

Give a good glass, and straight we'll praise you, one and
        all.   1900
Only let not your samples be too small ;
For if my judgment you desire,
Certes, an ample mouthful I require.

ALTMAYER (*aside*).

I guess, they're from the Rhenish land.

MEPHISTOPHELES.

Fetch me a gimlet here !

BRANDER.

        Say, what therewith to bore ?
You cannot have the wine-casks at the door?   1905

ALTMAYER.

Our landlord's tool-basket behind doth yonder stand.

MEPHISTOPHELES (*takes the gimlet*).
(*To* FROSCH).

Now only say ! what liquor will you take ?

FROSCH.

How mean you that ? have you of every sort?

MEPHISTOPHELES.

Each may his own selection make.   1910

ALTMAYER (*to* FROSCH).

Ha! Ha! You lick your lips already at the thought.

FROSCH.

Good, if I have my choice, the Rhenish I propose;
For still the fairest gifts the fatherland bestows.

MEPHISTOPHELES

(*boring a hole in the edge of the table opposite to where*
FROSCH *is sitting*).
Get me a little wax — and make some stoppers —
    quick!

ALTMAYER.

Why, this is nothing but a juggler's trick!   1915

MEPHISTOPHELES (*to* BRANDER).

And you?

BRANDER.

        Champagne's the wine for me;
Right brisk, and sparkling let it be!

(MEPHISTOPHELES *bores, one of the party has in the
    meantime prepared the wax-stoppers and stopped
    the holes.*)

BRANDER.

What foreign is one always can't decline,
What's good is often scattered far apart.
The French your genuine German hates with all his
    heart,
Yet has a relish for their wine.   1921

SIEBEL

(*as* MEPHISTOPHELES *approaches him*).
I like not acid wine, I must allow,
Give me a glass of genuine sweet!

MEPHISTOPHELES (*bores*).

        Tokay
Shall, if you wish it, flow without delay.

ALTMAYER.

Come! look me in the face! no fooling now!   1925
You are but making fun of us, I trow.

MEPHISTOPHELES.

Ah! ah! that would indeed be making free

With such distinguished guests. Come, no delay ;
What liquor can I serve you with, I pray ?

ALTMAYER.

Only be quick, it matters not to me.
  (*After the holes are all bored and stopped*) 1930

MEPHISTOPHELES (*with strange gestures*).

 Grapes the vine-stock bears,
 Horns the buck-goat wears !
 Wine is sap, the vine is wood,
 The wooden board yields wine as good.
 With a deeper glance and true 1935
 The mysteries of nature view !
 Have faith and here's a miracle !
 Your stoppers draw and drink your fill !

ALL

(*as they draw the stoppers and the wine chosen by each
 runs into his glass*).
Oh, beauteous spring, which flows so fair !

MEPHISTOPHELES.

Spill not a single drop, of this beware ! 1940
  (*They drink repeatedly.*)

ALL (*sing*).

 Happy as cannibals are we,
 Or as five hundred swine.

MEPHISTOPHELES.

They're in their glory, mark their elevation !

FAUST.

Let's hence, nor here our stay prolong.

MEPHISTOPHELES.

Attend, of brutishness ere long 1945
You'll see a glorious revelation.

SIEBEL

(*drinks carelessly; the wine is spilt upon the ground,
 and turns to flame*).
Help ! fire ! help ! Hell is burning !

MEPHISTOPHELES
(addressing the flames).
Stop,
Kind element, be still, I say!
(To the company.)
Of purgatorial fire as yet 'tis but a drop.

SIEBEL.
What means the knave!   For this you'll dearly pay!
Us, it appears, you do not know. 1950

FROSCH.
Such tricks a second time let him not show!

ALTMAYER.
Methinks 'twere well we packed him quietly away.

SIEBEL.
What, sir! with us your hocus-pocus play!

MEPHISTOPHELES.
Silence, old wine-cask!

SIEBEL.
How! add insult, too! 1955
Vile broomstick!

BRANDER.
Hold! or blows shall rain on you!

ALTMAYER
*(draws a stopper out of the table; fire springs
out against him).*
I burn! I burn!

SIEBEL.
'Tis sorcery, I vow!
Strike home! The fellow is fair game, I trow!
(They draw their knives and attack MEPHISTOPHELES).

MEPHISTOPHELES *(with solemn gestures).*
Visionary scenes appear!
Words delusive cheat the ear! 1960
Be ye there, and be ye here!
(They stand amazed and gaze on each other).

ALTMAYER.

Where am I?   What a beauteous land ! 30

FROSCH.

Vineyards! unless my sight deceives!

SIEBEL.

And clustering grapes too, close at hand!

BRANDER.

And underneath the spreading leaves,   1965
What stems there be!   What grapes I see!
    (*He seizes* SIEBEL *by the nose.   The others recip-*
    rocally do the same, and raise their knives).

MEPHISTOPHELES (*as above*).

Delusion, from their eyes the bandage take!
Note how the devil loves a jest to break !
    (*He disappears with* FAUST, *the fellows draw back*
    from one another.)

SIEBEL.

What was it?

ALTMAYER.

How?

FROSCH.

Was that your nose?

BRANDER (*to* SIEBEL).

And look, my hand doth thine enclose!   1970

ALTMAYER.

I felt a shock, it went through every limb!
A chair! I'm fainting! all things swim!

FROSCH.

Say what has happened, what's it all about?

SIEBEL.

Where is the fellow?   Could I scent him out,
His body from his soul I'd soon divide!   1975

ALTMAYER.

With my own eyes, upon a cask astride,
Forth through the cellar-door I saw him ride ——
Heavy as lead my feet are growing.

(*Turning to the table.*)
Would that the wine again were flowing!

SIEBEL.

'Twas all delusion, cheat and lie.   1980

FROSCH.

Twas wine I drank, most certainly.

BRANDER.

What of the grapes, too, — where are they?

ALTMAYER.

Who now will miracles gainsay?

WITCHES' KITCHEN. [31]

*A large caldron hangs over the fire on a low hearth;
various figures appear in the vapor arising from
it. A* FEMALE MONKEY *sits beside the caldron to
skim it, and watch that it does not boil over. The*
MALE MONKEY *with the young ones is seated
near, warming himself. The walls and ceiling are
adorned with the strangest articles of witch-furni-
ture.*

FAUST. MEPHISTOPHELES.

FAUST.

This senseless, juggling witchcraft I detest!
Dost promise that in this foul nest   1985
Of madness, I shall be restored?
Must I seek counsel from an ancient dame?
And can she, by these rites abhorred,
Take thirty winters from my frame?
Woe's me, if thou naught better canst suggest!   1990
Hope has already fled my breast.
Has neither nature nor a noble mind
A balsam yet devised of any kind?

MEPHISTOPHELES.

My friend, you now speak sensibly. In truth,
Nature a method giveth to renew thy youth: 1995
But in another book the lesson's writ; —
It forms a curious chapter, I admit.

FAUST.

I fain would know it.

MEPHISTOPHELES.

Good! a remedy
Without physician, gold, or sorcery:
Away forthwith, and to the fields repair, 2000
Begin to delve, to cultivate the ground,
Thy senses and thyself confine
Within the very narrowest round,
Support thyself upon the simplest fare,
Live like a very brute the brutes among, 2005
Neither esteem it robbery
The acre thou dost reap, thyself to dung
This the best method, credit me,
Again at eighty to grow hale and young.

FAUST.

I am not used to it, nor can myself degrade 2010
So far, as in my hand to take the spade.
For this mean life my spirit soars too high.

MEPHISTOPHELES.

Then must we to the witch apply!

FAUST.

Will none but this old beldame do?
Canst not thyself the potion brew? 2015

MEPHISTOPHELES.

A pretty play our leisure to beguile!
A thousand bridges I could build meanwhile.
Not science only and consummate art,
Patience must also bear her part. 2020
A quiet spirit worketh whole years long;
Time only makes the subtle ferment strong;
And all things that belong thereto,
Are wondrous and exceeding rare!
The devil taught her, it is true;
But yet the draught the devil can't prepare. 2025
(*Perceiving the beasts.*)
Look yonder, a dainty pair!
Here is the maid! the knave is there!

(*To the beasts.*)
It seems your dame is not at home?

THE MONKEYS.

Gone to carouse,
Out of the house,   2030
Thro' the chimney and away!

MEPHISTOPHELES.

How long is it her wont to roam?

THE MONKEYS.

While we can warm our paws she'll stay.

MEPHISTOPHELES (*to* FAUST).

What think you of the charming creatures?

FAUST.

I loathe alike their form and features!   2035

MEPHISTOPHELES.

Nay, such discourse, be it confessed,
Is just the thing that pleases me the best.

(*To the* MONKEYS.)

Tell me, ye whelps, accursed crew!
What stir ye in the broth about?

MONKEYS.

Coarse beggar's gruel here we stew. [32]   2040

MEPHISTOPHELES.

Of customers you'll have a rout.

THE HE-MONKEY

(*approaching and fawning on* MEPHISTOPHELES).

Quick! quick! throw the dice,
Make me rich in a trice,
Oh, give me the prize!
Alas, for myself!   2045
Had I plenty of pelf,
I then should be wise.

MEPHISTOPHELES.

How blest the ape would think himself, if he
Could only put into the lottery!

(*In the meantime the young* MONKEYS *have been playing with a large globe, which they roll forwards.*)

THE HE-MONKEY.

The world behold! 2050
Unceasingly rolled,
It riseth and falleth ever;
It ringeth like glass!
How brittle, alas!
'Tis hollow, and resteth never. 2055
How bright the sphere,
Still brighter here!
Now living am I!
Dear son, beware!
Nor venture there! 2060
Thou too must die!
It is of clay;
'Twill crumble away;
There fragments lie.

MEPHISTOPHELES.

Of what use is the sieve? 2065

THE HE-MONKEY (*taking it down*).

The sieve would show, [33]
If thou wert a thief or no?

(*He runs to the* SHE-MONKEY, *and makes her look
through it.*)

Look through the sieve!
Dost know him, the thief,
And dar'st thou not call him so? 2070

MEPHISTOPHELES (*approaching the fire*).

And then this pot?

THE MONKEYS.

The half-witted sot!
He knows not the pot!
He knows not the kettle!

MEPHISTOPHELES.

Unmannerly beast!   2075
Be civil at least!

THE HE-MONKEY.

Take the whisk and sit down in the settle!
(*He makes* MEPHISTOPHELES *sit down*).

FAUST.

(*Who all this time has been standing before a looking-
glass, now approaching, and now retiring from it.*)

What do I see? what form, whose charms transcend
The loveliness of earth, is mirrored here!
O Love, to waft me to her sphere,   2080
To me the swiftest of thy pinions lend!
Alas! If I remain not rooted to this place,
If to approach more near I'm fondly lured,
Her image fades, in veiling mist obscured!—
Model of beauty both in form and face!   2085
Is't possible? Hath woman charms so rare?
Is this recumbent form, supremely fair,
The very essence of all heavenly grace?
Can aught so exquisite on earth be found?

MEPHISTOPHELES.

The six days' labor of a god, my friend,   2090
Who doth himself cry bravo, at the end,
By something clever doubtless should be crowned.
For this time gaze your fill, and when you please
Just such a prize for you I can provide;
How blest is he to whom kind fate decrees,   2095
To take her to his home, a lovely bride!

(FAUST *continues to gaze into the mirror.* MEPHISTO-
PHELES, *stretching himself on the settle and playing
with the whisk, continues to speak.*)

Here sit I, like a king upon his throne;
My sceptre this; — the crown I want alone.

THE MONKEYS

*(who have hitherto been making all sorts of strange gest-
ures, bring* MEPHISTOPHELES *a crown, with loud
cries).*

> Oh, be so good,
> With sweat and with blood   2100
> The crown to lime!

*(They handle the crown awkwardly and break it in two
pieces, with which they skip about.)*

> 'Twas fate's decree!
> We speak and see!
> We hear and rhyme.

FAUST *(before the mirror).*

Woe's me! well-nigh distraught I feel.   2105

MEPHISTOPHELES

(pointing to the beasts).

And even my own head almost begins to reel,

THE MONKEYS.

> If good luck attend,
> If fitly things blend,
> Our jargon with thought
> And with reason is fraught!   2110

FAUST *(as above).*

A flame is kindled in my breast!
Let us begone! nor linger here!

MEPHISTOPHELES

(in the same position).

It now at least must be confessed,
That poets sometimes are sincere,

> *(The caldron which the* SHE-MONKEY *has neglected,
> begins to boil over; a great flame arises, which
> streams up the chimney. The* WITCH *comes
> down the chimney with horrible cries.)*

THE WITCH.

Ough! ough! ough! ough!   2115
Accursed brute! accursed sow!
Thou dost neglect the pot, for shame!
Accursed brute to scorch the dame!

(*Perceiving* FAUST *and* MEPHISTOPHELES.)

  Whom have we here?
  Who's sneaking here?   2120
  Whence are ye come?
  With what desire?
  The plague of fire
  Your bones consume!

(*She dips the skimming-ladle into the caldron and throws flames at* FAUST, MEPHISTOPHELES, *and the* MONKEYS. *The* MONKEYS *whimper.*)

MEPHISTOPHELES

(*twirling the whisk which he holds in his hand, and striking among the glasses and pots.*)

  Dash! Smash!   2125
  There lies the glass!
  There lies the slime!
  'Tis but a jest;
  I but keep time,
  Thou hellish pest,   2130
  To thine own chime!

(*While the* WITCH *steps back in rage and astonishment.*)

Dost know me! Skeleton! Vile scarecrow, thou!
Thy lord and master dost thou know?
What holds me, that I deal not now
Thee and thine apes a stunning blow?   2135
No more respect to my red vest dost pay?
Does my cock's feather no allegiance claim?
Have I my visage masked to-day?
Must I be forced myself to name?

THE WITCH.

Master, forgive this rude salute!   2140
But I perceive no cloven foot.
And your two ravens, where are they?

MEPHISTOPHELES.

This once I must admit your plea; —
For truly I must own that we
Each other have not seen for many a day.   2145
The culture, too, that shapes the world, at last

Hath e'en the devil in its sphere embraced;
The northern phantom from the scene hath pass'd,
Tail, talons, horns, are nowhere to be traced!
As for the foot, with which I can't dispense,　　2150
'Twould injure me in company, and hence,
Like many a youthful cavalier,
False calves I now have worn for many a year.

THE WITCH (dancing).

I am beside myself with joy,
To see once more the gallant Satan here!　　2155

MEPHISTOPHELES.

Woman, no more that name employ!

THE WITCH.

But why? what mischief hath it done?

MEPHISTOPHELES.

To fable it too long hath appertained;
But people from the change have nothing won.
Rid of the evil one, the evil has remained.[34]　　2160
Lord Baron call thou me, so is the matter good;
Of other cavaliers the mien I wear.
Dost make no question of my gentle blood;
See here, this is the scutcheon that I bear!
(He makes an unseemly gesture.)[35]

THE WITCH
(laughing immoderately).

Ha! Ha! Just like myself! You are, I ween, 2165
The same mad wag that you have ever been!

MEPHISTOPHELES (to FAUST).

My friend, learn this to understand, I pray!
To deal with witches this is still the way.

THE WITCH.

Now tell me, gentlemen, what you desire?

MEPHISTOPHELES.

Of your known juice a goblet we require.　　2170
But for the very oldest let me ask;
Double its strength with years doth grow.

THE WITCH.

Most willingly! And here I have a flask,
From which I've sipped myself ere now;
What's more, it doth no longer stink; 2175
To you a glass I joyfully will give.

(*Aside.*)

If unprepared, however, this man drink,
He hath not, as you know, an hour to live.

MEPHISTOPHELES.

He's my good friend, with whom 'twill prosper well;
I grudge him not the choicest of thy store. 2180
Now draw thy circle, speak thy spell,
And straight a bumper for him pour!

> (*The* WITCH, *with extraordinary gestures, de-
> scribes a circle, and places strange things
> within it. The glasses meanwhile begin to
> ring, the caldron to sound, and to make
> music. Lastly, she brings a great book;
> places the* MONKEYS *in the circle to serve
> her as a desk, and to hold the torches. She
> beckons* FAUST *to approach.*)

FAUST (*to* MEPHISTOPHELES).

Tell me, to what doth all this tend?
Where will these frantic gestures end?
This loathsome cheat, this senseless stuff 2185
I've known and hated long enough.

MEPHISTOPHELES.

Mere mummery, a laugh to raise!
Pray don't be so fastidious! She
But as a leech, her hocus-pocus plays,
That well with you her potion may agree. 2190
(*He compels* FAUST *to enter the circle.*)

> (*The* WITCH, *with great emphasis, begins to
> declaim from the book.*)

This must thou ken:
Of one make ten,
Pass two, and then

Make square the three,
So rich thou'lt be.   2195
Drop out the four!
From five and six,
Thus says the witch,
Make seven and eight.
So all is straight!   2200
And nine is one,
And ten is none,
This is the witch's one-time-one! [36]

FAUST.

The hag doth as in fever rave.

MEPHISTOPHELES.

To these will follow many a stave.   2205
I know it well, so rings the book throughout;
Much time I've lost in puzzling o'er its pages,
For downright paradox, no doubt,
A mystery remains alike to fools and sages.
Ancient the art and modern too, my friend.   2210
'Tis still the fashion as it used to be,
Error instead of truth abroad to send
By means of three and one, and one and three.
'Tis ever taught and babbled in the schools.
Who'd take the trouble to dispute with fools?   2215
When words men hear, in sooth, they usually believe
That there must needs therein be something to conceive.

THE WITCH (continues).

The lofty power
Of wisdom's dower,
From all the world conceal'd!   2220
Who thinketh not,
To him I wot,
Unsought it is revealed.

FAUST.

What nonsense doth the hag propound?
My brain it doth well-nigh confound.   2225
A hundred thousand fools or more,
Methinks I hear in chorus roar.

MEPHISTOPHELES.

Incomparable Sibyl, cease, I pray!
Hand us thy liquor without more delay.
And to the very brim the goblet crown!   2230
My friend he is, and need not be afraid;
Besides, he is a man of many a grade,
Who oft hath drunk good draughts.
(*The* WITCH, *with many ceremonies, pours the liquor
    into a cup; as* FAUST *lifts it to his mouth, a
    light flame arises.*)

MEPHISTOPHELES.

                    Gulp it down!
No hesitation!   It will prove
A cordial and your heart inspire!   2235
What? with the devil hand and glove,
And yet shrink back afraid of fire?
(*The* WITCH *dissolves the circle.*   FAUST *steps out*).

MEPHISTOPHELES.

Now forth at once! thou must not rest.

WITCH.

And much, sir, may the liquor profit you!

MEPHISTOPHELES. (*to the* WITCH).

And if to pleasure thee I aught can do,   2240
Pray on Walpurgis mention thy request.

WITCH.

Here is a song, sung o'er sometimes, you'll see,
That 'twill a singular effect produce.

MEPHISTOPHELES (*to* FAUST).

Come, quick, and let thyself be led by me;
Thou must perspire, in order that the juice   2245
Thy frame may penetrate through every part.
Thy noble idleness I'll teach thee then to prize,
And soon with ecstásy thou'lt recognize
How Cupid stirs and gambols in thy heart.

FAUST.

Let me but gaze one moment in the glass!   2250
Too lovely was that female form!

MEPHISTOPHELES.

> Nay! Nay!
A model which all women shall surpass,
In flesh and blood ere long thou shalt survey.
> (*Aside.*)
As works the draught, thou presently shalt greet
A Helen in each woman thou dost meet.   2255

——◆——

A Street.

Faust (Margaret *passing by*).

FAUST.

Fair lady, may I thus make free
To offer you my arm and company?

MARGARET.

I am no lady, am not fair,
Can without escort home repair.
> (*She disengages herself and exit.*)

FAUST.

By heaven!   This girl is fair indeed!   2260
No form like hers can I recall.
Virtue she hath, and modest heed,
Is piquant too, and sharp withal.
Her cheek's soft light, her rosy lips,
No length of time will e'er eclipse!   2265
Her downward glance in passing by,
Deep in my heart is stamped for aye;
How curt and sharp her answer too,
My ravished heart to rapture grew!
> (Mephistopheles *enters*).

FAUST.

This girl must win for me.   Dost hear?   2270

MEPHISTOPHELES.

Which?

FAUST.

She who but now passed.

MEPHISTOPHELES.

What! She?

She from confession cometh here,
From every sin absolved and free;
I crept near the confessor's chair.
All innocence her virgin soul, 2275
For next to nothing went she there;
O'er such as she I've no control!

FAUST.

She's past fourteen.

MEPHISTOPHELES.

You really talk
Like any gay Lothario,
Who every floweret from its stalk 2280
Would pluck, and deems nor grace, nor truth,
Secure against his arts, forsooth!
This ne'er the less won't always do.

FAUST.

Sir Moralizer, prithee, pause;
Nor plague me with your tiresome laws! 2285
To cut the matter short, my friend,
She must this very night be mine, —
And if to help me you decline,
Midnight shall see our compact end.

MEPHISTOPHELES.

What's possible just bear in mind! 2290
A fortnight's space, at least, I need,
A fit occasion but to find.

FAUST.

With but seven hours I could succeed,
Nor should I want the devil's wile,
So young a creature to beguile. 2295

MEPHISTOPHELES.

Like any Frenchman now you speak,
But do not fret, I pray; why seek
To hurry to enjoyment straight?
The pleasure is not half so great,

As when at first, around, above,　　　　　2300
With all the fooleries of love,
The puppet you can knead and mould
As in Italian story oft is told.

FAUST.

No such incentives do I need.

MEPHISTOPHELES.

But now, without offence or jest!　　　　2305
You cannot quickly, I protest,
In winning this sweet child succeed.
By storm we cannot take the fort,
To stratagem we must resort.

FAUST.

Conduct me to her place of rest!　　　　2310
Some token of the angel bring!
A kerchief from her snowy breast,
A garter bring me, — any thing!

MEPHISTOPHELES.

That I my anxious zeal may prove,
Your pangs to soothe, and aid your love,　　2315
A single moment will we not delay,
Will lead you to her room this very day.

FAUST.

And shall I see her? — Have her?

MEPHISTOPHELES.
　　　　　　　　　　No!
She to a neighbor's house will go;
But in her atmosphere alone,　　　　　2320
The tedious hours meanwhile you may employ,
In blissful dreams of future joy.

FAUST.

Can we go now?

MEPHISTOPHELES.
'Tis yet too soon.

FAUST.

Some present for my love procure!　　　(*Exit.*)

MEPHISTOPHELES.

Presents so soon! 'tis well! success is sure!　　　2325
I know full many a secret store
Of treasure, buried long before,
I must a little look them o'er.　　　　　(*Exit.*)

Evening.　A small and neat Room.

MARGARET

(*braiding and binding up her hair*).

I would give something now to know
Who yonder gentleman could be!　　　　　2330
He had a gallant air, I trow,
And doubtless was of high degree:
That written on his brow was seen —
Nor else would he so bold have been.　　　(*Exit.*)

MEPHISTOPHELES.

Come in! tread softly! be discreet!　　　　2335

FAUST (*after a pause*).

Begone, and leave me, I entreat!

MEPHISTOPHELES (*looking round*).

Not every maiden is so neat.　　　　　(*Exit.*)

FAUST (*gazing round*).

Welcome, sweet twilight gloom which reigns
Through this dim place of hallowed rest!
Fond yearning love, inspire my breast,　　　2340
Feeding on hope's sweet dew thy blissful pains!
What stillness here environs me!
Content and order brood around.
What fulness in this poverty!
In this small cell what bliss profound!　　　2345

(*He throws himself on the leather arm-chair beside
　the bed.*)

Receive me, thou, who hast in thine embrace,
Welcomed in joy and grief the ages flown!
How oft the children of a by-gone race
Have clustered round this patriarchal throne!
Haply she, also, whom I hold so dear,　　　2350

For Christmas gift, with grateful joy possessed,
Hath with the full, round cheek of childhood, here,
Her grandsire's withered hand devoutly pressed.
Maiden! I feel thy spirit haunt the place,
Breathing of order and abounding grace.   2355
As with a mother's voice it prompteth thee
The pure white cover o'er the board to spread,
To strew the crisping sand beneath thy tread.
Dear hand! so godlike in its ministry!
The hut becomes a paradise through thee!   2360
And here —   (*He raises the bed-curtain.*)

How thrills my pulse with strange delight!
Here could I linger hours untold;
Thou, Nature, didst in vision bright,
The embryo angel here unfold.   2365
Here lay the child, her bosom warm
With life; while steeped in slumber's dew,
To perfect grace, her godlike form,
With pure and hallowed weavings grew!

And thou! ah, here what seekest thou?   2370
How quails mine inmost being now!
What wouldst thou here? what makes thy heart so sore?
Unhappy Faust! I know thee now no more.

Do I a magic atmosphere inhale?
Erewhile, my passion would not brook delay!   2375
Now in a pure love-dream I melt away.
Are we the sport of every passing gale?

Should she return and enter now,
How wouldst thou rue thy guilty flame!
Great blockhead! thou wouldst hide thy brow,   2380
And at her feet sink down with shame.

MEPHISTOPHELES.

Quick! quick! below I see her there.

FAUST.

Away! I will return no more!

MEPHISTOPHELES.

Here is a casket, with a store
Of jewels, which I got elsewhere.   2385
Just lay it in the press; make haste!
I swear to you, 'twill turn her brain;
Therein some trifles I have placed,
Wherewith another to obtain.
But child is child, and play is play.   2390

FAUST.

I know not — shall I?

MEPHISTOPHELES.

        Do you ask?
Perchance you would retain the treasure?
If such your wish, why then, I say,
Henceforth absolve me from my task,
Nor longer waste your hours of leisure.   2395
I trust you're not by avarice led !
I rub my hands, I scratch my head, —
   (*He places the casket in the press and closes the lock.*)
Now quick!   Away!
That soon the sweet young creature may
The wish and purpose of your heart obey ;   2400
Yet stand you there
As would you to the lecture-room repair,
As if before you stood,
Arrayed in flesh and blood,
Physics and metaphysics weird and gray ! —   2405
Away !

     MARGARET (*with a lamp*).
   It is so close, so sultry now,
          (*She opens the window*).
Yet out of doors 'tis not so warm.
I feel so strange, I know not how —
I wish my mother would come home.
Through me there runs a shuddering —   2410
I'm but a foolish timid thing !
    (*While undressing herself she begins to sing.*)
    There was a king in Thule,[37]
    True even to the grave ;

To whom his dying mistress
A golden beaker gave.   2415

At every feast he drained it,
Naught was to him so dear,
And often as he drained it,
Gushed from his eyes the tear.

When death he felt approaching,   2420
His cities o'er he told ;
And grudged his heir no treasure
Except his cup of gold.

Girt round with knightly vassals
At a royal feast sat he,   2425
In yon proud hall ancestral
In his castle o'er the sea.

Up stood the jovial monarch,
And quaffed his last life's glow,
Then hurled the hallowed goblet   2430
Into the flood below.

He saw it splashing, drinking,
And plunging in the sea ;
His eyes meanwhile were sinking,
And never again drank he.   2435
(*She opens the press to put away her clothes,
and perceives the casket.*)
How comes this lovely casket here ?   The press
I locked, of that I'm confident.
'Tis very wonderful !   What's in it I can't guess ;
Perhaps 'twas brought by some one in distress,
And left in pledge for loan my mother lent.   2440
Here by a ribbon hangs a little key !
I have a mind to open it and see !
Heavens ! only look ! what have we here !
In all my days ne'er saw I such a sight !
Jewels ! which any noble dame might wear,   2445
For some high pageant richly dight !
How would the necklace look on me !
These splendid gems, whose may they be ?
(*She puts them on and steps before the glass.*)

Were but the earrings only mine!
Thus one has quite another air.   2450
What boots it to be young and fair?
It doubtless may be very fine;
But then, alas, none cares for you,
And praise sounds half like pity too.

Gold all doth lure,   2455
Gold doth secure
All things.   Alas, we poor!

Promenade.

(FAUST *walking thoughtfully up and down.   To
him* MEPHISTOPHELES.)

MEPHISTOPHELES.

By love despised.   By hell's fierce fires I curse,
Would I knew aught to make my imprecation worse!

FAUST.

What aileth thee? what chafes thee now so sore? 2460
A face like that I never saw before!

MEPHISTOPHELES.

I'd yield me to the devil instantly,
Did it not happen that myself am he!

FAUST.

There must be some disorder in thy wit!
To rave thus like a madman, is it fit?   2465

MEPHISTOPHELES.

Just think! The gems for Gretchen brought,
Them has a priest now made his own!—
A glimpse of them the mother caught,   2470
And 'gan with secret fear to groan.
The woman's scent is keen enough;
Doth ever in the prayer-book snuff;
Smells every article to ascertain
Whether the thing is holy or profane,
And scented in the jewels rare,
That there was not much blessing there.   2475

"My child," she cries, "ill-gotten good
Ensnares the soul, consumes the blood ;
With them we'll deck our Lady's shrine,
She'll cheer our souls with bread divine !"
At this poor Gretchen 'gan to pout;   2480
'Tis a gift-horse, at least, she thought,
And sure he godless cannot be,
Who brought them here so cleverly.
Straight for a priest the mother sent,
Who when he understood the jest,   2485
With what he saw was well content.
"This shows a pious mind !"   Quoth he :
"Self-conquest is true victory.
The church hath a good stomach, she, with zest,
Hath lands and kingdoms swallowed down,   2490
And never yet a surfeit known.
The Church alone, be it confessed,
Daughters, can ill-got wealth digest."

FAUST.

It is a general custom, too,
Practised alike by king and Jew.   2495

MEPHISTOPHELES.

With that, clasp, chain, and ring, he swept
As they were mushrooms ; and the casket,
Without one word of thanks, he kept,
As if of nuts it were a basket.
Promised reward in heaven, then forth he hied,   2500
And greatly they were edified.

FAUST.

And Gretchen ?

MEPHISTOPHELES,

In unquiet mood

Knows neither what she would or should ;
The trinkets night and day thinks o'er,
On him who brought them, dwells still more.   2505

FAUST.

The darling's sorrow grieves me, bring
Another set without delay !
The first, methinks, was no great thing.

MEPHISTOPHELES.

All's to my gentleman child's play!

FAUST.

Plan all things to achieve my end!   2510
Engage the attention of her friend!
No milk-and-water devil be,
And bring fresh jewels instantly!

MEPHISTOPHELES.

Ay, sir! most gladly I'll obey.

(FAUST *exit*.)

MEPHISTOPHELES.

Your doting love-sick fool, with ease,
Merely his lady-love to please,   2515
Sun, moon, and stars in sport would puff away.

(*Exit.*)

The Neighbor's House.

MARTHA (*alone*).

God pardon my dear husband, he
Doth not in truth act well by me!
Forth in the world abroad to roam,   2520
And leave me on the straw at home.
And yet his will I ne'er did thwart,
God knows, I loved him from my heart.

(*She weeps.*)

Perchance he's dead! — oh wretched state! —
Had I but a certificate!   2525

(MARGARET *comes*).

MARGARET.

Dame Martha!

MARTHA.

Gretchen?

MARGARET.

Only think!
My knees beneath me well nigh sink!
Within my press I've found to-day,
Another case, of ebony.
And things — magnificent they are,   2530
More costly than the first, by far.

MARTHA.

You must not name it to your mother!
It would to shrift, just like the other.

MARGARET.

Nay, look at them! now only see!

MARTHA (*dresses her up*).
Thou happy creature!

MARGARET.
   Woe is me!   2535
Them in the street I cannot wear,
Or in the church, or any where.

MARTHA.

Come often over here to me,   .
The gems put on quite privately;
And then before the mirror walk an hour or so,
Thus we shall have our pleasure too. 2540
Then suitable occasions we must seize,
As at a feast, to show them by degrees:
A chain at first, then ear-drops, — and your mother
Won't see them, or we'll coin some tale or other.
            2545

MARGARET.

But, who, I wonder, could the caskets bring?
I fear there's something wrong about the thing!
         (*A knock.*)
Good heavens! can that my mother be?

MARTHA (*peering through the blind*).
'Tis a strange gentleman, I see.
Come in!

(MEPHISTOPHELES *enters*).

MEPHISTOPHELES.

I've ventured to intrude to-day. 2550
Ladies, excuse the liberty, I pray.
 (*He steps back respectfully before* MARGARET.)
After Dame Martha Schwerdtlein I inquire!

MARTHA.

'Tis I. Pray what have you to say to me?

MEPHISTOPHELES (*aside to her*).

I know you now, — and therefore will retire ;
At present you've distinguished company.   2555
Pardon the freedom, madam, with your leave,
I will make free to call again at eve.

MARTHA (*aloud*).

Why, child, of all strange notions, he
For some grand lady taketh thee !

MARGARET.

I am, in truth, of humble blood —   2560
The gentleman is far too good —
Nor gems nor trinkets are my own.

MEPHISTOPHELES.

Oh, 'tis not the mere ornaments alone ;
Her glance and mien far more betray ;
Rejoiced I am that I may stay.   2565

MARTHA.

Your business, Sir?   I long to know —

MEPHISTOPHELES.

Would I could happier tidings show !
I trust mine errand you'll not let me rue ;
Your husband's dead, and greeteth you.

MARTHA.

Is dead ?   True heart!   Oh, misery !   2570
My husband dead !   Oh, I shall die !

MARGARET.

Alas! good Martha! don't despair !

MEPHISTOPHELES.

Now listen to the sad affair !

MARGARET.

I for this cause should fear to love.
The loss my certain death would prove.   2575

MEPHISTOPHELES.

Joy still must sorrow, sorrow joy attend.

MARTHA.

Proceed, and tell the story of his end!

MEPHISTOPHELES.

At Padua, in St. Anthony's,
In holy ground his body lies;
Quiet and cool his place of rest,   2580
With pious ceremonials blest.

MARTHA.

And had you nought besides to bring?

MEPHISTOPHELES.

Oh, yes! one grave and solemn prayer;
Let them for him three hundred masses sing!
But in my pockets I have nothing there.   2585

MARTHA.

No trinket! no love-token did he send!
What every journeyman safe in his pouch will hoard
There for remembrance fondly stored,
And rather hungers, rather begs than spend!

MEPHISTOPHELES.

Madam, in truth, it grieves me sore,   2590
But he his gold not lavishly hath spent.
His failings too he deeply did repent,
Ay! and his evil plight bewailed still more.

MARGARET.

Alas! that men should thus be doomed to woe!
I for his soul will many a requiem pray.   2595

MEPHISTOPHELES.

A husband you deserve this very day;
A child so worthy to be loved.

MARGARET.

               Ah no,
That time hath not yet come for me.

MEPHISTOPHELES.

If not a spouse, a gallant let it be.
Among heaven's choicest gifts, I place,   2600
So sweet a darling to embrace.

MARGARET.

Our land doth no such usage know.

MEPHISTOPHELES.

Usage or not, it happens so.

MARTHA.

Go on, I pray!

MEPHISTOPHELES.
　　　　I stood by his bedside.
Something less foul it was than dung;　　　2605
'Twas straw half rotten; yet he as a Christian died.
And sorely hath remorse his conscience wrung.
"Wretch that I was," quoth he, with parting breath,
"So to forsake my business and my wife!
Ah! the remembrance is my death.　　　2610
Could I but have her pardon in this life!" —

MARTHA (*weeping*).

Dear soul! I've long forgiven him, indeed!

MEPHISTOPHELES.

"Though she, God knows, was more to blame than I."

MARTHA.

What, on the brink of death assert a lie!

MEPHISTOPHELES.

If I am skilled the countenance to read,　　　2615
He doubtless fabled as he parted hence. —
"No time had I to gape or take my ease," he said,
"First to get children, and then get them bread;
And bread, too, in the very widest sense;
Nor could I eat in peace even my proper share." 2620

MARTHA.

What, all my truth, my love forgotten quite?
My weary drudgery by day and night!

MEPHISTOPHELES.

Not so!　He thought of you with tender care.
Quoth he: "Heaven knows how fervently I prayed,
For wife and children when from Malta bound;　2625
The prayer hath heaven with favor crowned;

We took a Turkish vessel which conveyed
Rich store of treasure for the Sultan's court;
Its own reward our gallant action brought;
The captured prize was shared among the crew,   2630
And of the treasure I received my due."

MARTHA.

How? Where? The treasure hath he buried, pray?

MEPHISTOPHELES.

Where the four winds have blown it, who can say?
In Naples as he strolled, a stranger there, —
A comely maid took pity on my friend;   2635
And gave such tokens of her love and care,
That he retained them to his blessed end.

MARTHA.

Scoundrel! to rob his children of their bread!
And all this misery, this bitter need,
Could not his course of recklessness impede!   2640

MEPHISTOPHELES.

Well, he hath paid the forfeit, and is dead.
Now were I in your place, my counsel hear;
My weeds I'd wear for one chaste year,
And for another lover meanwhile would look out.

MARTHA.

Alas, I might search far and near,   2645
Not quickly should I find another like my first!
There could not be a fonder fool than mine,
Only he loved too well abroad to roam;
Loved foreign women too, and foreign wine,
And loved besides the dice accursed.   2650

MEPHISTOPHELES.

All had gone swimmingly, no doubt,
Had he but given you at home,
On his side, just as wide a range.
Upon such terms, to you I swear,
Myself with you would gladly rings exchange!   2655

MARTHA.

The gentleman is surely pleased to jest!

MEPHISTOPHELES *(aside)*.

Now to be off in time, were best!
She'd make the very devil marry her.

(*To* MARGARET).

How fares it with your heart?

MARGARET.

How mean you, sir?

MEPHISTOPHELES *(aside)*.

The sweet young innocent!

(*Aloud.*)

Ladies, farewell!   2660

MARGARET.

Farewell!

MARTHA.

But ere you leave us, quickly tell!
I from a witness fain had heard,
Where, how, and when my husband died and was in-
    terred.
To forms I've always been attached indeed,
His death I fain would in the journals read.   2665

MEPHISTOPHELES.

Ay, madam, what two witnesses declare
Is held as valid everywhere;
A gallant friend I have, not far from here,
Who will for you before the judge appear.
I'll bring him straight.

MARTHA.

I pray you do!   2670

MEPHISTOPHELES.

And this young lady, we shall find her too?
A noble youth, far travelled, he,
Shows to the sex all courtesy.

MARGARET.

I in his presence needs must blush for shame.

MEPHISTOPHELES.

Not in the presence of a crowned king!   2675

MARTHA.

The garden, then, behind my house, we'll name,
There we'll await you both this evening.

A Street.

FAUST. MEPHISTOPHELES.

FAUST.

How is it now?   How speeds it?   Is't in train?

MEPHISTOPHELES.

Bravo!   I find you all aflame!
Gretchen full soon your own you'll name.   2680
This eve, at neighbor Martha's, her you'll meet again ;
The woman seems expressly made
To drive the pimp and gipsy's trade.

FAUST.

Good!

MEPHISTOPHELES.

But from us she something would request.

FAUST.

A favor claims return as this world goes.   2685

MEPHISTOPHELES.

We have an oath but duly to attest,
That her dead husband's limbs, outstretched, repose
In holy ground at Padua.

FAUST.

Sage indeed!
So I suppose we straight must journey there!

MEPHISTOPHELES.

Sancta simplicitas!   For that no need!   2690
Without much knowledge we have but to swear.

FAUST.

If that's your plan it will not do.

MEPHISTOPHELES.

Oh, holy man! that's truly you!
In all your life say, have you ne'er   2695
False witness borne, until this hour?
Have you of God, the world, and all it doth contain,
Of man, and that which worketh in his heart and
      brain,
Not definitions given, in words of weight and power,
With front unblushing, and a dauntless breast?   2700
Yet, if into the depth of things you go,
Touching these matters, it must be confessed,
As much as of Herr Schwerdtlein's death you know!

FAUST.

Thou art and dost remain a liar and sophist too.

MEPHISTOPHELES.

Ay, if one did not take a somewhat deeper view! 2705
To-morrow, in all honor, thou
Poor Gretchen wilt befool, and vow
Thy soul's deep love, in lover's fashion.

FAUST.

And from my heart.

MEPHISTOPHELES.

          All good and fair!
Then deathless constancy thou'lt swear!   2710
Speak of one all o'ermastering passion,—
Will that too issue from the heart?

FAUST.

          It will.   Forbear!
When passion sways me, and I seek to frame
Fit utterance for feeling, deep, intense,
And for my frenzy finding no fit name,   2715
Sweep round the ample world with every sense,
Grasp at the loftiest words to speak my flame,
And call the glow, wherewith I burn,
Quenchless, eternal, yea, eterne —
Is that of sophistry a devilish play?   2720

MEPHISTOPHELES.

Yet am I right!

FAUST.

Mark this, my friend,
And spare my lungs: whoe'er to have the right is fain,
If he have but a tongue, wherewith his point to gain,
Will gain it in the end.
But come, of gossip I am weary quite;   2725
Because I've no resource, thou'rt in the right.

MARGARET *on* FAUST's *arm.* MARTHA *with* MEPHIS-
TOPHELES *walking up and down.*

MARGARET.

I feel it, you but spare my ignorance,
To shame me, sir, you stoop thus low.
A traveller from complaisance,
Still makes the best of things; I know   2730
Too well, my humble prattle never can
Have power to entertain so wise a man.

FAUST.

One glance, one word of thine doth charm me more,
Than the world's wisdom or the sage's lore.
(He kisses her hand.)

MARGARET.

Nay! trouble not yourself!   A hand so coarse,   2735
So rude as mine, how can you kiss?
What constant work at home must I not do perforce!
My mother too exacting is.
(They pass on.)
MARTHA.

Thus, sir, unceasing travel is your lot?

MEPHISTOPHELES.

Traffic and duty urge us!   With what pain   2740
Are we compelled to leave full many a spot,
Where yet we may not once remain!

MARTHA.

In youth's wild years, with vigor crowned,
'Tis not amiss thus through the world to sweep;
But ah, the evil days come round!   2745

And to a lonely grave as bachelor to creep,
A pleasant thing has no one found.

MEPHISTOPHELES.

The prospect fills me with dismay.

MARTHA.

Therefore, in time, dear sir, reflect, I pray.
(*They pass on.*)

MARGARET.

Ay, out of sight is out of mind!   2750
Politeness easy is to you;
Friends everywhere, and not a few,
Wiser than I am, you will find.

FAUST.

Trust me, my angel, what doth pass for sense
Full oft is self-conceit and blindness!

MARGARET.

How ?   2755

FAUST.

Simplicity and holy innocence, —
When will ye learn your hallowed worth to know!
Ah, when will meekness and humility,
Kind and all-bounteous nature's loftiest dower —

MARGARET.

Only one little moment think of me!   2760
To think of you I shall have many an hour.

FAUST.

You are perhaps much alone?

MARGARET.

Yes, small our household is, I own,
Yet must I see to it. No maid we keep,
And I must cook, sew, knit, and sweep,   2765
Still early on my feet and late;
My mother is in all things, great and small,
So accurate!
Not that for thrift there is such pressing need;
Than others we might make more show indeed; 2770

My father left behind a small estate,
A house and garden near the city-wall.
Quiet enough my life has been of late;
My brother for a soldier gone;
My little sister's dead; the babe to rear   2775
Occasioned me some care and fond annoy;
But I would go through all again with joy,
The darling was to me so dear.

FAUST.

An angel, sweet, if it resembled thee!

MARGARET.

I reared it up, and it grew fond of me.   2780
After my father's death it saw the day;
We gave my mother up for lost, she lay
In such a wretched plight, and then at length
So very slowly she regained her strength.
Weak as she was, 'twas vain for her to try   2785
Herself to suckle the poor babe, so I
Reared it on milk and water all alone;
And thus the child became as 'twere my own;
Within my arms it stretched itself and grew,
And smiling, nestled in my bosom too.   2790

FAUST.

Doubtless the purest happiness was thine.

MARGARET.

But many weary hours, in sooth, were also mine.
At night its little cradle stood
Close to my bed; so I was wide awake
If it but stirred;   2795
One while I was obliged to give it food,
Or to my arms the darling take;
From bed full oft must rise, whene'er the cry I heard,
And, dancing it, must pace the chamber to and fro;
Stand at the wash-tub early; forthwith go   2800
To market, and then mind the cooking too —
To-morrow like to-day, the whole year through.
Ah, sir, thus living, it must be confessed
One's spirits are not always of the best;
Yet it a relish gives to food and rest. (*They pass on.*)

MARTHA.

Poor women! we are badly off, I own;   2806
A bachelor's conversion's hard, indeed!

MEPHISTOPHELES.

Madam, with one like you it rests alone,
To tutor me a better course to lead.

MARTHA.

Speak frankly, sir, none is there you have met?   2810
Has your heart ne'er attached itself as yet?

MEPHISTOPHELES.

One's own fireside and a good wife are gold
And pearls of price, so says the proverb old,

MARTHA.

I mean, has passion never stirred your breast?

MEPHISTOPHELES.

I've everywhere been well received, I own.   2815

MARTHA.

Yet hath your heart no earnest preference known?

MEPHISTOPHELES.

With ladies one should ne'er presume to jest.

MARTHA.

Ah! you mistake!

MEPHISTOPHELES.
I'm sorry I'm so blind!
But this I know — that you are very kind.
(They pass on.)
FAUST.

Me, little angel, didst thou recognize,   2820
When in the garden first I came?

MARGARET.

Did you not see it? I cast down my eyes.

FAUST.

Thou dost forgive my boldness, dost not blame
The liberty I took that day,
When thou from church didst lately wend thy way? 2825

MARGARET.

I was confused. So had it never been ;
No one of me could any evil say.
Alas, thought I, he doubtless in thy mien,
Something unmaidenly or bold hath seen ?
It seemed as if it struck him suddenly,   2830
Here's just a girl with whom one may make free !
Yet I must own that then I scarcely knew
What in your favor here began at once to plead ;
Yet I was angry with myself indeed,
That I more angry could not feel with you.   2835

FAUST.

Sweet love !

MARGARET.

Just wait awhile !
(*She gathers a star-flower and plucks off the leaves one
    after another.*)

FAUST.

A nosegay may that be ?

MARGARET.

No !   It is but a game.

FAUST.
How ?

MARGARET.

Go, you'll laugh at me !
(*She plucks off the leaves and murmurs to herself.*)

FAUST.

What murmurest thou ?

MARGARET (*half aloud*).

He loves me, — loves me not.

FAUST.

Sweet angel, with thy face of heavenly bliss !

MARGARET (*continues*).

He loves me — not — he loves me — not —
(*plucking off the last leaf with fond joy.*)
He loves me !

FAUST.

                    Yes!
And this flower-language, darling, let it be,   2841
A heavenly oracle! He loveth thee!
Know'st thou the meaning of, He loveth thee?
                  (*He seizes both her hands.*)

MARGARET.

I tremble so!

FAUST.

         Nay! do not tremble, love!
Let this hand-pressure, let this glance reveal   2845
Feelings, all power of speech above;
To give oneself up wholly and to feel
A joy that must eternal prove!
Eternal! — Yes, its end would be despair.
No end! — It cannot end?   2850
    (MARGARET *presses his hand, extricates herself, and*
      runs away. He stands a moment in thought, and
      then follows her.)

MARTHA (*approaching*).

Night's closing.

MEPHISTOPHELES.

Yes, we'll presently away.

MARTHA.

I would entreat you longer yet to stay;
But 'tis a wicked place, just here about;
It is as if the folk had nothing else to do,
Nothing to think of too,   2855
But gaping watch their neighbors, who goes in and out;
And scandal's busy still, do whatsoe'er one may.
And our young couple?

MEPHISTOPHELES.

         They have flown up there,
The wanton butterflies!

MARTHA.

         He seems to take to her.

MEPHISTOPHELES.

And she to him. 'Tis of the world the way!   2860

A Summerhouse.

(MARGARET *runs in, hides behind the door, holds
the tip of her finger to her lip, and peeps
through the crevice.*)

MARGARET.

He comes!

FAUST.

Ah, little rogue, so thou
Think'st to provoke me!   I have caught thee now!
(*He kisses her.*)

MARGARET

(*embracing him, and returning the kiss*).

Dearest of men!   I love thee from my heart!

(MEPHISTOPHELES *knocks.*)

FAUST (*stamping*).

Who's there?

MEPHISTOPHELES.

A friend!

FAUST.

A brute!

MEPHISTOPHELES.

'Tis time to part.

MARTHA (*comes*).

Ay, it is late, good sir.

FAUST.

Mayn't I attend you, then?   2865

MARGARET.

Oh, no — my mother would — adieu, adieu!

FAUST.

And must I really then take leave of you?
Farewell!

MARTHA.

Good-bye!

MARGARET.

Ere long to meet again!
(*Exeunt* FAUST *and* MEPHISTOPHELES.)

MARGARET.

Good heavens! how all things far and near
Must fill his mind, — a man like this!   2870
Abashed before him I appear,
And say to all things only, yes.
Poor simple child, I cannot see,
What 'tis that he can find in me.   (*Exit.*)

Forest and Cavern.

FAUST (*alone*).

Spirit sublime! Thou gavest me, gavest me all 2875
For which I prayed! Not vainly hast thou turned
To me thy countenance in flaming fire:
Gavest me glorious nature for my realm,
And also power to feel her and enjoy;
Not merely with a cold and wondering glance,   2880
Thou dost permit me in her depths profound,
As in the bosom of a friend to gaze.
Before me thou dost lead her living tribes,
And dost in silent grove, in air and stream
Teach me to know my kindred. And when roars 2885
The howling storm-blast through the groaning wood,
Wrenching the giant pine, which in its fall
Crashing sweeps down its neighboring trunks and
    boughs,
While with the hollow noise the hill resounds:
Then thou dost lead me to some sheltered cave,   2890
Dost there reveal me to myself, and show
Of my own bosom the mysterious depths.
And when with soothing beam, the moon's pure orb
Full in my view climbs up the pathless sky,
From crag and dewy grove, the silvery forms   2895
Of by-gone ages hover, and assuage
The joy austere of contemplative thought.

Oh, that naught perfect is assigned to man,
I feel, alas! With this exalted joy,
Which lifts me near and nearer to the gods,   2900
Thou gavest me this companion, unto whom
I needs must cling, though cold and insolent,
He still degrades me to myself, and turns
Thy glorious gifts to nothing, with a breath.

He in my bosom with malicious zeal   2905
For that fair image fans a raging fire;
From craving to enjoyment thus I reel,
And in enjoyment languish for desire.

(MEPHISTOPHELES *enters*.)

MEPHISTOPHELES.

Of this lone life have you not had your fill?
How for so long can it have charms for you?   2910
'Tis well enough to try it if you will;
But then away again to something new!

FAUST.

Would you could better occupy your leisure,
Than in disturbing thus my hours of joy.

MEPHISTOPHELES.

Well! Well! I'll leave you to yourself with pleasure,
A serious tone you hardly need employ.   2916
To part from one so crazy, harsh, and cross,
I should not find a grievous loss.
The live-long day, for you I toil and fret;
Ne'er from his worship's face a hint I get,   2920
What pleases him, or what to let alone.

FAUST.

Ay, truly! that is just the proper tone!
He wearies me, and would with thanks be paid!

MEPHISTOPHELES.

Poor Son of Earth, without my aid,
How would thy weary days have flown?   2925
Thee of thy foolish whims I've cured,
Thy vain imaginations banished,
And but for me, be well assured,
Thou from this sphere must soon have vanished.
In rocky hollows and in caverns drear,   2930
Why like an owl sit moping here?
Wherefore from dripping stones and moss with
      ooze embued,
Dost suck, like any toad, thy food?
A rare, sweet pastime.   Verily!
The doctor cleaveth still to thee.   2935

FAUST.

Dost comprehend what bliss without alloy
From this wild wandering in the desert springs? —
Couldst thou but guess the new life-power it brings,
Thou wouldst be fiend enough to envy me my joy.

MEPHISTOPHELES.

What super-earthly ecstasy! at night,   2940
To lie in darkness on the dewy height,
Embracing heaven and earth in rapture high,
The soul dilating to a deity;
With prescient yearnings pierce the core of earth,
Feel in your laboring breast the six-days' birth,   2945
Enjoy, in proud delight what no one knows,
While your love-rapture o'er creation flows, —
The earthly lost in beatific vision,
And then the lofty intuition —
                         (with a gesture)
I need not tell you how — to close!   2950

FAUST.

Fie on you!

MEPHISTOPHELES.

               This displeases you?   " For shame!"
You are forsooth entitled to exclaim;
We to chaste ears it seems must not pronounce
What, nathless, the chaste heart cannot renounce.
Well, to be brief, the joy as fit occasions rise,   2955
I grudge you not, of specious lies.
But soon the self-deluding vein
Is past, once more thou'rt whirled away,
And should it last, thou'lt be the prey
Of frenzy or remorse and pain.   2960
Enough of this!   Thy true love dwells apart,
And all to her seems flat and tame
Alone thine image fills her heart,
She loves thee with an all-devouring flame.
First came thy passion with o'erpowering rush,   2965
Like mountain torrent, swollen by the melted snow;
Full in her heart didst pour the sudden gush,
Now has thy brooklet ceased to flow.

Instead of sitting throned midst forests wild,
It would become so great a lord   2970
To comfort the enamored child,
And the young monkey for her love reward.
To her the hours seem miserably long;
She from the window sees the clouds float by
As o'er the lofty city-walls they fly.   2975
"If I a birdie were!" so runs her song,
Half through the night and all day long.
Cheerful sometimes, more oft at heart full sore;
Fairly outwept seem now her tears,
Anon she tranquil is, or so appears,   2980
And love-sick ever more.

FAUST.

Snake! Serpent vile!

MEPHISTOPHELES (aside).

Good!   If I catch thee with my guile!

FAUST.

Vile reprobate! go get thee hence;
Forbear the lovely girl to name!   2985
Nor in my half-distracted sense,
Kindle anew the smouldering flame!

MEPHISTOPHELES.

What would'st thou!   She thinks you've taken flight;
It seems, she's partly in the right.

FAUST.

I'm near her still — and should I distant rove,   2990
Her I can ne'er forget, ne'er lose her love;
And all things touched by those sweet lips of hers,
Even the very Host, my envy stirs.

MEPHISTOPHELES.

'Tis well!   I oft have envied you indeed,
The twin-pair that among the roses feed.   2995

FAUST.

Pander, avaunt!

MEPHISTOPHELES.

        Go to!   I laugh, the while you rail.
The power which fashioned youth and maid,

Well understood the noble trade;
So neither shall occasion fail.
But hence!—in truth a case for gloom!   3000
Bethink thee, to thy mistress' room
And not to death shouldst go!

FAUST.

What is to me heaven's joy within her arms?
What though my life her bosom warms!—
Do I not ever feel her woe?   3005
The outcast am I not, who knows no rest,
Inhuman monster, aimless and unblest,
Who like the greedy surge, from rock to rock,
Sweeps down the dread abyss with desperate shock?
While she, within her lowly cot, which graced   3010
The Alpine slope, beside the waters wild,
Her homely cares in that small world embraced.
Secluded lived, a simple artless child.
Was't not enough, in thy delirious whirl
To blast the steadfast rocks?   3015
Her, and her peace as well,
Must I, God-hated one, to ruin hurl!
Dost claim this holocaust, remorseless Hell!
Fiend, help me to cut short the hours of dread!
Let what must happen, happen speedily!   3020
Her direful doom fall crushing on my head,
And into ruin let her plunge with me.

MEPHISTOPHELES.

Why how again it seethes and glows!
Away, thou fool!   Her torment ease!
When such a head no issue sees,   3025
It pictures straight the final close.
Long life to him who boldly dares!
A devil's pluck thou'rt wont to show;
As for a devil who despairs,
There's naught so mawkish here below.   3030

MARGARET'S Room.

MARGARET (alone at her spinning wheel).

My peace is gone,
My heart is sore,

I find it never,
   And nevermore!

Where him I have not,   3035
   Is the grave to me;
And bitter as gall
   The whole world to me.

My wildered brain
   Is overwrought;   3040
My feeble senses
   Are distraught.

My peace is gone,
   My heart is sore,
I find it never,
   And nevermore!   3045

For him from the window
   I gaze, at home;
For him and him only
   Abroad I roam.   3050

His lofty step,
   His bearing high,
The smile of his lip,
   The power of his eye,

His witching words,   3055
   Their tones of bliss,
His hand's fond pressure,
   And ah — his kiss!

My peace is gone,
   My heart is sore,   3060
I find it never,
   And nevermore.

My bosom aches
   To feel him near;
Ah, could I clasp   3065
   And fold him here!

Kiss him and kiss him
   Again would I,
And on his kisses
   I fain would die!   3070

Martha's *Garden.*

Margaret *and* Faust.

MARGARET.

Promise me, Henry —

FAUST.

What I can!

MARGARET.

How is it with religion in thy mind?
Thou art a dear kind-hearted man,
But I'm afraid not piously inclined.

FAUST.

Forbear!   Thou feelest I love thee alone;   3075
For those I love my life I would lay down,
And none would of their faith or church bereave.

MARGARET.

That's not enough, we must ourselves believe!

FAUST.

Must we?

MARGARET.

Ah, could I but thy soul inspire!

Thou honorest not the sacraments, alas!   3080

FAUST.

I honor them.

MARGARET.

But yet without desire;

'Tis long since thou hast been either to shrift or mass.
Dost thou believe in God?

FAUST.

My darling, who dares say,

Yes, I in God believe?
Question or priest or sage, and they   3085
Seem, in the answer you receive,
To mock the questioner.

MARGARET.

Then thou dost not believe?

FAUST.

Sweet one! my meaning do not misconceive?
Him who dare name
And who proclaim,   3090
Him I believe?
Who that can feel,
His heart can steel,
To say: I believe him not?
The All-embracer,   3095
All-sustainer,
Holds and sustains he not?
Thee, me, himself?
Lifts not the Heaven its dome above?
Doth not the firm-set earth beneath us lie?   3100
And beaming tenderly with looks of love,
Climb not the everlasting stars on high?
Do I not gaze into thine eyes?
Nature's impenetrable agencies,
Are they not thronging on thy heart and brain,   3105
Viewless, or visible to mortal ken,
Around thee weaving their mysterious chain?
Fill thence thine heart, how large soe'er it be;
And in the feeling when thou utterly art blest,
Then call it, what thou wilt, —   3110
Call it Bliss! Heart! Love! God!
I have no name for it!
'Tis feeling all;
Name is but sound and smoke
Enclouding heaven's glow.   3115

MARGARET.

All this is doubtless good and fair;
Almost the same the parson says.
Only in slightly different phrase.

FAUST.

Beneath Heaven's sunshine, everywhere,
This is the utterance of the human heart;   3120
Each in his language doth the like impart;
Then why not I in mine?

MARGARET.

What thus I hear
Sounds plausible, yet I'm not reconciled;
There's something wrong about it, much I fear
That thou art not a Christian.

FAUST.

My sweet child!   3125

MARGARET.

Alas! long hath it sorely troubled me,
To see thee in such odious company.

FAUST.

How so?

MARGARET.

The man who comes with thee I hate,
Yea, in my spirit's inmost depths abhor;
As his loathed visage, in my life before,   3130
Naught to my heart e'er gave a pang so great.

FAUST.

Fear not, sweet love!

MARGARET.

His presence chills my blood.
Towards all beside I have a kindly mood;
Yet, though I yearn to gaze on thee, I feel
At sight of him strange horror o'er me steal;   3135
That he's a villain my conviction's strong.
May heaven forgive me if I do him wrong!

FAUST.

Yet such strange fellows in the world must be!

MARGARET.

I would not live with such an one as he.
If for a moment he but enter here,   3140
He looks around him with a mocking sneer,
And malice ill-concealed;
That he with naught on earth can sympathize is clear;
Upon his brow 'tis legibly revealed,
That to his heart no living soul is dear.   3145
So blest I feel, within thy arms,

So warm, so happy, — free from all alarms;
And still my heart doth close when he comes near.

FAUST.

Foreboding angel! check thy fear!

MARGARET.

It so o'ermasters me, that when,   3150
Or wheresoe'er, his step I hear,
I almost think, no more I love thee then.
Besides, when he is near, I ne'er could pray,
This eats into my heart; with thee
The same, my Henry, it must be.   3155

FAUST.

'Tis your antipathy!

MARGARET.

I must away.

FAUST.

For one brief hour then may I never rest,
And heart to heart, and soul to soul be pressed!

MARGARET.

Ah, if I slept alone, to-night
The bolt I fain would leave undrawn for thee;   3160
But then my mother's sleep is light,
Were we surprised by her, ah me!
Upon the spot I should be dead.

FAUST.

Dear angel! there's no cause for dread.
Here is a little phial, — if she take   3165
Mixed in her drink three drops, 'twill steep
Her nature in a deep and soothing sleep.

MARGARET.

What do I not for thy dear sake!
To her it will not harmful prove?

FAUST.

Should I advise else, sweet love?   3170

MARGARET.

I know not, dearest, when thy face I see,
What doth my spirit to thy will constrain;
Already I have done so much for thee,
That scarcely more to do doth now remain.

(*Exit*).

(MEPHISTOPHELES *enters*).

MEPHISTOPHELES.

The monkey!   Is she gone?

FAUST.

Again hast played the spy?   3175

MEPHISTOPHELES.

Of all that passed I'm well apprized,
I heard the doctor catechised,
And trust he'll profit much thereby!
Fain would the girls inquire indeed
Touching their lover's faith, if he   3180
Believe according to the ancient creed,
They think: if pliant there, to us he'll yielding be.

FAUST.

Thou monster, dost not see that this
Pure soul, possessed by ardent love,
Full of the living faith,   3185
To her of bliss
The only pledge, must holy anguish prove,
Holding the man she loves, fore-doomed to endless
        death!

MEPHISTOPHELES.

Most sensual, supersensualist?   The while
A damsel leads thee by the nose!   3160

FAUST.

Of filth and fire abortion vile!

MEPHISTOPHELES.

In physiognomy strange skill she shows;
She in my presence feels she knows not how;
My mask it seems a hidden sense reveals;
That I'm a genius she must needs allow,   3195

That I'm the very devil perhaps she feels.
So then to-night —

FAUST.

What's that to you?

MEPHISTOPHELES.

I've my amusement in it too!

At the Well.

MARGARET *and* BESSY *with pitchers.*

BESSY.

Of Barbara hast nothing heard?

MARGARET.

I rarely go from home, — no, not a word.   3200

BESSY.

'Tis true.   Sybilla told me so to-day!
That comes of being proud, methinks;
She played the fool at last.

MARGARET.

How so?

BESSY.

. They say
That two she feedeth when she eats and drinks.

MARGARET.

Alas!

BESSY.

She's rightly served, in sooth.   3205
How long she hung upon the youth!
What promenades, what jaunts there were,
To dancing booth and village fair!
The first she everywhere must shine,
He always treating her to pastry and to wine.   3210
Of her good looks she was so vain,
So shameless too, that she did not disdain
Even his presents to retain;
Sweet words and kisses came anon —
And then the virgin flower was gone!   3215

MARGARET.

Poor thing!

BESSY.

Forsooth dost pity her?
At night, when at our wheels we sat,
Abroad our mothers ne'er would let us stir.
Then with her lover she must chat,
Or on the bench, or in the dusky walk, [38] 3220
Thinking the hours too brief for their sweet talk;
Her proud head she will have to bow,
And in white sheet do penance now!

MARGARET.

But he will surely marry her?

BESSY.

Not he!
He won't be such a fool! a gallant lad 3225
Like him, can roam o'er land and sea,
Besides, he's off.

MARGARET.

That is not fair!

BESSY.

If she should get him, 'twere almost as bad!
Her myrtle wreath the boys would tear;
And then we girls would plague her too, 3230
For we chopped straw before her door would strew! [39]
    (*Exit.*)

MARGARET (*walking towards home*).

How stoutly once I could inveigh,
If a poor maiden went astray!
Not words enough my tongue could find,
'Gainst others' sin to speak my mind; 3235
Black as it seemed, I blackened it still more,
And strove to make it blacker than before.
And did myself securely bless —
Now my own trespass doth appear!
Yet ah! — what urged me to transgress. 3240
Sweet heaven, it was so good! so dear!

ZWINGER.

Enclosure between the City-wall and the Gate.
(In the niche of the wall a devotional image of the
Mater dolorosa, with flower-pots before it.)

MARGARET (*putting fresh flowers in the pots*).

Ah, rich in sorrow, thou,
Stoop thy maternal brow,
And mark with pitying eye my misery!

The sword in thy pierced heart,   3245
Thou dost with bitter smart,
Gaze upwards on thy Son's death agony.

To the dear God on high,
Ascends thy piteous sigh,
Pleading for his and thy sore misery.   3250

Ah, who can know
The torturing woe,
The pangs that rack me to the bone?
How my poor heart, without relief,
Trembles and throbs, its yearning grief   3255
Thou knowest, thou alone!

Ah, wheresoe'er I go,
With woe, with woe, with woe,
My anguished breast is aching!
When all alone I creep,   3260
I weep, I weep, I weep,
Alas! my heart is breaking!

The flower-pots at my window
Were wet with tears of mine,
The while I plucked these blossoms,   3265
At dawn to deck thy shrine!

When early in my chamber
Shone bright the rising morn,
I sat there on my pallet,
My heart with anguish torn.   3270

Help! from disgrace and death deliver me!
Ah! rich in sorrow, thou,
Stoop thy maternal brow,
And mark with pitying eye my misery!

Night.   Street before MARGARET'S *door.*

VALENTINE (*a soldier,* MARGARET'S *brother*).

When seated 'mong jovial crowd   3275
Where merry comrades boasting loud,
Each named with pride his favorite lass,
And in her honor drained his glass;
Upon my elbow I would lean,
With easy quiet view the scene,   3280
Nor give my tongue the rein, until
Each swaggering blade had talked his fill.
Then smiling I my beard would stroke,
The while, with brimming glass, I spoke;
"Each to his taste!—but to my mind,   3285
Where in the country will you find,
A maid, as my dear Gretchen fair,
Who with my sister can compare?"
Cling! Clang! so rang the jovial sound?
Shouts of assent went circling round;   3290
Pride of her sex is she!—cried some;
Then were the noisy boasters dumb.

And now!—I could tear out my hair,
Or dash my brains out in despair!—
Me every scurvy knave may twit,   3295
With stinging jest and taunting sneer!
Like skulking debtor I must sit,
And sweat each casual word to hear!
And though I smashed them one and all,—
Yet them I could not liars call.   3300

Who comes this way? who's sneaking here?
If I mistake not, two draw near.
If he be one, have at him;—well I wot
Alive he shall not leave this spot!

FAUST. MEPHISTOPHELES.

FAUST.

How from yon sacristy, athwart the night,   3305
Its beams the ever-burning taper throws,
While ever waning, fades the glimmering light,

As gathering darkness doth around it close!
So night-like gloom doth in my bosom reign.

MEPHISTOPHELES.

I'm like a tom-cat in a thievish vein,   3310
That up fire-ladders tall and steep,
And round the walls doth slyly creep;
Virtuous withal, I feel, with, I confess,
A touch of thievish joy and wantonness.
Thus through my limbs already there doth bound 3315
The glorious Walpurgis night!
After to-morrow it again comes round,
What one doth wake for, then one knows aright!

FAUST.

Meanwhile, the flame which I see glimmering there,
Is it the treasure rising in the air?   3320

MEPHISTOPHELES.

Ere long, I make no doubt, but you [40]
To raise the chest will feel inclined;
Erewhile I peeped within it too;
[41] With lion-dollars 'tis well lined.

FAUST.

And not a trinket? not a ring?   3325
Wherewith my lovely girl to deck?

MEPHISTOPHELES.

I saw among them some such thing,
A string of pearls to grace her neck.

FAUST.

'Tis well!   I'm always loath to go,
Without some gift my love to show.   3330

MEPHISTOPHELES.

Some pleasures gratis to enjoy,
Should surely cause you no annoy.
While bright with stars the heavens appear,
I'll sing a masterpiece of art:
A moral song shall charm her ear,   3335
More surely to beguile her heart.

(*Sings to the guitar.*[42])

Kathrina, say,
Why lingering stay
At dawn of day
Before your lover's door ?　　　　　3340
Maiden, beware,
Nor enter there,
Lest forth you fare,
A maiden nevermore.

Maiden, take heed !　　　　　3345
Reck well my rede !
Is't done, the deed ?
Good night, you poor, poor thing !
The spoiler's lies,
His arts despise,　　　　　3350
Nor yield your prize,
Without the marriage ring !

VALENTINE (*steps forward*).

Whom are you luring here ?　I'll give it you !
Accursed rat-catchers, your strains I'll end ! [43]
First, to the devil the guitar I'll send !　　　　　3355
Then to the devil with the singer too !

MEPHISTOPHELES.

The poor guitar ! 'tis done for now.

VALENTINE.

Your skull shall follow next, I trow !

MEPHISTOPHELES (*to* FAUST).

Doctor, stand fast ! your strength collect !
Be prompt, and do as I direct.　　　　　3360
Out with your whisk ! keep close, I pray,
I'll parry ! do you thrust away !

VALENTINE.

Then parry that !

MEPHISTOPHELES.
Why not?

VALENTINE.
That too !

MEPHISTOPHELES.

With ease!

VALENTINE.

The devil fights for you!
Why, how is this? my hand's already lamed!　　3365

MEPHISTOPHELES (*to* FAUST).

Thrust home!

VALENTINE (*falls*).

Alas!

MEPHISTOPHELES.

There! now the lubber's tamed!
But quick, away!　We must at once take wing;
A cry of murder strikes upon the ear;
With the police I know my course to steer,
But with the blood-ban 'tis another thing.　　3370

MARTHA (*at the window*).

Without! without!

MARGARET (*at the window*).

Quick, bring a light!

MARTHA (*as above*).

They rail and scuffle, scream and fight!

PEOPLE.

One lieth here already dead!

MARTHA (*coming out*).

Where are the murderers? are they fled?

MARGARET (*coming out*).

Who lieth here?

PEOPLE.

Thy mother's son!　　3375

MARGARET.

Almighty God! I am undone!

VALENTINE.

I'm dying—'tis a soon told tale,
And sooner done the deed.
Why, women, do ye howl and wail?　　3379
To my last words give heed!　(*All gather round him*).

Gretchen, thou'rt still of tender age,
And, well I wot, not over sage,
Thou dost thy matters ill;
Let this in confidence be said:
Since thou the path of shame dost tread,   3385
Tread it with right good will!

MARGARET.

My brother!   God! what can this mean?

VALENTINE.

Abstain,

Nor dare God's holy name profane!
What's done, alas, is done and past!
Matters will take their course at last;   3390
By stealth thou dost begin with one,
Others will follow him anon;
And when a dozen thee have known,
Thou'lt common be to all the town.
When infamy is newly born,   3395
In secret she is brought to light,
And the mysterious veil of night
O'er head and ears is drawn;
The loathsome birth men fain would slay;
But soon, full grown, she waxes bold,   .   3400
And though not fairer to behold,
With brazen front insults the day:
The more abhorrent to the sight,
The more she courts the day's pure light.

The time already I discern,   3405
When thee all honest folk will spurn,
And shun thy hated form to meet,
As when a corpse infects the street.
Thy heart will sink with thy despair,
When they shall look thee in the face!   3410
A golden chain no more thou'lt wear —
Nor near the altar take in church thy place —
In fair lace collar richly dight
Thou'lt dance no more with spirits light —
In darksome corners thou wilt bide,   3415
Where beggars vile and cripples hide —   .

And e'en though God thy crime forgive,
On earth, a thing accursed, thou'lt live.

MARTHA.

Your parting soul to God commend;
Your dying breath in slander will you spend?   3420

VALENTINE.

Could I but reach thy withered frame,
Thou wretched beldame, void of shame!
Full measure I might hope to win
Of pardon then for every sin.

MARGARET.

Brother! what agonizing pain!   3425

VALENTINE.

I tell thee! from vain tears abstain!
'Twas thy dishonor pierced my heart,
Thy fall the fatal death-stab gave.
Through the death-sleep I now depart
To God, a soldier true and brave.   (*dies.*)   3430

Cathedral.

Service, Organ, and Anthem.

MARGARET *amongst a number of people.*

EVIL SPIRIT *behind* MARGARET.

EVIL SPIRIT.

How different, Gretchen, was it once with thee,
When thou, still full of innocence,
Here to the altar camest,
And from the small and well-conned book
Didst lisp thy prayer,   3435
Half childish sport,
Half God in thy young heart!
Gretchen!
What thoughts are thine?
What deed of shame   3440
Lurks in thy sinful heart?

Is thy prayer uttered for thy mother's soul,
Who into long, long torment slept through thee?

Whose blood is on thy threshold?
— And stirs there not already 'neath thy heart   3445
Another quickening pulse, that even now
Tortures itself and thee
With its foreboding presence?

MARGARET.

Woe! Woe!
Oh, could I free me from the thoughts   3450
That hither, thither, crowd upon my brain,
Against my will!

CHORUS.

> *Dies iræ, dies illa,*
> *Solvet sæclum in favilla.*
>
> *(The organ sounds).*

EVIL SPIRIT.

Grim horror seizes thee!   3455
The trumpet sounds!
The graves are shaken!
And thy heart
From ashy rest
For torturing flames   3460
Anew created,
Trembles into life!

MARGARET.

Would I were hence!
It is as if the organ
Choked my breath,   3465
As if the choir
Melted my inmost heart!

CHORUS.

> *Judex ergo cum sedebit,*
> *Quidquid latet adparebit,*
> *Nil inultum remanebit.*   3470

MARGARET.

I feel oppressed!
The pillars of the wall
Imprison me!

The vaulted roof
Weighs down upon me!—air!   3475

EVIL SPIRIT.

Wouldst hide thee? sin and shame
Remain not hidden!
Air! light!
Woe's thee!

CHORUS.

> *Quid sum miser tunc dicturus?*   3480
> *Quem patronum rogaturus!*
> *Cum vix justus sit securus.*

EVIL SPIRIT.

The glorified their faces turn
Away from thee!
Shudder the pure to reach   3485
Their hands to thee!
Woe!

CHORUS.

> *Quid sum miser tunc dicturus —*

MARGARET.

Neighbor! your smelling bottle!
(*She swoons away*).

The Hartz Mountains.
District of Schierke and Elend.
FAUST *and* MEPHISTOPHELES.

MEPHISTOPHELES.

A broomstick dost thou not at least desire?   3490
The roughest he-goat fain would I bestride,
By this road from our goal we're still far wide.

FAUST.

While fresh upon my legs, so long I naught require,
Except this knotty staff. Beside,
What boots it to abridge a pleasant way?   3495
Along the labyrinth of these vales to creep,
Then scale these rocks, whence, in eternal spray,
Adown the cliffs the silvery fountains leap:
Such is the joy that seasons paths like these!
Spring weaves already in the birchen trees;   3500
E'en the late pine-grove feels her quickening powers;
Should she not work within these limbs of ours?

MEPHISTOPHELES.

Naught of this genial influence do I know!
Within me is all wintry. Frost and snow
I should prefer my dismal path to bound.   3505
How sadly, yonder, with belated glow
Rises the ruddy moon's imperfect round,
Shedding so faint a light at every tread
One's sure to stumble 'gainst a rock or tree!
An Ignis Fatuus I must call instead.   3510
Yonder one burning merrily, I see.
Holloa! my friend, may I request your light?
Why should you flare away so uselessly?
Be kind enough to show us up the height!

IGNIS FATUUS.

Through reverence I hope, I may subdue   3515

The lightness of my nature; true,
Our course is but a zigzag one.

MEPHISTOPHELES.

                            Ho! ho!
So man, forsooth, he thinks to imitate!
Now, in the devil's name, for once go straight,
Or out at once your flickering life I'll blow!   3520

IGNIS FATUUS.

That you are master here is obvious quite;
To do your will I'll cordially essay;
Only reflect!   The hill is magic-mad to-night;
And if to show the path you choose a meteor's light,
You must not wonder should we go astray.   3525

FAUST, MEPHISTOPHELES, IGNIS FATUUS

(*in alternate song*).

Through this dream and magic-sphere,
Lead us on, thou flickering guide.
Pilot well our bold career!
That we may with onward stride
Gain yon vast and desert waste!   3530

See how tree on tree with haste
Rush amain, the granite blocks
Make obeisance as they go!
Hark! the grim long-snouted rocks,
How they snort, and how they blow!   3535

Brook and brooklet hurrying flow
Through the turf and stones along;
Hark, the rustling!   Hark, the song!
Hearken to love's plaintive lays;
Voices of those heavenly days—   3540
What we hope and what we love!
Like the song of olden time,
Echo's voice repeats the chime.

To-whit!   To-whoo!   It sounds more near;
Pewit, owl, and jay appear,   3545
All awake, around, above!
Paunchy salamanders too
Crawl, long-limbed, the bushes through!

And, like snakes, the roots of trees
Coil themselves from rock and sand,   3550
Stretching many a wondrous band,
Us to frighten, us to seize;
From rude knots with life embued,
Polyp-fangs abroad they spread,
To snare the wanderer! 'Neath our tread,   3555
Mice, in myriads, thousand-hued,
Through the heath and through the moss!
And the fire-flies' glittering throng,
Wildering escort, whirls along,
Here and there, our path across.   3560

Tell me, stand we motionless,
Or still forward do we press?
All things round us whirl and fly
Rocks and trees make strange grimaces,
Dazzling meteors change their places,   3565
How they puff and multiply!

MEPHISTOPHELES.

Now grasp my doublet — we at last
Have reached a central precipice,
Whence we a wondering glance may cast,
How Mammon lights the dark abyss.   3570

FAUST.

How through the chasms strangely gleams,
A lurid light, like dawn's red glow,
Pervading with its quivering beams,
The gorges of the gulf below!
There vapors rise, there clouds float by,   3575
And here through mist the splendor shines;
Now, like a fount, it bursts on high,
Now glideth on in slender lines;
Far-reaching, with a hundred veins,
Through the far valley see it glide,   3580
Here, where the gorge the flood restrains,
At once it scatters far and wide;
Anear, like showers of golden sand
Strewn broadcast, sputter sparks of light:
And mark yon rocky walls that stand   3585
Ablaze, in all their towering height!

MEPHISTOPHELES.

Sir Mammon for this festival,
Grandly illumes his palace hall!
To see it was a lucky chance;
E'en now the boist'rous guests advance.   3590

FAUST.

How the fierce tempest sweeps around!
Upon my neck it strikes with sudden shock!

MEPHISTOPHELES.

Cling to these ancient ribs of granite rock,
Else it will hurl you down to yon abyss profound,
A murky vapor thickens night.   3595
Hark!   Through the woods the tempests roar!
The owlets flit in wild affright.
Split are the columns that upbore
The leafy palace, green for aye:
The shivered branches whirr and sigh,   3600
Yawn the huge trunks with mighty groan,
The roots, upriven, creak and moan!
In fearful and entangled fall,
One crashing ruin whelms them all,
While through the desolate abyss,   3605
Sweeping the wreck-strown precipice,
The raging storm-blasts howl and hiss!
Hear'st thou voices sounding clear,
Distant now and now more near?
Hark! the mountain ridge along,   3610
Streameth a raving magic-song!

WITCHES (*in chorus*).

Now to the Brocken the witches hie,
The stubble is yellow, the corn is green;
Thither the gathering legions fly,
And sitting aloft is Sir Urian seen: 3615
O'er stick and o'er stone they go whirling along,
Witches and he-goats, a motley throng. [45]

VOICES.

Alone old Baubo's coming now;
She rides upon a farrow sow.

CHORUS.

Honor to her, to whom honor is due! 3620
Forward, Dame Baubo! Honor to you
A goodly sow and mother thereon,
The whole witch chorus follows anon.

VOICE.

Which way didst come?

VOICE.

O'er Ilsenstein!
There I peeped in an owlet's nest. 3625
With her broad eye she gazed in mine

VOICE.

Drive to the devil, thou hellish pest!
Why ride so hard?

VOICE.

She has grazed my side,
Look at the wounds, how deep and how wide!

WITCHES (*in chorus*).

The way is broad, the way is long; 3630
What mad pursuit! What tumult wide!
Scratches the besom and sticks the prong;
Crushed is the mother, and stifled the child.

WIZARDS (*half chorus*).

Like house-encumbered snail we creep;
While far ahead the women keep, 3635
For when to the devil's house we speed,
By a thousand steps they take the lead.

THE OTHER HALF.

Not so, precisely do we view it; —
They with a thousand steps may do it;
But let them hasten as they can, 3640
With one long bound 'tis cleared by man.

VOICES (*above*).

Come with us, come with us from Felsensee.

VOICES (*from below*).

Aloft to you we would mount with glee.

We wash, and free from all stain are we,
Yet barren evermore must be!   3645

BOTH CHORUSES.

The wind is hushed, the stars grow pale,
The pensive moon her light doth veil;
And whirling on, the magic choir,
Sputter forth sparks of drizzling fire.

VOICE (*from below*).

Stay! stay!

VOICE (*from above*).

What voice of woe   3650
Calls from the caverned depths below?

VOICE (*from below*).

Take me with you!   Oh, take me too!
Three centuries I climb in vain,
And yet can ne'er the summit gain!
To be with my kindred I am fain.   3655

BOTH CHORUSES.

Broom and pitchfork, goat and prong,
Mounted on these we whirl along;
Who vainly strives to climb to-night,
Is evermore a luckless wight!

DEMI-WITCH (*below*).

I hobble after, many a day;   3660
Already the others are far away!
No rest at home can I obtain —
Here too my efforts are in vain!

CHORUS OF WITCHES.

Salve gives the witches strength to rise;
A rag for a sail does well enough;   3665
A goodly ship is every trough;
To-night who flies not, never flies.

BOTH CHORUSES.

And when the topmost peak we round,
Then alight ye on the ground;
The heath's wide regions cover ye   3670
With your mad swarms of witchery!

(*They let themselves down*).

MEPHISTOPHELES.

They crowd and jostle, whirl, and flutter!
They whisper, babble, twirl, and splutter!
They glimmer, sparkle, stink, and flare —
A true witch-element!   Beware!   3675
Stick close! else we shall severed be.
Where art thou?

FAUST (*in the distance*).
Here!

MEPHISTOPHELES.
Already, whirled so far away!
The master then indeed I needs must play.
Give ground! Squire Voland comes! Sweet folk,
    give ground! [46]
Here, doctor, grasp me!   With a single bound   3680
Let us escape this ceaseless jar;
Even for me too mad these people are.
Hard by there shineth something with peculiar glare,
Yon brake allureth me; it is not far;
Come, come along with me! we'll slip in there.   3685

FAUST.

Spirit of contradiction!   Lead! I'll follow straight!
'Twas wisely done, however, to repair
On May-night to the Brocken, and when there,
By our own choice ourselves to isolate!

MEPHISTOPHELES.

Mark, of those flames the motley glare!   3690
A merry club assembles there.
In a small circle one is not alone.

FAUST.

I'd rather be above, though, I must own!
Already fire and eddying smoke I view;
The impetuous millions to the devil ride;   3695
Full many a riddle will be there untied.

MEPHISTOPHELES.

Ay! and full many a one be tied anew.
But let the great world rave and riot!
Here will we house ourselves in quiet.

A custom 'tis of ancient date, 3700
Our lesser worlds within the great world to create!
Young witches there I see, naked and bare,
And old ones, veiled more prudently.
For my sake only courteous be!
The trouble's small, the sport is rare. 3705
Of instruments I hear the cursed din —
One must get used to it! Come in! come in!
There's now no help for it. I'll step before,
And introducing you as my good friend,
Confer on you one obligation more. 3710
How say you now? 'Tis no such paltry room;
Why only look, you scarce can see the end.
A hundred fires in rows disperse the gloom;
They dance, they talk, they cook, make love, and drink:
Where could we find aught better, do you think? 3715

FAUST.

To introduce us, do you purpose here
As devil or as wizard to appear?

MEPHISTOPHELES.

Though I am wont indeed to strict incognito,
Yet upon gala-days one must one's orders show.
No garter have I to distinguish me, 3720
Nathless the cloven foot doth here give dignity.
Seest thou yonder snail? Crawling this way she hies;
With searching feelers, she, no doubt,
Hath me already scented out;
Here, even if I would, for me there's no disguise. 3725
From fire to fire, we'll saunter at our leisure,
The gallant you, I'll cater for your pleasure.

(To a party seated round some expiring embers.)

Old gentlemen, apart, why sit ye moping here?
Ye in the midst should be of all this jovial cheer,
Girt round with noise and youthful riot; 3730
At home one surely has enough of quiet.

GENERAL.

In nations put his trust who may,
Whate'er for them one may have done;

The people are like women, they
Honor your rising stars alone!   3735

MINISTER.

Too far from truth and right they wander now;
I must extol the good old ways,
For truly when all spoke our praise,
Then was the golden age, I trow,

PARVENU.

Ne'er were we 'mong your dullards found,   3740
And what we ought not, that we did of old;
Yet now are all things turning round,
Just when we most desired them fast to hold.

AUTHOR.

Who, as a rule, a treatise now would care
To read, of even moderate sense?   3745
As for the rising generation, ne'er
Has youth displayed such arrogant pretence.

MEPHISTOPHELES

(suddenly appearing very old).
Since for the last time I the Brocken scale,
That folk are ripe for doomsday, now one sees;
And just because my cask begins to fail,   3750
So the whole world is also on the lees.

HUCKSTER-WITCH.

Stop, gentlemen, nor pass me by,
Of wares I have a choice collection;
Pray honor them with your inspection.
Lose not this opportunity!   3755
No fellow to my booth you'll find
On earth, for 'mong my store there's naught,
Which to the world, and to mankind,
Hath not some direful mischief wrought.
No dagger here, which hath not flowed with blood, 3760
No bowl, which hath not poured into some healthy
        frame
Hot poison's life-consuming flood,
No trinket but hath wrought some woman's shame,
No weapon but hath cut some sacred tie,
Or from behind hath stabbed an enemy.   3765

MEPHISTOPHELES.

Gossip! For wares like these the time's gone by.
What's done is past! what's past is done!
With novelties your booth supply;
Now novelties attract alone.

FAUST.

May this wild scene my senses spare!　　　　3770
This may in truth be called a fair!

MEPHISTOPHELES.

Upward the eddying concourse throng;
Thinking to push, thyself art pushed along.

FAUST.

Who's that, pray?

MEPHISTOPHELES.

Mark her well! That's Lilith.

FAUST.

Who?

MEPHISTOPHELES.

Adam's first wife. Of her rich locks beware!　　3775
That charm in which she's paralleled by few :
When in its toils a youth she doth ensnare,
He will not soon escape, I promise you.

FAUST.

There sit a pair, the old one with the young;
Already they have bravely danced and sprung!　3780

MEPHISTOPHELES.

Here there is no repose to-day.
Another dance begins; we'll join it, come away!

FAUST

(*dancing with the young one*).

Once a fair vision came to me;
Therein I saw an apple-tree,
Two beauteous apples charmed mine eyes;　3785
I climbed forthwith to reach the prize.

THE FAIR ONE.

Apples still fondly ye desire,
From paradise it hath been so.

Feelings of joy my breast inspire
That such too in my garden grow.   3790

MEPHISTOPHELES (*with the old one*).

Once a weird vision came to me;
Therein I saw a rifted tree.
It had a . . . . . ;
But as it was it pleased me too.

THE OLD ONE.

I beg most humbly to salute   3795
The gallant with the cloven foot!
Let him a . . . have ready here,
If he a . . . does not fear.

PROCTOPHANTASMIST. [47]

Accursed mob! How dare ye thus to meet?
Have I not shown and demonstrated too,   3800
That ghosts stand not on ordinary feet?
Yet here ye dance as other mortals do!

THE FAIR ONE (*dancing*).

Then at our ball, what doth he here?

FAUST (*dancing*).

Oh! he must everywhere appear.
He must adjudge, when others dance;   3805
If on each step his say's not said,
So is that step as good as never made.
He's more annoyed as soon as we advance;
If ye would circle in one narrow round,
As he in his old mill, then doubtless he   3810
Your dancing would approve, — especially
If ye forthwith salute him with respect profound!

PROCTOPHANTASMIST.

Still here! what arrogance! unheard of quite!
Vanish; we now have filled the world with light!
Laws are unheeded by the devil's host;   3815
Wise as we are, yet Tegel hath its ghost! [48]
How long at this conceit I've swept with all my might,
Lost is the labor: 'tis unheard of quite!

THE FAIR ONE.

Cease here to tease us any more, I pray.

PROCTOPHANTASMIST.

Spirits, I plainly to your face declare: 3820
No spiritual control myself will bear,
Since my own spirit can exert no sway.
                  (*The dance continues.*)
To-night, I see, I shall in naught succeed;
But I'm prepared my travels to pursue,
And hope, before my final step indeed,   3825
To triumph over bards and devils too.

MEPHISTOPHELES.

Now in some puddle will he take his station,
Such is his mode of seeking consolation;
Where leeches feasting on his blood, will drain
Spirit and spirits from his haunted brain.   3830
        (*To* FAUST, *who has left the dance.*)
But why the charming damsel leave, I pray,
Who to you in the dance so sweetly sang?

FAUST.

Ah, in the very middle of her lay,
Out of her mouth a small red mouse there sprang.

MEPHISTOPHELES.

Suppose there did! one must not be too nice: 3835
'Twas well it was not gray, let that suffice.
Who 'mid his pleasures for a trifle cares?

FAUST

Then saw I —

MEPHISTOPHELES.
    What?

FAUST.
           Mephisto, see'st thou there
Standing far off, a lone child, pale and fair?
Slow from the spot her drooping form she tears, 3840
And seems with shackled feet to move along;
I own, within me the delusion's strong,
That she the likeness of my Gretchen wears.

MEPHISTOPHELES.

Gaze not upon her! 'Tis not good! Forbear!
'Tis lifeless, magical, a shape of air,   3845

An idol.   Such to meet with bodes no good;
That rigid look of hers doth freeze man's blood,
And well nigh petrifies his heart to stone :—
The story of Medusa thou hast known.

FAUST.

Ay, verily! a corpse's eyes are those,   3850
Which there was no fond loving hand to close.
That is the bosom I so fondly pressed,
That my sweet Gretchen's form so oft caressed!

MEPHISTOPHELES.

Deluded fool!   'Tis magic, I declare!
To each she doth his loved one's image wear.   3855

FAUST.

What bliss! what torture! vainly I essay
To turn me from that piteous look away.
How strangely doth a single crimson line
Around that lovely neck its coil entwine,
It shows no broader than a knife's blunt edge!   3860

MEPHISTOPHELES.

Quite right.   I see it also, and allege
That she beneath her arm her head can bear,
Since Perseus cut it off. — But you I swear
Are craving for illusion still!
Come then, ascend yon little hill!   3865
As on the Prater all is gay,
And if my senses are not gone,
I see a theatre, — what's going on?

SERVIBILIS.

They are about to recommence; the play
Will be the last of seven, and spick-span new — 3870
'Tis usual here that number to present —
A dilettanti did the piece invent,
And dilettanti will enact it too.
Excuse me, gentlemen ; to me's assigned
As dilettante to uplift the curtain.   3875

MEPHISTOPHELES.

You on the Blocksberg I'm rejoiced to find,
That 'tis your most appropriate sphere is certain.

THE INTERMEZZO.

NOTE BY THE TRANSLATOR.

As without some key this scene is utterly incomprehensible to the English reader, a brief notice of some of the allusions it contains is here subjoined; they are dwelt upon at greater length in Düntzer's work.

It may be regarded as a kind of satirical *jeu d'esprit*, and consists of a series of epigrams directed against a variety of false tendencies in art, literature, religion, philosophy, and political life.

The introductory stanzas are founded upon the Midsummer Night's Dream, and Wieland's Oberon. To celebrate the reconciliation of the fairy king and queen a grotesque assemblage of figures appears upon the stage. Commonplace musicians and poetasters, having no conception that every poem must be an organic whole, are satirized as the bagpipe, the embryo spirit, and the little pair. Then follows a series of epigrams, having reference to the plastic arts, and directed against that false pietism and affected purity which would take a narrow and one-sided view of artistical creations. Nicolai, the sworn enemy of ghosts and Jesuits, is introduced as the inquisitive traveller, and Stolberg, who severely criticized Schiller's poem, "The Gods of Greece," is alluded to in the couplet headed "Orthodox."

Hennings, the editor of two literary journals, entitled the Musaget, and the Genius of the Age, had attacked the Xenien, a series of epigrams, published jointly by Goethe and Schiller; Goethe, in retaliation, makes him confess his own unfitness to be a leader of the Muses, and his readiness to assign a place on the German Parnassus to any one who was willing to bow to his authority. Nicolai again appears as the inquisitive traveller, and Lavater is said to be alluded to as the crane. The metaphysical philosophers are next the objects of the poet's satire; allusion is made to the bitter hostility manifested by the contending schools, the characteristics of which are so well known that it is needless to dwell upon them here. The philosophers are succeeded by the politicians; the "knowing ones," who in the midst of political revolutions, manage to keep in with the ruling party, are contrasted with those unfortunate individuals who are unable to accommodate themselves to the new order of things. In revolutionary times also, parvenus are raised to positions of eminence, while worthless notabilities, deprived of their hereditary splendor, are unable to maintain their former dignified position. "The massive ones," typify the men of the revolution, the leaders of the people, who, heedless of intervening obstacles, march straight on to their destined goal. Puck and Ariel, who had introduced the shadowy procession, again make their appearance, and the fairy pageant vanishes into air.

What relation this fantastic assemblage bears to Faust is not immediately obvious, unless, indeed, as Düntzer suggests, the poet meant to shadow forth the various distractions with which Mephistopheles endeavors to dissipate the mind of Faust, who had turned with disgust from the witch-society of the Brocken.

WALPURGIS-NIGHT'S DREAM;

OR,

OBERON AND TITANIA'S GOLDEN WEDDING-FEAST.

———

INTERMEZZO.

Theatre.

MANAGER.

Vales, where mists still shift and play.
   To ancient hill succeeding, —
These our scenes ;—so we, to-day,   3880
   May rest, brave sons of Mieding. [49]

HERALD.

That the marriage golden be,
   Must fifty years be ended ;
More dear this feast of gold to me,
   Contention now suspended.   3885

OBERON.

Spirits, are ye hovering near,
   Show yourselves around us!
King and queen behold ye here,
   Love hath newly bound us.

PUCK.

Puck draws near and wheels about,   3890
   In mazy circles dancing !
Hundreds swell his joyous shout,
   Behind him still advancing.

169

ARIEL.

Ariel wakes his dainty air,
　His lyre celestial stringing. —　　　　　3895
Fools he lureth, and the fair,
　With his celestial singing.

OBERON.

Wedded ones, would ye agree,
　We court your imitation:
Would ye fondly love as we,　　　　　3900
　We counsel separation.

TITANIA.

If husband scold and wife retort,
　Then bear them far asunder;
Her to the burning south transport,
　And him the North Pole under.　　　　3905

THE WHOLE ORCHESTRA (*fortissimo*).

Flies and midges all unite
　With frog and chirping cricket,
Our orchestra throughout the night,
　Resounding in the thicket!

(*Solo.*)

Yonder doth the bagpipe come!　　　　3910
　Its sack an airy bubble.
Schnick, schnick, schnack, with nasal hum,
　Its notes it doth redouble.

EMBRYO SPIRIT.

Spider's foot and midge's wing,
　A toad in form and feature;　　　　　3915
Together verses it can string,
　Though scarce a living creature.

A LITTLE PAIR.

Tiny step and lofty bound,
　Through dew and exhalation;
Ye trip it deftly on the ground,　　　　3920
　But gain no elevation.

INQUISITIVE TRAVELLER.

Can I indeed believe my eyes?
  Is't not mere masquerading?
What! Oberon in beauteous guise,
  Among the groups parading!   3925

ORTHODOX.

No claws, no tail to whisk about,
  To fright us at our revel; —
Yet like the gods of Greece, no doubt,
  He too's a genuine devil.

NORTHERN ARTIST.

These that I'm hitting off to-day   3930
  Are sketches unpretending;
Towards Italy without delay,
  My steps I think of bending.

PURIST.

Alas! ill-fortune leads me here,
  Where riot still grows louder;   3935
And 'mong the witches gathered here,
  But two alone wear powder!

YOUNG WITCH.

Your powder and your petticoat,
  Suit hags, there's no gainsaying;
Hence I sit fearless on my goat,   3940
  My naked charms displaying.

MATRON.

We're too well-bred to squabble here,
  Or insult back to render;
But may you wither soon, my dear,
  Although so young and tender.   3945

LEADER OF THE BAND.

Nose of fly and gnat's proboscis,
  Throng not the naked beauty!
Frogs and crickets in the mosses,
  Keep time and do your duty!

WEATHERCOCK (*towards one side*).

What charming company I view   3950
    Together here collected!
Gay bachelors, a hopeful crew,
    And brides so unaffected!

WEATHERCOCK (*towards the other side*)

Unless indeed the yawning ground
    Should open to receive them,   3955
From this vile crew, with sudden bound,
    To Hell I'd jump and leave them.

XENIEN.

With small sharp shears, in insect guise,
    Behold us at your revel!
That we may tender, filial-wise,   3960
    Our homage to the devil.

HENNINGS.

Look now at yonder eager crew,
    How naïvely they're jesting!
That they have tender hearts and true,
    They stoutly keep protesting!   3965

MUSAGET.

Oneself amid this witchery
    How pleasantly one loses!
For witches easier are to me
    To govern than the Muses!

CI-DEVANT GENIUS OF THE AGE.

With proper folks when we appear,   3970
    No one can then surpass us!
Keep close, wide is the Blocksberg here
    As Germany's Parnassus.

INQUISITIVE TRAVELLER.

How name ye that stiff formal man,
    Who strides with lofty paces?   3975
He tracks the game where'er he can,
    "He scents the Jesuits' traces."

CRANE.

Where waters troubled are or clear,
  To fish I am delighted;
Thus pious gentlemen appear   3980
  With devils here united.

WORLDLING.

By pious people, it is true,
  No medium is rejected;
Conventicles, and not a few,
  On Blocksberg are erected.   3985

DANCER.

Another choir is drawing nigh,
  Far off the drums are beating.
Be still! 'tis but the bittern's cry,
  Its changeless note repeating.

DANCING-MASTER.

Each twirls about and never stops,   3990
  And as he can advances.
The crooked leaps, the clumsy hops,
  Nor careth how he dances.

FIDDLER.

To take each other's life, I trow,
  Would cordially delight them!   3995
As Orpheus' lyre the beasts, so now
  The bagpipe doth unite them.

DOGMATIST.

My views, in spite of doubt and sneer,
  I hold with stout persistence,
Inferring from the devils here,   4000
  The evil one's existence.

IDEALIST.

My every sense rules Phantasy
  With sway quite too potential;
Sure I'm demented if the *I*
  Alone is the essential.   4005

REALIST.

This entity's a dreadful bore,
  And cannot choose but vex me;
The ground beneath me ne'er before
  Thus tottered to perplex me.

SUPERNATURALIST.

Well pleased assembled here I view   4010
  Of spirits this profusion;
From devils, touching angels too,
  I gather some conclusion.

SKEPTIC.

The ignis fatuus they track out,
  And think they're near the treasure.   4015
Devil alliterates with doubt,
  Here I abide with pleasure.

LEADER OF THE BAND.

Frog and cricket in the mosses, —
  Confound your gasconading!
Nose of fly and gnat's proboscis; —   4020
  Most tuneful serenading!

THE KNOWING ONES.

Sans-souci, so this host we greet,
  Their jovial humor showing!
There's now no walking on our feet,
  So on our heads we're going.   4025

THE AWKWARD ONES.

In seasons past we snatched, 'tis true,
  Some tit-bits by our cunning;
Our shoes, alas, are now danced through,
  On our bare soles we're running,

WILL-O'-THE-WISPS.

From marshy bogs we sprang to light,   4030
  Yet here behold us dancing;
The gayest gallants of the night,
  In glitt'ring rows advancing.

SHOOTING STAR.

With rapid motion from on high,
  I shot in starry splendor;   4035
Now prostrate on the grass I lie;—
  Who aid will kindly render?

THE MASSIVE ONES.

Room! wheel round! They're coming! lo!
  Down sink the bending grasses.
Though spirits, yet their limbs, we know, 4040
  Are huge substantial masses.

PUCK.

Don't stamp so heavily, I pray.
  Like elephants you're treading!
And 'mong the elves be Puck to-day,
  The stoutest at the wedding!   4045

ARIEL.

If nature boon, or subtle sprite,
  Endow your soul with pinions;—
Then follow to yon rosy height,
  Through ether's calm dominions!

ORCHESTRA (*pianissimo*).

Drifting cloud and misty wreathes   4050
  Are filled with light elysian;
O'er reed and leaf the zephyr breathes —
  So fades the fairy vision!

A gloomy Day. A Plain.

FAUST *and* MEPHISTOPHELES.

FAUST.

In misery! despairing! long wandering pitifully on
the face of the earth and now imprisoned! This gentle,
hapless creature, immured in the dungeon as a malefactor and reserved for horrid tortures! That it should
come to this! To this! — Perfidious, worthless spirit,
and this thou hast concealed from me! — Stand! ay,
stand! roll in malicious rage thy fiendish eyes! Stand

and defy me with thine insupportable presence! Imprisoned! In hopeless misery! Delivered over to the power of evil spirits and the judgment of unpitying humanity! — And me, the while, thou wert lulling with tasteless dissipation, concealing from me her growing anguish, and leaving her to perish without help! 4066

MEPHISTOPHELES.

She is not the first.

FAUST.

Hound! Execrable monster! — Back with him, oh, thou infinite spirit! back with the reptile into his dog's shape, in which it was his wont to trot before me at even-tide, to roll before the feet of the harmless wanderer, and to fasten on his shoulders when he fell! Change him again into his favorite shape, that he may crouch on his belly before me in the dust, whilst I spurn him with my foot, the reprobate! — Not the first! Woe! Woe! By no human soul is it conceivable, that more than one human creature has ever sunk into a depth of wretchedness like this, or that the first in her writhing death-agony, should not have atoned in the sight of all-pardoning Heaven, for the guilt of all the rest! The misery of this one pierces me to the very marrow, and harrows up my soul; thou art grinning calmly over the doom of thousands! 4082

MEPHISTOPHELES.

Now we are once again at our wits' end, just where the reason of you mortals snaps! Why dost thou seek our fellowship, if thou canst not go through with it? Wilt fly, and art not proof against dizziness? Did we force ourselves on thee, or thou on us? 4087

FAUST.

Cease thus to gnash thy ravenous fangs at me! I loathe thee! — Great and glorious spirit, thou who didst vouchsafe to reveal thyself unto me, thou who dost know my very heart and soul, why hast thou linked me with this base associate, who feeds on mischief and revels in destruction? . 4093

MEPHISTOPHELES.

Hast done?

FAUST.

Save her!—or woe to thee! The direst of curses
on thee for thousands of years!

MEPHISTOPHELES.

I cannot loose the bands of the avenger, nor withdraw his bolts.—Save her!—Who was it plunged her
into perdition? I or thou?   4099

FAUST (*looks wildly around*).

MEPHISTOPHELES.

Wouldst grasp the thunder? Well for you, poor
mortals, that 'tis not yours to wield! To smite to
atoms, the being, however innocent, who obstructs his
path, such is the tyrant's fashion of relieving himself in
difficulties!

FAUST.

Convey me thither! She shall be free!   4104

MEPHISTOPHELES.

And the danger to which thou dost expose thyself?
Know, the guilt of blood, shed by thy hand, lies yet
upon the town. Over the place where fell the murdered one, avenging spirits hover and watch for the
returning murderer.   4109

FAUST.

This too from thee? The death and downfall of a
world be on thee, monster. Conduct me thither, I say,
and set her free!   4112

MEPHISTOPHELES.

I will conduct thee. And what I can do,—hear!
Have I all power in heaven and upon earth? I'll cloud
the senses of the warder,—do thou possess thyself of
the keys and lead her forth with human hand! I will
keep watch! The magic steeds are waiting, I bear thee
off. Thus much is in my power.   4118

FAUST.

Up and away!

Night.   Open country.
FAUST.   MEPHISTOPHELES.
(*Rushing along on black horses.*)

FAUST.

What weave they yonder round the Ravenstone? 4120

MEPHISTOPHELES.

I know not what they shape and brew.

FAUST.

They're soaring, swooping, bending, stooping.

MEPHISTOPHELES.

A witches' pack.

FAUST.

They charm, they strew.

MEPHISTOPHELES.

On!   On!

Dungeon.

FAUST

(*with a bunch of keys and a lamp before a small iron
door*).

A fear unwonted o'er my spirit falls;   4125
Man's concentrated woe o'erwhelms me here!
She dwells immured within these dripping walls;
Her only trespass a delusion dear!
Thou lingerest at the fatal door?
Thou dread'st to see her face once more?   4130
On!   While thou dalliest, draws her death-hour near.
          (*He seizes the lock.   Singing within.*)
              My mother, the harlot,[50]
              She took me and slew!
              My father, the scoundrel,
              Hath eaten me too!   4135
              My sweet little sister
              Hath all my bones laid,
              Where soft breezes whisper
              All in the cool shade!

Then became I a wood-bird and sang on the spray,
Fly away! little bird, fly away! fly away!   4141

FAUST (*opening the lock*).
Ah! she forebodes not that her lover's near.
The clanking chains, the rustling straw, to hear.
(*He enters.*)

MARGARET
(*hiding her face in the bed of straw*).
Woe! woe! they come! oh, bitter 'tis to die!

FAUST (*softly*).
Hush! hush! be still! I come to set thee free?   4145

MARGARET (*throwing herself at his feet*).
If thou art human feel my misery!

FAUST.
Thou wilt awake the jailer with thy cry!
(*He grasps the chains to unlock them*).

MARGARET (*on her knees*).
Who, headsman, unto thee this power
O'er me could give?
Thou com'st for me at midnight hour.   4150
Be merciful, and let me live!
Is morrow's dawn not time enough?
(*She stands up.*)
I'm still so young, so young—
And must so early die!
Fair was I too, and that was my undoing.   4155
My love is now afar, he then was nigh;
Torn lies the garland, the fair blossoms strewed.
Nay, seize me not with hand so rude!
Spare me!   What harm have I e'er done to thee?
Oh, let me not in vain implore!   4160
I ne'er have seen thee in my life before!

FAUST.
Can I endure this bitter agony?

MARGARET.

I now am at thy mercy quite.
Let me my babe but suckle once again!
I fondled it the livelong night;   4165
They took it from me but to give me pain,
And now, they say that I my child have slain.
Gladness I ne'er again shall know.
Then they sing songs about me, — 'tis wicked of the
      throng —
An ancient ballad endeth so: 4170
Who bade them thus apply the song?

FAUST

(throwing himself on the ground).

A lover at thy feet bends low,
To loose the bonds of wretchedness and woe.

MARGARET

(throws herself beside him).

Oh, let us kneel and move the saints by prayer!
Look! look! yon stairs below,   4175
Under the threshold there,
Hell's flames are all aglow!
Beneath the floor,
With hideous noise,
The devils roar!   4180

FAUST (aloud).

Gretchen! Gretchen!

MARGARET (listening).

That was my loved one's voice!

(She springs up, the chains fall off.)

Where is he? I heard him calling me.
Free am I! There's none shall hinder me.
To his neck will I fly,   4185
On his bosom will lie!
Gretchen he called! — On yon threshold he stood;
Amidst all the howling of hell's fiery flood,
The scoff and the scorn of its devilish crew,
The tones of his voice, sweet and loving, I knew.   4190

FAUST.

'Tis I !

MARGARET.

'Tis thou !　O say so once again !

(Embracing him.)

'Tis he !　'Tis he !　Where's now the torturing pain ?
Where are the fetters ?　where the dungeon's gloom ?
'Tis thou !　To save me thou art come !
And I am saved !　　　　　　　　　　4195
Already now the street I see
Where the first time I caught a glimpse of thee.
There too the pleasant garden shade,
Where I and Martha for thy coming stayed.

FAUST

(endeavoring to lead her away).

Come !　come away !

MARGARET.

　　　　　Oh, do not haste !　　　　4200
I love to linger where thou stayest.

(Caressing him.)

FAUST.

Ah, haste !　For if thou still delayest,
Our lingering we shall both deplore.

MARGARET.

How, dearest ! canst thou kiss no more ?
So short a time away from me, and yet,　　4205
To kiss thou couldst so soon forget !
Why on thy neck so anxious do I feel —
When formerly a perfect heaven of bliss
From thy dear looks and words would o'er me steal ?
As thou wouldst stifle me thou then didst kiss !　4210
Kiss me !
Or I'll kiss thee !　　(She embraces him.)
Woe ! woe !　Thy lips are cold, —
Are dumb !

Thy love where hast thou left?   4215
Who hath me of thy love bereft?
(*She turns away from him.*)

FAUST.

Come! Follow me, my dearest love, be bold .
I'll cherish thee with ardor thousandfold ;
I but entreat thee now to follow me !

MARGARET
(*turning towards him*).

And art thou he? and art thou really he?   4220

FAUST.

'Tis I ! Oh come!

MARGARET.

Thou wilt strike off my chain,
And thou wilt take me to thine arms again.
How comes it that thou dost not shrink from me ?—
And dost thou know, love, whom thou wouldst set free?

FAUST.

Come! come! already night begins to wane.   4225

MARGARET.

I sent my mother to her grave,
I drowned my child beneath the wave.
Was it not given to thee and me — thee too ?
'Tis thou thyself ! I scarce believe it yet.
Give me thy hand ! It is no dream ! 'Tis true ! 4230
Thine own dear hand ! — But how is this ? 'Tis wet !
Quick, wipe it off ! Meseems that yet
There's blood thereon !
Ah, God ! What hast thou done ?
Put up thy sword,   4235
I beg of thee !

FAUST.

Oh, dearest, let the past forgotten be !
Death is in every word.

MARGARET.

No, thou must linger here in sorrow !

The graves I will describe to thee, 4240
And thou to them must see
To-morrow :
The best place give to my mother,
Close at her side my brother,
Me at some distance lay — 4245
But not too far away !
And the little one place on my right breast.
Nobody else will near me lie !
To nestle beside thee so lovingly,
That was a rapture, gracious and sweet ! 4250
A rapture I never again shall prove ;
Methinks I have to force myself on thee, love,
And thou dost spurn me, and back retreat —
Yet 'tis thyself, thy fond, kind looks I see.

FAUST.

If thou dost feel 'tis I, then come with me ! 4255

MARGARET.

What, there ? without ?

FAUST.

    Yes, forth in the free air.

MARGARET.

Ay, if the grave's without, — if death lurk there
Hence to the everlasting resting-place,
And not one step beyond ! — Thou'rt leaving me ?
Oh, Henry ! would that I could go with thee ! 4260

FAUST.

Thou canst ! But will it ! Open stands the door.

MARGARET.

I dare not go ! I've naught to hope for more.
What boots it to escape ? They lurk for me !
'Tis wretched to beg, as I must do,
And with an evil conscience thereto ! 4265
'Tis wretched, in foreign lands to stray ;
And me they will catch, do what I may !

FAUST.

With thee will I abide.

MARGARET.

Quick!   Quick!
Save thy poor child !   4270
Keep to the path
The brook along,
Over the bridge
To the wood beyond,
To the left, where the plank is,   4275
In the pond.
Seize it at once !
It fain would rise,
It struggles still !
Save it.   Oh, save!   4280

FAUST.

Dear Gretchen, more collected be !
One little step, and thou art free !

MARGARET.

Were we but only past the hill !
There sits my mother upon a stone —
My brain, alas, is cold with dread ! —   4285
There sits my mother upon a stone,
And to and fro she shakes her head ;
She winks not, she nods not, her head it droops sore ;
She slept so long, she waked no more ;
She slept, that we might taste of bliss :   4290
Ah ! those were happy times, I wis !

FAUST.

Since here avails nor argument nor prayer,
Thee hence by force I needs must bear.

MARGARET.

Loose me !   I will not suffer violence !
With murderous hand hold not so fast !   4295
I have done all to please thee in the past !

FAUST.

Day dawns. My love! My love!

MARGARET.

                          Yes! day draws near.
The day of judgment too will soon appear!
It should have been my bridal! No one tell,
That thou hast been already here.   4300
Woe to my garland!
Its bloom is o'er!
We shall meet once more
But not at the dance.
The crowd doth gather, in silence it rolls;   4305
The squares, the streets,
Scarce hold the throng.
51 The staff is broken, — the death-bell tolls, —
They bind and seize me! I'm hurried along,
To the seat of blood already I'm bound!   4310
Quivers each neck as the naked steel
Quivers on mine the blow to deal —
The silence of the grave now broods around!

FAUST.

Would I had ne'er been born!

MEPHISTOPHELES (*appears without*).

Up! or you're lost.   4315
Vain hesitation! Babbling, quaking! 52
My steeds are shivering,
Morn is breaking.

MARGARET.

What from the floor ascendeth like a ghost?
'Tis he! 'Tis he! Him from my presence chase! 4320
What would he in this holy place?
It is for me he cometh!

FAUST.
Thou shalt live!

MARGARET.
Judgment of God! To thee my soul I give!

MEPHISTOPHELES (*to* FAUST).

Come! come.   I'll leave thee else to share her doom!

MARGARET.

Father, I'm thine!   Save me!   To thee I come! 4325
Ye angels!   Ye angelic hosts! descend,
Encamp around to guard me and defend!—
Henry!   I shudder now to look on thee!

MEPHISTOPHELES.

She now is judged!

VOICES (*from above*).

Is saved!

MEPHISTOPHELES (*to* FAUST).

Come thou with me!

(*vanishes with* FAUST.)

VOICE (*from within, dying away*).

Henry!   Henry!   4330

NOTES TO PART I.

1. This Dedication was written, it is supposed, in 1797, seven years after the "Fragment" of Part I. was published, and twenty-four years after the first scenes were written. Several of Goethe's most intimate friends, among them his beloved sister Cornelia, had died meanwhile.

2. Literally, "Cheated of beautiful hours by fate."

3. An allusion to the temporary structures which served for theatres when the actors were mostly itinerant companies.

4. Literally, "when the stream presses toward our booth and with repeated violent pains squeezes through the narrow gate of grace."

5. The three archangels speak in the inverse order of their celestial rank. The editor offers the following version of their song in which the female rhyme of the original is preserved : —

RAPHAEL.

The sun with brother orbs is sounding
  Still, as of old, his rival song,
As on his destined journey bounding
  With thunder-step he sweeps along.
The sight gives angels strength though greater
  Than angels' utmost thought sublime,
And all thy lofty works, Creator!
  Are grand as in creation's prime.

GABRIEL.

And fleetly, thought transcending, fleetly
  The earth's green pomp is spinning round,
And paradise alternates sweetly
  With night terrific and profound.
There foams the sea, its broad wave beating
  Against the cliff's deep rocky base,
And rock and sea away are fleeting
  In everlasting spheral chase.

MICHAEL.

And storms with rival fury heaving
  From land to sea, from sea to land,
Still as they rave a chain are weaving
  Of linkèd efficacy grand.
There burning desolation blazes,
  Precursor of the thunder's way;
But, Lord, thy servants own with praises
  The gentle movement of thy day.

ALL THREE.

The sight gives angels strength though greater
  Than angels' utmost thought sublime,
And all thy lofty works, Creator,
  Are grand as in creation's prime!

187

6. More properly the rogue, or the mischief-maker.

7. Fancy myself.

8. Michel de Notre Dame, a French astrologer of the sixteenth century. He published in 1555 a collection of prophecies in verse which attracted much attention. One of these prophecies predicted the death of Henry II. of France which happened soon after. Another foretold the downfall of the papacy, which caused his book to be placed on the Index expurgatorius.

9.

> In floods of life, in action's storm,
> Above, beneath,
> To and fro I am weaving
> Now birth, now death, —
> A deep ever heaving,
> With change still flowing,
> With life all glowing —
> The whirring loom of time I ply,
> And weave the live garment of Deity.

10. Famulus. A functionary once common in German universities where indigent students received tuition and material aid in return for services rendered to professors. Wagner is mentioned in the Faust legend as the magician's attendant. Goethe uses him as type of the German pedant, contrasting the idealism of Faust.

11. Brede, old English for braid, more proper to textile fabrics than to metallic work. The literal rendering is : " the artistically rich splendor of the many pictures."

12. Translation of the Easter Song by the editor :

CHORUS OF ANGELS.

> Christ has arisen !
> Joy ! ye dispirited
> Mortals, whom merited,
> Trailing, inherited
> Woes did imprison.

CHORUS OF WOMEN.

> Costly devices we had prepared,
> Shroud and sweet spices,
> Linen and nard.
> Wo ! the disaster !
> Whom we here laid,
> Gone is the Master,
> Empty his bed !

CHORUS OF ANGELS.

> Christ has arisen
> Loving and glorious,
> Out of laborious
> Conflict victorious.
> Hail to the risen !

CHORUS OF DISCIPLES.

> Hath the inhumated,
> Upward aspiring, —

Hath he consummated
All his desiring ?
Is he in nascent bliss
Near to creative joy ?
Wearily we in this
Earthly house sigh.
Empty and hollow, us
Left he unblest ?
Master, thy followers
Envy thy rest.

CHORUS OF ANGELS.

Christ hath arisen
Out of corruption's womb !
Burst every prison !
Vanish death's gloom !
Active in charity
Praise him in verity !
His feast, prepare it ye !
His message, bear it ye !
His joy, declare it ye !
Then is the Master near,
Then is he here.

13. St Andrew's Night, the 29th of November, when, according to popular superstition, maidens, by use of certain ceremonies, could obtain a vision of their future husbands.

14. Literally, she (the sun) wills to enliven all with color.

15. The word "scornful" does not express the meaning of *Hohn* in this passage. Faust says, "The applause of the multitude sounds to me like mockery."

16. Goethe here uses the jargon of alchemy, with which his youthful studies had made him acquainted. The "red lion" is red sulphuret of mercury, called a "suitor bold," on account of the readiness with which mercury combines with other metals. The "lily" (lilium Paracelci) is antimony. The "bridal bed" is the retort. The "youthful queen" is the chemical product, the medicine required.

17. The dog as a form assumed by Mephistopheles figures in the old Faust legend. Here he appears to be sent in answer to Faust's invocation addressed to "spirits of the air."

18. The Gospel according to St. John was one of the books which Faust by his compact with Mephistopheles was forbidden to read. Hence the uneasiness of the dog.

19. Solomon was esteemed in Jewish lore, represented by the Kabbala, a mighty magician The formulæ of conjuration, in a work known by the title "Clavicula Salomonis," were used by medieval exorcists.

20. The pentagram represents three triangles in one figure, a symbol of the Trinity.

21. This wonderful song is known in German as the lullaby (Einschläferungs lied). Its art consists in a rapid succession of images

which pass before the mind like dissolving views.   No translation can do it justice.   That of Mr. C. T. Brooks in his " Faust," is the best I have seen.

22. The editor thus translates Faust's curse :

> Though the torn heart a moment's healing
>   Imbibed with that familiar strain,*
> And what remain'd of childish feeling
>   Echoed the dear old time again,
> Yet curst be henceforth all that borrows
>   A magic lure to charm the breast,
> That prisoned in this cave of sorrows —
>   Would dazzle me or lull to rest.
> Curst before all the high opinion
>   With which the mind itself deludes !
> Curst be Appearance, whose dominion
>   Its shows on human sense intrudes !
> Curst all that to ambition caters
>   With honor and a deathless name !
> Curst all that as possession flatters
>   As wife and child and goods and game !
> Curst when with hope of golden treasure
>   He spurs our spirits to the fight,
> And curst be Mammon when for pleasure
>   He lays the tempting pillow right !
> Curst be the grape's balsamic potion !
>   And curst be love's delicious thrall !
> And curst be hope and faith's devotion !
>   And curst be patience more than all !

23. Mephistopheles seeks to nullify the effect of this lament of good spirits over Faust's despair by claiming them as his own and misinterpreting their counsel.

24. This scene is introduced for the evident purpose of ridiculing the methods of instruction in the universities, and especially the study of logic and systems of metaphysic, for which the author has a great contempt.

25. The original recommends a somewhat different method of arriving at the same result.

26. Faust does not say, " despite my long beard," but *with* (bei) my long beard I lack, etc.

27. The phrase " Frau Nachtigall " occurs in the poetry of the old Minnesingers.

28. 'Tis a pity the translator did not render the refrain literally :

> " As if he had love in his body."

29. Rippach, a country town not far from Leipzig.   Hans von Rippach, a synonyme for a verdant rustic, with which newcomers were taunted by the more advanced students.

30. This feat of jugglery is attributed to Albertus Magnus.

* To wit, the Easter Song.

31. The satirical allusions in the following scene are too obscure to admit of satisfactory explanation. It has been surmised that some of the utterances of the monkeys are hits at the poorer sorts of writers of the day. Faust finds them insipid (abgeschmackt), but Mephistopheles, who delights in what is low, professes himself well pleased with them.

32. Not coarse but broad (breite) that is, thin. Liquors are said to be "extended" when their volume is increased by dilution. There may be here an allusion to weak poetry. Gœthe in one of his aphorisms says: "Modern poets put too much water in their ink."

33. Koskinomancy, or prophesying by the sieve, was an ancient method of vaticination.

34. The translation misses the point of the original. "They are rid of the Evil One, but the evil ones have remained."

35. A vulgar jest of the German *plebs* ascribes to the nobility black posteriors.

36. The Multiplication-table is called in German *das Einmaleins*, once one is one.

37. The King in Thule. (*Editor's translation.*)

> There was a King in Thule,
>   True while life's breath he breathed;
> To him his mistress duly
>   A golden cup bequeathed.
>
> That cup — his choicest treasure —
>   He drained at every bout;
> His eyes ran o'er with pleasure
>   Whene'er he drank thereout.
>
> His day of life declining,
>   His towns he reckoned up,
> All to his heirs resigning,
>   All but the golden cup.
>
> Once more he held high wassail
>   With all his chivalry
> In his ancestral castle,
>   His castle by the sea.
>
> The old toper ere he perished
>   There drank life's parting glow,
> Then flung the cup he cherished
>   Into the flood below.
>
> He saw it plunging, drinking,
>   And sinking in the sea;
> His eyes the while were sinking,
>   Ne'er another drop drank he.

38. In the dark passageway or entry of the house.

39. This was done in token of contempt when, on her first marriage, the bride was not a virgin.

40. "You will soon have the satisfaction of lifting the treasure." There went a superstition that the earth contained buried treasures which periodically, in iron pots, approached the surface where their presence was indicated by a pale flame. Unless lifted by human hands they sank back again into the earth where they remained until the next period arrived.

41. Dollars coined in Louvain; the German name is Löwen (lion). They were stamped with the figure of a lion.

42. This song is an imitation of the one sung by Ophelia. Hamlet, act IV., sc. 5.

43. Rats were said to be caught by the lure of music.

44. The night of the first of May was the time assigned by popular superstition to the annual meeting of the witches on the Brocken. The first of May was also the calendar day of St. Walpurga, who came to Germany with Boniface. Hence Walpurgis Night.

45. The word translated he-goat, here means the stick on which the witches were supposed to ride; otherwise the line is an improvement on the original.

46. Squire Voland is a popular synonyme for the Devil.

47. By this term the author satirizes Nicolai, the inveterate rationalist, noted for his zealous polemic against the belief in witchcraft and ghosts.

48. The castle of Tegel, not far from Berlin, had the reputation of being "haunted."

49. Mieding was the name of a favorite theatre-decorator in Weimar.

50. This song refers to an old fairy-tale concerning a child who was killed by her stepmother and afterwards transformed into a bird.

51. The judge in a German court of justice, when pronouncing a sentence of death, breaks a wand.

52. "Quaking" is too great a sacrifice to rhyme; the original is *zaudern*, lingering.

THE SECOND PART

OF

THE TRAGEDY OF FAUST.

DRAMATIS PERSONÆ.

Faust.
Mephistopheles in various disguises.

ALSO IN

Act I.

Ariel.
Emperor.
Fool (*Mephistopheles*).
Chancellor.

Commander-in-Chief.
Treasurer.
Marshal.
Astrologer.

Various Ladies, Gentlemen, and pages of the Court.   Also
 numerous male and female masks.

Scene.   Chiefly in the different apartments and Pleasure
 Garden of the Imperial Palace.

Act II.

Famulus.
Baccalaureus.

Wagner.
Homunculus.

Numerous mythical personages and monsters appearing in the
 Classical Walpurgis Night.

Scene.   Faust's Study; afterwards the Pharsalian Plains.

Act III.

Helen.
Phorkyad (*Mephistopheles*).
Lynceus, the watchman.

Euphorion, Helen's son.
Panthalis and Chorus of
 Trojan women.

Scene.   At first the supposed Palace of Menelaus in Sparta;
 afterwards the courtyard of a mediæval castle, and finally a
 rocky dell.

Act IV.

The three mighty men: Bully, Havequick, and Holdfast.
Speedquick.
The Emperor, and other officers of his Court, as in Act I.

Scene.   A high mountainous country and the adjacent
 neighborhood.

Act V.

Baucis.
Philemon.
A Wanderer.
Lynceus.
Lemures.

The four gray women: Want,
 Guilt, Care, and Need.
A Penitent, formerly Marga-
 ret.
Dr. Marianus.

Chorus of Angels and Penitents and various Heavenly characters.

Scene.   The neighborhood of Faust's Palace, afterwards rocky
 heights and the higher regions of the sky.

PART II

ACT THE FIRST.

A pleasing landscape.
*F*AUST *reclining upon flowery turf,*
restless, seeking sleep.

TWILIGHT.

Circle of spirits, hovering, flit around ; —
graceful, tiny forms.

ARIEL.

Song, accompanied by Æolian harps.
When, in vernal showers descending,
Blossoms gently veil the earth,
When the field's green wealth, uptending,
Gleams on all of mortal birth :
Tiny elves, where help availeth,
Large of heart, there fly apace ;
Pity they whom grief assaileth,
Be he holy, be he base.

Ye round this head on airy wing careering,
Attend, in noble Elfin guise appearing ;   10
Assuage the cruel strife that rends his heart,
The burning shaft remove of keen remorse,
From rankling horror cleanse his inmost part :
Four are the pauses of tht nightly course ;
Them, without rest, fill up with kindly art.   15
And first his head upon cool pillow lay,
Then, bathe ye him in dew from Lethe's stream ;
His limbs, cramp-stiffened, will more freely play,
If sleep-refreshed he wait morn's wakening beam.

Perform the noblest Elfin rite,   20
Restore ye him to the holy light !

CHORUS

(*singly, two or more, alternately and together*).
Softly when warm gales are stealing
O'er the green environed ground,
Twilight sheddeth all concealing
Mists and balmy odors round :   25
Whispers low sweet peace to mortals,
Rocks the heart to childlike rest,
And of daylight shuts the portals
To these eyes, with care oppressed.

Night hath now descended darkling,   30
Holy star is linked to star ;
Sovereign fires, or faintly sparkling,
Glitter near and shine afar ;
Glitter here lake-mirrored, yonder
Shine adown the clear night sky ;   35
Sealing bliss of perfect slumber,
Reigns the moon's full majesty.

Now the hours are cancelled ; sorrow,
Happiness, have passed away :
Whole thou shalt be on the morrow !   40
Feel it !   Trust the new-born day !
Swell the hills, green grow the valleys,
In the dusk ere breaks the morn ;
And in silvery wavelets dallies,
With the wind the ripening corn.   45

Cherish hope, let naught appall thee !
Mark the East, with splendor dyed !
Slight the fetters that enthrall thee ;
Fling the shell of sleep aside !
Gird thee for the high endeavor ;   50
Shun the crowd's ignoble ease !
Fails the noble spirit never,
Wise to think and prompt to seize.

(*A tremendous tumult announces the uprising of the
Sun.*)

ARIEL.

Hark ! the horal tempest nears !
Sounding but for spirit ears,   55
Lo ! the new-born day appears ;

Clang the rocky portals, climb
Phœbus' wheels with thund'rous chime:
Breaks with tuneful noise the light!

Blare of trumpet, clarion sounding,   60
Eye-sight dazing, ear astounding!
Hear not the unheard; take flight!
Into petalled blossoms glide
Deeper, deeper, still to bide,
In the clefts, 'neath thickets! ye,   65
If it strike you, deaf will be.

FAUST.

Life's pulses reawakened freshly bound,
The mild ethereal twilight fain to greet.
Thou, Earth, this night wast also constant found,
And, newly-quickened, breathing at my feet,   70
Beginnest now to gird me with delight;
A strong resolve dost rouse, with noble heat
Aye to press on to being's sovereign height.
The world in glimmering dawn still folded lies;
With thousand-voicèd life the woods resound;   75
Mist-wreaths the valley shroud; yet from the skies
Sinks heaven's clear radiance to the depths profound;
And bough and branch from dewy chasms rise,
Where they had drooped erewhile in slumber furled;
Earth is enamelled with unnumbered dyes.   80
Leaflet and flower with dew-drops are impearled;
Around me everywhere is paradise.

Gaze now aloft!   Each mountain's giant height
The solemn hour announces, herald-wise;
They early may enjoy the eternal light,   85
To us below which later finds its way.
Now are the Alpine slopes and valleys dight
With the clear radiance of the new-born day,
Which, downward, step by step, steals on apace. —
It blazes forth, — and, blinded by the ray,   90
With aching eyes, alas! I veil my face.

So when a hope, the heart hath long held fast,
Trustful, still striving towards its highest goal,
Fulfilment's portals open finds at last; —
Sudden from those eternal depths doth roll   95

An overpowering flame; — we stand aghast!
The torch of life to kindle we were fain; —
A fire-sea, — what a fire! — doth round us close;
Love is it? Is it hate? with joy and pain,
In alternation vast, that round us glows?   100
So that to earth we turn our wistful gaze,
In childhood's veil to shroud us once again!

So let the sun behind me pour its rays!
The cataract, through rocky cleft that roars,
I view, with growing rapture and amaze.   105
From fall to fall, with eddying shock, it pours,
In thousand torrents to the depths below,
Aloft in air up-tossing showers of spray.
But see, in splendor bursting from the storm,
Arches itself the many-colored bow,   110
An ever-changeful, yet continuous form,
Now drawn distinctly, melting now away,
Diffusing dewy coolness all around!
Man's efforts there are glassed, his toil and strife;
Reflect, more true the emblem will be found: 115
This bright reflected glory pictures life!

Imperial Palace.   Throne-Room.

Council of State, in expectation of the EMPEROR.

TRUMPETS.

Enter courtiers of every grade, splendidly attired.

The EMPEROR *ascends the throne; to the right
the* ASTROLOGER.

EMPEROR.

I greet you, trusty friends and dear,
Assembled thus from far and wide! —
I see the wise man at my side,
But wherefore is the fool not here?   120

PAGE.

Entangled in thy mantle's flow,
He tripped upon the stair below;
The mass of fat they bare away,
If dead or drunken — who can say?

SECOND PAGE.

Forthwith another comes apace, 125
With wondrous speed to take his place;
Costly, yet so grotesque his gear,
All start amazed as he draws near.
Crosswise the guards before his face,
Entrance to bar, their halberds hold— 130
Yet there he is, the fool so bold.

MEPHISTOPHELES

(kneeling before the throne).

What is accursed and gladly hailed?
What is desired and chased away?
What is upbraided and assailed?
What wins protection every day? 135
Whom darest thou not summon here?
Whose name doth plaudits still command?
What to thy throne now draweth near?
What from this place itself hath banned?

EMPEROR.

For this time thou thy words mayst spare! 140
This is no place for riddles, friend;
They are these gentlemen's affair,—
Solve them! an ear I'll gladly lend.
My old fool's gone, far, far away, I fear;
Take thou his place, come, stand beside me here! 145

MEPHISTOPHELES *ascends and places himself at the* EMPEROR's *left.*

Murmur of the crowd.

Here's a new fool—for plague anew!
Whence cometh he?—How passed he through?
The old one fell—he squandered hath.
He was a tub—now 'tis a lath.

EMPEROR.

So now, my friends, beloved and leal, 150
Be welcome all, from near and far!
Ye meet 'neath an auspicious star;
For us above are written joy and weal.

But tell me wherefore, on this day,
When we all care would cast away,   155
And don the masker's quaint array,
And naught desire but to enjoy,
Should we with state affairs ourselves annoy?
But if ye think it so must be indeed,
Why, well and good, let us forthwith proceed!   160

CHANCELLOR.

The highest virtue circles halo-wise
Our Cæsar's brow; virtue, which from the throne,
He validly can exercise alone:
Justice!— What all men love and prize,
What all demand, desire, and sorely want,   165
It lies with him, this to the folk to grant.
But ah! what help can intellect command,
Goodness of heart, or willingness of hand,
When fever saps the state with deadly power,
And mischief breedeth mischief, hour by hour?   170
To him who downward from this height supreme
Views the wild realm, 'tis like a troubled dream,
Where the deformed deformity o'ersways,
Where lawlessness, through law, the tyrant plays,
And error's ample world itself displays.   175

One steals a woman, one a steer,
Lights from the altar, chalice, cross,
Boasts of his deed full many a year,
Unscathed in body, without harm or loss.
Now to the hall accusers throng;   180
On cushioned throne the judge presides;
Surging meanwhile in eddying tides,
Confusion waxes fierce and strong.

He may exult in crime and shame,
Who on accomplices depends;   185
Guilty! the verdict they proclaim,
When Innocence her cause defends.
So will the world succumb to ill,
And what is worthy perish quite;
How then may grow the sense which still   190
Instructs us to discern the right?

E'en the right-minded man, in time,
To briber and to flatterer yields;
The judge, who cannot punish crime,
Joins with the culprit whom he shields.—   195
I've painted black, yet fain had been
A veil to draw before the scene.

Pause.

Measures must needs be taken; when
All injure or are injured, then
E'en Majesty becomes a prey.   200

FIELD MARSHAL.

In these wild days what tumults reign!
Each smitten is and smites again,
Deaf to command, will none obey.
The burgher, safe behind his wall,
Within his rocky nest, the knight,   205
Against us have conspired, and all
Firmly to hold their own unite.
Impatient is the hireling now,
With vehemence he claims his due;
And did we owe him naught, I trow,   210
Off he would run, nor bid adieu.
Who thwarts what fondly all expect,
He hath disturbed a hornet's nest;
The empire which they should protect,
It lieth plundered and oppressed.   215
Their furious rage may none restrain;
Already half the world's undone;
Abroad there still are kings who reign—
None thinks 'tis his concern, not one.

TREASURER.

Who will depend upon allies!   220
For us their promised subsidies
Like conduit-water, will not flow.
Say, Sire, through your dominions vast
To whom hath now possession passed!
Some upstart, wheresoe'er we go,   225
Keeps house, and independent reigns;
We must look on, he holds his own;
So many rights away we've thrown,

That for ourselves no right remains.
On so-called parties in the state   230
There's no reliance, nowadays;
They may deal out or blame or praise,
Indifferent are love and hate.
The Ghibelline as well as Guelph
Retire, that they may live at ease!   235
Who helps his neighbor now?   Himself
Each hath enough to do to please.
Barred are the golden gates; while each
Scrapes, snatches, gathers all within his reach —
Empty, meanwhile, our chest remains.   240

STEWARD.

What worry must I, also, bear!
Our aim each day is still to spare —
And more each day we need; my pains,
Daily renewed, are never o'er.
The cooks lack nothing; — deer, wild-boar,   245
Stags, hares, fowls, turkeys, ducks and geese, —
Tribute in kind, sure payment, these
Come fairly in, and none complains.
But now at last wine fails; and if of yore
Up-piled upon the cellar-floor,   250
Cask rose on cask, a goodly store,
From the best slopes and vintage; now
The swilling of our lords, I trow,
Unceasing, drains the very lees.
E'en the Town-council must give out   255
Its liquor; — bowls and cups they seize,
And 'neath the table lies the drunken rout.
Now must I pay, whate'er betides;
Me the Jew spares not; he provides
Anticipation-bonds which feed   260
Each year on that which must succeed;
The swine are never fattened now;
Pawned is the pillow or the bed,
And to the table comes fore-eaten bread.

EMPEROR
(after some reflection, to MEPHISTOPHELES).
Say, fool, another grievance knowest thou?   265

MEPHISTOPHELES.

I, nowise.   On this circling pomp to gaze,
On thee and thine!   There can reliance fail
Where majesty resistless sways,
And ready power makes foemen quail?
Where loyal will, through reason strong,   270
And prowess, manifold, unite.
What could together join for wrong.
For darkness, where such stars give light?

Murmur of the crowd.

He is a knave — he comprehends —
He lies — while lying serves his ends —   275
Full well I know — what lurks behind —
What next? — Some scheme is in the wind! —

MEPHISTOPHELES.

Where is not something wanting here on earth?
Here this, — there that: of gold is here the dearth.
It cannot from the floor be scraped, 'tis true;   280
But what lies deepest wisdom brings to view.
In mountain-veins, walls underground,
Is gold, both coined and uncoined, to be found.
And if ye ask me, — bring it forth who can?
Spirit and nature-power of gifted man.   285

CHANCELLOR.

Nature and spirit — Christians ne'er should hear
Such words, with peril fraught and fear.
These words doom atheists to the fire.
Nature is sin, spirit is devil; they,
Between them, doubt beget, their progeny,   290
Hermaphrodite, misshapen, dire.
Not so with us!   Within our Cæsar's land
Two orders have arisen, two alone,
Who worthily support his ancient throne:
Clergy and knights, who fearless stand,   295
Bulwarks 'gainst every storm, and they
Take church and state, as their appropriate pay
Through lawless men the vulgar herd
To opposition have of late been stirred;
The heretics these are, the wizards, who   300
The city ruin and the country too.

With thy bold jests to this high sphere,
Such miscreants will smuggle in ;
Hearts reprobate to you are dear ;
They to the fool are near of kin.						305

MEPHISTOPHELES.

Herein your learned men I recognize ?
What you touch not, miles distant from you lies ;
What you grasp not, is naught in sooth to you ;
What you count not, cannot you deem be true ;
What you weigh not, that hath for you no weight ; 310
What you coin not, you're sure is counterfeit.

EMPEROR.

Therewith our needs are not one whit the less.
What meaneth thou with this thy Lent-address ?
I'm tired of this eternal If and How.
'Tis gold we lack ; so good, procure it thou !			315

MEPHISTOPHELES.

I'll furnish more, ay, more than all you ask,
Though light it seem, not easy is the task.
There lies the gold, but to procure it thence,
That is the art : who knoweth to commence ?
Only consider in those days of terror,					320
When human floods swamped land and folk together,
How every, one how great soe'er his fear,
All that he treasured most, hid there or here ;
So was it 'neath the mighty Roman's sway,
So on till yesterday, ay, till to-day :					325
That all beneath the soil still buried lies —
The soil is Cæsar's; his shall be the prize.

TREASURER.

Now for a fool he speaketh not amiss ;
Our Cæsar's ancient right, in sooth, was this.

CHANCELLOR.

Satan for you spreads golden snares ; 'tis clear,		330
Something not right or pious worketh here.

STEWARD.

To us at court if welcome gifts he bring,
A little wrong is no such serious thing.

Shrewd is the fool, he bids what all desire;
The soldier, whence it comes, will not inquire.   335

MEPHISTOPHELES.

You think yourselves, perchance, deceived by me;
Ask the Astrologer!   This man is he!
Circle round circle, hour and house he knows.
Then tell us, how the heavenly aspect shows.

Murmur of the crowd.

Two rascals — each to other known —   340
Phantast and fool — so near the throne;
The old, old song, — now trite with age,
The fool still prompts — while speaks the sage.

ASTROLOGER

(speaks, MEPHISTOPHELES *prompts).*

The sun himself is purest gold; for pay
And favor serves the herald, Mercury;   345
Dame Venus hath bewitched you from above,
Early and late, she looks on you with love;
Chaste Luna's humor varies hour by hour;
Mars, though he strike not, threats you with his power;
And Jupiter is still the fairest star;   350
Saturn is great, small to the eye and far;
As metal him we slightly venerate,
Little in worth, though ponderous in weight.
Now when with Sol fair Luna doth unite,
Silver with gold, cheerful the world and bright!   355
Then easy 'tis to gain whate'er one seeks;
Parks, gardens, palaces, and rosy cheeks;
These things procures this highly learned man.
He can accomplish what none other can.

EMPEROR.

Double, methinks, his accents ring,   360
And yet they no conviction bring.

Murmur.

Of what avail! — a worn-out tale —
Calendery — and chemistry —
I the false word — full oft have heard —
And as of yore — we're hoaxed once more.   365

MEPHISTOPHELES.

The grand discovery they misprize,
As, in amaze, they stand around;
One prates of gnomes and sorceries,
Another of the sable hound.
What matters it, though witlings rail,   370
Though one his suit 'gainst witchcraft press,
If his sole tingle none the less,
If his sure footing also fail?
Ye of all swaying Nature feel
The secret working, never-ending,   375
And, from her lowest depths up-tending,
E'en now her living trace doth steal.
If sudden cramps your limbs surprise,
If all uncanny seem the spot —
There dig and delve, but dally not!   380
There lies the fiddler, there the treasure lies!

Murmur.

Like lead it lies my foot about —
Cramped is my arm — 'tis only gout —
Twitchings I have in my great toe —
Down all my back strange pains I know;   385
Such indications make it clear
That sumless treasuries are here.

EMPEROR.

To work — the time for flight is past. —
Put to the test your frothy lies!
These treasures bring before our eyes!   390
Sceptre and sword aside I'll cast,
And with these royal hands, indeed,
If thou lie not, to work proceed.
Thee, if thou lie, I'll send to hell!

MEPHISTOPHELES.

Thither to find the way I know full well! —   395
Yet can I not enough declare,
What wealth unowned lies waiting everywhere:
The countryman, who ploughs the land,
Gold-crocks upturneth with the mould;
Nitre he seeks in lime-walls old,   400

And findeth, in his meagre hand,
Scared, yet rejoiced, rouleaus of gold.
How many a vault upblown must be,
Into what clefts, what shafts, must he
Who doth of hidden treasure know,   405
Descend, to reach the world below!
In cellars vast, impervious made,
Goblets of gold he sees displayed,
Dishes and plates, row after row;
There beakers, rich with rubies, stand;   410
And would he use them, close at hand
Well stored the ancient moisture lies;
Yet — would ye him who knoweth, trust? —
The staves long since have turned to dust,
A tartar cask their place supplies!   415
Not gold alone and jewels rare, ·
Essence of noblest wines are there,
In night and horror veiled.   The wise,
Unwearied here pursues his quest.·
To search by day, that were a jest;   420
'Tis darkness that doth harbor mysteries.

EMPEROR.

What can the dark avail?   Look thou to that!
If aught have worth, it cometh to the light.
Who can detect the rogue at dead of night?
Black are the cows, and gray is every cat.   425
These pots of heavy gold, if they be there —
Come, drive thy plough, upturn them with thy share!

MEPHISTOPHELES.

Take spade and hoe thyself; — dig on —
Great shalt thou be through peasant toil —
A herd of golden calves anon   430
Themselves shall tear from out the soil;
Then straight, with rapture newly born,
Thyself thou canst, thy sweetheart wilt adorn.
A sparkling gem, lustrous, of varied dye,
Beauty exalts, as well as majesty.   435

EMPEROR.

To work, to work!   How long wilt linger?

MEPHISTOPHELES.

Sire,
Relax, I pray, such vehement desire!
First let us see the motley, joyous show!
A mind distraught conducts not to the goal.
First must we calmness win through self-control,   440
Through things above deserve what lies below.
Who seeks for goodness, must himself be good;
Who seeks for joy, must moderate his blood;
Who wine desires, the luscious grape must press;
Who craveth miracles, more faith possess.   445

EMPEROR.

So be the interval in gladness spent!
Ash-Wednesday cometh, to our hearts' content.
Meanwhile we'll solemnize, whate'er befall,
More merrily the joyous Carnival.
                        (*Trumpets.   Exeunt.*)

MEPHISTOPHELES.

That merit and success are linked together,   450
This to your fools occurreth never;
Could they appropriate the wise man's stone,
That, not the wise man, they would prize alone.

*A spacious Hall, with adjoining apartments, arranged
and decorated for a masquerade.*

HERALD.

Think not we hold in Germany our revels;
Where dances reign of death, of fools and devils;   455
You doth a cheerful festival invite.
Our Cæsar, Romeward turning his campaign,
Hath — for his profit, and for your delight —
Crossed the high Alps, and won a fair domain.
Before the sacred feet bowed down,   460
His right to reign he first hath sought,
And when he went to fetch his crown,
For us the fool's cap hath he brought.
Now all of us are born anew;
And every world-experienced man   465
Draws it in comfort over head and ears,
A fool beneath it, he appears,

And plays the sage as best he can.
I see them, how they form in groups,
Now they pair off, now wavering sever ;   470
Choir now with choir together troops,
Within, without, unwearied ever!
The world remaineth as of yore,
With fooleries, ten thousand score,
The one great fool forevermore !   475

GARDEN-GIRLS.

Song, accompanied by mandolins.

That to us ye praise may render,
Decked are we in festive sort ;
Girls of Florence, we the splendor
Follow of the German court.

Many a flower, we, Flora's vassals,   480
In our dark brown tresses wear ;
Silken threads and silken tassels,
Play their part and grace our hair.

For we hold ourselves deserving,
All your praises, full and clear ;   485
Since our flowers, their bloom preserving,
Blossom through the live-long year.

Cuttings divers-hued were taken,
And arranged with symmetry ;
Piece by piece they mirth awaken,   490
Yet the whole attracts the eye.

Garden-girls and fair to look on,
Fittingly we play our part ;
For the natural in woman,
Closely is allied to art.   495

HERALD.

Now from baskets richly laden,
Which, upon her head and arm,
Beareth every lovely maiden,
Let each choose what each doth charm !
Hasten ye, till bower and alley,   500
Aspect of a garden bears !
Worthy are the crowds to dally
Round the sellers and their wares.

GARDEN-GIRLS.

In this mart your flowers unscreening,
Cheapen not, as them you show! 505
With brief words, but full of meaning,
What he hath, let each one know.

OLIVE-BRANCH (*with fruit*).

I of blossoms envy none,
· Quarrels studiously I shun;
They against my nature are: 510
Marrow of the land, in sooth
Pledge I am of peace and ruth,
To all regions near and far.
Be it my good fortune now
To adorn the loveliest brow. 515

WHEAT-WREATH (*golden*).

Ceres' gift sweet peace expressing,
Would enhance thy charms; be wise!
What is useful, rich in blessing,
As thy best adornment prize!

FANCY-GARLAND.

Colored flowers, from moss out-peering, 520
Mallow-like, a wondrous show —
Not in Nature's guise appearing,
Fashion 'tis that makes them blow.

FANCY-NOSEGAY.

Theophastus would not venture
Names to give to flowers like these. 525
Yet, though some perchance may censure
Many still, I hope to please.

Who to wreathe her locks permits me
Straight shall win a heightened grace,
Or who near her heart admits me, 530
Finding on her breast a place.

CHALLENGE.

Be your motley fancies moulded,
For the fashion of the day.
Nature never yet unfolded
Wonders half so strange as they? 535

Golden bells, green stalks, forth glancing
From rich locks, their charm enhancing.
But we —

ROSEBUDS.

hide from mortal eyes.
Happy he who finds the prize !
When draws nigh once more the summer,   540
Rosebuds greet the bright new-comer.
Who such happiness would miss ?
Promise, then fulfilment, — this
Is the law in Flora's reign,
Swayeth too sense, heart, and brain.   545

*The flower-girls tastefully arrange their wares under
green, leafy arcades.*

GARDENERS.

Song, accompanied by Theorbos.
Mark the blossoms calmly sprouting,
Charmingly to wreathe your brow ;
Fruits will not deceive, I trow,
Taste, enjoy them, nothing doubting.

Magnum bonums, cherries, peaches,   550
Faces offer sun-embrowned ;
Buy, poor judge the eye is found ; —
Heed what tongue, what palate teaches.

Luscious fruits to taste invite them
Who behold these rich supplies ?   555
We o'er roses poetize ; —
As for apples, we must bite them.

Let us now, with your good pleasure,
Join your youthful choir, in pairs ;
And beside your flowery wares,   560
Thus adorn our riper treasure,

Under leaf-adornèd bowers,
'Mid the merry windings haste ;
Each will find what suits his taste ;
Buds or leafage, fruit or flowers.   565

*Amid alternate songs, accompanied by guitars and
Theorbos, the two choruses proceed to arrange their
wares, terrace-wise, and to offer them for sale.*

MOTHER *and* DAUGHTER.

Maiden, when thou cam'st to light,
Full thy tender form of grace;
In its tiny hood bedight,
Lovely was thy infant face.
Then I thought of thee with pride   570
Of some wealthy youth the bride,
Taking as his wife thy place.

Ah! full many a year in vain.
All unused away have passed;
Of the suitor's motley train   575
Quickly hath gone by the last!
Thou with one didst gaily dance,
One didst seek with quiet glance,
Or sly elbow-touch, to gain.

All the fêtes that we might plan,   580
Vainly did we celebrate;
Games of forfeit, or third man,
Fruitless were, they brought no mate;
Many a fool's abroad to-day,
Dear one, now thy charms display,   585
One thou mayest attach though late.

*Girlish playfellows, young and beautiful, enter and join
the groups; loud confidential chatting is heard.
Fishers and bird-catchers with nets, fishing-rods,
limed twigs, and other gear, enter and mingle with
the maidens. Reciprocal attempts to win, to catch,
to escape, and hold fast, give occasion to most
agreeable dialogues.*

WOOD-CUTTERS

(enter, boisterous and uncouth).

Place!   Give place!
We must have space'
Trees we level,
Down they fall,   590
Crashing to the ground;
As we bear them forth,
Blows we deal around.
To our praise, be sure;—
This proclaim aloud;—   595

Labored not the boor,
Where were then the proud!
How in idless revel
Could they at their ease!
Never then forget, —   600
If we did not sweat,
That ye all would freeze.

PUNCHINELLOS

(awkward and foolish).

Fools are ye, poor hacks!
Born with curvèd backs.
Prudent ones are we,   605
From all burdens free;
For our greasy caps,
Our jerkins and our traps
We bear right easily.
Forthwith at our leisure,   610
We with slippered feet,
Saunter at our pleasure,
On through mart and street,
Standing still or going,
At each other crowing;   615
When the folk around
Gather at the sound,
Slipping then aside,
Frolicking together,
Eel-like on we glide.   620
And we care not whether
Ye applaud or blame;
To us 'tis all the same.

PARASITES (flattering — lustful).

Porters brave, and you,
Charcoal-burners true,   625
Kinsmen, ye indeed
Are the men we need.

Bowings low,
Assenting smiles,
Long-drawn phrases,   630
Crooked wiles,

Double-breath,
That as you please,
Blows hot or cold;
What profit these?—   635

Down from heaven
Must fire be given,
Vast, enormous,
If, to warm us,
We no coal had got,   640
Nor of logs a heap,
Warm our hearth to keep,
Our furnace to make hot.

There is roasting,
There is brewing,   645
There is toasting,
There is stewing,
Your true taster
Licks the dish;
Sniffs the roast,   650
Forebodes the fish;
These for great deeds make him able.
Seated at his patron's table.

DRUNKEN MAN (*hardly conscious*).

Naught to-day shall mar my pleasure!
Frank I feel myself and free;   655
Cheerful songs and jovial leisure,
Both I hither bring with me;
Therefore drink I!   Drink ye, drink!
Strike your glasses!   Clink ye, clink!
You behind there join the fun!   660
Strike your glasses; so, 'tis done!

Let my wife, shrill-tongued, assail me,
Sneering at my colored vest,
And, despite my vaunting, hail me
Fool, like masquerader dressed;   665
Still I'll drink!   Come, drink ye, drink!
Strike your glasses!   Clink ye, clink!
Fools in motley, join the fun!
Strike your glasses; so, 'tis done!

Here I'm blest whoever chooses   670
Me, as erring, to upbraid :
If to score mine host refuses,
Scores the hostess, scores the maid ;
Always drink I! drink ye, drink!
Up, my comrades! clink ye, clink!   675
Each to other!   Join the fun!
To my thinking now 'tis done!

From this place there's now no flying,
Here where pleasures are at hand :
Let me lie, where I am lying,   680
For I can no longer stand.

CHORUS.

Brothers all, come drink ye, drink!
One more toast, now clink ye, clink!
Firmly sit on bench and board ?
'Neath the table lie who's floored!   685

The HERALD *announces various poets, the Poet of
Nature, Court-singers, and Ritter-singers, tender as
well as enthusiastic. In the throng of competitors of
every kind none will allow the others to be heard.
One sneaks past with a few words.*

SATIRIST.

Know ye what would me to-day,
The poet, most rejoice and cheer?
If I dared to sing and say,
That which none would like to hear.

*Poets of Night and of the Sepulchre send apologies, inas-
much as they are engaged in a most interesting conversation with a newly-arisen Vampire, wherefrom
a new kind of poetry may perhaps be developed ; the
HERALD must admit the excuse, and meanwhile summons the Greek Mythology, which, though in modern
masks, loses neither character nor charm.*

THE GRACES.

AGLAIA.

Charm we bring to life, and grace ;   690
In your gifts let both have place!

HEGEMONY.

In receiving let the twain,
Preside!   'Tis sweet our wish to gain.

EUPHROSYNE.

And when benefits you own
Chiefly be these graces shown!   695

THE FATES.

ATROPOS.

I, the Eldest, am from yonder
Realm invited, here to spin.
Much to think of, much to ponder,
Lieth life's frail thread within.

That it pliant be and tender,   700
Finest flax to choose be mine;
That it even be and slender,
Must the cunning finger twine.

If of festive dance and pleasure
Ye too wantonly partake,   705
Think upon this thread's just measure
O be cautious! It may break!

CLOTHO.

Know ye, to my guidance lately
They the fateful shears confide.
By our elder's doings greatly   710
None in sooth were edified.

Spinnings, to no issue tending,
Forth she drew to air and light;
Threads of noblest promise rending,
Down she sent to realms of night.   715

While a novice still in reigning,
I too erred in by-gone years;
But to-day, myself restraining,
In the sheath I plunge my shears.

Fain I am to wear the bridle,   720
Kindly I this place survey;
In these seasons, gay and idle,
Give your revelry full play!

LACHESIS.

Reason's laws alone obeying,
Order was to me decreed.   725
Mine the will that, ever-swaying,
Never errs through over-speed.

Threads are coming; threads are going;
Each one in its course I guide,
None permit I overflowing,   730
From its skein to swerve aside.

Were I only once to slumber! —
For the world my spirit quakes;
Years we measure, hours we number,
And the hank the weaver takes.   735

HERALD.

How versed soe'er in lore of ancient fame,
Those who are coming now ye would not know;
Gazing upon these workers of much woe,
Them, as your welcome guests, ye would proclaim.

The Furies these, — none will believe us; — kind, 740
Graceful in figure, pretty, young, and fair;
If their acquaintance ye would make, beware;
How serpent-like such doves can wound, ye'll find.

Cunning they are, yet now, when every clown
Boastful, his fallings shuns not to proclaim,   745
They too, desiring not angelic fame,
Own themselves plagues of country and of town.

ALECTO.

What help for you?   Since young we are and fair,
Ye in such flattering kittens will confide!
Has any here a sweetheart to his side,   750
Stealing, we gain his ear, until we dare

To tell him, face to face, *she* may be caught
Winking at this or that one; that 'tis plain,
She halts, is crooked-backed, and dull of brain,
And, if to him betrothed, is good for naught.   755

To vex the bride doth also tax our skill:
We tell what slighting things, some weeks agone,
Her lover said of her, to such an one. —
They're reconciled, yet something rankles still.

MEGARA.

That's a mere jest! Let them be mated, then   760
I go to work, and e'en the fairest joy,
In every case can through caprice destroy.
The hours are changeful, changeful too are men.

What was desired, once grasped, its charm hath lost;
Who firmly holds the madly longed-for prize,   765
Straight for some other blessing fondly sighs;
The sun he flieth, and would warm the frost.

How to arrange, I know, in such affairs;
And here Asmodi lead, my comrade true,
At the right time mischief abroad to strew;   770
And so destroy the human race in pairs.

TISIPHONE.

Poison, steel, I mix and whet,
Words abjuring, — for the traitor; —
Lov'st thou others, sooner, later,
Ruin shall o'erwhelm thee yet.   775

All transformed to gall and foam
Is the moment's sweetest feeling!
Here no higgling, here no dealing!
Sinned he hath, his sin comes home.

Let none say: " Forgiveness cherish!"   780
To the rocks my cause I bring;
Hark!   Revenge, the echoes ring!
Who betrayeth, he must perish!

HERALD.

Now may it please you, to retire behind;
For what now cometh is not of your kind. —   785
Ye see a mountain press the crowd among,
Its flanks with brilliant carpet proudly hung;
With lengthened tusks, and serpent-trunk below,
A mystery, but I the key will show.
Throned on his neck a gentle lady rides,   790
With a fine wand his onward course she guides.
Aloft the other stands, of stately height,
Girt with a splendor that o'erpowers the sight;
Beside him, chained, two noble dames draw near;
Sad is the one, the other blithe of cheer   795

The one for freedom yearns, the other feels she's free.
Let them declare in turn who they may be!

FEAR.

Torches, lamps, with lurid sheen,
Through the turmoil gleam around;
These deceitful forms between,   800
Fetters hold me firmly bound.

Hence, vain laughter-loving brood!
I mistrust your senseless grin!
All my foes, with clamor rude,
Strive to-night to hem me in.   805

Friend like foeman would betray me,
But his mask I recognize;
There is one who fain would slay me,
Now, unmasked, away he hies.

Ah, how gladly would I wander   810
Hence, and leave this lower sphere;
But destruction, threatening yonder,
Holds me 'twixt despair and fear.

HOPE.

Hail!   Beloved sisters, hail!
If to-day and yesterday   815
Ye have loved this masking play,
Yet to-morrow, trite the tale,
Will your masks aside be thrown;
And if 'neath the torches' glare,
We no special joy have known,   820
Yet will we, in daylight fair,
Just according to our pleasure,
Now with others, now alone.
Wander forth o'er lawn and mead;
Work at will, or take our leisure,   825
Careless live, exempt from need;
And at last we'll aye succeed.
Everywhere, as welcome guest,
Step we in, with easy mind;
Confident that we the best   830
Somewhere, certainly, may find.

PRUDENCE.

Fear and hope in chains thus guiding,
Two of man's chief foes, I bar
From the thronging crowds — dividing,
Clear the way ; — now saved ye are !   835

I this live colosse am leading,
Which, tower-laden, as ye gaze
Unfatigued is onward speeding,
Step by step, up steepest ways.

But, with broad and rapid pinion,   840
From the battlement on high,
Gazing on her wide dominion,
Turneth that divinity.

Fame, around her, bright and glorious,
Shining on all sides one sees :   845
Victory her name, — victorious
Queen of all activities.

ZOILO-THERSITES.

Bah ! Bah ! The very time I've hit !
You all are wrong, no doubt of it !
Yet what I make my special aim   850
Is victory, yon stately dame.
She, with her snowy wings, esteems,
Herself an eagle, and still deems
That wheresoe'er she bends her sight,
Peoples and lands are hers by right !   855
But, where a glorious deed is done,
My harness straight I buckle on ;
Where high is low, and low is high,
The crooked straight, the straight awry —
Then only am I wholly sound :   860
So be it on this earthly round.

HERALD.

So take thou then, thou ragged hound,
From my good staff, a master blow !
There crouch and wriggle, bending low !
The double dwarfish form, behold,   865
Itself to a vile ball hath rolled !

The ball becomes an egg! — strange wonder!
It now dilates and bursts asunder:
Thence falleth a twin-pair to earth,
Adder and bat; — a hideous birth; 870
Forth in the dust one creeps, his brother
Doth darkling to the ceiling flee;
Outside they haste to join each other —
The third I am not fain to be!

Murmur.

Come on! Behind their dancing — No, 875
Not I, from hence I fain would go —
Dost thou not feel the spectral rout
Is flitting everywhere about?
It whistled right above my hair —
Close to my feet, — I felt it there — 880
No one is hurt — 'tis not denied, —
But we have all been terrified —
Wholly the frolic now is ended —
'Tis what the brutish pair intended.

HERALD.

Since on me, at festive masque, 885
Laid hath been the Herald's task,
At the doors I watch with care,
Lest aught harmful, unaware,
Creep into this joyous space;
I nor waver, nor give place. 890
Yet I fear, the spectral brood,
Through the window may intrude,
And from trick and sorcery,
I know not how to keep you free.
First the dwarf awakened doubt, 895
Now streams in the spectral rout.
I would show you herald-wise,
What each figure signifies.
But what none can comprehend
I should strive to teach in vain. 900
All must help me to explain! —
Through the crowd behold ye it wend; —
A splendid car is borne along
By a team of four; the throng

Is not parted, nor doth reign 905
Tumult round the stately wain;
Bright it glitters from afar;
Shineth many a motley star,
As from magic-lantern cast;
On it snorts with stormful blast.— 910
I needs must shudder! Clear the way!

BOY-CHARIOTEER.

Stay your wings, ye coursers, stay!
Own the bridle's wonted sway!
Rein yourselves, as you I rein;
When I prompt you, rush amain!— 915
Honor we this festal ground.
See how press the folk around,
Ring in ring, with wondering eyes.—
Herald, as thy wont is, rise;
From you ere we flee afar, 920
Tell our name, our meaning show?
Since we allegories are,
'Tis thy duty us to know.

HERALD.

I cannot guess how I should name thee;
I to describe thee should prefer. 925

BOY-CHARIOTEER.

So, try it then?

HERALD.

We must proclaim thee,
Firstly to be both young and fair;
A half-grown boy;— yet women own
They fain would see thee fully grown;
A future wooer seemest thou to me, 930
A gay deceiver out and out to be.

BOY-CHARIOTEER.

Not badly spoken! Pray proceed!
The riddle's cheerful meaning strive to read.

HERALD.

Thine eyes swart flash, thy jewelled bandlet glowing
Starlike, amid thy night-like hair; 935

And what a graceful robe dost wear,
Down from thy shoulder to thy buskin flowing,
With purple hem and fringes rare!
Thee as a girl one might misprize;
Yet thou, for weal or woe, wouldst be,   940
E'en now of worth in maiden's eyes;
Thee they would teach the A B C.

BOY-CHARIOTEER.

And he whose stately figure gleams
Enthroned upon his chariot wain?

HERALD.

A monarch, rich and mild, he seems;   945
Happy who may his grace obtain,
Henceforth they've naught for which to strive!
His glance discerns if aught's amiss,
Greater his pleasure is to give,
Than to possess or wealth or bliss.   950

BOY-CHARIOTEER.

Suspend not here thy words, I pray,
Him thou more fully must portray.

HERALD.

The noble none can paint.   Yet there
Glows the round visage, hale and fair,
Full mouth, and blooming cheeks, descried   955
Beneath the turban's jewelled pride;
What ease his mantle folds display!
What of his bearing can I say?
As ruler seems he known to me.

BOY-CHARIOTEER.

Plutus, the god of wealth is he.   960
Hither he comes in royal state;
Of him the emperor's need is great.

HERALD.

Tell of thyself the what and how to me!

BOY-CHARIOTEER.

I am profusion, I am Poesie;
The bard am I who to perfection tends   965

When freely he his inner wealth expends.
I too have riches beyond measure,
And match with Plutus' wealth my treasure,
For him adorn and quicken dance and show,
And what he lacketh, that do I bestow. 970

HERALD.

Boasting to thee new charm imparts.
Now show us something of thine arts!

BOY-CHARIOTEER.

See me but snap my fingers, lo!
Around the car what splendors glow!
A string of pearls forth leapeth here; 975
(Continually snapping.)
Take golden clasps for neck and ear;
Combs too, and other precious things,
Crowns without flaw, and jewelled rings!
Flamelets I scatter too, in play,
Awaiting where they kindle may. 980

HERALD.

How the good people snatch and seize!
Almost the donor's self they squeeze.
As in a dream he gems doth rain,
In the wide space they snatch amain.
But — here new juggling meets mine eye: 985
What one doth grasp so eagerly,
Doth prove, in sooth, a sorry prize;
Away from him the treasure flies;
The pearls are loosened from their band,
Now beetles crawl within his hand; 990
He shakes them off; poor fool, instead,
Swarming, they buzz around his head;
Others, in place of solid things,
Catch butterflies, with lightsome wings.
Though vast his promises, the knave 995
To them but golden glitter gave!

BOY-CHARIOTEER.

Masks, I remark, thou canst announce full well;
Only to reach the essence 'neath the shell,

Is not the Herald's courtly task;
A sharper vision that dost ask.   1000
But I from every quarrel would be free.—
Master, I speech and question turn to thee.
          (*Turning to* PLUTUS.)
The storm-blast didst thou not confide
To me, of this four-yokèd car?
Lead I not well, as thou dost guide?   1005
Where thou dost point, thence am I far?
Have I not known, on daring wing
For thee the victor's crown to wring?
Full often as for thee I've fought,
Still have I conquered; and if now   1010
The laurel decorates thy brow,
Have not my hand and skill the chaplet wrought?

PLUTUS.

If need there be, that I should witness bear,—
Soul of my soul, thee gladly I declare:
According to my will thou actest ever;   1015
Art richer than myself indeed.
To give thy service its due meed,
Before all crowns the laurel wreath I treasure.
This truthful word let all men hear:
My son art thou, thee doth my soul hold dear.   1020

BOY-CHARIOTEER (*to the crowd*).

Now of my hand the choicest dower
I've scattered in this festive hour;
There glows on this or that one's head
A flame, which I abroad have shed;
From one to other now it hies,   1025
To this one cleaves, from that one flies,
Seldom aloft its flames aspire;
Sudden they gleam, with transient fire;
With many, ere they know the prize,
It mournfully burns out and dies.   1030

          Clamor of Women.

          He yonder, on the chariot-van,
          Is, without doubt, a charlatan.
          Behind him, crouching, is the clown,
          By thirst and hunger so worn down

The like was never seen till now; 1035
If pinched, he would not feel, I trow.

THE STARVELING.

Avaunt, ye loathèd women-kind!
With you I ne'er a welcome find. —
When ruled the hearth your thrifty dame,
Then Avaritia was my name; 1040
Then throve our household well throughout;
For much came in, and naught went out!
Great was my zeal for chest and bin —
And that, forsooth, you call a sin!
But in these later years, no more 1045
The wife is thrifty, as of yore;
She, like each tardy payer, owns
Far more desires than golden crowns;
This for her spouse much care begets;
Where'er he turneth, there are debts; 1050
What she by spinning earns, she spends
On gay attire, and wanton friends;
Better she feasts, and drinketh too
More wine, with her vile suitor crew:
That raised for me of gold the price. 1055
Now, male of sex, I'm Avarice!

Leader of the Women.

Dragon may still with dragon spare;
It's cheat and lies at last, no more!
He comes to rouse the men; beware!
Full troublesome they were before. 1060

WOMEN (*all together*).

The scarecrow! Box his ears! Make haste!
To threat us does the juggler dare?
Us shall his foolish prating scare?
The dragons are but wood and paste;
Press in upon him, do not spare! 1005

HERALD.

Now, by my staff! Keep quiet there!
Yet scarcely needed is my aid.
See, in the quickly opened space,
How the grim monsters move apace!

Their pinions' double pair displayed! 1070
The dragons shake themselves in ire,
Scale-proof, their jaws exhaling fire —
The crowd recedes; clear is the place.
(PLUTUS descends from the chariot.)

HERALD.

He steps below, a king confessed!
He nods, the dragons move; the chest 1075
They from the chariot, in a trice,
Have lowered, with gold and avarice;
Before his feet it standeth now:
How done a marvel is, I trow.

PLUTUS (to the CHARIOTEER).

Now from the burden that oppressed thee here 1080
Thou'rt frank and free; away to thine own sphere!
Here is it not; distorted, wild, grotesque,
Surrounds us here a motley arabesque.
There fly, where on thy genius thou canst wait,
Lord of thyself; where charm the good, the fair; 1085
Where clear thy vision in the clear, calm air;
To solitude — there thine own world create!

BOY–CHARIOTEER.

Myself as trusty envoy I approve;
Thee as my nearest relative I love.
Where thou dost dwell, is fulness; where I reign, 1090
Within himself each feeleth glorious gain;
And 'midst life's contradictions wavers he:
Shall he resign himself to thee, to me?
Thy votaries may idly rest, 'tis true;
Who follows me has always work to do. 1095
My deeds are not accomplished in the shade,
I only breathe, and fortwith am betrayed,
Farewell! My bliss thou grudgest not to me;
But whisper low, and straight I'm back with thee.
(Exit as he came.)

PLUTUS.

Now is the time the treasure to set free! 1100
The lock I strike, thus with the Herald's rod;

'Tis opened now!   In blazing caldrons, see,
It bubbles up, and shows like golden blood;
Next crowns, and chains, and rings a precious dower:
It swells and fusing threats the jewels to devour. 1105

Alternate cry of the Crowd.

Look here!   Look there!   How flows the treasure,
To the chest's brim in ample measure! —
Vessels of gold are melting, near
Up-surging, coined rouleaux appear,
And ducats leap as if impressed —   1110
O how the vision stirs my breast!
My heart's desire now meets my eye!
They're rolling on the floor hard by. —
To you 'tis proffered; do not wait,
Stoop only, you are wealthy, straight! —   1115
While, quick as lightning, we, anon,
The chest itself will seize upon.

HERALD.

Ye fools, what ails you?   What your quest?
'Tis but a masquerading jest.
To-night no more desire ye may;   1120
Think you that gold we give away,
And things of worth?   For such as you,
And at such foolish masking too,
E'en counters were too much to pay.
Blockheads a pleasing show, forsooth,   1125
Ye take at once for solid truth.
What's truth to you?   Delusion vain
By every turn ye clutch amain. —
Thou, Plutus, hero of the masque,
This folk to chase be now thy task!   .   1130

PLUTUS.

Ready at hand thy staff I see;
For a brief moment lend it me! —
Quickly in fire and seething glare
I'll dip it. — Now, ye masks, beware!
It sputters, crackles, flares outright!   1135
Bravely the torch is now alight;
And pressing round, who comes too nigh,

Is forthwith scorched relentlessly! —
Now then my circuit is begun.

Cries and Tumult.

O misery! We are undone. — 1140
Escape, let each escape who can!
Back! further back! thou hindmost man! —
Hot in my face it sputtered straight —
Of the red staff I felt the weight —
We all, alas! we all are lost! — 1145
Back, back, thou masquerading host! —
Back, back, unthinking crowd! — Ah me,
Had I but wings, I hence would flee! —

PLUTUS.

Back is the circle driven now;
And no one has been singed, I trow. 1150
The crowds give way,
Scared, with dismay. —
Yet, pledge of order and of law,
A ring invisible I draw.

HERALD.

Achieved thou hast a noble deed; 1155
For thy sage might be thanks thy meed!

PLUTUS.

Yet needs there patience, noble friend;
Still many a tumult doth impend.

AVARICE.

If it so please us, pleasantly,
We on this living ring may gaze around. 1160
For women ever foremost will be found,
If aught allure the palate or the eye.
Not yet am I grown rusty quite!
A pretty face must always please;
And since it nothing costs to night, 1165
We'll go a-wooing at our ease.
Yet as in this o'ercrowded sphere,
Words are not audible to every ear,
Deftly I'll try — and can but hope success —
In pantomime my meaning to express. 1170

Hand, foot, and gesture will not here suffice,
Hence I must strive to fashion some device :
Like moistened clay forthwith I'll knead the gold ;
This metal into all things we can mould.

HERALD.

The meagre fool, what doeth he ?   1175
Hath such a starveling humor ? See,
He kneadeth all the gold to dough,
Beneath his hand 'tis pliant too ;
Yet howsoe'er he squeeze and strain,
Misshapen it must still remain.   ·   1180
He to the women turns, but they
All scream, and fain would flee away,
With gestures of aversion. Still
Ready the rascal seems for ill ;
Happy, I fear, himself he rates,   1185
When decency he violates.
Silence were wrong in such a case ;
Give me my staff, him forth to chase !

PLUTUS.

What threats us from without, he bodeth not,
Let him play out his pranks a little longer !   1190
Room for his jests will fail him soon, I wot ;
Strong as is law, necessity is stronger.

Enter FAUNS, SATYRS, GNOMES, NYMPHS, *etc., attendants on* PAN, *and announcing his approach.*

Tumult and Song.

From forest-vale and mountain height,
Advancing with resistless might,
The savage host, it cometh straight :   1195
Their mighty Pan they celebrate.
They know, what none beside can guess,
Into the vacant ring they press.

PLUTUS.

You and your mighty Pan I recognize !
Conjoined you've entered on a bold emprize.   1200
Full well I know, what is not known to all,
And ope this narrow space, at duty's call. —

O may a happy Fate attend!
Wonders most strange may happen now;
They know not whereunto they tend;   1205
Forward they have not looked, I trow.

Wild Song.

Bedizened people, glittering brood!
They're coming rough, they're coming rude
With hasty run, with lofty bound,
Stalwart and strong they press around.   1210

FAUNS.

Fauns advance,
Their crisp locks bound
With oak-leaves round, —
In merry dance!
A fine and sharply-pointed ear,   1215
Forth from their clustering locks doth peer;
A stumpy nose, with breadth of face —
These forfeit not a lady's grace;
If but his paw the Faun advance,
Not lightly will the fairest shun the dance.   1220

SATYR.

The Satyr now comes hopping in,
With foot of goat, and withered shin;
These sinewy must be and thin.
In chamois-guise, on mountain height,
Around to gaze is his delight;   1225
In freedom's air, with freshness rife,
Child he despiseth, man and wife,
Who, 'mid the valley's smoke and steam,
That they too live, contented dream;
On those pure heights, sequestered, lone,   1230
The upper world is his alone!

GNOMES.

Tripping, here comes a tiny crew.
They like not keeping two and two;
In mossy dress, with lamplet clear,
Commingling swiftly, they career,   1235
Where for himself his task each plies,
Swarming they glitter, emmet-wise;

And ever busy, move about,
With ceaseless bustle in and out. —

We the "Good Folk" as kindred own,   1240
As rock-chirurgists well we're known;
Cupping the lofty hills, we drain,
With cunning, from each well-filled vein,
The metals, which aloft we pile,
Shouting, Good luck! Good luck! the while: 1245
Kindness at bottom we intend ;
Good men we evermore befriend.
Yet to the light we gold unseal,
That men therewith may pimp and steal.
Nor to the proud, who murder planned   1250
Wholesale, shall fail the iron brand :
These three commands who hath transgressed,
Will take small reckoning of the rest ;
Nathless for that we're not to blame :
Patient we are, be ye the same!   1255

GIANTS.

The wild men, such in sooth our name,
Upon the Hartzberg known to fame,
Naked, in ancient vigor strong,
Pell-mell we come, a giant throng ;
With pine-stem grasped in dexter hanu,   1260
And round the loins a padded band,
Apron of leaf and bough, uncouth, —
Such guards the Pope owns not, in sooth.

CHORUS OF NYMPHS.
(They surround the great PAN.)

He draweth near!
In mighty Pan   1265
The All we scan
Of this world-sphere.
All ye of gayest mood advance,
And him surround, in sportive dance!
For since he earnest is and kind,   1270
Joy everywhere he fain would find ;
E'en 'neath the blue o'erarching sky,
He watcheth still, with wakeful eye ;

Purling to him the brooklet flows,
And Zephyrs lull him to repose;   1275
And when he slumbers at midday,
Stirs not a leaf upon the spray;
Health-breathing plants, with balsams rare,
Pervade the still and silent air;
The nymph no more gay vigil keeps,   1280
And where she standeth, there she sleeps.
But if, at unexpected hour,
His voice resounds with mighty power,
Like thunder, or the roaring sea,
Then knoweth none, where he may flee;   1285
Panic the valliant host assails,
The hero in the tumult quails.
Then honor to whom honor is due!
And hail to him, who leads us unto you!

> *Deputation of* GNOMES (*to the great* PAN).
>
> When a treasure, richly shining,   1290
> Winds through clefts its threadlike way,
> Sole the cunning rod, divining,
> Can its labyrinth display.
>
> Troglodytes in caves abiding,
> We our sunless homes vault o'er: 1295
> Thou, 'mid day's pure airs presiding,
> Graciously thy gifts doth pour.
>
> Close at hand, a fount of treasure
> We have found a wondrous vein; —
> Promising in fullest measure,   1300
> What we scarce might hope to gain.
>
> Perfect thou alone canst make it;
> Every treasure in thy hand,
> Is a world-wide blessing; take it,
> Thine it is, Sire, to command!   1305

> PLUTUS (*to the* HERALD).

Our self-possession now must be displayed,
And come what may, we must be undismayed;
Still hast thou shown a strong courageous soul.
A dreadful incident will soon betide;

'Twill be by world and after-world denied;   1310
Inscribe it truly in thy protocol!

HERALD

(grasping the staff which Plutus *holds in his hand).*
The dwarfs conduct the mighty Pan
Softly the source of fire to scan;
It surges from the gulf profound,
Then downward plunges 'neath the ground;   1315
While dark the mouth stands, gaping wide,
Once more uprolls the fiery tide.

The mighty Pan stands well content,
Rejoicing in the wondrous sight,
While pearl-foam drizzles left and right.   1320
How may he trust such element!
Bending, he stoops to look within. —
But now his beard has fallen in!
Who may he be, with shaven chin?

His hand conceals it from our eyes. —   1325
Now doth a dire mishap arise;
His beard takes fire and backward flies;
Wreath, head and breast are all ablaze,
Joy is transformed to dire amaze. —
To quench the fire his followers run   1330
Free from the flames remaineth none;
Still as they strike from side to side,
New flames are kindled far and wide;
Enveloped in the fiery shroud,
Burns now the masquerading crowd.   1335

But what's the tale that's rumored here,
From mouth to mouth, from ear to ear!
O night, for aye with sorrow fraught,
To us what mischief hast thou brought!
The coming morn will tidings voice,   1340
At which, in sooth, will none rejoice.
From every side they cry amain,
"The Emperor suffers grievous pain!"
O were some other tidings true! —
The Emperor burns, his escort too,   1345
Accursed be they, forevermore,
Who him seduced, with noisy roar,

Abroad, begirt with pitchy bough,
To roam, for general overthrow!

O youth, O youth, and wilt thou never   1350
To joy assign its fitting bound?
O Majesty, with reason never
Will thy omnipotence be crowned?

The mimic forest hath caught fire;
Tongue-like the flame mounts high and higher;   1355
Now on the wood-bound roof it plays,
And threats one universal blaze!
O'erflows our cup of suffering;
I know not, who may rescue bring;
Imperial pomp, so rich o'er night,   1360
An ash-heap lies in morning's light.

PLUTUS.

Long enough hath terror swayed;
Hither now be help conveyed. —
Strike, thou hallowed staff, the ground,
Till earth tremble and resound!   1365
Cooling vapors everywhere
Fill the wide and spacious air!
Moisture-teeming mist and cloud
Draw anear, and us o'ershroud;
Veil the fiery tumult, veil!   1370
Curling, drizzling, breathing low,
Gracious cloudlets hither sail,
Shedding down the gentle rain!
To extinguish, to allay,
Ye, the assuagers, strive amain;   1375
Into summer-lightning's glow
Change our empty fiery play!—
Threaten spirits us to hurt,
Magic must its power assert.

Pleasure-garden.
Morning sun.

The Emperor, *his court, men and women;* Faust,
Mephistopheles *dressed becomingly, in the usual
fashion; both kneel.*

FAUST.

The flaming juggler's play dost pardon, Sire?   1380

EMPEROR.

I of such sports full many should desire. —
I saw myself within a glowing sphere;
Almost it seemed as if I Pluto were;
A rock abyss there lay, with fire aglow.
Gloomy as night; from many a gulf below,   1385
Seething, a thousand savage flames ascend,
And in a fiery vault together blend;
Up to the highest dome their tongues were tossed,
Which ever was, and evermore was lost.
In the far space, through spiral shafts of flame,   1390
Peoples I saw, in lengthened lines who came;
In the wide circles forward pressed the crowd,
And as their wont hath been, in homage bowed;
I seemed, surrounded by my courtly train,
O'er thousand Salamanders king to reign.   1395

MEPHISTOPHELES.

Such art thou, Sire?   For thee each element
To own as absolute is well content.
Obedient thou hast proven fire to be.
Where it is wildest, leap into the sea —
And scarce thy foot the pearl-strewn floor shall tread,
A glorious, billowy dome o'ervaults thy head;   1401
Wavelets of tender green thou seest swelling,
With purple edge, to form thy beauteous dwelling,
Round thee, the central point; where thou dost wend,
At every step, thy palace homes attend;   1405
The very walls, in life rejoicing, flow
With arrowy swiftness, surging to and fro;
Sea-marvels to the new the gentle light repair;
They dart along, to enter none may dare;
There sports, with scales of gold, the bright-hued snake,
Gapes the fell shark, his jaws thy laughter wake: 1411
Howe'er thy court may round thee now delight,
Such throng as this, before ne'er met thy sight.
Nor long shalt severed be from the most fair;
The curious Nereids, to thy dwelling rare,   1415
'Mid the eternal freshness, shall draw nigh;
The youngest, greedy like the fish, and shy;
The elder prudent.   Thetis hears the news,

Nor to the second Peleus will refuse
Or hand or lip. — Olympos' wide domain ——   1420

EMPEROR.

I leave to thee, thou o'er the air may'st reign ;
Full early every one must mount that throne.

MEPHISTOPHELES.

Earth, noblest Sire! already thou dost own.

EMPEROR.

Hither what happy Fate, with kindness fraught,
Thee from the thousand nights and one hath brought!
If thou, like Scheherazade, prolific art,   1426
To thee my highest favor I'll impart ;
Be ever near when, as is oft the case,
Most irksome is our world of commonplace!

MARSHAL (*entering in haste*).

Your Highness, never thought I in my life   1430
Tidings to give, with such good fortune rife
As these which, in thy presence, cheer
My raptured heart, absolved from fear ;
All reckonings paid, from debt we're eased ; —
The usurer's clutches are appeased —   1435
From such hell-torment I am free!
In Heaven can none more cheerful be.

COMMANDER-IN-CHIEF (*follows hastily*).

Paid in advance the soldiers' due,
Now the whole army's pledged anew.
Blood dances in the trooper's veins ;   1440
Vintner and damsel reap their gains.

EMPEROR.

How freely now your breast doth heave!
The marks of care your visage leave!
How hastily you enter!

TREASURER (*entering*).

Sire, proceed
These men to question who have done the deed.   1445

FAUST (*to the* CHANCELLOR).

To you it doth belong the case to state.

CHANCELLOR (*who advances slowly*).

In my old days I am with joy elate!
So hear and see this fortune-weighted scroll,
Which hath to happiness transformed our dole:

(*He reads.*)

"To all whom it concerneth, be it known: 1450
Who owns this note a thousand crowns doth own.
To him assured, as certain pledge, there lies,
Beneath the Emperor's land, a boundless prize;
It is decreed, this wealth without delay
To raise, therewith the promised sum to pay."   1455

EMPEROR.

Crime I suspect, some huge deceit!
The Emperor's name who here doth counterfeit?
Unpunished still remains such breach of right?

TREASURER.

Remember, Sire! Thyself but yesternight   1459
Didst sign the note. — Thou stood'st as mighty Pan;
Then spake the Chancellor, whose words thus ran:
"This festive pleasure for thyself obtain,
Thy people's weal, with a few pen-strokes gain!"
These mad'st thou clearly; thousand-fold last night
Have artists multiplied what thou didst write;   1465
And that to each alike might fall the aid,
To stamp the series, we have not delayed,
Ten, thirty, fifty, hundreds at a stroke.
You cannot guess how it rejoiced the folk:
Behold your town, mouldering half dead that lay,   1470
How full of life and bounding joy to-day!
Long as thy name hath blessed the world, till now
So gladly was it ne'er beheld, I trow.
The Alphabet is now redundant grown;
Each in this sign finds happiness alone.   1475

EMPEROR.

My people take it for true gold, you say?
In camp, at court, it passes for full pay?
Much as I wonder, it I must allow.

MARSHAL.

To stay the flying leaves were hopeless now;
With speed of lightning all abroad they float: 1480
The changers' banks stand open; every note
Is honored there with silver and with gold;
Discount deducted, if the truth were told.
To butcher, baker, vintner, thence they fare;
With half the world is feasting their sole care; 1485
The other half, new-vestured, bravely shows;
The mercer cuts away, the tailor sews.
In cellars still "The Emperor!" they toast,
While, amid clattering plates, they boil and roast.

MEPHISTOPHELES.

Alone who treads the terraced promenade, 1490
Sees there the fair one, splendidly arrayed;
One eye the peacock's fan conceals; the while
This note in view, she lures us with her smile,
And swifter than through eloquence or wit,
Love's richest favor may be won by it. 1495
Oneself with purse and scrip one need not tease.
Hid in the breast, a note is borne with ease,
And with the billet-doux is coupled there;
The priest conveys it in his book of prayer;
The soldier, that his limbs may be more free, 1500
Quickly his girdle lightens. Pardon me,
Your Majesty, if the high work I seem,
Dwelling on these details, to disesteem.

FAUST.

This superfluity of wealth, that deep
Imprisoned in its soil thy land doth keep, 1505
Lies all unused; wide-reaching thought profound
Is of such treasure but a sorry bound;
In loftiest flight, fancy still strives amain
To reach its limit, but still strives in vain —
Yet minds who dare behind the veil to press, 1510
In the unbounded, boundless faith possess.

MEPHISTOPHELES.

Such paper, in the place of pearls and gold,
Convenient is, we know how much we hold;

No need for change or barter, each at will
Of love and wine may henceforth drink his fill.   1515
If coin is needed, stands the changer nigh,
If there it faileth, straight the shovel ply:
Goblet and chain at auction fetch their price;
The paper, forthwith cancelled, in a trice
The skeptic shames, who us did erst deride;   1520
The people, used to it, wish naught beside:
So henceforth, through the realm, there's goodly store
Of jewels, gold, and paper, ever more.

EMPEROR.

You this high aid have rendered to our state;
Great is the service, be the meed as great!   1525
Our realm's subsoil confide we to your care;
Best guardians of the treasure buried there.
Full well ye know the vast, well-guarded hoard,
And when men dig, so be it at your word!

To Faust *and the* Treasurer.

Ally yourselves, ye masters of our treasure,   1530
The honors of your place fulfil with pleasure,
There where together joined in blest content,
The upper with the under world is blent!

TREASURER.

Not the most distant strife shall us divide;
As colleague be the conjuror at my side.   1535
(*Exit with* Faust.)

EMPEROR.

If I at court each man with gifts endow,
Whereto he'll use them, let each tell me now.

PAGE (*receiving*).
Merry I'll be, and taste life's pleasant things.

ANOTHER (*the same*).
I for my sweetheart will buy chain and rings.

CHAMBERLAIN (*accepting*).
Wine twice as good from this time forth I'll drink.   1540

ANOTHER (*the same*).
The dice already in my pocket clink.

BANNERET (*thoughtfully*).
My field and castle I from debt will free.

ANOTHER (*the same*).
I'll lay my treasure in my treasury.

EMPEROR.
Courage I hoped, and joy, for new emprize —
But whoso knows you straight will recognize;   1545
I mark it well, though wealth be multiplied,
Just what ye were, the same will ye abide!

FOOL (*approaching*).
Favors you scatter; grant me some, I pray!

EMPEROR.
What, living yet? Thou'lt drink them soon away.

FOOL.
These magic leaves! I comprehend not quite —   1550

EMPEROR.
That I believe : them thou'lt not spend aright.

FOOL.
There, others drop — I know not what to do —

EMPEROR.
Take them! They've fallen to thy share, adieu!
                                                (*Exit.*)
FOOL.
Five thousand crowns in hand! can it be true?

MEPHISTOPHELES.
Thou two-legged paunch, art thou then risen anew? 1555

FOOL.
As oft before, ne'er happily as now.

MEPHISTOPHELES.
So great thy joy, it makes thee sweat, I trow.

FOOL.
Is this indeed worth money? art thou sure?

MEPHISTOPHELES.
What throat and paunch desire it will procure.

FOOL.

Can I then field, and house, and cattle buy?　　1560

MEPHISTOPHELES.

Of course!　Bid only, thee it will not fail.

FOOL.

Castle with forest, chase, and fish-pond?

MEPHISTOPHELES.

Ay!
Thee as your worship I should like to hail!

FOOL.

As land-owner I'll rock myself ere eve!　　(*Exit*)

MEPHISTOPHELES.

In our fool's wit who will not now believe?　　1565

Dark Gallery.

FAUST, MEPHISTOPHELES.

MEPHISTOPHELES.

Why drag me these dark corridors along?
Within hast not enough of sport?
Occasion 'mid the motley throng
For jest and lie, hath not at court?

FAUST.

Speak not of that; in days of old hast thou　　1570
Outworn it to the very soles.　But now,
Thy shuffling is a mere pretext
How to evade my questions.　Sore perplexed,
I know not how to act or what to do;
The marshal urges me, the steward too,　　1575
The Emperor wills it — hence it straight must be —
Wills Helena and Paris here to see;
Of man and woman-kind the true ideal,
He fain would view, in forms distinct and real
Quick to the work!　My word I may not break. 1580

MEPHISTOPHELES.

Such promise it was weak, nay, mad to make.

FAUST.

Comrade, thou hast not thought, I trow,
Whither these arts of thine must lead:
First we have made him rich, and now
Him to amuse we must proceed.   1585

MEPHISTOPHELES.

Thou think'st no sooner said than done;
Here before steeper steps we stand,
A foreign realm must here be won,
New debts wilt add to those of old,
With the same ease dost think I can command   1590
Helen, as phantom-notes evoke for gold!
With wizard, witchery, or ghostly ghost,
Or goitred dwarf, I'm ready at my post,
But Devil's darlings, though we mayn't abuse them,
Yet cannot we as heroines produce them.   1595

FAUST.

Still harping on the ancient lyre!
The father thou of hindrances; — with thee
We needs must fall into uncertainty;
For each expedient thou dost claim new hire!
With little muttering, I know, 'tis done;   1600
Ere one looks round, thou'lt bring them to the spot.

MEPHISTOPHELES.

The Heathen-folk I'm glad to let alone,
In their own hell is cast their lot;
Yet are there means —

FAUST.

Speak quickly, naught withhold!

MEPHISTOPHELES.

Loth am I higher secrets to unfold.   1605
In solitude, where reigns nor space nor time,
Are goddesses enthroned from early prime;
'Tis hard to speak of beings so sublime —
The Mothers are they.

FAUST (terrified).
Mothers!

MEPHISTOPHELES.

Tremblest thou?

FAUST.

The Mothers! Mothers! strange it sounds, I trow! 1610

MEPHISTOPHELES.

And is so: Goddesses, to men unknown,
And by us named unwillingly, I own.
Their home to reach, full deeply must thou mine.
That we have need of them, the fault is thine!

FAUST.

The way?

MEPHISTOPHELES.

No way; to the untrodden none,   1615
Not to be trodden, neither to be won
By prayer!   Art ready for the great emprize?
No locks are there, no bolts thy way to bar,
By solitudes shalt thou be whirled afar:
Such void and solitude canst realize?   1620

FAUST.

To spare such speeches, it were well!
They of the witches' kitchen smell,
And of a time long past and gone.
To know the world have I not sought?
The empty learned, the empty taught?—   1625
Spake I out plainly, as in reason bound,
Then doubly loud the paradox would sound;
By Fortune's adverse buffets overborne
To solitude I fled, to wilds forlorn,
And not in utter loneliness to live,   1630
Myself at last did to the Devil give!

MEPHISTOPHELES.

And hadst thou swum to ocean's utmost verge,
And there the shoreless infinite beheld,
There hadst thou seen surge rolling upon surge,   1634
Though dread of coming doom thy soul had quelled,
Thou hadst seen something;—dolphins thou hadst seen
Cleaving the silent sea's pellucid green,
And flying cloud hadst seen, sun, moon, and star;
Naught, in the everlasting void afar,

Wilt see, nor hear thy footfall's sound,   1640
Nor for thy tread find solid ground!

FAUST.

Thou speakest of mystagogues the first,
True neophytes who gulled — only reversed:
I to vacuity by thee am sent,
That art as well as strength I may augment;   1645
Thou wouldest, like the cat, make use of me,
The chestnuts from the fire to snatch for thee.
We'll fathom it! come on, nor look behind!
In this thy naught, the All I hope to find.

MEPHISTOPHELES.

Before we part, thy bearing I commend;   1650
I see, the Devil thou dost comprehend
Here, take this key!

FAUST.
That little thing!

MEPHISTOPHELES.

First hold it fast, nor lightly valuing!

FAUST.

It waxes in my hand!   It flashes, glows!

MEPHISTOPHELES.

Soon shalt thou mark what virtue it bestows.   1655
The key will scent the very place you need;
Follow, thee to the Mothers it will lead.

FAUST (shuddering).

The Mothers!   Like a blow it strikes mine ear!
What is this word, it troubles me to hear?

MEPHISTOPHELES.

So narrow-minded, scared by each new word!   1660
Wilt only hear, thou hast already heard?
Inured to marvels, thee let nought astound;
Be not disturbed, how strange soe'er the sound!

FAUST.

My weal I seek not in torpidity
Humanity's best part in awe doth lie: 1665

Howe'er the world the sentiment disown,
Once seized — we deeply feel the vast, the unknown.

MEPHISTOPHELES.

Sink then!   Arise!   This also I might say ; —
'Tis all the same escaping from the real,
Seek thou the boundless realm of the ideal.   1670
Delight thyself in forms long past away!
The train, like cloud-procession, glides along ;
Swing thou the key, hold off the shadowy throng!

FAUST (*inspired*).

Good! firmly grasping it, new strength is mine,
My breast expands!   Now for the great design! 1675

MEPHISTOPHELES.

A glowing tripod teaches thee thou hast
The deep attained, the lowest deep, at last ;
There, by its light the Mothers thou wilt see ;
Some sit, while others, as the case may be,
Or stand, or walk ; formation, transformation,   1680
Of mind etern, eternal recreation!
While forms of being round them hover ; thee
Behold they not, phantoms alone they see.
Take courage, for the danger is not slight,
Straight to the tripod press thou on, be brave,   1685
And touch it with the key —

(FAUST, *with the key, assumes an attitude of deter-
mined authority*).

MEPHISTOPHELES (*observing him*).

So, that is right!

It cleaves to thee, it follows like a slave ;
Calmly dost mount, fortune doth thee upbear,
Back art thou with it, ere they are aware.
And hither hast thou brought it, by its might,   1690
Hero may'st call, and heroine from night ;
The first to venture in such enterprise ;
'Tis done — with thee the bold achievement lies
And then by spells, to sorcery allowed,
To gods shall be transformed the incense-cloud.   1695

FAUST.

And now what next?

MEPHISTOPHELES.

       Downward thy being strain.
Stamping descend, stamping thou'lt rise again.
       (FAUST *stamps and sinks.*)
In his behoof if worketh but the key!
Whether he will return, I'm fain to see.

Hall brilliantly lighted.

EMPEROR *and* PRINCES. *The court in movement.*

CHAMBERLAIN (*to* MEPHISTOPHELES).

You're still our debtors for the spirit-show;   1700
To work! The Emperor doth impatient grow.

STEWARD.

His Highness even now hath questioned me;
Delay not, nor affront his majesty!

MEPHISTOPHELES.

My comrade's for that very purpose gone;
How to commence he knows; he labors on,   1705
Secluded in his study, calm and still,
With mind intensely strung; for who the prize,
Ideal beauty, would evoke at will,
Needs highest art, the magic of the wise.

STEWARD.

To us it matters not, what arts you need;   1710
The Emperor wills that ye forthwith proceed.

A BLONDE (*to* MEPHISTOPHELES).

One word, good sir! My visage now is clear —
It is not so when baleful summer's here:
Then sprout a hundred freckles, brown and red,
Which, to my grief, the white skin overspread.   1715
A cure!

MEPHISTOPHELES.

   'Tis pity, face so fair to see,
In May like panther's cub should mottled be!

Take spawn of frog, and tongue of toad, the twain
Under the fullest moon distil with care;
Lay on the mixture, when the moon doth wane, 1720
The spring arrives, no blemishes are there.

BRUNETTE.

To fawn upon you how the crowds advance;
A remedy I ask! A frozen foot
Hinders me sorely when I walk or dance;
Awkward my movement e'en when I salute. 1725

MEPHISTOPHELES.

A single tread allow me with my foot!

BRUNETTE.

Well, betwixt lovers that might come to pass —

MEPHISTOPHELES.

A deeper meaning, child, my footprint has:
Like unto like, in sickness is the rede;
Foot healeth foot; with every limb 'tis so. 1730
Draw near! Give heed! My tread return not.

BRUNETTE (screaming).

Woe!

Ah, woe! It burns! A hard tread that indeed,
Like horse's hoof!

MEPHISTOPHELES.

Receive thy cure as meed.

Now may'st thou dance at pleasure! and salute,
Beneath the festal board, thy lover's foot. 1735

LADY (pressing forward).

Make way for me, too grievous is my smart,
Seething, it rankles in my deepest heart:
Bliss in my looks he sought till yesterday —
With her he talks, and turns from me away!

MEPHISTOPHELES.

The case is grave, but this my lore receive: 1740
Thou to his side must stealthily make way;
Take thou this coal, a mark upon his sleeve,
His cloak, or shoulder make, as happen may —

His heart repentant will be thine once more
The coal thou straight must swallow; after it,   1745
No water near thy lip, no wine, permit —
This very night he'll sigh before thy door.

LADY.

It is not poison?

MEPHISTOPHELES (*offended*).

Honor where 'tis due!
You for such coal much ground must wander o'er
It cometh from a pyre, that we of yore   1750
More fiercely stirred than now we do.

PAGE.

I love; as still unripe they scorn my youth!

MEPHISTOPHELES (*aside*).

I know not whom to listen to, in sooth.
          (*To the* PAGE.)
Not on the youngest set your happiness;
Those more in years your merits will confess.   1755
          (*Others press up to him.*)
Others are coming!   What a fearful rout!
Myself with truth I must at last help out —
The sorriest shift!   Great is the need!   Ah me!
O Mothers, Mothers!   Only Faust set free.
          (*Looking round.*)
The lights are burning dimly in the hall;   1760
At once the court is moving, one and all;
Advancing in due order them I see,
Through long arcade and distant gallery;
Now in the old baronial hall, the train
Assemble, them it scarcely can contain;   1765
Its ample walls rare tapestries enrich,
While armor decks each corner, every niche.
Here magic-words, methinks, are needed not,
Ghosts, of their own accord, would haunt this spot.

Baronial Hall.
Dimly illuminated.
EMPEROR *and* Court *have entered.*

HERALD.

Mine ancient usage, to announce the play,   1770
The spirits' secret working mars; in vain
The surging tumult to ourselves, to-day,
Would we, on reasonable ground, explain.
Seats are arranged, ready is every chair;
The Emperor sits before the wall, and there,   1775
On tapestry in comfort may behold
The battles of the glorious days of old.
All now are seated; prince and court around;
While crowded benches fill the hinder ground;
Your lovers too, in these dark hours, will find,   1780
Beside their sweethearts, places to their mind.
So now we're seated, ready for the play;
The phantoms may appear, without delay!

(Trumpets.)

ASTROLOGER.

Now let the drama, 'tis the Sire's command,
Begin forthwith its course! ye walls expand!   1785
Naught hinders; magic yields what we require.
The curtains vanish, as up rolled by fire;
The wall splits open, backward it doth wend;
An ample theatre appears to rise,
A mystic lustre gleams before our eyes;   1790
And I to the proscenium ascend.

MEPHISTOPHELES

(emerging from the prompter's box).

I hope for general favor in your eyes,
The Devil's rhetoric in prompting lies!

(To the ASTROLOGER.)

The time dost know, in which the stars proceed,
And, like a master, wilt my whispering read.   1795

ASTROLOGER.

Through magic power, appears before our gaze,
Massive enough, a fane of ancient days;

Like Atlas, who of old the heavens up-bare,
Columns, in goodly rows, are standing there;
They for their burden may suffice, when twain   1800
A mighty edifice might well sustain.

ARCHITECT.

That the antique — I cannot think it right;
It as unwieldy we should designate;
The rude is noble styled, the clumsy great!
Slim shafts I love, aspiring, infinite;   1805
The pointed zenith lifts the soul on high;
Such building us doth mostly edify.

ASTROLOGER.

Receive with reverence star-granted hours!
By magic word enthralled be reason's powers
Here on the other hand, let phantasy,   1810
Noble and daring, roam more wildly free!
What boldly you desired, he with your eyes perceived!
Impossible, and hence, by faith to be believed.

(FAUST rises at the other side of the proscenium.)

ASTROLOGER.

In priestly vesture, crowned, a wondrous man,
Who now achieves, what trustful he began;   1815
A tripod with him from the gulf ascends;
With the surrounding air the incense blends;
He arms himself, the lofty work to bless:
Henceforth we naught can augur but success.

FAUST.

In your name, Mothers, ye who on your throne   1820
Dwell in the Infinite, for aye alone,
Yet sociably!   Around your heads are rife
Life's pictures, restless yet devoid of life;
What was, there moveth, bright with lustrous sheen;
For deathless will abide what once hath been.   1825
This ye dispense, beings of matchless might,
To day's pavilion, to the vault of night;
Life in its gentle course doth some arrest;
Of others the bold magian goes in quest,
In rich profusion, fearless, he displays   1830
The marvels upon which each longs to gaze.

ASTROLOGER.

Scarcely the glowing key the censer nears,
When o'er the scene a misty shroud appears;
It creepeth in, cloudlike it onward glides,
Expands, up-curls, contracts, unites, divides.   1835
Now recognize a spirit masterpiece:
The clouds make music; wonders never cease,
The airy tones, one knows not how, float by:
Where'er they move, there all is melody;
The pillared shaft, the very triglyph rings;   1840
Yes, I believe that the whole temple sings!
The mist subsides; step forth, in measured time,
From the light veil, a youth in beauty's prime.
Silent mine office here; his name I need not show;
Who doth the gentle Paris fail to know!   1845

1st LADY.

Oh! in his youthful strength what lustrous grace!

2d LADY.

Fresh as a peach, and full of sap his face!

3d LADY.

The finely chiselled, sweetly swelling lip!

4th LADY.

At such a beaker fain wert thou to sip?

5th LADY.

Though handsome, quite unpolished is his mien. 1850

6th LADY.

A little more refined he might have been.

KNIGHT.

The shepherd youth, methinks, in him I trace;
Naught of the prince or of the courtier's grace!

ANOTHER KNIGHT.

Half naked, fair the stripling seems to be;
But clad in armor him we first must see!   1855

LADY.

Gently he seats himself, with easy grace.

KNIGHT.

For you his lap were pleasant resting-place?

ANOTHER.

Lightly his arm he bendeth o'er his head.

CHAMBERLAIN.

That is not here allowed.   'Tis underbred!

LADY.

You gentlemen are always hard to please.   1860

CHAMBERLAIN.

Before the Emperor to loll at ease!

LADY.

He only acts!   He thinks himself alone.

CHAMBERLAIN.

The drama should be courtly near the throne.

LADY.

Gently hath sleep o'ercome the gracious youth.

CHAMBERLAIN.

He snoreth now; 'tis nature, perfect truth.   1865

YOUNG LADY (*enraptured*).

What fragrance with the incense sweetly blends,
That to my inmost heart refreshment sends?

OLD LADY.

A breath the soul pervades with gracious power!
From him it comes.

OLDEST LADY.

   Of growth it is the flower;
It like ambrosia from the youth distils,   1870
And the whole atmosphere around him fills.

   (HELENA *steps forward*.)

MEPHISTOPHELES.

Such then she was!   She will not break my rest!
Fair, doubtless; but she is not to my taste.

ASTROLOGER.

For me remains no further duty now,
As man of honor, this I must allow.   1875

The fair one comes; and had I tongues of fire —
Beauty of old did many a song inspire —
Who sees her is enraptured; all too blest
Was he indeed by whom she was possessed.

FAUST.

Have I still eyes?   Is beauty's very spring,   1880
Full gushing, to mine inmost sense revealed?
Most blessed gain doth my dread journey bring.
How blank to me the world, its depths unsealed!
What is it since my priesthood's solemn hour!
Enduring, firmly-based, a precious dower!   1885
Vanish from me of life the breathing power,
If, e'en in thought, I e'er from thee decline! —
The gracious form that raptured once my sight,
That in the magic mirror waked delight,
Was a foam-image to such charms as thine! —   1890
'Tis thou, to whom as tribute now I bring
My passion's depth, of every power the spring,
Love, adoration, madness, heart and soul!

MEPHISTOPHELES
(from the prompter's box).

Collect yourself, and fall not from your rôle!

ELDERLY LADY.

Tall and well-shaped!   Only too small the head. 1895

YOUNGER LADY.

Her foot!   'Tis clumsy if the truth were said.

DIPLOMATIST.

Princesses of this kind I've seen; and she
From head to foot seems beautiful to me.

COURTIER.

Softly she nears the sleeper, artful, shy.

LADY.

How hateful near that form of purity!   1900

POET.

He is illumined by her beauty's sheen.

LADY.

Endymion!   Luna! — 'Tis the pictured scene!

POET.

Quite right!   The goddess downward seems to sink;
O'er him she bends, his balmy breath to drink;
A kiss! — The measure's full! — O envied youth!   1905

DUENNA.

Before the crowd — Too bold that is, in sooth!

FAUST.

A fearful favor to the boy! —

MEPHISTOPHELES.

                              Be still!
And let the phantom do whate'er it will.

COURTIER.

She steals away, light-footed; — he awakes.

LADY.

A backward glance, just as I thought, she takes!   1910

COURTIER.

He starts!   'Tis marvellous! he's all amaze.

LADY.

To her no marvel is what meets her gaze.

COURTIER.

To him with coy reserve she turneth now.

LADY.

She takes him into tutelage, it seems;
All men, in such a case, are fools, I trow;   1915
Himself to be the first, he fondly dreams!

KNIGHT.

Let me admire!   Majestically fair —

LADY.

The courtesan!   'Tis vulgar, I declare!

PAGE.

Now in his place to be, full fain I were!

COURTIER.

Who in such net would not be gladly caught? 1920

LADY.

From hand to hand the jewel hath been passed;
The very gilding is worn off at last.

ANOTHER.

From her tenth year she hath been good for naught.

KNIGHT.

Each takes the best that Fate to him hath sent: ·
With this fair ruin I were well content. 1925

LEARNED MAN.

Her I behold, yet to confess am free,
Doubts may arise, if she the right one be.
What's present doth into extremes betray;
Cling closely to the letter, that's my way;
I to what's written turn, and there I read: 1930
How she all Troya's gray-beards charmed indeed.
How perfectly this tallies here, I see —
I am not young, and yet she pleases me.

ASTROLOGER.

A boy no more! A man, heroic, brave,
He claspeth her, who scarce herself can save; 1935
With stalwart arm aloft he raises her.
Thinks he to bear her off?

FAUST.

    Rash fool! Beware!
Thou darest! Hearest not! Forbear, I say!

MEPHISTOPHELES.

Why thou thyself dost make the phantom-play!

ASTROLOGER.

Only one word! From what did her befall, 1940
"The rape of Helena," the piece I call.

FAUST.

The rape! Count I for nothing here? This key,
Do I not hold it still within my hand?
Through dreary wastes, through waves, it guided me,
Through solitudes, here to this solid land; 1945

Here is firm footing, here the actual, where
Spirit with spirits to contend may dare,
And for itself a vast, twin-realm prepare.
Far as she was, how can she be more near?
Saved, she is doubly mine! I'll dare it! Hear, 1950
Ye Mothers, Mothers, hear, and grant my quest!
Who once hath known, without her cannot rest!

ASTROLOGER.

What dost thou? Faustus! Faustus!—Her with
        might,
He seizes; fades the phantom from the sight;
Towards the youth he turneth now the key   1955
He touches him!—Presto! alas! Woe's me!
        (*Explosion,* FAUST *lies upon the ground.*)
        (*The phantoms vanish in the air.*)

MEPHISTOPHELES.

        (*taking* FAUST *upon his shoulders*).
You have it now! With fools oneself to burden,
May to the Devil prove a sorry guerdon.
        (*Darkness.   Tumult.*)

ACT THE SECOND.

*High-vaulted, narrow Gothic chamber,
formerly* FAUST'S, *unaltered.*

MEPHISTOPHELES.

(*Stepping from behind a curtain.   While he raises
    it and looks back,* FAUST *is seen, stretched upon
    an old-fashioned bed.*)
Lie there, ill-starred one! In love's chain,
Full hard to loose, he captive lies!
Not soon his senses will regain
Whom Helena doth paralyze.
        (*Looking round.*)
Above, around, on every side   5
I gaze, uninjured all remains:
Dimmer, methinks, appear the colored panes,

The spiders' webs are multiplied,
Yellow the paper, and the ink is dry;
Yet in its place each thing I find ;   10
And here the very pen doth lie,
Wherewith himself Faust to the Devil signed,
Yea, quite dried up, and deeper in the bore,
The drop of blood, I lured from him of yore —
O'erjoyed to own such specimen unique   15
Were he who objects rare is fain to seek —;
Here on its hook hangs still the old fur cloak,
Me it remindeth of that merry joke,
When to the boy I precepts gave, for truth,
Whereon, perchance, he's feeding now, as youth.   20
The wish comes over me, with thee allied,
Enveloped in thy worn and rugged folds,
Once more to swell with the professor's pride
How quite infallible himself he holds ;
This feeling to obtain your savans know;   25
The Devil parted with it long ago.

*(He shakes the fur cloak which he has taken down ;
crickets, moths, and chafers fly out.)*

CHORUS OF INSECTS.

We welcome thy coming,
Our patron of yore!
We're dancing and humming,
And know thee once more.   30
Us singly, in silence,
Hast planted, and lo!
By thousands, oh, father,
We dance to and fro.
The rogue hides discreetly   35
The bosom within ;
We looseskins fly rather
Forth from the fur skin.

MEPHISTOPHELES.

O'erjoyed I am my progeny to know !
We're sure to reap in time, if we but sow.   40
I shake the old fur mantle as before,
And here and there out-flutters one or more. —

Above, around, hasten, belovèd elves,
In hundred thousand nooks to hide yourselves!
'Mid boxes there of bygone time,   45
Here in these age-embrownèd scrolls,
In broken potsherds, foul with grime,
In yonder skulls' now eyeless holes!
Amid such rotten, mouldering life,
Must foolish whims for aye be rife.   50
                    (*Slips into the fur mantle.*)
Come, shroud my shoulders as of yore!
To-day I'm principal once more;
But useless 'tis, to bear the name:
Where are the folk to recognize my claim?
    (*He pulls the bell, which emits a shrill penetrating
        sound, at which the halls shake and the doors spring
        open.*)

FAMULUS
        (*tottering up the long dark passage*).
What a clamor!   What a quaking!   55
Stairs are rocking, walls are shaking,
Through the windows' quivering sheen,
Are the stormful lightnings seen;
Springs the ceiling, — thence, below,
Lime and mortar rattling flow: 60
And, though bolted fast, the door
Is undone by magic power!
There, in Faust's old fleece bedight,
Stands a giant, — dreadful sight!
At his glance, his beck, at me!   65
I could sink upon my knee.
Shall I fly, or shall I stay?
What will be my fate to-day!

MEPHISTOPHELES.
Come hither, friend! — Your name is Nicodemus?

FAMULUS.
Most honored Sir, such is my name. — Oremus!   70

MEPHISTOPHELES.
That we'll omit.

FAMULUS.
        O joy, me you do not forget.

MEPHISTOPHELES.

I know it well: old, and a student yet;
My mossy friend, even a learned man
Still studies on, because naught else he can:
Thus a card-house each builds of medium height;   75
The greatest spirit fails to build it quite.
Your master, though, that title well may claim —
The noble Doctor Wagner, known to fame,
First in the learned world!   'Tis he, they say,
Who holds that world together; every day   80
Of wisdom he augments the store!
Who crave omniscience, evermore
In crowds upon his teaching wait;
He from the rostrum shines alone;
The keys doth like Saint Peter own,   85
And doth of Hell and Heaven ope the gate;
As before all he glows and sparkles,
No fame, no glory but grows dim,
Even the name of Faustus darkles!
Inventor there is none like him.   90

FAMULUS.

Pardon, most honored Sir, excuse me, pray —
If I presume your utterance to gainsay —
This bears not on the question any way;
A modest mind is his allotted share.
The disappearance, unexplained as yet,   95
Of the great man, his mind doth sorely fret;
Comfort from his return and health are still his prayer.
The chamber, as in Doctor Faustus' day,
Maintains, untouched, its former state,
And for its ancient lord doth wait.   100
Venture therein I scarcely may.
What now the aspect of the stars ? —
Awe struck the very walls appear;
The door-posts quivered, sprang the bars —
Else you yourself could not have entered here.   105

MEPHISTOPHELES.

Where then bestowed himself hath he?
Lead me to him ! bring him to me !

FAMULUS.

Alas!   Too strict his prohibition,
Scarce dare I, without his permission.
Months, on his mighty work intent,   110
Hath he, in strict seclusion spent.
Most dainty 'mong your men of books,
Like charcoal-burner now he looks,
With face begrimed from ear to nose;
His eyes are bleared, while fire he blows;   115
Thus for the crisis still he longs;
His music is the clang of tongs.

MEPHISTOPHELES.

Admittance unto me deny?
To hasten his success, the man am I.
      (*Exit* FAMULUS. *Mephistopheles seats himself with
            a solemn air.*)
Scarce have I ta'en my post, when lo!   120
Stirs from behind a guest, whom well I know;
Of the most recent school, this time, is he,
And quite unbounded will his daring be.

BACCALAUREUS
(*storming along the passage*).

Open find I door and gate!
Hope at last springs up elate,   125
That the living shall no more
Corpse-like rot, as heretofore,
And, while breathing living breath,
Waste and moulder as in death.

Here partition, screen, and wall   130
Are sinking, bowing to their fall,
And, unless we soon retreat,
Wreck and ruin us will greet.
Me, though bold, nor soon afraid,
To advance shall none persuade.   135

What shall I experience next?
Years ago when sore perplexed,
Came I not a freshman here,
Full of anxious doubt and fear,
On these gray-beards then relied,   140
By their talk was edified?

What from musty tomes they drew,
They lied to me; the things they knew
Believed they not; with falsehood rife,
Themselves and me they robbed of life.　　145
How? — Yonder in the murky glare,
There's one still sitting in the chair —

Drawing near I wonder more —
Just as him I left of yore,
There he sits, in furry gown,　　150
Wrapped in shaggy fleece, the brown!
Then he clever seemed, indeed,
Him as yet I could not read;
Naught will it avail to-day;
So have at him, straight-away!　　155

If Lethe's murky flood not yet hath passed,
Old Sir, through your bald pate, that sideways bends,
The scholar recognize, who hither wends,
Outgrown your academic rods at last.
The same I find you, as of yore;　　160
But I am now the same no more.

MEPHISTOPHELES.

Glad am I that I've rung you here.
I prized you then not slightingly;
In grub and chrysalis appear
The future brilliant butterfly.　　165
A childish pleasure then you drew
From collar, lace, and curls. — A queue
You probably have never worn? —
Now to a crop I see you shorn.
All resolute and bold your air —　　170
But from the *absolute* forbear!

BACCALAUREUS.

We're in the ancient place, mine ancient Sir,
But think upon time's onward flow,
And words of double meaning spare!
Quite otherwise we hearken now.　　175
You fooled the simple, honest youth;
It cost but little art in sooth,
To do what none to-day will dare.

MEPHISTOPHELES.

If to the young the naked truth one speaks,
It pleases in no wise the yellow beaks;   180
But afterwards, when in their turn
On their own skin the painful truth they learn,
They think, forsooth, from their own head it came;
" The master was a fool," they straight proclaim.

BACCALAUREUS.

A rogue perchance! — For where's the teacher
    found   185
Who, to our face direct, will Truth expound?
Children to edify, each knows the way.
To add or to subtract, now grave, now gay.

MEPHISTOPHELES.

For learning there's in very truth a time;
For teaching, I perceive, you now are prime   190
While a few suns and many moons have waned,
A rich experience you have doubtless gained !

BACCALAUREUS.

Experience ! Froth and scum alone,
Not with the mind of equal birth !
Confess! what men have always known,   195
As knowledge now is nothing worth.

MEPHISTOPHELES (after a pause).

I long have thought myself a fool;
Now shallow to myself I seem, and dull.

BACCALAUREUS.

That pleases me ! like reason that doth sound;
The first old man of sense I yet have found !   200

MEPHISTOPHELES.

I sought for hidden treasures, genuine gold —
And naught but hideous ashes forth I bore !

BACCALAUREUS.

Confess that pate of yours, though bare and old,
Than yonder hollow skull is worth no more !

MEPHISTOPHELES.

Thou knowest not, friend, how rude is thy reply.   205

BACCALAUREUS.

In German to be courteous is to lie.

MEPHISTOPHELES

(still moving his wheel-chair ever nearer to the proscen-
ium, to the pit).

Up here I am bereft of light and air;
I perhaps shall find a refuge with you there?

BACCALAUREUS

When at their worst, that men would something be,
When they are naught, presumptuous seems to me. 210
Man's life is in the blood, and where, in sooth,
Pulses the blood so strongly as in youth?
That's living blood, which with fresh vigor rife,
The newer life createth out of life.
There all is movement, something there is done;   215
Falleth the weak, the able presses on!
While half the world we 'neath our sway have brought,
What have ye done?   Slept, nodded, dreamed, and
        thought,
Plan after plan rejected; — nothing won.
Age is, in sooth, a fever cold,   220
With frosts of whims and peevish need:
When more than thirty years are told,
As good as dead one is indeed:
You it were best, methinks, betimes to slay.

MEPHISTOPHELES.

The devil here has nothing more to say.   225

BACCALAUREUS.

Save through my will, no devil dares to be.

MEPHISTOPHELES *(aside).*

The devil now prepares a fall for thee!

BACCALAUREUS.

The noblest mission this of youth's estate.
The world was not, till it I did create;
The radiant Sun I lead from out the sea;   230
Her changeful course the Moon began with me;
The Day arrayed herself my steps to meet,
The earth grew green, and blossomed me to greet;

At my command, upon yon primal Night,
The starry hosts unveiled their glorious light.   235
Who, beside me, the galling chains unbound,
Which cramping thought had cast your spirits round ?
And I am free, as speaks my spirit-voice,
My inward light I follow, and rejoice ;
Swift I advance, enraptured, void of fear,   240
Brightness before me, darkness in the rear.   (*Exit.*)

MEPHISTOPHELES.

Go, in thy pride, original, thy way !—
True insight would, in truth, thy spirit grieve !
What wise or stupid thoughts can man conceive,
Unpondered in the ages passed away ?—   245
Yet we for him need no misgiving have ;
Changed will he be, when a few years are past ;
Howe'er absurdly may the must behave,
Nathless it yields a wine at last. —

   (*To the younger part of the audience, who do not
      applaud.*)

Though to my words you're somewhat cold,   250
Good children, me you don't offend ;
Reflect !   The devil, he is old ;
Grow old then, him to comprehend !

Laboratory.

(*After the fashion of the middle ages ; cumbrous, useless apparatus, for fantastic purposes.*)

WAGNER (*at the furnace*).

Soundeth the bell, a fearful clang
Thrills through these sooty walls ; no more   255
Upon fulfilment waits the pang
Of hope or fear ; — suspense is o'er ;
The darkness begins to clear,
Within the inmost phial glows
Radiance, like living coal, that throws,   260
As from a splendid carbuncle, its rays ;
Athwart the gloom its lightning plays.
A pure white lustre doth appear ;
O may I never lose it more !—
My God ! what rattles at the door ?   265

MEPHISTOPHELES (*entering*).
Welcome!   As friend I enter here.

WAGNER.
Hail to the star that rules the hour!
(*Softly.*)
On breath and utterance let a ban be laid!
Soon will be consummate a work of power.

MEPHISTOPHELES (*in a whisper*).
What is it, then?

WAGNER.
A man is being made.   270

MEPHISTOPHELES.
A man? and pray what loving pair
Have in your smoke-hole their abode?

WAGNER.
Nay!   Heaven forbid!   As nonsense we declare
The ancient procreative mode;
The tender point, life's spring, the gentle strength 275
That took and gave, that from within hath pressed,
And seized, intent itself to manifest.
The nearest first, the more remote at length, —
This from its dignity is now dethroned!
The brute indeed may take delight therein,   280
But man, by whom such mighty gifts are owned,
Must have a purer, higher origin.
(*He turns to the furnace.*)
It flashes, see! — Now may we trustful hold,
That if, of substances a hundred-fold,
Through mixture, — for on mixture it depends — 285
The human substance duly we compose,
And then in a retort enclose,
And cohobate; in still repose
The work is perfected, our labor ends.
(*Again turning to the furnace.*)
It forms!   More clear the substance grows!   290
Stronger, more strong, conviction grows!

What Nature's mystery we once did style,
That now to test our reason tries,
And what she organized erewhile,
We now are fain to crystallize.   295

MEPHISTOPHELES.

Who lives doth much experience glean ;
By naught in this world will he be surprised ;
Already in my travel-years I've seen,
Full many a race of mortals crystallized.

WAGNER (*still gazing intently on the phial*).
It mounts and glows and doth together run,   300
One moment, and the work is done !
As mad, a grand design at first is viewed ;
But we henceforth may laugh at fate,
And so a brain, with thinking-power embued,
Henceforth your living thinker will create.   305
(*Surveying the phial with rapture.*)
The glass resounds, with gracious power possessed ;
It dims, grows clear ; living it needs must be !
And now in form of beauty dressed,
A dainty mannikin I see.
What more can we desire, what more mankind ?   310
Unveiled is now what hidden was of late ;
Give ear unto this sound, and you will find,
A voice it will become, articulate. —

HOMUNCULUS
(*in the phial, to* WAGNER).
Now, fatherkin, how goes it ?   'Twas no jest !
Come, let me to thy heart be fondly pressed —   315
Lest the glass break, less tight be thine embrace !
This is the property of things : the All
Scarcely suffices for the natural ;
The artificial needs a bounded space.
(*to* MEPHISTOPHELES.)

But thou, Sir Cousin, Rogue, art thou too here ?   320
At the right moment ! Thee I thank.   'Tis clear
To us a happy fortune leadeth thee ;
While I exist still must I active be,

And to the work forthwith myself would gird
Thou'rt skilled the way to shorten.

WAGNER.

Just one word! 325
I oft have been ashamed that knowledge failed,
When old and young with problems me assailed.
For instance: no one yet could comprehend,
How soul and body so completely blend,
Together hold, as ne'er to part, while they   330
Torment each other through the live-long day.
So then —

MEPHISTOPHELES.

Forbear! The problem solve for me,
Why man and wife so wretchedly agree?
Upon this point, my friend, thou'lt ne'er be clear;
The mannikin wants work, he'll find it here.   335

HOMUNCULUS.

What's to be done?

MEPHISTOPHELES
(pointing to a side door).

Yonder thy gifts display!

WAGNER
(still gazing into the phial).

A very lovely boy, I needs must say!
(The side door opens; FAUST is seen stretched upon a
     couch.)

HOMUNCULUS (amazed).

Momentus!

(The phial slips from WAGNER'S hands, hovers over
     FAUST, and sheds a light upon him.)

Girt with beauty! — Water clear
In the thick grove; fair women, who undress;
Most lovely creatures! — grows their loveliness: 340
But o'er the rest one shines without a peer,
As if from heroes, nay, from gods she came;
In the transparent sheen her foot she laves;
The tender life-fire of her noble frame
She cools in yielding crystal of the waves.   345
Of swiftly moving wings what sudden noise?
What plash, what plunge the liquid glass destroys?

The maidens fly alarmed; alone, the queen,
With calm composure gazes on the scene;
With womanly and proud delight, she sees   350
The prince of swans press fondly to her knees,
Persistent, tame; familiar now he grows. —
But suddenly up-floats a misty shroud,
And with thick-woven veil doth overcloud
The loveliest of all lovely shows.   355

MEPHISTOPHELES.

Why, thou, in sooth, canst everything relate!
Small as thou art, as phantast thou art great.
I can see nothing —

HOMUNCULUS.

I believe it.   Thou,
Bred in the north, in the dark ages, how,
In whirl of priesthood and knight-errantry,   360
Have for such sights thy vision free!
In darkness only thou'rt at home.

(*Looking round.*)

Ye brown, repulsive blocks of stone,
Arch-pointed, low, with mould o'ergrown!
Should he awake, new care were bred,   365
He on the spot would straight be dead.
Wood-fountains, swans, fair nymphs undressed;
Such was his dream presageful, rare;
In place like this how could he rest,
Which I, of easy mood, scarce bear!   370
Away with him!

MEPHISTOPHELES.

I like your plan, proceed!

HOMUNCULUS.

Command the warrior to the fight,
The maiden to the dancers lead!
They're satisfied, and all is right.
E'en now a thought occurs, most bright;   375
'Tis classical Walpurgis night —
Most fortunate!   It suits his bent,
So bring him straightway to his element!

MEPHISTOPHELES.

Of such I ne'er have heard, I frankly own.

HOMUNCULUS.

Upon your ear indeed how should it fall?   380
Only romantic ghosts to you are known;
Your genuine ghost is also classical.

MEPHISTOPHELES.

But whitherward to travel are we fain?
Your antique colleagues are against my grain.

HOMUNCULUS.

Northwestward, Satan, lies thy pleasure-ground; 385
But, this time, we to the southeast are bound. —
An ample vale Peneios floweth through.
'Mid bush and tree its curving shores it laves;
The plain extendeth to the mountain caves,
Above it lies Pharsalus, old and new.   390

MEPHISTOPHELES.

Alas!   Forbear !   Forever be eschewed
Those wars of tyranny and servitude!
I'm bored with them: for they, as soon as done,
Straight recommence; and no one calls to mind
That he in sooth, is only played upon   395
By Asmodeus, who still lurks behind.
They battle, so 'tis said for freedom's rights —
More clearly seen, 'tis slave 'gainst slave who fights.

HOMUNCULUS.

Leave we to men their nature, quarrel-prone !
Each must defend himself, as best he can,   400
From boyhood up so he becomes a man.
The question here is how to cure this one?
(Pointing to FAUST.)
Hast thou a means, here let it tested be;
Canst thou do naught, then leave the task to me.

MEPHISTOPHELES.

Full many a Brocken-piece I might essay,   405
But bolts of heathendom foreclose the way.

The Grecian folk were ne'er worth much, 'tis true,
Yet with the senses' play they dazzle you;
To cheerful sins the human heart they lure,
While ours are reckoned gloomy and obscure.   410
And now what next?

HOMUNCULUS.

                    Of old thou wert not shy;
And if I name Thessalian witches, — why,
I something shall have said, — of that I'm sure.

MEPHISTOPHELES (lustfully).

Thessalian witches — well! the people they
Concerning whom I often have inquired.   415
Night after night, indeed, with them to stay,
That were an ordeal not to be desired;
But for a trial trip —

HOMUNCULUS.

                    The mantle there
Reach hither, wrap it round the knight!
As heretofore, the rag will bear   420
Both him and thee; the way I'll light.

WAGNER (alarmed).

And I?

HOMUNCULUS.

            At home thou wilt remain,
Thee most important work doth there detain;
The ancient scrolls unfolding, cull
Life's elements, as taught by rule,   425
And each with other then combine with care;
Upon the What, more on the How, reflect!
Meanwhile as through a piece of world I fare,
I may the dot upon the " I " detect.
Then will the mighty aim accomplished be;   430
Such high reward deserves such striving; — wealth,
Honor and glory, lengthened life, sound health,
Knowledge withal and virtue — possibly.
Farewell!

WAGNER.

            Farewell!   That grieves my heart full sore!
I fear, indeed, I ne'er shall see thee more.   435

MEPHISTOPHELES.

Now to Peneios forth we wend!
We must not slight our cousin's aid.
                (*To the spectators.*)
At last, in sooth, we all depend
On creatures we ourselves have made.

CLASSICAL WALPURGIS NIGHT.

Pharsalian Fields.

Darkness.

ERICHTHO.*

To this night's ghastly fête, as oftentimes before,   440
I hither come, Erichtho, I, the gloomy one ;
Not so atrocious, as the sorry poet-throng
Me in excess have slandered. . .   They no measure
    know
In censure and applause. . . O'erwhitened seems to me,
With waves of dusky tents, the valley, far and wide,
Night-phantom of that dire and most appalling night.
How often 'tis repeated !   Will for evermore   447
Repeat itself for aye. . . empire none gladly yields
To others; none to him, by force who mastered it
And forceful reigns.   For each, his inmost self to rule
How impotent soe'er, ruleth right joyously   451
His neighbor's will, as prompts his own imperious
    mind. . . .
Nathless a great example here was battled through ;
Here force 'gainst force more potent takes its stand,
Freedom's fair chaplet breaks, with thousand blossoms
    rife,   455
The stubborn laurel bends around the victor's brow.
Of greatness' budding-day here Pompey dreamed ; and
    there,
Watching the wavering balance, Cæsar wakeful lay !
Strength they shall measure.   Knows the world who
    here prevailed.
Brightly the watch-fires burn, diffusing ruddy flames ;
Reflex of blood, once spilt, does from the soil exhale,461
And by the night's most rare and wondrous splendor
    lured,
Hither the legions throng of Hellas' mythic lore.
Round every fire dim shapes, phantoms of ancient days
Flit wavering to and fro, or there recline at ease. . 465

* A Thessalian witch consulted by Pompey.

The moon, not fully orbed, of clearest light serene,
Uprising, lustre mild diffuses all around.
Vanish the spectral tents, the fires are burning blue.

But lo! above my head, what sudden meteor sails!
It shines, and doth illume a ball corporeal.　　　470
I snuff the scent of life.　Me it beseemeth not
The living to approach, to whom I noxious am ;
That brings me ill-repute, and nothing profits me.
Already it sinks down.　With caution I retire.

　　　　　　　　　　　(*Withdraws.*

The aerial travellers above.

HOMUNCULUS.

O'er the horror weird and blazing,　　　475
　Wing once more your circling flight ;
Down on vale and hollow gazing,
　All phantasmal is the sight.

MEPHISTOPHELES.

Hideous ghosts, as through the casement
　Old, 'mid northern waste and gloom,　480
I behold, — without amazement, —
　Here as there I am at home!

HOMUNCULUS.

Swiftly, there, before us striding,
　Mark yon tall, retreating shade!

MEPHISTOPHELES.

Seeing us through ether gliding,　　　485
　Troubled seems she, and afraid.

HOMUNCULUS.

Let her stride!　Set down thy burden, —
　Him, thy Knight ; — the while I speak,
Life to him returns, the guerdon,
　He in fable-land doth seek.　　　490

　　　　　　FAUST (*touching the ground*).
Where is she?

HOMUNCULUS.

　　　　That I cannot say,
But here perchance inquire for her you may.

Till breaks the dawn, with speed, do thou.
From fire to fire, still seeking, wend ;
He nothing more need fear, I trow,   495
Who, to the Mothers, ventured to descend.

MEPHISTOPHELES.

My part to play, I also claim ;
And for our weal naught better know,
Than that, forthwith, from flame to flame,
Seeking his own adventures each should go.
Then us once more to re-unite,   500
Show, little friend, thy sounding light!

HOMUNCULUS.

Thus shall it sound, thus glitter, too!
        (*The glass rings, and emits a powerful light.*)
And now away to marvels new!

FAUST (*alone*).

Where is she? — Now no further question make! 505
If this were not the sod, her form that bare,
This not the wave that brake to welcome her,
Yet 'tis the air, that once her language spake!
Here! through a wonder, here on Grecian land!
I felt at once the soil whereon I stand :   510
As me, the sleeper, a new spirit fired,
An Antæus in heart, I rise inspired.
Assembled here objects most strange I find.
Searching, through this flame-labyrinth I'll wind.
                                (*He retires.*)

MEPHISTOPHELES (*prying around*).

As I these little fires still wander through,   515
I find myself a stranger everywhere ;
Quite naked most, some shirted here and there :
The Sphinxes shameless, and the Griffins too,
And wingèd things, with tresses, hurrying past,
Before, behind, within mine eye are glassed . . .   520
At heart indecent are we, truth to speak,
Yet all too lifelike find I the Antique ;
It by the modern mind must be controlled,
And overglossed, in fashions manifold. . . .
A crew repulsive! Yet, a stranger guest,   525

In courteous phrase be my salute expressed. . . .
All hail! ye beauteous ladies, gray-beards wise!

GRIFFIN (*snarling*).

Not Gray-beards — Griffins! It the temper tries
To hear oneself styled gray. In every word
Some echo of its origin is heard:　　　　　　　530
Grim, grievous, grizzled, grimy, graveyards, gray,
In etymology accord, and they
Still put us out of tune.

MEPHISTOPHELES.

　　　　　　Yet all the same,
The " Gri " contents you in your honored name.

GRIFFIN (*as above*).

Of course! For the alliance proved may be,　　　535
Oft blamed, indeed, but praised more frequently
Let each one gripe at beauty, empire, gold,
Fortune still aids the Griper if he's bold.

ANTS (*of the colossal kind*).

Of gold ye speak. Thereof we much had stored,
And piled in rocks and caves our secret hoard;　　540
The Arimaspians found it, bore it off —
So far away that now at us they scoff.

GRIFFIN.

We'll bring them straightway to confession.

ARIMASPIAN.

Not on this night of jubilee!
Ere morning, all will squandered be;　　　　　545
For this time we retain possession.

MEPHISTOPHELES
(*who has seated himself between the Sphinxes*).
How soon, well-pleased, I grow familiar here!
I understand them, man by man.

SPHINX.

Our spirit-tones into your ear
We breathe, embody them you can.　　　　　550
Until we know thee better, tell thy name.

MEPHISTOPHELES.

Full many a title I 'mong men may claim.
Are Britons here?   They travel far to trace
Renownèd battle-fields and water-falls,
Old musty classic sites, and ruined walls.   555
A worthy goal for them this very place;
Of me their ancient plays would testify;
I there was seen as Old Iniquity.

SPHINX.

How came they upon that?

MEPHISTOPHELES.

I know not.

SPHINX.

That may be.
To read the starry volume hast thou power?   560
What sayest to the aspect of the hour?

MEPHISTOPHELES (looking up).

Star shooteth after star, bright the shorn moon doth
    shine,
And I'm content this cosy place within;
I warm myself against thy lion's skin.
Aloft to climb were hurtful, I opine.   565
Propose some riddles, some charades! — Begin!

SPHINX.

Thyself declare, a riddle that indeed.
Only essay thine inmost self to read:
" Needful to pious, as to bad men found;
Armor to those, ascetic fence to test,   570
Comrade to these, in every desperate quest.
And both alike to Zeus, a merry jest."

1st GRIFFIN (snarling).

I like him not!

2d GRIFFIN (snarling more loudly).
What wants he here?

BOTH.

The brute belongs not to this sphere!

MEPHISTOPHELES (*brutally*).

Thou thinkest, maybe, that the stranger's nail,   575
To scratch with, like thy talons, can't avail?
Let's try, forthwith!

SPHINX (*mildly*).

                    Here thou may'st ever dwell,
But from our midst thyself wilt soon expel.
In thine own land art wont thyself to please.
If I mistake not, here thou'rt ill at ease.   580

MEPHISTOPHELES.

Enticing art thou, when above descried;
But with the beast below, I'm horrified.

SPHINX.

Thou false one, thou shalt bitterly repent:
These paws are sound: but as for thee,
With thy shrunk hoof thou'rt not content,   585
It seems, in our society.

SIRENS (*preluding above*).

MEPHISTOPHELES.

What birds are those, on poplar bough
Swinging, the river banks along?

SPHINX.

Beware! the noblest have ere now
Been mastered by the Sirens' song!   590

SIRENS.

Ah! Misguided one, why linger,
'Mid these hideous wonders dwelling!
Cometh each melodious singer; —
Hark! our choral notes are swelling,
As beseems the Siren-throng.   595

SPHINXES

(*mocking them in the same melody*).

Force them downward, hither faring;
'Mid the boughs themselves concealing,
They to seize you are preparing;
Ugly falcon-claws revealing,
If ye hearken to their song.   600

SIRENS.

Envy, Hate, avaunt ye!   Listen!
All the brightest joys that glisten
'Neath the sky, assemble we!
Now with joy in every feature,
Hail we gladly every creature,   605
On the earth or in the sea!

MEPHISTOPHELES.

Dainty novelties, — there ring
From the throat and from the string
Tones that sweetly interweave.
Trills on me away are thrown;   610
Tickle they mine ear alone,
But untouched my heart they leave.

SPHINXES.

Speak not of hearts, for, I believe,
A leathern wallet in its place,
Shrivelled, would better suit thy face.   615

FAUST (*entering*).

The spectacle contents me; — wondrous creatures,
Ill-favored, yet with large and stalwart features.
E'en now, I augur an auspicious fate;
Whither doth me that earnest glance translate?
                    (*pointing to the* SPHINXES).
Once before such took Œdipus his stand;   620
                    (*pointing to the* SIRENS).
Writhed before such Ulyss in hempen band?
                    (*pointing to the* ANTS).
By such the mightiest treasure was upstored.
                    (*pointing to the* GRIFFINS).
With true and faithful watch, these kept the hoard.
I feel new life my being penetrate;
Great are the forms, the memories are great!   625

MEPHISTOPHELES.

Once thou such shapes had scouted, now
Thou seemest friendly to their kind;
E'en monsters welcome are, I trow,
To him who would the loved one find.

FAUST (*to the* SPHINXES).

Ye women shapes, straight must ye answer me: 630
Hath one of you chanced Helena to see?

SPHINX.

We reach not to her day; the last was slain
By Hercules; some tidings thou may'st gain
From Chiron, canst thou him detain.
Round on this ghostly night he doth career;   635
If he will answer thee, thy goal is near.

SIRENS.

Thou, for certain, shalt not fail! . . . .
When Ulysses, with us whiling,
Sped not forward, unreviling,
He hath told us many a tale.   640
All to thee we would confide,
If 'midst Ocean's purple tide,
To our seats thou would'st repair.

SPHINX.

Noble one, their guile beware!
As Ulysses to the mast, —   645
Thee let our good counsel bind.
Canst thou noble Chiron find,
Thy desire wilt gain at last.

(Exit FAUST.)

MEPHISTOPHELES (*peevishly*).

What croaks, on pinions rushing by?
So swiftly they elude the eye,   650
In single file they hurrying fly;
The hunter they would tire, I ween.

SPHINX.

Like storm of wintry tempest, these,
Scarce reach Alcides' arrows keen —
They are the swift Stymphalides;   655
Their croaking too is kindly meant,
With foot of goose and vulture beak;
To mingle in our sphere they seek,
Their cousinship to prove intent.

MEPHISTOPHELES (*scared*).

There whiz some other forms of ill —   660

SPHINX.

For fear of these you need not quake:
These are the heads of the Lernæan snake,
Shorn from the trunk, and think they're something still.
But say what meaneth this distress?
This troubled air, this restlessness?   665
Where would you go?   Be off, I say!
The group, that yonder meets mine eye,
Leads you to turn your neck awry.
Be not constrained!   Begone!   Away!
And greet full many a visage fair!   670
The Lamiæ, wantons sly, are there,
With forehead bold, and winning smile,
As they the Satyr-race beguile:
With them the goat's foot all may dare.

MEPHISTOPHELES.

You'll stay, that I may find you here again.   675

SPHINX.

Yea! mingle with the airy train!
From Egypt we the custom own,
That each a thousand years shall keep her throne.
And to our place, if due respect ye pay,
We rule the lunar, rule the solar day.   680

> We, the Pyramids before,
> Sit for judgment of the nations,
> War and peace and inundations —
> Change our features nevermore.

———

PENEIOS.
Surrounded by waters and NYMPHS.

PENEIOS.

> Sedgy whispers, gently flow;   685
> Sister reeds, breathe faint and low;
> Willows, lightly rustle ye,
> Lisp, each trembling poplar-tree.

To my interrupted dream!
Wakens me a tempest drear;   690
From my rest a trembling fear
Scares me, 'neath my flowing stream.

FAUST (*approaching the stream*).

By mine ear I must believe,
Where these arbors interweave
Bush and bough, there breathes around,   695
As of human voice the sound;
Prattling seems each wave to play,
And the breeze keeps holiday.

NYMPHS (*to* FAUST).

Oh, best were it for thee,
Way-weary and sore,   700
In coolness reclining,
Thy limbs to restore;—
The rest thus enjoying
That from thee doth flee;
We rustle, we murmur,   705
We whisper to thee!

FAUST.

Yes, I'm awake? Let them have sway
These peerless shapes, as in their play
Follows mine eye, in eager quest.
How strange the feeling! What are these?   710
Dreams are they? Are they memories?
Already once wert thou so blest.
Athwart thick-woven copse and bush
Still waters glide;— they do not rush,
Scarcely they rustle as they flow: 715
From every side their currents bright
A hundred crystal springs unite,
And form a sloping bath below.
Young nymphs, whose limbs of graceful mould,
The gazer's raptured eyes behold,   720
Are in the liquid mirror glassed!
Bathing with joyance all-pervading,
Now boldly swimming, shyly wading,
With shout and water-fight at last.

Contented might I be with these,   725
Mine eye be charmed with what it sees,
Yet to yon covert's leafy screen
My yearning glance doth forward press,
The verdant wealth of whose recess
Shrouds from my gaze the lofty queen.   730
Most wonderful!   Swans now draw near;
Forth from the bays their course they steer,
Oaring with majestic grace;
Floating, tenderly allied,
But with self-complacent pride,   735
Head and beak they move apace!
But one seems before the rest,
Joyfully the wave to breast,
Sailing swift, without a peer;
Swells his plumage, wave on wave,   740
That the answering flood doth lave; —
He the hallowed spot doth near. . . .
Now the others swim together,
To and fro, with shining feather;
Soon in splendid strife, they scare   745
All the timid maids away;
That, from duty swerving, they
For themselves alone may care.

NYMPHS.

Sisters, hearken, lay your ear
To the water's grassy bound!   750
Ringeth, if I rightly hear,
As of horse's hoof the sound.
Would I knew who, on this night,
Message bears in rapid flight.

FAUST.

As it seems, the earth indeed   755
Echoes 'neath a hurrying steed.
            Yonder turns my glance!
            Can such blessed chance
            Wait upon me here?
            Marvel without peer!   760
Hither a rider swift doth scour —
Endowed with spirit and with power —

Borne by a snow-white steed is he. . . .
I err not, him I seek is found —
Of Philyra the son renowned ! —   765
Halt ! Chiron ! Halt ! I'd speak with thee. . . .

CHIRON.

How now ! what wouldest thou ?

FAUST.

Thy course arrest !

CHIRON.

I pause not.

FAUST.

Take me with thee, grant my quest !

CHIRON.

Mount ! So I can inquire, as on we fare,
Whither art bound ? Thou standest on the banks ; 770
Prepared I am, thee through the stream to bear.

FAUST (*mounting*).

Where'er thou wilt.   Have evermore my thanks. . . .
The mighty man, the pedagogue of old
Whose fame it was, a hero-race to mould :
The noble Argonauts, with all their peers,   775
Who formed the poet's world, in bygone years —

CHIRON.

That pass we over.   Pallas' self indeed
As Mentor is not honored ; to my thought,
All, in the end, in their own way proceed,
As though, in sooth, they never had been taught. 780

FAUST.

The leech who names each plant, who knows
All roots, e'en that which deepest grows,
Wounds who assuageth, sickness who doth chase,
In mind and body's strength I here embrace —

CHIRON.

Were hero wounded on the field,   785
Counsel and aid I could impart ;
But, in the end, to priests I yield,
And women-herbalists my healing art.

In thee the truly great man speaks,
To words of praise who stops his ears;   790
Who acts, while privacy he seeks,
As were he one of many peers.

CHIRON.

Well skilled thou seemest, to beguile
People and prince with glozing wile.

FAUST.

At least by thee 'twill be confessed, —   795
The greatest of thy time hast seen, the best;
Hast with the noblest vied, in earnest strife,
And lived of demi-gods the arduous life!
But 'mong those figures of heroic mould,
In virtue whom pre-eminent didst hold?   800

CHIRON.

In the high circle of the Argonauts,
Each valiant was in fashion of his own,
And, by the virtue which inspired his thoughts,
Where others failed, he could suffice alone;
The Dioscuri ever did prevail   805
Where youthful bloom and beauty turned the scale;
Resolve, prompt deeds for others' welfare, these
The portion fair of the Boreades;
Reflective, wary, strong, in council wise,
So Jason lorded, dear to woman's eyes.   810
Then, Orpheus, tender, contemplative, still; —
Smote he the lyre, all owned his wondrous skill.
Lynceus, through rocks and shoals, who, keen of sight,
Guided the holy ship, by day and night.
In fellowship is danger fronted best,   815
Where one achieves, extolled by all the rest.

FAUST.

Of Hercules to me wilt naught impart?

CHIRON.

Alas! wake not the longing in my heart. . . .
Never had Phœbus met my gaze,
Ares, or Hermes, — such their name;   820

When, as divine what all men praise
Before my raptured vision came !
A monarch born, in youth arrayed
With glorious beauty ; homage due
He to his elder brother paid,   825
And to the loveliest women, too ;
His second bears not Mother Earth,
Nor Hebe leads to heaven again ;
Song strives in vain to tell his worth,
Tortured is marble, too, in vain !   830

FAUST.

To give such form to mortal ken
The sculptor's boasted power is weak.
The fairest hast portrayed of men,
Now of the loveliest woman speak !

CHIRON.

What !   Woman's beauty !   Empty phrase,   835
Too oft an image void of life ;
The being only can I praise,
Joy-giving and with gladness rife.
For beauty in herself is blest ;
Grace makes resistless, where possessed,   840
Like Helena, whom once I bare.

FAUST.

Her thou hast borne ?

CHIRON.
                    Yea !   On this back.

FAUST.

Was I not 'mazed enough ?   Alack !
And now such seat must bless me !

CHIRON.
                              By my hair
Me hath she grasped, as thou dost now.   845

FAUST.

I lose myself !   Oh, tell me, how ?
She is in truth my sole desire !
Her, whence and whither didst thou bear ?

CHIRON.

Easy to tell what you require.
Their little sister, then the robbers' prey,   850
The Dioscuri had redeemed; but they, —
The ravishers, not wont to be subdued,
Took courage, and with stormful rage pursued;
The brothers, with their sister, urged their way
Towards the marsh, that near Eleusis lay: 855
The brothers waded; plashing over it, I swam;
Then off she sprang, and fondly pressed
My mane, all-dripping; self-possessed,
She soothed and thanked, with sweet reserve and coy!
How charming was she!   Young, of eld the joy!   860

FAUST.

Just seven years old. . . .

CHIRON.

                          The philologues, I see,
As they themselves deceived, so have they thee.
Unique, in sooth, your mythologic dame:
After his pleasure her the poet shows;
Forever young, old age she never knows,   865
Her figure, love-inspiring, aye the same;
Ravished when young, courted when youth is flown —
Enough, no bonds of time the poets own.

FAUST.

So let her also by no time be bound!
At Pheræ by Achilles she was found   870
Beyond time's limits — happiness how rare!
In spite of destiny, love triumphed there;
And should I not, with powerful longing rife,
Draw forth that matchless figure into life,
The deathless being, born of gods the peer,   875
Tender as great, sublime, yet ever dear?
Thou sawest her once, whom I to-day have seen,
Charming as fair, fair as desired, I ween!
Enthralled is my whole being, heart and brain;
I cease to live, unless I her obtain!   880

CHIRON.

Stranger! thou art enraptured, as men deem;
Yet among spirits, brain-struck thou dost seem.

'Tis well this madness hath assailed thee here,
Since, only for some moments every year,
My wont it is to Manto to repair;   885
She, Æsculapius' child, in silent prayer
Implores her sire, who honor thus would gain,
Now to illumine the physicians' brain.
That from rash death-strokes they henceforth refrain —
To me the dearest of the Sybil's guild,   890
Not wildly moved, with helpful kindness filled;
After a brief delay thy perfect cure,
Through power of simples, cau her art secure.

FAUST.

But cured I would not be!   My mind is strong!
Then were I abject like the vulgar throng!   895

CHIRON.

Scorn not the healing of the noble fount.
We now are at the place; with speed, dismount.

FAUST.

Whither, upon this night, with horror fraught,
Me, through the pebbly stream, to land hast brought?

CHIRON.

Here Rome and Hellas madly spurned in fight,   900
(Olympus left, Peneios to the right,)
The mightiest realm that e'er in sand was lost;
The monarch flies, triumphs the burgher host.
Look up!   Here stands, significantly near,
The fane eternal, bathed in moonlight clear.   905

MANTO (dreaming within.)

Horse-hoofs shake the air,
Rings the sacred stair;
Demi-gods draw near.

CHIRON.

Right?   Open but thine eyes!   I'm here!

MANTO (awaking).

Welcome!   Thou hast not failed, I see.   910

CHIRON.

Still stands thy temple-home for thee!

MANTO.

Unwearied roam'st thou far and wide?

CHIRON.

In quiet dost thou aye abide,
While I in ceaseless change delight?

MANTO.

I wait, time circles me. — This wight?   915

CHIRON.

Him hath this ill-reputed night
Caught in its whirl, and hither brought.
Helen, with mind and sense distraught,
Helen, he for himself would win,
But how and where he knows not to begin;   920
Worthy is he thy healing art to prove.

MANTO.

Who the impossible desires, I love.
          (CHIRON *is already far away.*)
Enter, bold man, be joy thy meed!
This gloomy path to Proserpine doth lead,
She at Olympus' hollow foot   925
Doth lurk for unallowed salute.
In bygone time I Orpheus smuggled here;
Do thou fare better! Forward! Do not fear!
          (*They descend.*)

The Upper Peneios, as before.

SIRENS.

Plunge into Peneios' flood!
There beseems to swim rejoicing,   930
Song on song in chorus voicing,
For the unhallowed people's good.
Without water health is none!
In bright bands to the Ægean,
Speed we now with sounding pæan;   935
Every joy will then be won.
          (*Earthquake.*)

SIRENS.

Back the foaming wave is rushing,
In its bed it flows no more;
Quakes the earth, the floods are gushing,
Bursting smokes the pebbly shore.   940
Let us fly!   Come, every one!
Bodes this marvel good to none.

Hence! each noble, joyous guest,
Seaward to our gladsome fest,
Where the wavelets' glittering band   945
Lightly swelling, lave the strand;
There where Luna, mirrored true,
Moistens us with holy dew!
There is life's unfettered motion —
Here an earthquake's dire commotion!   950
Hence!   Ye wise ones, fly apace!
Horror reigneth in this place.

SEISMOS

(bellowing and blustering in the depths).

Once more heave with might and main,
With the shoulders bravely strain:
So the upper world we gain,   955
Where to us must all things bend!

SPHINX.

What a most unpleasant quaking,
Hideous storm-blast, awe-awaking!
What a heaving, what a throe,
Surging, swaying, to and fro!   960
Horror not to be endured!
But our post we'll not forsake,
Though all Hell were loose to break.

Now uprears itself a dome,
Wonderful.   With age long hoar,   965
He it is who built of yore
Delos' isle amid the foam,
Heaving it from out the sea,
For her, a mother soon to be;
Striving, pressing, upward-tending,   970
Arms wide-stretching, back low-bending,

Atlas-like, amid the surf
Shale he raises, grass and turf,
Pebbles, gravel, loam, and sand,
Tranquil cradle of our strand: 975
Crosswise, he a track did wrest
From the valley's tranquil vest:
Caryatid, of giant mould,
He, with strength that ne'er grows old,
Bears, half buried, earth his zone, 980
A huge scaffolding of stone —
But his course must here be stayed!
Sphinxes here their stand have made.

SEISMOS.

That have I wrought, myself alone,
This will mankind at last declare; 985
Had I not shaken and upthrown,
How had the world been now so fair?
Into the pure ethereal blue,
Their crests how should yon mountains raise,
Had I not heaved them forth to view, 990
To charm the painter's raptured gaze,
What time (my sires meanwhile surveying,
Chaos and Night), myself I bare
Stoutly, and, with the Titans playing,
Pelion and Ossa, tossed like balls in air? 995
Madly we raged, by youthful heat possessed,
Till, fairly wearied out at last,
With malice on Parnassus' crest,
We, like twin-caps both mountains cast. . . .
There with the Muses' hallowed choir, 1000
Apollo finds a glad retreat;
For Zeus, too, and his bolts of fire,
I raised aloft his glorious seat.
So now have I, with direful strain,
Pressed from the depths to upper air, 1005
And joyous dwellers call amain
New life henceforth with me to share.

SPHINXES.

Primeval had been deemed, I trow,
What here hath struggled into birth,

Had we ourselves not witnessed how   1010
It tore itself from out the earth.
Now upwards bushy groves themselves extend,
Rocks pressing upon rocks still forward tend;
Yet not for this shall any sphinx retreat:
Untroubled we retain our sacred seat.   1015

GRIFFINS.

Gold in leaflets, gold in flitters,   .
Through the crannies how it glitters,
Let none rob you of the prize—
Up! to seize it, Emmets, rise!

CHORUS OF ANTS.

Giants, the light to greet,   1020
Upward-aspiring
Hurled it; with pattering feet
Climb, never tiring!
Nimbly press out and in!
Each cleft is screening   1025
(Seek ye each crumb to win,)
Gold worth the gleaning;
Even the least of all
Must ye uncover;
Haste, in each cranny small   1030
Gold to discover.
Swarmers, in quest of pelf,
Toil without leisure!
Heed not the hill itself;
Gather the treasure!   1035

GRIFFINS.

In with it; pile the golden heap!
Upon it we our claws will lay;
Bolts of the surest fashion, they
The greatest treasure safe will keep.

PIGMIES.

We a footing here have got,   1040
How it chanced, doth not appear;

Whence we issued, question not;
Once for all we're settled here!
Seat for merry life doth yield,
Every country, every land; 1045
Is a rocky cleft revealed,
There the dwarf is straight at hand,
Dwarf and dwarfess, model pair,
Swiftly each its labor plies.
Know I cannot if it were 1050
So before in Paradise;
Here all find we for the best,
So our stars we thank; for still,
Mother Earth, in east and west,
Bringeth forth with right good will. 1055

DACTYLS.

Hath she, in a single night
Brought these tiny ones to light,
She the smallest will create;
Each forthwith will find his mate.

ELDEST OF THE PIGMIES.

Hasten, make ready, 1060
Prompt be, and steady!
Swift to the deed!
Let strength be for speed!
Peace still is reigning;
Build uncomplaining 1065
The smithy, to burnish
Armor, and furnish
All war's belongings
Now for the host!

Ants in swift throngings. 1070
Busily post; —
Metals procure, and you,
Dactyls, a tiny crew,
Yet an unnumbered band,
Hear our command; 1075
Wood bring with speed!
Flamelets in secret heap;

Them still alive to keep,
Coals too we need!

GENERALESSISSIMO. .

With arrow and bow 1080
Now march on the foe:
The herons that o'er
Yon fish-pond now soar,
Numberless nesting,
Haughtily breasting, 1085
Shoot altogether,
That so we may
With helm and feather
Ourselves array!

ANTS AND DACTYLS.

Deliverance is vain! 1090
The iron we bring,
They forge the chain;
Our freedom to wring
'Tis not yet the hour:
Crouch then to their power! 1095

THE CRANES OF IBYCUS.

Cry of murder, dying-wailing!
Wing-strokes, anguished, unavailing!
What lament, what agony,
Pierces to our realms on high!
All are murdered now; the water, 1100
Red with blood, betrays the slaughter;
Wanton lust of ornament
Hath the heron's plumage shent:
See it o'er the helmet wave
Of each greasy, crook-legged knave! 1105
Comrades of our army, ye
Heron-wanderers of the sea,
Be with us for vengeance mated;
In a cause so near related:
Let none spare or strength or blood! 1110
Deathless hatred to this brood!
(They disperse, croaking in the air.)

MEPHISTOPHELES (*on the plain*).

The northern witches I could curb; with these,
Your foreign spirits, I am ill at ease.
The Blocksberg is convenient when you roam:
Go where you may, you find yourself at home,   1115
For us Dame Ilsa watches on her stone,
Heinrich is cheerful on his mountain-throne,
The Snorers grunt if Elend but appears,
Yet all is settled for a thousand years;
But here, stand still or walk, and who can know 1120
Whether the ground up-heaves not from below?
Through a smooth valley merrily I wind,
And all at once there rises from behind
A mountain, — scarce a mountain, — yet of height
To intercept the sphinxes from my sight. . . .   1125
Adown the valley many a flame aspires;
Round some adventure quiver still the fires . . . .
Dances, and round me hovers to entice,
An amorous crew, with many a coy device.
But soft: — Accustomed to forbidden sweets,   1130
One seeks to snatch them, wheresoe'er one meets!

LAMIÆ

(*luring* MEPHISTOPHELES *after them*).

Fleeter, still fleeter!
Ever advancing!
Then again staying,
Prattling and playing!   1135
Nothing is sweeter
Than the hoar sinner,
After us dancing,
Thus to allure;
Limping and stumbling,   1140
Fretting and grumbling,
To penance sure,
Draweth he nigh;
His stiff leg dragging,
Comes he unflagging,   1145
As him we fly.

MEPIISTOPHELES (*standing still*).

Accursed Fate!   Dupes truly styled!
From Adam downward, fooled, beguiled!
We age — but who's in wisdom schooled?
Wert not enough already fooled ?   1150
We know how good for naught these creatures ;
Pinched at the waist, with painted features ;
No soundness in their bodies slim ; —
Grasp where we may, rotten is every limb :
We know, we see, we handle it in life —   1155
And yet we dance, if but the carrion fife!

LAMIÆ (*stopping*).

Hold !   He considers, lingers, stands ;
Meet him, lest he escape your hands !

MEPHISTOPHELES (*advancing*).

Push on ! nor, like a simpleton,
Let web of doubt entangle thee!   1160
For if of witches there were none,
The devil who would devil be !

LAMIÆ.

Round this hero circle we !
Love for one within his breast,
Soon itself will manifest.   1165

MEPIISTOPHELES.

By this light's uncertain gleam
Beauteous damosels ye seem,
So from blame shall you be free.

EMPUSA (*rushing in*).

And I also !   One with you,
Now admit me to your crew !   1170

LAMIÆ.

One too many, she I ween
Spoiler of our sport hath been.

EMPUSA (to MEPHISTOPHELES).

Thee doth thy cousin dear salute,
Empusa with the ass' foot!
Thine but a horse's hoof, yet thee,   1175
Cousin, I greet most courteously!

MEPHISTOPHELES.

Myself unknown I fancied here —
And yet, alas, near kinsfolk meet;
From Hartz to Hellas, far and near,
So runs the rede, you'll cousins greet!   1180

EMPUSA.

I with resolve can act, can take
Full many a shape; but for thy sake,
That I to thee due honor pay,
The ass' head I don to-day.

MEPHISTOPHELES.

I see, with people of this sort,   1185
Relationship doth much import;
Yet, come what may, 'tis all the same;
The ass' head I must disclaim.

LAMIÆ.

This hag avoid!   She comes to scare
Whatever lovely seems and fair;   1190
What lovely was and fair before,
When she draws near, is so no more.

MEPHISTOPHELES.

These smooth slim cousins, short or tall,
Make me suspicious, one and all;
I fear, those rosy cheeks behind,   1195
Some metamorphoses to find.

LAMIÆ.

Come, take thy choice; we many are.
Catch hold!   If reigns thy lucky star,
Thou of the lot may'st draw the best.
What means this hankering delay?   1200
The wooer wretchedly dost play.

With haughty mien and lofty crest!—
Amid our troop now see him glide;
Throw by degrees your masks aside,
And be your proper selves confessed!   1205

MEPHISTOPHELES.

I've made my choice, the fairest, she. . .
(*Embracing her.*)
Dry as a besom! Woe is me!
(*Seizing another.*)
And this?. . . a fright, oh wretched lot!

LAMIÆ.

Deserv'st thou better? Think it not!

MEPHISTOPHELES.

The little one I fain would clasp.   1210
A lizard glides from out my grasp,
And serpent-like her polished hair.
Anon a taller one I catch. . . . .
A thyrsus-staff alone I snatch,
That for a head doth a pine-cone wear.   1215
Where will this end?. . . One plump and round,
With whom some solace may be found —
I'll try my fortune once again!—
Right flabby, squashy; such a prize,
Your Oriental dearly buys.   1220
But ah! The puff-ball bursts in twain!

LAMIÆ.

Quick as lightning, disunite!
Hover ye, in dusky flight,
Round the intruding witch's son,
In uncertain, ghastly rings,   1225
Flitter-mice, on noiseless wings!
Too cheaply he'll escape anon.

MEPHISTOPHELES (*shaking himself*).

I have not grown much wiser, that is clear;
The North's absurd, absurd 'tis also here,
Ghosts here as there, a devilish crew,   1230
Folk are insipid, poets too!
'Tis here a masquerade as there,
A sensual dance, as everywhere;

At beauty's mask I clutched amain —
And seized, what made me stand aghast. 1235
Yet to deceive myself I'm fain,
If only longer it would last!
     (Losing his way among the rocks.)
Where am I? Whither tend my pains?
Where was a path, there chaos reigns,
I by smooth roads have hither sped,   1240
Rude bowlders now impede my tread;
I clamber up and down in vain —
My sphinxes, where shall I regain?
Ne'er had I dreamed so mad a thing:
Such mountain in a single night!   1245
A bold witch-journey is this flight,
Their Blocksberg with them here they bring!

        OREAD (*from the natural rock*).
Hither ascend! My mountain old
Its form primeval still doth hold —
My steep and rocky steps revere,   1250
Extremest branch of Pindus — here,
Unshaken have I reared my head,
When over me Pompeius fled;
Yon phantom shape that cheats the eye
Away, when crows the cock, will fly!   1255
Such fables oft arise, I see,
And disappear as suddenly.

        MEPHISTOPHELES.
Honor to thee, thou reverend head;
With lofty oak-strength garlanded,
Moonshine, however clear and bright,   1260
Faileth to pierce thy rayless night! —
But, 'mong the bushes, comes this way
A light, that gleams with modest ray.
How fitly all things happen thus;
In truth! it is Homunculus! —   1265
Whither away, thou tiny friend?

        HOMUNCULUS.
Flitting from place to place, I wend.
In the best sense full fain I am to be;

And long impatiently my glass to break;
Only from what I've seen and see,   1270
Courage I lack the step to take.
But, now, in confidence to speak,
Of two philosophers the track I seek;
I hearkened, their discourse I overheard;
And Nature — Nature — was their only word: 1275
Apart from these I would not go,
Somewhat of earthly being they must know,
And doubtless I at last shall learn
Whither most wisely I myself may turn.

MEPHISTOPHELES.

Thy course shape thou thyself.   Be wise!   1280
For where your ghosts find entrance, there
Welcome is your philosopher:
That you his art and favor may delight,
A dozen new ones he brings forth to light.
Unless thou errest, reason dormant lies;   1285
Wilt thou exist, through thine own effort rise!

HOMUNCULUS.

Such good advice should not neglected be.

MEPHISTOPHELES.

So now away!   Of this we more shall see,
                      (*They separate.*)

ANAXAGORAS (*to* THALES).

To yield is adverse to thy stubborn mind;
To bring conviction, needs there further proof? 1290

THALES.

The waves yield willingly to every wind,
But from the beetling crag still keep aloof.

ANAXAGORAS.

Through fiery vapor came this rock to birth.

THALES.

Moisture hath gendered all that lives on earth.

HOMUNCULUS (*between them*).

To walk beside you, suffer me!   1295
I also greatly long to be.

ANAXAGORAS.

Hast thou, O Thales, ever in one night,
Such mountain out of slime brought forth to light?

THALES.

Never was Nature, with her living powers,
Measured by scale of days and nights and hours;   1300
By law each shape she fashioneth, and hence,
E'en in the grand there is no violence.

ANAXAGORAS.

Yet such was here!   Plutonic savage fire,
Æolian vaporous force, explosive, dire,
Burst through the ancient crusts of level earth,   1305
And a new mountain came forthwith to birth.

THALES.

Why further press the case? at any rate,
'Tis there, and that is well.   In such debate,
Leisure and precious time away one flings,
Your patient folk to keep in leading-strings.   1310

• ANAXAGORAS.

Quickly with myrmidons the mountain teems,
The clefts to people: forth there streams
Of pigmies, ants, and gnomes, a living tide,
And other tiny bustling things beside.
(*To* Homunculus.)
After the Great hast ne'er aspired,   1315
But hermit-like hast lived retired;
To lordship if thyself canst bring,
Forthwith I'll have thee crowned as king.

HOMUNCULUS.

What says my Thales?

THALES.

                    Not with my consent;
With dwarfs we are with dwarfish deeds content: 1320
While with the great the dwarf doth greatness win.
See there: of cranes the swarthy cloud,
They threaten the excited crowd,

And so would threat the king; with beak
Sharp-pointed and with talons fierce,   1325
Down-swooping, they the pigmies pierce;
Fateful, their stormful ire they wreak;
A crime the herons doomed to slaughter,
Brooding around their tranquil water;
But that death-shower of arrowy rain,   1330
For bloody vengeance cries amain,
And doth with rage their kindred fill,
The pigmies' guilty blood to spill.
Of what avail helm, spear, and shield?
What helps the dwarf the heron's plume?   1335
How ant and dactyl shun their doom!
Wavers the host, — they fly, they yield.

ANAXAGORAS
(after a pause, solemnly).

If I, till now, the powers subterrain praise,
I, in this hour, my prayers to heaven upraise. . . .
Thou throned aloft, eternal, aye the same,   1340
Threefold in aspect, and threefold in name,
Amid my people's woe I cry to thee,
Diana, Luna, Hecatè!
Deep pondering mind, expander of the breast,
Mighty within, though outwardly at rest,   1345
Unclose the gulfs abysmal of thy shade,
Be without spells thine ancient might displayed.
(Pause.)
Am I too quickly heard?
And hath my prayer,
Ascending there,   1350
Marred Nature's order with a word?

And greater, ever greater draweth near
The goddess' throne, her full-orbed sphere,
Enormous, fearful to the gaze!
Its fire grows redder through the haze. . . .   1355
No nearer!   Threatening orb, I pray; —
Ourselves and land and sea thou'lt sweep away!
Was it then true that dames of Thessaly
Through sinful trust in magic, thee
Have downward from thy pathway sung,   1360
From thee have powers most baleful wrung? . . .

The glittering shield, behold, it darkles!
Sudden it splits, and flares and sparkles!
What a hissing! what a rattling!
Thunder and storm-blast fiercely battling!—   1365
Humbled I fall before thy throne —
Pardon! myself invoked it, I alone.
                    (*Throws himself on his face.*)

THALES.

What hath this man not seen and heard!
I know not rightly how with us it fared.
Like him I have not felt it.   Ne'ertheless   1370
The hours are out of tune, we must confess,
And Luna calmly as before,
In her own place aloft doth soar.

HOMUNCULUS.

Behold the pigmies' seat!   The mound
Is pointed now, before 'twas 'round.   1375
Convulsion huge I felt; a rock
Down from the moon, with sudden shock,
Hath fallen; and both friend and foe
Were crushed and slaughtered at a blow!
Yet arts like these I needs must praise,   1380
That, working with creative might,
Upwards and downwards, could upraise,
This mountain in a single night.

THALES.

Peace!   'Twas but fancy.   That vile brood, —
To swift destruction let them fare!   1385
That thou wert not their king, is good.
Now to the sea's glad feast repair!
Strange guests are honored and expected there.
                    (*They withdraw.*)

MEPHISTOPHELES
            (*clambering up the opposite side*).
Up rocky stairs and steep must I to-day,
Through ancient oaks' gnarled roots make toilsome way.
Upon my Hartz the piny atmosphere   1391
Savors of pitch, and that to me is dear,

'Tis next to brimstone. . . . Here, among the Greeks
E'en for a trace of it one vainly seeks.
Inquisitive I am, and must inquire   1395
Wherewith they feed hell-torment and hell-fire.

DRYAD.

In thine own land be prudently at home;
Thou hast not wit enough abroad to roam.
Towards home thou should'st not turn thy thought;
    while here
The honor of the sacred oaks revere.   1400

MEPHISTOPHELES.

The lost will aye in thought arise;
What we are used to, is our Paradise.
But say, what triple object do I trace,
By the dim light, in yonder cavern's shade?

DRYAD.

The Phorkyads! Go, venture to the place,   1405
And speak to them, if thou art undismayed!

MEPHISTOPHELES.

And wherefore not? . . . I see it with amaze.
Proud as I am, e'en I must needs confess,
Their like I ne'er have seen; their ugliness
That of our hellish hags o'ersways!   1410
Sins reprobated long, — will they
Waken henceforth the least dismay,
If men this threefold dread survey?
Would we not suffer them to dwell
On threshold of our dreariest Hell;   1415
Rooted in Beauty's land of fame,
Here to be styled antique they claim . . .
They stir themselves, to scent me they appear,
Like Vampire-Bats, their twitter meets mine ear.

PHORKYADS.

Give me the eye, my sisters, forth to gaze,   1420
So near our fane who boldly thus delays!

MEPHISTOPHELES.

Most honored! To approach you give me leave,
That I your threefold blessing may receive.

As still unknown, indeed, I come to you,
Yet am, methinks, a distant cousin too.   1425
Gods ancient and revered I've seen of yore,
Deeply have Ops and Rhea bowed before ;
Your own and Chaos' sisters, yesternight,
Or night before, the Parcæ met my sight ;
Yet on your like I ne'er before have gazed.   1430
Silent I am, delighted and amazed.

PHORKYADS.

Intelligent this spirit seems to be.

MEPHISTOPHELES.

That you no bard hath sung, surprises me.
And say, most worthy ones, how hath it been
That of your charms no pictured forms are seen? 1435
Your shapes should sculpture labor to retain,
Not Juno, Pallas, Venus, and their train !

PHORKYADS.

Immersed in solitude and night profound,
Such thought no entrance to our mind hath found !

MEPHISTOPHELES.

How should it, from the world retired, when ye, 1440
Yourselves by none beheld, can no one see !
You in such regions rather should reside
Where art and splendor reign in equal pride,
Where from a marble-block, with genius rife,
Steps forth each day a hero into life,   1445
Where ——

PHORKYADS.

        Silence ! in us wake no longings new :
What would it profit us, if more we knew ?
In night begot, to things of night allied,
Unto ourselves scarce known, unknown to all beside.

MEPHISTOPHELES.

Not much, indeed, in such case can one say.   1450
But each himself to others can convey :
One eye, one tooth suffices for you three ;
So would it tally with mythology,

In two the being of the three to blend,
And your third semblance unto me to lend,   1455
But for brief space.

ONE OF THE PHORKYADS.

What think you, may we try?

THE OTHER.

We'll venture — but without tooth or eye.

MEPHISTOPHELES.

With these the very best away you've ta'en;
Imperfect the stern image would remain!

ONE OF THE PHORKYADS.

Press one eye close — full easily 'tis done;   1460
Now of your canine teeth display but one —
Forthwith, in profile, perfect and complete,
Our sisterly resemblance we shall greet.

MEPHISTOPHELES.

Much honor!   Be it so!

PHORKYADS.

So be it!

MEPHISTOPHELES.

(as a PHORKYAD in profile).

Done!

Here stand I Chaos' well-beloved son!   1465

PHORKYADS.

Daughters of Chaos we, by ancient right.

MEPHISTOPHELES.

Me now they call, oh shame, hermaphrodite!

PHORKYADS.

What beauty our new triad gives to view!
Of eyes, and eke of teeth, we now have two.

MEPHISTOPHELES.

Now must I shroud myself from mortal sight,   1470
In pool of hell the devils to affright.

(Exit.)

Rocky Bays of the Ægean Sea.
The moon pausing in the zenith.

SIRENS

(reclined upon the cliffs around, fluting and singing).

Thou whom from thy realm supernal,
Downward drew, with rites nocturnal,
Weird Thessalian sorceresses,
With thy glance, all things that blesses,   1475
Now illume the throng that presses
Through the waves with billowy motion,
Flooding all the rippling ocean
With the splendor of thy light!
Luna fair, thy vassals greet thee;   1480
Be propitious, we entreat thee!

NEREIDS *and* TRITONS

(as wonders of the sea).

Sing aloud, with shriller singing,
Let it, through broad ocean ringing,
Call its people, far and near!—
From the storm's dread whirlpools hiding,   1485
We in stillest depths were biding;
Gracious song allures us here.

See, we deck ourselves enraptured,
With the treasures we have captured,
Golden chain and clasp and gem,   1490
Spangled zone and diadem;
All this fruitage is your prey;
Down to us these shipwrecked treasures,
You have lured with your sweet measures,
You, the Dæmons of our bay!   1495

SIRENS.

Well we know, through sea-waves gliding,
In their crystal depths abiding,
Live the fishes, sorrow-free;
Yet blithe roamers, hither thronging,
We to-day to know are longing   500
That ye more than fishes be.

NEREIDS *and* TRITONS.

Ere your song hath hither brought us,
Of this question we've bethought us;
Sisters, Brothers, hasten we!
Briefest journey, doubt dispelling,   1505
Yieldeth proof sufficing, telling
That we more than fishes be! (*They retire.*)

SIRENS.

In a twinkling, straight away,
Sped to Samothrace have they,
Vanished with a favoring wind!   1510
What their purpose? what to gain,
Where the high Cabiri reign?
Gods they are, the strangest, who,
Self-evolved, are ever new,
Yet to their own nature blind.   1515

Kindly linger on thy height,
Gracious Luna, that the night
Tarry may, lest daylight breaking
Drive us hence, our haunts forsaking!

THALES

(*on the shore, to* HOMUNCULUS).

Thee to old Nereus gladly would I lead; 1520
Not distant are we from his cave indeed;
But sour he is and obstinate,
Moreover hath a stubborn pate!
The race entire of mortal kind
Is never to the grumbler's mind.   1525
But he the future can disclose,
Hence each to him due reverence shows,
And gives him honor at his post;
To many he hath rendered aid.

HOMUNCULUS.

Let's knock, that trial may be made!   1530
At once my glass and flame it will not cost.

NEREUS.

Men's voices are they that mine ear hath heard?
With anger straight mine inmost heart is stirred!

Forms — striving still, who high as gods would soar,
Yet to be like themselves, doomed evermore.   1535
Long years could I have dwelt in godlike rest,
But ever was impelled to aid the best;
And when at last I saw the accomplished deed,
It was as though they ne'er had heard my rede.

THALES.

Yet people trust in thee, thou Ocean Seer;   1540
Wise art thou; chase us not!   This flamelet here,
That man's similitude doth wear, survey,
In everything thy counsel he'll obey.

NEREUS.

Counsel!   What good to men hath counsel brought?
On stubborn ears fall prudent words in vain;   1545
Oft as the deed dire punishment hath wrought,
Self-willed as ever mortals aye remain.
How fatherly I Paris warned, or e'er
His lust another's consort did ensnare!
On Hellas' shore fearless he stood and bold;   1550
What I in spirit saw, I there foretold:
The reeking winds, the upstreaming ruddy glow,
Rafters ablaze, murder and death below,
Troy's day of doom — fast bound in deathless rhyme,
A terror and a portent for all time.   1555
The scoffer mocked the old man's oracle;
He followed his own lust, and Ilion fell,
A giant corpse, slowly its death-pangs ceased, —
To Pindus' eagles a right welcome feast.
Ulysses, too — did I not oft presage   1560
To him dark Circe's wiles, the Cyclop's rage,
His own delay, his comrades' reckless vein,
And what not else?   And hath it brought him gain?
Till, sorely battered, he full late, at last,
By favoring wave on friendly shore was cast.   1565

THALES.

Such conduct to the sage must needs give pain;
Yet still the good man trieth once again.
A grain of thanks that richly him repays,
Tons of ingratitude still overweighs.

I and this youngster no slight boon require.   1570
Wisely *to be* is now his sole desire.

NEREUS.

Spoil not for me my present mood, most rare!
Far other aims to-day engross my care;
My daughters I've invoked to come to me,
The Dorides, the Graces of the sea.   1575
Neither Olympos nor your region bears
Form so replete with grace, so light as theirs.
From Dragons of the sea, with loveliest motion,
They cast themselves upon the steeds of Ocean,
One with the element that round them plays,   1580
The very foam would seem their forms to raise.
'Mid rainbow-hues of Venus' pearly car,
Comes Galatea, beauty's choicest star,
Who, since on us hath Cypris ceased to smile,
As goddess honored is on Paphos' isle;   1585
And so for long the gracious one doth own,
As heiress, temple-town and chariot-throne.

Away!   Harsh words, and hatred in the heart
Have in the Father's raptured hour no part.
Away to Proteus!   Ask that being strange   1590
The secret of existence and of change.
(*He retires towards the sea.*)

THALES.

We by this step, it seems, have nothing won;
For if we light on Proteus, straight he's gone,
And if he wait, he only says at last
Things that perplex, and make one stand aghast. 1595
Yet, once for all, such counsel thou dost need;
So then to try him, onward let us speed!
(*They retire.*)

SIRENS (*on the rocks above*).

What are these, far off appearing,
Through the billowy realm careering?
Like to sails of snowy whiteness,   1600
Zephyr-guided, such their brightness,
Hither borne with gentle motion,
These the lustrous nymphs of Ocean!

Downward climb we; hark!   They're singing;
Hear ye not their voices ringing?   1605

NEREIDS *and* TRITONS.

Those whom thus our hand upraises
Scatter blessings ; — sing their praises !
From Chelone's giant shield,
Shines an awful form revealed :
Gods they are whom we rejoicing   1610
Hither bring, glad pæans voicing.

SIRENS.

Little in height,
Potent in might,
Hoar gods from the wave
The shipwrecked who save!   1615

NEREIDS *and* TRITONS.

To our peaceful revel speeding,
The Cabiri we are leading;
Where their power the hapless shieldeth,
Kindly sway there Neptune wieldeth.

SIRENS.

Yield we must to you.   1620
Ye the sinking crew,
With resistless power,
Save in shipwreck's hour.

NEREIDS *and* TRITONS.

Three we bring, our triumph sharing,
But the fourth refused, declaring   1625
That for all abiding yonder,
He the sole one is to ponder.

SIRENS.

Thus one god doth jeer
At his fellows still.
All the good revere,   1630
Dread ye every ill!

NEREIDS *and* TRITONS.

There of them should seven be.

SIRENS.

Where then are the other three?

NEREIDS *and* TRITONS.

That we cannot answer: rather,
On Olympos' question farther: 1635
There the eighth perchance is pining,
Whom none thinks upon.   Inclining
Graciously, they us have greeted —
But all are not yet completed.

The incomparable, these; —   1640
Pressing onward, aye aspiring,
Full of longing, still desiring
What can ne'er be reached, to seize.

SIRENS.

Every power enthroned,
Sun or Moon that sways,   1645
In our prayers is owned;
'Tis our wont; it pays.

NEREIDS *and* TRITONS.

How brightly shines our fame, behold,
Leading this festivity!

SIRENS.

Heroes of the ancient days   1650
Lack henceforth their meed of praise,
How great soe'er their fame of old;
Though they have won the fleece of gold,
Ye have the Cabiri.
          (*Repeated in full Chorus.*)
Though they have won the fleece of gold,   1655
We! ye! have the Cabiri.
     (*The* NEREIDS *and* TRITONS *pass on.*)

HOMUNCULUS.

These uncouth figures, — I am fain
For earthen pots to take them,
'Gainst them the wise ones strike amain
Their stubborn heads, and break them!   1660

THALES.

The very thing they most desire.
The rusty coin is valued higher.

PROTEUS (*unperceived*).

This pleases me, the old in fable:
The stranger 'tis, the more respectable!

THALES.

Where art thou, Proteus?

PROTEUS
(*ventriloquizing, now near, now far away*).

      Here! and here! 1665

THALES.

I pardon the stale jest; appear,
And with a friend vain words forego!
From a false place dost speak, I know.

PROTEUS (*as from a distance*).

Farewell!

THALES (*softly to* HOMUNCULUS).

  He's close at hand.   Now brightly flare,
He's curious as a fish; where'er 1670
He hide himself, that flame, be sure,
Hither forthwith will him allure.

HOMUNCULUS.

Full light I'll pour, yet care must take
Lest with the shock the glass should break.

PROTEUS.
(*in the form of a gigantic porpoise*).

What shines with radiancy so dear? 1675

THALES
(*concealing* HOMUNCULUS).

Good!   If thou wish it, thou canst draw more near;
Let the slight trouble vex thee not, I pray,
Thyself upon two human feet display.
'Tis solely by our leave, and courtesy,
That what we now conceal, who wills may see. 1680

PROTEUS (*in a noble form*).
Thy sophist's tricks, it seems, dost still employ.

THALES.
Thy figure to transform still gives thee joy.
          (*He has uncovered* HOMUNCULUS).

PROTEUS (*astonished*).
A glittering dwarflein!   Ne'er beheld before!

THALES.
Fain to exist, he counsel doth implore.
He is, from him I heard it, come to earth   1685
Only half-formed, through some mysterious birth.
Fairly endowed with qualities ideal,
The power he lacks, firmly to grasp the real,
Till now the glass alone to him gives weight;
But he at once would be incorporate.   1690

PROTEUS.
A genuine virgin's son art thou;
Born ere thou shouldest be, I trow!

THALES (*in a whisper*).
Further it seemeth critical to me;
He an Hermaphrodite appears to be.

PROTEUS.
The sooner 'twill succeed; where'er   1695
He comes, he happily will fare.
With much reflection we may here dispense;
In the broad sea thy being must commence;
On a small scale one there begins,
Well pleased the smallest to devour;   1700
Till, waxing step by step, one wins,
For loftier achievement, ample power.

HOMUNCULUS.
A tender air is wafted here;
Dear is to me the breeze, the fragrance dear!

PROTEUS.
Right, dearest youth!   Farther away   1705
Still more delightful 'twill be found;
Ineffable the airs that play
This narrow tongue of land around.

Thence, near enough, the train we see,
Now floating hither.   Come with me!   1710

THALES.

I, too, will go with thee, proceed!

HOMUNCULUS.

A threefold spirit-step, wondrous indeed!

TELCHINES of RHODES.

(Upon hippocampi and sea-dragons, bearing
Neptune's trident.)

The trident we forged, wherewith Neptune assuages
Old Ocean's wild waves, when most fiercely he rages:
His clouds when the Thunderer spreads o'er the skies,
To their rolling terrific then Neptune replies;   1716
And when from on high the jagged lightning doth leap,
Then wave after wave dashes up from the deep;
And all that in anguish their joint rage o'erpowered,
Long whirled to and fro, by the depth is devoured;
To-day then the sceptre to us hath he lent.—   1721
Now joyously float we, serene and content!

SIRENS.

You, to Helios dedicated,
You, to bright day consecrated,
Hail we to this hour, whose light   1725
Doth to Luna's praise invite!

TELCHINES.

Thou loveliest Queen of yon o'ervaulting sphere,
The praise of thy brother with rapture dost hear:
To Rhodus' blest island an ear thou dost lend,
Thence one deathless pæan to him doth ascend. 1730
The day-course he opens and with fiery gaze,
When finished his journey, our troop he surveys;
The cities and hills, shore and wave, yield delight
To the glorious God, and are lovely and bright.
No mist hovers o'er us, and should one draw near, 1735
A ray and a zephyr—the island is clear:
His form the high god beholds multiplied there,
As stripling, as giant, the Mighty, the Fair—

The power of the gods it was we who began
To portray in the form, not unworthy, of man.   1740

PROTEUS.

Grudge them not their boastful singing,
To the holy sun, life-bringing.
Dead works are an idle jest.
Fusing mould they; when completed   1745
Stands their god with rapture greeted,
Straight with triumph swells their breast!
These proud gods so fondly cherished,—
What their doom, inquire ye?   Prone,
By an earthquake overthrown,
Melted, they long since have perished.   1750

Toil of earth, whate'er it be,
Nothing is but drudgery:
Life in ocean better fareth:
Thee to endless water beareth
Proteus-Dolphin.   (*He transforms himself.*)
                    Fairly sped!   1755
Bravely, on my back careering,
Thou shalt prosper, onward steering,
And to Ocean thee I'll wed.

THALES.

Obey the noble inspiration,
And at its source begin creation,   1760
Make ready for the great emprize!
By laws eternal still ascending,
Through myriad forms of being wending,
To be a man in time thou'lt rise.
        (HOMUNCULUS *mounts the* PROTEUS *dolphin.*)

PROTEUS.

In spirit come to boundless ocean: 1765
Unfettered there in every motion,
At thine own pleasure thou shalt wend;
But let not higher rank allure thee;
Attaining manhood, I assure thee,
Then all with thee is at an end!   1770

THALES.

As it may happen; good it seems to me,
In one's own day a stalwart man to be.

PROTEUS (*to* THALES).

One of your stamp, perchance!   For they
Abide awhile, nor pass away;
Since 'mong the troops of spirits pale,   1775
As pass the centuries, thy form I hail.

SIRENS (*on the rocks*).

See yon cloudlets, how they mingle
Round the moon in circlet bright!
Doves they are, whom love doth kindle,
With their pinions pure as light!   1780
Paphos hath her bird-choir sent us,
Girt with radiance they appear.
Now our fête may well content us,
    Fraught with rapture full and clear !

NEREUS (*approaching* THALES).

Yonder ring, an airy vision   1785
Nightly wanderer might maintain;
But with juster intuition,
Other views we entertain :
Doves they are, whose escort playeth
Round my daughter's pearly car;   1790
Wondrous art their movement swayeth,
Learned by them in days afar.

THALES.

That I also hold for best,
Peace that yieldeth to the good,
If in warm and silent nest   1795
Something holy still doth brood.

PSYLLI *and* MARSI

(*on sea-bulls, sea-calves, and sea-rams*).

In the rugged Cyprian caves,
Sheltered from the shocks of Ocean,
From the earthquake's dire commotion,
Fanned by Zephyr's viewless waves,   1800
There, as in the days afar,
We, with conscious rapture, are

Guardians of Cythera's car,
And through breathings of the night,
Through the rippling wavelets bright,　　1805
Viewless still to mortal sight,
We the loveliest daughter lead.
Us nor wingèd lion scares,
Nor eagle, as our task we ply,
Nor cross, nor crescent, though it flares　　1810
Aloft, emblazoned in the sky;
To and fro, alternate swaying,
Each the other driving, slaying,
Fields and towns in ashes laying:
Thus with joyous speed,　　1815
Onward our loveliest mistress we lead.

SIRENS.

Circling still, with gentle motion,
Round the chariot, line on line,
Gliding o'er the waves of ocean,
With your movements serpentine,　　1820
Come, ye stalwart Nereides,
Sturdy damsels, gracious, wild;
Bring ye, tender Dorides,
Galatea, fair and mild,
Image of her mother, she　　1825
Earnest is, of godlike mien,
Worthy immortality,
Yet, like earth's fair dames, your queen
Winsome is, with grace serene!

DORIDES

(passing in chorus before NEREUS, *mounted upon dolphins).*

Luna, light and shadow throwing,　　1830
Round this youthful band, shine clear!
For we come our Father showing
Prayerfully, our bridegrooms dear.
(*To* NEREUS.)
Them, soft pity's voice obeying,
From the rock's fell tooth we bore,　　1835
And on moss and seaweed laying,
Warmed them back to light once more;

Kisses upon us bestowing,
Thus their grateful temper showing,
View them kindly, we implore!   1840

NEREUS.

Precious indeed the twofold gain;
To show compassion, and delight obtain!

DORIDES.

Dost praise, O Father, our endeavor?
Grudge us not our joy, well-earned;
Deathless youth, enjoyed forever   1845
In the bliss of love returned!

NEREUS.

Would ye enjoy your captured treasure!
Then mould each youth to be a man;
Powerless am I to do your pleasure;
Accord your prayer Zeus only can.   1850
The waves, whose foam around you playeth,
All steadfastness in love ignore,
And if its spell no longer swayeth,
Then place them quietly ashore.

DORIDES.

Dear ye are, sweet youths, in sooth;   1855
Yet from you we needs must sever:
We have craved eternal truth,
But the Gods allow it never!

THE YOUTHS.

Gallant sailor-youths and true,
If ye still will fondly tend us;   1860
Life so fair we never knew,
Nor could fate a fairer send us.

(GALATEA *approaches in the shell chariot*).

NEREUS.

Tis thou, my beloved one!

GALATEA.

                    O Sire! what delight
Linger, ye dolphins, enchained is my sight.

NEREUS.

Gone already!   They forsake me,   1865
Speeding on with circling motion !
What to them the heart's emotion!
Oh! that with them they would take me !
Yet such rapture yields one gaze,
The livelong year it well repays.   1870

THALES.

Hail! all hail!   The cry renew!
Blooms my spirit, piercèd through
By the Beautiful, the True! . . . .
All from water sprang amain !
All things water doth sustain :   1875
Ocean, grant thy deathless reign !
Were no clouds by thee outspread,
No rich brooklets by thee fed,
On their course no rivers sped,
And no streamlets perfected,   1880
What then were the world, what were ocean and plain ?
'Tis thou, who the freshness of life doth maintain.

ECHO

(chorus of the collective circles).

'Tis thou, from whom freshness of life pours amain !

NEREUS.

Far distant now they wheel and turn,
And vainly glance for glance must yearn ;   1885
Circle in circle wide extending,
The countless throngs, in order blending,
Urge o'er the waves their glad career.
But Galatea's pearly throne,
Behold I still, behold ; alone   1890
Now it glitters like a star
'Midst the crowd ; with radiance tender,
Shines through the press the loved one's splendor ;
Though so far, so very far,
Still it shimmers bright and clear,   1895
Ever true and ever near!

HOMUNCULUS.

In this moisture calm and clear,
All I shine on doth appear
    Exquisitely fair!

PROTEUS.

In this living, dewy sphere,   1900
First thy flamelet shineth clear,
    Breathing tones most rare.

NEREUS.

But lo! what new mystery, fraught with surprise,
Reveals itself now, 'mid yon crowds, to our eyes?
What flames round the shell, round the feet of my
    child?
Now strongly it glitters, now sweetly, now mild, 1906
As if by the pulses of love it were swayed!

THALES.

Homunculus is it, by Proteus betrayed . . . .
A yearning majestic these symptoms disclose,
Presageful they tell of his passionate throes;   1910
Against the bright throne he'll be shattered! It grows,
It flashes, it sparkles, abroad now it flows!

SIRENS.

What marvel illumines the billows, which dash
Against one another in glory?   They flash,
They waver, they hitherward glitter, and bright   1915
All forms are ablaze in the pathway of night;
And all things are gleaming, by fire girt around,
Prime source of creation, let Eros be crowned!

Hail, ye billows!   Hail to thee,
Girt by holy fire, O sea!   1920
Water, hail!   Hail, fire's bright glare!
Hail to this adventure rare!

ALL TOGETHER.

Hail, each softly blowing gale!
Caverns rich in marvels, hail!
Highly honored evermore   1925
Be the elemental four!

ACT THE THIRD.

Before the Palace of Menelaus in Sparta.
Enter HELENA, *with a chorus of captive Trojan women.*
PENTHALIS, *leader of the chorus.*

HELENA.

The much admired and much upbraided, Helena,
From yonder strand I come, where erst we disembarked,
Still giddy from the roll of ocean's billowy surge,
Which, through Poseidon's favor and through Euros'
        might,
On lofty-crested backs hither hath wafted us,   5
From Phrygia's open field, to our ancestral bays.
Yonder King Menelaus, glad of his return,
With his brave men of war, rejoices on the beach.
But oh, thou lofty mansion, bid me welcome home,
Thou, near the steep decline, which Tyndareus, my sire,
From Pallas' hill returning, here hath builded up ;   11
Which also was adorned beyond all Sparta's homes,
What time with Clytemnestra, sister-like I grew,
With Castor, Pollux, too, playing in joyous sport.
Wings of yon brazen portals, you I also hail !   15
Through you, ye guest-inviting, hospitable gates,
Hath Menelaus once, from many princes chosen,
Shone radiant on my sight, in nuptial sort arrayed.
Expand to me once more, that I the king's behest
May faithfully discharge, as doth the spouse beseem. 20
Let me within, and all henceforth behind remain,
That, charged with doom, till now darkly hath round
        me stormed !
For since, by care untroubled, I these sites forsook,
Seeking Cythera's fane, as sacred wont enjoined,
And by the spoiler there was seized, the Phrygian, 25
Happened have many things, whereof men far and wide
Are fain to tell, but which not fain to hear is he
Of whom the tale, expanding, hath to fable grown.

CHORUS.

Disparage not, oh, glorious dame,
Honored possession of highest estate!   30
For sole unto thee is the greatest boon given;
The fame of beauty that all over-towers!
The hero's name before him resounds,
So strides he with pride;
Nathless at once the stubbornest yields   35
To beauty, the presence which all things subdues.

HELENA.

Enough! I with my spouse, ship-borne, have hither sped,
And to this city now by him before am sent.
But what the thought he harbors, that I cannot guess.
Come I as consort hither?   Come I as a queen?   40
Come I as victim for the prince's bitter pangs,
And for the evils dire, long suffered by the Greeks?
Conquered I am; but whether captive, know I not:
For the Immortal Powers fortune and fame for me
Have doomed ambiguous; direful ministers that wait
On beauty's form, who even on this threshold here, 46
With dark and threat'ning mien, stand bodeful at my
          side!
Already, ere we left the hollow ship, my spouse
Looked seldom on me, spake no comfortable word;
As though he mischief brooded, facing me he sat.   50
But now, when, to Eurotas' deeply curving shores
Steering our course, scarce had our foremost vessel's
          beak
The land saluted, spake he, as by God inspired;
"Here let my men of war, in ordered ranks, disbark;
I marshal them, drawn up upon the ocean strand;   55
But thou, pursue thy way, not swerving from the
          banks,
Laden with fruit, that bound Eurotas' sacred stream,
Thy coursers guiding o'er the moist, enamelled meads,
Until thou may'st arrive at that delightful plain,
Where Lacedæmon, once a broad fruit-bearing field, 60
By mountains stern surrounded lifteth now its walls.
Set thou thy foot within the tower-crowned princely
          house,
Assemble thou the maids, whom I at parting left,

And with them summon too the wise old stewardess.
Bid her display to thee the treasures' ample store,   65
As by thy sire bequeathed, and which, in peace and war,
Increasing evermore, I have myself up-piled.
All standing shalt thou find in ancient order; for,
This is the prince's privilege, that to his home,
When he returns at last, safe everything he finds,   70
Each in its proper place, as he hath left it there.
For nothing of himself the slave hath power to change."

CHORUS.

Oh, gladden now, with glorious wealth,
Ever increasing, thine eye and heart!
For beautiful chains, the adornment of crowns,   75
Are priding themselves, in haughty repose;
But step thou in, and challenge them all,
They arm themselves straight;
I joy to see beauty contend for the prize,   79
With gold, and with pearls, and with jewels of price.

HELENA.

Forthwith hath followed next this mandate of my lord:
" Now when in order thou all things hast duly seen,
As many tripods take, as needful thou may'st deem,
And vessels manifold, which he at hand requires,
Who duly would perform the sacrificial rite,   85
The caldrons, and the bowls, and shallow altar-plates;
Let purest water, too, from sacred fount be there,
In lofty pitchers; further, store of seasoned wood,
Quick to accept the flame, hold thou in readiness;
A knife, of sharpest edge, let it not fail at last.   90
But I all other things to thy sole care resign."
So spake he, urging me at once to part; but naught,
Breathing the breath of life, the orderer appoints,
That, to the Olympians' honor, he to slaughter doomed:
Suspicious seems it! yet, dismiss I further care;   95
To the high Gods' decree be everything referred,
Who evermore fulfil, what they in thought conceive;
It may, in sooth, by men, as evil or as good
Be counted, it by us, poor mortals, must be borne.
Full oft the ponderous axe on high the priest hath raised
In consecration o'er the earth-bowed victim's neck.101

Nor could achieve the rite, for he was hinderèd,
Or by approaching foe, or intervening God.

CHORUS.

What now will happen, canst thou not guess;
Enter, queen, enter thou in,   105
Strong of heart!
Evil cometh and good
Unexpected to mortals;
Though foretold, we credit it not.
Troya was burning, have we not seen   110
Death before us, terrible death!
And are we not here,
Bound to thee, serving with joy,
Seeing the dazzling sunshine of heaven,
And of earth, too, the fairest,   115
Kind one — thyself — happy are we!

HELENA.

Come what come may!   Whate'er impends, me it be-
     hoves
To ascend, without delay, into the royal house,
Long missed, oft yearned-for, well-nigh forfeited;
Before mine eyes once more it stands, I know not how.
My feet now bear me not so lightly as of yore,   121
When up the lofty steps I, as a child, have sprung.

CHORUS.

Fling now, O sisters, ye
Captives who mourn your lot,
All your sorrows far from you.   125
Share ye your mistress' joy!
Share ye Helena's joy,
Who to the dear paternal hearth,
Though returning full late in sooth,
Nathless with surer, firmer tread   130
Joyfully now approaches!

Praise ye the holy ones,
Happy restoring ones,
Gods, the home-leaders, praise ye.
Soars the enfranchised one,   135
As upon outspread wings,
Over the roughest fate, while in vain

Pines the captured one, yearning-fraught,
Over the prison-battlements
Arms outstretching, in anguish.   140

Nathless her a god hath seized,
The exiled one,
And from Ilion's wreck
Bare her hitherward back once more,
To the ancient, the newly-adornèd   145
Father-house,
After unspeakable
Pleasure and anguish,
Earlier youthful time,
Newly quickened, to ponder.   150

PENTHALIS (*as leader of the chorus*).

Forsake ye now of song the joy-surrounded path,
And toward the portal-wings turn ye forthwith your
          gaze!
What see I, sisters?   Here, returneth not the queen?
With step of eager haste, comes she not back to us?—
What is it, mighty queen, that in the palace-halls, 155
Instead of friendly hail, could there encounter thee,
And shatter thus thy being?   Thou conceal'st it not;
For I abhorrence see, impressed upon thy brow,
And noble anger, that contendeth with surprise.

HELENA

(*who has left the folded doors open, excited*).

No vulgar fear beseems the daughter of high Zeus, 160
And her no lightly-fleeting terror-hand may touch;
But that dire horror which, from womb of ancient
          Night,
In time primeval rising, still in divers shapes,
Like lurid clouds, from out the mountain's fiery gorge,
Whirls itself forth, may shake even the hero's breast.165
Thus have the Stygian Gods, with horror fraught, to-day
Mine entrance to the house so marked, that fain I am,
Back from the oft-time trod, long-yearned-for threshold,
          now,
Like to a guest dismissed, departing, to retire.
Yet no, retreated have I hither to the light;   170
No further shall ye drive me, Powers, whoe'er ye be!

Some expiation I'll devise, then purified,
The hearth-flame welcome may the consort as the lord.

LEADER OF THE CHORUS.

Discover, noble queen, to us thy handmaidens,
Devotedly who serve thee, what hath come to pass ! 175

HELENA.

What I have seen, ye too, with your own eyes, shall see,
If ancient Night, within her wonder-teeming womb,
Hath not forthwith engulfed, once more, her ghastly
        birth ;
But yet, that ye may know, with words I'll tell it you : —
What time the royal mansion's gloomy inner court,   180
Upon my task intent, with gloomy step I trod,
I wondered at the drear and silent corridors.
Fell on mine ear no sound of busy servitors,
No stir of rapid haste, officious, met my gaze ;
Before me there appeared no maid, no stewardess, 185
Who every stranger erst, with friendly greeting, hailed.
But when I neared at length the bosom of the hearth,
There saw I, by the light of dimly smouldering fire,
Crouched on the ground, a crone, close-veiled, of
        stature huge,
Not like to one asleep, but as absorbed in thought ! 190
With accent of command I summon her to work,
The stewardess in her surmising, whom perchance
My spouse, departing hence, with foresight there had
        placed ;
Yet, closely muffled up, still sits she, motionless;   194
At length, upon my threat, uplifts she her right arm,
As though from hearth and hall she motioned me away.
Wrathful from her I turn and forthwith hasten out,
Towards the steps, whereon aloft the Thalamos
Rises adorned, thereto the treasure-house hard by ;
When, on a sudden, starts the wonder from the floor ;
Barring with lordly mien my passage, she herself   201
In haggard height displays, with hollow eyes, blood-
        grimed,
An aspect weird and strange, confounding eye and
        thought.
Yet speak I to the winds; for language all in vain

Creatively essays to body forth such shapes.   205
There see herself !   The light she ventures to confront !
Here are we master, till the lord and monarch comes ;
The ghastly brood of Night doth Phœbus, beauty's
        friend,
Back to their caverns drive, or them he subjugates.
      (PHORKYAS *stepping on the threshold, between the
            door-posts*).

CHORUS.

Much have I lived through, although my tresses 210
Youthfully waver still round my temples ;
Manifold horrors have mine eyes witnessed ;
Warfare's dire anguish, Ilion's night,
When it fell ;

Through the o'erclouded, dust-overshadowed   215
Tumult of war, to gods have I hearkened,
Fearfully shouting ; hearkened while discord's
Brazen voices clang through the field
Rampart-wards.

Ah, yet standing were Ilion's   220
Ramparts ; nathless the glowing flames
Shot from neighbor to neighbor roof,
Ever spreading from here and there,
With their tempest's fiery blast,
Over the night-darkened city. —   225

Flying, saw I through smoke and glare,
And the flash of the tonguèd flames,
Dreadful, threatening Gods draw near ;
Wondrous figures, of giant mould,
Onward striding through the weird   230
Gloom of fire-luminous vapor.

Saw I them, or did my mind,
Anguish-torn, itself body forth
Phantoms so terrible — nevermore
Can I tell ; but that I this   235
Horrible shape with eyes behold,
This of a surety know I !
Yea, with my hands could clutch it even,
Did not fear, from the perilous
Venture, ever withhold me.   240

Tell me, of Phorkyas'
Daughters which art thou?
For to that family
Thee must I liken.
Art thou, maybe, one of the gray-born?   245
One eye only, and but one tooth
Using still alternately?
One of the Graiæ art thou?

Darest thou, Horror,
Thus beside beauty,   250
Or to the searching glance
Phœbus' unveil thee?
Nathless step thou forward undaunted;
For the horrible sees he not,
As his hallowed glances yet   255
Never gazed upon shadows.

But a tragical fate, alas,
Us, poor mortals, constrains to bear
Anguish of vision, unspeakable,
Which the contemptible, ever detestable,   260
Doth in lovers of beauty wake!

Yea, so hearken then, if thou dar'st
Us to encounter, hear our curse,
Hark to each imprecation's threat,
Out of the curse-breathing lips of the happy ones,
Who by the gods created are!   266

PHORKYAS.

Trite is the word, yet high and true remains the sense:
That shame and beauty ne'er together, hand in hand,
Their onward way pursue, earth's verdant path along.
Deep-rooted in these twain dwelleth an ancient grudge,
So that, where'er they happen on their way to meet,
Upon her hated rival turneth each her back;   272
Then onward speeds her course with greater vehemence,
Shame filled with sorrow, Beauty insolent of mood,
Till her at length embraces Orcus' hollow night,   275
Unless old age erewhile her haughtiness hath tamed.
You find I now, ye wantons, from a foreign shore,
With insolence o'erflowing, like the clamorous flight

Of cranes, with shrilly scream that high above our
    heads,
A long and moving cloud, croaking send down their
    noise,   280
Which the lone pilgrim lures, wending his silent way,
Aloft to turn his gaze; yet on their course they fare,
He also upon his: so will it be with us.

Who are ye, then, that thus around the monarch's house,
With Mænad rage, ye dare like drunken ones to rave?
Who are ye, then, that ye the house's stewardess 286
Thus bay, like pack of hounds hoarsely that bay the
    moon?
Think ye, 'tis hid from me, the race whereof ye are?
Thou youthful, war-begotten, battle-nurtured brood,
Lewd and lascivious thou, seducers and seduced,   290
Unnerving both, the soldier's and the burgher's strength!
Seeing your throng, to me a locust swarm ye seem,
Which, settling down, conceals the young green harvest-
    field.
Wasters of others' toil! ye dainty revellers,
Destroyers in its bloom of all prosperity!   295
Thou conquered merchandise, exchanged and marketed!

HELENA.

Who in the mistress' presence chides her handmaidens,
Audacious, doth o'erstep her household privilege;
For her alone beseems, the praiseworthy to praise,
As also that to punish which doth merit blame.   300
Moreover with the service am I well content,
Which these have rendered me, what time proud
    Ilion's strength
Beleaguered stood, and fell and sank; nor less indeed
When we, of our sea-voyage the dreary changeful woe
Endured, where commonly each thinks but of himself.
Here also I expect the like from this blithe train; 306
Not what the servant is, we ask, but how he serves.
Therefore be silent thou, and snarl at them no more!
If thou the monarch's house till now hast guarded well
Filling the mistress' place, that for thy praise shall
    count;   310
But now herself is come, therefore do thou retire,
Lest chastisement be thine, instead of well-earned meed!

PHORKYAS.

The menial train to threat, a sacred right remains,
Which the illustrious spouse of heaven-favored lord 314
Through many a year doth earn of prudent governance.
Since that, now recognized, thy ancient place as queen,
And mistress of the house, once more thou dost resume,
The long-time loosened reins grasp thou; be ruler here,
And in possession take the treasures, us with them!
Me before all protect, who am the elder-born,   320
From this young brood, who seem, thy swan-like
      beauty near,
But as a basely wingèd flock of cackling geese!

LEADER OF THE CHORUS.

How hideous beside beauty showeth hideousness!

PHORKYAS.

How foolish by discretion's side shows foolishness!
(*Henceforth the choristers respond in turn, stepping
      forth singly from the chorus.*)

1ST CHORISTER.

Tell us of Father Erebus, tell us of Mother Night! 325

PHORKYAS.

Speak thou of Scylla, speak of her, thy sister born!

2D CHORISTER.

From thy ancestral tree springs many a monster forth.

PHORKYAS.

To Orcus hence, away! Seek thou thy kindred there!

3D CHORISTER.

Who yonder dwell, in sooth, for thee are far too young.

PHORKYAS.

Tiresias, the hoary, go, make love to him!   330

4TH CHORISTER.

Orion's nurse of old, was thy great-granddaughter.

PHORKYAS.

Harpies, so I suspect, did rear thee up in filth.

5TH CHORISTER.

Thy cherished meagreness, whereon dost nourish that?

PHORKYAS.

'Tis not with blood, for which so keenly thou dost thirst.

6TH CHORISTER.   [335

For corpses dost thou hunger, loathsome corpse thyself!

PHORKYAS.

Within thy shameless jaw the teeth of vampires gleam.

7TH CHORISTER.

Thine I should stop were I to tell thee who thou art.

PHORKYAS.

First do thou name thyself; the riddle then is solved.

HELENA.

Not wrathful, but in grief, step I between you now,
Forbidding such alternate quarrel's angry noise;   340
For to the ruler naught more hurtful can befall,
Than 'mong his trusty servants, sworn and secret strife;
The echo of his mandate then to him no more,
In swift accomplished deed responsively returns;
No, stormful and self-willed, it rages him around, 345
The self-bewildered one, and chiding still in vain.
Nor this alone; ye have in rude unmannered wrath
Unblessèd images of dreadful shapes evoked,
Which so encompass me, that whirled I feel myself
To Orcus down, despite these my ancestral fields. 350
Is it remembrance? Was it frenzy seized on me?
Was I all that? and am I? shall I henceforth be
The dread and phantom-shape of those town-wasting
          ones?
The maidens quail: but thou, the eldest, thou dost stand,
Calm and unmoved; speak, then, to me some word of
          sense!   355

PHORKYAS.

Who of long years recalls the fortune manifold,
To him heaven's highest favor seems at last a dream.
But thou, so highly favored, past all bound or goal,
Saw'st, in thy life-course, none but love-inflamèd men,

Kindled by impulse rash to boldest enterprise.   360
Theseus by passion stirred full early seized on thee,
A man of glorious form and strong as Heracles.

HELENA.

Forceful he bore me off, a ten-year slender roe,
And in Aphidnus' keep, shut me, in Attica.

PHORKYAS.

But thence full soon set free, by Castor, Pollux too, 365
In marriage wast thou sought by chosen hero-band.

HELENA.

Yet hath Patroclus, he, Pelides' other self,
My secret favor won, as willingly I own.

PHORKYAS.

But thee thy father hast to Menelaus wed,
Bold rover of the sea and house-sustainer too.   370

HELENA.

His daughter gave he, gave to him the kingdom's sway;
And from our wedded union sprang Hermione.

PHORKYAS.

But while he strove afar, for Crete, his heritage,
To thee, all lonely, came an all too beauteous guest.

HELENA.

Wherefore the time recall of that half-widowhood, 375
And what destruction dire to me therefrom hath grown!

PHORKYAS.

That voyage unto me a free-born dame of Crete,
Hath also capture brought, and weary servitude.

HELENA.

As stewardess forthwith he did appoint thee here, 379
With much entrusted, — fort and treasure boldly won.

PHORKYAS.

All which thou didst forsake, by Ilion's tower-girt town
Allured, and by the joys, the exhaustless joys of love.

HELENA.

Remind me not of joys: no, an infinitude
Of all too bitter woe o'erwhelmed my heart and brain.

PHORKYAS.

Nathless 'tis said thou didst in twofold shape appear;
Seen within Ilion's walls, and seen in Egypt too.   386

HELENA.

Confuse thou not my brain, distraught and desolate!
Here even, who I am, in sooth, I cannot tell.

PHORKYAS.

'Tis also said, from out the hollow shadow-realm,
Achilles, passion-fired, hath joined himself to thee, 390
Whom he hath loved of old, 'gainst all resolves of Fate.

HELENA.

As phantom I myself, to him a phantom bound;
A dream it was — thus e'en the very words declare.
I faint, and to myself a phantom I become.
            (*She sinks into the arms of the semi-chorus.*)

CHORUS.

Silence!   Silence!   395
False-seeing one, false-speaking one, thou!
Through thy horrible, single-toothed lips,
Ghastly, what exhaleth
From such terrible loathsome gulf!

For the malignant one, kindliness feigning.   400
Rage of wolf 'neath the sheep's woolly fleece,
Far more terrible is unto me than
Jaws of the hound three-headed.
Anxiously watching stand we here:
When?   How?   Where of such malice   405
Bursteth the tempest
From this deep-lurking brood of Hell?

Now, 'stead of friendly words, freighted with comfort,
Lethe-bestowing, gracious and mild,
Thou art summoning from times departed,   410
Thoughts of the past most hateful,
Overshadowing not alone
All sheen gilding the present,

Also the future's
Mildly glimmering light of hope.   ·   415
Silence!   Silence!
That fair Helena's soul,
Ready e'en now to take flight,
Still may keep, yea firmly keep
The form of all forms, the loveliest,   420
Ever illumined of old by the sun.

(HELENA *has revived, and again stands in the midst.*)

PHORKYAS.

Forth emerge from fleeting cloudlets, sun resplendent
    of this day,
If when veiled thou couldst delight us, dazzling now
    thy splendor reigns.
As the world unfolds before thee, thou dost gaze with
    gracious look.
Though as hideous they revile me, well the beautiful I
    know.   425

HELENA.

Giddy from the void I issue, that in fainting round me
    closed,
Rest once more I fain would cherish, for sore-weary
    are my limbs;
Yet the queen it still beseemeth, yea all mortals it
    beseems,
Self-controlled, to man their spirits, whatsoe'er of ill
    may threat.

PHORKYAS.

In thy greatness now thou standest, in thy beauty 'fore
    us there,   430
Tells thy glance that thou commandest; what com-
    mandest thou? speak it forth!

HELENA.

The delay your strife occasioned, now prepare ye to
    retrieve:
Haste, a sacrifice to order, as the king commanded me!

PHORKYAS.

In the palace all is ready: censer, tripod, sharpened axe,
For lustration and for incense; now the destined vic-
    tim show!   435

HELENA.

That to me the king disclosed not.

PHORKYAS.

Spake it not?   O doleful word!

HELENA.

What the sorrow that o'erpowers thee?

PHORKYAS.

Queen, it is thyself art meant!

HELENA.

I?

PHORKYAS.

And these.

CHORUS.

Oh, woe and wailing!

PHORKYAS.

Thou wilt perish by the axe.

HELENA.

Dreadful—yet surmised!   Me wretched!

PHORKYAS.

Unavoidable it seems.

CHORUS.

And to us, ah, what will happen?

PHORKYAS.   440

She a noble death will die;
But upon the lofty rafter, that upholds the gable-roof,
As in fowling-time the thrushes, ye shall struggle in a
     row.
(HELENA *and the chorus stand astounded and terrified,*
     in striking, well-arranged groups.)

PHORKYAS.

Poor phantoms!—Stand ye there like figures petrified,
In deadly fear to part from day, which is not yours.
Mortals, who phantoms are together like as ye,   445
Not willingly renounce the sun's resplendent beams;

Yet from their doom may none save them by force or
  prayer;
All know it, yet can few with pleasure welcome it!
Enough, ye all are lost. So to the work forthwith! 449
(*She claps her hands; thereupon appear at the door*
  masked dwarfish figures, who execute with alacrity
  the orders as they are delivered).
Approach, thou swarthy, round, misshapen, goblin
  train!
Roll yourselves hither! Mischief work ye here at will.
The altar, golden-horned, bear ye, and give it place;
And let the gleaming axe o'erlay the silver rim!
The water-vessels fill, wherewith to wash away
Of black polluting gore, the horror-breathing stain; 455
The costly carpet here outspread upon the dust,
That so the victim may in royal fashion kneel,
And wrapt within its folds, although with severed head,
Sepulchred straight may be, with honorable rites!

LEADER OF THE CHORUS.

The queen, absorbed in thought, beside us stands apart;
Blenching the maidens droop, like meadow-grass when
  mown;   461
On me, the eldest, seems a sacred duty laid,
With thee to barter words, thou form of primal eld.
Experienced art thou, wise, well-minded seemest to us,
Although this brainless troop, misjudging, thee reviled:
Tell then, if thou dost know, of rescue possible.   466

PHORKYAS.

'Tis easy said.   Alone it resteth with the queen
Herself to save, and you her handmaidens with her.
Needful is prompt resolve, and of the quickest, too!

CHORUS.

Most revered among the Parcæ, wisest of the Sibyls thou,
Sheathèd hold the golden scissors, light and life to us
  proclaim!   471
For our tender limbs already, feel we dangling, un-
  rejoicing,
Swinging to and fro, that rather in the dance rejoiced
  of yore,
Resting then on lover's breast.

HELENA.

These tremblers leave ye; sorrow feel I, naught of fear;
Yet knowest thou rescue, straight be it with thanks
  received! 476
To sage, far-seeing minds, oft the impossible
As possible doth show. Speak on and tell thy thought!

CHORUS.

Speak and tell us, tell us quickly; how may we escape
  the ghastly,
Odious nooses, that, with menace, like to ornaments the
  vilest, 480
Round our necks themselves are coiling? We, poor
  victims, feel beforehand,
Feel the stifling, feel the choking, if of all the gods,
  thou, Rhea,
Lofty mother, feelest no pity!

PHORKYAS.

Have ye patience, to my story's course protracted
Still to hearken? Manifold its windings are. 485

CHORUS.

Patience enough! For while we hearken still we live.

PHORKYAS.

The man at home who tarries, noble wealth who guards,
And knoweth to cement his dwelling's lofty walls,
As also to secure his roof 'gainst stress of rain,
With him shall all go well, through the long day of life:
But lightly who o'ersteps, with rash and flying foot, 491
His threshold's sacred bounds, by guilty aim impelled,
Shall find, on his return, the ancient place, indeed,
But altered everything, if not completely wrecked.

HELENA.

Declare, whereto these trite and well-known proverbs
  here? 495
Thou shouldst relate; stir not what needs must give
  offence!

PHORKYAS.

True history it is, in no wise a reproof.
As pirate Menelaus steered from bay to bay;

Mainland and islands, all he ravaged as a foe,
With spoil returning home, as it within lies stored. 500
He before Ilion's walls hath wasted ten long years,
But on his homeward course how many know I not;
Meanwhile how fares it here where stands the lofty house
Of Tyndarus?   How fares it with the region round?

HELENA.

Is then reproach in thee so thoroughly ingraft,   505
That, save to utter blame, thy lips thou canst not move?

PHORKYAS.

Thus stood, for many years, forlorn the sloping ridge
That northwards to the height rises in Sparta's rear,
Behind Taygetus, whence, still a merry brook,
Downward Eurotas rolls, and then, along our vale,   510
Broad-flowing among reeds, gives nurture to your swans.
There in the mountain-vale, behind, a stalwart race
Themselves established, pressing from Cimmerian night,
And have upreared a fastness, inaccessible,   514
Whence land and folk around they harry, as they list.

HELENA.

This could they then achieve?   Impossible it seems.

PHORKYAS.

They ample time have had; haply, some twenty years.

HELENA.

Is one the lord?   Are they a numerous robber-horde?

PHORKYAS.

Not robbers are they, yet is one among them lord. 520
Of him I speak no blame, though once he sought me here;
He might have taken all, yet did content himself
With some few things — which he free gifts, not trib-
    ute, named.

HELENA.

And what his mien?

PHORKYAS.

                    Nowise amiss! He pleases me.
A cheerful man he is, courageous, and well-built,

With understanding dowered, as few among the Greeks.
As barbarous we brand the race, but yet, methinks,
So savage none can be as heroes, not a few,
Who man-devouring pests at Ilion showed themselves.
His greatness I respect; did trust myself to him.
His fortress! That should ye with your own eyes behold!
'Tis something different from clumsy mason-work,   531
The which your fathers have aloft, at random, piled,
Cyclopean like the cyclops, one unwieldy stone
On stone unwieldy hurling!   There quite otherwise,
Upright and level, all is fixed by square and rule. 535
Gaze on it from without; upward it strives toward
          heaven,
So straight, so well-adjusted, mirror-smooth like steel;
To clamber there, in sooth, your very thought slides
          down.
Within are ample courts, broad spaces girt around
With solid mason-work, of divers kinds and use; 540
Pillars, pilasters, arches, archlets, balconies,
Are there, and galleries, for peering out and in,
And scutcheons.

HELENA.

What are they?

PHORKYAS.

                              Ajax, upon his shield,
A coiled serpent bare, as ye yourselves have seen;
The seven chiefs at Thebes have figured emblems borne,
Each one upon his shield, significant and rich: 546
There moon and star were seen, on heaven's nightly field,
There goddess, hero, ladder, weapons, torches, too,
And what with violence still threatens goodly towns.
Devices of like sort beareth our hero-band,   550
In colored splendor, heired from primal ancestors;
There lions you behold, eagles, claw too and beak,
Then horns of buffalo, wings, roses, peacock-tails,
Bars also, gold and black and silver, blue and red. 554
Such symbols in their halls hang pendant, row on row,
In halls that know no bound, ample as is the world;
There might ye dance!

CHORUS.

O tell us, be there dancers there?

PHORKYAS.

The best; a youthful band, blooming and golden-haired;
Of youth they breathe!   Of yore so only Paris breathed,
What time he to the queen approached too near.

HELENA.

Thou fall'st   560
Quite from thy part!   To me declare the final word.

PHORKYAS.

That speakest thou; in earnest say distinctly yes!
Then with that fortress thee I'll straightway compass.

CHORUS.

Speak
That little word, and save thyself and us with thee!

HELENA.

How?   Shall I harbor fear lest Menelaus should   565
So ruthlessly transgress as rage to wreak on me?

PHORKYAS.

Hast thou forgotten, how he thy Deiphobus,
Thy slaughtered Paris' brother, in unheard-of guise,
Hath mangled, he who strove thy stubborn widowhood
To bend, and gained his purpose!   Nose and ears he
    lopped,   570
And mutilated sore; 'twas horror to behold!

HELENA.

That did he unto him; for my sake it was done.

PHORKYAS.

And for his sake, be sure, the like he'll do to thee.
Not to be shared is beauty; her who hath possessed
Entire, destroyeth rather, cursing partnership.   575
    (*Trumpets in the distance; the* CHORUS *shudders.*)
As the shrill trumpets' blare doth ear and entrails seize,
Rending asunder, so her talons jealousy
Fixes in that man's breast, who never can forget
What once he owned, now lost, by him possessed no
    more.

CHORUS.

Hear'st thou not the horns resounding?   See'st thou
    not the gleam of arms?   580

PHORKYAS.

Be thou welcome!   To thee, lord and monarch! gladly
    give I reckoning.

CHORUS.

But for us?

PHORKYAS.

    Ye know full surely: 'fore your eyes her
  . death you see,
Your own death mark, too, within there; no, for you
    there is no help.   (*Pause.*)

HELENA.

I have the course devised, which next I will pursue.
An adverse Demon art thou, that full well I feel; 585
And fear thou wilt convert even the good to ill.
Nathless to yonder keep I straight will follow thee.
The rest I know: but what in her deep breast the
    queen
As mystery conceals, let it remain to all
A secret unrevealed!   Now, ancient one, lead on!   590

CHORUS.

    O how gladly go we hence,
    Urging our footsteps:
    Death in our rear;
    Once more before us
    Rises a fortress,   595
    With unscalable ramparts;
    Us may they shelter as well,
    Even as Ilion's keep,
    Which succumbed at last
    Through contemptible craft alone!   600
(*Mists diffuse themselves, veiling the background; also
    the nearer portion of the scene.*)
    How!   Sisters, how!
    Sisters, gaze around!
    Was it not cheerfulest day?
    Mists are rising, wreathing aloft,
    From Eurotas' hallowed stream!   605
    Vanished hath the beautiful,
    Sedge-becrowned marge from the gaze;
    And the free, graceful swans,
    Proudly, silently, floating,

Joyfully together,   610
See I, ah! no more!

Yet, sisters, yet!
Singing hear I them,
Singing harsh tones from afar —
Death presaging, so mortals say;   615
Ah, that they to us may not,
'Stead of rescue's promised weal,
Ruin dire betoken at last,
Unto us, swan-like maids,
Fair, white-throated ones, and ah!   620
To our queen swan-gendered!
Woe to us, woe, woe!

All itself overshrouds,
Wrapt in vapor and mist;
Gaze on each other can we not!   625
What befalls?   Do we walk?
Hover we now,
Tripping with light steps over the ground?
Seest thou naught?   Floats not us before
Hermes perchance? Gleams not his golden wand, 630
Bidding, commanding us back to return,
Back to yon joyless realm, dusky and gray,
With intangible phantoms teeming,
The o'ercrowded, yet aye-empty Hades?

Deepens all at once the darkness.   Rayless now dis-
          solves the vapor,   635
Gray and murky brown as stone-work.   Walls ascend,
          our glances meeting,
Our free glances meeting sheer.   Court is it? deep
          moat? or cavern?
'Tis in every case appalling!   Sisters, ah, we are im-
          prisoned,
'Prisoned now as erst we were!

(*Inner court of the castle, surrounded with rich fan-
          tastic buildings of the middle ages.*)

LEADER OF THE CHORUS.

Foolish and overswift, true type of woman-kind, 640
Dependent on the moment, sport of every gust

Of bale or blessing!   Yet not either can ye bear
With constant courage.   One still fiercely contradicts
The others, crosswise she by others is gainsaid;
Only in joy and pain ye, with the self-same tone,   645
Or howl or laugh.   Be still and hearken what the queen,
High-souled, may here decide both for herself and us.

HELENA.

Where art thou, Pythonissa?   Whatsoe'er thy name,
From out the gloomy vaults step forth of this stern
        keep!   650
Perchance, art gone to seek this wondrous hero-lord,
To herald my approach, reception kind bespeaking!
So take my thanks and quickly lead me unto him!
My wanderings I would end, repose I wish alone.

LEADER OF THE CHORUS.

Vainly thou lookest, queen, round thee on every side;
The hateful form hath vanished, or perchance remained
In yonder mist, from forth whose bosom hitherward,
We came, I wist not how, swiftly without a step;   657
Perchance, indeed, in doubt, this labyrinth she treads,
Where many castles strangely mingle into one,
Greeting august and high demanding from its lord.   660
But yonder see above, where move in busy throngs,
In corridors, at casements, and through portals wide,
A crowd of menials passing, swiftly here and there;
Distinguished welcome this portends of honored guest.

CHORUS.

Expands now my heart!   O, yonder behold,   665
How modestly downward, with lingering step,
A fair youthful throng becomingly move
In march well appointed!   Say, by whose command
Now appeareth well-trained, and so promptly arrayed,
Of blooming boyhood, the glorious race?   670
What admire I the most?   Is it their elegant gait,
Or the tresses that curl round their dazzling white brow,
Or the twin-blooming cheeks, with the hue of the peach.
And shaded like it with soft tender down?
Fain would I bite, but I shrink back in fear;   675
For in similar venture, replete was the mouth,
I shudder to tell it, with ashes!

But the most beautiful
Hither are wending;
What are they bearing?   680
Steps for the throne,
Carpet and seat,
Hangings and tent-
Adorning gear?
Hover the folds on high,   685
Cloud-garlands forming
Over the head of our queen;
Lo! now invited,
Climbs she the stately couch.
Forward advancing,   690
Step by step, treading,
Range yourselves there!
Worthy, oh worthy, thrice worthy of her,
Be blessing on such a reception!

(*All that the* CHORUS *has indicated takes place by
    degrees.*)
(*After pages and squires have descended in long pro-
    cession,* FAUST *appears above, on the steps, in
    knightly court costume of the middle ages; he de-
    scends slowly and with dignity.*)

LEADER OF THE CHORUS.
(*attentively observing him*).
If to this man the gods have not, as is their wont, 695
But for a season lent this wonder-worthy form,
And if his lofty grace, his love-inspiring mien,
Be not their transient gift, success will sure attend
On all he undertakes, be it in strife with men,
Or in the petty war, with fairest women waged.   700
To many others him, in sooth, I must prefer,
Others, the highly prized, on whom mine eyes have gazed.
With slow, majestic step, by reverence withheld,
The prince do I behold.   Towards him turn, O queen!

FAUST
(*advancing, a man in fetters at his side*).
'Stead of most solemn greeting, as beseemeth,   705
'Stead of most reverent welcome, bring I thee,
In chains fast manacled, this varlet, who
In duty failing, wrested mine from me. —

Here bend thy knee, before this noblest dame,
To make forthwith confession of thy guilt!—   710
This is, exalted potentate, the man,
Of rarest vision, from the lofty tower
Appointed round to gaze, the expanse of heaven
Keenly to overlook, and breadth of earth,
If here or yonder aught present itself,   715
From the encircling hills, across the vale,
Towards this fortress moving; billowy herds,
Or warlike host perchance; those we defend,
These meet in fight.   To-day, what negligence!
Thou comest hither, he proclaims it not;   720
August reception faileth, honor due
To guest so noble.   Forfeited he hath
His guilty life, and in the blood of death,
Well-merited, should lie; but thou alone
May'st punish, or show mercy, at thy pleasure.   725

HELENA.

High as the honor thou accordest me,
As judge, as potentate, and were it but,
As I suspect, to try me—so will I
The judge's foremost duty now fulfil,
To give the accused a hearing.—Therefore speak! 730

LYNCEUS, THE TOWER-WARDER.

Let me kneel and gaze upon her,
Let me live or let me die:
Pledged to serve, with truth and honor,
The god-given dame, am I.

Watching for the morning, gazing   735
Eastward for its rising, lo!
In the south, my vision dazing,
Rose the sun a wondrous show.

Neither earth nor heavenward turning,
Depth nor height my vision drew;   740
Thitherward I gazed, still yearning,
Her, the peerless one, to view.

Eyesight keen to me is granted,
Like to lynx on highest tree;
From the dream, which me enchanted.   745
Hard I struggled to be free.

Could I the delusion banish —
Turret — tower — barred gateway see?
Vapors rise, and vapors vanish;
Forward steps this deity!   750

Eye and heart to her I tender!
I inhale her gentle light;
Blinding all, such beauty's splendor
Blinded my poor senses quite;

I forgot the warder's duty,   755
I forgot the entrusted horn;
Threaten to destroy me — Beauty
Tameth anger, tameth scorn.

HELENA.

The ill, myself occasioned, dare I not
Chastise. Ah, woe is me! What ruthless fate   760
Pursues me, everywhere the breasts of men
So to befool, that they nor spare themselves
Nor aught that claimeth reverence. Plundering now,
Seducing, fighting, harrying here and there,
Gods, heroes, demi-gods, yea, dæmons, too,   765
Perplexed have led me, wandering to and fro;
Singly, the world I maddened, doubly, more;
Now threefold, fourfold, bring I woe on woe! —
This guiltless man discharge, let him go free,
No shame should light upon the god-befooled.   770

FAUST.

Filled with amaze, O queen, I see at once
The unerring smiter, here the smitten one;
The bow I see, wherefrom hath sped the shaft
This man that wounded. Shaft doth follow shaft,
And me they smite. Them crosswise I perceive,   775
Feathered, and whirring round through court and keep.
What am I now? Thou makest, all at once,
My trustiest, rebellious; insecure
My very walls; henceforth my hosts, I fear,
Will serve the conquering unconquered queen.   780
What now remaineth, save myself to yield,
And all I fancied mine, to thy sole sway?
Freely and truly, let me at thy feet,

Acknowledge thee as queen, who, coming here,
Hath won forthwith possession and a throne.   785

LYNCEUS

(with a chest, followed by men bearing other chests).

Back, queen, thou seest me once more !
One glance the rich man doth implore ;
Poor as a beggar feeleth he,
Yet rich as prince — beholding thee.

What was I erst — what am I now ?   790
What can I wish — what aim avow ?
What boots it keenest sight to own ?
Its glance reboundeth from thy throne ?

We from the east still onward pressed,
And soon o'ermastered was the west ;   795
A host of nations, long and vast —
The foremost knew not of the last ;

The foremost fell ; the next advance ;
Ready the third with doughty lance —
Strengthened was each a hundredfold ;   800
Thousands, unmarked, lay stark and cold.

We rushed along, we stormed apace,
Lordship we won, from place to place ;
And where to-day I sway achieved,
Next day another sacked and reaved.   805

Rapid the glance we took — one laid
His hand upon the fairest maid,
The steer one seized of surest tread ;
The horses all with us were led.

But my delight was everywhere   810
To peer about for things most rare ;
And what another held in store,
To me was withered grass, no more.

On treasure's track I onward sped,
Only by my keen insight led ;   815
In every coffer I could see,
Transparent was each chest to me.

Thus heaps of gold at length were mine,
And jewel-stones, with lustrous shine ? —

The emerald's resplendent green   820
Alone may grace thy breast, fair queen.

Let pearl-drops hang 'twixt lip and ear,
The spoil of Ocean! rubies, near
Thy dainty cheeks, their radiance lose,
Quenched by their vermeil-tinctured hues.   825

The greatest treasures thus to-day,
Before thy presence here I lay;
And at thy feet, in homage yield
Harvest of many a bloody field.

Though I full many a chest have brought,   830
Yet more I have, with treasure fraught;
Let me attend thy path, and lo!
Thy treasure-vaults shall straight o'erflow.

For scarce dost thou the throne ascend,
Already bow, already bend,   835
Reason, and wealth, and sovereign power,
Before thy beauty's peerless dower.

All this I firmly held, as mine —
Freely relinquished, now 'tis thine!
Its worth I deemed both vast and high —   840
Its nothingness I now descry.

What once was mine, doth from me pass,
Scattered like mown and withered grass.
With one kind look, give back once more,
In full, the worth it owned before!   845

FAUST.

Hence quickly with the burden boldly earned,
Not blamed, in sooth, but yet without reward.
Already all is hers, which in its depths
The castle hides; to offer special gifts
Is bootless. Hence! Treasure on treasure heap, 850
In order due; of splendor yet unseen
Set forth the exalted pomp; and let the vaults
Glitter like heaven new-born; from lifeless life
A paradise prepare; before her steps,
With eager haste, let carpet, rich in flowers,   855
Unroll on flowery carpet! Let her tread

Meet dainty footing, and the brightest sheen,
Blinding to all but gods, her glance arrest!

LYNCEUS.

Slight is our lord's behest; 'tis play,
A pleasant pastime, to obey :   860
Not wealth alone, the blood no less
O'ersways this beauty's fond excess!
Tamed is the host, and falchions keen,
Now blunt and lame have lost their sheen ;
The sun beside her form divine,   865
Weary and cold, forgets to shine ;
While near the riches of her face,
Empty is all devoid of grace.   (*Exit.*)

HELENA (*to* FAUST).

With thee I fain would speak, therefore ascend,
And seat thee at my side!   The vacant place   870
Invites its owner, and secures me mine.

FAUST.

First, kneeling, let my true allegiance be
Accepted, noble lady ; let me kiss
The hand that now uplifts me to thy side!
Me as co-regent strengthen of thy realm,   875
No bound that knows ; and for thyself obtain
Adorer, liegeman, warder, all in one!

HELENA.

Full many a wonder do I see and hear;
Amazement strikes me, much I have to ask.
Yet fain I am to know wherefore the speech   880
Of yonder man sounds strangely, strange and sweet :
Each tone appears accordant with the next,
And hath a word found welcome in the ear,
Another woos caressingly the first.

FAUST.

If thee our people's utterance thus delights,   885
O then be sure, their song will ravish thee,
Appeasing to their depths both ear and mind.
Yet were it best this language to essay ;
Alternate speech invites it, calls it forth.

HELENA.

How thus to speak so sweetly I would know.   890

FAUST.

'Tis easy, from the heart the words must flow;
And when with fond desire the bosom yearns,
We look around and ask —

HELENA,
Who with us burns?

FAUST.

The spirit looks nor forward nor behind,
The present only —

HELENA.
There our bliss we find.   895

FAUST.

Wealth is it, pledge and fortune; I demand,
Who granteth confirmation?

HELENA.
This — my hand.

CHORUS.

Who would now upbraid our princess
Grant she to this castle's lord
Friendliest demeanor?   900
For confess, together are we
Captives now, as oft already,
Since the tragical overthrow
Ilios', and our piteous voyage
Labyrinthine, with sorrow fraught.   905

Women wont to men's affection,
Choosers are they not, in sooth,
Rather adepts are they;
And to gold-ringleted shepherds,
May be to Fauns darkly bearded,   910
As to them the occasion comes,
O'er thy delicate limbs must they
Yield completely an equal right,

Near and nearer sit they already,
Each on other reclining,   915

Shoulder to shoulder, knee to knee,
Hand in hand, rock they themselves
Over the throne's
High and loftily cushioned state;
For no scruple hath majesty,   920
Secretest raptures,
'Fore the eyes of the people,
All unblushingly thus to display,

HELENA.

I feel myself so distant, yet so near,
And all too gladly say: Here am I! here!   925

FAUST.

I tremble; scarcely breathe, words die away:
A dream it is, vanished have place and day!

HELENA.

Outworn I feel and yet as life were new,
With thee entwined; to thee, the unknown one, true.

FAUST.

Forbear to ponder thy strange destiny!   930
Being is duty, were it momently.

PHORKYAS (*entering impatiently*).

On love's primer cast your eyes,
Its sweet lessons analyze,
Fondly sport in lover-wise!
Yet thereto time fails, I ween.   935
Feel ye not the storm o'erhanging?
Hear ye not the trumpet clanging!
Ruin nears, with threatening mien.

Menelaus comes, and gleaming
With him waves of people streaming;   940
Arm ye for the conflict keen!
Girt by victors conquest heated,
Like Deiphobus, maltreated,
Forfeit thou must pay, O queen;
These light ware shall from the halter   945
Dangle; ready on the altar
Sharpened axe for thee is seen!

Bold interruption, she annoyingly intrudes!
Not e'en in peril brook I senseless violence.
Ill message hideous make the fairest messenger;   950
Most hideous thou who dost ill tidings gladly bring.
They shall not profit thee; ay, shatter thou the air
With empty breath. In sooth, no danger lurketh here,
And danger's self would seem but idle threatening.

*(Signals. Explosions from the towers, trumpets and
cornets, martial music, a powerful army marches
across the stage.)*

FAUST.

No, straight assembled thou shalt see   955
Our heroes' close united band!
For woman's grace none wins but he
Who knows to shield with forceful hand.

*(To the leaders, who separate themselves from their
columns and step forward.)*

With bridled rage and silent power,
Which victory must crown at length,   960
Ye of the north, the youthful flower,
Ye of the east, the blooming strength!

Steel-clad, with sunbeams round them breaking,
Empires they shatter with their spear;
They march — beneath them earth is shaking; —
They pass — it thunders in their rear.   966

At Pylos from our barques we landed —
The ancient Nestor was no more;
In vain their troops, the kinglings banded,
'Gainst our free host, on Hellas' shore.   970

Drive from these walls, my voice obeying,
King Menelaus back to sea;
There let him, sacking and waylaying,
Fulfil his will and destiny.

I hail you dukes, for so ordaineth   975
Sparta's fair queen; before her lay
Mountain and valley; while she reigneth,
Ye, too, shall profit by her sway.

Guard, German, wall and fence extending,
Corinthus' bay, whate'er assails;   980
Goths, I confide to your defending,
Achaia, with its hundred vales;

March, Franks, your course to Elis steering,
Messene be the Saxon's share;
Normans, the sea from pirates clearing,   985
Of Argolis the strength repair.

Then shall each one, at home abiding,
Prowess and strength abroad make known;
Yet Sparta shall, o'er all presiding,
Be still our queen's ancestral throne.   990

Rejoicing in their lands, each nation
She sees, with every blessing crowned;
Justice and light and confirmation,
Seek at her feet, with trust profound.

(FAUST *descends, the princes close a circle round him,
in order better to hear his instructions and commands.*)

CHORUS.

Who the fairest fain would possess,   995
Foremost, let him for weapons
Stoutly and wisely look all around!
Fond words for him may have won
What on earth is the highest:
Yet in peace possesseth he not;   1000
Fawners slyly entice her from him,
Spoilers daringly snatch her from him;
This to guard against be he prepared!

I for this commend our prince,
Prize him higher than others,   1005
Who, brave and prudent, himself hath leagued,
So that the stalwart obedient stand,
To his beck still attentive;
Loyally they his hests fulfil,
To his own profit, one and all,   1010
Having his guerdon in his lord's thanks,
And for the loftiest glory of both.

For who shall snatch her away
From her potent possessor ?
She is his, to him be she granted,   1015
Doubly granted by us, whom he
Within, e'en like her, with impregnable ramparts,
Without, by mightiest host, surrounds.

FAUST.

Our gifts to these are great and glorious:
To every one a goodly land   1020
Fertile and broad.   March on victorious!
Here in the midst take we our stand.

Girt round by waves in sunlight dancing,
Half island, thee — whose hill-chains blend
With Europe's mountains, widely branching —   1025
Will they in rivalry defend.

Blessed be this land, all lands transcending,
To every race, for evermore,
Which sees my queen the throne ascending,
As erst her birth it hailed of yore.   1030

When, 'mid Eurotas' reedy whisper,
Forth from the shell she burst to light,
Her mighty mother, brothers, sister,
Were blinded by the dazzling sight.

This land, her choicest bloom that layeth   1035
Before thee, waiting thy behest —
Though the wide earth thy sceptre swayeth,
Oh, love thy fatherland the best!

What though the sun's keen arrow coldly playeth,
Upon the mountain summits, jagged and bare   1040
Yet where the rocks the verdure overlayeth,
The wild-goat nibbling crops its scanty fare ;

The spring leaps forth, united plunge the fountains,
And meadow, gorge, and valley, all are green,
On broken pastures of a hundred mountains,   1045
Spread far and wide the woolly herds are seen ;

With measured tread, cautious, in line divided,
By the steep edge, the hornèd cattle wend ;
Yet for them all a shelter is provided,
O'er many a cave the vaulted rock doth bend !   1050

Pan shields them there, and many a nymph appeareth.
In moist and bushy caverns dwelling free;
And yearning after higher spheres, upreareth
Its leafy branches, tree close pressed to tree —

Primeval woods!   The giant oak there standing, 1055
Links bough to bough, a stubborn, tortuous, maze;
The gentle maple, with sweet juice expanding,
Shoots clear aloft and with its burden plays —

And motherly for child and lambkin streameth,
'Mid silent shades, warm milk prepared for them; 1060
Fruit close at hand, the plain's ripe nurture, gleameth,
And honey droppeth from the hollow stem.

Pleasure is here a birthright; vieing
In gladness cheek and lip are found,
Each in his station is undying,   1065
Content and blooming health abound.

And thus to all his father's strength unfoldeth
The gentle child, environed by sweet day.
Amazed we stand; each asks, as he beholdeth:
If gods they be, or men? so fair are they.   1070

So when the part of hind Apollo playeth,
Like him the fairest shepherd-youth appears;
For there where Nature in clear circle swayeth,
Harmoniously are linked her several spheres.

(Taking his seat beside Helena.)

Thus happy Fate hath me, hath thee attended;   1075
Behind us henceforth let the past be thrown!
From God supreme, oh, feel thyself descended:
Thou to the primal world belongest alone.

Thee shall no firm-built fortress capture;
Strong in eternal youth, expands   1080
For us a sojourn; fraught with rapture,
Arcadia, near to Sparta's lands.

Allured to this blest region, hither
Hast fled to brightest destiny:
Thrones change to bowers that never wither;   1085
Arcadian be our bliss and free!

(*The scene is entirely changed.   Close arbors recline
     against a series of rocky caverns.   A shady grove
     extends to the base of the encircling rocks.   FAUST
     and HELENA are not seen.   The CHORUS lies sleep-
     ing scattered here and there.*)

PHORKYAS.

How long these maids have slept, in sooth, I cannot tell;
Or whether they have dreamed what I before mine eyes
Saw bright and clear, to me is equally unknown.
So wake I them.   Amazed the younger folk shall be,
Ye too, ye bearded ones, who sit below and wait, 1091
Hoping to see at length these miracles resolved.
Arise! Arise! And shake quickly your crisped locks!
Shake slumber from your eyes! Blink not, and list to
     me!

CHORUS.

Only speak, relate, and tell us, what of wonderful hath
     chanced!   1095
We more willingly shall hearken that which we cannot
     believe;
For we are aweary, weary, gazing on these rocks around.

PHORKYAS.

Children, how, already weary, though you scarce have
     rubbed your eyes?
Hearken then! Within these caverns, in these grottoes,
     in these bowers,
Shield and shelter have been given, as to lover-twain
     idyllic,   1100
To our lord and to our lady —

CHORUS.

                         How, within there?

PHORKYAS.

                                     Yea, secluded
From the world; and me, me only, they to secret service
     called.
Highly honored stood I near them, yet, as one in trust
     beseemeth,
Round I gazed on other objects, turning hither, turning
     thither,

Sought for roots, for barks and mosses, with their prop-
    erties acquainted;   1105
And they thus remained alone.

CHORUS.

Thou wouldst make believe that yonder, world-wide
    spaces lie within,
Wood and meadow, lake and brooklet; what strange
    fable spinnest thou!

PHORKYAS.

Yea, in sooth, ye inexperienced, there lie regions un-
    discovered:
Hall on hall, and court on court; in my musings these
    I track.   1110
Suddenly a peal of laughter echoes through the caverned
    spaces;
In I gaze, a boy is springing from the bosom of the
    woman
To the man, from sire to mother: the caressing and
    the fondling,
All love's foolish playfulnesses, mirthful cry and shout
    of rapture,
Alternating, deafen me.   1115
Naked, without wings, a genius, like a faun, with
    nothing bestial,
On the solid ground he springeth; but the ground, with
    counter-action,
Up to ether sends him flying; with the second, third
    rebounding
Touches he the vaulted roof.
Anxiously the mother calleth: Spring amain, and at
    thy pleasure: 1120
But beware, think not of flying, unto thee is flight de-
    nied
And so warns the faithful father: In the earth the
    force elastic
Lies, aloft that sends thee bounding; let thy toe but
    touch the surface,
Like the son of earth, Antæus, straightway is thy
    strength renewed.
And so o'er these rocky masses, on from dizzy ledge
    to ledge,   1125

Leaps he ever, hither, thither, springing like a stricken
    ball.
But in cleft of rugged cavern suddenly from sight he
    vanished;
And now lost to us he seemeth, mother waileth, sire
    consoleth,
Anxiously I shrug my shoulders.   But again, behold,
    what vision!
Lie there treasures hidden yonder?   Raiment broidered
    o'er with flowers   1130
He becomingly hath donned;
Tassels from his arms are waving, ribbons flutter on
    his bosom,
In his hand the lyre all-golden, wholly like a tiny
    Phœbus,
Boldly to the edge he steppeth, to the precipice; we
    wonder,
And the parents, full of rapture, cast them on each
    other's heart;   1135
For around his brow what splendor!   Who can tell
    what there is shining?
Gold-work is it, or the flaming of surpassing spirit-
    power?
Thus he moveth, with such gesture, e'en as boy himself
    announcing
Future master of all beauty, through whose limbs,
    whose every member,
Flow the melodies eternal: and so shall ye hearken to
    him,   1140
And so shall ye gaze upon him, to your special wonder-
    ment.

CHORUS.

    This callest thou marvellous,
    Daughter of Creta?
    Unto the bard's pregnant word
    Hast thou perchance never listened?   1145
    Hast thou not heard of Ionia's,
    Ne'er been instructed in Hellas'
    Legends, from ages primeval,
    Godlike, heroical treasure?
    All, that still happeneth   1150
    Now in the present,

Sorrowful echo 'tis,
Of days ancestral, more noble;
Equals not, in sooth, thy story
That which beautiful fiction,   1155
Than truth more worthy of credence,
Chanted hath of Maia's offspring!

This so shapely and potent, yet
Scarcely-born delicate nursling,
Straight have his gossiping nurses   1160
Folded in purest swaddling fleece,
Fastened in costly swathings,
With their irrational notions.
Potent and shapely, ne'ertheless,
Draws the rogue his flexible limbs,   1165
Body firm yet elastic,
Craftily forth; the purple shell,
Him so grievously binding,
Leaving quietly in its place;
As the perfected butterfly,   1170
From the rigid chrysalid,
Pinion unfolding, rapidly glides,
Boldly and wantonly sailing through
Sun-impregnated ether.

So he, too, the most dexterous,   1175
That to robbers and scoundrels,
Yea, and to all profit-seekers,
He a favoring god might be,
This he straightway made manifest,
Using arts the most cunning.   1180

Swift from the ruler of ocean he
Steals the trident, yea, e'en from Arès
Steals the sword from the scabbard;
Arrow and bow from Phœbus, too,
Also his tongs from Hephæstos: 1185
Even Zeus', the father's, bolt,
Him had fire not scared, he had taken.
Eros also worsted he,
In limb-grappling, wrestling match;
Stole from Cypria as she caressed him,   1190
From her bosom, the girdle.

*(An exquisite, purely melodious lyre-music resounds
    from the cave.   All become attentive, and appear
    soon to be inwardly moved; henceforth, to the
    pause indicated, there is a full musical accompa-
    niment.)*

PHORKYAS.

Hark, those notes so sweetly sounding;
Cast aside your fabled lore:
Gods, in olden time abounding, —
Let them go! their day is o'er.   1195

None will comprehend your singing;
Nobler theme the age requires:
From the heart must flow, up-springing,
What to touch the heart aspires.
                    (She retires behind the rock.)

CHORUS.

To these tones, so sweetly flowing,   1200
Dire one! dost incline thine ears,
They in us, new health bestowing,
Waken now the joy of tears.

Vanish may the sun's clear shining,
In our soul if day arise,   1205
In our heart we, unrepining,
Find what the whole world denies. .

HELENA, FAUST, EUPHORION *in the costume indicated
                above.*

EUPHORION.

Songs of childhood hear ye ringing,
Your own mirth it seems; on me
Gazing, thus in measure springing,   1210
Leap your parent-hearts with glee.

HELENA.

Love, terrestrial bliss to capture,
Two in noble union mates;
But to wake celestial rapture,
He a precious three creates.   1215

FAUST.

All hath been achieved.   Forever
I am thine, and mine thou art,

Blent our blessings are — oh, never
May our present joy depart!

CHORUS.

Many a year of purest pleasure,   1220
In the mild light of their boy,
Crowns this pair in richest measure.
Me their union thrills with joy!

EUPHORION.

Now let me gambol,
Joyfully springing!   1225
Upward to hasten
Through ether winging,
This wakes my yearning,
This prompts me now!

FAUST.

Gently! son, gently!   1230
Be not so daring!
Lest ruin seize thee
Past all repairing,
And our own darling
Whelm us in woe!   1235

EUPHORION.

From earth my spirit
Still upward presses;
Let go my hands now,
Let go my tresses,
Let go my garments,   1240
Mine every one!

HELENA.

To whom, bethink thee,
Now thou pertainest!
Think how it grieves us
When thou disdainest   1245
Mine, thine, and his — the all
That hath been won.

CHORUS.

Soon shall, I fear me,
The bond be undone!

HELENA and FAUST.

Curb for thy parents' sake,	1250
To us returning,	
Curb thy importunate	
Passionate yearning!	
Make thou the rural plain	
Tranquil and bright.	1255

EUPHORION.

But to content you
Stay I my flight.
(*Winding among the* CHORUS *and drawing them forth
to dance.*)

Round this gay troop I flee	
With impulse light.	
Say is the melody,	1260
Say is the movement right?	

HELENA.

Yea, 'tis well done; advance,
Lead to the graceful dance
These maidens coy!

FAUST.

Could I the end but see!	1265
Me this mad revelry	
Fills with annoy.	

EUPHORION and the CHORUS.

(*Dancing and singing, they move about in interweav-
ing lines.*)

Moving thine arms so fair	
With graceful motion,	
Tossing thy curling hair	1270
In bright commotion;	
When thou with foot so light	
Over the earth doth skim,	
Thither and back in flight	
Moving each graceful limb;	1275
Thou hast attained thy goal,	
Beautiful child,	
All hearts thou hast beguiled,	
Won every soul.	(*Pause.*)

EUPHORION.

Gracefully sporting,   1280
Light-footed roes,
New frolic courting,
Scorn ye repose:
I am the hunter,
Ye are the game.   1285

CHORUS.

Us wilt thou capture,
Urge not thy pace;
For it were rapture
Thee to embrace;
Beautiful creature,   1290
This our sole aim!

EUPHORION.

Through trees and heather,
Bound all together,
O'er stock and stone!
Whate'er is lightly won,   1295
That I disdain;
What I by force obtain,
Prize I alone.

HELENA and FAUST.

What vagaries, sense confounding!
Naught of measure to be hoped for!   1300
Like the blare of trumpet sounding,
Over vale and forest ringing.
What a riot!   What a cry!

CHORUS (entering quickly one by one).

Us he passed with glance scorn-laden;
Hastily still onward springing,   1305
Bearing now the wildest maiden
Of our troop, he draweth nigh.

EUPHORION (bearing a young maiden).

I this wilful maid and coy
Carry to enforced caress;
For my pleasure, for my joy   1310
Her resisting bosom press,

Kiss her rebel lips, that so
She my power and will may know.

MAIDEN.

Loose me! in this frame residing,
Burns a spirit's strength and might;   1315
Strong as thine, our will presiding
Swerveth not with purpose light.
Thinkest, on thy strength relying,
That thou hast me in a strait?
Hold me, fool! thy strength defying,   1320
For my sport, I'll scorch thee yet!
          (*She flames up and flashes into the air.*)
Follow where light breezes wander,
Follow to rude caverns yonder,
Strive thy vanished prey to net!

EUPHORION
(*shaking off the last flames*).

Rocks all around I see,   1325
Thickets and woods among!
Why should they prison me?
Still am I fresh and young.
Tempests, they loudly roar,
Billows, they lash the shore;   1330
Both far away I hear;
Would I were near!
          (*He springs higher up the rock.*)

HELENA, FAUST, *and* CHORUS.

Wouldst thou chamois-like aspire?
Us thy threatened fall dismays!

EUPHORION.

Higher must I climb, yet higher,   1335
Wider still must be my gaze.

Know I now, where I stand:
'Midst of the sea-girt land,
'Midst of the great Pelops' reign,
Kin both to earth and main.   1340

CHORUS.

Canst not near copse and wold
Tarry, then yonder,

Ripe figs and apple-gold
Seeking, we'll wander;
Grapes too shall woo our hand,   1345
Grapes from the mantling vine.
Ah, let this dearest land,
Dear one, be thine!

EUPHORION.

Dream ye of peaceful day?
Dream on, while dream ye may!   1350
War! is the signal cry.
Hark! cries of victory!

CHORUS.

War who desireth
While peace doth reign,
To joy aspireth   1355
Henceforth in vain.

EUPHORION.

All whom this land hath bred;
Through peril onward led,
Free, of undaunted mood,
Still lavish of their blood,   1360
With soul untaught to yield,
Rending each chain!
To such the bloody field,
Brings glorious gain.

CHORUS.

High he soars, — mark, upward gazing, — 1365
And to us not small doth seem:
Victor-like, in harness blazing,
As of steel and brass the gleam!

EUPHORION.

Not on moat or wall relying,
On himself let each one rest!   1370
Firmest stronghold, all defying,
Ever is man's iron breast!

Dwell for aye unconquered would ye?
Arm, by no vain dreams beguiled!

Amazons your women should be,   1375
And a hero every child!

CHORUS.

O hallowed Poesie,
Heavenward still soareth she!
Shine on, thou brightest star,
Farther and still more far!   1380
Yet us she still doth cheer,
Ever her voice to hear,
Joyful we are.

EUPHORION.

Child no more; a stripling bearing
Arms appears, with valor fraught,   1385
Leagued with the strong, the free, the daring,
In soul already who hath wrought.
Hence, away!
No delay!
There where glory may be sought.   1390

HELENA *and* FAUST.

Scarcely summoned to life's gladness,
Scarcely given to day's bright gleam,
Downward now to pain and sadness
Wouldst thou rush, from heights supreme!
Are then we   1395
Naught to thee?
Is our gracious bond a dream?

EUPHORION.

Hark! What thunders seaward rattle,
Echoing from vale to vale!
'Mid dust and foam, in shock of battle,   1400
Throng on throng, to grief and bale!
And the command
Is, firm to stand;
Death to face, nor ever quail.

HELENA, FAUST, *and* CHORUS.

Oh, what horror? Hast thou told it!   1405
Is then death for thee decreed?

EUPHORION.

From afar shall I behold it ?
No ! I'll share the care and need !

HELENA, FAUST, *and* CHORUS.

Rashness to peril brings,
And deadly fate !   1410

EUPHORION.

Yet — see a pair of wings
Unfoldeth straight !
Thither — I must, I must —
Grudge not my flight !

(*He casts himself into the air ; his garments support him
for a moment ; his head flames, a trail of light
follows him.*)

CHORUS.

Icarus ! Icarus !   1415
Oh, woeful sight !

(*A beautiful youth falls at the parents' feet, we imagine
that in the dead we recognize a well-known form ;
yet suddenly the corporeal part vanishes ; the
aureole rises like a comet to heaven ; dress, mantle,
and lyre remain lying on the ground.*)

HELENA *and* FAUST.

Follows on joy new-born
Anguishful moan !

EUPHORION'S VOICE (*from the depths*).

Leave me in realms forlorn,
Mother, not all alone !   (*Pause.*)   1420

CHORUS (*dirge*).

Not alone — for hope we cherish,
Where thou bidest thee to know !
Ah, from daylight though thou perish,
Ne'er a heart will let thee go !
Scarce we venture to bewail thee,   1425
Envying we sing thy fate :
Did sunshine cheer, or storm assail thee,
Song and heart were fair and great.

Earthly fortune was thy dower,
Lofty lineage, ample might,   1430
Ah, too early lost, thy flower
Withered by untimely blight!
Glance was thine the world discerning,
Sympathy with every wrong.
Woman's love for thee still yearning,   1435
And thine own enchanting song.

Yet the beaten path forsaking,
Thou didst run into the snare:
So with law and usage breaking,
On thy wilful course didst fare;   1440
Yet at last high thought has given
To thy noble courage, weight,
For the loftiest thou hast striven —
It to win was not thy fate.

Who does win it?   Unreplying,   1445
Destiny the question hears,
When the bleeding people lying,
Dumb with grief, no cry uprears! —
Now new songs chant forth, in sorrow
Deeply bowed lament no more;   1450
Them the earth brings forth, to-morrow,
As she brought them forth of yore!
              (*Full pause.   The music ceases.*)

HELENA (to FAUST).

An ancient word, alas, approves itself in me:
That joy and beauty ne'er enduringly are linked!
Rent is the bond of life, with it the bond of love; 1455
Lamenting both, I say a sorrowful farewell,
And throw myself once more, once only, in thine
          arms. —
Persephoneia, take the boy, take also me!
(*She embraces* FAUST, *her corporeal part vanishes, her
          garment and veil remain in his arms.*)

PHORKYAS.

Hold fast what doth of all alone remain to thee,
The garment, loose it not!   Already hale   1460
The demons at its skirts, and it would fain
Drag to the nether regions.   Hold it fast!

The Goddess is it not, whom thou hast lost,
Yet godlike 'tis.   Avail thee of the high
Inestimable gift, and upward soar;   1465
Thee o'er all common things 'twill swiftly bear
Through ether, long as there thou canst abide.
We meet again, far, far away from here.

Helena's *garments dissolve into clouds, they envelop*
    Faust, *raise him aloft, and pass with him from*
    the scene.)

PHORKYAS

(*takes* Euphorion's *dress, mantle, and lyre from the*
    earth, steps into the proscenium ; holding up the
    spoils, she says).

    A happy find hath me bestead.
    The flame in sooth is vanishèd,   1470
    Yet for the world no grief I know:
    Enough remaineth bards to consecrate,
    Envy to scatter in their guild and hate;
    And am I powerless genius to bestow,
    Its vesture I can lend, at any rate.   1475
(*She sits down in the proscenium at the foot of a*
                    pillar.)

PENTHALIS.

Now hasten, girls !   At length we are from magic free,
From the soul-swaying spell of the Thessalian hag;
Free also from the blare confused of jangling tones,
The ear perplexing, and still worse the inner sense.
Away to Hades !   Thither hath in haste the queen, 1480
With earnest step, descended.   Now, ye faithful maids,
Do ye, without delay, follow upon her track.
Her at the throne we find of the Inscrutable.

CHORUS.

Royal ladies, certes, everywhere are content;
E'en in Hades places take they supreme,   1485
Proud to be with their peers allied,
With Persephone in friendship knit;
We, meanwhile, far off in meadows
Deep of asphodel abiding,
With far-reaching poplars,   1490

And unfruitful willows conjoined,
What amusement or joy have we!
Flitting batlike to twitter —
Whispering, undelightsome, and ghostlike!

LEADER of the CHORUS.

Who hath no name achieved, nor at the noble aims,
Belongs but to the elements; so hence, begone! 1496
My vehement desire is with my queen to be;
Not merit 'tis alone, fidelity as well,
Secure in yonder spheres, the individual life.   (*Exit.*)

ALL.

Back are we given now to the daylight;   1500
Certes, persons no more,
That feel we, that know we;
Nathless return we never to Hades!
Nature, eternally living,
Claims in us spirits,   1505
We in her, a title undoubted.

A portion of the CHORUS.

We, amid the wavy-trembling of these thousand rustling branches,
Gently lure with dalliance charming from the root the
  vital currents,
Up into the boughs; with foliage, soon with lavish
  wealth of blossoms,
We adorn our tresses, floating in the breeze for airy
  growth.   1510
Falls the fruit, forthwith assemble life-enjoying folk
  and cattle,
For the grasping, for the tasting, swiftly coming, onward pressing,
And, as 'fore the gods primeval, so all bend around us
  here.

ANOTHER PORTION.

Where these rocky walls are imaged in the smooth, far-
  gleaming mirror,
Moving in the gentle wavelets, soothingly we onward
  glide,   1515

Listen, hearken, to all music : birdie's singing, reedy-
    fluting,
Is it Pan's loud voice tremendous — voice responsive
    straight replies :
Whisper is it? — we too whisper; thunders it? — we
    roll our thunder
In o'erwhelming repercussion, threefold, tenfold, echo-
    ing back.

A THIRD PORTION.

Sisters, we, of spirit mobile, hasten with the brooklets
    onwards;   1520
For yon hill-slopes, richly mantled, charm us rising far
    away.
Ever downwards, ever deeper, in meandering course we
    water
Now the meadows, then the pastures, then the garden
    round the house;
There, across the landscape, slender cypress shafts our
    banks o'erpeering,
Telling of our crystal mirror, upwards into ether soar.

A FOURTH PORTION.

Roam ye others, at your pleasure; we will circle, we
    will rustle   1526
Round the slopes so richly planted, on its prop where
    sprouts the vine.
By the vintager's emotion, we throughout the live-long
    day,
See what doubtful issue waiteth on his busy loving care:
Now with hoe, and now with mattock, earth up-heap-
    ing, pruning, binding,   1530
Prayeth he to all celestials, chiefly to the Sun-God prays.

Bacchus frets himself, the weakling, little for his faith-
    ful vassal,
Rests in arbors, leans in grottoes, toying with the young-
    est faun;
For his visions what he lacketh, dreaming half-inebriate,
Stored in skins, in jars and vessels, ready for his use
    he finds,   1535
Right and left in cool recesses treasured for eternal
    time.

But at length have the Celestials, hath now Helios 'fore
    them all,
Breathing, moistening, warming, glowing, filled the
    berries' teeming horn:
Where the vintager in silence labored, there is sudden
    life,
Busy stir in every alley, rustles round from vine to
    vine;   1540
Baskets creak, and pitchers clatter, and the loaded
    vine-troughs groan,
All towards the mighty wine-press, to the presser's
    sturdy dance;

And so is the sacred fullness of the purely-nurtured
    berries
Rudely trodden; foaming, seething, now it mingles,
    foully squashed;
And now splits the ear the cymbal, with the beaker's
    brazen tones,   1545
For himself hath Dionysos from his mysteries revealed;
Comes he with goat-footed satyrs, reeling nymphs goat-
    footed, too,
And meanwhile unruly brayeth shrill Silenus' long-
    eared beast —
Naught is spared; all law and order cloven hoofs are
    treading down —
All the senses whirl distracted, hideously the ear is
    stunned;   1550
Drunkards for their cups are groping, over-full are head
    and paunch;
Careful one is, there another, yet the tumult waxes
    loud:
Since the newer must to garner, they the old skins
    quickly drain.
(*The curtain falls.* PHORKYAS, *in the proscenium,
    rises to a gigantic height, descends from the
    cothurni, lays aside mask and veil, and reveals
    herself as* MEPHISTOPHELES, *in order, so far as it
    may be necessary, to comment upon the piece by
    way of epilogue.*)

ACT THE FOURTH.

High Mountain.

*Strong jagged rocky summit. A cloud approaches,
leans against the rock, and sinks down upon a
projecting level. It divides.*

FAUST (*steps forth*).

On deepest solitudes down-gazing, far below my feet,
Full thoughtfully I tread this lofty mountain ridge,
My cloudy car forsaking, me which softly bare,
Through days of sunshine, hither over land and sea.
Slowly it melts from me, not scattered suddenly;   5
Towards the East the mass strives in its rolling march.
In admiration lost, the eye strives after it;
Moving it now divides, wavelike, and full of change;
Yet will it shape itself — mine eye deceives me not,
On sun-illumined pillows, gloriously reclines,   10
Of giant size, indeed, a godlike female form;
I see it, like to Juno, Leda, Helena;
In majesty and love before mine eye it floats!
Ah, now it scatters; formless, broad, up-towering,
Rests in the East, and there, like ice-hills far away, 15
Mirrors of fleeting life the deep significance.
Yet round me hovers still, a mist-wreath, tender, light,
Surrounding breast and brow, cheering, caressing, cool.
Lightly it rises now, still lingering, high and higher, —
Together draws. Doth me a rapturing form delude, 20
As youth's first fondly prized, long-yearn'd for, highest
     good?
Well up the earliest treasures of my deepest heart:
To me Aurora's love, so light of wing, it shows,
The swift-experienced glance, the first, scarce under-
     stood,
Which, long and firmly held, each treasure over-
     shone!   25
Like beauty of the soul rises the gracious form,

Dissolveth not, but upward into ether floats,
And with it, of my being draws the best away.
(*A seven-league boot tramps down, another immediately follows.* MEPHISTOPHELES *descends.* The
boots stride onward in haste.)

MEPHISTOPHELES.

That's forward striding, I must own!
But tell me, what dost thou intend,   30
That 'mid such horrors dost descend,
Such wilderness of yawning stone?
Though not precisely here, I know it well;
This was, in sooth, the very floor of Hell.

FAUST.

Of foolish legends never fails thy store;   35
Such to give forth dost thou begin once more?

MEPHISTOPHELES (*seriously*).

When God the Lord — the reason well I know, —
Us from the air had banned to depths profound,
There, where of fire eterne the central glow
With lurid flames still circles round and round.   40
By the too brilliant light, we found that we
O'ercrowded were, and placed unpleasantly.
Forthwith to cough the devils all were fain;
From top to bottom straight they spat amain;
With sulphur-stench and acids thus inflated,   45
Hell, with foul gas, so hugely was dilated,
That earth's smooth surface, by the fiery blast,
Thick as it was, cracking must burst at last.
That all things are reversed we now discern;
What bottom was, is summit in its turn;   50
Also in this the proper lore they base,
To give the undermost the highest place;
For from the hot and slavish cave we fare
Into the lordship of the boundless air;
An open secret, long time well concealed,   55
And to the folk only of late revealed.

FAUST.

To me are mountain-masses grandly dumb;
I question neither whence nor why they come.

Herself when Nature in herself had founded,
This globe of earth she then hath purely rounded, 60
Took both in summit and in gorge delight,
Piled rock on rock, and mountain-height on height;
The hills she fashioned next with gentle force,
And to the valleys sloped their downward course:
Then growth and verdure came, and for her joy 65
She needs no mad convulsive freak employ.

MEPHISTOPHELES.

Ay! so you say, sun-clear to you it lies;
But who was present there, knows otherwise.
I was at hand when, seething still below,
Swelled the abyss, belching a fiery tide, 70
When Moloch's hammer rocks, with thunderous blow
Welding, the fragments scattered far and wide.
'Neath massive foreign blocks still groans the land —
Such hurling-might say who can comprehend?
This your philosopher can't understand; 75
There lies the rock, must lie, and there's an end;
But to our shame doth all our thinking tend.
Your genuine common folk alone conceive,
And naught disturbs them in their creed;
Long since their wisdom ripened: they believe 80
A marvel 'tis, Satan receives his meed;
On crutch of faith my pilgrim hobbles on
To Devil's bridges, to the Devil's stone.

FAUST.

Noteworthy 'tis, Nature, as now I do,
To study from the Devil's point of view. 85

MEPHISTOPHELES.

Be Nature what she may, what do I care!
My honor's touched: the Devil, sooth, was there!
We are the folk, the mighty to attain:
Convulsion, madness, force. 'Tis written plain! —
But now, at last, to make my meaning clear, 90
Did nothing please thee in our upper sphere?
In boundless space the world thou hast surveyed,
Its kingdoms and their glory, all displayed.

And yet, insatiate as thou art,
To thee did they no joy impart?   95

FAUST.

A project vast allured me on ;
Divine it!

MEPHISTOPHELES.

That I'll do anon.
Some capital I'd choose ; therein a store
Of burgher-feeding rubbish at its core ;
With crooked alleys, gabled peaks,   100
Markets confined, kale, turnips, leeks,
And shambles where blue flies repair,
On well-fed joints to batten — there,
At any moment shalt thou find
Stench and activity combined ;   105
Wide squares, with spacious streets between,
Which arrogate a lordly mien ;
And lastly, boundless to the eye,
Beyond the gate the suburbs lie.
Of coaches, too, the eternal roar,   110
Still rattling, behind, before,
Would charm me, and the ceaseless flow
Of ant-swarms, running to and fro ;
And let me walk, or let me ride,
Their central point I should abide,   115
By thousands honored and admired.

FAUST.

Such things I slightly estimate.
That men, it is to be desired,
Should multiply, should live at ease,
Be taught, developed if you please ; —   120
More rebels thus you educate.

MEPHISTOPHELES.

Then, in grand style, with conscious power, I'd rear
A pleasure-castle, some fair pleasance near :
Hill, valley, meadow, forest, glade,
Into a splendid garden made,   125

With velvet lawns and verdurous walls,
Straight paths, art-guided shadows, waterfalls,
From rock to rock constrained to wind,
And water-jets of every kind;
Majestic soaring there while at the sides,   130
With whiz and gush, threadlike the stream divides.
Then for the loveliest women I'd prepare
A tiny lodge, cosy and quiet; there
The countless hours, according to my mood,
I'd spend in that sweet, social solitude —   135
Women, I say: since, once for all,
I in the plural think upon the Fair.

FAUST.

Modern and base Sardanapal!

MEPHISTOPHELES.

Might one but guess thy purpose? High,
Doubtless, and grandly bold! Since thou   140
By so much nearer to the moon didst fly,
Aptly thy choice might thither tend, I trow!

FAUST.

Not so. Upon this globe of ours
For grand achievement still there's space;
Something astounding shall take place;   145
For daring toil I feel new powers.

MEPHISTOPHELES.

Fame also to achieve thou'rt fain?
That thou hast been with heroines is plain.

FAUST.

Dominion and estate by me are sought.
The deed is everything, the fame is naught!   150

MEPHISTOPHELES.

Yet poets shall arise, thy fame
To after ages to proclaim,
Through folly, folly to inflame.

FAUST.

That is beyond thy scope, I ween;
How knowest thou what man desires?   155
Adverse thy nature, bitter, keen,
How knoweth it what man requires?

MEPHISTOPHELES.

Be thy will done, since yield I must.
Me with the circuit of thy whims entrust.

FAUST.

Mine eye was fixed upon the open sea: 160
Aloft it towered, upheaving; then once more
Withdrew, and shook its waves exultingly,
To storm the wide expanse of level shore —
That angered me, since arrogance of mood,
In the free soul, that values every right,   165
Through the impetuous passion of the blood,
Harsh feeling genders, in its own despite.
I deemed it chance; more keenly eyed the main:
The billow paused, and then rolled back again,
And from its proudly conquered goal withdrew;   170
The hour returns, the sport it doth renew —

MEPHISTOPHELES (ad spectatores)

For me there's nothing novel here, I own;
This for some hundred thousand years I've known.

FAUST (continues passionately).

On through a thousand channels it doth press,
Barren itself, and causing barrenness;   175
It waxes, swells, it rolls and spreads its reign
Over the waste and desolate domain.
There, power-inspired, wave upon wave sweeps on,
Triumphs awhile, retreats — and naught is done:
It to despair might drive me to survey   180
Of lawless elements the aimless sway!
To soar above itself then dared my soul;
Here would I strive, this force would I control!

And it is possible.   Howe'er the tide
May rise, it fawneth round each hillock's side;   185

However proudly it may domineer,
Each puny height its crest doth 'gainst it rear,
Each puny deep it forcefully allures.
So swiftly plan on plan my mind matures:
This glorious pleasure for thyself attain;   190
Back from the shore to bar the imperious main,
Narrow the limits of the watery deep,
Constrain it far into itself to sweep!
My purpose step by step I might lay bare:
That is my wish, to aid it boldly dare!   195
(*Drums and martial music behind the spectators, from
      the distance, on the right hand.*)

MEPHISTOPHELES.

How easy 'tis! — Hear'st thou the drums afar?

FAUST.

What, war again! — The prudent likes not war.

MEPHISTOPHELES.

In peace or war the prudent doth obtain
From every circumstance his proper gain.
We watch, we mark each favoring moment; now,   200
The occasion smileth — Faustus, seize it thou!

FAUST.

Me, I entreat, this riddling nonsense spare.
And short and good, speak out; — thyself declare.

MEPHISTOPHELES.

On my way hither I became aware
That the good emperor is vexed with care;   205
Thou knowest him. The while we him amused,
And with the show of riches him abused,
Then the whole world to him was cheap, since he
While young attained to regal dignity;
This false resolve did then beguile his leisure,   210
That possible it is and right
Together these two interests to unite,
At once to govern, and to take one's pleasure.

FAUST.

A grievous error! He who would command,
His highest bliss must in commanding find.   215

With lofty will his bosom must expand,
Yet what he willeth may not be divined ;
To trusty ear he whispers his intent,
'Tis realized, — all feel astonishment :
So holds he still the most exalted place,   220
The worthiest.   Enjoyment doth debase !

MEPHISTOPHELES.

Such is he not ; on pleasure he was bent !
Meanwhile the realm by anarchy was rent,
Where high and low were ranged against each other,
And brother still pursued and slaughtered brother, 225
Castle 'gainst castle, town 'gainst town had feud,
Guild against noble, too ; in conflict rude,
Chapter and flock against their bishop rose ;
Who on each other gazed, were foes ;
Within the churches death and murder reign,   230
Merchant and traveller at the gates were slain ;
All waxed in daring, nor to small extent ;
To live was self-defence. — So matters went.

FAUST.

They went, they limped, they fell, again they rose,
Were overturned, rolled headlong — such the close. 235

MEPHISTOPHELES.

And such condition no one dared to blame,
Authority each could and each would claim ;
The smallest even proudly reared his crest.
At length too mad it grew e'en for the best.
The able, they forthwith arose with might,   240
And said : Who gives us peace is lord, by right ;
The Emperor cannot, will not ! — Let us choose
Another, in the realm who shall infuse
Fresh life, and safety unto each assign,
Who in a world its vigor that renews,   245
Together peace and justice shall combine !

FAUST.

That sounds like priestcraft.

MEPHISTOPHELES.

Priests, in sooth, were there;

The well-fed paunch, that was their primal care;
They implicated were above the rest.
The tumult swelled, the priests the tumult blest; 250
Our Emperor, whom we beguiled, perchance
To his last battle hither doth advance.

FAUST.

I pity him — so frank, so kind of heart.

MEPHISTOPHELES.

Let us look on.   There's hope ere life depart.
Him from this narrow vale let us deliver! 255
If rescued now, he rescued is forever.
How yet the die may fall, who may divine!
Vassals he'll have, if Fortune on him shine.
(*They ascend the middle range of hills and survey
the disposition of the army in the valley.   Drums
and military music resound from below.*)

MEPHISTOPHELES.

Well chosen the position is, I see;
We'll join them, perfect then the victory. 260

FAUST.

What there may we expect?   Deceit!
Illusive sorcery!   A hollow cheat!

MEPHISTOPHELES.

Cunning to win war's lofty game!
Be constant to thy mighty aim,
The while thy goal dost bear in sight; 265
Secure we to the Emperor throne and land,
Then kneel, from him receiving as thy right,
The fief of the unbounded strand.

FAUST.

Already much for me hast done;
By thee be now a battle won! 270

MEPHISTOPHELES.

No, do thou win it; forthwith here
As general-in-chief appear.

FAUST.

To my true honor it would tend,
There to command where naught I comprehend!

MEPHISTOPHELES.

The general's staff, let that provide,   275
So the field-marshal's safe whate'er betide.
War's want of council to its source I've traced;
War's council I forthwith have based
On mountain's and on man's primeval force:
Blest who together draws their joint resource.   280

FAUST.

What yonder bearing arms appears?
Hast thou aroused the mountaineers?

MEPHISTOPHELES.

No, but like Master Peter Squenze,
Of the whole mass the quintessence.
                    (*The three mighty ones enter.*)
My fellows now are drawing near!   285
Divers the clothes, the arms, they wear,
Of different ages they appear;
With them not badly shalt thou fare.
                    (*ad spectatores.*)
There's not a child but loves to see
Harness and arms of warlike knight;   290
And, allegoric as the rascals be,
They, for that reason, give the more delight.

BULLY

                    (*young, lightly armed, in motley attire*).

If one but looks into my eyes,
Straight let his jaws my clenchèd fist beware,
And if a coward from me flies,   295
Forthwith I seize him by the hair!

HAVEQUICK

                    (*manly, well armed, in rich attire*).

Such brawls are foolish, are invidious,
They forfeit what the occasion brings;
In *taking* only be assiduous;
Hereafter look to other things.   300

HOLDFAST

(in years, strongly armed, without attire).

Not much by such a course is won;
Through great possessions soon we run,
Borne by the stream of life away.
To take is good, 'tis better fast to hold;
Be still by the gray carle controlled,   305
And none from thee takes aught away.
(They descend the mountain together.)

On the Headland.

*Drums and martial music from below. The Emperor's
tent is pitched.* EMPEROR, GENERAL-IN-CHIEF, AT-
TENDANTS.

GENERAL-IN-CHIEF.

Still duly weighed appears our course,
Back to this vale at hand that lies,
To lead when somewhat pressed our force;
Our choice of ground, I trust, is wise.   310

EMPEROR.

How it succeeds must soon be known.
Me this half flight, this yielding, grieves, I own.

GENERAL-IN-CHIEF.

On our right flank, my prince, now cast your eyes!
Such ground doth war's ideal realize:
Not steep the hills, nor yet too easy to ascend,   315
The enemy ensnaring, while they ours befriend;
We, on the wavelike plain, are half concealed —
No cavalry durst venture on such field.

EMPEROR.

Save to commend naught now remains for me;
Here strength and courage can well tested be.   320

GENERAL-IN-CHIEF.

There, where the middle plain allures the sight,
Behold the phalanx, eager for the fight;
In the bright sunshine, gilded by its rays,
The lances glitter through the morning haze.   325
How darkly waves the mighty square below!
For bold emprize its thousands all aglow.

The mass' strength thou thus canst comprehend;
To them I trust, the foemen's strength to rend.

EMPEROR.

So fair a sight ne'er have I seen before :
Such host is worth its number, twice told o'er.   330

GENERAL-IN-CHIEF.

Of our left flank naught have I to relate.
Holding the stubborn cliffs, stout heroes wait;
Ablaze with arms, the rocky height ascends,
Which the close entrance to the pass defends.
Here, where the bloody onslaught none expect,   335
The hostile force will, I foresee, be wrecked.

EMPEROR.

There march my lying kinsfolk, still who claimed,
As me they uncle, cousin, brother, named,
More and more license; till the sceptre's strength,
Its honor from the throne, they stole at length;   340
The empire, through their feuds, distracted lies,
Now, leagued as rebels, they against me rise!
The many waver, swayed from side to side;
Then headlong rush, borne onward by the tide.

GENERAL-IN-CHIEF.

A trusty man, abroad for tidings sent,   345
Hastes down the rocks; oh, happy be the event.

FIRST SPY.

Fair success on us hath waited;
Through our bold and crafty art,
Here and there we penetrated;
Little good can we impart: 350
Many pure allegiance proffered;
But for their inaction they,
In excuse, these pretexts offered,
Public danger, civil fray —

EMPEROR.

Self-seekers, caring for themselves alone,   355
To duty, honor, gratitude, are blind!
If full your measure, you ne'er call to mind,
Your neighbor's house-fire may consume your own.

GENERAL-IN-CHIEF.

The second comes, descending heavily;
Tremble his limbs, a weary man is he.   360

SECOND SPY.

First with pleasure we detected
The wild tumult's erring course.
Undelaying, unexpected,
A new emperor leads his force;
And with his behests complying,   365
O'er the plain the concourse sweep.
This false banner, proudly flying,
They all follow now — like sheep!

EMPEROR.

As gain a rival emperor I hail;
That I am emperor, now first I feel!   370
But as a soldier did I don the mail;
For higher purpose now I'm clad in steel.
At every festival, how bright soe'er,
Though naught was wanting — danger failed me there.
When to the ring-sport at your call I went;   375
My heart beat high, I breathed the tournament;
From war had ye not held me back, my name
For deeds heroic had been known to fame!
What self-reliance in my breast did reign,
When I stood mirrored in the fire-domain;   380
The ruthless element pressed on elate,
'Twas but a show, and yet the show was great.
Fame, victory, my troubled dreams displayed —
I'll now achieve, what basely I delayed!
        (*Heralds are dispatched to challenge the rival*
                        Emperor.)

Faust *in armor, with half-closed visor. The three*
        mighty ones, armed and clothed, as above.

FAUST.

We come, we hope uncensured — foresight here   385
May yet avail, though needless it appear.
Thoughtful, thou knowest, and wise the mountain-race,
Of rock and nature they the secrets trace;
Spirits, who long have left the level ground,
Are to their rocky heights more firmly bound   390

Through labyrinthine clefts they labor, where
Rich fumes metallic fill the gaseous air;
Untired they separate, combine and test;
The hidden to make known is their sole quest;
With the light touch of spirit-might, they rear   395
Transparent figures, then in crystal clear
And its eternal silence, mirrored true,
The doings of the upper world they view.

EMPEROR.

This I have heard, and think that it may be;
But, honest man, say: what is this to me: 400

FAUST.

The Norcian sorcerer, the Sabine, he
True honorable servant is to thee;
What ghastly fate appalled him, on the pyre!
Crackled the brushwood, rose the tongues of fire;
Dry fagots all around up-piled were seen,   405
Mingled with pitch, with brimstone bars between,
Man's, god's, or devil's aid had been in vain —
Your majesty then burst the fiery chain!
'Twas there, in Rome.   Deeply to thee he's bound,
And o'er thy path keeps watch with care profound;
Himself forgetting, from that moment he   411
Questions the stars, questions the depths for thee.
He bade us, at the swiftest, hither post,
To succor thee.   Great powers the mountains boast:
There Nature works, omnipotently free —   415
The priest's dull mind blames it as sorcery.

EMPEROR.

On festal day when guest on guest we greet,
Joyful themselves, who joyance come to meet,
Well pleased we see them enter, each and all,
And, man by man, contract the spacious hall;   420
Yet highest welcome is the brave man's dower,
Who, as ally to aid us, comes with power,
When morning breaks, which doubtful issues wait,
While over it are poised the scales of Fate.
Nathless withhold awhile thy stalwart hand,   425
In this high moment, from the willing brand!

Honor the hour, when many thousands wend
To battle, for or 'gainst me to contend!
Man's self is man!   Who would be throned and
        crowned,
Of the high honor must be worthy found.   430
Now may this phantom, that against us stands,
This self-styled emperor, ruler of our lands,
The army's duke, lord of our feudal train,
By my own hand, be thrust to death's domain!

FAUST.

Whate'er the need to end the glorious fight,   435
To peril thine own head cannot be right.
Is not the helm with crest and plumage decked?
The head, our zeal which fires, it doth protect.
Without the head what could the members do?
Let that but sleep, forthwith all slumber, too;   440
If it be injured, all are straight unsound,
And all revive, if it with health be crowned.
Promptly the arm its own strong right doth wield,
And to protect the skull uplifts the shield;
Its proper duty well the sword doth know,   445
Parries with strength, and then returns the blow;
The active foot shares in the common weal,
And on the slain foe's neck doth plant the heel.

EMPEROR.

Such is mine anger: him I thus would treat,
Make his proud head a footstool for my feet!   450

HERALDS (returning).

Little profit, little credit,
From our challenge did we gain;
Noble 'twas, yet while we read it,
Us they flouted with disdain:
"Spent your Emperor's power," — they say,   455
"Like echo in yon narrow vale;
Would we think of him to-day; —
Once there was :— so runs the tale."

FAUST.

What hath occurred doth with their wish accord,
Who firm and true for thee would draw the sword. 460

The foe approach; thy troops impatient stand;
The moment favors; straight the charge command!

EMPEROR.

To the command all claim I now resign.
    (*To the* GENERAL-IN-CHIEF.)
To execute that duty, prince, be thine!

GENERAL-IN-CHIEF.

March then our right wing onward to the field! 465
The foemen's left, who even now ascend,
Ere they complete their final step, shall yield
To their tried valor who the slope defend!

FAUST.

Permission grant that this blithe hero be
Enrolled among thy ranks, immediately,   470
That with thy ranks incorporate, he may
Have for his powerful nature ample play.
       (*He points to the right.*)

BULLY (*steps forward*).

His face to me who shows doth not escape,
Till both his jaws I've smashed with sudden bang;
His back to me who turns, I strike his nape, — 475
Dangling adown his back, neck, head, and top-knot hang!
And if, with sword and club, thy men
Will strike, as on I rage before,
Man over man down-smitten, then
The foe shall welter in their gore! (*Exit.*) 480

GENERAL-IN-CHIEF.

Now let the centre phalanx follow slow,
And in full force with caution meet the foe!
Distressed, they yield already on the right,
Their plan, by our attack, is shattered quite.

FAUST
(*pointing to the middle one*).

Let this one also thy command obey. 485

HAVEQUICK (*steps forward*)

Unto the host's heroic pride,
Shall thirst for booty be allied;

Upon this goal be all intent;
The rival emperor's sumptuous tent.
Not long upon his throne he'll boast indeed !   490
Myself to battle will this phalanx lead.

SPEED-BOOTY (a sutler woman)

(*fawning upon him*).

Although his wife I may not be,
A sweetheart dear is he to me.
For us what harvest now is ripe !
Woman is fierce when she doth gripe,   495
Is ruthless when she robs; press on,
All is allowed — when we have won.   (*Exeunt.*)

GENERAL-IN-CHIEF.

Upon our left, as was to be expected,
With furious charge, their right is now directed.
The defile's rocky path they hope to gain;   500
To thwart their purpose man for man must strain.

FAUST (*beckons to the left*).

Sire, I entreat you, look also on this one;
If strength be stronger made, no harm is done.

HOLDFAST (*steps forward*).

For the left wing dismiss all care !   505
For where I am, safe is possession there;
Herein doth age approve itself, we're told;
No lightning rendeth what I hold !   (*Exit.*)

MEPHISTOPHELES.

(*coming down from above*).

Now to the background turn your gaze;
Forth from the jagged and rocky ways,
See how the armèd warriors pour,   510
The narrow paths to straiten more,
With helm, shield, harness, sword and spear,
A wall they're forming in our rear,
Waiting the sign to strike the blow.
(*Aside to the knowing ones.*)
From whence they come, ask not to know.   515
No time I lost; where I appeared,
The armor-halls around were cleared.

Footmen and horsemen, stood they there,
As if yet lords of earth they were;
Knight, emperor, king, they were of yore,   520
Now they are empty snail-shells, nothing more, —
Full many a ghost, thus armed for strife,
The middle ages have brought back to life;
What devilkin therein may lurk,
For this time it may do its work.   525
(*Aloud.*)

Hark, in their anger, how they clatter,
And, like tin-plates, each other batter;
Torn banners, too, flapping aloft one sees,
That wait impatiently to catch the breeze.
Reflect, an ancient race stands ready there,   530
And in this modern combat fain would share.
(*Terrible flourish of trumpets from above ; perceptible
        wavering in the hostile army.*)

FAUST.

Now dark the whole horizon shows,
Yet here and there presageful glows
A ruddy and portentous ray;
The weapons gleam, distained with blood;   535
The atmosphere, the rock, the wood,
The heavens, mingle in the fray.

MEPHISTOPHELES.

Firmly the right flank holds its ground;
Among them towering there I see
Stout Hans, the nimble giant, he   540
His wonted strokes now deals around.

EMPEROR.

First on one lifted arm I gazed,
A dozen now I see upraised :
Not Nature's laws are working here!

FAUST.

Of mist-wreaths hast not heard, above   545
The coast of Sicily that rove?
There hovering in daylight clear,
Uplifted in the middle air,
Mirrored in exhalations rare,

A wondrous show the vision takes. 550
There cities waver to and fro,
There gardens rise, now high, now low,
As form on form through ether breaks.

EMPEROR.

It looks suspicious! For I there
See all the lofty spear-tops glare; 555
And through our phalanx, on each lance
I see a nimble flamelet dance:
Too spectral seems to me the sight!

FAUST.

Pardon, my lord! The traces they
Of spirit-natures passed away, 560
A reflex of the mighty Pair,
By whom were sailors wont to swear:
Here they collect their final might.

EMPEROR.

To whom are we beholden, say,
That Nature, for our weal to-day, 565
Her rarest powers should here unite?

MEPHISTOPHELES.

To whom save him, that master high,
Thy fate who bears within his breast?
The strong threat of thine enemy
His soul hath stirred to deep unrest. 570
His gratitude will see thee saved,
Though death in the attempt be braved.

EMPEROR.

They cheered, with pomp around my march they
    pressed;
I now was something: That I fain would test,
So, without thought, it pleased me, then and there, 575
To grant to that white beard the cooling air.
Thus of the clergy I the sport have crossed,
And have, in sooth, thereby their favor lost;
Now shall I, when so many years are passed,
Of that glad deed the fruitage reap at last? 580

FAUST.

Rich interest bears the generous deed.
Now heavenward be thy glance directed:
An omen he will send; give heed!
Straight it appears — as I expected.

EMPEROR.

An eagle hovers in the heavenly height;   585
A griffin, with wild threats, attends his flight.

FAUST.

Give heed!   Auspicious seems the sign.
Your griffin is of fabled line;
How, self-forgetting, can he dare
Himself with genuine eagle to compare!   590

EMPEROR.

Forthwith, in widespread circles wending,
Around they wheel; now, through the sky,
Impetuous, they together fly,
Each other's throat and plumage rending.

FAUST.

Mark how the sorry griffin, torn   595
And ruffled sore, his flight now steereth,
With drooping lion-tail, forlorn,
And 'mid the tree-tops disappeareth.

EMPEROR.

So be it, e'en as these portend!
With wonder filled, I wait the end.   600

MEPHISTOPHELES (*towards the right*).

Pressed by our onslaught, oft-repeated,
Our foes must yield, well nigh defeated,
Yet, waging still a dubious fight,
Onward they press toward their right,
And thus embarrass in the fray   605
The left flank of their chief array.

Our phalanx its firm point doth bring,
Like lightning 'gainst their dexter wing,
The foe, where weakest, they engage.
Now, as when storm-vexed billows rage,   610

Wildly contend, with equal might,
Both armies in the double fight.
More glorious deed was never done,
Ours is the field, the victory's won!

EMPEROR

(on the left side, to Faust).

Suspicious yonder it doth seem;   615
Our station hazardous I deem,
No stones they hurl against the foe,
Scaled are the lower rocks, and lo!
Deserted those above appear;
The foe, — in solid mass, draw near;   620
With might and main still pressing on,
Perchance the passage they have won:
Of skill unholy such the end!
Your arts to futile issues tend!   (*Pause.*)

MEPHISTOPHELES.

Hither, my ravens twain are winging!   625
For us what message are they bringing?
We are, I fear, in evil plight.

EMPEROR.

What want these birds, mischance portending?
They come their swarthy sails extending,
Straight from the hot and rocky fight.   630

MEPHISTOPHELES (to the ravens).

Close to mine ears now take your post.
Whom you protect, is never lost;
For shrewd your counsel is and right.

FAUST (to the EMPEROR).

Of pigeons thou hast heard, returning
Homeward, for nest and fledglings yearning,   635
Steering their flight from far off lands.
But here a difference obtaineth:
Pigeons suffice while peace still reigneth,
But war the raven-post demands.

MEPHISTOPHELES.

The message tells of sore distresses.   640
See yonder how the tumult presses

Our heroes' rocky wall around!
The nearest heights are now ascended,
Win they the pass by ours defended,
In sorry plight we should be found.   645

EMPEROR.

So I deluded am at last!
Around me you have drawn your net;
I've shuddered, since it held me fast!

MEPHISTOPHELES.

Take courage!   Naught is lost as yet;
Patience unties the hardest knot!   650
Still sharpest is the final stand.
My trusty messengers I've got;
Command me, that I may command.

GENERAL-IN-CHIEF
(*who meanwhile has arrived*).

With these thou hast thyself allied,
I long have grieved to see them at thy side;   655
No stable good doth conjuring earn.
To change the battle now I can't pretend;
They have begun it, they may end!
My staff I unto thee return.

EMPEROR.

It for some better hour retain,   660
Which Fate for us may have in store.
This fellow and his ravens twain,
His horrid comrades, I abhor!

(*To* MEPHISTOPHELES.)

The staff I can't on thee bestow,
Thou seemest not the proper man;   665
Command, and save us from the foe!
Then happen may what happen can.
(*Exit into the tent with the* GENERAL-IN-CHIEF.)

MEPHISTOPHELES.

Him may the stupid staff defend!
To us small profit would it lend;
There was a kind of cross thereon.   670

FAUST.

What is to do?

MEPHISTOPHELES.

Why, all is done!
Now haste, my cousins, swart and fleet,
To the great mountain lake; the Undines greet,
And for a seeming flood, entreat them fair!
The actual they indeed, through female art,   675
Hard to conceive, from semblance know to part;
That it the actual is, then each will swear. (*Pause.*)

FAUST.

The water-maidens must our raven-pair
Rightly have flattered and with cunning rare:
Yonder it drops already; see,   680
From many a bare rock's barren side,
Gushes the full, swift-flowing tide —
'Tis over with their victory.

MEPHISTOPHELES.

Strange greeting give the rushing streams —
Perplexed the boldest climber seems.   685

FAUST.

Already downward brook to brook is sweeping,
Doubled from many a gorge again they're leaping;
A stately water-arch one stream doth throw;
Now o'er the rock's broad level smoothly gliding,
Anon, with flash and roar, again dividing,   690
It plunges step-wise to the vale below.
To stem the flood what boots their brave endeavor?
Them from the mighty flood may none deliver.
Before the tumult wild myself must quail!

MEPHISTOPHELES.

Nothing I see of all these watery lies;   695
They bring illusion but to human eyes;
With joy the wondrous change I hail.
Headlong the masses pour, a shining throng;
The fools imagine they will soon be drowned,
And while they snort upon the solid ground,   700

Like swimmers laughably they move along.
Now reigns confusion all around. (*The ravens return.*)
To the high master you I will commend.
Yourselves, would ye as masters prove — attend;
Straight to the glowing smithy fare,   705
To the dwarf-folk, who tireless there
Strike sparks from metal and from stone —
With them, while chattering, desire
A shining, dazzling, bursting fire,
As to man's highest fancy shown.   710
True, lightning-flashes gleaming from afar,
And, swift as vision, fall of loftiest star,
May happen every summer night;
But flashes amid tangled bushes found,
And stars that hiss upon the humid ground —   715
These are, in sooth, no common sight:
So must ye, without much annoy,
Entreaties first, and then commands, employ.
    (*Exeunt the ravens.   All happens as prescribed.*)

MEPHISTOPHELES.

Thick darkness o'er the foe is spreading!
They in uncertainty are treading!   720
Deluding flashes everywhere;
Then blindness, from the sudden glare! —
All that has wondrously succeeded;
But now some terror-sound is needed.

FAUST.

The hollow weapons from the armories,   725
Feel themselves stronger in the open breeze;
They rattle there above, and clatter on —
A wonderful discordant tone.

MEPHISTOPHELES.

Quite right.   They can be reined no more;
As in the gracious times of yore,   730
The sound of knightly blows is rife;
Armlets and leg-protecting gear,
As Guelfs and Ghibellines appear,
Swift to renew the eternal strife:
Firm in transmitted hate, they close,   735

While far and wide resound their blows,
The rancor ending but with life.

At last, in every devil's fête
Most potently works party-hate,
Till the last horror closes all;   740
Discordant sounds of rout and panic,
Between whiles, piercing, shrill, Satanic,
Through the wide valley rise and fall.
    (*War tumult in the Orchestra, passing at last into
        cheerful military music.*)

The rival Emperor's tent.   Throne, rich surroundings.
HAVEQUICK, SPEED-BOOTY.

SPEED-BOOTY.

So here the first we are, I see!

HAVEQUICK.

No raven flies so fast as we.   745

SPEED-BOOTY.

What treasure-heaps lie here and there;
Where to begin?   To finish, where?

HAVEQUICK.

So full the space, I'm hard to please:
I know not what I first should seize!

SPEED-BOOTY.

This carpet is the thing for me,   750
My bed is apt too hard to be.

HAVEQUICK.

Here a steel-club is hanging, such,
Long, as mine own, I've wished to clutch.

SPEED BOOTY.

The mantle red, with golden seams —
I've seen its fellow in my dreams.   755

HAVEQUICK (*taking the weapon*).

With this full soon the work is done:
One strikes him dead, and passes on.
Much hast thou packed, yet, for thy pains,
Nothing of worth thy sack contains:

This plunder in its place may rest,   760
One among many, take this chest!
The host's appointed pay they hold;
Within its belly is pure gold.

SPEED-BOOTY.

A murderous weight is this! I may
Nor lift, nor carry it away.   765

HAVEQUICK.

Duck quickly!   Thou must bend!   I'll pack
The booty on thy stalwart back.

SPEED-BOOTY.

Alack! alack!   'Tis all in vain!
The load will break my back in twain.
                    (*The chest falls, and springs open.*)

HAVEQUICK.

There lies of ruddy gold a heap;   770
Be quick, the prize away to sweep!

SPEED-BOOTY (*stoops down*).

Now fling it in my lap with speed!
There's plenty to supply our need.

HAVEQUICK.

Now there's enough!   Away then pack!
                                    (*She rises.*)
The apron has a hole, alack!   775
Where thou dost stand, and where dost go,
The treasure lavishly dost sow.

HALBERDIERS (*of our* EMPEROR).

Sacred this place!   What do ye here?
Why pillage thus the Emperor's gear?

HAVEQUICK.

Cheaply we sold our limbs, I trow!   780
Our share of spoil we gather now,
In hostile tents, the victors' due;
And we — why we are soldiers, too.

HALBERDIERS.

It suits not in our ranks to be
Soldier at once and thief, for he   785

To serve our Emperor who would claim,
Must bear an honest soldier's name!

HAVEQUICK.

Such honesty we know, by you
'Tis Contribution styled!   Ye, too,
Upon the self-same footing live :   790
The password of your trade is — Give!
(*To* SPEED-BOOTY.)
Off with thy prey, right speedily!
For here no welcome guests are we.   (*Exeunt.*)

FIRST HALBERDIER.

Say, wherefore didst thou not bestow
Upon the rascal's cheek a blow?   795

SECOND.

I know not; me my strength forsook;
So phantom-like to me their look!

THIRD.

Something there came to mar my sight.
It glimmered — I saw naught aright.

FOURTH.

In sooth, I know not what to say.   800
So hot it was the live-long day!
Fearful, oppressive, close as well ;
While one man stood, another fell ;
We groped, still striking at the foe ;
Opponents fell at every blow —   805
Floated before our eyes a mist ;
Then in our ear it buzzed, hummed, hissed.
So on it went — now are we here ;
The manner of it is not clear!

Enter the EMPEROR, *with four* PRINCES.
(*The* HALBERDIERS *retire.*)

EMPEROR.

Be with him as it may, the day is ours.   Sore-battered,
Over the level plain the foe in flight are scattered.   811
Here stands the vacant throne; with tapestry hung
    round,
The traitor's treasure, too, narrows the tented ground.

By our own guards defended, we wait with exultation,
And with imperial pomp, the envoys of each nation. 815
Here from all sides arrive glad tidings hour by hour:
The realm is pacified, and gladly owns our power.
Though in our fight perchance some magic arts were
    wrought,
Yet at the last, ourselves — we, only we, have fought.
To combatants, in sooth, chance still may work for
    good —
From Heaven falls a stone, on foemen it rains blood; 821
Strange sounds of wondrous power from rocky caves
    may flow,
Which lift our courage high, and strike with fear the foe.
Object of lasting scorn, prostrate the vanquished lies,
While to the favoring God the victor's praises rise ;   825
All blend with him, nor need that he should give the
    word —
"We praise Thee, Lord our God !" from million throats
    is heard.
Yet as the highest praise, my own breast I'll explore,
Searching with pious glance, which rarely happed before.
A young and joyous prince, of time may waste the
    dower: 830
Him years will teach, at last, the importance of the hour.
Hence to ally myself with you, most worthy four,
For house, and court, and realm, will I delay no more.
(To the First.)
Thine was, O Prince, the wise arrangement of the host,
And in the crisis thou heroic skill couldst boast ;   835
Therefore work thou as may with times of peace accord.
Arch-Marshal name I thee; to thee I give the sword.

ARCH-MARSHAL.

Thy host, within the realm till now employed alone,
Shall on the border guard thy person and thy throne.
Then be it ours, when crowds make glad on festive day
Thy large ancestral hall, thy banquet to array.   841
I'll hold it at thy side, or bear it thee before,
Of highest majesty the escort evermore.

EMPEROR (to the SECOND).

With valor who, like thee, doth courtesy unite,
Arch-Chamberlain shall be.   The duties are not light.

Of all the house-retainers chief art thou; them I find 846
But sorry servants still, to household strife inclined:
In honor held, may they, from thy example, see
How they to prince, to court, to all, may gracious be:

ARCH-CHAMBERLAIN.

The master's lofty thought to further, bringeth grace:
Ever to aid the good, nor injure e'en the base;   851
Frank, without guile to be, and calm without disguise,
That thou shouldst know me, Sire, this boon alone I
      prize.
Dare fancy to that feast press on with pinions bold —
Thou goest to the board, I reach the ewer of gold,   855
Thy rings I take, that while joy reigneth and delight,
Thy hand may be refreshed, while gladdens me thy
      light

EMPEROR.

Too earnest feel I now to think of joyous fest;
Yet be it so — a glad commencement still is best!
            (*To the* THIRD.)
Arch-Steward thee I choose.   Therefore henceforth to
      thee   860
The chase, the poultry-yard, the farm shall subject be.
Choice of my favorite dishes still for me prepare,
As them the month brings round, and dressed with
      proper care.

ARCH-STEWARD.

Strict fasting be for me the duty that I boast,
Until before thee placed the dish to please thee most:
The kitchen-service shall with me co-operate,   866
The far to bring anear, seasons to ante-date.
Thee charm not viands rare, wherewith thy board is
      graced ;
Simple and racy food, thereto inclines thy taste.

EMPEROR (*to the* FOURTH).

Since festivals perforce alone engage us now,   870
To Cupbearer transformed, young hero, straightbe thou!
Arch-Cupbearer, henceforth the duty shall be thine
To see our cellars stored richly with generous wine.
Be temperate thyself; be not misled through mirth,
Howe'er allurements tempt, to which the hour gives
      birth !   875

ARCH-CUPBEARER.

Your highness, youth itself, if trust therein be shown,
Stands, ere one looks around, to man's full stature
    grown.
Myself I, too, transport to that great festive day:
The imperial sideboard then right nobly I'll array;
Of gold and silver there shall splendid vessels shine,
Yet first the loveliest cup will I select as thine — 881
A clear Venetian glass, wherein joy lurking waits:
The flavor it improves, yet ne'er inebriates.
In such a wondrous cup, too, great our trust may be:
Thy moderation, sire, still more protecteth thee.   885

EMPEROR.

What, in this solemn hour, I have conferred on you,
Receive with confidence, from valid lips and true;
Great is the Emperor's word, and every gift makes
    sure,
For confirmation yet there needs his signature.
This duty to prepare, and royal writ thereto,   890
The fitting man appears, at the fit moment, too.

(*The* ARCHBISHOP *and* ARCH-CHANCELLOR *enter*.)

If to the keystone trusts its weight the vaulted arch,
Securely built it then defies time's onward march.
Thou see'st four princes here.   E'en now we have
    decided   894
How governance shall be for house and court provided.
What the whole realm concerns, be that with weight
    and power,
To you, ye princes five, entrusted from this hour.
In landed wealth ye shall all others far excel;
Hence, with their heritage who from our standard fell,
The bounds of your possessions I forthwith expand:
Ye faithful ones, be yours full many a goodly land, 901
Also the lofty right, should time the occasion send,
Through purchase, chance, exchange, their limits to
    extend;
To practise undisturbed, this is secured to you,
What sovereign rights soe'er, as landlords, are your
    due;   905

As judges, be it yours to speak the final doom, —
From your high stations none will to appeal presume.
Then tribute, tax, and tithe, safe-conduct, toll, and fee,
Mine-salt, and coinage-dues, your property shall be.
That thus my gratitude may validly be shown,   910
In rank I you have raised next the Imperial throne.

ARCHBISHOP.

In name of all be given our depest thanks to thee!
Us makest thou strong and firm, — thy power shall
        strengthened be.

EMPEROR.

Yet higher dignities I to you five will give.
Still live I for my realm, and still rejoice to live; 915
Nathless of my great sires the chain withdraws my gaze,
From keen endeavor back, the coming doom to face:
I also, in *His* time, must bid my friends adieu;
The emperor to name shall then belong to you.
On the high altar raised, crown ye his sacred brow, 920
And peacefully shall end, what stormful was e'en now!

ARCH-CHANCELLOR.

With pride in their deep breasts, with lowly gestures,
        stand
Princes, before thee bowed, the foremost of the land.
So long as in our veins the faithful current plays, 924
The body we, which still thy lightest impulse sways!

EMPEROR.

And, to conclude, what we to-day have done, made sure,
Shall be henceforth for aye, by writ and signature;
Ye hold, indeed, as lords, possession, full and free,
Yet on these terms — that it partitioned ne'er shall be,
And howsoe'er increased, what ye from us receive 930
Ye to your eldest son shall undivided leave.

ARCH-CHANCELLOR.

For our weal and the realm's, to parchment will I
        straight,
With joyful mind, confide a statute of such weight;
The Chancery shall seal and document procure,
Then shall confirm it, Sire, thy sacred signature! 935

EMPEROR.

And so I you dismiss, that on this glorious day,
In solemn conclave met, deliberate ye may.
(*The temporal lords retire.   The* ARCHBISHOP *remains,
     and speaks in a pathetic tone.*)

ARCHBISHOP.

The chancellor is gone ; the bishop doth remain,
His father's heart for thee trembles with anxious pain :
Him a deep warning soul impels thine ear to seek. 940

EMPEROR.

What in this joyous hour is thy misgiving? Speak !

ARCHBISHOP.

With what a bitter pang find I, in such an hour,
Thy consecrated head in league with Satan's power !
Confirmed upon thy throne, as it appeareth, — true ;
But in despite of God, and Father Pontiff, too !   945
Hearing of this, forthwith, will he pronounce thy doom ;
With sacred fire thy realm, accursed, will he consume ;
For he forgets not how, the day when thou wast
     crowned,
E'en at that hour supreme, the sorcerer hast unbound ;
To Christendom's foul shame, on that accursed head,
From out thy diadem, mercy's first beam was shed. 951
Now smite upon thy breast, and from thy guilty prey
Back to our holy church some little share repay.
The broad hill-space whereon thy tent did lately stand,
Where, thee to aid, themselves did evil spirits band, 955
There, where the Prince of Lies did late thine ears abuse,
Taught piously, that spot devote to pious use, —
With mountains and thick wood, so far as they extend,
With verdant slopes which yield rich pasture, without
     end ;   959
Clear lakes, alive with fish, unnumbered brooks that
     flow,
With swift and snakelike course, down to the vale
     below ;
Then the broad vale itself, with meadow, hollow, plain,—
Let thy repentance speak, and mercy thou'lt obtain !

EMPEROR.

For this, my grievous fault, terror so fills my mind, 964
By thine own measure be the bounds by thee assigned.

ARCHBISHOP.

First shall the space defiled, by sin so desecrated,
To service of the Highest straight be consecrated!
Swift, to the spirit-eye, the massive walls aspire,
The morning sun's first beam already gilds the choir;
Crosswise the structure grows, the nave, in length and
        height   970
Expanding, straightway fills believers with delight.
Through the wide portal now, they throng with ardent
        zeal,
While over hill and vale resounds the bells' first peal —
From lofty towers they ring, which heavenward strive
        amain,
The penitent draws near, there to be born again.   975
On consecration day — that day soon may we see ! —
The highest ornament should then thy presence be.

EMPEROR.

And be my pious wish, through work so great made
        known,
The Lord our God to praise, and for my sin atone !
Enough !   Already raised my spirit now I feel.   980

ARCHBISHOP.

As chancellor, I claim both covenant and seal.

EMPEROR.

A deed which to the church shall all these rights
        secure —
Bring it, I will with joy affix my signature.

ARCHBISHOP
        (*takes leave, but turns back again at the door*).
Thou, as the work proceeds, to it must dedicate
The land's collective dues — tribute, and tithe, and
        rate —   985
Forever.   Ample wealth for due support we need,
And careful governance still heavy costs doth breed.
For swift erection, too, on spot so waste, some gold,
From thy rich plunder, thou from us wilt not withhold.
Moreover, we shall want — this I cannot disguise — 990
Timber, and lime, and slate, and such far-off supplies ;
Taught from the pulpit, these the willing people bears :
The church still blesses him, who for her service cares.
                                                (*Exit.*)

EMPEROR.

Heavy and sore the sin whose burden I bewail! 994
These odious sorcerers have wrought me grievous bale!

ARCHBISHOP

(returning once more with profound obeisance).
Pardon, O Sire, thou hast to that unworthy man
The realm's seashore conveyed; yet him shall smite
  the ban,
Unless with tithe and dues, with rent and taxes, thou,
Repentant, also there our holy church endow.

EMPEROR *(with ill-humor).*

The land is not yet there; broad in the sea it lies. 1000

ARCHBISHOP.

For him the time will come who potent is and wise,
For us still may your word in its full powers remain.
        (Exit.)

EMPEROR *(alone).*

So may I sign away the realm o'er which I reign!

ACT THE FIFTH.

Open country.

WANDERER.

Yes, 'tis they, their branches rearing,
Hoary lindens, strong in age; —
There I find them, reappearing,
After my long pilgrimage!
'Tis the very spot; — how gladly   5
Yonder hut once more I see,
By the billows raging madly,
Cast ashore, which sheltered me!
My old hosts, I fain would greet them,
Helpful they, an honest pair;   10
May I hope to-day to meet them?
Even then they aged were.
Worthy folk, in God believing!
Shall I knock? or raise my voice?

Hail to you if, guest receiving,   15
In good deeds ye still rejoice!

BAUCIS (*a very aged woman*).

Stranger dear, beware of breaking
My dear husband's sweet repose!
Strength for brief and feeble waking
Lengthened sleep on age bestows.   20

WANDERER.

Mother, say then, do I find thee,
To receive my thanks once more,
In my youth who didst so kindly,
With thy spouse, my life restore?
Baucis, to my lips half-dying,   25
Art thou, who refreshment gave?
(*The husband steps forth.*)
Thou Philemon, strength who plying,
Snatched my treasure from the wave?
By your flames, so promptly kindled,
By your bell's clear silver sound —   30
That adventure, horror-mingled,
Hath a happy issue found.
Forward let me step, and gazing
Forth upon the boundless main,
Kneel, and thankful prayers upraising,   35
Ease of my full heart the strain!
(*He walks forward upon the downs.*)

PHILEMON (*to* BAUCIS).

Haste to spread the table, under
The green leafage of our trees.
Let him run, struck dumb with wonder,
Scarce he'll credit what he sees.   40
(*He follows the wanderer.   Standing beside him.*)

Where the billows did maltreat you,
Wave on wave in fury rolled,
There a garden now doth greet you,
Fair as Paradise of old.
Grown more aged, as when stronger,   45
I could render aid no more;
And, as waned my strength, no longer

Rolled the sea upon the shore:
Prudent lords, bold serfs directing,
It with trench and dyke restrained;   50
Ocean's rights no more respecting,
Lords they were, where he had reigned.
See, green meadows far extending; —
Garden, village, woodland, plain.
But return we, homeward wending,   55
For the sun begins to wane.
In the distance sails are gliding,
Nightly they to port repair;
Bird-like, in their nests confiding,
For a haven waits them there.   60
Far away mine eye discerneth
First the blue fringe of the main;
Right and left, where'er it turneth,
Spreads the thickly-peopled plain.

In the Garden.   The three at table.

BAUCIS (*to the stranger*).

Art thou dumb?   No morsel raising   65
To thy famished lips?

PHILEMON.

I trow,
He of wonders so amazing
Fain would hear; inform him thou.

BAUCIS.

There was wrought a wonder truly,
Yet no rest it leaves to me;   70
Naught in the affair was duly
Done, as honest things should be!

PHILEMON.

Who as sinful can pronounce it?
'Twas the Emperor gave the shore;—
Did the trumpet not announce it   75
As the herald passed our door?
Footing firm they first have planted
Near these downs.   Tents, huts, appeared;

O'er the green, the eye, enchanted,
Saw ere long a palace reared.   80

BAUCIS.

Shovel, axe, no labor sparing,
Vainly plied the men by day;
Where the fires at night shone flaring,
Stood a dam, in morning's ray.
Still from human victims bleeding,   85
Wailing sounds were nightly borne;
Seaward sped the flames, receding;
A canal appeared at morn!
Godless is he, naught respecting;
Covets he our grove, our cot;   90
Though our neighbor, us subjecting,
Him to serve will be our lot.

PHILEMON.

Yet he bids, our claims adjusting,
Homestead fair in his new land.

BAUCIS.

Earth, from water saved, mistrusting,   95
On thine own height take thy stand.

PHILEMON.

Let us, to the chapel wending,
Watch the sun's last rays subside;
Let us ring, and prayerful bending,
In our fathers' God confide!   100

Palace.

Spacious ornamental garden; broad, straight canal.
FAUST, in extreme old age, walking about meditating.

LYNCEUS, THE WARDER
(*through a speaking trumpet*).

The sun sinks down, the ships belated
Rejoicing to the haven steer.
A stately galley, deeply freighted,
On the canal, now draweth near;
Her chequered flag the breeze caresses,   105
The masts unbending bear the sails:

Thee now the grateful seaman blesses,
Thee at this moment Fortune hails.
(The bell rings on the downs.)

FAUST (starting).

Accursed bell!   Its clamor sending,
Like spiteful shot it wounds mine ear!   110
Before me lies my realm unending;
Vexation dogs me in the rear;
For I, these envious chimes still hearing,
Must at my narrow bounds repine;
The linden grove, brown hut thence peering,   115
The mouldering church, these are not mine.
Refreshment seek I, there repairing?
Another's shadow chills my heart,
A thorn, nor foot nor vision sparing, —
O far from hence could I depart!   120

WARDER (as above).

How, wafted by the evening gales,
Blithely the painted galley sails;
On its swift course, how richly stored!
Chest, coffer, sack, are heaped aboard.

A splendid galley, richly and brilliantly laden with the
produce of foreign climes.

MEPHISTOPHELES.   The three mighty comrades.

CHORUS.

Here do we land,   125
Here are we now,
Hail to our lord;
Our patron, thou!

(They disembark.   The goods are brought ashore).

MEPHISTOPHELES.

So have we proved our worth — content
If we our patron's praises earn: 130
With but two ships abroad we went,
With twenty we to port return.
By our rich lading all may see
The great successes we have wrought.
Free ocean makes the spirit free: 135

There claims compunction ne'er a thought!
A rapid grip there needs alone;
A fish, a ship, on both we seize.
Of three if we the lordship own,
Straightway we hook a fourth with ease,   140
Then is the fifth in sorry plight —
Who hath the power, has still the right;
The *What* is asked for, not the *How*.
Else know I not the seaman's art:
War, commerce, piracy, I trow,   145
A trinity, we may not part.

THE THREE MIGHTY COMRADES.

No thank and hail;
No hail and thank!
As were our cargo
Vile and rank!   150
Disgust upon
His face one sees:
The kingly wealth
Doth him displease!

MEPHISTOPHELES.

Expect ye now   155
No further pay;
For ye your share
Have taken away.

THE THREE MIGHTY COMRADES.

To pass the time,
As was but fair;   160
We all expect
An equal share.

MEPHISTOPHELES.

First range in order,
Hall on hall,
These wares so costly,   165
One and all!
And when he steps
The prize to view,

And reckons all
With judgment true,   170
He'll be no niggard;
As is meet,
Feast after feast
He'll give the fleet.
The gay birds come with morning tide;   175
Myself for them can best provide,
                    (*The cargo is removed.*)

MEPHISTOPHELES (*to* FAUST).

With gloomy look, with earnest brow
Thy fortune high receivest thou.
Thy lofty wisdom has been crowned;
Their limits shore and sea have found;   180
Forth from the shore, in swift career,
O'er the glad waves, thy vessels steer;
Speak only of thy pride of place,
Thine arm the whole world doth embrace.
Here it began; on this spot stood   185
The first rude cabin formed of wood;
A little ditch was sunk of yore
Where plashes now the busy oar.
Thy lofty thought, thy people's hand,
Have won the prize from sea and land.   190
From here, too——

FAUST.

              That accursed here!
It weighs upon me! Lend thine ear;—
To thine experience I must tell,
With thrust on thrust, what wounds my heart,
To bear it is impossible——   195
Nor can I, without shame, impart:
The old folk there above must yield;
Would that my seat those lindens were;
Those few trees not mine own, that field,
Possession of the world impair.   200
There I, wide view o'er all to take,
From bough to bough would scaffolds raise;
Would, for the prospect, vistas make,
On all that I have done to gaze;

To see at once before me brought   205
The master-work of human thought,
Where wisdom hath achieved the plan,
And won broad dwelling-place for man. —
Thus are we tortured ; — in our weal,
That which we lack, we sorely feel!   210
The chime, the scent of linden-bloom,
Surround me like a vaulted tomb.
The will that nothing could withstand,
Is broken here upon the sand :
How from the vexing thought be safe?   215
The bell is pealing, and I chafe!

MEPHISTOPHELES.

Such spiteful chance, 'tis natural,
Must thy existence fill with gall.
Who doubts it!   To each noble ear,
This clanging odious must appear;   220
This cursed ding-dong, booming loud,
The cheerful evening-sky doth shroud,
With each event of life it blends,
From birth to burial it attends,
Until this mortal life doth seem,   225
Twixt ding and dong, a vanished dream!

FAUST.

Resistance, stubborn selfishness,
Can trouble lordliest success,
Till, in deep angry pain one must
Grow tired at last of being first!   230

MEPHISTOPHELES.

Why let thyself be troubled here?
Is colonizing not thy sphere?

FAUST.

Then go, to move them be thy care!
Thou knowest well the homestead fair,
I've chosen for the aged pair —   235

MEPHISTOPHELES.

We'll bear them off, and on new ground
Set them, ere one can look around.

The violence outlived and past,
Shall a fair home atone at last.
(*He whistles shrilly.*)

The THREE *enter.*

MEPHISTOPHELES.

Come! straight fulfil the lord's behest;   240
The fleet to-morrow he will feast.

THE THREE.

The old lord us did ill requite;
A sumptuous feast is ours by right.

MEPHISTOPHELES.

What happed of old, here happens, too:
Still Naboth's vineyard meets the view.   245
(1 *Kings* xvi.)

Deep night.

LYNCEUS THE WARDER (*on the watch-tower singing*).
 Keen vision my birth-dower,
 I'm placed on this height,
 Still sworn to the watch-tower,
 The world's my delight,
 I gaze on the distant,   250
 I look on the near,
 On moon and on planet,
 On wood and the deer:
 The beauty eternal
 In all things I see;   255
 And pleased with myself
 All bring pleasure to me.
 Glad eyes, look around ye
 And gaze, for whate'er
 The sight they encounter,   260
 It still hath been fair!
(*Pause.*)

Not alone for pleasure-taking
Am I planted thus on high;
What dire vision, horror-waking,
From yon dark world scares mine eye!   265
Fiery sparkles see I gleaming

Through the lindens' twofold night;
By the breezes fanned, their beaming
Gloweth now with fiercest light!
Ah! the peaceful hut is burning;   270
Stood its moss-grown walls for years;
They for speedy help are yearning —
And no rescue, none appears!
Ah! the aged folk, so kindly,
Once so careful of the fire,   275
Now to smoke a prey, they blindly
Perish, oh, misfortune dire!
'Mid red flames, the vision dazing,
Stands the moss-hut, black and bare;
From the hell, so fiercely blazing,   280
Could we save the honest pair!
Lightning-like the fire advances,
'Mid the foliage, 'mid the branches;
Withered boughs, — they flicker, burning,
Swiftly glow, then fall; — ah me!   285
Must mine eyes, this woe discerning,
Must they so far-sighted be!
Down the lowly chapel crashes
'Neath the branches' fall and weight;
Winding now, the pointed flashes   290
To the summit climb elate.
Roots and trunks the flames have blighted;
Hollow, purple-red, they glow!

(Long pause. Song.)

Gone, what once the eye delighted,
With the ages long ago!   295

FAUST (on the balcony towards the downs).

From above what plaintive whimper?
Word and tone are here too late!
Wails my warder; me, in spirit
Grieves this deed precipitate!
Though in ruin unexpected   300
Charred now lie the lindens old,
Soon a height will be erected,
Whence the boundless to behold.

I the home shall see, enfolding
In its walls, that ancient pair,　　　　　　305
Who, my gracious care beholding,
Shall their lives end joyful there.

MEPHISTOPHELES *and* THE THREE (*below*).

Hither we come full speed.　We crave
Your pardon!　Things have not gone right!
Full many a knock and kick we gave,　　　310
They opened not, in our despite;
Then rattled we and kicked the more,
And prostrate lay the rotten door;
We called aloud with threat severe,
Yet, sooth, we found no listening ear.　　315
And as in such case still befalls,
They heard not, would not hear our calls;
Forthwith thy mandate we obeyed,
And straight for thee a clearance made.
The pair — their sufferings were light,　320
Fainting they sank, and died of fright.
A stranger, harbored there, made show
Of force, full soon was he laid low;
In the brief space of this wild fray,
From coals, that strewn around us lay,　325
The straw caught fire; 'tis blazing free,
As funeral death-pyre for the three.

FAUST.

To my commandments deaf were ye!
Exchange I wished, not robbery.
For this your wild and ruthless part; —　330
I curse it!　Share it and depart!

CHORUS.

The ancient saw still rings to-day:
Force with a willing mind obey;
If boldly thou canst stand the test,
Stake house, court, life, and all the rest!　335
(*Exeunt.*)

FAUST.

The stars their glance and radiance veil;
Smoulders the sinking fire, a gale

Fans it with moisture-laden wings,
Vapor to me and smoke it brings.
Rash mandate! — rashly, too, obeyed! —   340
What hither sweeps like spectral shade?

Midnight.

Four gray women enter.

FIRST.

My name, it is Want.

SECOND.

And mine, it is Blame.

THIRD.

My name, it is Care.

FOURTH.

Need, that is my name.

THREE (*together*).

The door is fast-bolted, we cannot get in;
The owner is wealthy, we may not within.   345

WANT.

There fade I to shadow.

BLAME.

There cease I to be.

NEED.

His visage the pampered still turneth from me.

CARE.

Ye sisters, ye cannot, ye dare not go in;
But Care through the keyhole an entrance may win.

(CARE *disappears.*)

WANT.

Sisters, gray sisters, away let us glide!   350

BLAME.

I bind myself to thee, quite close to thy side.

NEED.

And Need at your heels doth with yours blend her
        breath.*

* Noth and Tod, the German equivalents for Need and Death, form
a rhyme. As this cannot be rendered in English, I have introduced a
slight alteration in my translation.

THE THREE.

Fast gather the clouds, they eclipse star on star.
Behind there, behind, from afar, from afar,
There comes he, our brother, there cometh he —
    Death.   355

FAUST (in the palace).

Four saw I come, but only three went hence.
Of their discourse I could not catch the sense;
There fell upon mine ear a sound like breath,
Thereon a gloomy rhyme-word followed — Death;
Hollow the sound, with spectral horror fraught! 360
Not yet have I, in sooth, my freedom wrought;
Could I my pathway but from magic free,
And quite unlearn the spells of sorcery,
Stood I, oh, nature, man alone 'fore thee.
Then were it worth the trouble man to be! 365
Such was I once, ere I in darkness sought,
And curses dire, through words with error fraught,
Upon myself and on the world have brought;
So teems the air with falsehood's juggling brood,
That no one knows how them he may elude! 370
If but one day shines clear, in reason's light —
In spectral dream envelopes us the night;
From the fresh fields, as homeward we advance —
There croaks a bird : what croaks he? some mischance!
Ensnared by superstition, soon and late; 375
As sign and portent, it on us doth wait —
By fear unmanned, we take our stand alone;
The portal creaks, and no one enters, — none.

(Agitated.)

Is some one here?

CARE.

The question prompteth, yes!

FAUST.

What art thou, then?

CARE.

Here, once for all, am I. 380

FAUST.

Withdraw thyself!

CARE.

My proper place is this.

FAUST

(*first angry, then appeased.   Aside*).

Take heed, and speak no word of sorcery.

CARE.

Though by outward ear unheard,
By my moan the heart is stirred;
And in ever-changeful guise,   385
Cruel force I exercise;
On the shore and on the sea,
Comrade dire hath man in me,
Ever found, though never sought,
Flattered, cursed, so have I wrought.   390
Hast thou as yet Care never known?

FAUST.

I have but hurried through the world, I own.
I by the hair each pleasure seized;
Relinquished what no longer pleased,
That which escaped me I let go,   395
I've craved, accomplished, and then craved again;
Thus through my life I've stormed — with might and
    main,
Grandly, with power, at first; but now, indeed,
It goes more cautiously, with wiser heed.
I know enough of earth, enough of men;   400
The view beyond is barred from mortal ken;
Fool, who would yonder peer with blinking eyes,
And of his fellows dreams above the skies!
Firm let him stand, the prospect round him scan,
Not mute the world to the true-hearted man.   405
Why need he wander through eternity?
What he can grasp, that only knoweth he.
So let him roam adown earth's fleeting day;
If spirits haunt, let him pursue his way;
In joy or torment ever onward stride,   410
Though every moment still unsatisfied!

CARE.

To him whom I have made mine own
All profitless the world hath grown:
Eternal gloom around him lies;
For him suns neither set nor rise;   415
With outward senses perfect, whole,
Dwell darknesses within his soul;
Though wealth he owneth, ne'ertheless
He nothing truly can possess.
Weal, woe, become mere phantasy;   420
He hungers 'mid satiety;
Be it joy or be it sorrow,
He postpones it till the morrow;
Of the future thinking ever,
Prompt for present action never.   425

FAUST.

Forbear!   Thou shalt not come near me!
I will not hear such folly.   Hence!
Avaunt!   This evil litany
The wisest even might bereave of sense.

CARE.

Shall he come or go?   He ponders;—   430
All resolve from him is taken;
On the beaten path he wanders,
Groping on as if forsaken.
Deeper still himself he loses,
Everything his sight abuses,   435
Both himself and others hating,
Taking breath — and suffocating,
Without life — yet scarcely dying,
Not despairing — not relying.
Rolling on without remission: 440
Loathsome ought, and sad permission,
Now deliverance, now vexation,
Semi-sleep — poor recreation,
Nail him to his place and wear him,
And at last for hell prepare him.   445

FAUST.

Unblessèd spectres! Ye mankind have so
Treated a thousand times, their thoughts deranging;
E'en uneventful days to mar ye know,
Into a tangled web of torment changing!
'Tis hard, I know, from demons to get free,   450
The mighty spirit-bond by force untying;
Yet Care, I never will acknowledge thee,
Thy strong in-creeping, potency defying.

CARE.

Feel it then now; as thou shalt find
When with a curse from thee I've wended: 455
Through their whole lives are mortals blind —
So be thou, Faust, ere life be ended!

(She breathes on him.)

FAUST (blind).

Deeper and deeper night is round me sinking;
Only within me shines a radiant light.
I haste to realize, in act, my thinking;   460
The master's word, that only giveth might.
Up, vassals, from your couch! my project bold,
Grandly completed, now let all behold!
Seize ye your tools; your spades, your shovels ply;
The work laid down, accomplish instantly!   465
Strict rule, swift diligence — these twain
The richest recompense obtain.
Completion of the greatest work demands
One guiding spirit for a thousand hands.

Great fore-court of the Palace.

Torches.

MEPHISTOPHELES (as overseer leading the way).

This way! this way! Come on! come on!   470
Ye Lemures, loose of tether,
Of tendon, sinew, and of bone,
Half natures, patched together!

LEMURES (*in chorus*).

At thy behest we're here at hand;
Thy destined aim half guessing —   475
It is that we a spacious land
May win for our possessing.
Sharp-pointed stakes we bring with speed,
Long chains wherewith to measure,
But we've forgotten why, indeed,   480
To call us was thy pleasure.

MEPHISTOPHELES.

No artist-toil we need to-day;
Sufficeth your own measure here:
At his full length the tallest let him lay!
Ye others round him straight the turf uprear;   485
As for our sires was done of yore,
An oblong square delve ye once more.
Out of the palace to the narrow home —
So at the last the sorry end must come!

LEMURES

(*digging, with mocking gestures*).

In youth when I did live and love,   490
Methought, it was very sweet!
Where frolic rang and mirth was rife,
Thither still sped my feet.

Now with his crutch hath spiteful age
Dealt me a blow full sore: 495
I stumbled o'er a yawning grave,
Why open stood the door!

FAUST

(*comes forth from the palace, groping his way by the
door-posts*).

How doth the clang of spades delight my soul!
For me my vassals toil, the while
Earth with itself they reconcile,   500
The waves within their bounds control,
And gird the sea with steadfast zone —

MEPHISTOPHELES (*aside*).

And yet for us dost work alone,

While thou for dam and bulwark carest;
Since thus for Neptune thou preparest,   505
The water-fiend, a mighty fête;
Before thee naught but ruin lies;
The elements are our allies;
Onward destruction strides elate.

FAUST.

Inspector!

MEPHISTOPHELES.

  Here.

FAUST.

     As many as you may,   510
Bring crowds on crowds to labor here;
Then by reward and rigor cheer;
Persuade, entice, give ample pay!
Each day be tidings brought me at what rate
The moat extends which here we excavate.   515

MEPHISTOPHELES (half aloud).

They speak, as if to me they gave
Report, not of a moat — but of a grave.*

FAUST.

A marsh along the mountain chain
Infecteth what's already won;
Also the noisome pool to drain —   520
My last best triumph then were won:
To many millions space I thus should give,
Though not secure, yet free to toil and live;
Green fields and fertile; men, with cattle blent,
Upon the newest earth would dwell content,   525
Settled forthwith upon the firm-based hill,
Uplifted by a valiant people's skill;
Within, a land like Paradise; outside,
E'en to the brink, roars the impetuous tide,
And as it gnaws, striving to enter there,   530
All haste, combined, the damage to repair.

* The play of words contained in the original cannot be reproduced
in translation, the German for moat being Graben, and for grave Grab.

Yea, to this thought I cling, with virtue rife,
Wisdom's last fruit, profoundly true:
Freedom alone he earns as well as life,
Who day by day must conquer them anew.   535
So girt by danger, childhood bravely here,
Youth, manhood, age, shall dwell from year to year;
Such busy crowds I fain would see,
Upon free soil stand with a people free;
Then to the moment might I say: 540
Linger awhile, so fair thou art!
Nor can the traces of my earthly day
Through ages from the world depart!
In the presentiment of such high bliss,
The highest moment I enjoy — 'tis this.   545
    (FAUST *sinks back, the* LEMURES *lay hold of him
       and lay him upon the ground.*)

MEPHISTOPHELES.

Him could no pleasures sate, no joys appease,
So wooed he ever changeful phantasies;
The last worst empty moment to retain,
E'en to the last, the sorry wretch was fain.
Me who so stoutly did withstand —   550
Time conquers, — lies the old man on the sand!
The clock stands still —

CHORUS.
      Stands still, no sound is heard;
The index falls —

MEPHISTOPHELES.
    It falls, 'tis finished now.

CHORUS.
Yes, it is past!

MEPHISTOPHELES.
    Past, 'tis a stupid word.
Why past?   555
Past and pure nothingness are one, I trow.
Of what avail creation's ceaseless play?
Created things forthwith to sweep away?
"There, now 'tis past." — 'Tis past, what may it mean?
It is as good as if it ne'er had been,   560

And yet as if it Being did possess,
Still in a circle it doth ceaseless press:
I should prefer the Eternal — Emptiness.

[*BURIAL.*]

LEMUR (*solo*).

Who hath the house so badly built,
With shovel and with spade?   565

LEMURES (*in chorus*).

For thee, sad guest, in hempen vest,
'Tis all too deftly made.

LEMUR (*solo*).

Who furnished hath so ill the place?
Chair, table, where are they?

LEMURES (*in chorus*).

Short was the let; there came apace   570
New claimants, day by day.

MEPHISTOPHELES.

There lies the body, would the spirit flee,
I'd show him speedily the blood-signed scroll —
Yet they've so many methods, woe is me,
To cheat the devil now of many a soul!   575
On the old way one is not sure;
Upon the new we're not commended
Else had I done it unattended,
Assistants must I now procure.
In all things we're in evil plight!   580
Transmitted usage, ancient right —
In these the time for confidence is past.
With the last breath once sped the soul away;
And like the nimblest mouse, I watched my prey;
Snap! Locked within my claws I held it fast;   585
Now she delays, nor will the dismal cell,
The loathsome body, leave, though reft of life,
The elements, in ceaseless strife,
Her, in the end, disgracefully expel.
For days and hours I've plagued myself ere now; — 590
Abides the sorry question; — when? where? how?

Old death has lost his power, once swift and strong;
If dead or no? in doubt we tarry long;
On rigid members oft I've lustful gazed ;   594
'Twas but a feint, it stirred, once more itself upraised !

(Fantastic gestures of conjuration.)

Come swiftly on !   Double your speed ; no pause !
Lords of the straight, lords of the crooked horn !
Chips of the ancient block, true devils born,
Hither bring ye forthwith Hell's murky jaws.
Hell, to be sure, full many jaws may claim ;   600
Which gape as rank enjoins, and dignity ;
But we however in this final game,
Not so particular henceforth will be.

(The ghastly jaws of Hell open on the left.)

Clatter the corner-teeth ; the fire-stream whirling,
The vault's abyss doth overflow,   605
And through the background-smoke up-curling
The town of flame I see in endless glow ;
Up to the very teeth the ruddy billow dashes ;
The damned, salvation hoping, swim amain,
Them in his jaws the huge hyæna crashes,   610
Then they retrace their path of fiery pain.
In nooks fresh horrors lurk to scare the sight,
In narrowest space supremest agony :
Full well ye do, thus sinners to affright,
They hold it but for dream, deceit and lie.   615

(To the stout devils, with short straight horns.)

Now, paunchy slaves, with cheeks that hotly burn,
On hellish brimstone richly fed, ye glow,
Clumsy and short, with necks that never turn —
For gleam like phosphor-light, watch here below :
It is the soul, Psyche, with soaring wing ;   620
The wings pluck off, so 'tis a sorry worm.
First with my seal I'll stamp the ugly thing,
Then off with it to fiery whirling-storm !

Mark ye the lower regions duly,
Ye bladders ! 'tis your duty so !   625
If there she likes to harbor, — truly,
We cannot accurately know ;

She in the navel loves to bide:
Take heed, lest from you thence away she glide!

(To the lean devils, with long crooked horns.)

Buffoons, ye fuglemen, a giant crew,   630
Grasp in the air, still clutch without repose,
With outstretched arms, claws sharp and pliant, too,
The fluttering, fleeing creature to enclose!
In her old home she rests uneasily,
Genius aspires, it fain would soar on high.   635

(Glory from above, on the right.)

THE HEAVENLY HOST.

Follow, ye envoys blest,
Leave, brood of heaven, your rest,
Earthward to steer:
Sinners do ye forgive,
Dust cause ye now to live!   640
Floating on outspread wing
Through nature's sphere,
Kindliest traces bring
Of your career!

MEPHISTOPHELES.

Discordant tones I hear, an odious noise   645
Comes with unwelcome daylight from above:
A mawkish whimper, fit for girls and boys,
Such as a canting taste doth still approve.
Ye know how we, in hours with curses fraught,
Planned the destruction of the human race: 650
The most atrocious product of our thought
In their devotion finds a fitting place.

They come, the fools, in hypocritic guise!
Full many a soul from us they've snatch'd away —
With our own weapons warring 'gainst us, they   655
Are devils also, only in disguise.
Here your defeat eternal shame would bring;
On to the grave, and to the margin cling!

CHORUS OF ANGELS (*scattering roses*).

Roses, with dazzling sheen,
Balsam outpouring!   660

Float heaven and earth between,
Sweet life restoring!
Branchlets with plumy wing,
Buds softly opening
Hasten to blow!   665
Burst into verdure, Spring,
Purple and green!
To him who sleeps below,
Paradise bring!

MEPHISTOPHELES (*to the Satans*).

Why duck and shrink? Is this hell's wonted way? 670
Stand firm, and let them scatter to and fro.
Back to his place each fool!   Imagine they,
Forsooth, with such a pretty flowery show,
To cover the hot devils, as with snow?
They'll shrink and shrivel where your breathings play.

Blow now, ye Blowers!   Hold! not quite so fast! 676
Pales the whole bevy 'neath your fiery blast.
Not quite so fiercely!   Mouth and nostril close!
Your breathing now too strongly blows.
O that ye never the just mean will learn!   680
That shrivels not alone, 'twill scorch and burn.

Floating they come, with poisonous flames and clear;
Stand firm against them, press together here! —

Force is extinguished, courage all is spent;
A strange alluring glow the devils scent.   685

ANGELS.

Blossoms, with rapture crowned,
Flames fraught with gladness,
Love they diffuse around,
Banishing sadness,
As the heart may: 690
Words, blessed truth that tell,
Give, by their potent spell,
Spirits eterne to dwell
In endless day!

MEPHISTOPHELES.

A curse upon the idiot band!   695
Upon their heads the Satans stand!

Tail foremost down the hellward path
Plunge round and round the clumsy host.
Enjoy your well-earned fiery bath!
But, for my part, I'll keep my post.   700

(*Striking aside the hovering roses.*)

Off, will o' the wisp!   How bright soe'er thy ray,
Captured, thou'rt but an odious, pulpy thing;
Why flutterest?   Wilt vanish, straight away!—
Like pitch and brimstone to my neck doth cling?

ANGELS (*chorus*).

Doth aught thy nature mar?   705
Cease to endure it;
If 'gainst thy soul it war,
Must ye abjure it;
If to press in it try,
Quell it right valiantly!   710
'Tis love the loving-one
Leadeth on high.

MEPHISTOPHELES.

I'm all aflame, head, heart, and liver burn—
An over-devilish element,
Than hellish fire more sharp by far!   715
Hence ye so mightily lament,
Unhappy lovers, who, when scorned ye are,
After your sweethearts still your necks must turn.

Thus, too, with me, what draws my head aside?
Them have I not to deadly war defied?   720
My fiercest hate their aspect waked of yore;
Hath something alien pierced me through and through?
These gracious youths, them am I fain to view!—
What now restrains me that I curse no more?
And if befooled I now should be,   725
Who may henceforth " the fool " be styled?—
The rascals, whom I hate, for me
Too lovely are, I fairly am beguiled!

Sweet children, tell me, to the race
Belong ye not of Lucifer?   730
So fair ye seem, you I would fain embrace!

At the right moment ye appear;
So pleasant 'tis, so natural, as though
I you had seen a thousand times before,
So lustfully alluring now ye show.   735
With every look your beauty charms me more!
O nearer come!   O grant me but one glance!

ANGEL.

We come, why dost thou shrink as we advance?
So, if thou canst, abide; go not away.
(*The angels hover round, and occupy the entire space.*)

MEPHISTOPHELES

(who is pressed into the proscenium).
As spirits damned we're blamed by you —   740
Yourselves are yet the sorcerers true,
For man and maid ye lead astray. —
A cursed adventure this, I trow!
Is this love's element?   My frame
In fire is plunged, I scarcely now   745
Feel on my neck the scorching flame! —

Ye hover to and fro; with pinions furled
Float downward, after fashion of the world
Move your sweet limbs; in sooth, that earnest style
Becomes you, yet, for once, I fain would see you smile;
That were for me a rapture unsurpassed, —   751
A glance, I mean, like that which lovers cast:
A slight turn of the mouth, so is it done. —
Thee, tall and stately youth, most dearly thee I prize;
But ill beseemeth thee that priestly guise,   755
Give me one loving glance, I crave but one!
Ye might, with decency, less clothed appear,
O'er modest in such lengthened drapery. —
They wheel around, to see them in the rear!
All too enticing are the rogues for me!   760

CHORUS OF ANGELS.

Love now with lustrous ray
Thy fires reveal!
Those to remorse a prey
Truth's power can heal;

No longer evil's thrall,   765
Joyful and blest,
One with the All-in-all,
Henceforth they rest!

MEPHISTOPHELES (*collecting himself*).

How is't with me?   The man entire, like Job,
Must loathe himself, cleft through with boil on boil,—
Yet triumphs, too, after the first recoil,   771
If he his inward nature fairly probe,
And in himself confides and in his kin:
Saved are the noble devil parts within.
This love attack he casts upon the skin,—   775
Burnt out already are the cursed flames,
And, one and all, I curse you, as the occasion claims!

CHORUS OF ANGELS.

Whom ye with hallowed glow,
Pure fires, o'erbrood,
Blest in love's overflow,   780
Lives with the good.
Singing with voices clear,
Soar from beneath;
Pure is the atmosphere,
Breathe, spirit, breathe!   785

(*They rise, bearing with them the immortal part of*
FAUST.)

MEPHISTOPHELES (*looking around*).

How is it?   Whither are they gone?
Me have ye cozened, young things though ye be!
They with their booty now are heavenward flown.
Therefore they nibbled at this grave!   From me
A great rare prize they've captured: the high soul, 790
That pledged itself to me with written scroll,—
This have they filched away, right cunningly!
From whom shall I now seek redress?
Who can secure my well-earned right?
In thine old days thou'rt cheated!   Yet confess,   795
Thou hast deserved it, art in sorry plight;
Mismanaged have I in disgraceful sort,
Vast outlay shamefully away have thrown;

The devil's sense, though seasoned well, the sport
Of common lust!—a love absurd I own.   800
And if the shrewd old devil chose
Himself to busy with this childish freak,
Not small the foolishness, the truth to speak,
Which him hath thus o'ermastered at the close.

*Mountain defiles, Forest, Rock, Wilderness.
Holy Anchorites, dispersed up the hill, stationed
among the clefts.*

CHORUS and ECHO.

Forests are waving here,   805
Rocks their huge fronts uprear,
Roots round each other coil,
Stems thickly crowd the soil;
Wave gusheth after wave,
Shelter yields deepest cave;   810
Lions, in silence round
Tamely that rove,
Honor the hallowed ground,
Refuge of love.

PATER ECSTATICUS.

(floating up and down).

Joy's everlasting fire,   815
Love's glow of pure desire,
Pang of the seething breast,
Rapture, a hallowed guest!
Darts, pierce me through and through,
Lances, my flesh subdue,   820
Clubs, me to atoms dash,
Lightnings, athwart me flash,
That all the worthless may
Pass like a cloud away,
While shineth from afar   825
Love's germ, a deathless star.

PATER PROFUNDUS.

(Lower region.)

As the rock-chasm, sheer descending,
On chasm resteth more profound,
As thousand sparkling streamlets blending,
Foam in the torrent's headlong bound;   830

As soars, the realm of air invading,
The stem, impelled by inward strain;
So love, almighty, all-pervading,
Doth all things mould, doth all sustain.

A roaring that the heart appalleth 835
Sounds as if shook the wood-crowned steep;
Yet, lovely in its plashing, falleth
The wealth of water to the deep,
Refreshment to the valley bearing;
The atmosphere, with poison fraught, 840
The lightning cleareth, wildly flaring,
Whose deadly flash dire ruin brought —
Love's heralds these, His purpose telling
Who, ever-working, us surrounds.
Come, holy fire, within me dwelling, 845
Where, tortured in the senses' bounds,
Fetters of pain my soul enclosing,
Hold it immured in rayless gloom!
O God, my troubled thoughts composing,
My needy heart do thou illume! 850

PATER SERAPHINUS.
(*Middle region.*)

Through the pine-trees' waving tresses,
What bright cloud floats high and higher?
What it shrouds my spirit guesses!
Soars from earth and youthful choir.

CHORUS OF BLESSED BOYS.

Whither, father, are we hieing? 855
Tell us, kind one, who are we?
Happy are we, upward flying;
Unto all 'tis bliss to be!

PATER SERAPHINUS.

Boys, ere soul or sense could waken,
Ye were born at midnight hour; 860
From your parents straightway taken,
For the angels a sweet dower.
You a loving one embraces,
This ye feel — then hither fare!

But of earth's rude paths no traces,   865
Blessed ones, your spirits bear.
In the organ now descending
Of my worldly, earth-born, eyes;
Use them, thus thy need befriending —
View the sphere that round you lies: 870

    (*He takes them into himself.*)

There are trees; there rocks up-soaring;
Headlong there the flood doth leap;
Cleaves the torrent, loudly roaring,
Shorter passage to the deep.

     BLESSED BOYS (*from within*).

Grand the scene, but fear awaking: —   875
Desolate the spot and drear,
Us with dread and horror shaking.
Hold us not, kind father, here!

     PATER SERAPHINUS.

Rise to higher spheres, and higher!
Unobserved your growth, yet sure,   880
As God's presence doth inspire
Strength, by laws eternal, pure.
This the spirit's nurture, stealing
Through the ether's depths profound:
Love eternal, self-revealing,   885
Sheds beatitude around.

    CHORUS OF BLESSED BOYS
     (*circling round the highest summit*).

 Through ether winging,
 Hands now entwine,
 Joyfully singing
 With feelings divine!   890
 Taught by the Deity,
 Trust in his grace;
 Whom ye adore shall ye
 See face to face!

ANGELS

(hovering in the higher atmosphere, bearing the immortal part of FAUST).

Saved is this noble soul from ill,   895
  Our spirit-peer.   Whoever
Strives forward with unswerving will, —
  Him can we aye deliver;
And if with him celestial love
Hath taken part, — to meet him   900
Come down the angels from above;
  With cordial hail they greet him.

THE YOUNGER ANGELS.

Roses, from fair hands descending,
Holy, penitent, and pure,
Our high mission gladly ending,   905
Helped our conquest to secure,
Making ours this spirit-treasure.
Demons shrank, in sore displeasure,
Devils fled, as we assailed them,
Hell's accustomed torture failed them,   910
They by pangs of love were riven;
The old Satan-master even,
Piercèd was by sharp annoyance.
Conquered have we! shout with joyance!

THE MORE PERFECT ANGELS.

Sad 'tis for us to bear   915
Spirit earth-encumbered;
Though of asbest he were,
Yet is he numbered
Not with the pure.   For where
Worketh strong spirit-force,   920
Elements blending,
No angel may divorce
Natures thus tending
Of twain to form but one;
Parts them God's love, alone,   925
Their union ending.

THE YOUNGER ANGELS.

Mistlike, with movement rife
Rock-summits veiling,

Near us a spirit-life
Upwards is sailing;   930
Now grow the vapors clear;
Yonder blest boys appear,
In chorus blending; .
They from earth's pressure free
Circle united;   935
Still upward tending,
In the new spring with glee
Bathe they delighted:
Here let him then begin,
Yet fuller life to win,   940
With these united.

BLESSED BOYS.

Him as a chrysalis
Joyful receive we:
Pledge of angelic bliss
In him achieve we.   945
Loosen the flakes of earth
That still enfold him!
Great through the heavenly birth,
And fair, now behold him.

DOCTOR MARIANUS

(in the highest, purest cell).

Here is the prospect free,   950
The soul subliming.
Yonder fair forms I see,
Heavenward they're climbing;
In starry wreath is seen,
Lofty and tender,   955
Midmost the heavenly Queen,
Known by her splendor.
(Enraptured.)
In thy tent of azure hue,
Queen supremely reigning,
Let me now thy secret view,   960
Vision high obtaining!
With the holy joy of love,
In man's breast, whatever
Lifts the soul to thee above,
Kind one, foster ever!   965

All invincible we feel,
If our arm thou claimest;
Suddenly assuaged our zeal
If our breast thou tamest.
Virgin, pure from taint of earth,   970
Mother, we adore thee,
With the Godhead one by birth,
Queen, we bow before thee!

   Cloudlets are pressing,
   Gently around her;   975
   Her knee caressing
   Cloudlets surround her; —
   Penitents are they;
   Ether inhaling,
   Their sins bewailing.   980

Passionless and pure, from thee
Hath it not been taken,
That poor frail ones may to thee
Come, with trust unshaken.
In their weakness snatched away,   985
Hard it is to save them;
By their own strength rend who may
Fetters that enslave them?
Glide on slippery ground the feet
Swiftly downward sailing!   990
Whom befool not glances sweet,
Flattery's breath inhaling?
   (Mater Gloriosa *soars forward.*)

CHORUS OF FEMALE PENITENTS.

   To realms eternal
   Upward art soaring;
   Peerless, supernal,   995
   Hear our imploring,
   Thy grace adoring.
      (*St. Luke* vii. 36.)

MAGNA PECCATRIX.

By the love, warm tears outpouring,
Laving as with balsam sweet,

Pharisaic sneers ignoring,   1000
Of thy godlike Son the feet;
By the vase, rich odor breathing,
Lavishing its costly store;
By the locks, that gently wreathing,
Dried his holy feet once more —   1005

MULIER SAMARITANA (*St. John* iv.)

By the well, whereto were driven
Abram's flocks in ancient days;
By the cooling draught thence given,
Which the Saviour's thirst allays;
By the fountain, still outsending   1010
Thence its waters, far and wide,
Overflowing, never-ending,
Through all worlds it pours its tide —

MARIA AEGYPTIACA (*Acta Sanctorum*).

By the hallowed grave, whose portal
Closed upon the Lord of yore;   1015
By the arm, unseen by mortal,
Back which thrust me from the door;
By my penance, slowly fleeting,
Forty years amid the waste;
By the blessèd farewell greeting,   1020
Which upon the sand I traced —

THE THREE.

Thou, unto the greatly sinning,
Access who dost not deny,
By sincere repentance winning
Bliss throughout eternity,   1025
So from this good soul thy blessing,
Who but once itself forgot,
Sin who knew not, while transgressing,
Gracious One, withhold thou not!

UNA POENITENTIUM

(*formerly named* GRETCHEN, *pressing towards her*).
Incline, oh, incline,   1030
All others excelling,
In glory are dwelling,
Unto my bliss thy glance benign!

The loved one, ascending,
His long trouble ending,
Comes back, he is mine! 1035

BLESSED BOYS.

(*They approach, hovering in a circle.*)
Mighty of limb, he towers
E'en now above us,
He for this care of ours
Richly will love us. 1040
Dying, ere we could reach
Earth's pain or pleasure;
What he hath learned he'll teach
In ample measure.

A PENITENT

(*formerly named* GRETCHEN.)
Encircled by the choirs of heaven, 1045
Scarcely himself the stranger knows;
Scarce feels the existence newly given,
So like the heavenly host he grows.
See, how he every band hath riven!
From earth's old vesture freed at length, 1050
Now clothed upon by garb of heaven,
Shines forth his pristine youthful strength,
To guide him, be it given to me;
Still dazzles him the new-born day.

MATER GLORIOSA.

Ascend, thine influence feeleth he, 1055
He'll follow on thine upward way.

DOCTOR MARIANUS

(*adoring, prostrate on his face.*)
Penitents, her Saviour-glance
Gratefully beholding
To beatitude advance,
Still new powers unfolding! 1060
Thine each better thought shall be
To thy service given!
Holy Virgin, gracious be,
Mother, Queen of Heaven!

CHORUS MYSTICUS.

All of mere transient date   1065
As symbol showeth;
Here, the inadequate
To fulness groweth;
Here the ineffable
Wrought is in love;   1070
The ever-womanly
Draws us above.

ANNOTATIONS

SECOND PART OF FAUST.

ON the first appearance of the "Helena," Goethe declared with reference to the completion of "Faust," that in the second part the hero must be introduced into a higher sphere, and be brought into social relations of a more elevated character. This purpose is manifest in each act of the second part. It may be well, however, before entering upon the study of the poem, to bear in mind that Goethe repudiated the notion that "the rich, varied, and highly diversified life which he has brought to view in Faust is strung upon the slender thread of one pervading idea." His utterance with reference to "Helena" is, in a certain degree, applicable to the other scenes of the drama; "it forms," he says, "an independent little world, and is only connected with the whole by a slight reference to what precedes and follows;" "the only matter of importance in such compositions," he adds, "is, that the single masses should be clear and significant, while the whole remains incommensurable; and even on that account, like an unsolved problem, constantly lures mankind to study it again and again." *

ACT I.
A Pleasing Landscape.

Faust's remorseful agony, and his resolve to venture his life for the deliverance of Gretchen, as portrayed in the concluding scene of the first part, indicate that the voice of conscience is not stifled in his soul. In the opening scene of the second part he is represented as coming under the healing influences of time and of nature, typified by Ariel and the Elfin choir. They allay the anguish of remorse; soothe and tranquillize the troubled spirit; summon him to cast aside the shell of sleep, and to return to the active duties of life. The break of day, heralded by the rising sun, symbolizes the new life-career upon which he is about to enter, inspired by the high resolve.

"Aye to press on to being's sovereign height."

The Imperial Court.

The visit of Mephistopheles to the imperial court, suggested by the old Faust-book, affords Goethe the opportunity of exhibiting, in the

---

* "Conversations of Goethe with Eckermann" (Bohn Trans., p. 507).

reckless expenditure which there prevails, while the people perish for lack of food and of justice, the evils which threaten the fall of an empire, together with their cause.

"In the Emperor," he said, "I have endeavored to represent a prince who has all the necessary qualities for losing his land, and at last succeeds in so doing. He does not concern himself about the welfare of his kingdom and his subjects; he only thinks of himself and how he can amuse himself from day to day. The land is without law and justice; the judge himself is on the side of the criminals; the most atrocious crimes are committed without check and with impunity. The army is without pay and without discipline. . . . . The state treasury is without money. . . . . In the Emperor's own household things are no better. . . . . The councillor of state wishes to remonstrate with his majesty upon all these evils, and advises as to their remedy; but the gracious sovereign is unwilling to lend his sublime ear to anything so disagreeable; he prefers amusing himself. Here now is the true element of Mephisto, who quickly supplants the former fool, and is at once at the side of the Emperor as new fool and counsellor." *   The greatest embarrassment is caused by the want of money, which Mephistopheles promises to provide. This theme continues through the masquerade.

The Carnival Masquerade.

In this scene a series of groups is introduced, representing manifold aspects of human society, and intended possibly to exhibit the progress of civilization, together with the agencies by which it is retarded or advanced. It also serves to introduce the paper-money device, which forms the subject of the following scene.

The first group brings before the eyes some features of the golden age, when the human race, free from selfishness and greed, lived together in joyous liberty; the peace and plenty, the richness of imagination and love, which characterized that idyllic period, are aptly symbolized by the Olive-branch, the Wheat-sheaf, the Fancy-nosegay, and the Budding Roses, in the hands of the Florentine Garden-girls.

In the succeeding group of the Mother and Daughter, this picture of primeval simplicity is contrasted with life under a more conventional aspect. As civilization advances the fruits of the field no longer suffice for human nourishment. Fishermen and Bird-catchers are introduced, and the Wood-cutters appear as representatives of manly toil. It is not difficult to discern the social classes represented by the Pulcinelli and the Parasites, while the Drunken Man exhibits the debasing influence of sensual indulgence.

The figures of Grecian mythology, which next appear, represent those spiritual forces and qualities which permanently manifest themselves in civilized society, under all its various aspects. The Graces, through the courteous interchange of kindly aid, restore to life its freedom and its charm. The Fates are the representatives of law, of just measure and established order; while the Furies, appearing not as the avengers but as the authors of crime, under the guise of evil passions, calumny, and slander, are the destroyers alike of public and domestic peace.

In order to bridle these unruly elements, firm Authority is needed, and accordingly one of the most significant groups is next introduced. A living Colossus symbolizes the State, guided by Prudence, while delusive Hope, and desponding Fear, two of the most potent disturbers of public tranquillity, walk chained on either side; Victoria, queen of all activities, is enthroned upon the summit.

* Conversations of Goethe with Eckermann.

The accompanying figure of Zoilo-Thersites (a combination formed from the Thersites of the Iliad and Zoilus, a grammarian of the third century before Christ, known as the defamer of Homer) represents the spirit of envious detraction, manifested more especially in public life.

Drawn by dragons and guided by the Boy-Charioteer, Faust appears as the god of wealth, spiritual as well as material, while Mephistopheles is introduced, seated upon the chariot, as Avarice. By means of a magic lantern the picture of the dragon-team has passed in rapid flight over and through the crowd.

Düntzer sees in Faust the symbol of prosperity as the result of well-directed activity in the state, while art, which is closely connected with it, which reconciles the useful and the beautiful, and is itself a source of national wealth, is typified by the Boy-Charioteer; as the spirit of poetry, he is the first appearance of the genius subsequently embodied in Euphorion. Of the latter, Goethe is reported to have said, " he is not a human, but an allegorical being. In him is personified Poetry, which is bound to neither time, place, nor person. The same spirit who afterwards chooses to be Euphorion, appears here as the Boy-Charioteer, and is so far like a spectre, that he can be present everywhere and at all times."

Poetry and art, which prepare for life its richest embellishments, must seek their inspiration far from the bustle of resort; the Boy-Charioteer is accordingly dismissed by Plutus, that " in solitude he may create his own world; " thither, to the realms of The Mothers, he will soon be followed by Faust himself. The relation between Goethe and Karl August, the Grand Duke of Weimar, are supposed to be represented in those between the Boy-Charioteer and Plutus. The interpretation of the allegory in its details must be left to the penetration of the reader; suffice it to say that therein is portrayed the vulgar crowd, who, incapable of appreciating the beautiful and the true, mistake appearance for reality, and are unable to reach the idea which underlies it. By them gold is prized as the means of purchasing the frivolous enjoyments of sense, and thus, instead of raising the national life to a higher level, it becomes a source of immorality and corruption. In the final group the Emperor appears in the mask of Pan, "the All of the world," reminding us of Louis XIVth's celebrated exclamation : " The state, it is I." The Fauns, Satyrs, Gnomes and Giants, supposed by some commentators to symbolize the privileged classes attendant upon royalty, are represented by his courtiers. The Emperor is conducted to the fount of gold; the fiery catastrophe may be regarded as a delusive magic show, which has its counterparts in the old Faust-book. It probably symbolizes the revolution caused by misgovernment, and may have been designed by Faust as a warning to the pleasure-loving Emperor. The moral of the show is embodied in the words of the Herald.

> " O youth, O youth, and wilt thou never
> To joy assign its fitting bound ?
> O Majesty, with reason never
> Will thy omnipotence be crowned ? "

The Pleasure Garden.

The paper-money device, the subject of this scene, shows that a corrupt society is stimulated by the acquisition of wealth, not to the accomplishment of noble deeds, but to idleness and self-indulgence. The sudden influx of riches, instead of being employed in making available, through labor and skill, the undeveloped resources of the country, tends to relax the energies of the nation, and thus prepares the way for the dangers which threaten it, as represented in the fourth act.

Dark Gallery.   (The Mothers.)

Goethe, when asked by Eckermann for an explanation of this scene, replied, "I can only reveal that I found it mentioned in Plutarch, that in Grecian antiquity certain goddesses were revered under the name of 'The Mothers.'" These Mothers were old Pelasgian Nature-deities, who were superseded by the great goddesses, Demeter and Persephone.

Of special significance in this connection is the following passage from Plutarch ("De Defect.," chap. 22). "There are 183 worlds; they were arranged in the figure of a triangle, and every side contained sixty worlds, the remaining three occupy the corners; in this order they gently touch each other, and ceaselessly revolve as in a dance. The space within the triangle is to be regarded as a common hearth for all, and is called the field of Truth. Within lie, motionless, the causes, forms, and original images of all things, which have been and which shall be. Eternity surrounds them, from which Time, as an effluence, flows over the worlds. Human souls of transcendent excellence, obtain permission, every thousand years, to contemplate the spectacle, and the most glorious mysteries on earth are simply dreams of such contemplation."

The realm of "The Mothers" is that field of Truth; they are its imaginary guardians; the conceptions, causes, energies of all created things repose in its mysterious depths, issue thence, and are developed in time and space; it is the realm of the infinite as opposed to the finite; of the ideal as opposed to the real.

As in everything which receives new life on earth, the female principle is most in operation; these creating divinities are rightly thought of as female, and the august title of "The Mothers" may be given to them not without reason.

Faust is required to invoke Helena and Paris, in whom he recognizes the ideal impersonation of womanly and manly beauty, whose forms had been embodied in Grecian art. In order to reproduce them he must forget the region of actuality, and enter that of the Infinite and the Eternal; he must, moreover, realize in the depths of his spiritual consciousness the sentiments and ideas from which they originally sprang. This can only be accomplished by an intense effort of mental abstraction, combined with the patient study of classical antiquity. It is given to creative genius alone to unlock with its glowing key the treasury of the past, to summon thence the spirits of a bygone age, and to breathe into them the breath of life. This intellectual process is typified by Faust's descent to "The Mothers." At first he shrinks back appalled from the effort; having, however, at length entered the realm of the invisible, the contemplation of the divine ideal is for him a spiritual new-birth. The tripod appears to have a double signification, and to symbolize at the same time the original creative energy subsisting at the heart of things, and also the inspiration of genius, which is alone the source of ideal impersonation.

The Brilliantly-lighted Hall.

This and the following scene exhibit the contrast between the frivolous impulses of the courtly throng, and Faust's earnest devotion to his ideal aim. Genuine art is regarded by them simply as an amusement, and their contemplation of its masterworks is accompanied by the shallowest remarks.

Hall of the Knights.

What to the audience is merely a charming spectacle is to Faust a profound experience. His ideal, conceived in the innermost depths of his spirit, meets his enraptured gaze; with that passionate desire, which is characterized by Plato as a divine madness, he seeks to grasp it, to retain it as an enduring possession. Without this fiery enthusiasm nothing great is accomplished either in life or in art; it is, however, the beginning, not the end; perfection can be achieved only by long and patient labor; to him who thinks to hold the ideal with a sudden grasp, it vanishes in mist. Faust falls prostrate to the ground as, in the first act, at the appearance of the Earth-spirit. Now, however, he will follow the star which has arisen within him; he will prepare " the twofold realm; " the spirit-realm of antiquity, which has vanished from his consciousness, will again arise within him, and will combine with the actual to form an ideal world, over which beauty and order shall reign supreme, as symbolically portrayed in the picture of Arcadia, in the " Helena."

Act II.

Faust's Study.

Faust has seen his ideal; paralyzed by the vision he is borne sleeping by Mephistopheles to the study from which he had escaped in bygone years, and from which, lighted by Homunculus, he is speedily to issue forth in quest of Helena. The poet here symbolizes his own experience; like Faust, he drew his ideals from the depth of his inner consciousness. How earnestly he devoted himself to the study of nature, art, and antiquity, as the necessary condition for their realization, is revealed by the whole course of his biography.

During Faust's absence his chamber has remained undisturbed, and amidst its dust and mould are generated the whims and crotchets typified by the chorus of insects. Mephisto assumes Faust's furry gown; that he first shakes thence the chafers and other insects is not without significance. When the contemner of ancient authority, the Voltaire of the age, occupies the professor's chair, a revolution is at hand; the bell sounds which announces the advent of a new epoch; the walls tremble, the doors spring open, giving access to the fresh air of independent thought.

Genuine knowledge requires that careful observation and reverence for the past shall be combined with freedom from prejudice, and perfect liberty of thought; these elements are here disjoined, the former having their representatives in Wagner and his Famulus, the latter in the character of the Baccalaureus, in whom is personified, as Goethe himself said, the arrogance peculiar to youth. The conversation between him and Mephisto is a satirical comment upon the philosophy of Fichte, whose extravagant idealism found no favor with Goethe.

The Laboratory.

Antiquity was acquainted with certain small waxen figures, in the human shape, called Homunculi, which were employed by dealers in magical arts. The name also occurs in the writings of Paracelsus, which contain a curious receipt for the " *generatio Homunculorum.*" The passage is quoted by Düntzer, who adds that through the lectures of the philosopher, John Jacob Wagner, who maintained that all organisms were developed metals, the assertion was disseminated throughout Germany that chemists could succeed in producing organized bodies, and in creating men through crystallization. The name of this philosopher may have suggested to Goethe to ascribe the attempt to his Wagner. Through the co-operation of Mephistopheles he succeeds: Homunculus appears like a small human form in the phial; being a product of the understanding, without any physical attributes, he may fairly be represented as desiring incorporation. With regard to the signification of the Homunculus various interpretations have been suggested. He has been supposed to symbolize the truth that reflection and study, of which he is the product, must be associated with inspiration and genius for the accomplishment of any great master-work. By Düntzer he is regarded as the type of thoughtful, self-conscious striving after the ideal, which cannot be conquered by storm, but can be won only by sustained and patient effort. Hermann Küntzel gives a wider application to the symbol. After alluding to the Darwinian theory, that all organized beings have their origin in a primal cell, so Homunculus, he says, may be regarded as the spiritual protoplasma of the anticipated new epoch.

"As a being to whom the present is perfectly clear and transparent, the Homunculus sees into the soul of the sleeping Faust, who, enraptured by a lovely dream, beholds Leda visited by swans while she is bathing in a pleasant spot." With reference to this dream, Eckermann remarked to Goethe, "It is wonderful to me how the several parts of such a work bear upon, perfect, and sustain one another! By this dream of Leda, ' Helena ' gains its proper foundation." Goethe acquiesced, and said in reply : " Thus you will see that in these earlier acts the chords of the classic and romantic are constantly struck, so that, as on a rising ground, where both forms of poetry are brought out, and in some sort balance one another, we may ascend to ' Helena.' "*

The Classical Walpurgis-Night.

The scene is laid in the Pharsalian field where, 48 B.C., the triumph of Cæsar over Pompey put an end to the Roman republic and inaugurated a new epoch in the history of the world. It represents Faust's passionate striving after the realization of his ideal, together with the transition from lower to higher forms of being, as manifested more especially in the history of Grecian art. With these motives are associated two others, namely, the search of Mephistopheles for an appropriate form which brings out the repulsive elements in classical mythology, where supreme ugliness, in contrast with ideal beauty, has its type in the Phorkyads; and also the striving of Homunculus after organic existence.

We are presented at the opening of the scene with figures from the East, which were adopted and developed by the Greeks, the Assyrian Griffin and the Egyptian Sphinx, together with the Arimaspians, who were of Scythian origin. To these strange beings Mephistopheles introduces himself as the Old Iniquity ; he is, however, soon recognized by the Sphinxes, who tell him that he himself is the greatest riddle. While Mephistopheles feels not quite at home among these antique forms, Faust awakens to new life upon the classic soil. He inquires from the Sphinxes the way to Helena, and is referred by them to Chiron, the Centaur, the teacher of Æsculapius, who carries him to the Prophetess Manto. This venerable sybil sympathized with his striving to win the apparently impossible; she suffers him to descend through the temple of Apollo to the depths of Olympus, where Persephone sits enthroned queen of the dead. With reference to this scene Goethe is reported by Eckermann to have spoken as follows: " Then only think what is to be said on that mad night! Faust's speech to Proserpine when he would move her to give him Helena, what a speech that would be when Proserpine herself is moved to tears ! " We cannot but regret that the poet was never inspired to embody his

* " Conversations of Goethe with Eckermann."

conception, but has left its realization to the imagination of the reader.

Faust here withdraws from the scene, in order to prepare for the consummation in the following act, when, through the union between classical and mediæval culture, a new epoch is to be inaugurated.

The idea of Being and Development is now transferred to the history of the earth; in geological phenomena Goethe preferred the theory which refers to water as the chief agency in modifying the surface of the globe; alike in the moral and the material world he was opposed to everything violent and explosive; hence, when he wished to picture a period of transition under the image of a struggle between the elements, he would naturally give the victory to water and to air.

While the Sirens sing the praise of water, the soil is upheaved by an earthquake, personified by the giant Seismos. Rafael, in a picture of the imprisonment of St. Paul, has similarly represented an earthquake under the form of a powerful giant, who, with his broad shoulders presses upward through the earth. The process of transition from lower to higher forms of being, alike in nature and in history, is accompanied not unfrequently by seasons of revolution and disruption; such a period seems to be indicated by the Seismos episode, with the Pigmies and Dactyles, the slaughter of the Herons, and the subsequent attack of the avenging Cranes: it would be beyond the scope of these notes to attempt any elaborate interpretation of the scene. It is regarded by Hermann Küntzel as typifying a political insurrection; and to his work I must refer for a fuller exposition of his views. I will accordingly pass on to the moonlit bay, where the festival prepared by the Nereids indicates the transition from a period of anarchy and confusion to one of happiness and peace.

They hasten to Samothrace to bring thence the venerable Cabiri, which they carry upon the giant shield of Chelone (the ancient shell of the turtle covered with hieroglyphics). The Cabiri, according to Hermann Küntzell, indicate the religious element; they are mentioned by Strabo as primeval Pelasgian divinities, who sat in council with the greater gods; they were the mediators between the gods and men, and as such it is striking that Goethe should have introduced them as symbols of the great religions of the world; their likenesses are found only on coins and pottery; they also appeared as figures on the bowsprits of Phœnician vessels, and were supposed by the mariners to insure protection against shipwreck.

Three only of the Cabiri are brought by the Nereids and Tritons upon their hieroglyphic-covered shield; the ancient Indian, the Egyptian, and the Grecian Mythus are probably indicated. The fourth god, who was not willing to come, must be regarded as the Mosaic Monotheistic religion, which in its abhorrence of symbols would fain keep aloof from the mythological festivity of the Walpurgis-night.

The Cabiri were regarded as seven in number, which, with the introduction of the Egyptian god, was increased to eight. Four have been accounted for; the Sirens inquire "Where are the other three?" They are yet concealed in Olympus; the Buddhist, Mohammedan, and Christian religions belong to the future; they are not yet ready; and there in Olympus abides the eighth god, of whom as yet no one thinks. Goethe may be supposed to refer to his own religious conceptions, which combined the idea of a self-acting nature pervaded by the Deity, with belief in a personal God who could be apprehended by thought, and who comes into direct relation with the human soul. How strongly was Goethe possessed by the idea of the Divine love appears from the following dialogue between Eckermann and himself; the former, struck with admiration at seeing a bird which had been set free re-

turn through the window to fed its young, remarked, " Such parental
love, superior to danger and imprisonment, moved me deeply, and I
expressed my surprise to Goethe."

" Foolish man !" he replied, with a meaning smile ; " if you believed
in God you would not wonder.   Did not God inspire the bird with
this all-powerful love for its young, and did not similar impulses
pervade all animate nature, the world could not subsist. But thus
is the Divine energy everywhere diffused, and Divine love everywhere
active."

To return, however, to the Ægean Sea. The religious element having been introduced by the arrival of the Cabiri, the peaceful festival
proceeds, heralded by the Telchines of Rhodes, the mythological fire-
workers who forged the trident of Neptune.

Proteus transforms himself into a dolphin, in order to carry Homunculus to the sea ; the words which follow are of interest as bearing upon
the Darwinian theory.   Thales commends the praiseworthy desire to
commence creation at the beginning, and assures Homunculus that he
shall progress, by eternal laws, through a thousand and still a thousand
forms towards his goal, in order eventually to become a man. Thales,
the materialistic philosopher, is in error.   He regards Homunculus as
an organic, whereas he is a spiritual protoplasma. Proteus takes a
juster view of the matter, and assures him that if he once becomes a
man there will be an end of him. The true destination of ideas is their
diffusion, not their incorporation, in individual forms, where they are
liable to perish. Meanwhile appear new messengers of peace, the
love-enkindled doves sent by Paphos, the island of Galatea.

Should aught of danger threaten, in water or on land, the Pselli and
Marsè, the serpent-destroyers, draw near, to establish security and to
purify the way for the approach of Galatea.   The female element is
represented by the Nereids and the Dorides, both daughters of Nereus ;
the former strong and sturdy, resembling their father, the latter graceful and tender, like their mother Doris.   Galatea now draws near,
advancing with her innumerable host, in extended chain-circles, symbolizing the path of culture and of progress ; such spiral lines were
before indicated as described by the Paphian doves, who, in wonderful
flight learned in olden time, accompanied the chariot of the goddess.
Thus with a revolving, yet ever-advancing motion, comes Galatea, as
portrayed in Rafael's beautiful fresco on the walls of the Farnesina
Palace at Rome. The lovely sea nymph, being the successor of Aphro-
dite, the queen of beauty, her apparition forms a fitting prelude to the
Helena.

Fain would she stay to greet her aged father ; in vain ; time's onward
movement knows no pause ; her innumerable attendants, the representatives of the new epoch, festively follow in her train.   Meanwhile
the glass of Homunculus gives forth a beautiful sound, and glitters
like a flame. He feels the presence of Eros, the primeval god, the
origin of all things ; he feels the constraining power of infinite longing ; he renounces his self-existence ; his glass is shattered against the
throne of Galatea, and the ideas which constituted his essence are far
and wide diffused over the waves. It is interesting to compare the
concluding chorus, which celebrates the praise of Eros, with the final
chorus of the poem, where Divine love, symbolized as the Mater Gloriosa, is represented as the pervading, all-inspiring principle of the
universe.

ACT III.

The marriage of Faust with Helena, forming, as it does, a prominent
feature of the mediæval legend, belongs to the oldest of Goethe's con-

ceptions, a sketch of it having been brought with him to Weimar in 1775. After his Italian journey, the thought occurred to him that this element of the old legend might be employed to symbolize the union between classical and romantic poetry. In 1825 Byron's individuality and tragic fate, having supplied him with the long-sought motive for his Euphorion, the child of Helena and Faust, the type of modern poetic genius, he applied himself to the completion of the work. Goethe himself directs attention to the fundamental idea which underlies it: " It is time," he says, " that the passionate conflict between the classic and the romantic should at last be reconciled; " and adds, " the delivery of the human mind from the monkish barbarism of the fifteenth and sixteenth centuries was largely due to the extended survey then obtained over Greek and Roman literature." We are, moreover, justified, by the poet's own words, in saying that his own inward experience is embodied in this poem; that it symbolizes the union of his own spirit with classical antiquity, together with the refining of his poetic genius, the perfection of artistic form, and the spiritual new birth to which it conducted him.

Thus Helena and Faust represent the culture of two distinct world-epochs, from whose union was to spring a new form of spiritual development, wherein the depth and intensity of sentiment and other characteristics of Mediævalism were to be associated with the harmony, the moderation, the plastic clearness of conception, which formed the chief elements of Grecian art, a spirit which was to exert an enlightening and emancipating influence, not only over poetry, but over life.

This thought finds expression in the description of Arcadia, the imaginary realm over which Faust and Helena are to exercise their united sway. The state of things here described forms a striking contrast to the lawlessness and disorder portrayed in the scene at the Emperor's court, and exhibits the purifying and regenerating influences of ideal beauty, when regarded as the crowning glory of the reign of law.

Act IV.

A Mountain Ridge.

Helena's veil has wafted Faust from the imaginary realms of Arcadia and set him down on German soil; how great has been the distance thus traversed is symbolized by the seven-league boots employed by Mephistopheles to overtake him. The veil dissolves to a cloud, which, mirroring the affections of his soul, take the forms of Helena and Gretchen; art and early love are thus recognized as the ideal powers which raise the spirit above the vulgar and the mean.

Through the contemplation of ideal beauty, Faust has won for his guidance in actual life, the conception of moderation and self-restraint; an aimless activity, the alternate reeling from desire to enjoyment, these have become repulsive to him; this idea underlies the word wherein he gives expression to Goethe's idea of creation, as a process of orderly development as opposed to the Plutonic theory, symbolized by the action of Moloch and other Satanic agencies described by Mephistopheles.

Faust strives no longer after the vague and the undefined; he desires a distinct, practical aim for his activity. Mephistopheles endeavors to divert him from his purpose by the prospect of sensual enjoyment and the lure of fame; Faust, however, does not swerve from his ideal; not art, but life, is the true aim of life; to realize man's highest welfare is the problem of humanity. The sea-waves, breaking with unfettered violence upon the strand, barren themselves and causing barrenness, are the symbols of the ungoverned impulses of his early life; both shall now be restrained, and a region recovered from the lawless elements where a free people may dwell upon a free soil. Faust is no longer the type of isolated genius; he has learned the great lesson that "man is made for man," and that all efforts must be glorified by consecration to the service of humanity.

Upon the Headland.

Here the masquerade of the first act is realized in actual life; the Emperor, made apparently rich by the influx of paper money, has, in accordance with the character there attributed to him, let things take their course, till the insurrection, symbolized by the magical conflagration, has actually broken out. Faust helps to suppress it, that he may thus obtain the privilege of reclaiming a tract of land from the sea. In his description of the battle and its accompaniments, Goethe directs his irony against the admirers of Mediævalism, with its party hatreds, gross popular superstitions, and strange military parapharnalia. The three mighty men represent the more brutal aspects of war.

The Rival Emperor's Tent.

In the hour of victory the Emperor speaks proud words, and tells how he had turned his gaze inward, and has learnt through the experience of years the value of the moment. Nevertheless, in this crisis of his affairs, instead of applying himself to the establishment of good government, he forthwith augments the power of the princes, and, that they may give lustre to his court, he allows them to oppress the people by the arbitrary imposition of taxes. Goethe here exhibits the Golden Bull, by which the Emperor, Charles VI., in the Reichtag at Mainz, 1356, defined the hereditary offices of the Kurfursts. Hollow pomp and artificial ceremonialism take the place of genuine political activity. The insurrection had been promoted by the clergy, whose bigotry and rapacity are strikingly exhibited in the person of the Archbishop. We have here a picture of the political state of Germany from the days of Faust to the days of Goethe. Such a state of things offered no sphere for the high and earnest purpose of Faust, which, for its realization, must create for itself a new and appropriate sphere.

ACT V.

Open Country.

The names of Philemon and Baucis recall the ancient pair whose piety is celebrated by Ovid. "These names," said Eckermann to Goethe, "transport me to the Phrygian coast, and remind me of the famous couple of antiquity. But our scene belongs to modern days, and a Christian landscape."

"My Philemon and Baucis," said Goethe, "have nothing to do with that renowned ancient couple and the tradition connected with them. I gave this couple the names merely to elevate the characters."

The return of the wanderer to the scene of his shipwreck in bygone years shows us the magnitude of the work accomplished by Faust, in reclaiming from the now distant sea a vast area of fertile and thickly-peopled land.

The Palace.

"Faust," said Goethe to Eckermann, "when he appears in the fifth act, should, according to my design, be exactly a hundred years old; and I rather think it would be well expressly to say so in some passage." His desire to appropriate the cottage of the aged pair exemplifies the familiar experience that new desires are awakened by the consciousness of success; that the lust for power is too often generated by the possession of power. Thus Faust grows weary of being just; he cannot brook opposition. The aged pair are to be deprived of their inheritance, and to receive in compensation a new estate.

Deep Night.

Such unrestrained self-will is, however, sinful egotism, and its exercise is often attended by consequences more disastrous than were anticipated. The cottage, the chapel, and the linden-trees perish in the flames. Faust vainly laments the impatient deed, still hoping that the aged couple, in the enjoyment of their new estate, will forgive the destruction of their property; he has to learn, however, that the arrow when it has left the bow is no longer under the control of the archer. On hearing from Mephistopheles that the aged pair, together with their guest, have perished in the flames, he curses the savage execution of his command. He cannot, however, prevent that the smoke of the murderous conflagration shall shape itself into vague shadowy figures, tormenting spirits that hover round him, presageful of approaching death.

Midnight.

Faust now recognizes that he has not yet attained true freedom, perfect self-control; that imperious interference with the established order, expressed by magic, has become habitual to him; he would now fain stand face to face with the world in simple humanity, and with that very patience which had been the object of his special curse. Nevertheless he manfully fights with Care, which now seeks to embitter his last hours; he abides by his resolve to speak no magic word, no longer through self-will forcefully to interrupt the established order; and thus, though the outward power of vision is extinguished, a spiritual light arises within his soul. The fact that he does not murmur against his calamity, that he patiently bears it and elevates himself above it, in the joy of beneficial activity, reveals that his reconciliation with the moral order has been achieved.

Fore-court of the Palace.

Faust recognizes in his dying speech that genuine freedom is no external possession; that it is the permanent enfranchisement of the human spirit, which can only be achieved and maintained through constantly repeated effort. He hopes to stand with a free people upon a free soil; he recognizes that he has labored for the highest welfare of humanity, and inspired by such thoughts he can address to the moment the fateful words, " Linger awhile, so fair thou art! " In accordance with his compact, this should be his death-hour; there is here a direct allusion to his curse in the first part; " The clock stands still, the index falls " — as there indicated, his earthly career is ended.

We must now inquire into the significance of the compact, one condition of which is thus fulfilled. As the wager between the Lord and Mephistopheles had preceded the compact, Faust could not unconditionally sign away his soul. Mephistopheles was to be Faust's servant here, and in return Faust was to be surrendered to him when they met in the world beyond. Would this come to pass? That is the question. The answer depends upon whether Mephistopheles has succeeded in dragging Faust upon the downward way, or whether the higher elements of Faust's nature have eventually triumphed over the lower.

The moment which he would fain arrest finds him possessed not by sinful egotistic desires, but by aspirations in harmony with the highest moral order.

In speaking of the conclusion of "Faust," Goethe directed Eckermann's attention to the following passage : —

> "Saved is this noble soul from ill,
> Our spirit peer.   Whoever
> Strives forward with unswerving will,
> Him can we aye deliver ;
> And if with him celestial love
> Hath taken part, — to meet him
> Come down the angels from above ;
> With cordial hail they greet him."

" In these lines," said he, " is contained the key to Faust's salvation. In Faust himself there is an activity which becomes constantly higher and purer to the end, and from above there is eternal love coming to his aid.   This harmonizes perfectly with our religious views, according to which we cannot obtain heavenly bliss through our own strength alone, but with the assistance of Divine grace."

Goethe recognized that the human spirit is an imperishable essence, an ever-unfolding energy, which, like the sun, appears only to the bodily eye to set, but in reality shines on without intermission; he maintained that the best proof of our immortality is that we cannot do without it.   So Kant also named it a postulate of the practical reason, a necessary condition of our moral self-consciousness.   The traditional conceptions of heaven and hell, of devil and angels, are accepted by him as mythical symbols of ideal truth ; as he himself said, " amid such supersensual matters, I might easily have lost myself in the vague, if I had not, by means of sharply drawn figures and images from the Christian church, given my poetical design a desirable form and substance."

The contest between devils and angels for the soul of the dying, as portrayed in mediæval pictures and wood-carvings, formed the kernel of the "Moralities."   In the letter of Judas, verse 9, it is mentioned that the archangel Michael quarrelled with the devil over the soul of Moses; a legend to which Goethe alludes in the " Xenien."

Hell yawns below, heaven opens above, and the angels descend to awaken life, to bring aid and salvation to the sinner, and to manifest to all nature the richness of Divine grace.

How often in pictures angels are represented scattering roses, which however become burning flames to the devils; just as in the depraved soul, which has lost the capacity for ideal enjoyment, the vision of pure beauty awakens only the torment of ungratified desire.   This is experienced by Mephistopheles.

The form of the mediæval Latin hymns is reproduced in the angels' songs, which intentionally echo those of the Easter morning of the first part.

Between the musical harp-like tones of the angels' songs are heard in wonderful contrast the discordant utterances of Mephistopheles, as he now exhorts the devils to pluck off the Psyche-wings of Faust's soul, now recognizes and deplores his own lustful and futile cravings.   Thus he retires, like the stupid devil in the popular religious plays, self-deceived, rather than deceived by others.

In Goethe's treatment of the subject, as in the mediæval dramas, the humorous element is associated with the earnest conception of the struggle between heaven and hell; the poet has ventured to blend together the sublime and the burlesque, heavenly peace and demoniacal desire, and has succeeded.

Mountain-gorge, Woods, Rocks, and Desert-place.

The song of the angels who bear aloft the immortal part of Faust contains, according to Goethe's own confession to Eckermann (ii. 350), the key to his deliverance : the providence of God, guiding men from error and perplexity to freedom and light, corresponds to the innate tendency to goodness and truth implanted in the human soul. This thought embodied in the Prologue in Heaven, finds expression also in the Epilogue.

As the Prologue in Heaven was suggested to Goethe by the Book of Job, so the Epilogue reminds us of Dante. If the poet desired to bring the supersensual sphere before the spiritual gaze, and at the same time poetically to represent the blessed immortality of the human soul, his object was most effectually accomplished by freely employing the conceptions wherewith Christianity, from the earliest times, had endeavored to symbolize the infinite and unseen, and which no one has set forth with greater nobleness than Dante. As the Florentine bard is conducted by Beatrice, the beloved of his youth, so Faust is led to higher spheres by Gretchen. Both symbolize the glorified spirit, a ray of the everlasting truth and love. As in the vision of Dante, the mountain of purification rises from earth to heaven, from the summit of which the purified spirits soar aloft, while angels descend from the celestial spheres, so Goethe transports us to an eminence, where anchorites and hermits, hovered round by glorified spirits, dedicate themselves to the worship of the Divine. The mountains of Montserrat, near Barcelona, with its hermitages, nestling amid the loftiest and most rugged summits, of which William von Humboldt had sent the poet a masterly description, doubtless hovered before his mental eye.

Pater Ecstaticus, lifted above the earth by the heavenward impulse of his soul, as is related of St. Theresa and Philip Neri, together with expressions of sorrow for sin and heavenly rapture, blends the passionate longing to be redeemed from everything transient, and purified from all earthly dross.

Pater Profundus (who recalls Bernhard of Clairvaux or Thomas of Bradwardyne), in strains which harmonize with the song of the Archangels in the Prologue, gives expression to the hope that the Eternal Love, all-embracing, all-sustaining, ever actively beneficent, may deliver him from the earthly limitations which imprison his spirit as with bonds of pain, and lead him to freedom and to light.

Pater Seraphicus (the representative, perchance, of Francis of Assisi or Bonaventura) offers his eyes as organs of sense to the blessed boys, early deceased, that they may thus acquire some knowledge of the earth, which they were obliged to forsake before they had attained to perfect consciousness. He intimates that God's presence, pervading all things, is the eternal source of strength, and that to recognize the revelation of His love, whose goal is the blessedness of His creatures, is the spirit's true nourishment.

Emanuel Swedenborg imagined himself to be in communication with spirits, who entered into him in order, through his senses, to obtain the perception and knowledge of earthly things.

Faust's association with the blessed boys recalls the words of Jesus, that we must become as little children, in order to enter into the kingdom of heaven; while their desire to learn from him, and the rapidity with which he outgrows them, indicate the signifiance which attaches to our earthly existence, with its intellectual and moral striving, for all futurity.

The soul of Faust is not yet free from the dross of earth, and it is intimated by the more perfect angels that God's eternal love is alone able to purify the spirit from the lower elements with which it has been associated, and to bring it into harmony with the eternal goodness. Faust is at length freed from the old coil of earthly bondage, and Gretchen can exclaim with joy, that his first truthful strength shines forth, full and beautiful, from its ethereal robes.

It is the privilege of poetry thus to give expression to the deepest yearning of the human heart. Doctor Marianus, like the scholastic doctor, Duns Scotus, derives his name from the worship of the Virgin Mary. The womanly element, impersonating Love, as an essential principle in the divine nature, has manifested itself in all ancient religions. Goethe has here followed the symbolism of mediæval art. The Mater Gloriosa is here introduced as the manifestation of Divine mercy, which, with saving power, is near to all those who confidingly seek it.

Three pardoned sinners implore that Gretchen, who has sinned without evil intention, may be received into eternal blessedness; Mary Magdalene and the woman of Samaria are known to us from the Gospels; the story of the Egyptian Mary (Mary Ægyptiaca) is related in the legend of the saints.

Gretchen's rapturous words, intentionally on the part of the poet, recalls the prayer of anguish addressed by her to the Mater Dolorosa, in the first part. The whole image is bathed in light. The Mystical Chorus (Chorus Mysticus) reminds us that all things visible and transient are only types of the unseen and eternal; only symbolically can the world beyond be represented. There will be perfected what on earth is fragmentary or incomplete. The ever-womanly, type of pure, self-sacrificing love, the innermost core of woman's nature, makes us one with God.

FAUST:

A DRAMATIC POEM.

TRANSLATED INTO ENGLISH PROSE, BY A. HAYWARD, Esq.

FAUST.

PROLOGUE IN HEAVEN.

The Lord; the Heavenly Hosts; *afterwards* Mephis-
TOPHELES.

The three Archangels come forward.

Raphael. The sun chimes in, as ever, with the emulous
music of his brother spheres, and performs his prescribed
journey with thunder-speed. His aspect gives strength to
the angels, though none can fathom him. Thy inconceivably sublime works are glorious as on the first day.

Gabriel. And rapid, inconceivably rapid, the pomp of
the earth revolves; the brightness of paradise alternates
with deep, fearful night. The sea foams up in broad waves
at the deep base of the rocks; and rock and sea are whirled
on in the ever rapid course of the spheres.

Michael. And storms are roaring as if in rivalry, from
sea to land, from land to sea, and form all around a chain of
the deepest ferment in their rage. There, flashing desolation flares before the path of the thunder-clap. But thy
messengers, Lord, respect the mild going of thy day.

The Three. Thy aspect gives strength to the angels,
though none can fathom thee, and all thy sublime works are
glorious as on the first day.

Mephistopheles. Since, Lord, you approach once again,
and inquire how things are going on with us, and on other
occasions were not displeased to see me — therefore is it
that you see me also amongst your suite. Excuse me, I
cannot talk fine, not though the whole circle should cry
scorn on me. My pathos would certainly make you laugh,
had you not left off laughing. I have nothing to say about
suns and worlds; I only mark how men are plaguing themselves. The little god of the world continues ever of the
same stamp, and is as odd as on the first day. He would
lead a somewhat better life of it had you not given him a

glimmering of heaven's light. He calls it reason, and uses it only to be the most brutal of brutes. He seems to me, with your Grace's leave, like one of the long-legged grass-hoppers, which is ever flying, and bounding as it flies, and then sings its old song in the grass; — and would that he did but lie always in the grass! He thrusts his nose into every puddle.

THE LORD. Have you nothing else to say to me? Are you always coming to me for no other purpose than to complain? Is nothing ever to your liking upon earth?

MEPHISTOPHELES. No, Lord! I find things there, as ever, miserably bad. Men, in their days of wretchedness, move my pity; even I myself have not the heart to torment the poor things.

THE LORD. Do you know Faust?

MEPHISTOPHELES. The Doctor?

THE LORD. My servant!

MEPHISTOPHELES. Verily! he serves you after a fashion of his own. The fool's meat and drink are not of earth. The ferment of his spirit impels him towards the far away. He himself is half conscious of his madness. Of heaven — he demands its brightest stars; and of earth — its very highest enjoyment; and all the near, and all the far, content not his deeply-agitated breast.

THE LORD. Although he does but serve me in perplexity now, I shall soon lead him into light. When the tree buds, the gardener knows that blossom and fruit will deck the coming years.

MEPHISTOPHELES. What will you wager? you shall lose him yet, if you give me leave to guide him quietly my own way.

THE LORD. So long as he lives upon the earth, so long be it not forbidden to thee. Man is liable to error whilst his struggle lasts.

MEPHISTOPHELES. I am much obliged to you for that; for I have never had any fancy for the dead. I like plump, fresh cheeks the best. I am not at home to a corpse. I am like the cat to the mouse.

THE LORD. Enough, it is permitted thee. Divert this spirit from his original source, and bear him, if thou canst seize him, down on thy own path with thee. And stand abashed, when thou art compelled to own — a good man, in his dark strivings, may still be conscious of the right way.

Mephistopheles.   Well, well — only it will not last long.
I am not at all in pain for my wager.   Should I succeed,
excuse my triumphing with my whole soul.   Dust shall he
eat, and with a relish, like my cousin, the renowned snake.

The Lord.   There also you are free to act as you like.   I
have never hated the like of you.   Of all the spirits that
deny, the scoffer is the least offensive to me.   Man's activity
is all too prone to slumber: he soon gets fond of unconditional repose; I am, therefore, glad to give him a companion,
who stirs and works, and must, as devil, be doing.   But ye,
the true children of heaven, rejoice in the living profusion
of beauty.   The creative essence, which works and lives
through all time, embrace you within the happy bounds of
love; and what hovers in changeful seeming do ye fix firm
with everlasting thoughts.   (*Heaven·closes, the archangels
disperse.*)

Mephistopheles *alone*.   I like to see the Ancient One
occasionally, and take care not to break with him.   It is
really civil in so great a Lord to speak so kindly with the
Devil himself.

FAUST.

NIGHT.

FAUST *in a high-vaulted, narrow, Gothic chamber, seated restlessly at his desk.*

FAUST. Have now, alas! by zealous exertion, thoroughly mastered philosophy, the jurist's craft, and medicine, — and, to my sorrow, theology, too. Here I stand, poor fool that I am, just as wise as before. I am called Master, ay, and Doctor, and have now for nearly ten years been leading my pupils about — up and down, cross-ways and crooked ways — by the nose; and see that we can know nothing! This it is that almost burns up the heart within me. True, I am cleverer than all the solemn triflers — doctors, masters, writers, and priests. No doubts nor scruples of any sort trouble me; I fear neither hell nor the devil. For this very reason is all joy torn from me. I no longer fancy I know anything worth knowing; I no longer fancy I could reach anything to better and convert mankind. Then I have neither land nor money, nor honor and rank in the world. No dog would like to live so any longer. I have therefore devoted myself to magic — whether, through the power and voice of the Spirit, many a mystery might not become known to me; that I may no longer, with bitter sweat, be obliged to speak of what I do not know; that I may learn what it is that holds the world together in its inmost core, see all the springs and seeds of production, and drive no longer a paltry traffic in words.

Oh! would that thou, radiant moonlight, wert looking for the last time upon my misery; thou, for whom I have sat watching so many a midnight at this desk; then, over books and papers, melancholy friend, didst thou appear to me! — Oh! that I might wander on the mountain-tops in thy loved light — hover with spirits around the mountain caves — flit over the fields in thy glimmer, and, disencumbered from all the fumes of knowledge, bathe myself sound in thy dew!

462

Woe is me! am I still penned up in this dungeon?—accursed, musty, walled hole!—where even the precious light of heaven breaks mournfully through painted panes, tinted by this heap of books,—which worms eat—dust begrimes—which, up to the very top of the vault, a smoke-smeared paper encompasses; with glasses and boxes ranged round, with instruments piled up on all sides, ancestral lumber stuffed in with the rest! This is thy world, and a precious world it is!

And dost thou still ask, why thy heart flutters so confinedly in thy bosom?—Why a vague aching deadens within thee every stirring principle of life?—Instead of the animated nature, for which God made man, thou hast naught around thee but beasts' skeletons and dead men's bones, in smoke and mould.

Up! away! out into the wide world! And this mysterious book, from Nostradamus' own hand, is it not guide enough for thee? Thou then knowest the course of the stars, and, when nature instructs thee, the soul's essence then rises up to thee, as one spirit speaks to another. Vain! that dull poring here expounds the holy signs to thee! Ye are hovering, ye Spirits, near me; answer me, if you hear. (*He opens the book and perceives the sign of the Macrocosm.*)

Ah! what rapture thrills at once through all my senses at his sight! I feel a fresh, hallowed life-joy, new-glowing, shoot through nerve and vein. Was it a god that traced these signs?—which still the storm within me, fill my poor heart with gladness, and, by a mystical inspiration, unveil the powers of nature all around me. Am I a god? All grows so bright! I see, in these pure lines, nature herself working in my soul's presence. Now for the first time do I conceive what the sage saith,—"The spirit-world is not closed. Thy sense is shut, thy heart is dead! Up, acolyte! bathe, unired, thy earthly breast in the morning-red." (*He contemplates the sign.*)

How all weaves itself into the whole; one works and lives in the other. How heavenly influences ascend and descend, and reach each other the golden buckets,—on bliss-exhaling pinions, press from heaven through earth, all ringing harmoniously through *the* All.

What a show! but, ah! a show only! Where shall I seize thee, infinite nature? Ye breasts, where? ye sources of all life, on which hang heaven and earth, towards which the blighted breast presses—ye gush, ye suckle, and am I thus languishing in vain? (*He turns over the book indignantly, and sees the sign of the Spirit of the Earth.*)

How differently this sign affects me! Thou, Spirit of the Earth, art nearer to me! Already do I feel my energies exalted, already glow as with new wine; I feel courage to venture into the world; to endure earthly weal, earthly woe; to wrestle with storms, and stand unshaken 'mid the ship-wreck's crash. — Clouds thicken over me; the moon pales her light; the lamp dies away; exhalations arise; red beams flash round my head; a cold shuddering flickers down from the vaulted roof and fastens on me! I feel it — thou art flitting round me, prayer-compelled Spirit. Unveil thyself! Ah! what a tearing in my heart — all my senses are up-stirring to new sensations! I feel my whole heart surrendered to thee. Thou must — thou must! — should it cost me my life. (*He seizes the book and pronounces mystically the sign of the Spirit. A red flame flashes up; the* SPIRIT *appears in the flame.*)

SPIRIT. Who calls me?

FAUST (*averting his face*). Horrible vision!

SPIRIT. Thou hast compelled me hither, by dint of long sucking at my sphere. And now —

FAUST. Torture! I endure thee not.

SPIRIT. Thou prayest, panting, to see me, to hear my voice, to gaze upon my face. Thy powerful invocation works upon me. I am here! What a pitiful terror seizes thee, the demi-god! Where is the soul's calling? Where the breast that created a world in itself, and upbore and cherished it? which, with tremors of delight swelled to lift itself to a level with us, the Spirits. Where art thou, Faust? — whose voice rang to me, who pressed towards me with all his energies! Art thou he? thou, who, at the bare perception of my breath art shivering through all the depths of life, a trembling, writhing worm?

FAUST. Shall I yield to thee, child of fire? I am he, am Faust, thy equal.

SPIRIT.

In the tides of life,
In the storm of action,
I am tossed up and down,
I drift hither and thither,
Birth and grave,
An eternal sea,
A changeful weaving,
A glowing life —
Thus I work at the whizzing loom of time,
And weave the living clothing of the Deity.

FAUST. Busy Spirit, thou who sweepest round the wide world, how near I feel to thee!

SPIRIT. Thou art mate for the spirit whom thou conceivest, not for me. (*The Spirit vanishes.*)

FAUST, *collapsing.* Not for thee! For whom then? I, the image of the Deity, and not mate for even thee! (*A knocking at the door.*) Oh, death! I know it: that is my amanuensis. My fairest fortune is turned to naught. That the unidea'd groveller must disturb this fulness of visions! (WAGNER *enters in his dressing-gown and night-cap, with a lamp in his hand.* FAUST *turns round in displeasure.*)

WAGNER. Excuse me—I hear you declaiming; you were surely reading a Greek tragedy. I should like to improve myself in this art, for nowadays it influences a good deal. I have often heard say, a player might instruct a priest.

FAUST. Yes, when the priest is a player, as may likely enough come to pass occasionally.

WAGNER. Ah! when a man is so confined to his study, and hardly sees the world of a holiday—hardly through a telescope, only from afar—how is he to lead it by persuasion?

FAUST. If you do not feel it, you will not get it by hunting for it,—if it does not gush from the soul, and subdue the hearts of all hearers with original delight. Sit at it forever—glue together—cook up a hash from the feast of others, and blow the paltry flames out of your own little heap of ashes! You may gain the admiration of children and apes, if you have a stomach for it; but you will never touch the hearts of others, if it does not flow fresh from your own.

WAGNER. But it is elocution that makes the orator's success. I feel well that I am still far behindhand.

FAUST. Try what can be got by honest means.—Be no tinkling fool!—Reason and good sense express themselves with little art. And when you are seriously intent on saying something, is it necessary to hunt for words? Your speeches, I say, which are so highly polished, in which ye crisp the shreds of humanity, are unrefreshing as the mistwind which whistles through the withered leaves in autumn.

WAGNER. Oh, God! art is long, and our life is short. Often, indeed, during my critical studies do I suffer both in head and heart. How hard it is to compass the means by which one mounts to the fountain-head; and before he has got half way, a poor devil must probably die!

FAUST.   Is parchment the holy well, a drink from which allays the thirst forever?   Thou hast not gained the cordial. if it gushes not from thy own soul.

WAGNER.   Excuse me! it is a great pleasure to transport one's self into the spirit of the times; to see how a wise man has thought before us, and to what a glorious height we have at last carried it.

FAUST.   Oh, yes, far up to the very stars.   My friend, the past ages are to us a book with seven seals.   What you term the spirit of the times, is at bottom only your own spirit, in which the times are reflected.   A miserable exhibition, too, it frequently is!   One runs away from it at the first glance!   A dirt-tub and a lumber-room! — and, at best, a puppet-show play, with fine pragmatical saws, such as may happen to sound well in the mouths of the puppets!

WAGNER.   But the world! the heart and mind of man! every one would like to know something about that.

FAUST.   Ay, what is called knowing!   Who dares call the child by its true name?   The few who have ever known anything about it, who sillily enough did not keep a guard over their full hearts, who revealed what they had felt and seem to the multitude, — these, time immemorial, have been crucified and burned.   I beg, friend — the night is far advanced — for the present we must break off.

WAGNER.   I could fain have kept waking to converse with you so learnedly.   To-morrow, however, the first day of Easter, permit me a question or two more.   Zealously have I devoted myself to study.   True I know much; but I would fain know all.   (*Exit.*)

FAUST, *alone.*   How all hope only quits not the brain, which clings perseveringly to trash, — gropes with greedy hand for treasures, and exults at finding earth-worms!

Dare such a human voice sound here, where all around me teemed with spirits?   Yet, ah! this once I thank thee, thou poorest of all the sons of earth.   Thou hast snatched me from despair, which had well-nigh got the better of sense.   Alas! the vision was so giant-great that I felt quite shrunk into a dwarf.

I, formed in God's own image, who already thought myself near to the mirror of eternal truth; who revelled in heaven's lustre and clearness, with the earthly part of me stripped off; I, more than cherub, whose free spirit already, in its imaginative soarings, aspired to glide through nature's veins, and in creating, enjoy the life of gods —

how must I atone for it! a thunder-word has swept me
wide away.

I dare not presume to mate myself with thee. If I have
possessed the power to draw thee to me, I had no power to
hold thee. In that blest moment, I felt so little, so great;
you fiercely thrust me back upon the uncertain lot of
humanity. Who will teach me? What am I to shun?
Must I obey that impulse? Alas! our actions, equally with
our sufferings, clog the course of our lives.

Something foreign, and more foreign, is ever clinging to
the noblest conception the mind can form. When we have
attained to the good of this world, what is better is termed
falsehood and vanity. The glorious feelings which gave us
life grow torpid in the worldly throng.

If phantasy at one time, on daring wing and full of hope,
dilates to infirmity, — a little space is now enough for her,
when venture after venture has been wrecked in the whirlpool of time. Care straightway builds her nest in the
depth of the heart, hatches vague tortures there, rocks herself restlessly, and frightens joy and peace away. She is
ever putting on some new mask; she may appear as house
and land, as wife and child, as fire, water, dagger, poison.
You tremble before all that does not befall you, and must be
always wailing what you never lose.

I am not like the heavenly essences; I feel it but too
deeply. I am like the worm, which drags itself through the
dust, — which, as it seeks its living in the dust, is crushed
and buried by the step of the passer-by.

Is it not dust? all that in a hundred shelves contracts
this lofty wall — the frippery, which, with its thousand
forms of emptiness, cramps me up in this world of moths?
Is this the place for finding what I want? Must I go on
reading, in a thousand books, that men have everywhere
been miserable, and now and then there has been a happy
one?

Thou hollow skull, what mean'st thou by that grin?
but that thy brain, like mine, was once bewildered, — sought
the bright day, and, with an ardent longing after truth,
went miserably astray in the twilight?

Ye instruments, too, forsooth, are mocking me, with your
wheels and cogs, cylinders and collars. I stood at the gate,
ye were to be the key; true, your wards are curiously
twisted, but you raise not the bolt. Inscrutable at broad
day, nature does not suffer herself to be robbed of her veil;

and what she does not choose to reveal to thy mind thou wilt not wrest from her by levers and screws.

Thou, antiquated lumber, which I have never used, thou art here, only because my father had occasion for you. Thou, old roll, hast been growing smoke-besmeared since the dim lamp first smouldered at this desk. Far better would it be for me to have squandered away the little I possess than to be sweating here under the burden of that little. To possess what thou hast inherited from thy sires, enjoy it. What one does not profit by, is an oppressive burden; what the moment brings forth, that only can it profit by.

But why are my looks fastened on that spot? is that phial there a magnet to my eyes? Why, of a sudden, is all so exquisitely bright, as when the moonlight breathes round one benighted in the wood? I hail thee, thou precious phial, which I now take down with reverence; in thee I honor the wit and art of man. Thou abstraction of kind soporific juices, thou concentration of all refined deadly essences, vouchsafe thy master a token of thy grace! I see thee, and the pang is mitigated; I grasp thee, and the struggle abates; the spirit's flood-tide ebbs by degrees. I am beckoned out into the wide sea; the glassy wave glitters at my feet; another day invites to other shores. A chariot of fire waves, on light pinions, down to me. I feel prepared to permeate the realms of space on a new track, to new spheres of pure activity. This sublime existence, this godlike beatitude! And thou, worm as thou wert but now, dost thou merit it? Ay, only resolutely turn thy back on the lovely sun of this earth! Dare to tear up the gates which each willingly slinks by! Now is the time to show by deeds that man's dignity yields not to God's sublimity, — to quail not in the presence of that dark abyss, in which phantasy damns itself to its own torments — to struggle onwards to that pass, round whose narrow mouth all Hell is flaming; calmly to resolve upon the step, even at the risk of dropping into nothingness.

Now come down, pure crystal goblet, on which I have not thought for many a year, — forth from your old receptacle! You glittered at my father's festivities; you gladdened the grave guests, as one pledged you to the other. The gorgeousness of the many artfully-wrought images, — the drinker's duty to explain them in rhyme, and empty the contents at a draught, — remind me of many a night of my youth.   I shall not now pass you to a neighbor; I shall not now display my wit on your devices.   Here is a juice which soon intoxicates.   It fills your cavity with its brown flood. Be this last draught — which I have brewed, which I choose —quaffed, with my whole soul, as a solemn festal greeting to the morn.   (*He places the goblet to his mouth.*)

(*The ringing of bells and singing of choruses.*)

CHORUS OF ANGELS.

Christ has arisen!
Joy to the mortal,
Whom the corrupting,
Creeping, hereditary
Imperfections enveloped.

FAUST.   What deep humming, what clear strain, draws irresistibly the goblet from my mouth?   Are ye hollow sounding bells already proclaiming the first festal hour of Easter?   Are ye choruses already singing the comforting hymn, which once, round the night of the sepulchre, pealed forth, from angel lips, the assurance of a new covenant?

CHORUS OF WOMEN.

With spices
Had we embalmed him;
We, his faithful ones,
Had laid him out.
Clothes and bands
Cleanlily swathed we round;
Ah! and we find
Christ no longer here!

CHORUS OF ANGELS.

Christ is arisen!
Happy the loving one,
Who the afflicting,
Wholesome and chastening
Trial hath stood!

FAUST.   Why, ye heavenly tones, subduing and soft, do you seek me out in the dust?   Peal out, where weak men are to be found!   I hear the message, but want faith.   I dare not aspire to those spheres from whence the glad tidings sound; and yet, accustomed to this sound from infancy, it even now calls me back to life.   In other days, the kiss of heavenly love descended upon me in the solemn stillness of the Sabbath; then the full-toned bell sounded so fraught with mystic meaning, and a prayer was burning enjoyment. A longing, inconceivably sweet, drove me forth to wander over wood and plain, and amidst a thousand burning tears, I felt a world rise up to me. This anthem harbingered the gay sports of youth, the unchecked happiness of spring festivity. — Recollection now holds me back, with childlike feeling, from the last decisive step. Oh! sound on, ye sweet heavenly strains! The tear is flowing, earth has me again.

CHORUS OF DISCIPLES.

The Buried One,
Already on high,
Living, sublime,
Has gloriously raised himself!
He is, in reviving bliss,
Near to creating joy.
Ah! on earth's bosom
Are we for suffering here.
He left us, his own,
Languishing here below!
Alas! we weep over,
Master, thy happy lot.

CHORUS OF ANGELS.

Christ is arisen
Out of corruption's lap.
Joyfully tear yourselves
Loose from your bonds!
Ye, in deeds giving praise to him
Love manifesting,
Living brethren-like,
Travelling and preaching him,
Bliss promising—
You is the Master nigh,
For you is he here!

BEFORE THE GATE.

Promenaders of all kinds pass out.

SOME MECHANICS. Why that way?
OTHERS. We are going up to Jagerhaus.
THE FORMER. But we are going to the mill.
A MECHANIC. I advise you to go to the Wasserhof.
A SECOND. The road is not pleasant.
THE OTHERS. What shall you do?

A Third. I am going with the others.

A Fourth. Come up to Burgdorf; you are there sure of finding the prettiest girls and best beer, and rows of the first order.

A Fifth. You wild fellow, is your skin itching for the third time? I don't like going there; I have a horror of the place.

Servant Girl. No, no, I shall return to the town.

Another. We shall find him to a certainty by those poplars.

The First. That is no great gain for me. He will walk by your side. With you alone does he dance upon the green. What have I to do with your pleasures?

The Second. He is sure not to be alone to-day. The curly head, he said, would be with him.

Student. The devil! how the brave wenches step out; come along, brother, we must go with them. Strong beer, stinging tobacco, and a girl in full trim, — that now is my taste.

Citizens' Daughters. Now do you but look at those fine lads! It is really a shame. They might have the best of company, and are running after these servant-girls.

Second Student to the First. Not so fast! there are two coming up behind; they are trimly dressed out. One of them is my neighbor; I have a great liking for the girl. They are walking in their quiet way, and yet will suffer us to join them in the end.

The First. No, brother. I do not like to be under restraint. Quick, lest we lose the game. The hand that twirls the mop on a Saturday will fondle you best on Sundays.

Townsman. No, the new Burgomaster is not to my taste; now that he has become so, he is daily getting bolder; and what is he doing for the town? Is it not growing worse every day? One is obliged to submit to more restraints than ever, and pay more than in any time before.

Beggar, *sings*. Ye good gentlemen, ye lovely ladies, so trimly dressed and rosy cheeked, be pleased to look upon me, to regard and relieve my wants. Do not suffer me to sing here in vain. The free-handed only is light-hearted. Be the day, which is a holiday to all, a harvest-day to me.

Another Townsman. I know nothing better on Sundays and holidays than a chat of war and war's alarms, when people are fighting, behind, far away in Turkey. A man stands at the window, takes off his glass, and sees the painted vessels glide down the river; then returns home glad at heart at eve, and blesses peace and times of peace.

THIRD TOWNSMAN. Ay, neighbor, I have no objection to that; they may break one another's heads, and turn everything topsy turvy, for aught I care, only let things at home remain as they are.

AN OLD WOMAN TO THE CITIZENS' DAUGHTERS. Heydey: how smart! the pretty young creatures. Who would not fall in love with you? Only not so proud! it is all very well; and what you wish, I should know how to put you in the way of getting.

CITIZEN'S DAUGHTER. Come along, Agatha. I take care not to be seen with such witches in public; true, on St. Andrew's eve, she showed me my future sweetheart in flesh and blood.

THE OTHER. She showed me mine in the glass, soldierlike, with other bold fellows; I looked around, I seek him everywhere, but I can never meet with him.

SOLDIER.

Towns with lofty
Walls and battlements
Maidens with proud
Scornful thoughts,
I fain would win.
Bold the adventure,
Noble the reward.

And the trumpets
Are our summoners
As to joy
So to death.
That is storming,
That is life for you!

Maidens and towns
Must surrender.
Bold the adventure,
Noble the reward —
And the soldiers
Are off.

FAUST *and* WAGNER.

FAUST. River and rivulet are freed from ice by the gay, quickening glance of the spring. The joys of hope are budding in the dale. Old Winter, in his weakness, has retreated to the bleak mountains; from thence he sends, in his flight, nothing but impotent showers of hail, in flakes, over the green-growing meadows. But the Sun endures no white. Production and growth are everywhere stirring; he is about to enliven everything with colors. The landscape wants flowers; he takes gaily-dressed men and women instead. Turn and look back, from this rising ground, upon the town. Forth from the gloomy portal presses a motley crowd. Every one suns himself so willingly to-day. They celebrate the rising of the Lord, for they themselves have arisen ; — from the damp rooms of mean houses, from the bondage of mechanical drudgery, from the confinement of gables and roofs, from the stifling narrowness of streets, from the venerable gloom of churches, are they raised up to the open light of day. But look, look! how quickly the mass scatters itself through the gardens and fields; how the river, broad and long, tosses many a merry bark upon its surface, and how this last wherry, overladen almost to sinking, moves off! Even from the farthest paths of the mountain gay-colored dresses glance upon us. I hear already the bustle of the village; this is the true heaven of the multitude; big and little are huzzaing joyously. Here, I am a man — here I may be one.

WAGNER. To walk with you, Sir Doctor, is honor and profit. But I would not lose myself alone, because I am an enemy to coarseness of every sort. Fiddling, shouting, skittle-playing, are sounds thoroughly detestable to me. People run riot as if the devil was driving them, and call it merriment, call it singing.

Rustics under the Lime Tree.

DANCE AND SONG.

The swain dressed himself out for the dance.
With parti-colored jacket, ribbon and garland,
Smartly was he dressed!
The ring round the lime-tree was already full,
And all were dancing like mad.
 Huzza! Huzza!
 Tira-lira-hara-la!
Merrily went the fiddle-stick.

He pressed eagerly in,
Gave a maiden a push
With his elbow:
The buxom girl turned round
And said — "Now that I call stupid."
 Huzza! Huzza!
 Tira-lira-hara-la!
"Don't be so rude."

> Yet nimbly sped it in the ring;
> They turned right, they turned left,
> And all the petticoats were flying.
> They grew red, they grew warm,
> And rested panting arm-in-arm,
>> Huzza! Huzza!
>> Tira-lira-hara-la!
> And elbow on the hip.
>
> "Have done now! don't be so fond!
> How many a man has cajoled and
> Deceived his betrothed!"
> But he coaxed her aside,
> And far and wide echoed from the lime-tree
>> Huzza! Huzza!
>> Tira-lira-hara-la!
> Shouts and fiddle-sticks.

OLD PEASANT. Doctor, this is really good of you, not to scorn us to-day, and, great scholar as you are, to mingle in this crowd. Take, then, the fairest jug, which we have filled with fresh liquor: I pledge you in it, and pray aloud that it may do more than quench your thirst — may the number of drops which it holds be added to your days!

FAUST. I accept the refreshing draught, and wish you all health and happiness in return. (*The people collect round him.*)

OLD PEASANT. Of a surety it is well done of you to appear on this glad day. You have been our friend in evil days, too, before now. Many a one stands here alive whom your father tore from the hot fever's rage, when he stayed the pestilence. You, too, at that time a young man, went into every sick house: many a dead body was borne forth, but you came out safe. You endured many a sore trial. The Helper above helped the helper.

ALL. Health to the tried friend — may he long have the power to help!

FAUST. Bend before Him on high, who teaches how to help, and sends help. (*He proceeds with Wagner.*)

WAGNER. What a feeling, great man, must you experience at the honors paid you by this multitude! Oh, happy he who can turn his gifts to so good an account! The father points you out to his boy; all ask, and press, and hurry round. The fiddle stops, the dancer pauses. As you go by, they range themselves in rows, caps fly into the air, and they all but bend the knee as if the Host were passing.

FAUST. Only a few steps further, up to that stone yonder! Here we will rest from our walk. Here many a time have I sat, thoughtful and solitary, and mortified myself with prayer and fasting. Rich in hope, firm in faith, I thought to extort the stoppage of that pestilence from the Lord of heaven with tears, and sighs, and wringing of hands. The applause of the multitude now sounds like derision in my ears. Oh! couldst thou read in my soul how little father and son merited such an honor! My father was a worthy, sombre man, who, honestly but in his own way, meditated, with whimsical application, on nature and her hallowed circles; who, in the company of adepts, shut himself up in the dark laboratory, and fused contraries together after numberless recipes. There was a red lion, a bold lover, married to the lily in the tepid bath, and then both, with open flame, tortured from one bridal chamber to another. If the young queen, with varied hues, then appeared in the glass — this was the medicine; the patients died, and no one inquired who recovered. Thus did we, with our hellish electuaries, rage in these vales and mountains far worse than the pestilence. I myself have given the poison to thousands; they pined away, and I must survive to hear the reckless murderers praised!

WAGNER. How can you make yourself uneasy on that account? Is it not enough for a good man to practise conscientiously and scrupulously the art that has been entrusted to him? If, in youth, you honor your father, you will willingly learn from him: if, in manhood, you extend the bonds of knowledge, your son may mount still higher than you.

FAUST. Oh, happy he, who can still hope to emerge from this sea of error! We would use the very thing we know not, and cannot use what we know. But let us not embitter the blessing of this hour by such melancholy reflections. See, how the green-girt cottages shimmer in the setting Sun! He bends and sinks — the day is over-lived. Yonder he hurries off, and quickens other life. Oh! that I have no wing to lift me from the ground, to struggle after, forever after, him! I should see, in everlasting evening beams, the stilly world at my feet, — every height on fire, — every vale in repose, — the silver brook flowing into golden streams. The rugged mountain, with all its dark defiles, would not then break my god-like course. Already the sea, with its heated bays, opens on my enraptured sight. Yet, the god seems at last to sink away. But the new impulse wakes. I hurry on to drink his everlasting light, — the day before me and the night behind — the heavens above, and under me the waves. A glorious dream! as it is passing, he is gone. Alas! no bodily wing will so easily keep pace with the wings of the mind. Yet it is the inborn tendency of our being for feeling to strive upwards and onwards; when, over us, lost in the blue expanse, the lark sings its trilling lay: when, over rugged, pine-covered heights, the outspread eagle soars; and, over marsh and sea, the crane struggles onward to her home.

WAGNER. I myself have often had my capricious moments, but I never yet experienced an impulse of the kind. One soon looks one's fill of woods and fields. I shall never envy the wings of the bird. How differently the pleasures of the mind bear us, from book to book, from page to page! With them, winter nights become cheerful and bright, a happy life warms every limb, and, ah! when you actually unroll a precious manuscript, all heaven comes down to you.

FAUST. Thou art conscious only of one impulse. Oh, never became acquainted with the other! Two souls, alas, dwell in my breast; the one struggles to separate itself from the other. The one clings with persevering fondness to the world, with organs like cramps of steel; the other lifts itself energetically from the mist to the realms of an exalted ancestry. Oh! if there be spirits hovering in the air, ruling 'twixt earth and heaven, descend ye, from your golden atmosphere, and lead me off to a new, variegated life! Ay, were but a magic mantle mine, and could it bear me into foreign lands, I would not part with it for the costliest garments — not for a king's mantle.

WAGNER. Invoke not the well-known troop, which diffuses itself, streaming, through the atmosphere, and prepares danger in a thousand forms, from every quarter, to man. The sharp-fanged spirits, with arrowy tongues, press upon you from the north; from the east, they come parching, and feed upon your lungs. If the south sends from the desert those which heap fire after fire upon thy brain, the west brings the swarm which only refreshes to drown fields, meadows, and yourself. They are fond of listening, ever keenly alive for mischief: they obey with pleasure, because they take pleasure to delude: they feign to be sent from heaven, and lisp like angels when they lie. But let us be going; the earth is already grown gray, the air is chill, the mist is falling; it is only in the evening that we set a proper value on our homes. Why do you stand still and gaze with astonishment thus? What can thus attract your attention in the gloaming?

Faust. Seest thou the black dog ranging through the corn and stubble?

Wagner. I saw him long ago; he did not strike me as anything particular.

Faust. Mark him well! for what do you take the brute?

Wagner. For a poodle, who, poodle-fashion, is puzzling out the track of his master.

Faust. Dost thou mark how, in wide spiral curves, he quests round and ever nearer us? and, if I err not, a line of fire follows upon his track.

Wagner. I see nothing but a black poodle; you may be deceived by some optical illusion.

Faust. It appears to me that he is drawing light magical nooses, to form a toil around our feet.

Wagner. I see him bounding hesitatingly and shyly around us, because, instead of his master, he sees two strangers.

Faust. The circle grows narrow; he is already close.

Wagner. You see it is a dog, and no spirit. He growls and hesitates, crouches on his belly and wags with his tail — all as dogs are wont to do.

Faust. Come to us! — Hither!

Wagner. It's a droll creature. Stand still, and he will sit on his hind legs; speak to him, and he will jump up on you; lose aught, and he will fetch it to you, and jump into the water for your stick.

Faust. I believe you are right; I find no trace of a spirit, and all is the result of training.

Wagner. Even a wise man may become attached to a dog when he is well brought up. And he richly deserves all your favor, — he, the accomplished pupil of your students, as he is. (*They enter the gate of the town.*)

STUDY.

Faust (*entering with the poodle*). I have left plain and meadow veiled in deep night, which wakes the better soul within us with a holy feeling of foreboding awe. Wild desires are now sunk in sleep, with every deed of violence:

the love of man is stirring — the love of God is stirring now.

Be quiet, poodle, run not hither and thither. What are you snuffing at on the threshold? Lie down behind the stove; there is my best cushion for you. As without, upon the mountain-path, you amused us by running and gambolling, so now receive my kindness as a welcome quiet guest.

Ah! when the lamp is burning again friendly in our narrow cell, then all becomes clear in our bosom, — in the heart that knows itself. Reason begins to speak, and hope to bloom, again; we yearn for the streams — oh, yes! for the fountain of life.

Growl not, poodle; the brutish sound ill harmonizes with the hallowed tones which now possess my whole soul. We are accustomed to see men deride what they do not understand — to see them snarl at the good and beautiful, which is often troublesome to them. Is the dog disposed to snarl at it like them? But, ah! I feel already that, much as I may wish for it, contentment wells no longer from my breast. Yet why must the stream be so soon dried up, and we again lie thirsting? I have had so much experience of that! This want, however, admits of being compensated. We learn to prize that which is not of this earth; we long for revelation, which nowhere burns more majestically or more beautifully than in the new Testament. I feel impelled to open the original text — to translate for once, with upright feeling, the sacred original into my darling German. (*He opens a volume, and disposes himself for the task.*)

It is written: "In the beginning was the Word." Here I am already at a stand — who will help me on? I cannot possibly value the Word so highly; I must translate it differently, if I am truly inspired by the spirit. It is written: "In the beginning was the Sense." Consider well the first line, that your pen be not over-hasty. Is it the sense that influences and produces everything? It should stand thus: "In the beginning was the Power." Yet, even as I am writing down this, something warns me not to keep to it. The spirit comes to my aid! At once I see my way, and write confidently: "In the beginning was the Deed."

If I am to share the chamber with you, poodle, cease your howling — cease your barking. I cannot endure so troublesome a companion near to me. One of us two must quit the cell. It is with reluctance that I withdraw the rites of hospitality; the door is open — the way is clear for you. But what do I see? Can that come to pass by natural means? Is it shadow — is it reality? How long and broad my poodle grows! He raises himself powerfully; that is not the form of a dog! What a phantom I have brought into the house! — he looks already like a hippopotamus, with fiery eyes, terrific teeth. Ah! I am sure of thee! Solomon's key is good for such a half-hellish brood.

Spirits in the Passage.

One is caught within!
Stay without, follow none!
As in the gin the fox,
Quakes an old lynx of hell.
    But take heed!
Hover hither, hover back,
    Up and down,
And he is loose!
If ye can aid him,
Leave him not in the lurch,
For he has already done
Much to serve us.

Faust.

First to confront the beast,
Use I the spell of the four:
  Salamander shall grow,
  Undine twine,
  Sylph vanish,
  Kobold stir himself.
Who did not know
  The elements,
Their power and properties,
  Were no master
  Over the spirits.
Vanish in flame,
  Salamander!
Rushingly flow together
  Undine!
Shine in meteor beauty,
  Sylph!
Bring homely help,
Incubus! Incubus!
Step forth and make an end of it.

No one of the four sticks in the beast. He lies undisturbed and grins at me. I have not yet made him feel. Thou shalt hear me conjure stronger.

Art thou, fellow,
A scapeling from hell?
Then see this sign!
To which bend the dark troop.

He is already swelling, and bristling his hair.

> Reprobate!
> Canst thou read him? —
> The unoriginated,
> Unpronounceable,
> Through all heaven diffused,
> Vilely transpierced?

Driven behind the stove, it is swelling like an elephant; it fills the whole space; it is about to vanish in the mist. Rise not to the ceiling! Down at thy master's feet! Thou seest I do not threaten in vain. I will scorch thee with holy fire. Wait not for the thrice-glowing light. Wait not for the strongest of my spells.

MEPHISTOPHELES. (*Comes forward as the mist sinks, in the dress of a travelling scholar, from behind the stove.*) Wherefore such a fuss? What may be your pleasure?

FAUST. This, then, was the kernel of the poodle. A travelling scholar? The *casus* makes me laugh.

MEPHISTOPHELES. I salute your learned worship. You have made me sweat with a vengeance.

FAUST. What is thy name?

MEPHISTOPHELES. The question strikes me as trifling for one who rates the Word so low; who, far estranged from all mere outward seeming, looks only to the essence of things.

FAUST. With such gentlemen as you one may generally learn the essence from the name, since it appears but too plainly if your name be fly-god, destroyer, liar. Now, in a word, who art thou, then?

MEPHISTOPHELES. A part of that power which is ever willing evil and ever producing good.

FAUST. What is meant by this riddle?

MEPHISTOPHELES. I am the spirit that constantly denies, and that rightly; for everything that has originated, deserves to be annihilated. Therefore, better were it that nothing should originate. Thus, all that you call sin, destruction, in a word, Evil, is my proper element.

FAUST. You call yourself a part, and yet stand whole before me.

MEPHISTOPHELES. I tell thee the modest truth. Although man, that microcosm of folly, commonly esteems himself a whole, I am a part of the part which in the beginning was all; a part of the darkness which brought forth light, — the proud light, which now contests her ancient rank and space with mother night. But he succeeds not; since, strive as he will, he cleaves, as if bound, to bodies, he streams from bodies, he gives beauty to bodies, a body stops him in his course, and so, I hope, he will perish with bodies before long.

Faust. Now I know thy dignified calling. Thou art not able to destroy on a great scale, and so art just beginning on a small one.

Mephistopheles. And, to say truth, I have made little progress in it. That which is opposed to nothing — the something, this clumsy world, much as I have tried already, I have not yet learnt how to come at it, — with waves, storms, earthquakes, fire. Sea and land remain undisturbed, after all! And the damned set, the brood of brutes and men, there is no such thing as getting the better of them, neither. How many I have already buried! And new, fresh blood is constantly circulating! Things go on so — it is enough to make one mad! From air, water, earth, in wet, dry, hot, cold — germs by thousands evolve themselves. Had I not reserved fire, I should have nothing apart for myself.

Faust. So thou opposest thy cold devil's fist, clenched in impotent malice, to the ever-stirring, the beneficent creating power. Try thy hand at something else, wondrous son of Chaos.

Mephistopheles. We will think about it in good earnest — more of that anon! Might I be permitted this time to depart?

Faust. I see not why you ask. I have now made acquaintance with you ; call on me in future as you feel inclined. Here is the window, here the door ; there is also a chimney for you.

Mephistopheles. To confess the truth, a small obstacle prevents me from walking out — the wizard-foot upon your threshold.

Faust. The Pentagram embarrasses you ? Tell me, then, thou child of hell, if that repels thee, how camest thou in ? How was such a spirit entrapped?

Mephistopheles. Mark it well; it is not well drawn ; one angle, the outward one, is, as thou seest, a little open.

Faust. It is a lucky accident. Thou shouldst be my prisoner, then? This is a chance hit.

Mephistopheles. The poodle observed nothing when he jumped in. The thing looks differently now ; the devil cannot get out.

Faust. But why do you not go through the window?

MEPHISTOPHELES. It is a law, binding on devils and phantoms, that they must go out the same way they stole in. The first is free to us; we are slaves as regards the second.

FAUST. Hell itself has its laws? I am glad of it; in that case a compact, a binding one, may be made with you gentlemen?

MEPHISTOPHELES. What is promised, that shalt thou enjoy to the letter; not the smallest deduction shall be made from it. But this is not to be discussed so summarily, and we will speak of it the next time. But I must earnestly beg of you to let me go this once.

FAUST. Wait yet another moment, and tell me something worth telling.

MEPHISTOPHELES. Let me go now! I will soon come back; you may then question me as you like.

FAUST. I have laid no snare for thee; thou hast run into the net of thy own free will. Let whoever has got hold of the devil keep hold of him; he will not catch him a second time in a hurry.

MEPHISTOPHELES. If you like, I am ready to stay and keep you company here, but upon condition that I may beguile the time properly for you by my arts.

FAUST. I shall attend with pleasure; you may do so, provided only that the art be an agreeable one.

MEPHISTOPHELES. My friend, you will gain more for your senses in this one hour than in the whole year's monotony. What the delicate spirits sing to you, the lovely images which they call up, are not an unsubstantial play of enchantment. Your smell will be charmed, you will then delight your palate, and then your feelings will be entranced. No preparation is necessary; we are all assembled — strike up!

SPIRITS.

Vanish, ye dark
Arched ceilings above,
More charmingly look in
The friendly blue sky,
Were the dark clouds
Melted away.
Little stars sparkle,
Softer suns shine in.
Ethereal beauty
Of the children of heaven,
Tremulous bending
   Hovers across;
Longing desire
   Follows after.

And the fluttering
Ribbons of drapery
Cover the plains,
Cover the bower,
Where lovers,
Deep in thought,
Give themselves for life,
Bower on bower!
Sprouting tendrils!
Down-weighing grapes
Gush into the vat
Of the hard-squeezing press.
The foaming wines
Gush in brooks,
Rustle through
Pure, precious stones,
Leave the heights
Behind them lying,
Broaden to seas
Around the charm of
Green-growing hill.
And the winged throng
Sips happiness,
Flies to meet the sun,
Flies to meet the bright
Isles, which dancingly
Float on the waves;
Where we hear
Shouting in choruses,
Where we see
Dancers on meads;
In the open air
All disporting alike.
Some are clambering
Over the heights,
Others are swimming
Over the seas,
Others are hovering —
All towards the life,
All towards the far away
Loving stars of
Bliss-giving grace.

MEPHISTOPHELES. He slumbers! Well done, my airy, delicate youngsters! Ye have fairly sung him to sleep. I am your debtor for this concert. Thou art not yet the man to hold fast the devil! Play round him with sweet dreamy visions; plunge him in a sea of illusion. But to break the spell of this threshold I need a rat's tooth. I have not to conjure long; one is already rustling hither, and will hear me in a moment. The lord of rats and mice, of flies, frogs, bugs, and lice, commands thee to venture forth and gnaw this threshold so soon as he has smeared it with oil. Thou comest hopping forth already! Instantly to the work! The point which repelled me is towards the front on the ledge; one bite more, and it is done. — Now, Faust, dream on, till we meet again.

FAUST, *waking*. Am I, then, once again deceived? Does the throng of spirits vanish thus? Was it in a lying dream that the devil appeared to me, and was it a poodle that escaped?

STUDY.

FAUST; MEPHISTOPHELES.

FAUST. Does any one knock? Come in! Who wants to disturb me again?

MEPHISTOPHELES. It is I.

FAUST. Come in.

MEPHISTOPHELES. You must say so three times.

FAUST. Come in, then!

MEPHISTOPHELES. So far, so good. We shall go on very well together, I hope; for, to chase away your fancies, I am here, like a youth of condition, in a coat of scarlet laced with gold, a mantle of stiff silk, a cock's feather in my hat, and a long pointed sword at my side. And, to make no more words about it, my advice to you is to array yourself in the same manner immediately, that, unrestrained, emancipated, you may try what life is.

FAUST. In every dress, I dare say, I shall feel the torture of the contracted life of this earth. I am too old for mere play, too young to be without a wish. What can the world afford me? — "Thou shalt renounce!" "Thou shalt renounce!" — That is the eternal song which is rung in every one's ears; which, our whole life long, every hour is hoarsely singing to us. In the morning I wake only to horror. I would fain weep bitter tears to see the day, which, in its course, will not accomplish a wish for me; no, not one; which, with wayward captiousness, weakens even the presentiment of every joy, and disturbs the creation of my busy breast by a thousand ugly realities. Then again, at the approach of night, I must stretch myself in anguish on my couch; here, too, no rest is vouchsafed to me; wild dreams are sure to harrow me up. The God that dwells in my bosom, that can stir my inmost soul, that sways all my energies — he is powerless as regards things without; and thus existence is a load to me, death an object of earnest prayer, and life detestable.

MEPHISTOPHELES. And yet death is never an entirely welcome guest.

FAUST. Oh! happy the man around whose brow he wreathes the bloody laurel in the glitter of victory — whom, after the maddening dance, he finds in a maiden's arms. Oh, that I had sunk away, enrapt, exanimate, before the great spirit's power.

MEPHISTOPHELES. And yet a certain person did not drink a certain brown juice on a certain night.

FAUST. Playing the spy, it seems, is thy amusement.

MEPHISTOPHELES. I am not omniscient, but I know much.

FAUST. Since a sweet familiar tone drew me from those thronging horrors, and played on what of childlike feeling remained in me with the concording note of happier times, — my curse on everything that entwines the soul with its jugglery, and chains it to this den of wretchedness with blinding and flattering influences. Accursed, first, be the lofty opinion in which the mind wraps itself! Accursed, the blinding of appearances, by which our senses are oppressed! Accursed, what plays the pretender to us in dreams, — the cheat of glory, of the lasting of a name! Accursed, wha flatters us as property, as wife and child, as slave and plough! Accursed be Mammon when he stirs us to bold deeds with treasures, when he smooths our couch for indolent delight! Accursed, the balsam-juice of the grape! Accursed, that highest grace of love! Accursed be Hope, accursed be Faith, and accursed, above all, be Patience!

CHORUS OF SPIRITS (*invisible*).

Woe, woe,
Thou hast destroyed it,
The beautiful world,
With violent hands;
It tumbles, it falls abroad.
A demi-god has shattered it to pieces!
We bear away
The wrecks into nothingness,
And wail over
The beauty that is lost.
Mighty
Among the sons of earth,
Proudlier
Build it again,
Build it up in thy bosom!

A new career of life,
With unstained sense
Begin,
And new lays
Shall peal out thereupon.

MEPHISTOPHELES.   These are the little ones of my train. Listen, how, with wisdom beyond their years, they counsel you to pleasure and action.   Out into the world, away from solitariness, where the senses and the juices of life stagnate — would they fain lure you.   Cease to trifle with your grief, which, like the vulture, feeds upon your vitals.   The worst company will make you feel that you are a man amongst men.   Yet I do not mean to thrust you amongst the pack. I am none of your great men ; but if, united with me, you will wend your way through life, I will readily accommodate myself to be yours upon the spot.   I am your companion ; and, if it suits you, your servant, your slave !

FAUST.   And what am I to do for you in return ?

MEPHISTOPHELES.   For that you have still a long day of grace.

FAUST.   No, no ; the devil is an egotist, and is not likely to do for God's sake what may advantage another.   Speak the condition plainly out ; such a servant is a dangerous inmate.

MEPHISTOPHELES. I will bind myself to your service *here*, and never sleep nor slumber at your call.   When we meet on *the other side*, you shall do as much for me.

FAUST. I care little about *the other side ;* if you first knock this world to pieces, the other may arise afterwards if it will. My joys flow from this earth, and this sun shines upon my sufferings : if I can only separate myself from them, what will and can may come to pass.   I will hear no more about it — whether there be hating and loving in the world to come, and whether there be an Above or Below in those spheres like our own.

MEPHISTOPHELES. In this sense, you may venture.   Bind yourself ; and during these days you shall be delighted by my arts ; I will give thee what no human being ever saw yet.

FAUST. What, poor devil, wilt thou give ?   Was the mind of a man, in its high aspiring, ever comprehended by the like of thee ?   But if thou hast food which never satisfies ; ruddy gold, which, volatile like quicksilver, melts away in the hand ; a game at which one never wins ; a maiden, who, on my breast, is already ogling my neighbor; the bright god-like joy of honor, which vanishes like a meteor! — Show me the fruit that rots before it is plucked, and trees which every day grow green anew.

Mephistopheles. Such a task affrights me not. I have such treasures at my disposal. But, my good friend, the time will come round when we may feast on what is really good in peace.

Faust. If ever I stretch myself, calm and composed, upon a couch, be there at once an end of me. If thou canst ever flatteringly delude me into being pleased with myself — if thou canst cheat me with enjoyment, be that day my last. I offer the wager.

Mephistopheles. Done!

Faust. And my hand upon it! If I ever say to the passing moment — "Stay, thou art so fair!" then mayest thou cast me into chains; then will I readily perish; then may the death-bell toll; then art thou free from thy service. The clock may stand, the index hand may fall: be time a thing no more for me!

Mephistopheles. Think well of it; we shall bear it in mind.

Faust. You have a perfect right so to do. I have formed no rash estimate of myself. As I remain I am a slave; what care I whether thine or another's?

Mephistopheles. This very day, at the doctor's feast, I shall enter upon my duty as servant. Only one thing — to guard against accidents, I must trouble you for a line or two.

Faust. Pedant, dost thou, too, require writing? Hast thou never known man nor man's word? Is it not enough that my word of mouth disposes of my days for all eternity? Does not the world rave on in all its currents, and am I to be bound by a promise? Yet this prejudice is implanted in our hearts: who would willingly free himself from it? Happy the man who bears truth pure in his breast; he will never have cause to repent any sacrifice! But a parchment, written and stamped, is a spectre which all shrink from. The word dies away in the very pen; in wax and leather is the mastery. What, evil spirit, wouldst thou of me? Brass, marble, parchment, paper? Shall I write with style, graver, pen? I leave the choice to thee.

Mephistopheles. How can you put yourself in a passion and overwork your oratory in this manner? Any scrap will do: you will subscribe your name with a drop of blood.

Faust. If this will fully satisfy you, the whim shall be complied with.

Mephistopheles. Blood is quite a peculiar sort of juice.

Faust. But fear not that I shall break this compact. What I promise, is precisely what all my energies are striving for. I have aspired too high: I belong only to thy class. The Great Spirit has spurned me; Nature shuts herself against me. The thread of thought is snapped; I have long loathed every sort of knowledge. Let us quench our glowing passions in the depths of sensuality; let every wonder be forthwith prepared beneath the hitherto impervious veil of sorcery. Let us cast ourselves into the rushing of time, into the rolling of accident. There pain and pleasure, success and disappointment, may succeed each other as they will — man's proper element is restless activity.

Mephistopheles. Nor end nor limit is prescribed to you. If it is your pleasure to sip the sweets of everything, to snatch at all as you fly by, much good may it do you — only fall to, and don't be coy.

Faust. I tell thee again, pleasure is not the question: I devote myself to the intoxicating whirl; — to the most agonizing enjoyment — to enamored hate — to animating vexation. My breast, cured of the thirst of knowledge, shall henceforth bare itself to every pang. I will enjoy in my own heart's core all that is parcelled out amongst mankind; grapple in spirit with the highest and deepest; heap the weal and woe of the whole race upon my breast, and thus dilate my own individuality to theirs and perish also, in the end, like them.

Mephistopheles. Oh, believe me, who many thousand years have chewed the cud on this hard food, that, from the cradle to the bier, no human being digests the old leaven. Believe a being like me, this Whole is only made for a god. *He* exists in an eternal halo; *us* he has brought forth in darkness; and only day and night are proper for *you.*

Faust. But I will.

Mephistopheles. That is well enough to say! But I am only troubled about one thing; time is short, art is long. I should suppose you would suffer yourself to be instructed. Take a poet to counsel; make the gentleman set his imagination at work, and heap all noble qualities on your honored head, — the lion's courage, the stag's swiftness, the fiery blood of the Italian, the enduring firmness of the North. Make him find out the secret of combining magnanimity with cunning, and of being in love, after a set plan, with the burning desires of youth. I myself should like to know such a gentleman — I would call him Mr. Microcosm.

FAUST. What, then, am I, if it be not possible to attain the crown of humanity, which every sense is striving for?

MEPHISTOPHELES. Thou art in the end — what thou art. Put on wigs with millions of curls — set thy foot upon ell-high socks, — thou abidest ever what thou art.

FAUST. I feel it; in vain have I scraped together and accumulated all the treasures of the human mind upon myself; and when I sit down at the end, still no new power wells up within : I am not a hair's breadth higher, nor a whit nearer the Infinite.

MEPHISTOPHELES. My good sir, you see things precisely as they are ordinarily seen ; we must manage matters better, before the joys of life pass away from us. What the deuce! you have surely hands and feet and head and — And what I enjoy with spirit, is that, then, the less my own? If I can pay for six horses, are not their powers mine? I dash along and am a proper man, as if I had four-and-twenty legs. Quick, then, have done with poring, and straight away into the world with me. I tell you, a fellow that speculates is like a brute driven in a circle on a barren heath by an evil spirit, whilst fair green meadow lies everywhere around.

FAUST. How shall we set about it?

MEPHISTOPHELES. We will just start and take our chance. What a place of martyrdom! what a precious life to lead! — wearying one's self and a set of youngsters to death. Leave that to your neighbor, Mr. Paunch! Why will you plague yourself to thrash straw? The best that you can know, you dare not tell the lads. Even now I hear one in the passage.

FAUST. I cannot possibly see him.

MEPHISTOPHELES. The poor boy has waited long; he must not be sent away disconsolate. Come, give me your cap and gown : the mask will become me to admiration. (*He changes his dress.*) Now trust to my wit. I require but a quarter of an hour. In the meantime prepare for our pleasant trip. (*Exit* FAUST.)

MEPHISTOPHELES, *in* FAUST's *gown*. Only despise reason and knowledge, the highest strength of humanity ; only permit thyself to be confirmed in delusion and sorcery-work by the spirit of lies, — and I have thee unconditionally. Fate has given him a spirit which is ever pressing onwards uncurbed, — whose overstrained striving o'erleaps the joys of earth. Him will I drag through the wild passages of life, through vapid unmeaningness. He shall sprawl, stand amazed, stick fast, — and meat and drink shall hang, for his insatiableness, before his craving lips: he shall pray for refreshment in vain; and had he not already given himself up to the devil, he would, notwithstanding, inevitably be lost. (*A* STUDENT *enters.*)

STUDENT. I am but just arrived, and come, full of devotion, to address and know a man whom all name to me with reverence.

MEPHISTOPHELES. I am flattered by your politeness. You see a man like many others. Have you yet made any inquiry elsewhere?

STUDENT. Interest yourself for me, I pray you. I come with every good disposition, a little money, and youthful spirits; my mother could hardly be brought to part with me, but I would fain learn something worth learning in the world.

MEPHISTOPHELES. You are here at the very place for it.

STUDENT. Honestly speaking, I already wish myself away. These walls, these halls, are by no means to my taste. The space is exceedingly confined; there is not a tree, nothing green, to be seen; and in the lecture-rooms, on the benches, — hearing, sight, and thinking fail me.

MEPHISTOPHELES. It all depends on habit. Thus, at first, the child does not take kindly to the mother's breast, but soon finds a pleasure in nourishing itself. Just so will you daily experience a greater pleasure at the breasts of wisdom.

STUDENT. I shall hang delightedly upon her neck; do but tell me how I am to attain it.

MEPHISTOPHELES. Tell me, before you go further, what faculty you fix upon?

STUDENT. I should wish to be profoundly learned, and should like to comprehend what is upon earth or in heaven, science and nature.

MEPHISTOPHELES. You are here upon the right scent; but you must not suffer your attention to be distracted.

STUDENT. I am heart and soul in the cause. A little relaxation and pastime, to be sure, would not come amiss on bright summer holidays.

MEPHISTOPHELES. Make the most of time, it glides away so fast. But method teaches you to gain time. For this reason, my good friend, I advise you to begin with a course of logic. In this study, the mind is well broken in, — laced up in Spanish boots, so that it creeps circumspectly along the path of thought, and runs no risk of flickering, ignis fatuus-like, in all directions. Then many a day will be spent in teaching you that one, two, three — is necessary for that which formerly you hit off at a blow, as easily as eating and drinking. It is with the fabric of thought as with a weaver's masterpiece; where one treadle moves a thousand threads: the shuttles shoot backwards and forwards; the threads flow unseen: ties, by thousands, are struck off at a blow. Your philosopher, — he steps in and proves to you, it must have been so: the first would be so, the second so, and therefore the third and fourth so: and if the first and second were not, the third and fourth would never be. The students of all countries put a high value on this, but none have become weavers. He who wishes to know and describe anything living, seeks first to drive the spirit out of it; he has then the parts in his hand; only, unluckily, the spiritual bond is wanting. Chemistry terms it *encheiresis n aturæ*, and mocks herself without knowing it.

STUDENT. I cannot quite comprehend you.

MEPHISTOPHELES. You will soon improve in that respect, if you learn to reduce and classify all things properly.

STUDENT. I am so confounded by all this; I feel as if a mill-wheel was turning round in my head.

MEPHISTOPHELES. In the next place, before everything else, you must set to at metaphysics. There see that you conceive profoundly what is not made for human brains. A fine word will stand you in stead for what enters and what does not enter there. And be sure, for this half-year, to adopt the strictest regularity. You will have five lectures every day. Be in as the clock strikes. Be well prepared beforehand with the paragraphs carefully conned, that you may see the better that he says nothing but what is in the book; yet write away as zealously as if the Holy Ghost were dictating to you.

STUDENT. You need not tell me that a second time. I can imagine how useful it is. For what one has in black and white one can carry home in comfort.

MEPHISTOPHELES. But choose a faculty.

STUDENT. I cannot reconcile myself in jurisprudence.

MEPHISTOPHELES. I cannot much blame you. I know the nature of this science. Laws descend, like an inveterate hereditary disease ; they trail from generation to generation, and glide imperceptibly from place to place. Reason becomes nonsense; beneficence a plague. Woe to thee that thou art a grandson ! Of the law that is born with us — of that, unfortunately, there is never a question.

STUDENT. You increase my repugnance. Oh, happy he whom you instruct ! I should almost like to study theology.

MEPHISTOPHELES. I do not wish to mislead you. As for this science, it is so difficult to avoid the wrong way ; there is so much hidden poison in it, which is hardly to be distinguished from the medicine. Here, again, it is best to attend but one master, and swear by his words. Generally speaking, stick to words ; you will then pass through the safe gate into the temple of certainty.

STUDENT. But there must be some meaning connected with the word.

MEPHISTOPHELES. Right ! only we must not be too anxious about that ; for it is precisely where meaning fails that a word comes in most opportunely. Disputes may be admirably carried on with words ; a system may be built with words ; words form a capital subject for belief ; a word admits not of an iota being taken from it.

STUDENT. Your pardon, I detain you by my many questions, but I must still trouble you. Would you be so kind as to add a pregnant word or two on medicine? Three years is a short time, and the field, God knows, is far too wide. If one has but a hint, one can feel one's way along further.

MEPHISTOPHELES (*aside*). I begin to be tired of the prosing style. I must play the devil properly again (*aloud*). The spirit of medicine is easy to be caught ; you study through the great and little world, and let things go on in the end — as it pleases God. It is vain that you wander scientifically about ; no man will learn more than he can ; he who avails himself of the passing moment — that is the proper man. You are tolerably well built, nor will you be wanting in boldness, and if you do but confide in yourself other souls will confide in you. In particular, learn how to treat the women : their eternal ohs ! and ahs ! so thousandfold, are to be cured from a single point, and if you only assume a moderately demure air, you will have them all under your thumb. You must have a title to convince them that your art is superior to most others, and then you are admitted from the first to all those little privileges which another spends years in coaxing for.—Learn how to feel the pulse adroitly, and boldly clasp them, with hot wanton looks, around the tapering hip, to see how tightly it is laced.

STUDENT. There is some sense in that; one sees, at any rate, the where and the how.

MEPHISTOPHELES. Gray, my dear friend, is all theory, and green the golden tree of life.

STUDENT. I vow to you all is a dream to me. Might I trouble you another time to hear your wisdom speak upon the grounds?

MEPHISTOPHELES. I am at your service, to the extent of my poor abilities.

STUDENT. I cannot possibly go away without placing my album in your hands. Do not grudge me this token of your favor.

MEPHISTOPHELES. With all my heart. (*He writes and gives it back.*)

STUDENT *reads*. Eritis sicut Deus, scientes bonum et malum. (*He closes the book reverentially, and takes his leave.*)

MEPHISTOPHELES. Only follow the old saying and my cousin the snake, and some time or other you, with your likeness to God, will be sorry enough.

FAUST *enters*. Whither now?

MEPHISTOPHELES. Where you please; to see the little, then the great world. With what joy, what profit, will you revel through the course.

FAUST. But with my long beard, I want the easy manners of society. I shall fail in the attempt. I never knew how to present myself in the world; I feel so little in the presence of others. I shall be in a constant state of embarrassment.

MEPHISTOPHELES. My dear friend, all that will come of its own accord; so soon as you feel confidence in yourself you know the art of life.

FAUST. How, then, are we to start? Where are your carriages, horses, and servants?

MEPHISTOPHELES. We have but to spread out this mantle that shall bear us through the air. Only you will have no heavy baggage on this bold trip. A little inflammable air, which I will get ready, will lift us quickly from this earth; and if we are light, we shall mount rapidly. I wish you joy of your new course of life.

AUERBACH'S CELLAR IN LEIPSIC.

(Drinking bout of merry fellows.)

FROSCH. Will no one drink? No one laugh? I will teach you to grin. Why, you are like wet straw to-day, yet at other times you blaze brightly enough.

BRANDER. That is your fault, you contribute nothing towards it : no nonsense, no beastliness ——

FROSCH (*throws a glass of wine over* BRANDER'S *head*). There are both for you!

BRANDER. You double hog!

FROSCH. Why, you wanted me to be so.

SIEBEL. Out with him who quarrels! With open heart strike up the song! swill and shout! holla, holla, ho!

ALTMAYER. Woe is me, I am a lost man. Cotton, here! the knave splits my ears.

SIEBEL. It is only when the vault echoes again that one feels the true power of the bass.

FROSCH. Right : out with him who takes anything amiss. A! taralara, da!

ALTMAYER. A! taralara!

FROSCH. Our throats are tuned. (*He sings.*) The dear holy Romish empire, how holds it still together?

BRANDER. A nasty song! psha, a political song! an offensive song! Thank God every morning of your life that you have not the Roman empire to care for. I, at least, esteem it no slight gain that I am not emperor nor chancellor. But we cannot do without a head. We will choose a pope. You know what sort of qualification turns the scale and elevates the man.

FROSCH *sings*. Soar up, Madam Nightingale, give my sweetheart ten thousand greetings for me.

SIEBEL. No greeting to the sweetheart; I will not hear of it.

FROSCH. Greeting to the sweetheart, and a kiss, too! Thou shalt not hinder me.

(He sings.)

Open bolts! in stilly night.
Open bolts! the lover wakes.
Shut bolts! at morning's dawn.

SIEBEL. Ay, sing, sing on, and praise and celebrate her; my turn for laughing will come, She has taken me in; she will do the same for you. May she have a hobgoblin for a lover! He may toy with her on a cross way. An old he-goat, on his return from the Blocksberg, may wicker good night to her on the gallop. A hearty fellow of genuine flesh and blood is far too good for the wench. I will hear of no greeting, unless it be to smash her windows.

BRANDER (*striking on the table*). Attend, attend; listen to me! You gentlemen must allow me to know something of life. Lovesick folks sit here, and I must give them something suitable to their condition by way of good night. Attend! a song of the newest cut! and strike boldly in with the chorus.

(He sings.)

There was a rat in the cellar, who lived on nothing but fat and butter, and had raised himself up a paunch fit for Doctor Luther himself. The cook had laid poison for him, then the world became too hot for him, as if he had love in his body.

CHORUS. — As if he had love in his body.

He ran round, he ran out, he drank of every puddle; he gnawed and scratched the whole house, but his fury availed nothing; he gave many a bound of agony; the poor beast was soon done for, as if he had love in his body,

CHORUS. — As if, etc.

He came running into the kitchen, for sheer pain, in open daylight, fell on the earth, and lay convulsed, and panted pitiably. Then the poisoner exclaimed, with a laugh — Ha! he is at his last gasp, as if he had love in his body.

CHORUS. — As if, etc.

SIEBEL. How the flats chuckle! It is a fine thing, to be sure, to lay poison for the poor rats.

BRANDER. They stand high in your favor, I dare say.

ALTMAYER. The bald-pated paunch! The misadventure makes him humble and mild. He sees in the swollen rat his own image drawn to the life.

FAUST and MEPHISTOPHELES.

MEPHISTOPHELES. Before all things else, I must bring you into merry company, that you may see how lightly life may be passed. These people make every day a feast. With little wit and much self-complacency, each turns round in the narrow circle-dance, like kittens playing with their tails. So long as they have no headache to complain of, and so long as they can get credit from their host, they are merry and free from care.

BRANDER. They are just off their journey; one may see as much from their strange manner. They have not been here an hour.

FROSCH. Thou art right; Leipsic is the place for me: it is a little Paris, and gives its folks a finish.

SIEBEL. What do you take the strangers to be?

FROSCH. Let me alone; in the drinking of a bumper I will worm it out of them as easily as draw a child's tooth. They appear to me to be noble; they have a proud and discontented look.

BRANDER. Mountebanks to a certainty, I wager.

ALTMAYER. Likely enough.

FROSCH. Now mark; I will smoke them.

MEPHISTOPHELES *to* FAUST. These people would never scent the devil if he had them by the throat.

FAUST. Good morrow, gentlemen.

SIEBEL. Thanks, and good morrow to you. (*Aside, looking at* MEPHISTOPHELES *askance.*) Why does the fellow halt on one foot?

MEPHISTOPHELES. Will you permit us to sit down with you? We shall have company to cheer us, instead of good liquor, which is not to be had.

ALTMAYER. You seem a very dainty gentleman.

FROSCH. I dare say you are lately from Rippach. Did you sup with Mr. Hans before you left?

MEPHISTOPHELES. We passed him without stopping to-day. The last time we spoke to him, he had much to say of his cousins; he charged us with compliments to each. (*With an inclination towards* FROSCH.)

ALTMAYER (*aside*). Thou hast it there! he knows a thing or two.

SIEBEL. A knowing fellow.

FROSCH. Only wait, I shall have him presently.

MEPHISTOPHELES. If I am not mistaken, we heard some practised voices singing in chorus? No doubt singing must echo admirably from this vaulted roof.

FROSCH. I dare say you are a dilettante.

MEPHISTOPHELES. Oh, no! The power is weak, but the desire is strong.

ALTMAYER. Give us a song.

MEPHISTOPHELES. As many as you like.

SIEBEL. Only let it be bran new.

MEPHISTOPHELES. We are just returned from Spain, the fair land of wine and song. (*He sings.*) There was once upon a time a king who had a great flea ——

FROSCH. Hark! A flea! Did you catch that? A flea is a fine sort of chap.

Mephistopheles *sings.* There was once upon a time a king; he had a great flea, and was as fond of it as if it had been his own son. Then he called his tailor; the tailor came. "There, measure the youngster for clothes, and measure him for breeches."

Brander. Only don't forget to impress it on the tailor to measure with the greatest nicety, and, as he loves his head, to make the breeches sit smoothly.

Mephistopheles *sings.* He was now attired in velvet and silk, had ribbons on his coat, had a cross besides, and was forthwith made minister, and had a great star. Then his brothers and sisters also became great folks. And the ladies and gentlemen at court were dreadfully tormented; from the queen to the waiting-women they were pricked and bitten, yet dared not crack nor scratch them away. But we crack and stifle fast enough when one pricks. Chorus.— But we crack, etc.

Frosch. Bravo! bravo! That was capital.

Siebel. So perish every flea.

Brander. Point your fingers, and nick them cleverly.

Altmayer. Liberty forever! Wine forever!

Mephistopheles. I would willingly drink a glass in honor of liberty, were your wine a thought better.

Siebel. You had better not let us hear that again!

Mephistopheles. I am afraid of giving offence to the landlord, or I would treat these worthy gentlemen out of our own stock.

Siebel. O, bring it in; I take the blame upon myself.

Frosch. Give us a good glass, and we shall not be sparing of our praise; only don't let your samples be too small; for, if I am to give an opinion, I require a regular mouthful.

Altmayer (*aside*). They are from the Rhine, I guess.

Mephistopheles. Bring a gimlet.

Brander. What for? You surely have not the casks at the door?

Altmayer. Behind there, is a tool-chest of the landlord's.

Mephistopheles (*taking the gimlet*) *to* Frosch. Now say, what wine do you wish to taste?

Frosch. What do you mean? Have you so many sorts?

Mephistopheles. I give every man his choice.

Altmayer *to* Frosch. Ah! you begin to lick your lips already.

Frosch. Well! if I am to choose, I will take Rhine wine. Our fatherland affords the best of gifts.

Mephistopheles (*boring a hole in the edge of the table where* Frosch *is sitting*). Get a little wax to make stoppers, immediately.

Altmayer. Ah! these are juggler's tricks.

Mephistopheles *to* Brander. And you?

Brander. I choose champagne, and right sparkling it must be. (Mephistopheles *bores again; one of the others has in the meantime prepared the wax-stoppers and stopped the holes.*) One cannot always avoid what is foreign; what is good often lies so far off. A true German cannot abide Frenchmen, but has no objection to their wine.

Siebel (*as* Mephistopheles *approaches him*). I must own I do not like acid wine; give me a glass of genuine sweet.

Mephistopheles (*bores*). You shall have Tokay in a twinkling.

Altmayer. No, gentlemen, look me in the face. I see plainly you are only making fun of us.

Mephistopheles. Ha! ha! that would be taking too great a liberty with such distinguished guests. Quick! only speak out at once. What wine can I have the pleasure of serving you with?

Altmayer. With any; there is no need of much questioning. (*After all the holes are bored and stopped*)

Mephistopheles (*with strange gestures*).

The vine bears grapes.
The he-goat bears horns.
Wine is juicy,
Vines are wood;
The wooden table can also give wine.
A deep insight into nature:
Behold a miracle, only have faith;
Now draw the stoppers, and drink.

All (*as they draw the stoppers, and the wine he chose runs into each man's glass*). Oh, beautiful spring that flows for us!

Mephistopheles. Only take care not to spill any of it. (*They drink repeatedly.*)

All *sing.* We are as happy as cannibals — as five hundred swine.

Mephistopheles. These people are now in their glory; mark, how merry they are.

Faust. I should like to be off now.

Mephistopheles. But first attend; their brutishness will display itself right gloriously.

Siebel. (*Drinks carelessly; the wine is spilt upon the ground, and turns to flame.*) Help! fire, help! Hell is burning.

Mephistopheles (*conjuring the flame*). Be quiet, friendly element! (*To* Siebel.) This time it was only a drop of the fire of purgatory.

Siebel. What may that be? Hold! you shall pay dearly for it. It seems that you do not know us.

Frosch. He had better not try that a second time.

Altmayer: I think we had better send him packing quietly.

Siebel. What, sir, you dare play off your hocus-pocus here?

Mephistopheles. Silence, old wine-butt!

Siebel. Broomstick! will you be rude to us, too?

Brander. But hold! or blows shall rain.

Altmayer. (*Draws a stopper from the table; fire flies out against him.*) I burn! I burn!

Siebel. Sorcery! thrust home! the knave is fair game. (*They draw their knives and attack* Mephistopheles.)

Mephistopheles (*with solemn gestures*).

> False form and word,
> Change sense and place,
> Be here, be there!

(*They stand amazed, and gaze on each other.*)

Altmayer. Where am I? What a beautiful country!

Frosch. Vineyards! Can I believe my eyes?

Siebel. And grapes close at hand!

Brander. Here, under these green leaves, see, what a stem! see what a bunch! (*He seizes* Siebel *by the nose. The others do the same one with the other, and brandish their knives.*)

Mephistopheles (*as before*). Error, loose the bandage from their eyes! And do ye remember the devil's mode of jesting. (*He disappears with* Faust. *The fellows start back from one another.*)

Siebel. What's the matter?

Altmayer. How?

Frosch. Was that your nose?

Brander *to* Siebel. And I have yours in my hand!

Altmayer. It was a shock that thrilled through **every** limb! Give me a chair; I am sinking.

Frosch. No, do but tell me what has happened?

Siebel. Where is the fellow? If I meet with him, it shall be as much as his life is worth.

Altmayer. I saw him with my own eyes riding out of the cellar door upon a cask. My feet feel as heavy as lead. (*Turning towards the table.*) My! I wonder whether the wine is flowing still?

Siebel. It was all a cheat, a lie, a make-believe. Yet it seemed to me as if I was drinking wine.

Brander. But how was it with the grapes?

Altmayer. Let any one tell me, after that, that one is not to believe in wonders!

WITCHES' KITCHEN.

A large caldron is hanging over the fire on a low hearth. Different figures are seen in the fumes which rise from it. A female monkey is sitting by the caldron and skimming it, and taking care that it does not run over. The male monkey is seated near with the young ones, and warming himself. The walls and ceiling are hung with the strangest articles of witch furniture.

Faust. I loathe this mad concern of witchcraft. Do you promise me that I shall recover in this chaos of insanity? Do I need an old hag's advice? And will this mess of cookery really take thirty years from my body? Woe is me, if you know of nothing better! Hope is already gone. Has nature and has a noble spirit discovered no sort of balsam?

Mephistopheles. My friend, now again you speak wisely! There is also a natural mode of renewing youth. But it is in another book, and is a strange chapter.

Faust. Let me know it.

Mephistopheles. Well, to have a mean without money, physician, or sorcery; betake thyself straightway to the field, begin to back and dig, confine thyself and thy sense within a narrow circle; support thyself on simple food; live with beasts as a beast, and think it no robbery to manure the land you crop. That is the best way, believe me, to keep a man young to eighty.

Faust. I am not used to it. I cannot bring myself to take the spade in hand. The confined life does not suit me at all.

Mephistopheles. Then you must have recourse to the witch, after all.

Faust. But why the old woman in particular? Cannot you brew the drink yourself?

Mephistopheles. That were a pretty pastime! I could build a thousand bridges in the time. Not art and science only, but patience is required for the job. A quiet spirit is busy at it for years; time only makes this fine liquor strong. And the ingredients are exceedingly curious. The devil, it is true, has taught it to her, but the devil cannot make it. (*Perceiving the* Monkeys.) See what a pretty breed! That is the lass — that the lad. (*To the* Monkeys.) — It seems your mistress is not at home?

The Monkeys.

At the feast,
Out of the house,
Out and away by the chimney-stone!

Mephistopheles. How long does she usually rake!

The Monkeys. Whilst we are warming our paws.

Mephistopheles (*to* Faust). What think you of the pretty creatures?

Faust. The most disgusting I ever saw.

Mephistopheles. Nay, a discourse like the present is precisely what I am fondest of engaging in. (*To the* Monkeys.) Tell me, accursed whelps, what are ye stirring up with the porridge?

Monkeys. We are cooking coarse beggars' broth.

Mephistopheles. You will have plenty of customers.

The He-Monkey. (*Approaches and fawns on* Mephistopheles.)

Oh, quick, throw the dice,
And make me rich —
And let me win!
My fate is a sorry one,
And had I money
I should not want for consideration.

Mephistopheles. How happy the monkey would think himself, if he could only put into the lottery.

(*The* Young Monkeys *have in the meantime, begun playing with a large globe, and roll it forwards.*)

THE HE-MONKEY.

That is the world;
It rises and falls,
And rolls unceasingly.
It rings like glass:
How soon breaks that?
It is hollow within;
It glitters much here,
And still more here—
I am alive!
My dear son,
Keep thee aloof;
Thou must die!
It is of clay,
This makes potsherds.

MEPHISTOPHELES. What is the sieve for?

THE HE-MONKEY (*takes it down*). Wert thou a thief, I should know thee at once. (*He runs to the female and makes her look through.*)

Look through the sieve!
Dost thou recognize the thief?
And darest not name him?

MEPHISTOPHELES (*approaching the fire*). And this pot?

THE MONKEYS.

The half-witted sot!
He knows not the pot!
He knows not the kettle!

MEPHISTOPHELES. Uncivil brute!

THE HE-MONKEY. Take the brush here and sit down on the settle. (*He makes* MEPHISTOPHELES *sit down.*)

FAUST (*who all this time has been standing before a looking-glass, now approaching and now standing off from it*). What do I see? What heavenly image shows itself in this magic mirror! O love! lend me the swiftest of thy wings, and bear me to her region. Ah! when I stir from this spot, when I venture to go near, I can only see her as in a mist. The loveliest image of a woman! Is it possible — is woman so lovely? Must I see in these recumbent limbs the innermost essence of all heavens? Is there anything like it upon earth?

MEPHISTOPHELES. When a God first works hard for six days, and himself says bravo at the end, it is but natural that something clever should come of it. For this time look your fill. I know where to find out such a love for you, and happy he whose fortune it is to bear her home as a bridegroom. (FAUST *continues looking into the mirror.* ME-PHISTOPHELES, *stretching himself on the settle, and playing with the brush, continues speaking.*)   Here I sit, like the king upon his throne; here is my sceptre — I only want the crown.

THE MONKEYS (*who have hitherto been playing all sorts of strange antics, bring* MEPHISTOPHELES *a crown, with loud acclamations*).   O be so good as to glue the crown with sweat and blood.   (*They handle the crown awkwardly, and break it into two pieces, with which they jump about.*)

> Now it is done.
> We speak and see ;
> We hear and rhyme —

FAUST (*before the mirror*). Woe is me!   I am becoming almost mad!

MEPHISTOPHELES (*pointing to the* MONKEYS).   My own head begins to totter now.

THE MONKEYS.

> — And if we are lucky —
> And if things fit,
> Then there are thoughts.

FAUST (*as before*). My heart is beginning to burn.   Do but let us be gone immediately.

MEPHISTOPHELES (*in the same position*). Well, no one can deny, at any rate, that they are sincere poets.   (*The caldron, which the* SHE-MONKEY *has neglected, begins to boil over ; a great flame arises, and streams up the chimney. The* WITCH *comes shooting down through the flame with horrible cries.*)

THE WITCH.

> Ough, ough, ough, ough!
> Damned beast! accursed sow!
> Neglecting the caldron, scorching your dame —
> Cursed beast!

> *Espying* FAUST *and* MEPHISTOPHELES.)

> What now ?
> Who are ye ?
> What would ye here ?
> Who hath come slinking in ?
> The red plague of fire
> Into your bones!

(*She dips the skimming ladle into the caldron, and sprinkles flames at* FAUST, MEPHISTOPHELES, *and the* MONKEYS. *The* MONKEYS *whimper.*)

MEPHISTOPHELES (*who inverts the brush which he holds in his hand, and strikes amongst the glasses and pots*).

To pieces!
To pieces!
There lies the porridge!
There lies the glass!

It is only carrying on the jest — beating time, thou carrion, to thy melody. (*As the* WITCH *steps back in rage and amazement.*) Dost thou recognize me, thou atomy, thou scare-crow? Dost thou recognize thy lord and master? What is there to hinder me from striking in good earnest, from dashing thee and thy monkey-spirits to pieces? Hast thou no more any respect for the red doublet? Canst thou not distinguish the cock's feather? Have I concealed this face? Must I then name myself?

THE WITCH. O master, pardon this rough reception. But I see no cloven foot. Where, then, are your two ravens?

MEPHISTOPHELES. This once the apology may serve. For, to be sure, it is long since last we met. The march of intellect, too, which licks all the world into shape has even reached the devil. The northern phantom is no more to be seen. Where do you now see horns, tail and claws? And as for the foot, which I cannot do without, it would prejudice me in society; therefore, like many a gallant, I have worn false calves these many years.

THE WITCH (*dancing*). I am almost beside myself to see the gallant Satan here again.

MEPHISTOPHELES. The name, woman, I beg to be spared.

THE WITCH. Wherefore? What has it done to you?

MEPHISTOPHELES. It has long been written in story-books; but men are not the better for that; they are rid of the wicked one, the wicked have remained. You may call me Baron, that will do very well. I am a cavalier, like other cavaliers. You doubt not of my gentle blood; see here, these are the arms I bear! (*He makes an unseemly gesture.*)

THE WITCH *laughs immoderately*. Ha, ha! That is in your way. You are the same mad wag as ever.

MEPHISTOPHELES (*to* FAUST). My friend, attend to this. This is the way to deal with witches.

THE WITCH. Now, sirs, say what you are for.

MEPHISTOPHELES. A good glass of the juice you wot of. I must beg you to let it be of the oldest. Years double its power.

THE WITCH. Most willingly. Here is a bottle out of which I sometimes sip a little myself; which, besides, no longer stinks in the least. I will give you a glass with pleasure. (*Aside.*) But if this man drinks it unprepared, you well know he cannot live an hour.

MEPHISTOPHELES. He is a worthy friend of mine, on whom it will have a good effect. I grudge him not the best of my kitchen. Draw thy circle, spell thy spells, and give him a cup full. (*The* WITCH, *with strange gestures, draws a circle and places rare things in it; in the meantime, the glasses begin to ring and the caldron to sound and make music. Lastly, she brings a great book, and places the* MONKEYS *in the circle, who are made to serve her for a reading-desk and hold the torches. She signs to* FAUST *to approach.*)

FAUST (*to* MEPHISTOPHELES). But tell me, what is to come of all this? This absurd apparatus, these frantic gestures, this most disgusting jugglery — I know them of old, and thoroughly abominate them.

MEPHISTOPHELES. Pooh! that is only fit to laugh at. Don't be so fastidious. As mediciner, she is obliged to play off some hocus-pocus that the dose may operate well on you. (*He makes* FAUST *enter the circle.*)

THE WITCH, *with a strong emphasis, begins to declaim from the book.*

> You must understand,
> Of one make ten,
> And let two go,
> And three make even;
> Then art thou rich.
> Lose the four!
> Out of five and six,
> So says the Witch,
> Make seven and eight,
> Then it is done,
> And nine is one,
> And ten is none.
> That is the witches' one-times-one.

FAUST. It seems to me that the hag is raving.

MEPHISTOPHELES. There is a good deal more of it yet — I know it well; the whole book is to the same tune. I have wasted many an hour upon it, for a downright contradiction remains equally mysterious to wise folks and fools. My friend, the art is old and new. It has ever been the fashion to spread error instead of truth by three and one, and one and three. It is taught and prattled uninterruptedly. Who will concern themselves about dolts? Men are wont to believe, when they hear only words, that there must be something in it.

THE WITCH *continues.*

The high power
Of knowledge,
Hidden from the whole world!
And he who thinks not,
On him is it bestowed;
He has it without trouble.

FAUST. What sort of nonsense is she reciting to us? My head is splitting! I seem to hear a hundred idiots declaiming in full chorus.

MEPHISTOPHELES. Enough, enough, incomparable Sybil! Hand us thy drink, and fill the cup to the brim without more ado; for this draught will do my friend no harm. He is a man of many grades, who has taken many a good gulp already. (*The* WITCH *with many ceremonies pours the liquor into a cup; as* FAUST *lifts it to his mouth, a light flame arises.*)

MEPHISTOPHELES. Down with it at once. Do not stand hesitating. It will soon warm your heart. Are you hail-fellow well-met with the devil, and afraid of fire? (*The* WITCH *dissolves the circle —* FAUST *steps out.*)

MEPHISTOPHELES. Now forth at once! You must not rest.

THE WITCH. Much good may the draught do you.

MEPHISTOPHELES (*to the* WITCH). And if I can do anything to pleasure you, you need only mention it to me on Walpurgis' night.

THE WITCH. Here is a song! if you sing it occasionally, it will have a particular effect on you.

MEPHISTOPHELES (*to* FAUST). Come quick, and be guided by me; you must necessarily expire, to make the spirit work through blood and bone. I will afterwards teach you to value the nobility of idleness, and you will feel ere long, with heartfelt delight, how Cupid bestirs himself and bounds hither and thither.

FAUST. Let me only look another moment in the glass. That female form was too, too lovely.

MEPHISTOPHELES. Nay, nay; you shall soon see the model of all womankind in flesh and blood. (*Aside.*) With this draught in your body, you will soon see a Helen in every woman you meet.

THE STREET.

FAUST. (MARGARET *passing by*.) My pretty lady, may I take the liberty of offering you my arm and escort?

MARGARET. I am neither lady, nor pretty, and can go home without an escort. (*She disengages herself and exit*.)

FAUST. By heaven this girl *is* lovely! I have never seen the like of her. She is so well-behaved and virtuous, and something snappish, withal. The redness of her lip, the light of her cheek — I shall never forget them all the days of my life. The manner in which she cast down her eyes is deeply stamped upon my heart: and how tart she was — it was absolutely ravishing!

MEPHISTOPHELES *enters*.

FAUST. Hark, you must get me the girl.

MEPHISTOPHELES. Which?

FAUST. She passed but now.

MEPHISTOPHELES. What, she? She came from her confessor, who absolved her from all her sins. I stole up close to the chair. It is an innocent little thing, that went for next to nothing to the confessional. Over her I have no power.

FAUST. Yet she is past fourteen!

MEPHISTOPHELES. You positively speak like Jack Rake, who covets every sweet flower for himself, and fancies that there is neither honor nor favor which is not to be had for the plucking. But this will not always do.

FAUST. My good Mr. Sermonizer, don't plague me with your morality. And, in a word, I tell you this : if the sweet young creature does not lie this very night in my arms at midnight our compact is at an end.

MEPHISTOPHELES. Consider what is possible. I need a fortnight, at least, to find an opportunity.

FAUST. Had I but seven hours clear, I should not want the devil's assistance to seduce such a child.

MEPHISTOPHELES. You talk now almost like a Frenchman : but don't fret about it, I beg. What boots it to go straight to enjoyment? The delight is not so great by far, as when you have kneaded and molded the doll on all sides with all sorts of nonsense, as many a French story teaches.

FAUST. But I have appetite without all that.

MEPHISTOPHELES. Now seriously, and without offence, I tell you, once for all, that the lovely girl is not to be had in such a hurry; nothing here is to be taken by storm; we must have recourse to stratagem.

FAUST. Get me something belonging to the angel. Carry me to her place of repose; get me a kerchief from her bosom, a garter of my love.

MEPHISTOPHELES. That you may see my anxiety to minister to your passion, — we will not lose a moment; this very day I will conduct you to her chamber.

FAUST. And shall I see her? have her? —

MEPHISTOPHELES. No. She will be at a neighbor's. In the meantime, you, all alone, and in her atmosphere, may feast to satiety on anticipated joy.

FAUST. Can we go now?

MEPHISTOPHELES. It is too early.

FAUST. Get me a present for her.   [*Exit.*

MEPHISTOPHELES. Presents directly! Now that's capital! That's the way to succeed! I know many a fine place, and many a long-buried treasure. I must look them over a bit. [*Exit.*

EVENING.

A neat little Room.

MARGARET (*braiding and binding up her hair.*) I would give something to know who that gentleman was to-day! He had a gallant bearing, and is of a noble family, I am sure. I could read that on his brow; he would not else have been so impudent.   [*Exit.*

MEPHISTOPHELES — FAUST.

MEPHISTOPHELES. Come in — as softly as possible — only come in!

FAUST (*after a pause*). Leave me alone, I beg of you.

MEPHISTOPHELES (*looking round*). It is not every maiden that is so neat.   [*Exit.*

FAUST (*looking round*). Welcome, sweet twilight, that pervades this sanctuary! Possess my heart, delicious pangs of love, you who live languishing on the dew of hope! What a feeling of peace, order, and contentment breathes round! What abundance in this poverty! What bliss in this cell! (*He throws himself upon the leathern easy-chair by the side of the bed.*) Oh! receive me, thou, who hast welcomed with open arms, in joy and sorrow, the generations that are past. Ah, how often has a swarm of children clustered about this patriarchal throne. Here, perhaps, in gratitude for her Christmas-box, with the warm round cheek of childhood — has my beloved piously kissed the withered hand of her grandsire. Maiden, I feel thy spirit of abundance and order flutter around me — that spirit which daily instructs thee like a mother — which bids thee spread the neat cloth upon the table and curl the sand upon the floor. Dear hand! so godlike; you make the hut a heaven; and here —(*He lifts up a bed-curtain*), what blissful tremor seizes me! Here could I linger for hours! Nature, here, in light dreams, you matured the born angel. Here lay the child! its gentle bosom filled with warm life; and here, with weavings of hallowed purity, the divine image developed itself. And thou, what has brought thee hither? How deeply moved I feel! What wouldst thou here? Why grows thy heart so heavy? Poor Faust, I no longer know thee. Am I breathing an enchanted atmosphere? I panted so for instant enjoyment, and feel myself dissolving into a dream of love. Are we the sport of every pressure of the air? And if she entered this very moment, how wouldst thou atone for thy guilt! The big boaster, alas, how shrunk! would lie, dissolved away, at her feet.

MEPHISTOPHELES. Quick! I see her coming below.

FAUST. Away, away! I return no more.

MEPHISTOPHELES. Here is a casket tolerably heavy. I took it from somewhere else. Place it instantly in the press. I promise you she will be fairly beside herself. I put baubles in it to gain another; but children are children, and play is play, all the world over.

FAUST. I know not — shall I?

MEPHISTOPHELES. Is that a thing to ask about? Perchance you mean to keep the treasure for yourself, in that case, I advise, you to spare the precious hours for your lusts, and further trouble to me. I hope you are not avaricious. I scratch my head, rub my hands — (*He places the casket in the press and closes the lock.*) But quick, away to bend the sweet young creature to your heart's desire; and now you look as if you were going to the lecture-room — as if Physic and Metaphysic were standing gray and bodily before you there. But away!   [*Exeunt.*

MARGARET (*with a lamp.*) It feels so close, so sultry here. (*She opens the window.*) And yet it is not so very warm without. I begin to feel I know not how. I wish my mother would come home. I tremble all over; but I am a silly, timid woman. (*She begins to sing as she undresses herself.*)

Song. There was a king in Thule, faithful even to the grave, to whom his dying mistress gave a golden goblet.

He prized nothing above it; he emptied it at every feast; his eyes overflowed as often as he drank out of it.

And when he came to die, he reckoned up the cities in his kingdom; he grudged none of them to his heir, but not so with the goblet.

He sat at the royal banquet, with his knights around him, in his proud ancestral hall, there in his castle on the sea.

There stood the old toper, took a parting draught of life's glow, and threw the hallowed goblet down into the waves.

He saw it splash, fill, and sink deep into the sea; his eyes fell, he never drank a drop more. (*She opens the press to put away her clothes, and perceives the casket.*) How came this beautiful casket here? I am sure I locked the press. It is very strange! What is in it I wonder? Perhaps some one brought it as a pledge, and my mother lent money upon it. A little key hangs by the ribbon: I have a good mind to open it. What is here? Good heavens! look! I have never seen anything like it in all my born days! A set of trinkets a countess might wear on the highest festival. How would the chain become me? To whom can such finery belong? (*She puts them on and walks before the looking-glass.*) If the earrings were but mine! one cuts quite a different figure in them. What avails your beauty, poor maiden? That may be all very pretty and good, but they let it all be. You are praised, half in pity; but after gold presses — on gold hangs — everything, — Alas, for us poor ones!

PROMENADE.

Faust, *walking up and down thoughtfully. To him* Mephistopheles. By all despised love! By the elements of hell! Would that I know something worse to curse by!

Faust. What is the matter? What is it that pinches you so sharply? I never saw such a face in my life!

Mephistopheles. I could give myself to the devil directly were I not the devil myself.

Faust. Is your brain disordered? It becomes you truly to rave like a madman.

Mephistopheles. Only think! A priest has carried off the jewels provided for Margaret. The mother gets sight of the thing, and begins at once to have a secret horror of it. Truly the woman hath a fine nose, is ever snuffling in her prayer-book, and smells in every piece of furniture, whether the thing be holy or profane; and she plainly smells out in the jewels that there was not much blessing connected with them. "My child," said she, "ill-gotten wealth ensnares the soul, consumes the blood. We will consecrate it to the Mother of God; she will gladden us with heavenly manna." Margaret made a wry face; it is, after all, thought she, a gift-horse; and truly, he cannot be godless, who brought it here so handsomely. The mother sent for a priest. — Scarcely had he heard the jest, but he seemed well pleased with the sight. He spoke, "This shows a good disposition; who conquers himself, — he is the gainer. The church has a good stomach; she has eaten up whole countries, and has never yet overeaten herself. The church alone, my good woman, can digest unrighteous wealth."

Faust. That is a general custom; a Jew and a king can do it, too.

Mephistopheles. So saying, he swept off clasp, chain, and ring, as if they were so many mushrooms; thanked them neither more nor less than if it had been a basket of nuts; promised them all heavenly reward — and very much edified they were.

Faust. And Margaret——

Mephistopheles. Is now sitting full of restlessness, not knowing what to do with herself; thinks day and night on the trinkets, and still more on him who gave them to her.

Faust. My love's grief distresses me. Get her another set immediately. The first were no great things after all.

Mephistopheles. Oh! to be sure, all is child's play to the gentleman!

Faust. Do it, and order it as I wish. Stick close to her neighbor. Don't be a milk-and-water devil; and fetch a fresh set of jewels.

Mephistopheles. With all my heart, honored sir. (Faust *exit*.) A love-sick fool like this puffs away sun, moon, and all the stars indifferently, by way of pastime for his mistress.

THE NEIGHBOR'S HOUSE.

MARTHA (*alone*). God forgive my dear husband; he has not acted well towards me. He goes straight away into the world, and leaves me widowed and lonely. Yet truly I never did anything to vex him; God knows I loved him to my heart. (*She weeps.*) Perhaps he is actually dead. Oh, torture! Had I but a certificate of his death!

MARGARET (*enters*). Martha!

MARTHA. What is the matter, Margaret?

MARGARET. My knees almost sink under me! I have found just such another ebony casket in my press — and things absolutely magnificent, far costlier than the first.

MARTHA. You must say nothing about it to your mother. She would carry it to the confessional again.

MARGARET. Now, only see! only look at them!

MARTHA (*dresses her up in them*). Oh! you happy creature.

MARGARET. Unfortunately, I must not be seen in them in the street, nor in the church.

MARTHA. Do but come over frequently to me, and put on the trinkets here in private. Walk a little hour up and down before the looking-glass; we shall have our enjoyment in that. And then an occasion offers, a festival occurs, where, little by little, one lets folks see them; — first a chain, then the pearl earrings. Your mother, perhaps, will not observe it, or one may make some pretence to her.

MARGARET. But who could have brought the two caskets? There is something not right about it. (*Some one knocks.*) Good God! can that be my mother?

MARTHA (*looking through the blinds*). It is a stranger — come in.

MEPHISTOPHELES (*enters*). I have made free to come in at once; I have to beg pardon of the ladies. (*He steps back respectfully before Margaret.*) I came to inquire after Mrs. Martha Schwerdtlein.

MARTHA. I am she; what is your pleasure, sir?

MEPHISTOPHELES (*aside to her*). I know you now — that is enough. You have a visitor of distinction there. Excuse the liberty I have taken. I will call again in the afternoon.

MARTHA (*aloud*). Only think, child — of all things in the world! this gentleman takes you for a lady.

MARGARET. I am a poor young creature. Oh! heavens, the gentleman is too obliging. The jewels and ornaments are none of mine.

Mephistopheles. Ah! it is not the jewels alone. She has a mien, a look, so striking. How glad I am that I may stay.

Martha. What do you bring, then? I am very curious —

Mephistopheles. I wish I had better news. I hope you will not make me suffer for it. Your husband is dead, and sends you his compliments.

Martha. Is dead! the good soul! Oh, woe is me! My husband is dead! Ah, I shall die!

Margaret. Dear, good Martha, don't despair.

Mephistopheles. Listen to the melancholy tale.

Margaret. For this reason I should wish never to be in love for all the days of my life. The loss would grieve me to death.

Mephistopheles. Joy must have sorrow — sorrow joy.

Martha. Relate to me the close of his life.

Mephistopheles. He lies buried in Padua, at St. Antony's, in a spot well consecrated for a bed of rest, — eternally·cool.

Martha. Have you nothing else for me?

Mephistopheles. Yes, a request, big and heavy! be sure to have three hundred masses sung for him. For the rest, my pockets are empty.

Martha. What! not a coin by way of token? Not a trinket? what every journeyman mechanic husbands at the bottom of his pouch, saved as a keepsake, and rather starves, rather begs —

Mephistopheles. Madam, I am very sorry. But he really has not squandered away his money. He, too, bitterly repented of his sins; aye, and bewailed his ill-luck still more.

Margaret. Ah! that mortals should be so unlucky. Assuredly I will sing many a *requiem* for him.

Mephistopheles. You deserve to be married directly. You are an amiable girl.

Margaret. Oh, no, there is time enough for that.

Mephistopheles. If not a husband, then a gallant in the meantime. It were one of the best gifts of heaven to have so sweet a thing in one's arms.

Margaret. That is not the custom in this country.

Mephistopheles. Custom or not, such things do come to pass, though.

Martha. But relate to me —

Mephistopheles. I stood by his death-bed. It was

somewhat better than dung, — of half-rotten straw; but he died like a Christian, and found that he had still much more upon his score. "How thoroughly," he cried, "must I detest myself — to run away from my business and my wife in such a manner. Oh! the recollection is death to me. If she could but forgive me in this life!"

MARTHA (*weeping*). The good man! I have long since forgiven him.

MEPHISTOPHELES. "But, God knows, she was more in fault than I."

MARTHA. He lied, then! What, tell lies on the brink of the grave!

MEPHISTOPHELES. He certainly fabled with his last breath, if I am but half a connoisseur. "I," said he, "had no occasion to gape for pastime — first to get children, and then bread for them, and bread in the widest sense, — and could not even eat my share in peace."

MARTHA. Did he thus forget all my faith, all my love — my drudgery by day and night?

MEPHISTOPHELES. Not so; he affectionately reflected on it. He said: "When I left Malta, I prayed fervently for my wife and children; and heaven was so far favorable that our ship took a Turkish vessel, which carried a treasure of the great Sultan. Bravery had its reward, and, as was no more than right, I got my fair share of it."

MARTHA. How! where! Can he have buried it?

MEPHISTOPHELES. Who knows where it is now scattered to the four winds of heaven? A fair damsel took an interest in him as he was strolling about, a stranger, in Naples. She manifested great fondness and fidelity towards him; so much so that he felt it even unto his blessed end.

MARTHA. The villain! the robber of his children! And all the wretchedness, all the poverty, could not check his scandalous life.

MEPHISTOPHELES. But consider, he has paid for it with his life. Now, were I in your place, I would mourn him for one chaste year, and have an eye towards a new sweetheart in the meantime.

MARTHA. Oh, God! but I shall not easily in this world find another like my first. There could hardly be a kinderhearted fool; he only loved being away from home too much, and stranger women, and stranger wine, and the cursed dicing.

MEPHISTOPHELES. Well, well, things might have gone on very well if he, on his part, only winked at an equal number of peccadillos in you. I protest, upon this condition, I would change rings with you myself!

MARTHA. Oh, the gentleman is pleased to jest.

MEPHISTOPHELES (*aside*). Now it is full time to be off. I dare say she would take the devil himself at his word. (*To* MARGARET.) How feels your heart?

MARGARET. What do you mean?

MEPHISTOPHELES (*aside*). Good, innocent child. (*Aloud.*) Farewell, ladies!

MARGARET. Farewell!

MARTHA. Oh, but tell me quickly! I should like to have a certificate where, how, and when my love died and was buried. I was always a friend to regularity, and should like to read his death in the weekly papers.

MEPHISTOPHELES. Ay, my good madam, the truth is manifested by the testimony of two witnesses all the world over; and I have a gallant companion whom I will bring before the judge for you. I will fetch him here.

MARTHA. Oh, pray do!

MEPHISTOPHELES. And the young lady will be here, too? —a fine lad! has travelled much, and shows all possible politeness to the ladies.

MARGARET. I should be covered with confusion in the presence of the gentleman.

MEPHISTOPHELES. In the presence of no king on earth.

MARTHA. Behind the house there, in my garden, we shall expect you both this evening.

THE STREET.

FAUST — MEPHISTOPHELES.

FAUST. How have you managed? Is it in train? Will it soon do?

MEPHISTOPHELES. Bravo! Do I find you all on fire? Margaret will very shortly be yours. This evening you will see her at her neighbor Martha's. That is a woman especially chosen, as it were, for the procuress and gypsy calling.

FAUST.   So far so good.

MEPHISTOPHELES.   Something, however, is required of us.

FAUST.   One good turn deserves another.

MEPHISTOPHELES.   We have only to make a formal deposition that the extended limbs of her lord repose in holy ground in Padua.

FAUST.   Wisely done!   We shall first be obliged to take the journey thither, I suppose.

MEPHISTOPHELES.   *Sancta simplicitas!*   There is no necessity for that.   Only bear witness without knowing much about the matter.

FAUST.   If you have nothing better to propose, the scheme is at an end.

MEPHISTOPHELES.   Oh, holy man!   There's for you now! Is it the first time in your life that you have borne false testimony?   Have you not confidently given definitions of God, of the world, and of whatever moves in it — of man, and of the working of his head and heart — with unabashed front, dauntless breast?   And, looking fairly at the real nature of things, did you — you must confess you did not — did you know as much of these matters as of Mr. Schwerdtlein's death?

FAUST.   Thou art and ever wilt be a liar, a sophist.

MEPHISTOPHELES.   Ay, if one did not look a little deeper. To-morrow, too, will you not, in all honor, make a fool of poor Margaret, and swear to love her with all your soul?

FAUST.   And truly from my heart.

MEPHISTOPHELES.   Fine talking!   Then will you speak of eternal truth and love — of one exclusive, all-absorbing passion; will that also come from the heart?

FAUST.   Peace — it will! — when I feel, and seek a name for the passion, the frenzy, but find none; then range with all my senses through the world, grasp at all the most sublime expressions, and call this flame, which is consuming me, endless, eternal, eternal! — is that a devilish play of lies?

MEPHISTOPHELES.   I am right, for all that.

FAUST.   Hark! mark this, I beg of you, and spare my lungs.   He who is determined to be right, and has but a tongue, will be right undoubtedly.   But, come, I am tired of gossiping.   For you are right, particularly because I cannot help myself.

GARDEN.

Margaret *on* Faust's *arm*, Martha *with* Mephistopheles, *walking up and down.*

Margaret.   I am sure that you are only trifling with me
— letting yourself down to shame me.   Travellers are wont
to put up with things out of complacency.   I know too well
that my poor prattle cannot entertain a man of your experience.

Faust.   A glance, a word from thee, gives greater pleasure than all the wisdom of this world. (*He kisses her hand.*)

Margaret.   Don't inconvenience yourself!   How can
you kiss it?   It is so coarse, so hard.   I have been obliged
to do — heaven knows what not; my mother is indeed too
close. (*They pass on.*)

Martha.   And you, sir, are always travelling in this manner?

Mephistopheles.   Alas, that business and duty should
force us to it!   How many a place one quits with regret, and
yet may not tarry in it!

Martha.   It does very well, in the wild years of youth, to
rove about freely through the world.   But the evil day comes
at last, and to sneak a solitary old bachelor to the grave —
that was never well for any one yet.

Mephistopheles.   I shudder at the distant view of it.

Martha.   Then, worthy sir, think better of it in time.
(*They pass on.*)

Margaret.   Ay! out of sight out of mind!   Politeness
sits easily on you.   But you have friends in abundance: they
are more sensible than I am.

Faust.   O, thou excellent creature! believe me, what is
called sensible often better deserves the name of vanity and
narrow-mindedness.

Margaret.   How?

Faust.   Alas, that simplicity, that innocence, never ap-
preciates itself and its own hallowed worth!   That humility,
lowliness — the highest gifts of love-fraught, bounteous nature —

Margaret.   Only think of me one little minute; I shall
have time enough to think of you.

Faust.   You are much alone, I dare say?

Margaret.   Yes, our household is but small, and yet it
must be looked after.   We keep no maid; I am obliged to

cook, sweep, knit, and sew, and run early and late. And my mother is so precise in everything! Not that she has such pressing occasion to restrict herself. We might do more than many others. My father left a nice little property — a small house and garden near the town. However, my days at present are tolerably quiet. My brother is a soldier; my little sister is dead. I had my full share of trouble with her, but I would gladly take all the anxiety upon myself again so dear was the child to me.

FAUST. An angel, if it resembled thee!

MARGARET. I brought it up, and it loved me dearly. It was born after my father's death. We gave up my mother for lost, so sad was the condition she then lay in; and she recovered very slowly, by degrees. Thus she could not think of suckling the poor little worm, and so I brought it up, all by myself, with milk and water. It thus became my own. On my arm, in my bosom it smiled and sprawled and grew.

FAUST. You have felt, no doubt, the purest joy.

MARGARET. And many anxious hours, too. The little one's cradle stood at night by my bedside; it could scarcely move but I was awake; now obliged to give it drink; now to take it to bed to me; now, when it would not be quiet, to rise from bed and walk up and down in the room, dandling it; and early in the morning, stand already at the wash-tub; then go to market, and see to the house; and so on, day after day. Under such circumstances, sir, one is not always in spirits; but food and rest relish the better for it. (*They pass on.*)

MARTHA. The poor women have the worst of it. It is no easy matter to convert an old bachelor.

MEPHISTOPHELES. It only depends on one like you to teach me better.

MARTHA. Tell me plainly, sir, have you never met with any one? Has your heart never attached itself anywhere?

MEPHISTOPHELES. The proverb says — a hearth of one's own, a good wife, are worth pearls and gold.

MARTHA. I mean, have you never had an inclination?

MEPHISTOPHELES. I have been in general very politely received.

MARTHA. I wished to say — was your heart never seriously affected?

MEPHISTOPHELES. One should never venture to joke with women.

MARTHA. Ah, you do not understand me.

MEPHISTOPHELES. I am heartily sorry for it. But I understand — that you are very kind. (*They pass on.*)

FAUST. You knew me again, you little angel, the moment I entered the garden.

MARGARET. Did you not see it? I cast down my eyes.

FAUST. And you forgive the liberty I took — my imprudence, as you were leaving the cathedral?

MARGARET. I was quite abashed. Such a thing had never happened to me before; no one could say anything bad of me. Alas, thought I, has he seen anything bold, unmaidenly, in thy behavior? It seemed as if the thought suddenly struck him, "I need stand on no ceremony with this girl." I must own I knew not what began to stir in your favor *here;* but certainly I was right angry with myself for not being able to be more angry with you.

FAUST. Sweet love!

MARGARET. Wait a moment! (*She plucks a star-flower and picks off the leaves one after the other.*)

FAUST. What is that for — a nosegay?

MARGARET. No, only for a game.

FAUST. How!

MARGARET. Go! You will laugh at me. (*She plucks off the leaves, and murmurs to herself.*)

FAUST. What are you murmuring?

MARGARET (*half aloud*). He loves me — he loves me not!

FAUST. Thou angelic being!

MARGARET *continues.* Loves me — not — loves me — not — (*Plucking off the last leaf with fond delight.*) He loves me!

FAUST. Yes, my child. Let this flower-prophecy be to thee as a judgment from heaven. He loves thee! Dost thou understand what that means? He loves thee! (*He takes both her hands.*)

MARGARET. I tremble all over!

FAUST. Oh, tremble not. Let this look, let this pressure of the hand, say to thee what is unutterable! — to give ourselves up wholly, and feel a bliss which must be eternal! Eternal! — its end would be despair! No, no end! no end! (*MARGARET presses his hand, breaks from him, and runs away. He stands a moment in thought, and then follows her.*)

MARTHA (*approaching*). The night is coming on.

MEPHISTOPHELES.   Ay, and we will away.

MARTHA.   I would ask you to stay here longer, but it is a wicked place.   One would suppose no one had any other object or occupation than to gape after his neighbor's in-comings and outgoings.   And one comes to be talked about, behave as one will.   And our pair of lovers?

MEPHISTOPHELES.   Have flown up the walk yonder. Wanton butterflies!

MARTHA.   He seems fond of her.

MEPHISTOPHELES.   And she of him.   Such is the way of the world.

A SUMMER-HOUSE.

(MARGARET *runs in, gets behind the door, holds the tip of her finger to her lips, and peeps through the crevice.*)

MARGARET.   He comes!

FAUST (*enters*).   Ah, rogue, is it thus you trifle with me? I have caught you at last.   (*He kisses her.*)

MARGARET (*embracing him, and returning the kiss*). Dearest! from my heart I love thee!   (MEPHISTOPHELES *knocks.*)

FAUST (*stamping*).   Who is there?

MEPHISTOPHELES.   A friend.

FAUST.   A brute.

MEPHISTOPHELES.   It is time to part, I believe.

MARTHA (*comes up*).   Yes, it is late, sir.

FAUST.   May I not accompany you?

MARGARET.   My mother would—farewell!

FAUST.   Must I then go?   Farewell!

MARTHA.   Adieu!

MARGARET.   Till our next speedy meeting!   (FAUST *and* MEPHISTOPHELES *exeunt.*)

MARGARET.   Gracious God!   How many things such a man can think about!   How abashed I stand in his pres-ence, and say yea to everything!   I am but a poor, silly girl; I cannot conceive what he sees in me.

FOREST AND CAVERN.

Faust (*alone*). Sublime spirit! thou gavest me, gavest me everything I prayed for. Not in vain didst thou turn thy face in fire to me. Thou gavest me glorious nature for a kingdom, with power to feel, to enjoy her. It is not merely a cold, wondering visit that thou permittest me; thou grudgest me not to look into·her deep bosom, as into the bosom of a friend. Thou passest in review before me the whole series of animated things, and teachest me to know my brothers in the still wood, in the air, and in the water. And when the storm roars and creaks in the forest, and the giant pine, precipitating its neighbor-boughs and neighbor-stems, sweeps, crushing, down — and the mountain thunders with a dead hollow muttering to the fall, — then thou bearest me off to the sheltered cave; then thou showest me to myself, and deep mysterious wonders of my own breast reveal themselves. And when the clear moon, with its soothing influences, rises full in my view, — from the wall-like rocks, out of the damp underwood, the silvery forms of past ages hover up to me, and soften the austere pleasure of contemplation. Oh, now I feel that nothing perfect falls to the lot of man! With this beatitude, which brings me nearer and nearer to the gods, thou gavest me the companion, whom already I cannot do without; although, cold and insolent, he degrades me in my own eyes, and turns thy gifts to nothing with a breath. He is ever kindling a wild-fire in my heart for that lovely image. Thus do I reel from desire to enjoyment, and in enjoyment languish for desire.

Mephistopheles (*enters*). Have you not had enough of this kind of life? How can you delight in it so long? It is all well enough to try once, but then on again to something new.

Faust. I would you had something else to do than to plague me in my happier hour.

Mephistopheles. Well, well! I will let you alone, if you wish. You need not say so in earnest. Truly, it is little to lose an ungracious, peevish, and crazy companion in you. The livelong day one has one's hands full. One cannot read in your worship's face what pleases you, and what to let alone.

Faust. That is just the right tone! He would fain be thanked for wearying me to death.

Mephistopheles. Poor son of earth! what sort of life would you have led without me! I have cured you, for some time to come, of the crotchets of imagination, and, but for me, you would already have taken your departure from this globe. Why mope in caverns and fissures of rocks, like an owl? Why sip in nourishment from sodden moss and dripping stone, like a toad? A fair, sweet pastime! The doctor still sticks to you.

Faust. Dost thou understand what new life-power this wandering in the desert procures for me? Ay, couldst thou have but a dim presentiment of it, thou wouldst be devil enough to grudge me my enjoyment.

Mephistopheles. A super-earthly pleasure! To lie on the mountains in darkness and dew — clasp earth and heaven ecstatically — swell yourself up to a godhead — rake through the earth's marrow with your thronging presentiments — feel the whole six days' work in your bosom — in haughty might enjoy I know not what — now overflow in love's raptures, into all, with your earthly nature cast aside — and then the lofty intuition (*with a gesture*) — I must not say how — to end!

Faust. Fie upon you!

Mephistopheles. That is not your mind. You are entitled to cry fie! so morally! We must not name to chaste ears what chaste hearts cannot renounce. And, in a word, I do not grudge you the pleasure of lying to yourself occasionally. But you will not keep it up long. You are already driven back into your old course, and, if this holds much longer, will be fretted into madness or torture and horror. Enough of this! your little love sits yonder at home, and all to her is confined and melancholy. You are never absent from her thoughts. She loves you all subduingly. At first, your passion came overflowing, like a snow-flushed rivulet; you have poured it into her heart and, lo! your rivulet is dry again. Methinks, instead of reigning in the woods, your worship would do well to reward the poor young monkey for her love. The time seems lamentably long to her; she stands at the window and watches the clouds roll away over the old walls of the town. "Were I a bird!" so runs her song, during all the day and half the night. One while she is cheerful, mostly sad, — one while fairly outwept; — then, again, composed, to all appearance — and ever lovesick!

Faust. Serpent! serpent!

Mephistopheles (*aside*). Good! if I can but catch you!

Faust. Reprobate! take thyself away, and name not the lovely woman. Bring not the desire for her sweet body before my half-distracted senses again!

MEPHISTOPHELES. What is to be done, then? She thinks that you are off, and in some manner you are.

FAUST. I am near her, and were I ever so far off I can never forget, never lose her. Nay, I already envy the very body of the Lord when her lips are touching it.

MEPHISTOPHELES. Very well, my friend. I have often envied you the twin-pair, which feed among roses.

FAUST. Pander! begone.

MEPHISTOPHELES. Good again! You rail, and I cannot help laughing. The God who made lad and lass well understood the noble calling of making opportunity, too. But away, it is a mighty matter to be sad about! You should betake yourself to your mistress' chamber — not, I think, to death.

FAUST. What are the joys of heaven in her arms? Let me kindle on her breast! Do I not feel her wretchedness unceasingly? Am I not the outcast — the houseless one? — the monster without aim or rest, — who, like a cataract, dashed from rock to rock, in devouring fury towards the precipice? And she, upon the side, with childlike simplicity, in her little cot upon the little mountain field, and all her homely cares embraced within that little world! And I, the hated of God — it was not enough for me to grasp the rocks and smite them to shatters! Her, her peace, must I undermine! — Hell, thou couldst not rest without this sacrifice. Devil, help me to shorten the pang! Let what must be, be quickly! Let her fate fall crushing upon me, and both of us perish together!

MEPHISTOPHELES. How it seethes and glows again! Get in, and comfort her, you fool! — When such a noddle sees no outlet it immediately represents to itself the end. He who bears himself bravely, forever! And yet, on other occasions, you have a fair spice of the devil in you. I know nothing in the world more insipid than a devil that despairs.

MARGARET'S ROOM.

MARGARET *alone, at the spinning-wheel.*

My peace is gone;
My heart is heavy;
I shall find it never,
And never more.

Where I have him not,
Is the grave to me.
The whole world
Is embittered to me.

My poor head
Is wandering,
My feeble sense
Distraught.

My peace is gone;
My heart is heavy;
I shall find it never,
And never more.

For him alone look I
Out at the window!
For him alone go I
Out of the house!

His stately step,
His noble form;
The smile of his mouth,
The power of his eyes,

And of his speech
The witching flow;
The pressure of his hand,
And, ah! his kiss!

My peace is gone;
My heart is heavy;
I shall find it never,
And never more.

My bosom struggles
After him.
Ah! could I enfold him
And hold him! and kiss him
As I would!
On his kisses,
Would I die away.

MARTHA'S GARDEN.

MARGARET — FAUST.

MARGARET. Promise me, Henry!
FAUST. What I can!
MARGARET. Now, tell me, how do you feel as to religion?
You are a dear, good man, but I believe you don't think
much of it.

Faust. No more of that, my child! you feel I love you; I would lay down my life for those I love, nor would I deprive any of their feeling and their church.

Margaret. That is not right; we must believe in it.

Faust. Must we?

Margaret. Ah! if I had any influence over you! Besides, you do not honor the holy sacraments.

Faust. I honor them.

Margaret. But without desiring them. It is long since you went to mass or confession. Do you believe in God?

Faust. My love, who dares say I believe in God? You may ask priests and philosophers, and their answer will appear but a mockery of the questioner.

Margaret. You don't believe, then?

Faust. Mistake me not, thou lovely one! Who dare name him? and who avow: "I believe in him?" Who feel — and dare to say; "I believe in him not?" The All-embracer, the All-sustainer, does he not embrace and sustain thee, me, himself? Does not the heaven arch itself there above? — Lies not the earth firm here below? — And do not eternal stars rise, kindly twinkling, on high? — Are we not looking into each other's eyes, and is not all thronging to thy head and heart, and weaving in eternal mystery, invisibly — visibly, about thee? With it fill thy heart, big as it is, and when thou art wholly blest in the feeling, then call it what thou wilt! Call it Bliss! — Heart! — Love! — God! I have no name for it! Feeling is all in all. Name is sound and smoke, clouding heaven's glow.

Margaret. That is all very fine and good. The priest says nearly the same, only with somewhat different words.

Faust. All hearts in all places under the blessed light of day say it, each in its own language — why not in mine?

Margaret. Thus taken, it may pass; but, for all that, there is something wrong about it, for thou hast no Christianity.

Faust. Dear child!

Margaret. I have long been grieved at the company I see you in.

Faust. How so?

Margaret. The man you have with you is hateful to me in my inmost soul. Nothing in the whole course of my life has given my heart such a pang as the repulsive visage of that man.

FAUST. Fear him not, dear child.

MARGARET. IIis presence makes my blood creep. With this exception, I have kind feelings towards everybody. But, much as I long to see you, I have an unaccountable horror of that man, and hold him for a rogue besides, God forgive me if I do him wrong.

FAUST. There must be such oddities, notwithstanding.

MARGARET. I would not live with the like of him. Whenever he comes to the door, he looks in so mockingly, and with fury but half-suppressed; one sees that he sympathizes with nothing. It is written on his forehead that he can love no living soul. I feel so happy in thy arms — so unrestrained — in such glowing abandonment; and his presence closes up my heart's core.

FAUST. You misgiving angel, you!

MARGARET. It overcomes me to such a degree that when he but chances to join us, I even think I do not love you any longer. And in his presence I should never be able to pray; and this eats into my heart. You, too, Henry, must feel the same.

FAUST. You have an antipathy, that is all.

MARGARET. I must go now.

FAUST. Ah, can I never recline one little hour undisturbed upon thy bosom, and press heart to heart, and soul to soul!

MARGARET. Ah! did I but sleep alone! I would gladly leave the door unbolted for you this very night. But my mother does not sleep sound, and were she to catch us I should die upon the spot.

FAUST. Thou angel, there is no fear of that. You see this phial? Only three drops in her drink will gently envelop nature in deep sleep.

MARGARET. What would I not do for thy sake? It will do her no harm, I hope.

FAUST. Would I recommend it to you, my love, if it could?

MARGARET. If, best of men, I do but look on you, I know not what drives me to comply with your will. I have already done so much for you that next to nothing now remains for me to do. (*Exit.*)

(MEPHISTOPHELES *enters.*)

MEPHISTOPHELES. The silly monkey! is she gone.

FAUST. Hast thou been playing the spy again?

MEPHISTOPHELES. I heard what passed, plainly enough. You were catechized, doctor. Much good may it do you.

The girls are certainly deeply interested in knowing whether a man be pious and plain after the old fashion. They say to themselves: "If he is pliable in that matter, he will also be pliable to us."

FAUST. Thou, monster as thou art, canst not conceive how this fond, faithful soul, full of her faith, which, according to her notions, is alone capable of conferring eternal happiness, feels a holy horror to think that she must hold her best beloved for lost.

MEPHISTOPHELES. Thou super-sensual, sensual lover, a chit of a girl leads thee by the nose.

FAUST. Thou abortion of dirt and fire!

MEPHISTOPHELES. And she is knowing in physiognomy, too. In my presence she feels she knows not how. This little mask betokens some hidden sense. She feels that I am most assuredly a genius — perhaps the devil himself. To-night, then — ?

FAUST. What is that to you?

MEPHISTOPHELES. I have my pleasure in it, though.

———

AT THE WELL.

MARGARET and BESSY with pitchers.

BESSY. Have you heard nothing of Barbara?

MARGARET. Not a word. I go very little abroad.

BESSY. Certainly, Sybella told it me to-day. She has even made a fool of herself at last. That comes of playing the fine lady.

MARGARET. How so?

BESSY. It is a bad business. She feeds two now when she eats and drinks.

MARGARET. Ah!

BESSY. She is rightly served at last. What a time she has hung upon the fellow! There was a promenading and a gallanting to village junketings and dancing booths — she, forsooth, must be the first in everything — he was ever treating her to tarts and wine. She thought great things of her beauty, and was so lost to honor as not to be ashamed to receive presents from him. There was then a hugging and kissing — and, lo, the flower is gone!

MARGARET. Poor thing!

BESSY. You really pity her! When the like of us were at the spinning our mothers never let us go down at night. She stood sweet with her lover; on the bench before the door, and in the dark walk, the time was never too long for them. But now she may humble herself, and do penance in a white sheet, in the church.

MARGARET. He will surely make her his wife.

BESSY. He would be a fool if he did. A brisk young fellow has the world before him. Besides he's off.

MARGARET. That's not handsome.

BESSY. If she gets him, it will go ill with her. The boys will tear her garland for her, and we will strew cut straw before her door. (*Exit.*)

MARGARET (*going home*). How stoutly I could formerly revile, if a poor maiden chanced to make a slip! How I could never find words enough to speak of another's shame! How black it seemed to me! and, blacken it as I would, it was never black enough for me — and blessed myself and felt so grand, and am now myself a prey to sin? Yet — all that drove me to it, was, God knows, so sweet, so dear!

ZWINGER.

(*In the niche of the wall a devotional image of the Mater Dolorosa, with pots of flowers before it.*)

MARGARET *places fresh flowers in the pots.*

Ah, incline,
Thou full of pain,
Thy countenance graciously to my distress.

The sword in thy heart,
With thousand pangs
Up-lookest thou to thy Son's death.

To the Father look'st thou,
And sendest sighs
Aloft for his and thy distress.
Who feels
How rages
My torment to the quick?
How the poor heart in me throbbeth,
How it trembleth, how it yearneth
Knowest thou, and thou alone!

Whithersoc'er I go,
What woe, what woe, what woe,
Grows within my bosom *here!*
Hardly, alas, am I alone,
I weep, I weep, I weep,
My heart is bursting within me.
The flower-pots on my window-sill
Bedewed I with my tears, alas!
When I at morning's dawn
Plucked these flowers for thee.
When brightly in my chamber
The rising sun's rays shone,
Already, in all wretchedness,
Was I sitting up in my bed.
Help! rescue me from shame and death!
Ah, incline,
Thou full of pain,
Thy countenance graciously to my distress!

NIGHT.

STREET BEFORE MARGARET'S DOOR.

VALENTINE (*a soldier*, MARGARET'S *brother*). When I made one of a company, where many like to show off, and the fellows were loud in their praises of the flower of maidens, and drowned their commendation in bumpers, — with my elbows leaning on the board, I sat in quiet confidence, and listened to all their swaggering! then I stroke my beard with a smile, and take the bumper in my hand, and say: "All very well in its way! but is there one in the whole country to compare with my dear Margaret; — who is fit to hold a candle to my sister?" Hob and nob, kling! klang! so it went round! Some shouted, "He is right; she is the pearl of the whole sex;" and all those praisers were dumb. And now — it is enough to make one tear out one's hair by the roots, and run up the walls — I shall be twitted by the sneers and taunts of every knave, shall sit like a bankrupt debtor, and sweat at every chance word. And though I might crush them at a blow, yet I could not call them liars. Who comes there? Who is slinking this way? If I mistake not, there are two of them. If it is he, I will have at him at once; he shall not leave this spot alive.

FAUST. How, from the window of the sacristy there, the light of the eternal lamp flickers upwards, and glimmers weaker and weaker at the sides, and darkness thickens round! Just so is all night-like in my breast.

MEPHISTOPHELES. And I feel languishing like the tom-cat, that sneaks along the fire-ladders and then creeps stealthily round the walls. I feel quite virtuously, — with a spice of thievish pleasure, a spice of wantonness. In such a manner does the glorious Walpurgis night already thrill me through every limb. The day after to-morrow it comes round to us again; there one knows what one wakes for.

FAUST. In the meantime, can that be the treasure ris-ing, — that which I see glimmering yonder?

MEPHISTOPHELES. You will soon enjoy the lifting up of the casket. I lately took a squint at it. There are capital lion-dollars within.

FAUST. Not a trinket — not a ring — to adorn my lovely mistress with?

MEPHISTOPHELES. I think I saw some such thing there as a sort of pearl necklace.

FAUST. That is well. I feel sorry when I go to her without a present.

MEPHISTOPHELES. You ought not to regret having some enjoyment gratis. Now that the heavens are studded thick with stars, you shall hear a true piece of art. I will sing her a moral song, to make a fool of her the more certainly. (*He sings to the guitar.*) What are you doing here, Cath-erine, before your lover's door at morning dawn? Stay, and beware! he lets thee in a maid, not to come out a maid. Beware! If it be done, then good night to you, you poor, poor things. If you love yourselves, do nothing to pleasure any spoiler, except with the ring on the finger.

VALENTINE (*comes forward*). Whom art thou luring here? by God! thou cursed rat-catcher! First, to the devil with the instrument, then to the devil with the singer.

MEPHISTOPHELES. The guitar is broken to pieces! It is all up with it!

VALENTINE. Now, then, for a skull-cracking.

MEPHISTOPHELES (*to* FAUST). Don't give way, doctor! Courage! Stick close, and do as I tell you. Out with your toasting-iron! Thrust away, and I will parry.

VALENTINE. Parry that!

MEPHISTOPHELES. Why not?

VALENTINE. And that!

MEPHISTOPHELES. To be sure.

VALENTINE. I believe the devil is fighting. What is that? My hand is already getting powerless.

MEPHISTOPHELES (*to* FAUST). Thrust home!

VALENTINE (*falls*). Oh, torture!

MEPHISTOPHELES. The clown is tamed now. But away! We must vanish in a twinkling, for a horrible outcry is already raised. I am perfectly at home with the police, but should find it hard to clear scores with the criminal courts.

MARTHA (*at the window*). Out! out!

MARGARET (*at the window*). Bring a light!

MARTHA (*as before*). They are railing and scuffling, screaming and fighting.

PEOPLE. Here lies one dead, already!

MARTHA (*coming out*). Have the murderers escaped?

MARGARET (*coming out*). Who lies here?

PEOPLE. Thy mother's son.

MARGARET. Almighty God! what misery!

VALENTINE. I am dying! that is soon said, and sooner still done. What are you women howling and wailing about? Approach and listen to me. (*All come round him.*) Look ye, Margaret! you are still young! you are not yet adroit enough, and manage your matters ill. I tell it you in confidence; since you are, once for all, a whore, be one in good earnest.

MARGARET. Brother! God! What do you mean?

VALENTINE. Leave God out of the game. What is done, alas! cannot be undone, and things will take their course. You begin privately with one; more of them will soon follow; and when a dozen have had you, the whole town will have you, too.

When first shame is born, she is brought into the world clandestinely, and the veil of night is drawn over her head and ears. Ay, people would fain stifle her. But when she grows and waxes big, she walks flauntingly in open day, and yet is not a whit the fairer. The uglier her face becomes the more she courts the light of day.

I already see the time when all honest citizens will turn aside from you, you whore, as from an infected corpse. Your heart will sink within you when they look you in the face. You will wear no golden chain again! No more will you stand at the altar in the church, or take pride in a fair lace collar at the dance. You will hide yourself in some dark, miserable corner, amongst beggars and cripples, and, even should God forgive you, be cursed upon earth!

MARTHA. Commend your soul to God's mercy. Will you yet heap the sin of slander upon your soul?

VALENTINE. Could I but get at thy withered body, thou shameless bawd, I should hope to find a full measure of pardon for all my sins!

MARGARET. My brother! Oh this agonizing pang!

VALENTINE. Have done with tears, I tell you. When you renounced honor, you gave me the deepest heart-stab of all. I go through death's sleep unto God, a soldier and a brave one. (*He dies.*)

CATHEDRAL.

SERVICE, ORGAN, AND ANTHEM.

MARGARET *amongst a number of People.* EVIL SPIRIT *behind* MARGARET.

EVIL SPIRIT.

How different was it with thee, Margaret,
When still full of innocence
Thou camest to the altar there —
Out of the well-worn little book,
Lispedst prayers,
Half child-spirit,
Half God in the heart!
Margaret!
Where is thy head?
In thy heart
What crime?
Prayest thou for thy mother's soul — who
Slept over into long, long pain through thee?
Whose blood on thy threshold?
—— And under thy heart
Stirs it not quickening, even now,
Torturing itself and thee
With its foreboding presence?

MARGARET.

Woe! woe!——
Would that I were free from the thoughts
That come over and across me
Despite of me!

CHORUS.

Dies iræ, dies illa
Solvet sæclum in favilla.　　　　(*Organ plays.*)

EVIL SPIRIT.

Horror seizes thee!
The trump sounds!
The graves tremble!
And thy heart
From the repose of its ashes
For fiery torment
Brought to life again
Trembles up!

MARGARET.

Would that I were hence.
I feel as if the organ
Stifled my breath,
As if the anthem
Dissolved my heart's care!

CHORUS.

Judex ergo cum cedebit
Quidquid latet adparebit
Nil inultum remanebit.

MARGARET.

I feel so thronged!
The wall-pillars
Close on me!
The vaulted roof
Presses on me! — Air!

EVIL SPIRIT.

Hide thyself! sin and shame
Remain unhidden.
Air?   Light?
Woe to thee!

CHORUS.

Quid sum miser tunc dicturus ?
Quem patronum rogaturus ?
Cum vix justus sit securus.

EVIL SPIRIT.

The glorified from thee
Avert their faces.
The pure shudder
To reach thee their hands.
Woe!

CHORUS.

Quid sum miser tunc dicturus ?

MARGARET.

Neighbor; your smelling-bottle!
(She swoons away.)

MAY–DAY NIGHT.

THE HARTZ MOUNTAINS.

District of Schirke and Elend.

Faust — Mephistopheles.

Mephistopheles. Do you not long for a broomstick? For my part I should be glad of the roughest he-goat. By this road we are still far from our destination.

Faust. So long as I feel fresh upon my legs this knotted stick suffices me. What is the use of shortening the way? To creep along the labyrinth of the vales, and then ascend these rocks, from which the ever-bubbling spring precipitates itself, — this is the pleasure which gives zest to such a path. The spring is already weaving in the birch-trees, and even the pine is beginning to feel it, — ought it not to have some effect upon our limbs?

Mephistopheles. Verily, I feel nothing of it. All is wintry in my body, and I should prefer frost and snow upon my path. How melancholy the imperfect disk of the red moon rises with belated glare! and gives so bad a light, that, at every step, one runs against a tree or a rock. With your leave, I will call a will-o'-the-wisp. I see one yonder, burning right merrily. Holloa, there, my friend! may I entreat your company? Why wilt thou blaze away so uselessly? Be so good as to light us up along here.

Will-o'the-Wisp. Out of reverence, I hope, I shall succeed in subduing my unsteady nature. Our course is ordinarily but a zigzag one.

Mephistopheles. Ha! ha! you think to imitate men. But go straight, in the devil's name, or I will blow your flickering life out.

Will-o'-the-Wisp. I see well that you are master here, and will willingly accommodate myself to you. But consider! the mountain is magic-mad to-night, and if a will-o'-the-wisp is to show you the way you must not be too particular.

Faust, Mephistopheles, Will-o'-the-Wisp (*in alternate song*). Into the sphere of dreams and enchantments, it seems, have we entered. Lead us right, and do yourself credit! — that we may advance betimes in the wide, desolate regions.

See trees after trees, how rapidly they move by; and the cliffs, that bow, and the long-snouted rocks, how they snort, how they blow!

Through the stones, through the turf, brook and brookling hurry down. Do I hear rustling? do I hear songs? do I hear the sweet plaint of love? — voices of those blest days — what we hope, what we love! And Echo, like the tale of old times, sends back the sound.

Tu-whit-tu-whoo — it sounds nearer; the owl, the pewit, and the jay, — have they all remained awake? Are those salamanders through the brake, with their long legs, thick paunches? And the roots, like snakes, wind from out of rock and sand, and stretch forth strange filaments to terrify, to seize us: from coarse speckles, instinct with life, they set polypus-fibres for the traveller. And the mice, thousand-colored, in whole tribes, through the moss and through the heath! And the glow-worms fly, in crowded swarms, a confounding escort.

But tell me whether we stand still, or whether we are moving on. Everything seems to turn round, — rocks and trees, which make grimaces, and the will-o'-the-wisps, which multiply, which swell themselves out.

MEPHISTOPHELES. Keep a stout hold of my skirt! Here is a central peak, from which one sees with wonder how Mammon is glowing in the mountain.

FAUST. How strangely a melancholy light, of morning red, glimmers through the mountain gorges, and quivers even to the deepest recesses of the precipice! Here rises a mine-damp, there float exhalations. Here the glow sparkles out of gauze-like vapor, then steals along like a fine thread, and then again bursts forth like a fountain. Here it winds, a whole track, with a hundred veins, through the valley; and here, in the compressed corner, it scatters itself at once. There sparks are sputtering near, like golden sand unsprinkled in the air. But, see the wall of rocks is on fire in all its height.

MEPHISTOPHELES. Does not Sir Mammon illuminate his palace magnificently for this festival? It is lucky that you have seen it. I already see traces of the boisterous guests.

FAUST. How the storm-blast is raging through the air. With what thumps it strikes against my neck!

MEPHISTOPHELES. You must lay hold of the old ribs of the rock or it will hurl you down into this abyss. A mist thickens the night. Hark! what a crashing through the forest! The owls fly scared away. Hark, to the splintering of the pillars of the evergreen palaces! the crackling and snapping of the boughs, the mighty groaning of the trunks, the creaking and yawning of the roots! — All come crashing down, one over the other, in fearfully-confused fall; and the winds hiss and howl through the wreck-covered cliffs! Dost thou hear voices aloft? — in the distance? — close at hand? — Ay, a raving witch-song streams along the whole mountain.

The Witches (*in chorus*). To the Brocken the witches repair! The stubble is yellow, the sown-fields are green. — There the huge multitude is assembled. Sir Urian sits at the top. On they go, over stone and stock; the witch ——s, the he-goat ——s.

Voices. Old Baubo comes alone; she rides upon a farrow sow.

Chorus. Then honor to whom honor is due! Mother Baubo to the front, and lead the way! A proper sow and mother upon her, — then follows the whole swarm of witches.

Voice. Which way did you come?

Voice. By Ilsenstein. I there peeped into the owl's nest. She gave me such a look!

Voice. Oh, drive to hell! What a rate you are riding at!

Voice. She has grazed me in passing; only look at the wound!

Chorus of Witches. The way is broad — the way is long. What mad throng is this? The fork sticks — the besom scratches: the child is suffocated — the mother bursts.

Wizards — Half-Chorus. We steal along like snails in their house; the women are all before; for, in going to the house of the wicked one, woman is a thousand steps in advance.

The other Half. We do not take that so, precisely. The woman does it with a thousand steps; but, let her make as much haste as she can, the man does it at a single bound.

Voices (*above*). Come with us, come with us, from Felsensee!

Voices (*from below*). We should like to mount with you. We wash and are thoroughly clean, but we are ever barren.

Both Choruses. The wind is still, the stars fly, the melancholy moon is glad to hide herself. The magic-choir sputters forth sparks by thousands in its whizzing.

Voice (*from below*). Hold! hold!

Voice (*from above*). Who calls there, from the cleft in the rock?

Voice (*from below*). Take me with you! take me with you! I have been mounting for three hundred years already, and cannot reach the top. I would fain be with my fellows.

Both Choruses. The besom carries, the stick carries, the fork carries, the he-goat carries. Who cannot raise himself to-night is lost forever.

Demi-Witch (*below*). I have been tottering after such a length of time, — how far the others are ahead already! I have no rest at home, — and don't get it here, neither.

Chorus of Witches. The salve gives courage to the witches; a rag is good for a sail; every trough makes a good ship; he will never fly who flew not to-night.

Both Choruses. And when we round the peak, sweep along the ground, and cover the heath far and wide with your swarm of witch-hood. (*They let themselves down.*)

Mephistopheles. There's crowding and pushing, rustling and clattering! There's whizzing and twirling, bustling and babbling! There's glittering, sparkling, stinking, burning! A true witch-element! But stick close to me, or we shall be separated in a moment. Where art thou?

Faust (*in the distance*). Here!

Mephistopheles. What! already torn away so far? I must exert my authority as master. Room! Squire Voland comes! Make room, sweet people, make room! Here, Doctor, take hold of me! and now, at one bound, let us get clear of the crowd. It is too mad, even for the like of me. Hard by there, shines something with a peculiar light. Something attracts me towards those bushes. Come along, we will slip in there.

Faust. Thou spirit of contradiction! But go on! thou may'st lead me. But it was wisely done, to be sure! We repair to the Brocken on Walpurgis night — to try and isolate ourselves when we get there.

Mephistopheles. Only see what variegated flames! A merry club is met together. One is not alone in a small company.

Faust. I should prefer being above, though! I already see flame and eddying smoke. Yonder the multitude is streaming to the Evil One. Many a riddle must there be untied.

Mephistopheles. And many a riddle is also tied anew.

Let the great world bluster as it will, we will here house ourselves in peace. It is an old saying, that in the great world one makes little worlds. Yonder I see young witches, naked and bare, and old ones who prudently cover themselves. Be compliant, if only for my sake; the trouble is small, the sport is great. I hear the tuning of instruments. Confounded jangle! One must accustom one's self to it. Come along, come along! it cannot be otherwise. I will go forward and introduce you, and I shall lay you under fresh obligation. What sayest thou, friend? This is no trifling space. Only look? you can hardly see the end. A hundred fires are burning in a row. People are dancing, talking, cooking, drinking, love-making! Now, tell me where anything better is to be found!

FAUST. To introduce us here, do you intend to present yourself as wizard or devil?

MEPHISTOPHELES. In truth, I am much used to go *incognito*. But one shows one's orders on gala days. I have no garter to distinguish me, but the cloven foot is held in high honor here. Do you see the snail there? she comes creeping up, and with her feelers has already found out something in me. Even if I would, I could not deny myself here. But come! we will go from fire to fire; I will be the pander, and you shall be the gallant. (*To some who are sitting round some expiring embers.*) Old gentlemen, what are you doing here at the extremity? I should commend you, did I find you nicely in the middle, in the thick of the riot and youthful revelry. Every one is surely enough alone at home.

GENERAL. Who can put his trust in nations, though he has done ever so much for them? For with the people, as with the women, youth has always the upper hand.

MINISTER. At present, people are wide astray from the right path — the good old ones for me! For verily, when we were all in all, that was the true golden age.

PARVENU. We, too, were certainly no fools, and often did what we ought not. But now, everything is turned topsy-turvy, and just when we wished to keep it firm.

AUTHOR. Who nowadays, speaking generally, likes to read a work of even moderate sense? And as for the rising generation they were never so malapert.

MEPHISTOPHELES (*who all at once appears very old*). I feel the people ripe for doomsday, now that I ascend the witch-mountain for the last time; and because my own cask runs thick, the world also is come to the dregs.

A Witch (*who sells old clothes and frippery*). Do not pass by in this manner, gentlemen! Now is your time. Look at my wares attentively; I have them of all sorts. And yet there is nothing in my shop which has not its fellow upon earth — that has not, at some time or other, wrought proper mischief to mankind and to the world. There is no dagger here from which blood has not flowed; no chalice from which hot consuming poison has not been poured into a healthy body; no trinket which has not seduced some amiable woman; no sword which has not cut some tie asunder, which has not perchance stabbed an adversary from behind.

Mephistopheles. Cousin, you understand but ill the temper of the times. Done, happened! Happened, done! Take to dealing in novelties; novelties only have any attraction for us.

Faust. If I can but keep my senses! This is a fair with a vengeance!

Mephistopheles. The whole throng struggles upwards. You think to shove, and you yourself are shoved.

Faust. Who, then, is that?

Mephistopheles. Mark her well, that is Lilith.

Faust. Who?

Mephistopheles. Adam's first wife. Beware of her fair hair, of that ornament in which she shines pre-eminent. When she ensnares a young man with it she does not let him off again so easily.

Faust. There sit two, the old one with the young one. They have already capered a good bit!

Mephistopheles. That has neither stop nor stay to-night. A new dance is beginning; come we will set to.

Faust (*dancing with the young one*). I had once upon a time a fair dream. In it I saw an apple-tree; two lovely apples glittered on it; they enticed me, I climbed up.

The Fair One. You are very fond of apples, and have been so from Paradise downwards. I feel moved with joy that my garden also bears such.

Mephistopheles (*with the old one*). I had once upon a time a wild dream. In it I saw a cleft tree. It had a —— —— ——; —— as it was it pleased me, notwithstanding.

The Old One. I present my best respects to the knight of the cloven foot. Let him have a —— —— ready, if he does not fear —— —— ——.

PROCTOPHANTASMIST. Confounded mob! how dare you? Was it not long since demonstrated to you? A spirit never stands upon ordinary feet; and you are actually dancing away like us other mortals!

THE FAIR ONE. What does he come to our ball for, then?

FAUST (*dancing*). Ha! He is absolutely everywhere. He must appraise what others dance. If he cannot talk about every step, the step is as good as never made at all. He is most vexed when we go forwards. If you would but turn round in a circle, as he does in his old mill, he would term that good, I dare say; particularly were you to consult him about it.

PROCTOPHANTASMIST. You are still there, then! No, that is unheard of! But vanish! We have enlightened the world, you know. That devil's crew, they pay no attention to rules. We are so wise, and Tegel is haunted, notwithstanding! How long have I been sweeping away at the delusion; and it never becomes clean? It is unheard of!

THE FAIR ONE. Have done boring us here at any rate, then!

PROCTOPHANTASMIST. I tell you, spirits, to your faces, I endure not the despotism of the spirit. My spirit cannot exercise it. (*The dancing goes on.*) To-night I see I shall succeed in nothing; but I am always ready for a journey; and still hope, before my last step, to get the better of devils and poets.

MEPHISTOPHELES. He will forthwith seat himself in a puddle; that is his mode of soothing himself; and when leeches have amused themselves on his rump, he is cured of spirits and spirit. (*To* FAUST, *who has left the dance.*) Why do you leave the pretty girl who sung so sweetly to you in the dance?

FAUST. Ah! in the middle of the song a red mouse jumped out of her mouth.

MEPHISTOPHELES. There is nothing out of the way in that. One must not be too nice about such matters. Enough that the mouse was not gray. Who cares for such things in a moment of enjoyment?

FAUST. Then I saw —

MEPHISTOPHELES. What?

FAUST. Mephisto, do you see yonder a pale, fair girl, standing alone and far off? She drags herself but slowly from the place; she seems to move with fettered feet. I must own, she seems to me to resemble poor Margaret.

MEPHISTOPHELES. Have nothing to do with that! no good can come of it to any one. It is a creation of enchantment, is lifeless, — an idol. It is not well to meet it; the blood of man thickens at its chill look, and he is well-nigh turned to stone. You have heard, no doubt, of Medusa.

FAUST. In truth they are the eyes of a corpse, which there was no fond hand to close. That is the bosom, which Margaret yielded to me; that is the sweet body which I enjoyed.

MEPHISTOPHELES. *That* is sorcery, thou easily deluded fool! for she wears to every one the semblance of his beloved.

FAUST. What bliss! what suffering! I cannot tear myself from that look. How strangely does a single red line, no thicker than the back of a knife, adorn that lovely neck!

MEPHISTOPHELES. Right! I see it, too. She can also carry her head under her arm, for Perseus has cut it off for her. But ever this fondness for delusion! Come up the hill, however; here all is as merry as in the Prater; and, if I am not bewitched, I actually see a theatre. What is going on here, then?

SERVIBILIS. They will recommence immediately. A new piece, the last of seven; — it is the custom here to give so many. A dilettante has written it, and dilettanti play it. Excuse me, gentlemen, but I must be off. It is my dilettante office to draw up the curtain.

MEPHISTOPHELES. When I find you upon the Blocksberg, — that is just what I approve; for this is the proper place for you.

WALPURGIS-NIGHT'S DREAM.

THEATRE-MANAGER. To-day we rest for once; we, the brave sons of Mieding. Old mountain and damp dale — that is the whole scenery.

HERALD. That the wedding-feast may be golden, fifty years are to be past; but if the quarrel is over, I shall like the golden the better.

OBERON. If ye spirits are with me, this is the time to show it: the king and the queen, they are united anew.

PUCK. When Puck comes and whirls himself about and his foot goes whisking in the dance, — hundreds come after to rejoice along with him.

ARIEL. Ariel awakes the song, in tones of heavenly purity; his music lures many trifles, but it also lures the fair.

OBERON. Wedded ones, who would agree, — let them take a lesson from us two. To make a couple love each other it is only necessary to separate them.

TITANIA. If the husband looks gruff, and the wife be whimsical, take hold of both of them immediately. Conduct me her to the South, and him to the extremity of the North.

ORCHESTRA TUTTI.

FORTISSIMO. Flies' snouts, and gnats' noses, with their kindred! Frog in the leaves, and cricket in the grass : they are the musicians.

SOLO. See, here comes the bagpipe! It is the soap-bubble. Hark to the Schnecke-schnicke-schnack through its snub-nose.

SPIRIT THAT IS FASHIONING ITSELF. Spider's foot and toad's belly, and little wings for the little wight! It does not make an animalcula, it is true, but it makes a little poem.

A PAIR OF LOVERS. Little step and high bound, through honey-dew and exhalations. Truly, you trip it me enough, but you do not mount into the air.

INQUISITIVE TRAVELLER. Is not this masquerading-mockery? Can I believe my eyes? To see the beauteous god, Oberon, here to-night, too!

ORTHODOX. No claws, no tail! Yet it stands beyond a doubt, that, even as "The Gods of Greece," so is he too a devil.

NORTHERN ARTIST. What I catch is at present only sketch-ways, as it were; but I prepare myself betimes for the Italian journey.

PURIST. Ah! my ill-fortune brings me hither; what a constant scene of rioting! and of the whole host of witches, only two are powdered.

YOUNG WITCH. Powder as well as petticoats are for little old and gray women. Therefore I sit naked upon my he-goat, and show a stout body.

MATRON. We have too much good breeding to squabble with you here. But I hope you will rot, young and delicate as you are.

LEADER OF THE BAND. Flies' snouts and gnats' noses, don't swarm so about the naked. Frog in leaves, and cricket in the grass! Continue, however, to keep time, I beg of you.

WEATHERCOCK (*towards one side*). Company to one's heart's content! Truly, nothing but brides! and young bachelors, man for man! the hopefullest people!

WEATHERCOCK (*towards the other side*). And if the ground does not open, to swallow up all of them — with a quick run, I will immediately jump into hell.

XENIEN. We are here as insects, with little sharp nebs, to honor Satan, our worshipful papa, according to his dignity.

HENNINGS. See! how naively they joke together in a crowded troop. They will e'en say, in the end, that they had good hearts.

MUSAGET. I like full well to lose myself in this host of witches; for, truly, I should know how manage these better than Muses.

CI-DEVANT GENIUS OF THE AGE. With proper people, one becomes somebody. Come, take hold of my skirt! The Blocksberg, like the German Parnassus, has a very broad top.

INQUISITIVE TRAVELLER. Tell me, what is the name of that stiff man? He walks with stiff steps. He snuffles everything he can snuffle. "He is scenting out Jesuits."

THE CRANE. I like to fish in clear and even in troubled waters. On the same principle you see the pious gentleman associate even with devils.

WORLDLING. Ay, for the pious, believe me, everything is a vehicle. They actually form many a conventicle here upon the Blocksberg.

DANCER. Here is surely a new choir coming! I hear distant drums. But don't disturb yourselves! there are single-toned bitterns among the reeds.

DANCING-MASTER.* How each throws up his legs! gets on as best he may! The crooked jumps, the clumsy hops, and asks not how it looks.

FIDDLER. How deeply this pack of ragamuffins hate each other, and how gladly they would give each other the finishing blow! the bagpipe unites them here, as Orpheus' lyre the beasts.

DOGMATIST. I will not be put out of my opinion, not by either critics or doubts. The devil, though, must be something; for how else could there be devils?

---

* This and the following stanza were added in the last complete edition of Goethe's Works.

IDEALIST. Phantasy, this once, is really too masterful in my mind. Truly, if I be that All, I must be beside myself to-day.

REALIST. Entity is a regular plague to me, and cannot but vex me much. I stand here, for the first time, not firm upon my feet.

SUPERNATURALIST. I am greatly pleased at being here, and am delighted with these; for, from devils, I can certainly draw conclusions as to good spirits.

SKEPTIC. They follow the track of the flame, and believe themselves near the treasure. Only doubt (*zweifel*) rhymes to devil (*teufel*). Here I am quite at home.

LEADER OF THE BAND. Frog in the leaves, and cricket in the grass! Confounded dilettanti! Flies' snouts and gnats' noses; you are fine musicians!

THE KNOWING ONES. *Sansouci*, that is the name of the host of merry creatures. There is no longer any walking upon feet, wherefore we walk upon our heads.

THE MALADROIT ONES. In times past we have sponged many a tit-bit; but now, good-bye to all that! Our shoes are danced through; we run on bare soles.

WILL-O'-THE-WISPS. We come from the bog, from which we are just sprung; but we are the glittering gallants here in the dance directly.

STAR-SHOOT. From on high, in star-and-fire-light, I shot hither. I am now lying crooked-ways in the grass; who will help me upon my legs?

THE MASSIVE ONES. Room! room! and round about! so down go the grass-stalks. Spirits are coming, but, spirits as they are, they have plump limbs.

PUCK. Don't tread so heavily, like elephants' calves; and the plumpest on this day be the stout Puck himself.

ARIEL. If kind nature gave — if the spirit gave you wings, follow my light track up to the hill of roses!

ORCHESTRA (*pianissimo*). Drifting clouds, and wreathed mists, brighten from on high! Breeze in the leaves, and wind in the rushes, and all is dissipated!

A GLOOMY DAY. — A PLAIN.

Faust — Mephistopheles.

Faust. In misery! Despairing! Long a wretched wanderer upon the earth, and now a prisoner! The dear, unhappy being, cooped up in the dungeon, as a malefactor for horrid tortures. Even to that! to that! Treacherous, worthless Spirit, and this hast thou concealed from me! Stand, only stand? roll thy devilish eyes infuriated in thy head! Stand and brave me with thy unbearable presence! A prisoner! In irremediable misery! Given over to evil spirits, and to sentence-passing, unfeeling man! And me, in the meantime, hast thou been lulling with tasteless dissipations, concealing her growing wretchedness from me, and leaving her to perish without help.

Mephistopheles. She is not the first.

Faust. Dog! horrible monster! Turn him, thou Infinite Spirit! turn the reptile back again into his dog's shape, in which he was often pleased to trot before me by night, to roll before the feet of the harmless wanderer, and fasten on his shoulders when he fell. Turn him again into his favorite shape, that he may crouch on his belly before me in the sand, whilst I spurn him with my foot, the reprobate! Not the first! Woe! woe! It is inconceivable by any human soul, that more than one creature can have sunk into such a depth of misery, — that the first in its writhing death-agony was not sufficient to atone for the guilt of all the rest in the sight of the Ever-pardoning. It harrows up my marrow and my very life, — the misery of this one: thou art grinning calmly at the fate of thousands.

Mephistopheles. Now are we already at our wits' end again! just where the sense of you mortals snaps with over-straining. Why dost thou enter into fellowship with us, if thou canst not go through with it? Will'st fly, and art not safe from dizziness? Did we force ourselves on thee, or thou thyself on us?

Faust. Gnash not thy greedy teeth thus defyingly at me! I loathe thee? Great, glorious Spirit, thou who deignest to appear to me, thou who knowest my heart and my soul, why yoke me to this shame-fellow, who feeds on mischief, and battens on destruction!

Mephistopheles. Hast done?

FAUST. Save her! or woe to thee! The most horrible curse on thee for thousands of years!

MEPHISTOPHELES. I cannot loosen the shackles of the avenger, nor undo his bolts. — Save her! Who was it that plunged her into ruin? I or thou? (FAUST *looks wildly around.*) Art thou grasping after the thunder? Well, that it is not given to you wretched mortals! To dash to pieces one who replies to you in all innocence — that is just the tyrant's way of venting himself in perplexities.

FAUST. Bring me thither! She shall be free!

MEPHISTOPHELES. And the danger to which you expose yourself! Know, the guilt of blood, from your hand, still lies upon the town. Avenging spirits hover over the place of the slain, and lie in wait for the returning murderer.

FAUST. That, too, from thee? Murder and death of a world upon thee, monster! Conduct me thither, I say, and free her!

MEPHISTOPHELES. I will conduct thee, and what I can, hear! Have I all power in heaven and upon earth? I will cloud the jailer's senses; do you possess yourself of the keys, and bear her off with human hand. I will watch! The magic horses will be ready; I will bear you off. This much I can do.

FAUST. Up and away!

NIGHT. — OPEN PLAIN.

FAUST *and* MEPHISTOPHELES *rushing along upon black horses.*

FAUST. What are they working — those about the Raven-stone yonder?

MEPHISTOPHELES. Can't tell what they're cooking and making.

FAUST. Are waving upwards — waving downwards — bending — stooping.

MEPHISTOPHELES. A witch company.

FAUST. They are sprinkling and charming.

MEPHISTOPHELES. On! on!

DUNGEON.

FAUST (*with a bunch of keys and a lamp, before an iron wicket*). A tremor, long unfelt, seizes me; the concentrated misery of mankind fastens on me. Here, behind these damp walls, is her dwelling-place, and her crime was a good delusion! Thou hesitatest to go to her! Thou fearest to see her again! On! thy irresolution lingers death hitherwards. (*He takes hold of the lock. — Singing within.*)

> My mother, the whore,
> That killed me!
> My father, the rogue,
> That ate me up!
> My little sister
> Picked up the bones
> At a cool place!
> There I became a beautiful little wood-bird.
> Fly away! fly away!

FAUST (*opening the lock*). She has no presentiment that her lover is listening, hears the chains clank, the straw rustle. (*He enters.*)

MARGARET (*hiding her face in the bed of straw*). Woe! woe! They come. Bitter death!

FAUST (*softly*). Hush! hush! I come to free thee.

MARGARET (*throwing herself before him*). If thou art human, feel for my wretchedness.

FAUST. You will wake the guard by your cries! (*He takes hold of the chains to unlock them.*

MARGARET (*on her knees*). Who has given you, headsman, this power over me? You come for me whilst it is yet midnight. Be merciful and let me live. Is not to-morrow morning soon enough? (*She stands up.*) I am yet so young, so young! and am to die already! I was fair, too, and that was my undoing! My true-love was near — he is now far away. Torn lies my garland, scattered the flowers. Don't take hold of me so roughly! Spare me! What have I done to you? Let me not implore in vain! I never saw you before in all my life, you know!

FAUST. Can I endure this misery?

MARGARET. I am now entirely in thy power. Only let me first give suck to the child. I pressed it this whole night to my heart. They took it away to vex me, and now say I killed it. And I shall never be happy again. They sing songs upon me! It is wicked of the people. An old tale ends so, — who bids them apply it?

FAUST (*throws himself on the ground*). A lover lies at thy feet, to unloose the bonds of wretchedness.

MARGARET (*throws herself by his side*). Ay, let us kneel to invoke the saints. See under these steps, under the threshold, hell is seething! The Evil One, with fearful fury, is making a din.

FAUST (*passionately*). Margaret! Margaret!

MARGARET (*listening*). That was my true-love's voice. (*She springs up. The chains fall off.*) Where is he! I heard him call. I am free! Nobody shall hinder me. I will fly to his neck! lie on his bosom! He called Margaret! He stood upon the threshold. In the midst, through the howling and clattering of hell, through the grim, devilish scoffing, I knew the sweet, the loving tone again.

FAUST. 'Tis I.

MARGARET. 'Tis thou! Ah, say so once again! (*Clasping him.*) 'Tis he!' 'Tis he! Whither is all my wretchedness! Whither the agony of the dungeon!—the chains! 'Tis thou! Thou comest to save me. I am saved!— There again already is the street, where I saw thee for the first time; and the cheerful garden where I and Martha waited for thee.

FAUST (*striving to take her away*). Come! come with me!

MARGARET. Oh, stay! I like to stay where thou stayest. (*Caressing him.*)

FAUST. Haste! If you do not make haste we shall pay dearly for it.

MARGARET. What! You can no longer kiss? So short a time away from me, my love, and already forgotten how to kiss! Why do I feel so sad upon your neck? when in other times a whole heaven came over me from your words, your looks; and you kissed me as if you were going to smother me! Kiss me! or I will kiss you! (*She embraces him.*) O woe! your lips are cold,—are dumb. Where have you left your love? Who has robbed me of it? (*She turns from him.*)

FAUST. Come! follow me! take courage, my love. I will press thee to my heart with a thousandfold warmth — only follow me! I ask thee but this.

MARGARET (*turning to him*). And is it thou, then? And is it thou, indeed?

FAUST. 'Tis I. Come along.

MARGARET. You undo my fetters, you take me to your bosom again! How comes it that you are not afraid of me? And do you then know, my love, whom you are freeing?

FAUST. Come, come! the depth of night is already passing away.

MARGARET. I have killed my mother, I have drowned my child. Was it not bestowed on thee and me?—on thee, too? 'Tis thou! I scarcely believe it. Give me thy hand. It is no dream—thy dear hand!—but oh, 'tis damp! Wipe it off. It seems to me as if there was blood on it. Oh, God! what hast thou done! Put up thy sword! I pray thee, do!

FAUST. Let what is past be past. Thou wilt kill me.

MARGARET. No, you must remain behind. I will describe the graves to you! you must see to them the first thing to-morrow. Give my mother the best place;—my brother close by;—me a little on one side, only not too far off. And the little one on my right breast; no one else will lie by me. To nestle to *thy* side,—that was a sweet, a dear delight! But it will never be mine again! I fear as if I were irresistibly drawn to you, and you were thrusting me off. And yet, 'tis you; you look so good, so kind.

FAUST. If you feel that 'tis I, come along.

MARGARET. Out there?

FAUST. Into the free air!

MARGARET. If the grave is without, if death lies in wait,—then come! Hence into the eternal resting-place, and not a step further.—Thou art now going away? O Henry, could I but go, too!

FAUST. Thou canst! Only consent! The door stands open.

MARGARET. I dare not go out; there is no hope for me! What avails it flying? They are lying in wait for me. It is so miserable to be obliged to beg,—and, what is worse, with an evil conscience, too. It is so miserable to wander in a strange land,—and they will catch me, do as I will.

FAUST. I shall be with thee.

MARGARET. Quick, quick! Save thy poor child. Away! Keep the path up by the brook—over the bridge—into the wood—to the left where the plank is—in the pond. Only quick and catch hold of it! it tries to rise! it is still struggling! Help! help!

FAUST. Be calm, I pray! Only one step, and thou art free.

MARGARET. Were we but past the hill! There sits my mother on a stone — my brain grows chill! — there sits my mother on a stone, and waves her head to and fro. She beckons not, she nods not, her head is heavy; she slept so long, she'll wake no more. She slept that we might enjoy ourselves. Those were pleasant times!

FAUST. As no prayer, no persuasion, is here of any avail, I will risk the bearing thee away.

MARGARET. Let me go! No, I endure no violence! Lay not hold of me so murderously! Time was, you know, when I did all to pleasure you.

FAUST. The day is dawning! My love! my love!

MARGARET. Day! Yes, it is growing day! The last day is breaking in! My wedding-day it was to be! Tell no one that thou hadst been with Margaret already. Woe to my garland! It is all over now! We shall meet again, but not at the dance. The crowd thickens; it is not heard. The square, the streets, cannot hold them. The bell tolls — the staff breaks! How they bind and seize me! Already am I hurried off to the blood-seat! Already quivering for every neck is the sharp steel which quivers for mine. Dumb lies the world as the grave.

FAUST. O that I had never been born!

MEPHISTOPHELES (*appears without*). Up! or you are lost. Vain hesitation! Lingering and prattling! My horses shudder; the morning is gloaming up.

MARGARET. What rises up from the floor? He! He! Send him away! What would he at the holy place? He would me!

FAUST. Thou shalt live!

MARGARET. Judgment of God! I have given myself up to thee.

MEPHISTOPHELES (*to* FAUST). Come! come! I will leave you in the scrape with her.

MARGARET. Thine am I, Father! save me, ye angels! Ye holy hosts, range yourselves round about to guard me! Henry! I tremble to look upon thee.

MEPHISTOPHELES. She is judged!

VOICE (*from above*). Is saved!

MEPHISTOPHELES (*to* FAUST). Hither to me! (*Disappears with* FAUST.

VOICE (*from within, dying away*). Henry! Henry!

CLAVIGO:

A TRAGEDY IN FIVE ACTS.

Clavigo was written in 1774, a few months before the publication of The Sorrows of Young Werther, and a year after the appearance of Goetz von Berlichingen. It has always been popular in Germany, where it still holds a place on the stage ; but it has not been translated into English before.

INTRODUCTION TO CLAVIGO.

THE story on which Clavigo is founded is not only an authentic one, but the circumstances occurred only ten years before the publication of the play. They are as follows : — Beaumarchais (the well-known French writer) had two sisters living in Madrid, one married to an architect, the other, Marie, engaged to Clavijo, a young author without fortune, No sooner had Clavijo obtained an office which he had long solicited than he refused to fulfil his promise. Beaumarchais hurried to Madrid ; his object was twofold ; to save the reputation of his sister, and to put a little speculation of his own on foot. He sought Clavijo, and by his *sang-froid* and courage extorted from him a written avowal of his contemptible conduct. No sooner is this settled than Clavijo, alarmed at the consequences, solicits a reconciliation with Marie, offering to marry her. Beaumarchais consents, but just as the marriage is about to take place he learns that Clavijo is secretly conspiring against him, accusing him of having extorted the marriage by force, in consequence of which he has procured an order from the government to expel Beaumarchais from Madrid. Irritated at such villainy, Beaumarchais goes to the Ministers, reaches the King, and avenges himself by getting Clavijo dismissed from his post.

This story was published by Beaumarchais under title of a " Mémoire, " in the year 1774 ; the circumstances having occurred in 1764. Goethe once, at a friendly meeting, read the recently published Mémoire, and in the conversation that ensued promised to produce a play on the subject in the course of the following week. He fulfilled his promise, and it will be seen how closely, with the exception of the tragic *dénouement,* he adhered to the original story. The real Clavijo subsequently became a man of considerable eminence in Madrid, though Goethe could not have been aware of his existence when he wrote the play.*

* The above details are derived from Mr. G. H. Lewes' "Life of Goethe."

It belongs to the period just after the composition of *Werther*, and is one of the less important of his literary works; but the exceedingly dramatic presentation of the incidents has given it great popularity on the German stage, and helped considerably to establish the fame of the author.

———◆———

DRAMATIS PERSONÆ.

CLAVIGO.
CARLOS, *his friend.*
BEAUMARCHAIS.
MARIE BEAUMARCHAIS.
SOPHIE GUILBERT (*née* BEAUMARCHAIS).
GUILBERT, *her husband.*
BUENCO.
ST. GEORGE.

The scene is at Madrid.

CLAVIGO.

ACT I.

SCENE I. CLAVIGO'S *Dwelling*.

Enter CLAVIGO *and* CARLOS.

CLAVIGO (*rising up from the writing-table*). The journal will do a good work, it must charm all women. Tell me, Carlos, do you not think that my weekly periodical is now one of the first in Europe ?

CARLOS. We Spaniards, at least, have no modern author who unites such great strength of thought, so much florid imagination, with so brilliant and easy a style.

CLAVIGO. Please don't. I must still be among the people the creator of the good style ; people are ready to take all sorts of impressions ; I have a reputation among my fellow-citizens, their confidence : and, between ourselves, my acquirements extend daily ; my experience widens, and my style becomes ever truer and stronger.

CARLOS. Good, Clavigo ! Yet, if you will not take it ill, your paper pleased me far better when you yet wrote it at Marie's feet, when the lovely cheerful creature had still an influence over you. I know not how, the whole had a more youthful blooming appearance.

CLAVIGO. Those were good times, Carlos, which are now gone. I gladly avow to thee, I wrote then with opener heart ; and, it is true, she had a large share in the approbation which the public accorded me at the very beginning. But at length, Carlos, one becomes very soon weary of women ; and were you not the first to applaud my resolution, when I determined to forsake her ?

CARLOS. You would have become rusty. Women are far too monotonous. Only, it seems to me, it were again time that you cast about for a new plan, for it is all up when one is so entirely aground.

CLAVIGO. My plan is the Court ; there there is no leisure nor holiday. For a stranger, who, without standing, without name, without fortune, came here, have I not already advanced far enough? Here in a Court! amid the throng of men, where it is not easy to attract attention? I do so rejoice, when I look on the road I have left behind me. Loved by the first in the kingdom! Honored for my attainments, my rank! Recorder of the king! Carlos, all that spurs me on; I were nothing if I remained what I am. Forward! forward! There it costs toil and art! One needs all his wits; and the women! the women! one loses far too much time with them.

CARLOS. Simpleton, that is your fault. I can never live without women, and they are not in my way at all. Moreover, I do not say so very many fine things to them, I do not amuse myself entire months with sentiment and such like; for I do not at all like to have to do with prudish girls. One has soon said his say with them: afterwards, if you have carried on with them for a while, scarcely have they been warmed up a little, when straightway — the deuce — you are pestered with thoughts of marriage and promises of marriage, which I fear as the plague. You are pensive, Clavigo?

CLAVIGO. I cannot get rid of the recollection that I jilted, deceived Marie, call it as you will.

CARLOS. Wonderful! It seems to me, however, that one lives only once in this world, has only once this power, these prospects, and he who does not make the most of them, and rise as high as possible, is a fool. And to marry! to marry just at the time when life is for the first time about to soar aloft on widespread pinions! to bury one's self in domestic repose, to shut one's self up when one has not traversed the half of his journey — has not yet achieved the half of his conquests! To love her was natural; to promise her marriage was folly, and if you had kept your word it would have been downright madness.

CLAVIGO. Hold! I do not understand men. I loved her truly, she drew me to her, she held me, and as I sat at her feet I vowed to her — I vowed to myself — that it should ever be so, that I would be hers as soon as I had an office, a position — and now, Carlos!

CARLOS. It will be quite time enough when you are a made man, when you have reached the desired goal, if then — to crown and confirm all your happiness — you seek to ally yourself by a prudent marriage with a family of wealth and consequence.

CLAVIGO. She has vanished! quite out of my heart vanished, and if her unhappiness does not sometimes remind me — strange that one is so changeable!

CARLOS. If one were constant I should wonder. Look, pray, does not everything in the world change? Why should our passions endure? Be tranquil; she is not the first jilted girl, nor the first that has consoled herself. If I were to advise you, there is the young widow over the way ——

CLAVIGO. You know I do not set much store on such proposals. A love affair which does not come of its own accord has no charm for me.

CARLOS. So dainty people!

CLAVIGO. Be it so, and forget not that our chief work at present is, to render ourselves necessary to the new minister That Whal resigns the government of India is troublesome enough for us. In truth, otherwise it does not disquiet me; his influence abides — Grimaldi and he are friends, and we know how to talk and manœuvre.

CARLOS. And think and do what we will.

CLAVIGO. That is the grand point in the world. (*Rings for the servant.*) Take this sheet to the printing-office.

CARLOS. Are you to be seen in the evening?

CLAVIGO. I do not think so. However, you can inquire.

CARLOS. This evening I should like to undertake something which gladdened my heart; all this afternoon I must write again, there is no end of it.

CLAVIGO. Have patience. If we did not toil for so many persons we would not get the ascendancy over so many. [*Exit.*

SCENE II. GUILBERT'S *Dwelling.*

SOPHIE GUILBERT, MARIE, *and* DON BUENCO.

BUENCO. You have had a bad night?

SOPHIE. I told her so yesterday evening. She was so foolishly merry and prattled till eleven, then she was overheated, could not sleep, and now again she has no breath and weeps the whole morning.

MARIE. Strange that our brother comes not! It is two days past the time.

SOPHIE. Only have patience, he will not fail us.

MARIE (*rising*). How anxious I am to see this brother, my avenger and my saviour. I scarcely remember him.

SOPHIE. Indeed! Oh, I can well picture him to myself; he was a fiery, open, brave boy of thirteen when our father sent us here.

MARIE. A noble great soul. You have read the letter which he wrote when he learnt my unhappiness; each character of it is enshrined in my heart. "If you are guilty," writes he, "expect no forgiveness; over and above your misery the contempt of a brother will fall heavy upon you, and the curse of a father. If you are innocent, oh, then, all vengeance, all, all glowing vengeance on the traitor!"—I tremble! He will come. I tremble, not for myself, I stand before God in my innocence! You must, my friends—I know not what I want! O Clavigo!

SOPHIE. You will not listen! You will kill yourself.

MARIE. I will be still. Yes, I will not weep. It seems to me, however, I could have no more tears. And why tears? I am only sorry that I make my life bitter to you. For when all is said and done, what have I to complain of? I have had much joy as long as our old friend still lived. Clavigo's love has caused me much joy, perhaps more than mine for him. And now what is it after all? of what importance am I? What matters it if a girl's heart is broken? What matters it whether she pines away and torments her poor young heart?

BUENCO. For God's sake, Mademoiselle!

MARIE. Whether it is all one to *him*—that he loves me no more? Ah! why am I not more amiable? But *he* should pity, at least pity me!—that the hapless girl, to whom he had made himself so needful, now without him should pine and weep her life away—Pity! I wish not to be pitied by this man.

SOPHIE. If I could teach you to despise him—the worthless, detestable man.

MARIE. No, sister, worthless he is not; and must I then despise him whom I hate? Hate! Indeed, sometimes I can hate him—sometimes, when the Spanish spirit possesses me. Lately, oh! lately, when we met him, his look wrought full, warm love in me! And as I again came home, and his manner recurred to me, and the calm, cold glance that he cast over me, while beside the brilliant donna; then I became a Spaniard in my heart, and seized my dagger and poison, and disguised myself. Are you amazed, Buenco? All in thought only, of course!

Sophie. Foolish girl!

Marie. My imagination led me after him. I saw him as he lavished all the tenderness, all the gentleness at the feet of his new love — the charms with which he poisoned me —I aimed at the heart of the traitor! Ah! Buenco!— all at once the good-hearted French girl was again there, who knows of no love-sickness, and no daggers for revenge. We are badly off! Vaudevilles to entertain our lovers, fans to punish them, and, if they are faithless?— Say, sister, what do they do in France when lovers are faithless?

Sophie. They curse them.

Marie. And——

Sophie. And let them go their ways.

Marie. Go!—and why shall not I let Clavigo go? If that is the French fashion, why shall it not be so in Spain? Why shall a Frenchwoman not be a Frenchwoman in Spain? We will let him go, and take to ourselves another; it appears to me they do so with us, too.

Buenco. He has broken a sacred promise, and no light love-affair, no friendly attachment. Mademoiselle, you are pained, hurt even to the depths of your heart. Oh! never was my position of an unknown, peaceful citizen of Madrid so burdensome, so painful as at this moment, in which I feel myself so feeble, so powerless to obtain justice for you against the treacherous courtier!

Marie. When he was still Clavigo, not yet Recorder of the King; when he was still the stranger, the guest, the new-comer in our house, how amiable he was, how good! How all his ambition, all his desire to rise, seemed to be a child of his love! For me he struggled for name, rank, fortune; he has all now, and I !——

Guilbert comes.

Guilbert (*privately to his wife*). Our brother is coming?

Marie. My brother! (*She trembles; they conduct her to a seat*). Where? where? Bring him to me! Take me to him!

Beaumarchais comes.

Beaumarchais. My sister! (*Quitting the eldest to rush towards the youngest*). My sister! My friends! O my sister!

Marie. Is it you, indeed? God be thanked it is you! ·

Beaumarchais. Let me regain composure.

MARIE. My heart!—my poor heart!

SOPHIE. Be calm. Dear brother, I hoped to see you more tranquil.

BEAUMARCHAIS. More tranquil! Are you, then, tranquil? Do I not behold in the wasted figure of this dear one, in your tearful eyes, your sorrowful paleness, in the dead silence of your friends, that you are as wretched as I have imagined you to be during all the long way? and more wretched; for I see you, I hold you in my arms; your presence redoubles my sufferings. O my sister!

SOPHIE. And our father?

BEAUMARCHAIS. He blesses you, and me, if I save you.

BUENCO. Sir, permit one unknown who, at the first look, recognizes in you a noble, brave man, to bear witness to the deep interest which all this matter inspires in me. Sir, you undertake this long journey to save, to avenge your sister! Welcome! be welcome as a guardian angel, though, at the same time, you put us all to the blush!

BEAUMARCHAIS. I hoped, sir, to find in Spain such hearts as yours; that encouraged me to take this step. Nowhere, nowhere in the world are feeling, congenial souls wanting, if only one steps forward whose circumstances leave him full freedom to carry his courage through. And oh, my friends, I feel full of hope! Everywhere there are men of honor among the powerful and great, and the ear of Majesty is rarely deaf; only our voice is almost always too weak to reach to their height.

SOPHIE. Come, sister! come, rest a moment. She is quite beside herself. (*They lead her away.*)

MARIE. My brother!

BEAUMARCHAIS. God willing if you are innocent, then all, all vengeance on the traitor! (*Exeunt* MARIE *and* SOPHIE.) My brother!—my friends!—I see it in your looks that you are so. Let me regain composure and then!—a pure impartial recital of the whole story. This must determine my actions. The feeling of a good cause shall confirm my courage; and, believe me, if we are right, we shall get justice.

ACT II.

Scene I. Clavigo's *House.*

Clavigo. Who may these Frenchmen be, that have got themselves announced in my house? Frenchmen! In former days this nation was welcome to me! And why not now? It is singular that a man who sets so much at naught is yet bound with feeble thread to a single point. It is too much! And did I owe more to Marie than to myself? and is it a duty to make myself unhappy because a girl loves me?

A Servant.

Servant. The foreign gentlemen, sir.

Clavigo. Bid them enter. Pray, did you tell their servant that I expect them to breakfast?

Servant. As you ordered.

Clavigo. I shall be back presently. [*Exit.*

Beaumarchais — St. George.

The Servant places chairs for them and withdraws.

Beaumarchais. I feel so much at ease; so content, my friend, to be at length here, to hold him; he shall not escape me. Be calm: at least show him a calm exterior. My sister! my sister! who could believe that you are as innocent as you are unhappy? It shall come to light; you shall be terribly avenged! And Thou, good God! preserve to me the tranquillity of soul which Thou accordest to me at this moment, that, amid this frightful grief, I may act as prudently as possible and with all moderation.

St. George. Yes; this wisdom — all the prudence, my friend, you have ever shown — I claim now. Promise me once more, dear friend, that you will reflect where you are. In a strange kingdom, where all your protectors, all your money cannot secure you from the secret machinations of worthless foes.

Beaumarchais. Be tranquil: play your part well; he shall not know with which of us he has to do. I will torture him! Oh, I am just in a fine humor to roast this fellow over a slow fire!

Clavigo *returns.*

Clavigo. Gentlemen, it gives me joy to see in my house men of a nation that I have always esteemed.

BEAUMARCHAIS. Sir, I wish that we, too, may be worthy of the honor which you are good enough to confer on our fellow-countrymen.

ST. GEORGE. The pleasure of making your acquaintaince has surmounted the fear of being troublesome to you.

CLAVIGO. Persons, whom the first look recommends, should not push modesty so far.

BEAUMARCHAIS. In truth it cannot be a novelty to you to be sought out by strangers; for by the excellence of your writings, you have made yourself as much known in foreign lands as the important offices which his majesty has entrusted to you distinguish you in your fatherland.

CLAVIGO. The king looks with much favor on my humble services, and the public with much indulgence on the trifling essays of my pen; I have wished that I could contribute in some measure to the improvement of taste, to the propagation of the sciences in my country; for they only unite us with other nations, they only make friends of the most distant spirits, and maintain the sweetest union among those even, who, alas! are too often disunited through political interests.

BEAUMARCHAIS. It is captivating to hear a man so speak who has equal influence in the state and in letters. I must also avow you have taken the word out of my mouth and brought me straight to the purpose, on account of which you see me here. A society of learned, worthy men has commissioned me, in every place through which I travel and find opportunity, to establish a correspondence between them and the best minds in the kingdom. As no Spaniard writes better than the author of the journal called the *Thinker* — a man with whom I have the honor to speak (CLAVIGO *makes a polite bow*), and who is an especial ornament of learned men, since he has known how to unite with his literary talents so great a capacity for political affairs, he cannot fail to climb the highest steps of which his character and acquirements render him worthy. I believe I can perform no more acceptable service to my friends than to put them in connection with a man of such merit.

CLAVIGO. No proposal in the world could be more agreeable to me, gentlemen; I thereby see fulfilled the sweetest hopes, with which my heart was often occupied without any prospect of their happy accomplishment. Not that I believe I shall be able, through my correspondence, to satisfy the wishes of your learned friends; my vanity does not go so far. But as I have the happiness to be in accordance with the best minds in Spain, as nothing can remain unknown to me which is achieved in our vast kingdom by isolated, often obscure, individuals for the Arts and Sciences, I have looked upon myself, till now, as a kind of colporteur, who possesses the feeble merit of rendering the inventions of others generally useful; but now I become, through your intervention, a merchant, happy enough through the exportation of native products to extend the renown of his fatherland and thereby to enrich it with foreign treasures. So then, allow me, sir, to treat as not a stranger a man who, with such frankness, brings such agreeable news; allow me to ask what business — what project made you undertake this long journey? It is not that I would, through this officiousness, gratify vain curiosity; no, believe rather that it is with the purest intention of exerting in your behalf all the resources, all the influence which I may perchance possess; for I tell you beforehand, you have come to a place where countless difficulties encounter a stranger in the prosecution of his business, especially at the Court.

BEAUMARCHAIS. I accept so obliging an offer with warmest thanks. I have no secrets with you, sir, nor will this friend be in the way during my statement; he is sufficiently acquainted with what I have to say. (CLAVIGO *looks at* ST. GEORGE *with attention.*) A French merchant, with a large family and a limited fortune, had many business friends in Spain. One of the richest came to Paris fifteen years ago, and made him this proposal: "Give me two of your daughters, and I shall take them with me to Madrid and provide for them. I am not married, am getting old and have no relatives; they will form the happiness of my declining years, and after my decease I shall leave them one of the most considerable establishments in Spain. The eldest and one of the younger sisters were confided to his care. The father undertook to supply the house with all kinds of French merchandise which might be required, and so all went well till the friend died without the least mention of the Frenchwomen in his will, who then saw themselves in the embarrassing position of superintending alone a new business. The eldest had meanwhile married, and notwithstanding their moderate fortune, they secured through their good conduct and varied accomplishments a multitude o friends who were eager to extend their credit and business. (CLAVIGO *becomes more and more attentive*.) About the same time a young man, a native of the Canary Islands, had got himself introduced into the family. (CLAVIGO's *countenance loses all cheerfulness, and his seriousness changes gradually into embarrassment, more and more visible*.) Despite his humble standing and fortune they receive him kindly. The Frenchwomen, remarking in him a great love of the French language, favored him with every means of making rapid progress in its study. Extremely anxious to make himself known, he forms the design of giving to the city of Madrid the pleasure, hitherto unknown to Spain, of reading a weekly periodical in the style of the English *Spectator*. His lady friends fail not to aid him in every way; they do not doubt that such an undertaking would meet with great success; in short, animated by the hope of soon becoming a man of some consequence, he ventures to make an offer of marriage to the younger. Hopes are held out to him. "Try to make your fortune," quoth the elder, "and if an appointment, the favor of the Court, or any other means of subsistence shall have given you a right to think of my sister, if she still prefers you to other suitors, I cannot refuse you my consent." (CLAVIGO, *covered with confusion, moves uneasily on his seat*.) The younger declines several advantageous offers; her fondness for the man increases, and helps her to bear the anxiety of an uncertain expectation; she interests herself for his happiness as for her own, and encourages him to issue the first number of his periodical, which appears under an imposing title. (CLAVIGO *is terribly embarrassed*. BEAUMARCHAIS, *icy cold*.) The success of the journal was astonishing; the King even, delighted with this charming production, gave the author public tokens of his favor. He was promised the first honorable office that might be vacant. From that moment he removed all rivals from his beloved, while quite openly striving hard to win her good graces. The marriage was delayed only in expectation of the promised situation. At last, after six years' patient waiting, unbroken friendship, aid, and love on the part of the girl; after six years' devotion, gratitude, attentions, solemn assurances on the part of the man, the office is forthcoming — and he vanishes. (CLAVIGO *utters a deep sigh, which he tries to stifle, and is quite overcome*.) The matter had made so great a noise in the world that the issue could not be regarded with indifference. A house had been rented for two families. The whole town was talking of it. The hearts of all friends were wrung and sought revenge. Application was made to powerful protectors; but the worthless fellow, already initiated in the cabals of the Court, knew how to render fruitless all their efforts, and went so far in his insolence as to dare to threaten the unhappy ladies; to dare to say, in the very face of those friends who had gone to find him, that the Frenchwomen should take care; he defied them to injure him, and if they made bold to undertake aught against him, it would be easy for him to ruin them in a foreign land, where they would be without protection and help. At this intelligence the poor girl fell into convulsions, which threatened death. In the depth of her grief, the elder wrote to France about the public outrage which had been done to them. The news most powerfully moves her brother; he demands leave of absence to obtain counsel and aid in so complicated an affair, he flies from Paris to Madrid, and the brother — it is I! who have left all — my country, duties, family, standing, pleasures, in order to avenge, in Spain, an innocent, unhappy sister. I come, armed with the best cause and firm determination to unmask a traitor, to mark with bloody strokes his soul on his face, and the traitor — art thou!

CLAVIGO. Hear me, sir — I am — I have — I doubt not ——

BEAUMARCHAIS. Interrupt me not. You have nothing to say to me and much to hear from me. Now, to make a beginning, have the goodness, in the presence of this gentleman, who has come from France expressly with me, to declare whether my sister has deserved this public outrage from you through any treachery, levity, weakness, rudeness, or any other blemish.

CLAVIGO. No, sir. Your sister, Donna Maria, is a lady overflowing with wit, amiability, and goodness.

BEAUMARCHAIS. Has she ever during your acquaintance given you any occasion to complain of her or to esteem her less?

CLAVIGO. Never! never!

BEAUMARCHAIS (*rising*). And why, monster, had you the barbarity to torture the girl to death? Only because her heart preferred you to ten others, all more honorable and richer than you?

CLAVIGO. Ah, sir! If you knew how I have been instigated; how I, through manifold advisers and circumstances ——

BEAUMARCHAIS. Enough! (*To* ST. GEORGE.) You have heard the vindication of my sister; go and publish it. What I have further to say to the gentleman, needs no witnesses. (CLAVIGO *rises*. ST. GEORGE *retires*.) Stay! Stay! (*Both sit down again*.) Having now got so far, I shall make a proposal to you, which I hope you will accept. It is equally agreeable to you and to me that you do not wed Marie, and you are deeply sensible that I have not come to play the part of a theatrical brother, who will unravel the drama, and present a husband to his sister. You have cast a slur upon an honorable lady in cold blood because you supposed that in a foreign land she was without prop and avenger. Thus acts a base, worthless fellow. And so, first of all, testify with your own hand, spontaneously, with open doors, in presence of your servants, that you are an abominable man, who have deceived, betrayed my sister without the least cause; and with this declaration I will set out for Aranjuez, where our ambassador resides; I will show it, get it printed, and the day after to-morrow the court and the town shall be flooded with it. I have powerful friends here, I have time and money, and of all shall I avail myself to pursue you in the most furious manner possible till the resentment of my sister is appeased and satisfied, and she herself says, "Stop."

CLAVIGO. I will not make such a declaration.

BEAUMARCHAIS. I believe you, for in your place I should, perhaps, not make it either. But here is the reverse of the medal. If you do not write it I shall remain beside you, from this moment I shall not quit you. I shall follow you everywhere, till you, disgusted with such society, will have sought to get rid of me behind Buenretiro. If I am more fortunate than you, without seeing the ambassador, without speaking here with any one, I take my dying sister in my arms, place her in my carriage, and return to France with her. Should fate favor you, I am played out, and you may have a laugh at our expense. Meanwhile, breakfast. (BEAUMARCHAIS *rings the bell. An* ATTENDANT *brings the chocolate.* BEAUMARCHAIS *takes a cup, and walks in the adjoining gallery, examining the pictures*.)

CLAVIGO. Air! air! I have been surprised and seized like a boy. Where are you then, Clavigo? How will you end this? How can you end it? Frightful position, into which your folly, your treachery has plunged you? (*He seizes his sword on the table*.) Ha! short and good! (*Lays it down*.) And is there no way, no means, but death?—or murder?—horrible murder! To deprive the hapless lady of her last solace, her only stay, her brother! To see gushing out the blood of a noble, brave man! And to draw upon yourself the double, insupportable curse of a ruined family! O, this was not the prospect when this amiable creature, even from your first meeting, attracted you with so many winsome ways! And when you abandoned her, did you not see the frightful consequences of your crime? What blessedness awaited you in her arms! in the friendship of such a brother! Marie! Marie! O that you could forgive! that at your feet I could atone for all by my tears!— And why not? —My heart overflows; my soul mounts up in hope! Sir!

BEAUMARCHAIS. What is your determination?

CLAVIGO. Hear me! My deceit towards your sister is unpardonable. Vanity has misled me. I feared by this marriage to ruin all my plans, all my projects for a world-wide celebrity. Could I have known that she had such a brother she would have been in my eyes no unimportant stranger; I should have expected from our union very considerable advantages. You inspire me, sir, with the highest esteem, and, in making me so keenly sensible of my errors, you impart to me a desire, a power, to make all good again. I throw myself at your feet! Help! help, if it is possible, to efface my guilt and put an end to unhappiness. Give your sister to me, again, sir, give me to her! How happy were I to receive from your hand a wife and the forgiveness of all my faults!

BEAUMARCHAIS. It is too late! My sister loves you no more, and I detest you. Write the desired declaration, that is all that I exact from you, and leave me to provide for a choice revenge.

CLAVIGO. Your obstinacy is neither right nor prudent. I grant you that it does not depend on me, whether I will make good again so irremediable an evil. Whether I can make it good? That rests with the heart of your excellent sister, whether she may again look upon a wretch who does not deserve to see the light of day. Only it is your duty to ascertain that and to conduct yourself accordingly, if your demeanor is not to resemble the inconsiderate passion of a young man. If Donna Maria is immovable. O, I know her heart! O, her good, heavenly soul hovers before me quite vividly! If she is inexorable, then it is time, sir.

BEAUMARCHAIS. I insist on the vindication.

CLAVIGO (*approaching the table*). And if I seize the sword?

BEAUMARCHAIS (*advancing*). Good, sir! Excellent, sir!

CLAVIGO (*holding him back*). One word more! You have the better case; let me have prudence for you. Consider what you are doing. Whether you or I fall, we are irrecoverably lost. Should I not die of pain, of remorse, if your blood were to stain my sword, if I, to complete her wretchedness, bereft her of her brother; and on the other hand — the murderer of Clavigo would not re-cross the Pyrenees.

BEAUMARCHAIS. The vindication, sir, the vindication!

CLAVIGO. Well! be it so. I will do all to convince you of the upright feeling with which your presence inspires me. I will write the vindication, I will write it at your dictation. Only promise me not to make use of it till I am able to convince Donna Maria of the change and repentance of my heart, till I have spoken to her elder sister; till she has put in a good word for me with my beloved one. Not before, sir.

BEAUMARCHAIS. I am going to Aranjuez.

CLAVIGO. Well, then, till your return, let the vindication remain in your portfolio; if I have not been forgiven, then let your vengeance have full swing. This proposal is just, fair, and prudent; and if you do not agree to it let us then play the game of life and death. And whichever of us two become the victim of his own rashness, you and your poor sister will suffer in any case.

BEAUMARCHAIS. It becomes you to pity those you have made wretched.

CLAVIGO (*sitting down*). Are you satisfied?

BEAUMARCHAIS. Well, then, I yield the point. But not a moment longer. I shall come back from Aranjuez, shall ask, shall hear! And if they have not forgiven you, which is what I hope and desire, I am off directly with the paper to the printing-office.

CLAVIGO (*sitting down*). How do you demand it?

BEAUMARCHAIS. Sir! in presence of your attendants.

CLAVIGO. Why?

BEAUMARCHAIS. Command only that they be present in the adjoining gallery. It shall not be said that I have constrained you.

CLAVIGO. What scruples!

BEAUMARCHAIS. I am in Spain and have to deal with you.

CLAVIGO. Now then! (*Rings. A* SERVANT.) Call my attendants together, and betake yourselves to the gallery there. (*The* Servant *retires. The rest come and occupy the gallery.*) You allow me to write the vindication?

Beaumarchais. No, sir! Write it, I must beg of you, write it as I dictate it to you. (Clavigo *writes.*) "I, the undersigned, Joseph Clavigo, Recorder of the King"——

Clavigo. "Of the King."

Beaumarchais. "Acknowledge that after I was received into the family of Madame Guilbert as a friend "——

Clavigo. "As a friend."

Beaumarchais. "I made her sister, Mademoiselle de Beaumarchais, a promise of marriage, repeated many times, which I have unscrupulously broken." Have you got it down?

Clavigo. But, sir!

Beaumarchais. Have you another expression for it?

Clavigo. I should think ——

Beaumarchais. "Unscrupulously broken." What you have done you need not hesitate to write.—"I have abandoned her, without any fault or weakness on her part having suggested a pretext or an excuse for this perfidy."

Clavigo. Well!

Beaumarchais. "On the contrary, the demeanor of the lady has been always pure, blameless, and worthy of all honor."

Clavigo. —" Worthy of all honor."

Beaumarchais. "I confess that, through my deceit, the levity of my conversations, the construction of which they were susceptible, I have publicly humiliated this virtuous lady; and on this account I entreat her forgiveness, although I do not regard myself as worthy of receiving it." (Clavigo *stops.*) Write! write! "And this testimony of my own free will, and unforced, I have given, with this especial promise, that if this satisfaction should not please the injured lady, I am ready to afford it in every other way required. Madrid."

Clavigo (*rises, beckons to the servants to withdraw, and hands him the paper*). I have to do with an injured, but a noble man. You will keep your word, and put off your vengeance. Only on this consideration, in this hope, I have granted you the shameful document, to which nothing else would have reduced me. But before I venture to appear before Donna Maria, I have resolved to engage some one to put in a word for me, to speak in my behalf — and you are the man.

BEAUMARCHAIS.　Do not reckon on that.

CLAVIGO.　At least make her aware of the bitter heart-felt repentance which you have seen in me.　That is all, all, that I beg of you; do not deny me this; I should have to choose another less powerful intercessor, and even you owe her anyhow a faithful account.　Do tell her how you have found me!

BEAUMARCHAIS.　Well! this I can do, this I shall do. Good-bye, then.

CLAVIGO.　Farewell! (*He wishes to take his hand;* BEAUMARCHAIS *draws it back.*)

CLAVIGO (*alone*).　So unexpectedly from one position into the other.　It is an infatuation, a dream!—I should not have given this vindication.—It came so quickly, so suddenly, like a thunder-storm!

CARLOS enters.

CARLOS.　What visit is this you have had?　The whole house is astir.　What is the matter?

CLAVIGO.　Marie's brother.

CARLOS.　I suspected it.　This old dog of a servant, who was formerly with Guilbert, and who at present acts the spy for me, knew yesterday that he was expected, and found me only this moment.　He was here then?

CLAVIGO.　An excellent young man.

CARLOS.　Of whom we shall soon be rid.　Already I have spread nets on his way!—What, then, was the matter?　A challenge?　An apology?　Was he very hot, the fellow?

CLAVIGO.　He demanded a declaration, that his sister gave me no occasion for the change in my feelings towards her.

CARLOS.　And have you granted it?

CLAVIGO.　I thought it was best.

CARLOS.　Well, very well!　Was that all?

CLAVIGO.　He insisted on a duel or the vindication.

CARLOS.　The latter was the more judicious.　Who will risk his life for a boy so romantic?　And did he exact the paper with violence?

CLAVIGO.　He dictated it to me, and I had to call the servants into the gallery.

CARLOS.　I understand! ah! now I have you, little master!　That will prove his ruin.　Call me a scrivener if in two days I have not the varlet in prison and off for India by the next transport.

CLAVIGO.　No, Carlos.　The matter stands otherwise than as you think.

Carlos.   What?

Clavigo.   I hope through his intervention, through my earnest endeavors, to obtain forgiveness from the unhappy girl.

Carlos.   Clavigo!

Clavigo.   I hope to efface all the past, to heal the breach, and so in my own eyes and in the eyes of the world again to become an honorable man.

Carlos.   The devil! Have you become childish? One can still detect the bookworm in you. — To let yourself be so befooled ! Do you not see that that is a stupidly laid plan to entrap you ?

Clavigo.   No, Carlos, he does not wish marriage; they are even opposed to it ; she will not listen to aught from me.

Carlos.   That is the very point. No, my good friend, take it not ill ; I may, perhaps, in plays have seen a country squire thus cheated.

Clavigo.   You pain me. I beg you will reserve your humor for my wedding. I have resolved to marry Marie, of my own accord, from the impulse of my heart. All my hope, all my felicity, rests on the thought of procuring her forgiveness. And then away, Pride! Heaven still lies, as before, in the breast of this loved one. All the fame which I acquire, all the greatness to which I rise, will fill me with double joy, for it is shared by the lady who makes me twice a man. Farewell! I must hence. I must at least speak with Guilbert.

Carlos.   Wait only till after dinner.

Clavigo.   Not a moment.   [*Exit.*

Carlos (*looking after him in silence for some time*). There, some one is going to burn his fingers again !

ACT III.

Scene I.   Guilbert's *abode.*

Sophie Guilbert, Marie, Beaumarchais.

Marie.   You have seen him? All my limbs tremble! You have seen him? I had almost fainted when I heard he was come; and you have seen him? No, I can — I will — no — I can never see him again.

SOPHIE. I was beside myself when he stepped in. For ah! did not I love him as you did, with the fullest, purest, most sisterly love? Has not his estrangement grieved, tortured me? And now, the returning, the repentent one, at my feet! Sister, there is something so charming in his look, in the tone of his voice. He ——

MARIE. Never, never more!

SOPHIE. He is the same as ever; has still that good, soft, feeling heart; still even that impetuosity of passion. There is still even the desire to be loved, and the excruciatingly painful torture when love is denied him. All! all! and of thee he speaks, Marie! as in those happy days of the most ardent passion. It is, as if your good genius had even brought about this interval of infidelity and separation to break the uniformity and tediousness of a prolonged attachment, and impart to the feeling a fresh vivacity.

MARIE. Do you speak a word for him?

SOPHIE. No, sister. Nor have I promised to do so. Only, dearest, I see things as they are. You and your brother see them in a light far too romantic. You have this experience in common with many a very good girl, that your lover became faithless and forsook you. And that he comes again penitent, will amend his fault, revive all old hopes — that is a happiness which another would not lightly reject.

MARIE. My heart would break!

SOPHIE. I believe you. The first moment must make a sensible impression on you — and then, my dear, I beseech you, regard not this anxiety, this embarrassment, which seems to overpower all your senses, as a result of hatred and ill-will. Your heart speaks more for him than you suppose, and even on that account you do not trust yourself to see him, because you so anxiously desire his return.

MARIE. Spare me, dearest!

SOPHIE. You should be happy. Did I feel that you despise him, that he is indifferent to you, I would not say another word, he should see my face no more. Yet, as it is, my love, you will thank me that I have helped you to overcome this painful irresolution, which is a token of the deepest love.

GUILBERT, BUENCO.

SOPHIE. Come, Buenco! Guilbert, come! Help me to give this darling courage, resolution, now while we may.

BUENCO. Would that I dared say — receive him again.

SOPHIE. Buenco!

BUENCO. The thought makes my blood boil — that he should still possess this angel, whom he has so shamefully injured, whom he has dragged to the grave. He — possess her? Why? How does he repair all that he has violated? He returns; once more it pleases him to return and say: "Now I may; now I will," just as if this excellent creature were suspected wares, which in the end you toss to the buyer after he has tormented you to the marrow by the meanest offers, and haggling like a Jew. No, my voice he will never obtain, not even if the heart of Marie herself should speak for him. To return; and why, then, now? — now? — Must he wait till a valiant brother come, whose vengeance he must fear, and, like a schoolboy, come and crave pardon? Ha! he is as cowardly as he is worthless.

GUILBERT. You speak like a Spaniard, and as if you did not know Spaniards. This moment we are in greater danger than any of you perceive.

MARIE. Good Guilbert!

GUILBERT. I honor our brother's bold soul. In silence I have observed his heroic conduct. That all may turn out well, I wish that Marie could resolve to give Clavigo her hand; for — *(smiling)* — her heart he has still.

MARIE. You are cruel.

SOPHIE. Listen to him, I beseech you, listen to him!

GUILBERT. Your brother has wrung from him a declaration which will vindicate you in the eyes of the world and ruin us.

BUENCO. What?

MARIE. O God!

GUILBERT. He gave it in the hope of touching your heart. If you remain unmoved, then he must with might and main destroy the paper. This he can do; this he will do. Your brother will print and publish it immediately after his return from Aranjuez. I fear, if you persist, he will not return.

SOPHIE. My dear Guilbert!

MARIE. It is killing me!

GUILBERT. Clavigo cannot let the paper be published. If you reject his offer and he is a man of honor he goes to meet your brother, and one of them falls; and whether your brother perish or triumph he is lost. A stranger in Spain! The murderer of this beloved courtier! My sister, it is all very well to think and feel nobly, but to ruin yourself and yours ——

MARIE. Advise me, Sophie; help me!

GUILBERT. And Buenco, contradict me, if you can.

BUENCO. He dares not; he fears for his life; otherwise he would not have written at all; he would not have offered Marie his hand.

GUILBERT. So much the worse. He will get a hundred to lend him their arm; a hundred to take away our brother's life on the way. Ha! Buenco, are you then so young? Should not a courtier have assassins in his pay?

BUENCO. The king is great and good.

GUILBERT. Go, then, traverse the walls which surround him, the guards, the ceremonial, and all that his courtiers have put between his people and him; press through and save us. Who comes?

CLAVIGO appears.

CLAVIGO. I must! I must! (MARIE utters a shriek, and falls into SOPHIE'S arms.)

SOPHIE. Cruel man, in what a position you place us! (GUILBERT and BUENCO draw near to her.)

CLAVIGO. Yes, it is she! it is she! and I am Clavigo! Listen to me, gentle Marie, if you will not look on me. At the time that Guilbert received me as a friend into his house, when I was a poor unknown youth, and when in my heart I felt for you an overpowering passion, was that any merit in me? or was it not rather an inner harmony of characters, a secret union of soul, so that you neither could remain unmoved by me, and I could flatter myself with the sole possession of this heart? And now — am I not even the same? Are you not even the same? Why should I not venture to hope? Why not entreat? Would you not once more take to your bosom a friend, a lover, whom you had long believed lost, if after a perilous, hapless voyage he returned unexpectedly and laid his preserved life at your feet? And have I not also tossed upon a raging sea? Are not our passions, with which we live in perpetual strife, more terrible and indomitable than those waves which drive the unfortunate far from his fatherland? Marie! Marie! How can you hate me when I have never ceased to love you? Amid all infatuation, and in the very lap of all the enchanting seductions of vanity and pride, I have ever remembered those happy days of liberty, which I spent at your feet in sweet retirement, as we saw lie before us a succession of blooming prospects. And now why would you not realize with me all that we hoped? Will you now not enjoy the happiness of life because a gloomy interval has deferred our hopes? No, my love, believe that the best friends in the world are not quite pure; the highest joy is also interrupted through our passions, through fate. Shall we complain that it has happened to us as to all others, and shall we chastise ourselves in casting away this opportunity of repairing the past, of consoling a ruined family, of rewarding the heroic deed of a noble brother, and of establishing our own happiness forever? My friends! from whom I deserve nothing; my friends, who must be so, because they are the friends of virtue, to which I return, unite your entreaties with mine, Marie! (*He falls on his knees.*) Marie! Do you no longer recognize my voice? Do you no more feel the pulse of my heart? Is it so? Marie! Marie!

MARIE. O Clavigo!

CLAVIGO (*leaps up and kisses her hand with transport*). She forgives me! She loves me! (*He embraces* GUILBERT *and* BUENCO.) She loves me still! O Marie, my heart told me so! I might have thrown myself at your feet silently, uttered with tears my anguish, my penitence; without words you would have understood me, as I without words receive my forgiveness. No, this intimate union of our souls is not destroyed; no, still they understand each other as in the olden time, in which no sound, no sign was needful to impart our deepest emotions. Marie! Marie! Marie!

BEAUMARCHAIS advances.

BEAUMARCHAIS. Ha!

CLAVIGO (*rushing towards him*). My brother!

BEAUMARCHAIS. Do you forgive him?

MARIE. No more, no more! my senses abandon me. (*They lead her away.*)

BEAUMARCHAIS. Has she forgiven him?

BUENCO. It seems so.

BEAUMARCHAIS. You do not deserve your happiness.

CLAVIGO. I feel it, believe me.

SOPHIE (*returns*). She forgives him. A stream of tears broke from her eyes. Let him withdraw, said she, sobbing, till I recover! I forgive him. — "Ah, my sister!" she exclaimed, and fell upon my neck, "whereby knows he that I love him so?"

CLAVIGO (*kissing her hand*). I am the happiest man under the sun. My brother!

BEAUMARCHAIS (*embraces him*). With all my heart then. Although I must tell you: even yet I cannot be your friend, even yet I cannot love you. So now you are one of us, and let all be forgotten. The paper you gave me — here it is. (*He takes it from his portfolio, tears it, and gives it to him.*)

CLAVIGO. I am yours, ever yours.

SOPHIE. I beseech you to retire, that she may not hear your voice, that she may rest.

CLAVIGO (*embracing them in turn*). Farewell! Farewell! A thousand kisses to the angel. [*Exit.*

BEAUMARCHAIS. After all, it may be for the best, although I should have preferred it otherwise (*smiling*). A girl is a good-natured creature, I must say — and, my friends, I should tell you, too, it was truly the thought, the wish of our ambassador, that Marie should forgive him, and that a happy marriage might end this vexatious business.

GUILBERT. I, too, am taking heart again.

BUENCO. He is your brother-in-law, and so, good-bye! You shall see me in your house no more.

BEAUMARCHAIS. Sir!

GUILBERT. Buenco!

BUENCO. I hate him, and shall hate him till the day of judgment. And look out with what kind of a man you have to deal. [*Exit.*

GUILBERT. He is a melancholy bird of ill-omen. But yet in time he will be persuaded, when he sees that all goes well.

BEAUMARCHAIS. Yet it was hasty to return him the paper.

GUILBERT. No more! no more! no visionary cares. [*Exit.*

ACT IV.

SCENE I. CLAVIGO's *abode.* CARLOS, *alone.*

CARLOS. It is praiseworthy to place under guardianship a man, who, by his dissipation or other follies, shows that his reason is deranged. If the magistrate does that, who otherwise does not much concern himself about us, why should not we do it for a friend? Clavigo, you are in a bad position; but there is still hope. And, provided that you retain a little of your former docility, there is time yet to keep you from a folly which, with your lively and sensitive character, will cause the misery of your life and lead you to an untimely grave. He comes.

CLAVIGO (*thoughtful*). Good day, Carlos.

CARLOS. A very sad, dull . . . Good day! Is that the mood in which you come from your bride?

CLAVIGO. She is an angel! They are excellent people!

CARLOS. You will not so hasten with the wedding that we cannot get an embroidered dress for the occasion?

CLAVIGO. Jest or earnest, at our wedding no embroidered dresses will make a parade.

CARLOS. I believe it, indeed.

CLAVIGO. Pleasure in each other's society, friendly harmony, shall constitute the splendor of this festival.

CARLOS. You will have a quiet little wedding.

CLAVIGO. As those who feel that their happiness rests entirely with themselves.

CARLOS. In those circumstances it is very proper.

CLAVIGO. Circumstances! What do you mean by "those circumstances?"

CARLOS. As the matter now stands and remains.

CLAVIGO. Listen, Carlos, I cannot bear a tone of reserve between friends. I know you are not in favor of this marriage; notwithstanding, if you have aught to say against it, you may say it; come, out with it. How then does the matter stand? how goes it?

CARLOS. More things, unexpected, astonishing, happen to one in life, and it were not well if all went smoothly. Society would have nothing to wonder at, nothing to whisper in the ear, nothing to pull to pieces.

CLAVIGO. It will make some stir.

CARLOS. Clavigo's wedding! that is a matter of course. How many a girl in Madrid waits for thee to make her an offer, and if you now play them this trick?

CLAVIGO. That cannot be helped now.

CARLOS. 'Tis strange, I have known few men who make so great and general an impression on women as you. In all ranks there are good girls who occupy their time with plans and projects to become yours. One relies on her beauty, another on her riches, another on her rank,

another on her wit, and another on her connections. What
compliments have been paid to me on your account! For,
indeed, neither my flat nose, nor crisp hair, nor my known
contempt for women can bring me such good luck.

CLAVIGO. You mock.

CARLOS. As if I have not already had in my hands dec-
larations, offers, written with their own white fond little
fingers, as badly spelt as an original love-letter of a girl can
only be! How many pretty duennas have come under my
thumb on this account!

CLAVIGO. And you did not say a word of all this?

CARLOS. I did not wish to trouble you with mere trifles,
and I could not have advised you to take any matter
seriously. O Clavigo, my heart has watched over your fate
as over my own! I have no other friend but you; all men
are not to be tolerated and you even begin to be unbearable.

CLAVIGO. I entreat you, be calm.

CARLOS. Burn the house of a man who has taken ten
years to build it, and then send him a confessor to recommend Christian patience! A man ought to look out for
no one but himself; people do not deserve ———

CLAVIGO. Are your misanthropic visions returning?

CARLOS. If I harp anew on that string who is to blame
but you? I said to myself: What would avail him at
present the most advantageous marriage? him, who for an
ordinary man has doubtless advanced far enough? But
with his genius, with his gifts, it is not probable, it is not
possible that he can remain stationary. I concerted my
plans. There are so few men at once so enterprising and so
supple, so highly gifted and so diligent. He is well qualified
in all departments. As Recorder, he can rapidly acquire
the most important knowledge; he will make himself
necessary; and should a change take place, he becomes
minister.

CLAVIGO. I avow it. Often, too, were these my dreams.

CARLOS. Dreams! As surely as I should succeed in
reaching the top of a tower, if I set off with the firm determination not to yield till I had carried my point, so surely
would you have overcome all obstacles; and afterwards the
rest would have given me no disquietude. You have no
fortune from your family, so much the better! You would
have become more zealous to acquire, more attentive to
preserve. Besides, he who sits at the receipt of custom with-

out enriching himself is a great fool; and I do not see why the country does not owe taxes to the minister as well as to the king. The latter gives his name, and the former the power. When I had arranged all that, I then sought out a fit match for you. I saw many a proud family which would have shut their eyes to your origin, many of the richest, who would have gladly supported the maintenance of your rank, to share the dignity of the second king — and now —

CLAVIGO. You are unjust, you lower my actual condition too much; and do you fancy then that I cannot rise higher, and advance still further.

CARLOS. My dear friend, if you lop off the heart of a young plant, in vain will it afterwards and incessantly put forth countless shoots; it will form, perhaps, a large bush, but it is all over with the kingly attempt of its first growth. And think not that at the court this marriage is regarded with indifference. Have you forgotten what sort of men disapproved your attachment, your union with Marie? Have you forgotten who inspired you with the wise thought of abandoning her? Must I count them all on my fingers?

CLAVIGO. This thought has already distressed me; yes, few will approve this step.

CARLOS. Nobody; and will not your powerful friends be indignant that you, without asking their leave, without consulting them, should have hastily sacrificed yourself like a thoughtless child, who throws away his money in the market on worm-eaten nuts?

CLAVIGO. That is impolite, Carlos, and exaggerated.

CARLOS. Not at all. Let one commit an egregious error through passion, I allow it. To marry a chambermaid because she is as beautiful as an angel! Well, the man is blamed, and yet people envy him.

CLAVIGO. People, always the people!

CARLOS. You know I do not inquire very curiously after the success of others; but it is ever true that he who does nothing for others does nothing for himself; and if men do not wonder at or envy you you are not happy either.

CLAVIGO. The world judges by appearances. Oh! he who possesses Marie's heart is to be envied.

CARLOS. Things appear what they are; but, frankly, I have always thought that there were hidden qualities that render your happiness enviable; for what one sees with his eyes and can comprehend with his understanding ——

CLAVIGO. You wish to make me desperate.

CARLOS. "How has that happened?" they will ask in the town. "How has that happened?" they will ask at court. "But, good God! how has that happened? She is poor, without position. If Clavigo had not had an intrigue with her one would not have known that she is in the world; she is said to be well-bred, agreeable, witty!" But who takes to himself a wife for that? That passes away in the first years of marriage. "Ah!" says some one, "she must be beautiful, charmingly, ravishingly beautiful." "That explains the matter," says another.

CLAVIGO (*troubled, lets a deep sigh escape*). Alas!

CARLOS. "Beautiful? Oh," says one lady, "very good! I have not seen her for six years." "She may well be altered," says another.. "One must, however, see her, he will soon bring her forth," says a third. People ask, look, are eager, wait, and are impatient; they recall the ever-proud Clavigo, who never let himself be seen in public without leading out in triumph some stately, splendid, haughty Spaniard lady, whose full bosom, blooming checks, impassioned eyes — all, all, seemed to ask the world encircling her: "Am not I worthy of my companion?" and who in her pride lets flaunt so widely in the breeze the train of her silken robe, to render her appearance more imposing and remarkable. And now appears the gentleman — and surprise renders the people dumb — he comes accompanied by his tripping little Frenchwoman, whose hollow eyes, whose whole appearance announces consumption, in spite of the red and white with which she has daubed her death-pale countenance. Yes, brother! I become frantic, I run away, when people stop me now and ask, and question, and say they cannot understand ——

CLAVIGO (*seizing his hand*). My friend, my brother, I am in a frightful position. I tell you, I avow, I was horror-struck when I saw Marie again. How changed she is! — how pale and exhausted! Oh! it is my fault, my treacheries! ——

CARLOS. Follies! visions! She was in consumption when the romance of your love was still unfolding. I told you a thousand times, and . . . But you lovers have your eyes, nay, all your senses closed. Clavigo, it is a shame. All, yes all to forget thus! A sick wife, who will plague all your posterity, so that all your children and grandchildren will in a few years be politely extinguished, like the sorry lamp of a beggar. — A man who could have been the founder of a family, which perhaps in future . . . Ah! I shall yet turn crazy, my reason fails me.

CLAVIGO. Carlos, what shall I say to thee? When I saw her again, in the first transport, my heart went out towards her; and alas! when that was gone, compassion — a deep, heartfelt pity was breathed into me: but love . . . Lo! in the warm fullness of joy, I seemed to feel on my neck the cold hand of death, I strove to be cheerful; to play the part of a happy man again, in presence of those who surrounded me: it was all gone, all so stiff, so painfully anxious! Had they not somewhat lost their self-possession they would have remarked it.

CARLOS. Hell! death and devil! and you are going to marry her! (CLAVIGO *remains absorbed, without giving any answer.*) It is all over with thee; lost for ever. Farewell, brother, and let me forget all; let me, all the rest of my solitary life, furiously curse your fatal blindness. Ah! to sacrifice all, to render oneself despicable in the eyes of the world, and not even then satisfy thereby a passion, a desire! To contract a malady voluntarily, which, while undermining your inmost strength, will make you hideous in the eyes of men!

CLAVIGO. Carlos! Carlos!

CARLOS. Would that you had never been elevated, at least you would never have fallen! With what eyes will they look on all this! "There is the brother," they will say; "he must be a lad of spirit; he has put to the last shift Clavigo, who dared not draw the sword." "Ah!" our flaunting courtiers will say, "'Twas to be seen all along that he was not a gentleman." "Ah, ah!" exclaims another, while drawing his hat over his eyes, "the Frenchman should have come to me!" And he claps himself on the paunch — a fellow, who perhaps were not worthy of being your groom!

CLAVIGO (*expresses the most acute distress, and falls into the arms of* CARLOS *amid a torrent of tears*). Save me! My friend! my best friend, save me! Save me from a double perjury! from an unutterable disgrace, from myself. I am undone!

CARLOS. Poor, hapless fellow! I hoped that these youthful furies, these stormy tears, this absorbing melancholy would have been gone; I hoped to behold you, as a man, agitated no more, no more plunged in that overwhelming sorrow, which in other days you so often uttered on my breast with tears. Be a man, Clavigo, quit yourself like a man!

Clavigo. Let me weep! (*Throws himself into a chair.*)

Carlos. Alas for you, that you have entered on a career which you will not pursue to the end! With your heart, with your sentiments, which would make a tranquil citizen happy, you must unite this unhappy hankering after greatness! And what is greatness, Clavigo? To raise oneself above others in rank and consequence? Believe it not. If your heart is not greater than that of others; if you are not able to place yourself calmly above the circumstances which would embarrass an ordinary man, then with all your ribbons, all your stars, even with the crown itself, you are but an ordinary man. Take heart, compose your mind! (Clavigo *rises, looks on* Carlos, *and holds out his hand, which* Carlos *eagerly seizes.*) Come, come, my friend! make up your mind. Look, I will put everything aside, and will say to you: Here lie two proposals on equal scales; either you marry Marie and find your happiness in a quiet citizen-like life, in tranquil homely joys; or you bend your steps along the path of honor to a near goal. — I will put all aside, and say : The beam of the balance is in equilibrium ; your decision will settle which of the two scales will carry the day! Good! But decide! There is nothing in the world so pitiable as an undecided man, who wavers between two feelings, hoping to reconcile them, and does not understand that nothing can unite them except the doubt, the disquietude, which rack him. Go, and give Marie your hand, act as an honorable man, who, to keep his word, sacrifices the happiness of his life, who regards it a duty to repair the wrong he has committed ; but who, on the other hand, has never extended the sphere of his passions and activity further than to be in a position to repair the wrong he has committed; and thus enjoy the happiness of a tranquil retirement, the approval of a peaceful conscience, and all the blessedness belonging to those who are able to create their own happiness and provide the joy of their families. Decide, and then shall I say — You are every inch a man.

Clavigo. Carlos! Oh, for a spark of your strength — of your courage!

Carlos. It slumbers in thee, and I will blow till it burst forth into flames. Behold on the one side the fortune and the greatness which await you. I shall not set off this future with the variegated hues of poetry; represent it to yourself with such vivacity as it clearly appeared before your mind till the hot-headed Frenchman made you lose your wits. But there, too, Clavigo, be a man thoroughly, and take your way straight, without looking to the right or left. May your soul expand, and this great idea become deeply rooted there, that extraordinary men are extraordinary, precisely because their duties differ from the duties of ordinary men; that he, whose task it is to watch over, to govern, to preserve a great whole, needs not reproach himself with having overlooked trifling circumstances, with having sacrificed small matters to the good of the whole. Thus acts the Creator in nature, and the king in the state; why should not we do the same, in order to resemble them?

CLAVIGO. Carlos, I am a little man.

CARLOS. We are not little when circumstances trouble us, only when they overpower us. Yet another breath, and you are yourself again. Cast away the remnant of a pitiable passion, which in these days as little becomes you as the little gray jacket and modest mien with which you arrived at Madrid. What the poor girl has done for you, you have long ago returned; and that your first friendly reception was from her hands. Oh, another would, for the pleasure of your acquaintance, have done as much and more, without putting forth such pretensions . . . and would you take it into your head to give your schoolmaster the half of your fortune because he taught you the alphabet thirty years ago? What say you, Clavigo!

CLAVIGO. That is all very well. On the whole you may be right, it may be so; only how are we to get out of the embarrassment in which we stick fast? Advise me there, help me there, and then lecture.

CARLOS. All right! You are, then, resolved.

CLAVIGO. Give me the power and I shall exert it. I am not able to think; think for me.

CARLOS. Thus then. First you will go and meet this person, and then you will demand, sword in hand, the vindication which you inconsiderately and involuntarily gave.

CLAVIGO. I have it already; he tore it and returned it to me.

CARLOS. Excellent! excellent! That step taken already —and you have let me speak so long?—Your course is so much the shorter! Write him quite coolly: "You find it inconvenient to marry his sister; the reason he can learn if he will repair to-night to a certain place, attended by a friend, and armed with any weapons he likes." And then follows the signature. Come, Clavigo, write that; I shall be your second — and the devil is in it if —— (CLAVIGO *approaches the table.*) Listen! A word! If I think aright of it, it is an extravagant proposal. Who are we to risk our lives with a mad adventurer? Besides, the man's conduct, his standing, do not deserve that we regard him as an equal, Listen, then! Now if I were to bring forward a criminal charge against him, that he arrived secretly at Madrid, got himself announced under a pseudonym with an accomplice, at first gained your confidence with friendly words, and thereafter fell upon you all of a sudden, forcibly obtained a declaration, and afterwards went off to spread it abroad — that will prove his ruin: he shall learn what it means — to invade the tranquillity of a Spaniard under his own roof.

CLAVIGO. You are right.

CARLOS. But till the lawsuit has begun, in which interval the gentleman might play all sorts of tricks, if now we could meanwhile play a dead-sure game, and seize him tight by the head.

CLAVIGO. I understand, and know you are the man to carry it out.

CARLOS. Ah! well! if I, who have been at it for five-and-twenty years, and have witnessed tears of anguish trickling down the cheeks of the foremost men, if I cannot unravel such child's play! So then, give me full power; you need do nothing, write nothing. He, who orders the imprisonment of the brother, pantomimically intimates that he will have nothing to do with the sister.

CLAVIGO. No, Carlos! Let it go as it may, I cannot, I will not suffer that. Beaumarchais is a worthy man, and he shall not languish in an ignominious prison on account of his righteous cause. Another plan, Carlos, another!

CARLOS. Bah! bah! Stuff and nonsense! We will not devour him. He will be well lodged and well cared for, and thereafter he cannot hold out long: for, observe, when he perceives that we are in earnest, all his theatrical rage will cease; he will come to terms, return smarting to France, and be only too thankful, if we secure a yearly pension for his sister — perhaps the only thing he had in view.

CLAVIGO. So be it then! Only let him be kindly dealt with.

CARLOS. Leave that to me. — One precaution more! We

cannot know but that it may be blabbed out — that the thing may get wind, and then he gets over you, and all is lost. Therefore, leave your house, so that not even your servants know where you have gone. Take with you only absolute necessaries. I shall despatch you a fellow, who will conduct you and bring you to a place where the holy Hermandad herself will not find you. I have always in readiness a few of these mouse-holes. Adieu!

CLAVIGO. Good bye!

CARLOS. Cheer up! cheerily! When it is all over, brother, we will enjoy ourselves.   [*Exit.*

SCENE II.   GUILBERT's *abode.*

SOPHIE GUILBERT, MARIE BEAUMARCHAIS *at work.*

MARIE. With such violence did Buenco depart?

SOPHIE. It was natural. He loves you, and how could he endure the sight of the man whom he must doubly hate?

MARIE. He is the best, most upright citizen I have ever known. (*Showing her work to her sister.*) It seems to me I must do it thus. I shall take in that and turn the end up. That will do nicely.

SOPHIE. Very well. And I am going to put a straw-colored ribbon on my bonnet; it becomes me best. Do you smile?

MARIE. I am laughing at myself. We girls are a queer set of people, I must say : hardly are our spirits but a little raised when straightway we are busy with finery and ribbons.

SOPHIE. You cannot well apply that to yourself; from the moment Clavigo forsook you, nothing could give you the least pleasure. (MARIE *starts up and looks towards the door.*) What is the matter?

MARIE (*anxious*). I thought I heard some one come in! My poor heart! O, it will destroy me yet! Feel how it beats with that groundless terror!

SOPHIE. You look pale. Be calm, I beseech you, my love!

MARIE (*pointing to her chest*). I feel here an oppression — a sudden pain. It will kill me.

SOPHIE. Be careful.

MARIE. I am a foolish, hapless girl. Pain and joy with all their force have undermined my poor life. I tell you 'tis but half a joy that I have him again. Little shall I enjoy the happiness that awaits me in his arms; perhaps not at all.

SOPHIE. My sister, my only love! You are wearing yourself out with these visions.

MARIE. Why shall I deceive myself?

SOPHIE. You are young and happy, and can hope for all.

MARIE. Hope! O the only sweet balm of life! How often it charms my soul! Happy youthful dreams hover before me and accompany the beloved form of the peerless one, who now is mine again. O Sophie, he is so winsome! Whilst I saw him not, he has—I know not how I shall express it;—all the qualities which in former days lay hid in him through his diffidence, have unfolded themselves. He has become a man, and must with this pure feeling of his, with which he advances, that is so entirely devoid of pride and vanity—he must captivate all hearts.—And he shall be mine? No, my sister, I was not worthy of him— and now I am much less so!

SOPHIE. Take him, however, and be happy. I hear your brother!

BEAUMARCHAIS enters.

BEAUMARCHAIS.   Where is Guilbert?

SOPHIE.   He has been gone some time; he cannot be much longer.

MARIE. What is the matter, brother? (Springing up and falling on his neck.) Dear brother, what is the matter?

BEAUMARCHAIS. Nothing, nothing at all, my Marie!

MARIE. If I am thy Marie, do tell me what is on thy mind!

SOPHIE. Let him be. Men often look vexed without having aught particular on their mind!

MARIE. No, no. I have seen thy face only a little while; but already I read all thy thoughts, all the feelings of thy pure and sincere soul are stamped on thy brow. There is somewhat which makes thee anxious. Speak, what is it?

BEAUMARCHAIS. It is nothing, my love. I hope that at bottom it is nothing. Clavigo—

MARIE. How?

BEAUMARCHAIS. I was at Clavigo's house. He is not at home.

SOPHIE. And does that perplex you?

BEAUMARCHAIS. His porter says he has gone he knows not where; no one knows how long. If he should be hiding himself! If he be really gone! Whither? for what reason?

MARIE. We will wait.

BEAUMARCHAIS. Thy tongue lies. Ah! the paleness of thy cheeks, the trembling of thy limbs, all speaks and testifies that thou canst not wait. Dear sister! (*Clasps her in his arms.*) On this beating, painfully trembling heart I vow,—hear me, O God, who art righteous! hear me, all His saints!—thou shalt be avenged if he—my senses abandon me at the thought—if he fail, if he make himself guilty of a frightful, double perjury; if he mock at our misery ... No, it is, it is not possible, not possible—Thou shalt be avenged.

SOPHIE. All too soon, too precipitate. Be careful of her health, I beseech you, my brother. (MARIE *sits down.*) What ails thee? You are fainting.

MARIE. No, no. You are so anxious.

SOPHIE (*gives her water*). Take this glass.

MARIE. No, no! what avails that? Well, for my own sake, give it me.

BEAUMARCHAIS. Where is Guilbert? Where is Buenco? Send for them, I entreat you. (SOPHIE *exit.*) How dost thou feel, Marie?

MARIE. Well, quite well! Think'st thou then, bro-ther——

BEAUMARCHAIS. What, my love?

MARIE. Ah!

BEAUMARCHAIS. Is your breathing painful?

MARIE. The disordered beating of my heart oppresses me.

BEAUMARCHAIS. Have you then no remedy? Do you use no anodyne?

MARIE. I know of only one remedy, and for that I have prayed to God many a time and oft.

BEAUMARCHAIS. Thou shalt have it, and I hope from my hand.

MARIE. That will do well.

SOPHIE enters.

SOPHIE. A courier has just brought this letter; he comes from Aranjuez.

BEAUMARCHAIS. That is the seal and the hand of our ambassador.

SOPHIE. I bade him dismount and take some refreshment; he would not, because he had yet more dispatches.

MARIE. Will you, my love, send the servant for the physician?

SOPHIE. Are you ill? Holy God! what ails thee?

MARIE. You will make me so anxious that at last I shall scarcely dare ask for a glass of water ... Sophie! Brother! — What is in the letter? See, how he trembles! how all courage leaves him!

SOPHIE. Brother, my brother! (BEAUMARCHAIS *throws himself speechless into a chair and lets the letter fall.*) My brother! (*Lifts up the letter and reads it.*)

MARIE. Let me see it! I must — (*tries to rise*). Alas! I feel it. It is the last. Oh, sister, spare not, for mercy's sake, the last quick death-stroke! — He betrays us!

BEAUMARCHAIS (*springing up*). He betrays us! (*Beating on his brow and breast.*) Here! here! All is as dumb, as dead before my soul, as if a thunder-clap had disordered my senses. Marie! Marie! thou art betrayed! — and I stand here! Whither? — What? — I see nothing, nothing! no way, no safety! (*Throws himself into a seat.*)

GUILBERT *enters.*

SOPHIE. Guilbert! Counsel! Help! We are lost!

GUILBERT. My wife!

SOPHIE. Read! read! The ambassador makes known to our brother: that Clavigo has made a criminal complaint against him, under the pretext that he introduced himself into his house under a false name; and that, taking him by surprise in bed and presenting a pistol, he compelled him to sign a disgraceful vindication; and if he do not quickly withdraw from the kingdom they will get him thrown into prison, from which the ambassador himself, perhaps, will not be able to deliver him.

BEAUMARCHAIS (*springing up*). Indeed, they shall do so! they shall do so! shall get me imprisoned; but from his corpse, from the place where I shall have glutted my vengeance with his blood. Ah! the stern, frightful thirst after his blood fills my whole soul. Thanks to Thee, God in heaven, that Thou vouchsafest to man, amid burning, insupportable wrongs, a solace, a refreshment! What a thirst for vengeance I feel in my breast! how the glorious feeling, the lust for his blood, raises me out of my utter dejection, out of my sluggish indecision; raises me above myself! Vengeance! How I rejoice in it! how all within me strives after him, to seize him, to destroy him.

SOPHIE. Thou art terrible, brother!

BEAUMARCHAIS. So much the better. — Ah! No sword, no weapon! with these hands will I strangle him, that the triumph may be mine! all my own the feeling: I have destroyed him!

MARIE. My heart! my heart!

BEAUMARCHAIS. I have not been able to save thee, so thou shalt be avenged. I pant after his footsteps, my teeth lust after his flesh, my gums after his blood. Have I become a frantic wild beast! There burns in every vein, there glows in every nerve, the desire after him, after him! — I could hate forever, who should make away with him by poison, who should rid me of him by assassination. Oh, help me, Guilbert, to seek him out. Where is Buenco? Help me to find him!

GUILBERT. Save yourself! save yourself! you have lost your reason.

MARIE. Flee, my brother!

SOPHIE. Take him away; he will cause his sister's death.

BUENCO appears.

BUENCO. Up, sir! away! I foresaw it. I gave heed to all. And now they are in hot pursuit; you are lost if you do not leave the town this moment.

BEAUMARCHAIS. Never! where is Clavigo?

BUENCO. I do not know.

BEAUMARCHAIS. Thou knowest. I entreat you on my knees, tell me.

SOPHIE. For God's sake, Buenco!

MARIE. Ah! air! air! (*Falls back.*) Clavigo! —

BUENCO. Help! she is dying!

SOPHIE. Forsake us not, God in heaven; — Hence, my brother, away!

BEAUMARCHAIS (*falls down before* MARIE, *who despite every aid does not recover*). To forsake thee! to forsake thee!

SOPHIE. Stay, then, and ruin us all, as you have killed Marie. You are gone, then, O my sister, through the heedlessness of your own brother!

BEAUMARCHAIS. Stop, sister!

SOPHIE (*mocking*). Saviour! — Avenger! — help yourself!

BEAUMARCHAIS. Do I deserve this?

SOPHIE. Give her to me again! And then go to the prison, to the stake; go, pour forth thy blood and give me her again.

BEAUMARCHAIS. Sophie!

SOPHIE. Ha! and she is gone; she is dead — save yourself for us! (*falling on his neck*) my brother, for us! for our father! Haste, haste! That was her fate! she has met it! And there is a God in Heaven; to Him leave vengeance.

BUENCO. Hence! away! Come with me; I will hide you till we find means to get you out of the kingdom.

BEAUMARCHAIS (*falls on* MARIE *and kisses her*). Sister dear! (*They tear him away, he clasps* SOPHIE, *she disengages herself. They remove* MARIE, *and* BUENCO *and* BEAUMARCHAIS *retire.*)

GUILBERT, *a* PHYSICIAN.

SOPHIE (*returning from the room to which they had taken* MARIE). Too late! She is gone! she is dead!

GUILBERT. Come in, sir! See for yourself! It is not possible! [*Exit.*

ACT V.

SCENE I. *The Street before the house of* GUILBERT. *Night.* (*The house is open, and before the door stand three men clad in black mantles, holding torches.* CLAVIGO *enters, wrapped in a cloak, his sword under his arm; a* SERVANT *goes before him with a torch.*)

CLAVIGO. I told you to avoid this street.

SERVANT. We must have gone a great way round, sir, and you are in such haste. It is not far hence where Don Carlos is lodged.

CLAVIGO. Torches there!

SERVANT. A funeral. Come on, sir.

CLAVIGO. Marie's abode! A funeral! A death-agony shudders through all my limbs! Go, ask whom they are going to bury.

SERVANT (*to the men*). Whom are you going to bury?

THE MEN. Marie de Beaumarchais.

(CLAVIGO *sits down on a stone and covers himself with a cloak.*)

SERVANT (*comes back*). They are going to bury Marie de Beaumarchais.

CLAVIGO (*springing up*). Must thou repeat it? Repeat that word of thunder which strikes all the marrow out of my bones?

Servant. Peace, sir! Come on, sir. Consider the danger by which you are surrounded.

Clavigo. To hell with thee, reptile! I remain.

Servant. O Carlos! O that I could find thee! — Carlos! — he has lost his reason.   [*Exit.*

SCENE II. Clavigo. *The Mutes in the distance.*

Clavigo. Dead! Marie dead! Torches! her dismal attendants! it is a trick of enchantment, a night vision, that terrifies me; that holds up to me a mirror, in which I may see foreboded the end of all my treacheries. But there is still time. Still! — I tremble! — my heart melts with horror! No! no! thou shalt not die — I come, I come! Vanish, ye spirits of the night, who with your horrible terrors set yourselves in my way. (*He goes up to them.*) Vanish — they remain! Ha! they look round after me! Woe! woe is me! They are men like myself. It is true! true! Canst thou comprehend it? She is dead. It seizes me amid all the horrors of midnight — the feeling — she is dead. There she lies, the flower at your feet! and thou — O have mercy on me, God in heaven — I have not killed her! Hide yourselves, ye stars; look not down! Ye, who have so often beheld the villain, with feelings of the most heartfelt happiness, leave this threshold; through this very street float along in golden dreams, with music and song, and enrapture his maiden listening at the secret casement and lingering in transport. And now I fill the house with wailing and sorrow — and this scene of my bliss with the funeral song — Marie! Marie! take me with thee! take me with thee! (*Mournful music breathes forth a few sounds from within.*) They are setting out on the way to the grave. Stop! stop! Shut not the coffin. Let me see her once more. (*He runs up to the house.*) Ha! into whose presence am I rushing? Whom to face in his terrible sorrow? Her friends! her brother! whose breast is panting with raving grief! (*The music recommences.*) She calls me! she calls me! I come! What anguish is this which overwhelms me? What shuddering withholds me?

(*The music begins for the third time and continues. The torches move before the door; three others come out to them, who range themselves in order to enclose the funeral procession, which now comes out of the house. Six bearers carry the bier, upon which lies the coffin, covered.*)

SCENE III.   GUILBERT *and* BUENCO (*in deep mourning.*)

CLAVIGO (*coming forward*).   Stay!
GUILBERT.   What voice is that?
CLAVIGO.   Stay!   (*The bearers stop.*)
BUENCO.   Who dares to interrupt the solemn funeral?
CLAVIGO.   Set it down.
GUILBERT.   Ha!
BUENCO.   Wretch! are thy deeds of shame not yet ended?   Is thy victim not safe from thee in the coffin?
CLAVIGO.   No more!   Make me not frantic.   The wretched are dangerous; I must see her.   (*He tears off the pall and the lid of the coffin.   MARIE is seen lying within it, clad in white, her hands clasped before her; CLAVIGO steps back and covers his face.*)
BUENCO.   Wilt thou awake her to murder her again?
CLAVIGO.   Poor mocker!   Marie!   (*He falls down before the coffin.*)

SCENE IV.   *Enter* BEAUMARCHAIS.   *The preceding.*

BEAUMARCHAIS.   Buenco has left me.   They say she is not dead.   I must see, spite of hell, I must see her.   Ha! torches! a funeral!   (*He runs hastily up to it, gazes on the coffin, and falls down speechless.   They raise him up; he is as if deprived of sense; GUILBERT holds him.*)
CLAVIGO (*who is standing on the other side of the coffin*). Marie! Marie!
BEAUMARCHAIS (*springing up*).   That is his voice.   Who calls Marie?   At the sound of that voice what burning rage starts into my veins!
CLAVIGO.   It is I.   (BEAUMARCHAIS *staring wildly around and grasping his sword.   GUILBERT holds him.*)   I fear not thy blazing eyes, nor the point of thy sword.   Oh! look here, here, on these closed eyes — these clasped hands!
BEAUMARCHAIS.   Dost *thou* show *me* that sight?   (*He tears himself loose, runs upon CLAVIGO, who instantly draws; they fight; BEAUMARCHAIS pierces him through the breast.*)
CLAVIGO (*falling*).   I thank thee, brother; thou marriest us.   (*He falls upon the coffin.*)
BEAUMARCHAIS (*tearing him away*).   Hence from this saint, thou fiend!
CLAVIGO.   Alas!   (*The bearers raise up his body and support him.*)

Beaumarchais. His blood! Look up, Marie, look upon thy bridal ornaments, and then close thine eyes forever. See how I have consecrated thy place of rest with the blood of thy murderer! Charming! Glorious!

Scene V. *Enter* Sophie. *The preceding.*

Sophie. My brother? O my God, what is the matter?

Beaumarchais. Draw nearer, my love, and see! I hoped to have strewn her bridal bed with roses; see the roses with which I adorn her on her way to heaven!

Sophie. We are lost!

Clavigo. Save yourself, rash one! save yourself, ere the dawn of day. May God, who sent you for an avenger, conduct you! Sophie, forgive me. Brothers, friends, forgive me.

Beaumarchais. How the sight of his gushing blood extinguishes all the glowing vengeance within me! how with his departing life vanishes all my rage! (*Going up to him.*) Die, I forgive thee.

Clavigo. Your hand! and yours, Sophie! and yours! (Buenco *hesitates.*)

Sophie. Give it him, Buenco.

Clavigo. I thank you; you are as good as ever; I thank you. And thou, O spirit of my beloved, if thou still hoverest around this place, look down, see these heavenly favors, bestow thy blessing, and do thou too forgive me. I come! I come! Save yourself, my brother. Tell me, did she forgive me? How did she die?

Sophie. Her last word was thy unhappy name. She departed without taking leave of us.

Clavigo. I will follow her and bear your farewells to her.

Scene VI. Carlos, *a* Servant. *The preceding.*

Carlos. Clavigo! murderers!

Clavigo. Hear me, Carlos! Thou seest here the victim of thy prudence; and now, I conjure thee, for the sake of that blood, in which my life irrevocably flows away, save my brother.

Carlos. O my friend! (*to the* Servant). You standing there? Fly for a surgeon. [*Exit* Servant.

CLAVIGO. It is in vain; save, save my unhappy brother! thy hand thereon. They have forgiven me, and so forgive I thee. Accompany him to the frontiers, and — oh!

CARLOS (*stamping with his feet*). Clavigo! Clavigo!

CLAVIGO (*drawing nearer to the coffin, upon which they lay him down*). Marie! Thy hand! (*He unfolds her hands and grasps the right hand.*)

SOPHIE (*to* BEAUMARCHAIS). Hence, unhappy one, away!

CLAVIGO. I have her hand, her cold, dead hand. Thou art mine. Yet this last bridal kiss! Alas!

SOPHIE. He is dying! Save thyself, brother! (BEAU-MARCHAIS *falls on* SOPHIE'S *neck. She returns the embrace and makes a sign for him to withdraw.*)

EGMONT:

A TRAGEDY IN FIVE ACTS.

TRANSLATED BY ANNA SWANWICK.

This tragedy was commenced in the year 1775, when Goethe was twenty-six years of age — but it was not finished until eleven years later. A rough draft of the whole was made in 1782, but it was only completed and finally re-written during Goethe's residence in Rome, in 1786.

INTRODUCTION TO EGMONT.

In Schiller's critique upon the tragedy of *Egmont*, Goethe is censured for departing from the truth of history in the delineation of his hero's character, and also for misrepresenting the circumstances of his domestic life. The Egmont of history left behind him a numerous family, anxiety for whose welfare detained him in Brussels when most of his friends sought safety in flight. His withdrawal would have entailed the confiscation of his property, and he shrank from exposing to privation those whose happiness was dearer to him than life; — a consideration which he repeatedly urged in his conferences with the Prince of ·Orange, when the latter insisted upon the necessity of escape. We see here, not the victim of a blind and foolhardy confidence, as portrayed in Goethe's drama, but the husband and father, regardless of his personal safety in anxiety for the interests of his family.

I shall not inquire which conception is best suited for the purposes of art, but merely subjoin a few extracts from the same critique, in which Schiller does ample justice to Goethe's admirable delineation of the age and country in which the drama is cast, and which are peculiarly valuable from the pen of so competent an authority as the historian of the Fall of the Netherlands.

"Egmont's tragical death resulted from the relation in which he stood to the nation and the government; hence the action of the drama is intimately connected with the political life of the period — an exhibition of which forms its indispensable groundwork. But if we consider what an infinite number of minute circumstances must concur in order to exhibit the spirit of an age, and the political condition of a people, and the art required to combine so many isolated features into an intelligible and organic whole; and if we contemplate, moreover, the peculiar character of the Netherlands, consisting not of one nation, but of an aggregate of many smaller states, separated from each other by the sharpest contrasts, we shall not cease to wonder at the creative genius, which, triumphing over all these difficulties, conjures up before us, as with an enchanter's wand, the Netherlands of the sixteenth century.

"Not only do we behold these men living and working before us, we dwell among them as their familiar associates ; we see, on the other hand, the joyous sociability, the hospitality, the loquacity, the somewhat boastful temper of the people, their republican spirit, ready to boil up at the slightest innovation, and often subsiding again as rapidly on the most trivial grounds ; and, on the other hand, we are made acquainted with the burdens under which they groaned, from the new mitres of the bishops, to the French psalms which they were forbidden to sing ; — nothing is omitted, no feature introduced which does not bear the stamp of nature and of truth. Such delineation is not the result of premeditated effort, nor can it be commanded by art ; it can only be achieved by the poet whose mind is thoroughly imbued with his subject ; from him such traits escape unconsciously, and without design, as they do from the individuals whose characters they serve to portray.

"The few scenes in which the citizens of Brussels are introduced appear to us to be the result of profound study, and it would be difficult to find, in so few words, a more admirable historical monument of the Netherlands of that period.

"Equally graphic is that portion of the picture which portrays the spirit of the government, though it must be confessed that the artist has here somewhat softened down the harsher features of the original. This is especially true in reference to the character of the Duchess of Parma. Before his Duke of Alva we tremble, without ever turning from him with aversion ; he is a firm, rigid, inaccessible character ; 'a brazen tower without gates, the garrison of which must be furnished with wings.' The prudent forecast with which he makes his arrangements for Egmont's arrest excites our admiration, while it removes him from our sympathy. The remaining characters of the drama are delineated with a few masterly strokes. The subtle, taciturn Orange, with his timid, yet comprehensive and all-combining mind, is depicted in a single scene. Both Alva and Egmont are mirrored in the men by whom they are surrounded. This mode of delineation is admirable. The poet, in order to concentrate the interest upon Egmont, has isolated his hero, and omitted all mention of Count Horn, who shared the same melancholy fate."

The Appendix to Schiller's "History of the Fall of the Netherlands" contains an interesting account of the trial and execution of the Counts Egmont and Horn, which is, however, too long for insertion here.

DRAMATIS PERSONÆ.

MARGARET OF PARMA, *Daughter of Charles V., and Regent of the Netherlands.*

COUNT EGMONT, *Prince of Gaure.*

WILLIAM OF ORANGE.

THE DUKE OF ALVA.

FERDINAND, *his Natural Son.*

MACHIAVEL, *in the service of the Regent.*

RICHARD, *Egmont's Private Secretary.*

SILVA,
GOMEZ, } *in the service of Alva.*

CLARA, *the beloved of Egmont.*

HER MOTHER.

BRACKENBURG, *a Citizen's Son.*

SOEST, *a Shopkeeper,*
JETTER, *a Tailor.*
A CARPENTER,
A SOAPBOILER, } *Citizens of Brussels.*

BUYCK, *a Hollander, a Soldier under Egmont.*

RUYSUM, *a Frieslander, an invalid Soldier and deaf.*

VANSEN, *a Clerk.*

People, Attendants, Guards, etc.

The Scene is laid in Brussels.

EGMONT.

ACT I.

Scene I. *Soldiers and Citizens (with cross-bows).*

Jetter (*steps forward, and bends his cross-bow*). Soest, Buyck, Ruysum.

Soest. Come, shoot away, and have done with it! You won't beat me! Three black rings, you never made such a shot in all your life. And so I'm master for this year.

Jetter. Master and king to boot; who envies you? You'll have to pay double reckoning; 'tis only fair you should pay for your dexterity.

Buyck. Jetter, I'll buy your shot, share the prize, and treat the company. I have already been here so long, and am a debtor for so many civilities. If I miss, then it shall be as if you had shot.

Soest. I ought to have a voice, for in fact I am the loser. No matter! Come, Buyck, shoot away.

Buyck (*shoots*). Now, corporal, look out! — One! Two! Three! Four!

Soest. Four rings! So be it!

All. Hurrah! Long live the king! Hurrah! Hurrah!

Buyck. Thanks, sirs, master even were too much! Thanks for the honor.

Jetter. You have no one to thank but yourself.

Ruysum. Let me tell you! ——

Soest. How now, gray-beard?

Ruysum. Let me tell you! — He shoots like his master, he shoots like Egmont.

Buyck. Compared with him I am only a bungler. He aims with the rifle as no one else does. Not only when he's lucky or in the vein; no! he levels, and the bull's-eye is pierced. I have learned from him. He were, indeed, a blockhead, who could serve under him and learn nothing! — But,

601

sirs, let us not forget: A king maintains his followers; and so, wine here, at the king's charge!

JETTER. We have agreed among ourselves that each—

BUYCK. I am a foreigner and a king, and care not a jot for your laws and customs.

JETTER. Why you are worse than the Spaniard, who has not yet ventured to meddle with them.

RUYSUM. What does he say?

SOEST (*loud to* RUYSUM). He wants to treat us; he will not hear of our clubbing together, the king paying only a double share.

RUYSUM. Let him! under protest, however! 'Tis his master's fashion, too, to be munificent, and to let the money flow in a good cause. (*Wine is brought.*)

ALL. Here's to his majesty! Hurrah!

JETTER (*to* BUYCK). That means your majesty, of course.

BUYCK. My hearty thanks, if it be so.

SOEST. Assuredly! A Netherlander does not find it easy to drink the health of his Spanish majesty from his heart.

RUYSUM. Who?

SOEST (*aloud*). Philip the Second, King of Spain.

RUYSUM. Our most gracious king and master! Long life to him.

SOEST. Did you not like his father, Charles the Fifth, better?

RUYSUM. God bless him! He was a king, indeed! His hand reached over the whole earth, and he was all in all. Yet, when he met you, he'd greet you just as one neighbor greets another,—and if you were frightened, he knew so well how to put you at your ease—ay, you understand me —he walked out, rode out, just as it came into his head, with very few followers. We all wept when he resigned the government here to his son. You understand me—he is another sort of man, he's more majestic.

JETTER. When he was here, he never appeared in public, except in pomp and royal state. He speaks little, they say.

SOEST. He is no king for us Netherlanders. Our princes must be joyous and free like ourselves, must live and let live. We will neither be despised nor oppressed, good-natured fools though we be.

JETTER. The king, methinks, were a gracious sovereign enough, if he had only better counsellors.

SOEST. No, no! He has no affection for us Netherlanders; he has no heart for the people; he loves us not; how then can we love him? Why is everybody so fond of Count Egmont? Why are we all so devoted to him? Why, because one can read in his face that he loves us; because joyousness, open-heartedness, and good-nature speak in his eyes; because he possesses nothing that he does not share with him who needs it, ay, and with him who needs it not. Long live Count Egmont! Buyck, it is for you to give the first toast; give us your master's health.

BUYCK. With all my heart; here's to Count Egmont! Hurrah!

RUYSUM. Conqueror of St. Quintin.

BUYCK. The hero of Gravelines.

ALL. Hurrah!

RUYSUM. St. Quintin was my last battle. I was hardly able to crawl along, and could with difficulty carry my heavy rifle. I managed, notwithstanding, to singe the skin of the French once more, and, as a parting gift, received a grazing shot in my right leg.

BUYCK. Gravelines! Ha, my friends, we had sharp work of it there! The victory was all our own. Did not those French dogs carry fire and desolation into the very heart of Flanders? We gave it them, however! The old, hard-fisted veterans held out bravely for a while, but we pushed on, fired away, and laid about us till they made wry faces, and their lines gave way. Then Egmont's horse was shot under him; and for a long time we fought pell-mell, man to man, horse to horse, troop to troop, on the broad, flat sea-sand. Suddenly, as if from heaven, down came the cannon-shot from the mouth of the river, bang, bang, right into the midst of the French. These were English who, under Admiral Malin, happened to be sailing past from Dunkirk. They did not help us much, 'tis true; they could only approach with their smallest vessels, and that not near enough;—besides, their shot fell sometimes among our troops. It did some good, however! It broke the French lines, and raised our courage. Away it went. Helter-skelter! topsy-turvy! all struck dead, or forced into the water; the fellows were drowned the moment they tasted the water, while we Hollanders dashed in after them. Being amphibious, we were as much in our element as frogs, and hacked away at the enemy, and shot them down as if they had been ducks. The few who struggled through were struck dead in their flight by the peasant women, armed with hoes and pitchforks. His Gallic majesty was compelled at once to hold out his paw and make peace. And that peace you owe to us, to the great Egmont.

ALL. Hurrah for the great Egmont! Hurrah! Hurrah!

JETTER. Had they but appointed him Regent instead of Margaret of Parma!

SOEST. Not so! Truth is truth! I'll not hear Margaret abused. Now it is my turn. Long live our gracious lady!

ALL. Long life to her!

SOEST. Truly, there are excellent women in that family. Long live the Regent!

JETTER. Prudent she is, and moderate in all she does; if she would only not hold so fast and stiffly with the priests. It is partly her fault, too, that we have the fourteen new mitres in the land. Of what use are they, I should like to know? Why, that foreigners may be shoved into the good benefices, where formerly abbots were chosen out of the chapters! And we're to believe it's for the sake of religion. We know better. Three bishops were enough for us; things went on decently and reputably. Now each must busy himself as if he were needed; and this gives rise every moment to dissensions and ill-will. And the more you agitate the matter, so much the worse it grows. (*They drink.*)

SOEST. But it was the will of the king; she cannot alter it, one way or another.

JETTER. Then we may not even sing the new psalms; but ribald songs, as many as we please. And why? There is heresy in them, they say, and heaven knows what. I have sung some of them, however; they are new, to be sure, but I see no harm in them.

BUYCK. Ask their leave, forsooth! In our province we sing just what we please. That's because Count Egmont is our stadtholder, who does not trouble himself about such matters. In Ghent, Ypres, and throughout the whole of Flanders, anybody sings them that chooses. (*Aloud to* RUYSUM.) There is nothing more harmless than a church hymn — is there, father?

RUYSUM. What, indeed! It is a godly work, and truly edifying.

JETTER. They say, however, that they are not of the right sort, not of their sort, and, since it is dangerous, we had better leave them alone. The officers of the Inquisition are always lurking and spying about; many an honest fellow has already fallen into their clutches. They had not gone so far as to meddle with conscience! If they will not allow me to do what I like, they might at least let me think and sing as I please.

SOEST. The Inquisition won't do here. We are not made like the Spaniards, to let our consciences be tyrannized over. The nobles must look to it, and clip its wings betimes.

JETTER. It is a great bore. Whenever it comes into their worships' heads to break into my house, and I am sitting there at my work, humming a French psalm, thinking nothing about it, neither good nor bad — singing it just because it is in my throat; — forthwith I am a heretic, and am clapped into prison. Or, if I am passing through the country, and stand near a crowd listening to a new preacher, one of those who have come from Germany; instantly I am called a rebel, and am in danger of losing my head! Have you ever heard one of these preachers?

SOEST. A worthy set of people! Not long ago I heard one of them preach in a field, before thousands and thousands of people. He gave us a sort of dish very different from that of our humdrum preachers, who, from the pulpit, choke their hearers with scraps of Latin. He spoke from his heart; told us how we had till now been led by the nose, how we had been kept in darkness, and how we might procure more light; — ay, and he proved it all out of the Bible.

JETTER. There may be something in it. I always said as much, and have often pondered over the matter. It has long been running in my head.

BUYCK. All the people run after them.

SOEST. No wonder, since they hear both what is good and what is new.

JETTER. And what is it all about? Surely they might let every one preach after his own fashion.

BUYCK. Come, sirs! While you are talking, you forget the wine and the Prince of Orange.

JETTER. We must not forget him. He's a very wall of defence. In thinking of him, one fancies that if one could only hide behind him, the devil himself could not get at one. Here's to William of Orange! Hurrah!

ALL. Hurrah! Hurrah!

SOEST. Now, gray-beard, let's have your toast.

RUYSUM. Here's to old soldiers! To all soldiers! War forever!

BUYCK.   Bravo, old fellow.   Here's to all soldiers.   War forever!

JETTER.   War! War!   Do ye know what ye are shouting about?   That it should slip glibly from your tongue is natural enough; but what wretched work it is for us, I have not words to tell you.   To be stunned the whole year round by the beating of the drum; to hear of nothing except how one troop marched here, and another there; how they came over this height, and halted near that mill; how many were left dead on this field, and how many on that; how they press forward, and how one wins, and another loses, without being able to comprehend what they are fighting about; how a town is taken, how the citizens are put to the sword, and how it fares with the poor women and innocent children.   This is a grief and a trouble, and then one thinks every moment, " Here they come!   It will be our turn next."

SOEST.   Therefore every citizen must be practised in the use of arms.

JETTER.   Fine talking, indeed, for him who has a wife and children.   And yet I would rather hear of soldiers than see them.

BUYCK.   I might take offence at that.

JETTER.   It was not intended for you, countryman. When we got rid of the Spanish garrison we breathed freely again.

SOEST.   Faith! they pressed on you heavily enough.

JETTER.   Mind your own business.

SOEST.   They came to sharp quarters with you.

JETTER.   Hold your tongue.

SOEST.   They drove him out of kitchen, cellar, chamber — and bed.   (*They laugh.*)

JETTER.   You are a blockhead.

BUYCK.   Peace, sirs!   Must the soldier cry peace? Since you will not hear anything about us, let us have a toast of your own — a citizen's toast.

JETTER.   We're all ready for that!   Safety and peace!

SOEST.   Order and freedom!

BUYCK.   Bravo!   That will content us all.

(*They ring their glasses together, and joyously repeat the words, but in such a manner that each utters a different sound, and it becomes a kind of chant.   The old man listens, and at length joins in.*)

ALL.   Safety and peace!   Order and freedom!

Scene II. *Palace of the Regent.*

Margaret of Parma (*in a hunting dress*). Courtiers, Pages, Servants.

Regent. Put off the hunt, I shall not ride to-day. Bid Machiavel attend me. [*Exeunt all but the* Regent.

The thought of these terrible events leaves me no repose! Nothing can amuse, nothing divert my mind. These images, these cares are always before me. The king will now say that these are the natural fruits of my kindness, of my clemency; yet my conscience assures me that I have adopted the wisest, the most prudent course. Ought I sooner to have kindled and spread abroad these flames with the breath of wrath? my hope was to keep them in, to let them smoulder in their own ashes. Yes, my inward conviction, and my knowledge of the circumstances, justify my conduct in my own eyes; but in what light will it appear to my brother? For can it be denied that the insolence of these foreign teachers waxes daily more audacious? They have desecrated our sanctuaries, unsettled the dull minds of the people, and conjured up amongst them a spirit of delusion. Impure spirits have mingled among the insurgents, horrible deeds have been perpetrated, which to think of makes one shudder, and of these a circumstantial account must be transmitted to court instantly. Prompt and minute must be my communication, lest rumor outrun my messenger, and the king suspect that some particulars have been purposely withheld. I can see no means, severe or mild, by which to stem the evil. Oh, what are we great ones on the waves of humanity? We think to control them, and are ourselves driven to and fro, hither and thither.

Enter Machiavel

Regent. Are the despatches to the king prepared?

Machiavel. In an hour they will be ready for your signature.

Regent. Have you made the report sufficiently circumstantial?

Machiavel. Full and circumstantial, as the king loves to have it. I relate how the rage of the iconoclasts first broke out at St. Omer. How a furious multitude, with staves, hatchets, hammers, ladders and cords, accompanied by a few armed men, first assailed the chapels, churches, and convents, drove out the worshippers, forced the barred gates, threw everything into confusion, tore down the altars, destroyed the statues of the saints, defaced the pictures, and dashed to atoms, and trampled under foot whatever that was consecrated and holy came in their way. How the crowd increased as it advanced, and how the inhabitants of Ypres opened their gates at its approach. How, with incredible rapidity, they demolished the cathedral, and burned the library of the bishop. How a vast multitude, possessed by the like frenzy, dispersed themselves through Menin, Comines, Verviers, Lille, nowhere encountered opposition; and how, through almost the whole of Flanders, in a single moment, the monstrous conspiracy declared itself and was accomplished.

REGENT. Alas! Your recital rends my heart anew; and the fear that the evil will wax greater and greater adds to my grief. Tell me your thoughts, Machiavel!

MACHIAVEL. Pardon me, your Highness, my thoughts will appear to you but as idle fancies; and though you always seem well satisfied with my services, you have seldom felt inclined to follow my advice. How often have you said in jest: "You see too far, Machiavel! You should be an historian; he who acts must provide for the exigency of the hour." And yet, have I not predicted this terrible history? Have I not foreseen it all?

REGENT. I, too, foresee many things without being able to avert them.

MACHIAVEL. In one word, then: — you will not be able to suppress the new faith. Let it be recognized, separate its votaries from the true believers, give them churches of their own, include them within the pale of social order, subject them to the restraints of law, — do this, and you will at once tranquillize the insurgents. All other measures will prove abortive, and you will depopulate the country.

REGENT. Have you forgotten with what aversion the mere suggestion of toleration was rejected by my brother? Know you not, how in every letter he urgently recommends to me the maintenance of the true faith? That he will not hear of tranquillity and order being restored at the expense of religion? Even in the provinces, does he not maintain spies, unknown to us, in order to ascertain who inclines to the new doctrines? Has he not, to our astonishment, named to us this or that individual residing in our very neighborhood, who, without its being known, was obnoxious to the charge of heresy? Does he not enjoin harshness and severity? and am I to be lenient? Am I to recommend for his adoption measures of indulgence and toleration? Should I not thus lose all credit with him, and at once forfeit his confidence?

MACHIAVEL. I know it. The king commands, and puts you in full possession of his intentions. You are to restore tranquillity and peace by measures which cannot fail still more to embitter men's minds, and which must inevitably kindle the flames of war from one extremity of the country to the other. Consider well what you are doing. The principal merchants are infected — nobles, citizens, soldiers. What avails persisting in our opinion when everything is changing around us? Oh, that some good genius would suggest to Philip that it better becomes a monarch to govern burghers of two different creeds, than to excite them to mutual destruction!

REGENT. Never let me hear such words again. Full well I know that the policy of statesmen rarely maintains truth and fidelity; that it excludes from the heart candor, charity, toleration. In secular affairs, this is, alas! only too true; but shall we trifle with God as we do with each other? Shall we be indifferent to our established faith, for the sake of which so many have sacrificed their lives? Shall we abandon it to these far-fetched, uncertain, and self-contradicting heresies?

MACHIAVEL. Think not the worse of me for what I have uttered.

REGENT. I know you and your fidelity. I know, too, that a man may be both honest and sagacious, and yet miss the best and nearest way to the salvation of his soul. There are others, Machiavel, men whom I esteem, yet whom I needs must blame.

MACHIAVEL. To whom do you refer?

REGENT. I must confess that Egmont caused me to-day deep and heartfelt annoyance

MACHIAVEL. How so?

REGENT. By his accustomed demeanor, his usual indifference and levity. I received the fatal tidings as I was leaving church, attended by him and several others. I did not restrain my anguish, I broke forth into lamentations, loud and deep, and turning to him, exclaimed, "See what is going on in your province! Do you suffer it, Count, you in whom the king confided so implicitly?"

MACHIAVEL. And what was his reply?

REGENT. As if it were a mere trifle, an affair of no moment, he answered: "Were the Netherlanders but satisfied as to their constitution, the rest would soon follow."

MACHIAVEL. There was, perhaps, more truth than discretion or piety in his words. How can we hope to acquire and to maintain the confidence of the Netherlander when he sees that we are more interested in appropriating his possessions than in promoting his welfare, temporal or spiritual? Does the number of souls saved by the new bishops exceed that of the fat benefices they have swallowed? And are they not for the most part foreigners? As yet, the office of stadtholder has been held by Netherlanders; but do not the Spaniards betray their great and irresistible desire to possess themselves of these places? Will not people prefer being governed by their own countrymen, and according to their ancient customs, rather than by foreigners, who, from their first entrance into the land, endeavor to enrich themselves at the general expense, who measure everything by a foreign standard, and exercise their authority without cordiality or sympathy?

REGENT. You take part with our opponents?

MACHIAVEL. Assuredly not in my heart. Would that with my understanding I could be wholly on our side.

REGENT. If such is your opinion, it were better I should resign the regency to them; for both Egmont and Orange entertained great hopes of occupying this position. Then they were adversaries; now they are leagued against me, and have become friends — inseparable friends.

MACHIAVEL. A dangerous pair.

REGENT. To speak candidly, I fear Orange. — I fear for Egmont. — Orange meditates some dangerous scheme, his thoughts are far-reaching, he is reserved, appears to accede to everything, never contradicts, and while maintaining the show of reverence, with clear foresight accomplishes his own designs.

MACHIAVEL. Egmont, on the contrary, advances with a bold step, as if the world were all his own.

REGENT. He bears his head as proudly as if the hand of majesty were not suspended over him.

MACHIAVEL. The eyes of all the people are fixed upon him, and he is the idol of their hearts.

REGENT. He has never assumed the least disguise, and carries himself as if no one had a right to call him to account. He still bears the name of Egmont. Count Egmont is the title by which he loves to hear himself addressed, as though he would fain be reminded that his ancestors were masters of Guelderland. Why does he not assume his proper title, — Prince of Gaure? What object has he in view? Would he again revive extinguished claims?

MACHIAVEL. I hold him to be a faithful servant of the king.

REGENT. Were he so inclined, what important service he could render to the government! Whereas now, without benefiting himself, he has caused us unspeakable vexation. His banquets and entertainments have done more to unite the nobles and to knit them together than the most dangerous secret associations. With his toasts his guests have drunk in a permanent intoxication, a giddy frenzy, that never subsides. How often have his facetious jests stirred up the minds of the populace? and what an excitement was produced among the mob by the new liveries and the extravagant devices of his followers!

MACHIAVEL. I am convinced he had no design.

REGENT. Be that as it may, it is bad enough. As I said before, he injures us without benefiting himself. He treats as a jest matters of serious import; and, not to appear negligent and remiss, we are forced to treat seriously what he intended as a jest. Thus one urges on the other; and what we are endeavoring to avert is actually brought to pass. He is more dangerous than the acknowledged head of a conspiracy; and I am much mistaken if it is not all remembered against him at court. I cannot deny that scarcely a day passes in which he does not wound me — deeply wound me.

MACHIAVEL. He appears to me to act on all occasions according to the dictates of his conscience.

REGENT. His conscience has a convenient mirror. His demeanor is often offensive. He carries himself as if he felt he were the master here, and were withheld by courtesy alone from making us feel his supremacy; as if he would not exactly drive us out of the country; there'll be no need for that.

MACHIAVEL. I entreat you, put not too harsh a construction upon his frank and joyous temper, which treats lightly matters of serious moment. You but injure yourself and him.

REGENT. I interpret nothing. I speak only of inevitable
consequences, and I know him. His patent of nobility and
the Golden Fleece upon his breast strengthen his confidence,
his audacity. Both can protect him against any sudden outbreak of royal displeasure. Consider the matter closely, and
he is alone responsible for the whole mischief that has broken
out in Flanders. From the first, he connived at the proceedings of the foreign teachers, avoided stringent measures,
and perhaps rejoiced in secret that they gave us so much to
do. Let me alone; on this occasion, I will give utterance to
that which weighs upon my heart; I will not shoot my arrow
in vain. I know where he is vulnerable. For he is vulnerable.

MACHIAVEL. Have you summoned the council? Will
Orange attend?

REGENT. I have sent for him to Antwerp. I will lay
upon their shoulders the burden of responsibility; they shall
either strenuously co-operate with me in quelling the evil, or
at once declare themselves rebels. Let the letters be completed without delay, and bring them for my signature.
Then hasten to despatch the trusty Vasca to Madrid; he is
faithful and indefatigable; let him use all diligence, that he
may not be anticipated by common report, that my brother
may receive the intelligence first through him. I will myself
speak with him ere he departs.

MACHIAVEL. Your orders shall be promptly and punctually obeyed.

SCENE III. *Citizen's House.*

CLARA, *her* MOTHER, BRACKENBURG.

CLARA. Will you not hold the yarn for me, Brackenburg?

BRACKENBURG. I entreat you, excuse me, Clara.

CLARA. What ails you? Why refuse me this trifling service?

BRACKENBURG. When I hold the yarn, I stand as it
were spell-bound before you, and cannot escape your eyes.

CLARA. Nonsense! Come and hold!

MOTHER (*knitting in her arm-chair*). Give us a song!
Brackenburg sings so good a second. You used to be merry
once, and I had always something to laugh at.

BRACKENBURG. Once!

CLARA. Well, let us sing.

BRACKENBURG. As you please.

CLARA. Merrily, then, and sing away. 'Tis a soldier's song, my favorite. (*She winds yarn, and sings with BRACK-ENBURG.*)

> The drum is resounding,
> And shrill the fife plays;
> My love, for the battle,
> His brave troop arrays;
> He lifts his lance high,
> And the people he sways.
> My blood it is boiling!
> My heart throbs pit-pat!
> Oh, had I a jacket,
> With hose and with hat!
>
> How boldly I'd follow,
> And march through the gate;
> Through all the wide province
> I'd follow him straight.
> The foe yield, we capture
> Or shoot them! Ah, me!
> What heart-thrilling rapture
> A soldier to be!

(*During the song, BRACKENBURG has frequently looked at CLARA; at length his voice falters, his eyes fill with tears, he lets the skein fall, and goes to the window. CLARA finishes the song alone, her mother motions to her, half displeased, she rises, advances a few steps towards him, turns back as if irresolute, and again sits down.*)

MOTHER. What is going on in the street, Brackenburg? I hear soldiers marching.

BRACKENBURG. It is the Regent's body-guard.

CLARA. At this hour? What can it mean? (*She rises and joins BRACKENBURG at the window.*) That is not the daily guard; it is more numerous! almost all the troops! Oh, Brackenburg, go! Learn what it means. It must be something unusual. Go, good Brackenburg, do me this favor.

BRACKENBURG. I am going! I will return immediately. (*He offers his hand to CLARA, and she gives him hers.*)

[*Exit* BRACKENBURG.

MOTHER. Thou sendest him away so soon!

CLARA. I am curious; and, besides — do not be angry, mother — his presence pains me. I never know how I ought to behave towards him. I have done him a wrong, and it goes to my very heart to see how deeply he feels it. Well, it can't be helped now!

MOTHER. He is such a true-hearted fellow!

CLARA. I cannot help it, I must treat him kindly. Often, without a thought, I return the gentle, loving pressure of his hand. I reproach myself that I am deceiving him, that I am nourishing in his heart a vain hope. I am in a sad plight! God knows I do not willingly deceive him. I do not wish him to hope, yet I cannot let him despair!

MOTHER. That is not as it should be.

CLARA. I liked him once, and in my soul I like him still. I could have married him; yet I believe I was never really in love with him.

MOTHER. Thou wouldst always have been happy with him.

CLARA. I should have been provided for, and have led a quiet life.

MOTHER. And through thy fault it has all been trifled away.

CLARA. I am in a strange position. When I think how it has come to pass, I know it, indeed, and I know it not. But I have only to look upon Egmont, and I understand it all; ay, and stranger things would seem natural then. Oh, what a man he is! All the provinces worship him. And in his arms should not I be the happiest creature in the world?

MOTHER. And how will it be in the future?

CLARA. I only ask does he love me? — does he love me? — as if there were any doubt about it.

MOTHER. One has nothing but anxiety of heart with one's children. Always care and sorrow, whatever may be the end of it! It cannot come to good! Thou hast made thyself wretched! Thou hast made thy mother wretched, too.

CLARA (*quietly*). Yet thou didst allow it in the beginning.

MOTHER. Alas! I was too indulgent; I am always too indulgent.

CLARA. When Egmont rode by, and I ran to the window, did you chide me then? Did you not come to the window yourself? When he looked up, smiled, nodded, and greeted me, was it displeasing to you? Did you not feel yourself honored in your daughter?

MOTHER. Go on with your reproaches.

CLARA (*with emotion*). Then, when he passed more frequently, and we felt sure that it was on my account that he came this way, did you not remark it yourself with secret joy? Did you call me away when I stood behind the window-pane and awaited him?

MOTHER. Could I imagine that it would go so far?

CLARA (*with faltering voice, and repressed tears*). And then, one evening, when, enveloped in his mantle, he surprised us as we sat at our lamp, who busied herself in receiving him, while I remained, lost in astonishment, as if fastened to my chair?

MOTHER. Could I imagine that the prudent Clara would so soon be carried away by this unhappy love? I must now endure that, my daughter ——

CLARA (*bursting into tears*). Mother! How can you? You take pleasure in tormenting me!

MOTHER (*weeping*). Ay, weep away! Make me yet more wretched by thy grief. Is it not misery enough that my only daughter is a castaway!

CLARA (*rising, and speaking coldly*). A castaway! The beloved of Egmont a castaway!—What princess would not envy the poor Clara a place in his heart? Oh, mother,— my own mother, you were not wont to speak thus! Dear mother, be kind!—Let the people think, let the neighbors whisper, what they like — this chamber, this lowly house, is a paradise since Egmont's love has had its abode in it.

MOTHER. One cannot help liking him, that is true. He is always so kind, frank, and open-hearted.

CLARA. There is not a drop of false blood in his veins. And then, mother, he is indeed the great Egmont; yet, when he comes to me, how tender he is, how kind! How he tries to conceal from me his rank, his bravery! How anxious he is about me! so entirely the man, the friend, the lover.

MOTHER. Do you expect him to-day?

CLARA. Have you not seen how often I go the window? Have you not noticed how I listen to every noise at the door?—Though I know that he will not come before night, yet, from the time when I rise in the morning, I keep expecting him every moment. Were I but a boy, to follow him always, to the court and everywhere! Could I but carry his colors in the field!——

MOTHER. You were always such a lively, restless creature; even as a little child, now wild, now thoughtful. Will you not dress yourself a little better?

CLARA. Perhaps, mother, if I have nothing better to do. — Yesterday, some of his people went by singing songs in his honor. At least his name was in the songs! The rest I could not understand. My heart leaped up into my throat, — I would fain have called them back if I had not felt ashamed.

MOTHER. Take care! Thy impetuous nature will ruin all. Thou wilt betray thyself before the people; as, not long ago, at thy cousin's, when thou foundest out the woodcut with the description, and didst exclaim, with a cry: "Count Egmont!" — I grew as red as fire.

CLARA. Could I help crying out? It was the battle of Gravelines, and I found in the picture the letter C. and then looked for it in the description below. There it stood, "Count Egmont, with his horse shot under him." I shuddered, and afterwards I could not help laughing at the woodcut figure of Egmont, as tall as the neighboring tower of Gravelines, and the English ships at the side. —When I remember how I used to conceive of a battle, and what an idea I had, as a girl, of Count Egmont; when I listened to descriptions of him, and of all the other earls and princes; — and think how it is with me now!

Enter BRACKENBURG.

CLARA. Well, what is going on?

BRACKENBURG. Nothing certain is known. It is rumored that an insurrection has lately broken out in Flanders; the Regent is afraid of its spreading here. The castle is strongly garrisoned, the burghers are crowding to the gates, and the streets are thronged with people. I will hasten at once to my old father. (*As if about to go.*)

CLARA. Shall we see you to-morrow? I must change my dress a little. I am expecting my cousin, and I look too untidy. Come, mother, help me a moment. Take the book, Brackenburg, and bring me such another story.

MOTHER. Farewell.

BRACKENBURG (*extending his hand*). Your hand!

CLARA (*refusing hers*). When you come next.

[*Exeunt* MOTHER *and* DAUGHTER.]

BRACKENBURG (*alone*). I had resolved to go away again at once; and yet, when she takes me at my word, and lets me leave her, I feel as if I could go mad.—Wretched man! Does the fate of thy fatherland, does the growing disturbance fail to move thee?—Are countryman and Spaniard the same to thee? and carest thou not who rules, and who is in the right?—I was a different sort of fellow as a school-boy!—Then, when an exercise in oratory was given; "Brutus' Speech for Liberty," for instance, Fritz was ever the first, and the rector would say: "If it were only spoken more deliberately, the words not all huddled together."— Then my blood boiled, and longed for action.—Now I drag along, bound by the eyes of a maiden. I cannot leave her! yet she, alas, cannot love me!—ah—no—she—she cannot have entirely rejected me—not entirely—yet half love is no love!—I will endure it no longer!—Can it be true what a friend lately whispered in my ear, that she secretly admits a man into the house by night, when she always sends me away modestly before evening? No, it cannot be true! It is a lie! A base, slanderous lie! Clara is as innocent as I am wretched.—She has rejected me, has thrust me from her heart—and shall I live on thus? I cannot, I will not endure it. Already my native land is convulsed by internal strife, and do I perish abjectly amid the tumult? I will not endure it! When the trumpet sounds, when a shot falls, it thrills through my bone and marrow! But, alas, it does not rouse me! It does not summon me to join the onslaught, to rescue, to dare.—Wretched, degrading position! Better end it at once! Not long ago I threw myself into the water; I sank—but nature in her agony was too strong for me; I felt that I could swim, and saved myself against my will. Could I but forget the time when she loved me, seemed to love me!—Why has this happiness penetrated my very bone and marrow? Why have these hopes, while disclosing to me a distant paradise, consumed all the enjoyment of life? —And that first, that only kiss!—Here (*laying his hand upon the table*), here we were alone,—she had always been kind and friendly towards me,—then she seemed to soften, —she looked at me,—my brain reeled,—I felt her lips on mine,—and—and now?—Die, wretch! Why dost thou hesitate? (*He draws a phial from his pocket.*) Thou healing poison, it shall not have been in vain that I stole thee from my brother's medicine chest? From this anxious fear, this dizziness, this death-agony, thou shalt deliver me at once.

ACT II.

SCENE I. *Square in Brussels.*

JETTER *and a* MASTER CARPENTER *(meeting).*

CARPENTER. Did I not tell you beforehand? Eight days ago at the guild I said there would be serious disturbances?

JETTER. Is it really true that they have plundered the churches in Flanders?

CARPENTER. They have utterly destroyed both churches and chapels. They have left nothing standing but the four bare walls. The lowest rabble! And this it is that damages our good cause. We ought rather to have laid our claims before the Regent, formally and decidedly, and then have stood by them. If we speak now, if we assemble now, it will be said that we are joining the insurgents.

JETTER. Ay, so every one thinks at first. Why should you thrust your nose into the mess? The neck is closely connected with it.

CARPENTER. I am always uneasy when tumults arise among the mob — among people who have nothing to lose. They use as a pretext that to which we also must appeal, and plunge the country in misery.

Enter SOEST.

SOEST. Good-day, sirs? What news? Is it true that the image-breakers are coming straight in this direction?

CARPENTER. Here they shall touch nothing at any rate.

SOEST. A soldier came into my shop just now to buy tobacco! I questioned him about the matter. The Regent, though so brave and prudent a lady, has for once lost her presence of mind. Things must be bad, indeed, when she thus takes refuge behind her guards. The castle is strongly garrisoned. It is even rumored that she means to flee from the town.

CARPENTER. Forth she shall not go! Her presence protects us, and we will insure her safety better than her mustachioed gentry. If she only maintains our rights and privileges, we will stand faithfully by her.

Enter a SOAPBOILER.

SOAPBOILER. An ugly business this! a bad business! Troubles are beginning; all things are going wrong! Mind you keep quiet, or they'll take you also for rioters.

Soest. Here come the seven wise men of Greece.

Soapboiler. I know there are many who in secret hold with the Calvinists, abuse the bishops, and care not for the king. But a loyal subject, a sincere Catholic!—— (*By degrees others join the speakers and listen.*)

Enter Vansen.

Vansen. God save you, sirs! What news?

Carpenter. Have nothing to do with him, he's a dangerous fellow.

Jetter. Is he not secretary to Dr. Wiets?

Carpenter. He has had several masters. First he was a clerk, and as one patron after another turned him off, on account of his roguish tricks, he now dabbles in the business of notary and advocate, and is a brandy-drinker to boot. (*More people gather round and stand in groups.*)

Vansen. So here you are putting your heads together. Well, it is worth talking about.

Soest. I think so, too.

Vansen. Now, if only one of you had heart and another head enough for the work, we might break the Spanish fetters at once.

Soest. Sirs! you must not talk thus. We have taken our oath to the king.

Vansen. And the king to us. Mark that!

Jetter. There's sense in that? Tell us your opinion.

Others. Hearken to him; he's a clever fellow. He's sharp enough.

Vansen. I had an old master once, who possessed a collection of parchments, among which were charters of ancient constitutions, contracts, and privileges. He set great store too, by the rarest books. One of these contained our whole constitution; how, at first we Netherlanders had princes of our own, who governed according to hereditary laws, rights, and usages; how our ancestors paid due honor to their sovereign so long as he governed them equitably; and how they were immediately on their guard the moment he was for overstepping his bounds. The states were down upon him at once; for every province, however small, had its own chamber and representatives.

Carpenter. Hold your tongue! we knew that long ago! Every honest citizen learns as much about the constitution as he needs.

Jetter. Let him speak; one may always learn something.

Soest. He is quite right.

Several Citizens. Go on! Go on! One does not hear this every day.

Vansen. You, citizens, forsooth! You live only in the present; and as you tamely follow the trade inherited from your fathers, so you let the government do with you just as it pleases. You make no inquiry into the origin, the history, or the rights of a Regent; and, in consequence of this negligence, the Spaniard has drawn the net over your ears.

Soest. Who cares for that, if one only has daily bread?

Jetter. The devil! Why did not some one come forward and tell us this in time?

Vansen. I tell it you now. The King of Spain, whose good fortune it is to bear sway over these provinces, has no right to govern them otherwise than the petty princes who formerly possessed them separately. Do you understand that?

Jetter. Explain it to us.

Vansen. Why it is as clear as the sun. Must you not be governed according to your provincial laws? How comes that?

A Citizen. Certainly!

Vansen. Has not the burgher of Brussels a different law from the burgher of Antwerp? The burgher of Antwerp from the burgher of Ghent? How comes that?

Another Citizen. By heaven!

Vansen. But if you let matters run on thus they will soon tell you a different story. Fie on you! Philip, through a woman, now ventures to do what neither Charles the Bold, Frederick the Warrior, nor Charles the Fifth could accomplish.

Soest. Yes, yes! The old princes tried it also.

Vansen. Ay! but our ancestors kept a sharp lookout. If they thought themselves aggrieved by their sovereign, they would perhaps get his son and heir into their hands, detain him as a hostage, and surrender him only on the most favorable conditions. Our fathers were men! They knew their own interests! They knew how to lay hold on what they wanted, and to get it established! They were men of the right sort; and hence it is that our privileges are so clearly defined, our liberties so well secured.

Soest. What are you saying about our liberties?

All. Our liberties! our privileges! Tell us about our privileges.

VANSEN. All the provinces have their peculiar advantages, but we of Brabant are the most splendidly provided for. I have read it all.

SOEST. Say on.

JETTER. Let us hear.

A CITIZEN. Pray do.

VANSEN. First, it stands written: — The Duke of Brabant shall be to us a good and faithful sovereign.

SOEST. Good! Stands it so?

JETTER. Faithful? Is that true?

VANSEN. As I tell you. He is bound to us as we are to him. Secondly: in the exercise of his authority he shall neither exert arbitrary power nor exhibit caprice himself, nor shall he, either directly or indirectly, sanction them in others.

JETTER. Bravo! Bravo! Not exert arbitrary power.

SOEST. Nor exhibit caprice.

ANOTHER. And not sanction them in others! That is the main point. Not sanction them, either directly or indirectly.

VANSEN. In express words.

JETTER. Get us the book.

A CITIZEN. Yes, we must see it.

OTHERS. The book! The book!

ANOTHER. We will to the Regent with the book.

ANOTHER. Sir doctor, you shall be spokesman.

SOAPBOILER. Oh, the dolts!

OTHERS. Something more out of the book!

SOAPBOILER. I'll knock his teeth down his throat if he says another word.

PEOPLE. We'll see who dares to lay hands upon him. Tell us about our privileges! Have we any more privileges?

VANSEN. Many, very good and very wholesome ones, too. Thus it stands: The sovereign shall neither benefit the clergy, nor increase their number, without the consent of the nobles and of the states. Mark that! Nor shall he alter the constitution of the country.

SOEST. Stands it so?

VANSEN. I'll show it you, as it was written down two or three centuries ago.

A CITIZEN. And we tolerate the new bishop? The nobles must protect us, we will make a row else!

OTHERS. And we suffer ourselves to be intimidated by the Inquisition?

VANSEN. It is your own fault.

PEOPLE. We have Egmont! We have Orange! They will protect our interests.

VANSEN. Your brothers in Flanders are beginning the good work.

SOAPBOILER. Dog! (*Strikes him.*)

OTHERS *oppose the* SOAPBOILER, *and exclaim*, Are you also a Spaniard?

ANOTHER. What! This honorable man?

ANOTHER. This learned man?

> (*They attack the* SOAPBOILER.)

CARPENTER. For heaven's sake, peace!

> (*Others mingle in the fray.*)

CARPENTER. Citizens, what means this?

> (*Boys whistle, throw stones, set on dogs; citizens stand and gape, people come running up, others walk quietly to and fro, others play all sorts of pranks, shout and huzza.*)

OTHERS. Freedom and privilege! Privilege and freedom!

Enter EGMONT, *with followers*

EGMONT. Peace! Peace! good people. What is the matter? Peace, I say! Separate them.

CARPENTER. My good lord, you come like an angel from heaven. Hush! See you nothing? Count Egmont! Honor to Count Egmont!

EGMONT. Here, too! What are you about? Burgher against burgher! Does not even the neighborhood of our royal mistress oppose a barrier to this frenzy? Disperse yourselves, and go about your business. 'Tis a bad sign when you thus keep holiday on working days. How did the disturbance begin?

> (*The tumult gradually subsides, and the people gather around* EGMONT.)

CARPENTER. They are fighting about their privileges.

EGMONT. Which they will forfeit through their own folly — and who are you? You seem honest people.

CARPENTER. 'Tis our wish to be so.

EGMONT. Your calling?

CARPENTER. A carpenter, and master of the guild.

EGMONT. And you?

SOEST. A shopkeeper.

EGMONT. And you?

JETTER. A tailor.

EGMONT. I remember, you were employed upon the liveries of my people. Your name is Jetter.

JETTER. To think of your grace remembering it!

EGMONT. I do not easily forget any one whom I have seen or conversed with. Do what you can, good people, to keep the peace; you stand in bad enough repute already. Provoke not the king still farther. The power, after all, is in his hands. An honest burgher, who maintains himself industriously, has everywhere as much freedom as he needs.

CARPENTER. To be sure; that is just our misfortune! With all due deference, your grace, 'tis the idle portion of the community, your drunkards and vagabonds, who quarrel for want of something to do, and clamor about privilege because they are hungry; they impose upon the curious and the credulous, and, in order to obtain a pot of beer, excite disturbances that will bring misery upon thousands. That is just what they want. We keep our houses and chests too well guarded; they would fain drive us away from them with firebrands.

EGMONT. You shall have all needful assistance; measures have been taken to stem the evil by force. Make a firm stand against the new doctrines, and do not imagine that privileges are secured by sedition. Remain at home; suffer no crowds to assemble in the streets. Sensible people can accomplish much. (*In the meantime the crowd has for the most part dispersed.*)

CARPENTER. Thanks, your excellency — thanks for your good opinion! We will do what in us lies. (*Exit* EGMONT.) A gracious lord! A true Netherlander! Nothing of the Spaniard about him.

JETTER. If we had only him for a regent. 'Tis a pleasure to follow him.

SOEST. The king won't hear of that. He takes care to appoint his own people to the place.

JETTER. Did you notice his dress? It was of the newest fashion — after the Spanish cut.

CARPENTER. A handsome gentleman.

JETTER. His head now were a dainty morsel for a headsman.

SOEST. Are you mad? What are you thinking about?

JETTER. It is stupid enough that such an idea should come into one's head! But so it is. Whenever I see a fine, long neck, I cannot help thinking how well it would suit the block. These cursed executions! One cannot get them out of one's head. When the lads are swimming, and I chance to see a naked back, I think forthwith of the dozens I have seen beaten with rods. If I meet a portly gentleman, I fancy I already see him being roasted at the stake. At night, in my dreams, I am tortured in every limb; one cannot have a single hour's enjoyment; all merriment and fun have long been forgotten. These terrible images seem burnt in upon my brain.

SCENE II. EGMONT's *residence*.

His SECRETARY (*at a desk with papers. He rises impatiently*).

SECRETARY. He is not yet here! And I have been waiting already full two hours, pen in hand, the paper before me; and just to-day I am anxious to be off early. The floor burns under my feet. I can with difficulty restrain my impatience. "Be punctual to the hour." Such was his parting injunction; now he comes not. There is so much business to get through, I shall not have finished before midnight. He overlooks one's faults, it is true; methinks it would be better, though, were he more strict, so he dismissed one at the appointed time. One could then arrange one's plans. It is now full two hours since he came away from the Regent; who knows whom he may have chanced to meet by the way?

Enter EGMONT.

EGMONT. Well, how do matters look?

SECRETARY. I am ready, and three couriers are waiting.

EGMONT. I have detained you too long; you look somewhat out of humor.

SECRETARY. In obedience to your command I have been in attendance for some time. Here are the papers.

EGMONT. Donna Elvira will be angry with me when she learns that I have detained you.

SECRETARY. You are pleased to jest.

EGMONT. No, no. Be not ashamed. I admire your taste. She is pretty, and I have no objection that you should have a friend at the castle. What say the letters?

SECRETARY. Much, my lord, but withal little that is satisfactory.

EGMONT. 'Tis well that we have pleasures at home; we have the less occasion to seek them from abroad. Is there much that requires attention?

Secretary. Enough, my lord; three couriers are in attendance.

Egmont. Proceed! The most important.

Secretary. All are important.

Egmont. One after the other; only be prompt.

Secretary. Captain Breda sends an account of the occurrences that have further taken place in Ghent and the surrounding districts. The tumult is for the most part allayed.

Egmont. He doubtless reports individual acts of folly and temerity?

Secretary. He does, my lord.

Egmont. Spare me the recital.

Secretary. Six of the mob who tore down the image of the Virgin at Verviers have been arrested. He inquires whether they are to be hanged like the others.

Egmont. I am weary of hanging; let them be flogged and discharged.

Secretary. There are two women; are they to be flogged also?

Egmont. He may admonish them and let them go.

Secretary. Brink, of Breda's company, wants to marry; the captain hopes you will not allow it. There are so many women among the troops, he writes, that when on the march they resemble a gang of gypsies rather than regular soldiers.

Egmont. We must overlook it in his case. He is a fine young fellow, and moreover entreated me so earnestly before I came away. This must be the last time, however; though it grieves me to refuse the poor fellows their best pastime; they have enough without that to torment them.

Secretary. Two of your people, Seter and Hart, have ill-treated a damsel, the daughter of an inn-keeper. They got her alone, and she could not escape from them.

Egmont. If she be an honest maiden, and they used violence, let them be flogged three days in succession; and if they have any property, let him retain as much as will portion the girl.

Secretary. One of the foreign preachers has been discovered passing secretly through Comines. He swore that he was on the point of leaving for France. According to orders, he ought to be beheaded.

Egmont. Let him be conducted quietly to the frontier, and there admonished that the next time he will not escape so easily.

SECRETARY. A letter from your steward. He writes that money comes in slowly; he can with difficulty send you the required sum within the week; the late disturbances have thrown everything into the greatest confusion.

EGMONT. Money must be had! It is for him to look to the means.

SECRETARY. He says he will do his utmost, and at length proposes to sue and imprison Raymond, who has been so long in your debt.

EGMONT. But he has promised to pay!

SECRETARY. The last time he fixed a fortnight himself.

EGMONT. Well, grant him another fortnight; after that he may proceed against him.

SECRETARY. You do well. His non-payment of the money proceeds not from inability, but from want of inclination. He will trifle no longer when he sees that you are in earnest. The steward further proposes to withhold, for half a month, the pensions which you allow to the old soldiers, widows, and others. In the meantime some expedient may be devised; they must make their arrangements accordingly.

EGMONT. But what arrangements can be made here? These poor people want the money more than I. He must not think of it.

SECRETARY. How then, my lord, is he to raise the required sum?

EGMONT. It is his business to think of that. He was told so in a former letter.

SECRETARY. And therefore he makes these proposals.

EGMONT. They will never do; — he must think of something else. Let him suggest expedients that are admissible, and, above all, let him procure the money.

SECRETARY. I have again before me the letter from Count Oliva. Pardon my recalling it to your remembrance. Above all others, the aged count deserves a detailed reply. You proposed writing to him with your own hand. Doubtless, he loves you as a father.

EGMONT. I cannot command the time; — and of all detestable things, writing is to me the most detestable. You imitate my hand so admirably, do you write in my name. I am expecting Orange. I cannot do it; — I wish, however, that something soothing should be written to allay his fears.

SECRETARY. Just give me a notion of what you wish to communicate; I will at once draw up the answer, and lay it before you. It shall be so written that it might pass for your hand in a court of justice.

EGMONT. Give me the letter. (*After glancing over it.*) Good, honest, old man! Wert thou so cautious in thy own youth? Didst thou never mount a breach? Didst thou remain in the rear of battle at the suggestion of prudence? — What affectionate solicitude! He has, indeed, my safety and happiness at heart, but considers not that he who lives but to save his life is already dead. — Charge him not to be anxious on my account; I act as circumstances require, and shall be upon my guard. Let him use his influence at court in my favor, and be assured of my warmest thanks.

SECRETARY. Is that all? He expects still more.

EGMONT. What can I say? If you choose to write more fully, do so. The matter turns upon a single point; he would have me live as I cannot live. That I am joyous, live fast, take matters easily, is my good fortune; nor would I exchange it for the safety of a sepulchre. My blood rebels against the Spanish mode of life, nor have I the least inclination to regulate my movements by the new and cautious measures of the court. Do I live only to think of life? Am I to forego the enjoyment of the present moment in order to secure the next? And must that in its turn be consumed in anxieties and idle fears?

SECRETARY. I entreat you, my lord, be not so harsh towards the venerable man. You are wont to be friendly towards every one. Say a kindly word to allay the anxiety of your noble friend. See how considerate he is, with what delicacy he warns you.

EGMONT. Yet he harps continually on the same string. He knows of old how I detest these admonitions. They serve only to perplex and are of no avail. What if I were a somnambulist, and trod the giddy summit of a lofty house, — were it the part of friendship to call me by my name, to warn me of my danger, to waken, to kill me? Let each choose his own path, and provide for his own safety.

SECRETARY. It may become you to be without a fear, but those who know and love you ——

EGMONT (*looking over the letter*). Then he recalls the old story of our sayings and doings one evening in the wantonness of conviviality and wine; and what conclusions and inferences were thence drawn and circulated throughout the whole kingdom! Well, we had a cap and bells embroidered on the sleeves of our servants' liveries, and afterwards exchanged this senseless device for a bundle of arrows; — a still more dangerous symbol for those who are bent upon discovering a meaning where nothing is meant. These and similar follies were conceived and brought forth in a moment of merriment. It was at our suggestion that a noble troop, with beggars' wallets and a self-chosen nick-name, with mock humility recalled the king's duty to his remembrance. It was at our suggestion, too — well, what does it signify? Is a carnival jest to be construed into high treason? Are we to be grudged the scanty, variegated rags, wherewith a youthful spirit and heated imagination would adorn the poor nakedness of life? Take life too seriously, and what is it worth? If the morning wake us to no new joys, if in the evening we have no pleasures to hope for, is it worth the trouble of dressing and undressing? Does the sun shine on me to-day that I may reflect on what happened yesterday? That I may endeavor to foresee and control what can neither be foreseen nor controlled, — the destiny of the morrow? Spare me these reflections, we will leave them to scholars and courtiers. Let them ponder and contrive, creep hither and thither, and surreptitiously achieve their ends. — If you can make use of these suggestions, without swelling your letter into a volume, it is well. Everything appears of exaggerated importance to the good old man. 'Tis thus the friend, who has long held our hand, grasps it more warmly ere he quits his hold.

SECRETARY. Pardon me, the pedestrian grows dizzy when he beholds the charioteer drive past with whirling speed.

EGMONT. Child! Child! Forbear! As if goaded by invisible spirits, the sun-steeds of time bear onward the light car of our destiny; and nothing remains for us, but, with calm self-possession, firmly to grasp the reins, and now right, now left, to steer the wheels here from the precipice and there from the rock. Whither he is hasting, who knows? He hardly remembers whence he came?

SECRETARY. My lord! my lord!

EGMONT. I stand high, but I can and must rise yet higher. Courage, strength, and hope possess my soul. Not yet have I attained the height of my ambition; that once achieved, I want to stand firmly and without fear. Should I fall, should a thunder-clap, a storm-blast, ay, a false step of my own, precipitate me into the abyss, so be it! I shall lie there with thousands of others. I have never disdained, even for a trifling stake, to throw the bloody die with my gallant comrades; and shall I hesitate now, when all that is most precious in life is set upon the cast?

SECRETARY. Oh, my lord! you know not what you say! May Heaven protect you!

EGMONT. Collect your papers. Orange is coming. Despatch what is most urgent, that the couriers may set forth before the gates are closed. The rest may wait. Leave the Count's letter till to-morrow. Fail not to visit Elvira, and greet her from me. Inform yourself concerning the Regent's health. She cannot be well, though she would fain conceal it. [*Exit* SECRETARY.

Enter ORANGE.

EGMONT. Welcome, Orange; you appear somewhat disturbed.

ORANGE. What say you to our conference with the Regent?

EGMONT. I found nothing extraordinary in her manner of receiving us. I have often seen her thus before. She appeared to me to be somewhat indisposed.

ORANGE. Marked you not that she was more reserved than usual? She began by cautiously approving our conduct during the late insurrection; glanced at the false light in which, nevertheless, it might be viewed; and finally turned the discourse to her favorite topic — that her gracious demeanor, her friendship for us Netherlanders, had never been sufficiently recognized, never appreciated as it deserved; that nothing came to a prosperous issue; that for her part she was beginning to grow weary of it; that the king must at last resolve upon other measures. Did you hear that?

EGMONT. Not all; I was thinking at the time of something else. She is a woman, good Orange, and all women expect that every one shall submit passively to their gentle yoke; that every Hercules shall lay aside his lion's skin, assume the distaff, and swell their train; and, because they are themselves peaceably inclined, imagine, forsooth, that the ferment which seizes a nation, the storm which powerful rivals excite against one another, may be allayed by one soothing word, and the most discordant elements be brought to unite in tranquil harmony at their feet. 'Tis thus with her; and since she cannot accomplish her object, why she has no resource left but to lose her temper, to menace us with direful prospects for the future, and to threaten to take her departure.

ORANGE. Think you not that this time she will fulfil her threat?

EGMONT. Never! How often have I seen her actually prepared for the journey? Whither should she go? Being here a stadtholder, a queen, think you that she could endure to spend her days in insignificance at her brother's court, or to repair to Italy, and there drag on her existence among her old family connections?

ORANGE. She is held incapable of this determination, because you have already seen her hesitate and draw back; nevertheless, it is in her to take this step; new circumstances may impel her to the long-delayed resolve. What if she were to depart, and the king to send another?

EGMONT. Why, he would come, and he also would have business enough upon his hands. He would arrive with vast projects and schemes to reduce all things to order, to subjugate, and combine; and to-day he would be occupied with this trifle, to-morrow with that, and the day following have to deal with some unexpected hinderance. He would spend one month in forming plans, another in mortification at their failure, and half a year would be consumed in cares for a single province. With him also time would pass, his head grow dizzy, and things hold on their ordinary course, till, instead of sailing into the open sea, according to the plan which he had previously marked out, he might thank God if, amid the tempest, he were able to keep his vessel off the rocks.

ORANGE. What if the king were advised to try an experiment?

EGMONT. Which should be —— ?

ORANGE. To try how the body would get on without the head.

EGMONT. What?

ORANGE. Egmont, our interests have for years weighed upon my heart; I ever stand as over a chess-board, and regard no move of my adversary as insignificant; and as men of science carefully investigate the secrets of nature, so I hold it to be the duty, ay, the very vocation of a prince, to acquaint himself with the dispositions and intentions of all parties. I have reason to fear an outbreak. The king has long acted according to certain principles; he finds that they do not lead to a prosperous issue; what more probable than that he should seek it some other way?

EGMONT. I do not believe it! When a man grows old, has attempted much, and finds that the world cannot be made to move according to his will, he must needs grow weary of it at last.

ORANGE. One thing he has not yet attempted.

EGMONT. What?

ORANGE. To spare the people, and to put an end to the princes.

EGMONT. How many have long been haunted by this dread? There is no cause for such anxiety.

ORANGE. Once I felt anxious; gradually I became suspicious; suspicion has at length grown into certainty.

EGMONT. Has the king more faithful servants than ourselves?

ORANGE. We serve him after our own fashion; and, between ourselves, it must be confessed that we understand pretty well how to make the interests of the king square with our own.

EGMONT. And who does not? He has our duty and submission in so far as they are his due.

ORANGE. But what if he should arrogate still more, and regard as disloyalty what we esteem the maintenance of our just rights?

EGMONT. We shall know in that case how to defend ourselves. Let him assemble the Knights of the Golden Fleece; we will submit ourselves to their decision.

ORANGE. What if the sentence were to precede the trial? punishment the sentence?

EGMONT. It were an injustice of which Philip is incapable; a folly which I cannot impute either to him or to his counsellors.

ORANGE. And what if they were both unjust and foolish?

EGMONT. No, Orange, it is impossible. Who would venture to lay hands on us? The attempt to capture us were a vain and fruitless enterprise. No, they dare not raise the standard of tyranny so high. The breeze that should waft these tidings over the land would kindle a mighty conflagration. And what object would they have in view? The king alone has no power either to judge or to condemn us; and would they attempt our lives by assassination? They cannot intend it. A terrible league would unite the entire people. Direful hate and eternal separation from the crown of Spain would, on the instant, be forcibly declared.

ORANGE. The flames would then rage over our grave, and the blood of our enemies flow, a vain oblation. Let us consider, Egmont.

EGMONT. But how could they effect this purpose?

ORANGE. Alva is on the way.

EGMONT. I do not believe it.

ORANGE. I know it.

EGMONT. The Regent appeared to know nothing of it.

ORANGE. And, therefore, the stronger is my conviction. The Regent will give place to him. I know his bloodthirsty disposition, and he brings an army with him.

EGMONT. To harass the provinces anew? The people will be exasperated to the last degree.

ORANGE. Their leaders will be secured.

EGMONT. No! No!

ORANGE. Let us retire, each to his province. There we can strengthen ourselves; the duke will not begin with open violence.

EGMONT. Must we not greet him when he comes?

ORANGE. We will delay.

EGMONT. What if, on his arrival, he should summon us in the king's name?

ORANGE. We will answer evasively.

EGMONT. And if he is urgent?

ORANGE. We will excuse ourselves.

EGMONT. If he insist?

ORANGE. We shall be the less disposed to come.

EGMONT. Then war is declared; and we are rebels. Do not suffer prudence to mislead you, Orange. I know it is not fear that makes you yield. Consider this step.

ORANGE. I have considered it.

EGMONT. Consider for what you are answerable if you are wrong. For the most fatal war that ever yet desolated a country. Your refusal is the signal that at once summons the provinces to arms, that justifies every cruelty for which Spain has hitherto so anxiously sought a pretext. With a single nod you will excite to the direst confusion what, with patient effort, we have so long kept in abeyance. Think of the towns, the nobles, the people; think of commerce, agriculture, trade! Realize the murder, the desolation! Calmly the soldier beholds his comrade fall beside him in the battlefield. But towards you, carried down by the stream, will float the corpses of citizens, of children, of maidens, till, aghast with horror, you shall no longer know whose cause you are defending, since you will see those for whose liberty you drew the sword perish around you. And what will be your emotions when conscience whispers, "It was for my own safety that I drew it?"

ORANGE. We are not ordinary men, Egmont. If it becomes us to sacrifice ourselves for thousands, it becomes us no less to spare ourselves for thousands.

EGMONT. He who spares himself becomes an object of suspicion even to himself.

ORANGE. He who is sure of his own motives can with confidence advance or retreat.

EGMONT. Your own act will render certain the evil that you dread.

ORANGE. Wisdom and courage alike prompt us to meet an inevitable evil.

EGMONT. When the danger is imminent the faintest hope should be taken into account.

ORANGE. We have not the smallest footing left; we are on the very brink of the precipice.

EGMONT. Is the king's favor on ground so narrow?

ORANGE. Not narrow, perhaps, but slippery.

EGMONT. By heavens! he is belied. I cannot endure that he should be so meanly thought of! He is Charles' son, and incapable of meanness.

ORANGE. Kings of course do nothing mean.

EGMONT. He should be better known.

ORANGE. Our knowledge counsels us not to wait the result of a dangerous experiment.

EGMONT. No experiment is dangerous the result of which we have the courage to meet.

ORANGE. You are irritated, Egmont.

EGMONT. I must see with my own eyes.

ORANGE. Oh, that for once you saw with mine! My friend, because your eyes are open you imagine that you see. I go! Await Alva's arrival, and God be with you! My refusal to do so may perhaps save you. The dragon may deem the prey not worth seizing if he cannot swallow us both. Perhaps he may delay in order more surely to execute his purpose; in the meantime you may see matters in their true light. But, then, be prompt! Lose not a moment! Save, — oh, save yourself! Farewell! — Let nothing escape your vigilance : — how many troops he brings with him; how he garrisons the town; what force the Regent retains; how your friends are prepared. Send me tidings — Egmont ——

EGMONT. What would you?

ORANGE (*grasping his hand*). Be persuaded! Go with me!

EGMONT. What? Tears, Orange?

ORANGE. To weep for a lost friend is not unmanly.

EGMONT. You deem me lost?

ORANGE. You are lost! Consider! Only a brief respite is left you. Farewell. [*Exit.*

EGMONT. Strange that the thoughts of other men should exert such an influence over us. These fears would never have entered my mind; and this man infects me with his solicitude. Away! 'Tis a foreign drop in my blood! Kind nature cast it forth! And to erase the furrowed lines from my brow there yet remains, indeed, a friendly means.

ACT III.

SCENE I. *Palace of the Regent.*

MARGARET OF PARMA.

REGENT. I might have expected it. Ha! when we live immersed in anxiety and toil we imagine that we achieve the utmost that is possible; while he, who, from a distance, looks on and commands, believes that he requires only the possible. Oh, ye kings! I had not thought it could have galled me thus. It is so sweet to reign! — and to abdicate? I know not how my father could do so; but I will also.

MACHIAVEL *appears in the background.*

REGENT. Approach, Machiavel. I am pondering over my brother's letter.

MACHIAVEL. May I know what it contains?

REGENT. As much tender consideration for me as anxiety for his states. He extols the firmness, the industry, the fidelity, with which I have hitherto watched over the interests of his majesty in these provinces. He condoles with me that the unbridled people occasion me so much trouble.

He is so thoroughly convinced of the depth of my views, so extraordinarily satisfied with the prudence of my conduct, that I must almost say the letter is too politely written for a king — certainly for a brother.

MACHIAVEL. It is not the first time that he has testified to you his just satisfaction.

REGENT. But the first time that it is a mere rhetorical figure.

MACHIAVEL. I do not understand you.

REGENT. You soon will. For after this preamble he is of opinion that without soldiers, without a small army, indeed, I shall always cut a sorry figure here! We did wrong, he says, to withdraw our troops from the provinces at the remonstrance of the inhabitants; a garrison, he thinks, which shall press upon the neck of the burgher, will prevent him, by its weight, from making any lofty spring.

MACHIAVEL. It would irritate the public mind to the last degree.

REGENT. The king thinks, however, do you hear? — he thinks that a clever general, one who never listens to reason, will be able to deal promptly with all parties; — people and nobles, citizens and peasants; he therefore sends, with a powerful army, the Duke of Alva.

MACHIAVEL. Alva?

REGENT. You are surprised.

MACHIAVEL. You say he sends, he asks, doubtless, whether he should send.

REGENT. The king asks not, he sends.

MACHIAVEL. You will then have an experienced warrior in your service.

REGENT. In my service? Speak your mind, Machiavel.

MACHIVEL. I would not anticipate you.

REGENT. And I would I could dissimulate. It wounds me — wounds me to the quick. I had rather my brother would speak his mind than attach his signature to formal epistles drawn up by a secretary of state.

MACHIAVEL. Can they not comprehend?

REGENT. I know them both within and without. They would fain make a clean sweep; and since they cannot set about it themselves, they give their confidence to any one who comes with a besom in his hand. Oh, it seems to me as if I saw the king and his council worked upon this tapestry.

MACHIAVEL. So distinctly!

REGENT. No feature is wanting. There are good men among them. The honest Roderigo, so experienced and so moderate, who does not aim too high, yet lets nothing sink too low; the upright Alonzo, the diligent Freneda, the steadfast Las Vargas, and others who join them when the good party are in power. But there sits the hollow-eyed Toledan, with brazen front and deep fire-glance, muttering between his teeth about womanish softness, ill-timed concession, and that women can ride trained steeds well enough, but are themselves bad masters of the horse, and the like pleasantries, which in former times I have been compelled to hear from political gentlemen.

MACHIAVEL. You have chosen good colors for your picture.

REGENT. Confess, Machiavel, among the tints from which I might select, there is no hue so livid, so jaundice-like as Alva's complexion, and the color he is wont to paint with. He regards every one as a blasphemer or traitor; for under this head they can all be racked, impaled, quartered, and burnt at pleasure. The good I have accomplished here appears as nothing seen from a distance, just because it is good. Then he dwells on every outbreak that is past, recalls every disturbance that is quieted, and brings before the king such a picture of mutiny, sedition, and audacity, that we appear to him to be actually devouring one another, when with us the transient explosion of a rude people has been long forgotten. Thus he conceives a cordial hatred for the poor people; he views them with horror, as beasts and monsters; looks around for fire and sword, and imagines that by such means human beings are subdued.

MACHIAVEL. You appear to me too vehement; you take the matter too seriously. Do you not remain Regent?

REGENT. I am aware of that. He will bring his instructions. I am old enough in state affairs to understand how people can be supplanted without being actually deprived of office. First, he will produce a commission couched in terms somewhat obscure and equivocal; he will stretch his authority, for the power is in his hands; if I complain, he will hint at secret instructions; if I desire to see them, he will answer evasively; if I insist, he will produce a paper of totally different import; and if this fail to satisfy me, he will go on precisely as if I had never interfered. Meanwhile he will have accomplished what I dread, and will have frustrated my most cherished schemes.

MACHIAVEL. I wish I could contradict you.

REGENT. His harshness and cruelty will again arouse the turbulent spirit, which, with unspeakable patience, I have succeeded in quelling; I shall see my work destroyed before my eyes, and have besides to bear the blame of his wrong-doing.

MACHIAVEL. Await it, your highness.

REGENT. I have sufficient self-command to remain quiet. Let him come; I will make way for him with the best grace ere he pushes me aside.

MACHIAVEL. So important a step thus suddenly?

REGENT. 'Tis harder than you imagine. He who is accustomed to rule, to hold daily in his hand the destiny of thousands, descends from the throne as into the grave. Better thus, however, than linger a spectre among the living, and with hollow aspect endeavor to maintain a place which another has inherited, and already possesses and enjoys.

SCENE II. CLARA's *dwelling*

CLARA *and her* MOTHER.

MOTHER. Such a love as Brackenburg's I have never seen; I thought it was to be found only in romance books.

CLARA (*walking up and down the room, humming a song*).

> With love's thrilling rapture
> What joy can compare!

MOTHER. He suspects thy intercourse with Egmont; and yet, if thou wouldst but treat him somewhat kindly, I do believe he would marry thee still, if thou wouldst have him.

CLARA (*sings*).

> Blissful
> And tearful,
> With thought-teeming brain;
> Hoping
> And fearing
> In wavering pain;
> Now shouting in triumph,
> Now sunk in despair;—
> With love's thrilling rapture
> What joy can compare!

MOTHER. Have done with such baby nonsense!

CLARA. Nay, do not abuse it; 'tis a song of marvellous virtue. Many a time have I lulled a grown child to sleep with it.

Mother. Ay! Thou canst think of nothing but thy love. If only it did not put everything else out of thy head. Thou shouldst have more regard for Brackenburg, I tell thee. He may make thee happy yet some day.

Clara. He?

Mother. Oh, yes! A time will come! You children live only in the present, and give no ear to our experience. Youth and happy love, all has an end; and there comes a time when one thanks God if one has any corner to creep into.

Clara (*shudders, and after a pause starts up*). Mother, let that time come — like death. To think of it beforehand is horrible! And if it come! If we must — then — we will bear ourselves as we may. Live without thee, Egmont! (*Weeping.*) No! It is impossible.

Enter Egmont (*enveloped in a horseman's cloak, his hat drawn over his face*).

Egmont. Clara!

Clara (*utters a cry and starts back*). Egmont! (*She hastens towards him.*) Egmont! (*She embraces and leans upon him.*) O thou good, kind, sweet Egmont! Art thou come? Art thou here, indeed!

Egmont. Good evening, mother?

Mother. God save you, noble sir! My daughter has well-nigh pined to death because you have stayed away so long; she talks and sings about you the livelong day.

Egmont. You will give me some supper?

Mother. You do us too much honor. If we only had anything ——

Clara. Certainly! Be quiet, mother; I have provided everything; there is something prepared. Do not betray me, mother.

Mother. There's little enough.

Clara. Never mind! And then I think when he is with me I am never hungry; so he cannot, I should think, have any great appetite when I am with him.

Egmont. Do you think so? (Clara *stamps with her foot and turns pettishly away*.) What ails you?

Clara. How cold you are to-day! You have not yet offered me a kiss. Why do you keep your arms enveloped in your mantle, like a new-born babe? It becomes neither a soldier nor a lover to keep his arms muffled up.

Egmont. Sometimes, dearest, sometimes. When the soldier stands in ambush and would delude the foe, he collects his thoughts, gathers his mantle around him, and matures his plan; and a lover ——

MOTHER. Will you not take a seat and make yourself comfortable? I must to the kitchen, Clara thinks of nothing when you are here. You must put up with what we have.

EGMONT. Your good-will is the best seasoning.

[*Exit* MOTHER.

CLARA. And what then is my love?

EGMONT. Just what thou wilt.

CLARA. Liken it to anything, if you have the heart.

EGMONT. But first. (*He flings aside his mantle, and appears arrayed in a magnificent dress.*)

CLARA. Oh, heavens!

EGMONT. Now my arms are free! (*Embraces her.*)

CLARA. Don't! You will spoil your dress. (*She steps back.*) How magnificent! I dare not touch you.

EGMONT. Art thou satisfied! I promised to come once arrayed in Spanish fashion.

CLARA. I had ceased to remind you of it; I thought you did not like it — ah, and the Golden Fleece!

EGMONT. Thou seest it now.

CLARA. And did the emperor really hang it round thy neck!

EGMONT. He did, my child! And this chain and Order invest the wearer with the noblest privileges. On earth I acknowledge no judge over my actions, except the grand master of the Order, with the assembled chapter of knights.

CLARA. Oh, thou mightest let the whole world sit in judgment over thee. The velvet is too splendid! and the braiding! and the embroidery! One knows not where to begin.

EGMONT. There, look thy fill.

CLARA. And the Golden Fleece! You told me its history, and said it is the symbol of everything great and precious, of everything that can be merited and won by diligence and toil. It is very precious — I may liken it to thy love; — even so I wear it next my heart; — and then —

EGMONT. What wilt thou say?

CLARA. And then again it is not like.

EGMONT. How so?

CLARA. I have not won it by diligence and toil, I have not deserved it.

Egmont. It is otherwise in love. Thou dost deserve it because thou hast not sought it — and, for the most part, those only obtain who seek it not.

Clara. Is it from thine own experience that thou hast learned this? Didst thou make that proud remark in reference to thyself? Thou, whom all the people love?

Egmont. Would that I had done something for them! That I could do anything for them! It is their own good pleasure to love.

Clara. Thou hast doubtless been with the Regent to-day?

Egmont. I have.

Clara. Art thou upon good terms with her?

Egmont. So it would appear. We are kind and serviceable to each other.

Clara. And in thy heart?

Egmont. I like her. True, we have each our own views; but that is nothing to the purpose. She is an excellent woman, knows with whom she has to deal, and would be penetrating enough were she not quite so suspicious. I give her plenty of employment, because she is always suspecting some secret motive in my conduct when, in fact, I have none.

Clara. Really none?

Egmont. Well, with one little exception, perhaps. All wine deposits lees in the cask in the course of time. Orange furnishes her still better entertainment, and is a perpetual riddle. He has got the credit of harboring some secret design; and she studies his brow to discover his thoughts, and his steps, to learn in what direction they are bent.

Clara. Does she dissemble?

Egmont. She is Regent — and do you ask?

Clara. Pardon me; I meant to say, is she false?

Egmont. Neither more nor less than every one who has his own objects to attain.

Clara. I should never feel at home in the world. But she has a masculine spirit, and is another sort of woman than we housewives and seamstresses. She is great, steadfast, resolute.

Egmont. Yes, when matters are not too much involved. For once, however, she is a little disconcerted.

Clara. How is that?

Egmont. She has a moustache, too, on her upper lip, and occasionally an attack of the gout. A regular Amazon,

CLARA.   A majestic woman! I should dread to appear before her.

EGMONT.   Yet thou art not wont to be timid! It would not be fear, only maidenly bashfulness.

(*CLARA casts down her eyes, takes his hand, and leans upon him.*)

EGMONT.   I understand thee, dearest! Thou mayest raise thine eyes.   (*He kisses her eyes.*)

CLARA.   Let me be silent! Let me embrace thee! Let me look into thine eyes, and find there everything — hope and comfort, joy and sorrow! (*She embraces and gazes on him.*) Tell me! Oh, tell me! It seems so strange — art thou, indeed, Egmont! Count Egmont! The great Egmont, who makes so much noise in the world, who figures in the newspapers, who is the support and stay of the provinces?

EGMONT.   No, Clara, I am not he.

CLARA.   How?

EGMONT.   Seest thou, Clara! Let me sit down! (*He seats himself, she kneels on a footstool before him, rests her arms on his knees, and looks up in his face.*) That Egmont is a morose, cold, unbending Egmont, obliged to be upon his guard, to assume now this appearance and now that; harassed, misapprehended and perplexed, when the crowd esteem him light-hearted and gay; beloved by a people who do not know their own mind; honored and extolled by the intractable multitude; surrounded by friends in whom he dares not confide; observed by men who are on the watch to supplant him; toiling and striving, often without an object, generally without a reward. O let me conceal how it fares with him, let me not speak of his feelings! But this Egmont, Clara, is calm, unreserved, happy, beloved and known by the best of hearts, which is also thoroughly known to him, and which he presses to his own with unbounded confidence and love. (*He embraces her.*) This is thy Egmont.

CLARA.   So let me die! The world has no joy after this!

ACT IV.

Scene I. *A Street.*

Jetter, Carpenter.

Jetter.   Hist! neighbor,—a word!

Carpenter.   Go your way and be quiet.

Jetter.   Only one word.   Is there nothing new?

Carpenter.   Nothing, except that we are anew forbidden to speak.

Jetter.   How?

Carpenter.   Step here, close to this house.   Take heed! Immediately on his arrival, the Duke of Alva published a decree, by which two or three, found conversing together in the streets, are, without trial, declared guilty of high treason.

Jetter.   Alas!

Carpenter.   To speak of state affairs is prohibited on pain of perpetual imprisonment.

Jetter.   Alas for our liberty!

Carpenter.   And no one, on pain of death, shall censure the measures of government.

Jetter.   Alas for our heads!

Carpenter.   And fathers, mothers, children, kindred, friends, and servants are invited, by the promise of large rewards, to disclose what passes in the privacy of our homes, before an expressly appointed tribunal.

Jetter.   Let us go home.

Carpenter.   And the obedient are promised that they shall suffer no injury either in person or estate.

Jetter.   How gracious!—I felt ill at ease the moment the duke entered the town.   Since then it has seemed to me as though the heavens were covered with black crape, which hangs so low that one must stoop down to avoid knocking one's head against it.

Carpenter.   And how do you like his soldiers?   They are a different sort of crabs from those we have been used to.

Jetter.   Faugh!   It gives one the cramp at one's heart to see such a troop march down the street.   As straight as tapers, with fixed look, only one step, however many there may be; and when they stand sentinel, and you pass one of them, it seems as though he would look you through and through; and he looks so stiff and morose that you fancy you see a task-master at every corner. They offend my sight. Our militia were merry fellows; they took liberties, stood their legs astride, their hats over their ears, they lived and let live! these fellows are like machines with a devil inside them.

CARPENTER. Were such an one to cry "Halt!" and to level his musket, think you one would stand?

JETTER. I should fall dead upon the spot.

CARPENTER. Let us go home!

JETTER. No good can come of it. Farewell.

Enter SOEST.

SOEST. Friends! Neighbors!

CARPENTER. Hush! Let us go.

SOEST. Have you heard?

JETTER. Only too much!

SOEST. The Regent is gone.

JETTER. Then Heaven help us.

CARPENTER. She was some stay to us.

SOEST. Her departure was sudden and secret. She could not agree with the duke; she has sent word to the nobles that she intends to return. No one believes it, however.

CARPENTER. God pardon the nobles for letting this new yoke be laid upon our necks. They might have prevented it. Our privileges are gone.

JETTER. For Heaven's sake not a word about privileges. I already scent an execution; the sun will not come forth; the fogs are rank.

SOEST. Orange, too, is gone.

CARPENTER. Then are we quite deserted

SOEST. Count Egmont is still here.

JETTER. God be thanked! Strengthen him, all ye saints, to do his utmost; he is the only one who can help us.

Enter VANSEN.

VANSEN. Have I at length found a few, brave citizens who have not crept out of sight?

JETTER. Do us the favor to pass on.

VANSEN. You are not civil.

JETTER. This is no time for compliments. Does your back itch again? are your wounds already healed?

VANSEN. Ask a soldier about his wounds! Had I cared for blows, nothing good would have come of me.

JETTER. Matters may grow more serious.

VANSEN. You feel from the gathering storm a pitiful weakness in your limbs it seems.

CARPENTER. Your limbs will soon be in motion elsewhere if you do not keep quiet.

VANSEN. Poor mice! The master of the house procures a new cat, and ye are straight in despair! The difference is very trifling; we shall get on as we did before, only be quiet.

CARPENTER. You are an insolent knave.

VANSEN. Gossip! Let the duke alone. The old cat looks as though he had swallowed devils instead of mice, and could not now digest them. Let him alone, I say; he must eat, drink, and sleep like other men. I am not afraid if we only watch our opportunity. At first he makes quick work of it; by-and-by, however, he too will find that it is pleasanter to live in the larder, among flitches of bacon, and to rest by night, than to entrap a few solitary mice in the granary. Go to! I know the stadtholders.

CARPENTER. What such a fellow can say with impunity! Had I said such a thing I should not hold myself safe a moment.

VANSEN. Do not make yourselves uneasy! God in heaven does not trouble himself about you poor worms, much less the Regent.

JETTER. Slanderer!

VANSEN. I know some for whom it would be better if, instead of their own high spirits, they had a little tailor's blood in their veins.

CARPENTER. What means you by that?

VANSEN. Hum! I mean the count.

JETTER. Egmont! What has he to fear?

VANSEN. I'm a poor devil, and could live a whole year round on what he loses in a single night; yet he would do well to give me his revenue for a twelvemonth, to have my head upon his shoulders for one quarter of an hour.

JETTER. You think yourself very clever; yet there is more sense in the hairs of Egmont's head than in your brains.

VANSEN. Perhaps so! Not more shrewdness, however. These gentry are the most apt to deceive themselves. He should be more chary of his confidence.

JETTER. How his tongue wags! Such a gentleman!

VANSEN. Just because he is not a tailor.

JETTER. You audacious scoundrel!

VANSEN. I only wish he had your courage in his limbs for an hour to make him uneasy, and plague and torment him till he were compelled to leave the town.

JETTER. What nonsense you talk; why he's as safe as a star in heaven.

VANSEN. Have you ever seen one snuff itself out? Off it went!

CARPENTER. Who would dare to meddle with him?

VANSEN. Will you interfere to prevent it? Will you stir up an insurrection if he is arrested?

JETTER. Ah!

VANSEN. Will you risk your ribs for his sake?

SOEST. Eh!

VANSEN (*mimicking them*). Eh! Oh! Ah! Run through the alphabet in your wonderment. So it is, and so it will remain. Heaven help him!

JETTER. Confound your impudence. Can such a noble, upright man have anything to fear?

VANSEN. In this world the rogue has everywhere the advantage. At the bar, he makes a fool of the judge; on the bench, he takes pleasure in convicting the accused. I have had to copy out a protocol, where the commissary was handsomely rewarded by the court, both with praise and money, because, through his cross-examination, an honest devil, against whom they had a grudge, was made out to be a rogue.

CARPENTER. Why, that again is a downright lie. What can they want to get out of a man if he is innocent?

VANSEN. Oh, you blockhead! When nothing can be worked out of a man by cross-examination they work it into him. Honesty is rash and withal somewhat presumptuous; at first they question quietly enough, and the prisoner, proud of his innocence, as they call it, comes out with much that a sensible man would keep back; then, from these answers the inquisitor proceeds to put new questions, and is on the watch for the slightest contradictions; there he fastens his line; and, let the poor devil lose his self-possession, say too much here or too little there, or, Heaven knows from what whim or other, let him withhold some trifling circumstance, or at any moment give way to fear — then we're on the right track, and I assure you no beggar-woman seeks for rags among the rubbish with more care than such a fabricator of rogues, from trifling, crooked, disjointed, misplaced, misprinted, and concealed facts and information, acknowledged or denied, endeavors at length to patch up a scare-crow, by means of which he may at least hang his victim in effigy: and the poor devil may thank Heaven if he is in a condition to see himself hanged.

JETTER. He has a ready tongue of his own.

CARPENTER. This may serve well enough with flies. Wasps laugh at your cunning web.

VANSEN. According to the kind of spider. The tall duke, now, has just the look of your garden-spider; not the large-bellied kind — they are less dangerous; but your long-footed, meagre-bodied gentleman, that does not fatten on his diet, and whose threads are slender, indeed, but not the less tenacious.

JETTER. Egmont is knight of the Golden Fleece; who dares lay hands on him? He can be tried only by his peers, by the assembled knights of his Order. Your own foul tongue and evil conscience betray you into this nonsense.

VANSEN. Think you that I wish him ill? I like it well enough. He is an excellent gentleman. He once let off with a sound drubbing some good friends of mine who would else have been hanged. Now take yourselves off! begone, I advise you! Yonder I see the patrol again commencing their round. They do not look as if they would be willing to fraternize with us over a glass. We must wait, and bide our time. I have a couple of nieces and a tapster; if after enjoying themselves in their company, they are not tamed, they are regular wolves.

SCENE II.   *The Palace of Eulenberg, Residence of the* DUKE OF ALVA.

SILVA *and* GOMEZ (*meeting*).

SILVA. Have you executed the duke's commands?

GOMEZ. Punctually. All the day-patrols have received orders to assemble at the appointed time, at the various points that I have indicated. Meanwhile, they march as usual through the town to maintain order. Each is ignorant respecting the movements of the rest, and imagines the command to have reference to himself alone; thus in a moment the cordon can be formed, and all the avenues to the palace occupied. Know you the reason of this command?

SILVA. I am accustomed blindly to obey; and to whom

can one more easily render obedience than to the duke, since the event always proves the wisdom of his commands?

Gomez. Well! Well! I am not surprised that you are become as reserved and monosyllabic as the duke, since you are obliged to be always about his person; to me, however, who am accustomed to the lighter service of Italy, it seems strange enough. In loyalty and obedience, I am the same old sailor as ever; but I am wont to indulge in gossip and discussion; here you are all silent, and seem as though you knew not how to enjoy yourselves. The duke, methinks, is like a brazen tower without gates, the garrison of which must be furnished with wings. Not long ago I heard him say at the table of a gay, jovial fellow that he was like a bad spirit-shop, with a brandy sign displayed, to allure idlers, vagabonds, and thieves.

Silva. And has he not brought us hither in silence?

Gomez. Nothing can be said against that. Of a truth, we, who witnessed the address with which he lead the troops hither out of Italy, have seen something. How he advanced warily through friends and foes; through the French, both royalists and heretics; through the Swiss and their confederates; maintained the strictest discipline, and accomplished with ease, and without the slightest hinderance, a march that that was esteemed so perilous! — We have seen and learned something.

Silva. Here, too! Is not everything as still and quiet as though there had been no disturbance?

Gomez. Why, as for that, it was tolerably quiet when we arrived.

Silva. The provinces have become much more tranquil; if there is any movement now it is only among those who wish to escape; and to them, methinks, the duke will speedily close every outlet.

Gomez. This service cannot fail to win for him the favor of the king.

Silva. And nothing is more expedient for us than to retain his. Should the king come hither, the duke doubtless and all whom he recommends will not go without their reward.

Gomez. Do you really believe then that the king will come?

Silva. So many preparations are made that the report appears highly probable.

Gomez. I am not convinced, however.

Silva. Keep your thoughts to yourself then. For if it should not be the king's intention to come it is at least certain that he wishes the rumor to be believed.

Enter Ferdinand.

Ferdinand. Is my father not yet abroad?
Silva. We are waiting to receive his commands.
Ferdinand. The princes will soon be here.
Gomez. Are they expected to-day?
Ferdinand. Orange and Egmont.
Gomez (aside to Silva). A light breaks in upon me.
Silva. Well, then, say nothing about it.

Enter the Duke of Alva (as he advances the rest draw back).

Alva. Gomez.
Gomez (steps forward). My lord.
Alva. You have distributed the guards and given them your instructions?
Gomez. Most accurately. The day-patrols ——
Alva. Enough. Attend in the gallery. Silva will announce to you the moment when you are to draw them together, and to occupy the avenues leading to the palace. The rest you know.
Gomez. I do, my lord. [Exit.
Alva. Silva.
Silva. Here, my lord.
Alva. I shall require you to manifest to-day all the qualities I have hitherto prized in you: courage, resolve, unswerving execution.
Silva. I thank you for the opportunity of showing that your old servant is unchanged.
Alva. The moment the princes enter my cabinet hasten to arrest Egmont's private secretary. You have made all needful preparations for securing the others who are specified?
Silva. Rely upon us. Their doom, like a well-calculated eclipse, will overtake them with terrible certainty.
Alva. Have you had them all narrowly watched?
Silva. All. Egmont especially. He is the only one whose demeanor since your arrival remains unchanged. The livelong day he is now on one horse and now on another; he invites guests as usual, is merry and entertaining at table, plays at dice, shoots, and at night steals to his

mistress. The others, on the contrary, have made a manifest pause in their mode of life; they remain at home, and, from the outward aspect of their houses, you would imagine that there was a sick man within.

ALVA. To work then ere they recover in spite of us.

SILVA. I shall bring them without fail. In obedience to your commands we load them with officious honors; they are alarmed; cautiously, yet anxiously they tender their thanks, feel that flight would be the most prudent course, yet none venture to adopt it; they hesitate, are unable to work together, while the bond which unites them prevents their acting boldly as individuals. They are anxious to withdraw themselves from suspicion, and thus only render themselves more obnoxious to it. I already contemplate with joy the successful realization of your scheme.

ALVA. I rejoice only over what is accomplished, and not easily over that; for there ever remains ground for serious and anxious thought. Fortune is capricious; the common, the worthless, she oft-times ennobles, while she dishonors with a contemptible issue the most maturely-considered schemes. Await the arrival of the princes, then order Gomez to occupy the streets, and hasten yourself to arrest Egmont's secretary, and the others who are specified. This done, return, and announce to my son that he may bring me the tidings of the council.

SILVA. I trust this evening I shall dare to appear in your presence. (ALVA *approaches his son, who has hitherto been standing in the gallery.*) I dare not whisper it even to myself my mind misgives me. The event will, I fear, be different from what he anticipates. I see before me spirits who, still and thoughtful, weigh in ebon scales the doom of princes and of many thousands. Slowly the beam moves up and down; deeply the judges appear to ponder; at length one scale sinks, the other rises, breathed on by the caprice of destiny, and all is decided. [*Exit.*

ALVA (*advancing with his son*). How did you find the town?

FERDINAND. All is quiet again. I rode, as for pastime, from street to street. Your well-distributed patrols hold Fear so tightly yoked that she does not venture even to whisper. The town resembles a plain when the lightning's glare announces the impending storm: no bird, no beast is to be seen, that is not stealing to a place of shelter.

ALVA. Has nothing further occurred?

FERDINAND. Egmont, with a few companions, rode into the market-place; we exchanged greetings; he was mounted on an unbroken charger, which excited my admiration, "Let us hasten to break in our steeds," he exclaimed; "we shall need them ere long!" He said that he should see me again to-day; he is coming here at your desire to deliberate with you.

ALVA. He will see you again.

. FERDINAND. Among all the knights whom I know here he pleases me the best. I think we shall be friends.

ALVA. You are always rash and inconsiderate. I recognize in you your mother's levity, which threw her unconditionally into my arms. Appearances have already allured you precipitately into many dangerous connections.

FERDINAND. You will find me ever submissive.

ALVA. I pardon this inconsiderate kindness, this heedless gaiety, in consideration of your youthful blood. Only forget not on what mission I am sent, and what part in it I would assign to you.

FERDINAND. Admonish me, and spare me not, when you deem it needful.

ALVA (*after a pause*). My son!

FERDINAND. Father!

ALVA. The princes will be here anon; Orange and Egmont. It is not mistrust that has withheld me till now from disclosing to you what is about to take place. They will not depart hence.

FERDINAND. What do you purpose?

ALVA. It has been resolved to arrest them. You are astonished! Learn what you have to do; the reasons you shall know when all is accomplished. Time fails now to unfold them. With you alone I wish to deliberate on the weightiest, the most secret matters; a powerful bond holds us linked together; you are dear and precious to me; on you I would bestow everything. Not the habit of obedience alone would I impress upon you; I desire also to implant within your mind the power to realize, to command, to execute; to you I would bequeath a vast inheritance, to the king a most useful servant; I would endow you with the noblest of my possessions, that you may not be ashamed to appear among your brethren.

FERDINAND. How deeply I am indebted to you for this love, which you manifest for me alone, while a whole kingdom stands in fear of you!

ALVA. Now hear what is to be done. As soon as the princes have entered every avenue to the palace will be guarded. This duty is confided to Gomez. Silva will hasten to arrest Egmont's secretary, together with those whom we hold most in suspicion. You, meanwhile, will take the command of the guards stationed at the gates and in the courts. Above all, take care to occupy the adjoining apartment with the trustiest soldiers. Wait in the gallery till Silva returns, then bring me any unimportant paper, as a signal that his commission is executed. Remain in the antechamber till Orange retires; follow him; I will detain Egmont here as though I had some further communication to make to him. At the end of the gallery demand Orange's sword, summon the guards, secure promptly the most dangerous man; I meanwhile will seize Egmont here.

FERDINAND. I obey, my father — for the first time with a heavy and an anxious heart.

ALVA. I pardon you; this is the first great day of your life.

Enter SILVA.

SILVA. A courier from Antwerp. Here is Orange's letter. He is not coming.

ALVA. Says the messenger so?

SILVA. No, my own heart tells me.

ALVA. In thee speaks my evil genius. (*After reading the letter he makes a sign to the two, and they retire to the gallery.* ALVA *remains alone in front of the stage.*) He comes not! Till the last moment he delays declaring himself. He dares not to come! So, then, the cautious man, contrary to all expectation, is for once cautious enough to lay aside his wonted caution. The hour moves on. Let the hand travel but a short space over the dial, and a great work is done or lost — irrevocably lost; for the opportunity can never be retrieved, nor can our intention remain concealed. Long had I maturely weighed everything, foreseen even this contingency, and firmly resolved in my own mind what in that case was to be done; and now, when I am called upon to act, I can with difficulty guard my mind from being again distracted by conflicting doubts. Is it expedient to seize the others if he escape me? Shall I delay, and suffer Egmont to elude my grasp, together with his friends, and so many others who now, and perhaps for to-day only, are in my hands? Thus destiny controls even thee — the uncontrollable! How long matured! How well prepared!

How great, how admirable the plan!　How nearly had hope attained the goal!　And now, at the decisive moment, thou art placed between two evils; as into a lottery thou dost grasp into the dark future; what thou hast drawn remains still unrolled, to thee unknown whether it is a prize or a blank!　(*He becomes attentive, like one who hears a noise, and steps to the window.*)　'Tis he!　Egmont!　Did thy steed bear thee hither so lightly, and started not at the scent of blood, at the spirit with the naked sword who received thee at the gate?　Dismount!　Lo, now thou hast one foot in the grave!　And now both!　Aÿe, caress him, and for the last time stroke his neck for the gallant service he has rendered thee.　And for me no choice is left.　The delusion in which Egmont ventures here to-day cannot a second time deliver him into my hands!　Hark!　(FERDINAND *and* SILVA *enter hastily.*)　Obey my orders.　I swerve not from my purpose.　I shall detain Egmont here as best I may till you bring me tidings from Silva.　Then remain at hand.　Thee, too, fate has robbed of the proud honor of arresting with thine own hand the king's greatest enemy. (*To* SILVA.)　Be prompt!　(*To* FERDINAND.)　Advance to meet him.　(ALVA *remains some moments alone, pacing the chamber in silence.*)

Enter EGMONT.

EGMONT.　I come to learn the king's commands; to hear what service he demands from our loyalty, which remains eternally devoted to him.

ALVA.　He desires above all to hear your counsel.

EGMONT.　Upon what subject?　Does Orange come also? I thought I should find him here.

ALVA.　I regret that he fails us at this important crisis. The king desires your counsel, your opinion as to the best means of tranquillizing these states.　He trusts, indeed, that you will zealously co-operate with him in quelling these disturbances, and in securing to these provinces the benefit of complete and permanent order.

EGMONT.　You, my lord, should know better than I that tranquillity is already sufficiently restored, and was still more so till the appearance of fresh troops again agitated the public mind, and filled it anew with anxiety and alarm.

ALVA.　You seem to intimate that it would have been more advisable if the king had not placed me in a position to interrogate you.

EGMONT. Pardon me! It is not for me to determine whether the king acted advisedly in sending the army hither, whether the might of his royal presence alone would not have operated more powerfully. The army is here, the king is not. But we should be most ungrateful were we to forget what we owe to the Regent. Let it be acknowledged! By her prudence and valor, by her judicious use of authority and force, of persuasion and finesse, she pacified the insurgents, and, to the astonishment of the world, succeeded, in the course of a few months, in bringing a rebellious people back to their duty.

ALVA. I deny it not. The insurrection is quelled; and the people appear to be already forced back within the bounds of obedience. But does it not depend upon their caprice alone to overstep these bounds? Who shall prevent them from again breaking loose? Where is the power capable of restraining them? Who will be answerable to us for their future loyalty and submission? Their own goodwill is the sole pledge we have.

EGMONT. And is not the good-will of a people the surest, the noblest pledge? By heaven! when can a monarch hold himself more secure, ay, against both foreign and domestic foes, than when all can stand for one, and one for all?

ALVA. You would not have us believe, however, that such is the case here at present?

EGMONT. Let the king proclaim a general pardon; he will thus tranquillize the public mind; and it will be seen how speedily loyalty and affection will return when confidence is restored.

ALVA. How! And suffer those who have insulted the majesty of the king, who have violated the sanctuaries of our religion, to go abroad unchallenged! living witnesses that enormous crimes may be perpetrated with impunity!

EGMONT. And ought not a crime of frenzy, of intoxication, to be excused rather than cruelly chastised? Especially when there is the sure hope, nay, more, where there is positive certainty, that the evil will never again recur? Would not sovereigns thus be more secure? Are not those monarchs most extolled by the world and by posterity who can pardon, pity, despise an offence against their dignity? Are they not on that account likened to God himself, who is far too exalted to be assailed by every idle blasphemy?

ALVA. And, therefore, should the king contend for the honor of God and of religion, we for the authority of the king. What the supreme power disdains to avert, it is our duty to avenge. Were I to counsel, no guilty person should live to rejoice in his impunity.

EGMONT. Think you that you will be able to reach them all? Do we not daily hear that fear is driving them to and fro, and forcing them out of the land? The more wealthy will escape to other countries with their property, their children, and their friends; while the poor will carry their industrious hands to our neighbors.

ALVA. They will, if they cannot be prevented. It is on this account that the king desires counsel and aid from every prince, zealous co-operation from every stadtholder; not merely a description of the present posture of affairs, or conjectures as to what might take place were events suffered to hold on their course without interruption. To contemplate a mighty evil, to flatter oneself with hope, to trust to time, to strike a blow, like the clown in a play, so as to make a noise and appear to do something, when in fact one would fain do nothing; is not such conduct calculated to awaken a suspicion that those who act thus contemplate with satisfaction a rebellion, which they would not indeed excite, but which they are by no means unwilling to encourage?

EGMONT (*about to break forth, restrains himself, and after a brief pause, speaks with composure*). Not every design is obvious, and many a man's design is misconstrued. It is widely rumored, however, that the object which the king has in view is not so much to govern the provinces according to uniform and clearly-defined laws, to maintain the majesty of religion, and to give his people universal peace, as unconditionally to subjugate them, to rob them of their ancient rights, to appropriate their possessions, to curtail the fair privileges of the nobles, for whose sake alone they are ready to serve him with life and limb. Religion, it is said, is merely a splendid device, behind which every dangerous design may be contrived with the greater ease; the prostrate crowds adore the sacred symbols pictured there, while behind lurks the fowler ready to ensnare them.

ALVA. This I must hear from you?

EGMONT. I speak not my own sentiments! I but repeat what is loudly rumored, and uttered now here and now there by great and by humble, by wise men and fools. The Netherlanders fear a double yoke, and who will be surety to them for their liberty?

ALVA. Liberty! A fair word when rightly understood. What liberty would they have? What is the freedom of the most free? To do right! And in that the monarch will not hinder them. No! No! They imagine themselves enslaved when they have not the power to injure themselves and others. Would it not be better to abdicate at once rather than rule such a people? When the country is threatened by foreign invaders, the burghers, occupied only with their immediate interests, bestow no thought upon the advancing foe, and when the king requires their aid, they quarrel among themselves, and thus, as it were, conspire with the enemy. Far better is it to circumscribe their power, to control and guide them for their good, as children are controlled and guided. Trust me, a people grows neither old nor wise, a people remains always in its infancy.

EGMONT. How rarely does a king attain wisdom! And is it not fit that the many should confide their interests to the many rather than to the one? And not even to the one, but to the few servants of the one, men who have grown old under the eyes of their master. To grow wise, it seems, is the exclusive privilege of these favored individuals.

ALVA. Perhaps for the very reason that they are not left to themselves.

EGMONT. And therefore they would fain leave no one else to his own guidance. Let them do what they like, however; I have replied to your questions, and I repeat, the measures you propose will never succeed! They cannot succeed! I know my countrymen. They are men worthy to tread God's earth; each complete in himself, a little king, steadfast, active, capable, loyal, attached to ancient customs. It may be difficult to win their confidence, but it is easy to retain it. Firm and unbending! They may be crushed but not subdued.

ALVA (*who during this speech has looked round several times*). Would you venture to repeat what you have uttered in the king's presence?

EGMONT. It were the worse, if in his presence I were restrained by fear! The better for him and for his people if he inspired me with confidence, if he encouraged me to give yet freer utterance to my thoughts.

ALVA. What is profitable I can listen to as well as he.

EGMONT. I would say to him — 'Tis easy for the shepherd to drive before him a flock of sheep; the ox draws the plough without opposition; but if you would ride the noble steed, you must study his thoughts, you must require nothing unreasonable, nor unreasonably, from him. The burgher desires to retain his ancient constitution; to be governed by his own countrymen; and why? Because he knows in that case how he shall be ruled, because he can rely upon their disinterestedness, upon their sympathy with his fate.

ALVA. And ought not the Regent to be empowered to alter these ancient usages? Should not this constitute his fairest privilege? What is permanent in this world? And shall the constitution of a state alone remain unchanged? Must not every relation alter in the course of time, and, on that very account, an ancient constitution become the source of a thousand evils, because not adapted to the present condition of the people? These ancient rights afford, doubtless, convenient loopholes, through which the crafty and the powerful may creep, and wherein they may lie concealed to the injury of the people and of the entire community; and it is on this account, I fear, that they are held in such high esteem.

EGMONT. And these arbitrary changes, these unlimited encroachments of the supreme power, are they not indications that one will permit himself to do what is forbidden to thousands? The monarch would alone be free, that he may have it in his power to gratify his every wish, to realize his every thought. And though we should confide in him as a good and virtuous sovereign, will he be answerable to us for his successors? That none who come after him shall rule without consideration, without forbearance! And who would deliver us from absolute caprice, should he send hither his servants, his minions, who, without knowledge of the country and its requirements, should govern according to their own good pleasure, meet with no opposition, and know themselves exempt from all responsibility?

ALVA (*who has meanwhile again looked round*). There is nothing more natural than that a king should choose to retain the power in his own hands, and that he should select as the instruments of his authority those who best understand him, who desire to understand him, and who will unconditionally execute his will.

EGMONT. And just as natural is it that the burgher should prefer being governed by one born and reared in the same land, whose notions of right and wrong are in harmony with his own, and whom he can regard as his brother.

ALVA. And yet the noble, methinks, has shared rather unequally with these brethren of his.

EGMONT. That took place centuries ago, and is now submitted to without envy. But should new men, whose presence is not needed in the country, be sent to enrich themselves a second time at the cost of the nation; should the people see themselves exposed to their bold, unscrupulous rapacity, it would excite a ferment that would not soon be quelled.

ALVA. You utter words to which I ought not to listen; — I, too, am a foreigner.

EGMONT. That they are spoken in your presence is a sufficient proof that they have no reference to you.

ALVA. Be that as it may, I would rather not hear them from you. The king sent me here in the hope that I should obtain the support of the nobles. The king wills, and will have his will obeyed. After profound deliberation, the king at length discerns what course will best promote the welfare of the people; matters cannot be permitted to go on as heretofore; it is the king's intention to limit their power for their own good; if necessary, to force upon them their salvation: to sacrifice the more dangerous burghers in order that the rest may find repose, and enjoy in peace the blessing of a wise government. This is his resolve; this I am commissioned to announce to the nobles; and in his name I require from them advice, not as to the course to be pursued — on that he is resolved — but as to the best means of carrying his purpose into effect.

EGMONT. Your words, alas, justify the fears of the people, the universal fear! The king then has resolved as no sovereign ought to resolve. In order to govern his subjects more easily, he would crush, subvert, nay, ruthlessly destroy, their strength, their spirit, and their self-respect! He would violate the inmost core of their individuality, doubtless with the view of promoting their happiness. He would annihilate them, that they may assume a new, a different form. Oh! if his purpose be good, he is fatally misguided! It is not the king whom we resist; — we but place ourselves in the way of the monarch, who, unhappily, is about to take the first rash step in a wrong direction.

ALVA. Such being your sentiments, it were a vain attempt for us to endeavor to agree. You must, indeed, think poorly of the king, and contemptibly of his counsellors, if you imagine that everything has not already been thought of and maturley weighed. I have no commission a second time to balance conflicting arguments. From these people I demand submission;—and from you, their leaders and princes, I demand counsel and support as pledges of this unconditional duty.

EGMONT. Demand our heads, and your object is attained; to a noble soul it must be indifferent whether he stoop his neck to such a yoke or lay it upon the block. I have spoken much to little purpose. I have agitated the air, but accomplished nothing.

Enter FERDINAND.

FERDINAND. Pardon my intrusion. Here is a letter, the bearer of which urgently demands an answer.

ALVA. Allow me to peruse its contents. (*Steps aside*).

FERDINAND (*to* EGMONT). 'Tis a noble steed that your people have brought to carry you away.

EGMONT. I have seen worse. I have had him some time; I think of parting with him. If he pleases you we shall probably soon agree as to the price.

FERDINAND. We will think about it.

(ALVA *motions to his son, who retires to the background.,*

EGMONT. Farewell! Allow me to retire; for, by heaven, I know not what more I can say.

ALVA. Fortunately for you, chance prevents you from making a fuller disclosure of your sentiments. You incautiously lay bare the recesses of your heart, and your own lips furnish evidence against you more fatal than could be produced by your bitterest adversary.

EGMONT. This reproach disturbs me not. I know my own heart; I know with what honest zeal I am devoted to the king; I know that my allegiance is more true than that of many who, in his service, seek only to serve themselves. I regret that our discussion should terminate so unsatisfactorily, and trust that, in spite of our opposing views, the service of the king, our master, and the welfare of our country, may speedily unite us; another conference, the presence of the princes who to-day are absent, may, perchance, in a more propitious moment, accomplish what at present appears impossible. In this hope I take my leave.

ALVA (*who at the same time makes a sign to* FERDINAND). Hold, Egmont!—Your sword!—(*The centre door opens and discloses the gallery, which is occupied with guards, who remain motionless.*)

EGMONT (*after a pause of astonishment*). This was the intention? For this thou hast summoned me? (*Grasping his sword as if to defend himself.*) Am I then weaponless?

ALVA. The king commands. Thou art my prisoner. (*At the same time guards enter from both sides.*)

EGMONT (*after a pause*). The king?—Orange! Orange! (*After a pause, resigning his sword.*) Take it! It has been employed far oftener in defending the cause of my king than in protecting this breast. (*He retires by the centre door, followed by the guard and* ALVA'S *son.* ALVA *remains standing while the curtain falls.*)

ACT V.

SCENE I. *A Street. Twilight.*

CLARA, BRACKENBURG, BURGHERS.

BRACKENBURG. Dearest, for heaven's sake, what wouldst thou do?

CLARA. Come with me, Brackenburg! Thou canst not know the people, we are certain to rescue him; for what can equal their love for him? Each feels, I could swear it, the burning desire to deliver him, to avert danger from a life so precious, and to restore freedom to the most free. Come! A voice only is wanting to call them together. In their souls the memory is still fresh of all they owe him, and well they know that his mighty arm alone shields them from destruction. For his sake, for their own sake, they must peril everything. And what do we peril? At most our lives, which, if he perish, are not worth preserving.

BRACKENBURG. Unhappy girl! Thou seest not the power that holds us fettered as with bands of iron.

CLARA. To me it does not appear invincible. Let us not lose time in idle words. Here comes some of our old, honest, valiant burghers! Hark ye, friends! Neighbors! Hark!—Say, how fares it with Egmont?

CARPENTER. What does the girl want? Tell her to hold her peace.

CLARA. Step nearer, that we may speak low, till we are united and more strong. Not a moment is to be lost!

Audacious tyranny, that dared to fetter him, already lifts the dagger against his life. Oh, my friends! With the advancing twilight my anxiety grows more intense. I dread this night. Come! Let us disperse; let us hasten from quarter to quarter, and call out the burghers. Let every one grasp his ancient weapons. In the market-place we meet again, and every one will be carried onward by our gathering stream. The enemy will see themselves surrounded, overwhelmed, and be compelled to yield. How can a handful of slaves resist us? And he will return among us, he will see himself rescued, and can for once thank us, us, who are already so deeply in his debt. He will behold, perchance, ay, doubtless, he will again behold the morn's red dawn in the free heavens.

CARPENTER. What ails thee, maiden?

CLARA. Can ye misunderstand me? I speak of the Count! I speak of Egmont.

JETTER. Speak not the name! 'tis deadly.

CLARA. Not speak his name? How? Not Egmont's name? Is it not on every tongue? Where stands it not inscribed? Often have I read it emblazoned with all its letters among these stars. Not utter it? What mean ye? Friends! good, kind neighbors, ye are dreaming; collect yourselves. Gaze not upon me with those fixed and anxious looks! Cast not such timid glances on every side! I but give utterance to the wish of all. Is not my voice the voice of your own hearts? Who, in this fearful night, ere he seeks his restless couch, but on bended knee will, in earnest prayer, seek to wrest his life as a cherished boon from heaven? Ask each other! Let each ask his own heart! And who but exclaims with me,—"Egmont's liberty, or death!"

JETTER. God help us! This is a sad business.

CLARA. Stay! Stay! Shrink not away at the sound of his name, to meet whom ye were wont to press forward so joyously!—When rumor announced his approach, when the cry arose, "Egmont comes! He comes from Ghent!"—then happy, indeed, were those citizens who dwelt in the streets through which he was to pass. And when the neighing of his steed was heard, did not every one throw aside his work, while a ray of hope and joy, like a sunbeam from his countenance, stole over the toil-worn faces that peered from every window. Then, as ye stood in the doorways, ye would lift up your children in your arms, and, pointing to him, exclaim: "See, that is Egmont, he who towers above the rest? 'Tis from him that ye must look for better times than those your poor fathers have known." Let not your children inquire at some future day, "Where is he? Where are the better times ye promised us?"— Thus we waste the time in idle words! do nothing,—betray him.

SOEST. Shame on thee, Brackenburg! Let her not run on thus! Prevent the mischief!

BRACKENBURG. Dear Clara! Let us go! What will your mother say? Perchance ——

CLARA. Thinkest thou I am a child, or frantic? What avails perchance?—With no vain hope canst thou hide from me this dreadful certainty . . . Ye shall hear me and ye will: for I see it, ye are overwhelmed, ye cannot hearken to the voice of your own hearts. Through the present peril cast but one glance into the past,—the recent past. Send your thoughts forward into the future. Could ye live, would ye live, were he to perish? With him expires the last breath of freedom. What was he not to you? For whose sake did he expose himself to the direst perils? His blood flowed, his wounds were healed for you alone. The mighty spirit that upheld you all a dungeon now confines, while the horrors of secret murder are hovering around. Perhaps he thinks of you—perhaps he hopes in you,—he who has been accustomed only to grant favors to others and to fulfil their prayers.

CARPENTER. Come, gossip.

CLARA. I have neither the arms nor the vigor of a man; but I have that which ye all lack—courage and contempt of danger. Oh, that my breath could kindle your souls! That, pressing you to this bosom, I could arouse and animate you! Come! I will march in your midst!—As a waving banner, though weaponless, leads on a gallant army of warriors, so shall my spirit hover, like a flame, over your ranks, while love and courage shall unite the dispersed and wavering multitude into a terrible host.

JETTER. Take her away; I pity her, poor thing!

[*Exeunt* BURGHERS.

BRACKENBURG. Clara! Seest thou not where we are?

CLARA. Where! Under the dome of heaven, which has so often seemed to arch itself more gloriously as the noble Egmont passed beneath it. From these windows I have seen them look forth, four or five heads one above the

other; at these doors the cowards have stood, bowing and
scraping, if he but chanced to look down upon them! Oh,
how dear they were to me when they honored him. Had
he been a tyrant they might have turned with indifference
from his fall! But they loved him! Oh, ye hands so
prompt to wave caps in his honor, can ye not grasp a
sword? Brackenburg, and we? — do we chide them?
These arms that have so often embraced him, what do they
for him now? Stratagem has accomplished so much in the
world. Thou knowest the ancient castle, every passage,
every secret way. Nothing is impossible, — suggest some
plan ——

BRACKENBURG. That we might go home!

CLARA. Well.

BRACKENBURG. There, at the corner, I see Alva's guard;
let the voice of reason penetrate to thy heart! Dost thou
deem me a coward? Dost thou doubt that for thy sake
I would peril my life? Here we are both mad, I as well as
thou. Dost thou not perceive that thy scheme is imprac-
ticable? Oh, be calm! Thou art beside thyself.

CLARA. Beside myself! Horrible. You, Brackenburg,
are beside yourself. When you hailed the hero with loud
acclaim, called him your friend, your hope, your refuge,
shouted vivats as he passed; — then I stood in my corner,
half-opened the window, concealed myself while I listened,
and my heart beat higher than yours who greeted him so
loudly. Now it again beats higher! In the hour of peril
you conceal yourselves, deny him, and feel not, that if he
perish, you are lost.

BRACKENBURG. Come home.

CLARA. Home?

BRACKENBURG. Recollect thyself! Look around thee!
These are the streets in which thou wert wont to appear
only on the Sabbath-day, when thou didst walk modestly to
church; where, over-decorous perhaps, thou wert displeased
if I but joined thee with a kindly greeting. And now thou
dost stand, speak, and act before the eyes of the whole
world. Recollect thyself, love! How can this avail us?

CLARA. Home! Yes, I remember. Come, Brackenburg, let us go home! Knowest thou where my home lies?

[Exeunt.

Scene II. *A Prison.*

Lighted by a lamp, a couch in the back-ground.

Egmont (*alone*). Old friend! Ever faithful sleep, dost thou, too, forsake me like my other friends? How thou wert wont of yore to descend unsought upon my free brow, cooling my temples as with a myrtle wreath of love! Amidst the din of battle, on the waves of life, I rested in thine arms, breathing lightly as a growing boy. When tempests whistled through the leaves and boughs, when the summits of the lofty trees swung creaking in the blast, the inmost core of my heart remained unmoved. What agitates thee now? What shakes thy firm and steadfast mind? I feel it; 'tis the sound of the murderous axe gnawing at thy root. Yet I stand erect, but an inward shudder runs through my frame. Yes, it prevails, this treacherous power; it undermines the firm, the lofty stem, and ere the bark withers thy verdant crown falls crashing to the earth.

Yet wherefore now, thou who hast so often chased the weightiest cares like bubbles from thy brow, wherefore canst thou not dissipate this dire foreboding which incessantly haunts thee in a thousand different shapes? Since when hast thou trembled at the approach of death, amid whose varying forms thou wert wont calmly to dwell, as with the other shapes of this familiar earth? But 'tis not he, the sudden foe, to encounter whom the sound bosom emulously pants; — 'tis the dungeon, emblem of the grave, revolting alike to the hero and the coward. How intolerable I used to feel it, in the stately hall, girt round by gloomy walls, when, seated on my cushioned chair in the solemn assembly of the princes, questions which scarcely required deliberation were overlaid with endless discussions, while the rafters of the ceiling seemed to stifle and oppress me. Then I would hurry forth as soon as possible, fling myself upon my horse with deep-drawn breath, and away to the wide champaign, man's natural element, where, exhaling from the earth, nature's richest treasures are poured forth around us, while, from the wide heavens, the stars shed down their blessings through the still air; where, like earth-born giants, we spring aloft, invigorated by our mother's touch; where our entire humanity and our human desires throb in every vein; where the desire to press forward, to vanquish, to snatch, to use his clenched fist, to possess, to conquer, glows through the soul of the young hunter; where the warrior, with rapid stride, assumes his inborn right to dominion over the world, and, with terrible liberty, sweeps like a desolating hail-storm over field and grove, knowing no boundaries traced by the hand of man.

Thou art but a shadow, a dream of the happiness I so long possessed; where has treacherous fate conducted thee? Did she deny thee to meet the rapid stroke of never-shunned death in the open face of day only to prepare for thee a foretaste of the grave, in the midst of this loathsome corruption? How revoltingly its rank odor exhales from these damp stones! Life stagnates, and my foot shrinks from the couch as from the grave.

O care, care! Thou who dost begin prematurely the work of murder, forbear;—since when has Egmont been alone, so utterly alone in the world? 'Tis doubt renders thee insensible, not happiness. The justice of the king, in which through life thou hast confided, the friendship of the regent, which, thou may'st confess it, was akin to love,—have these suddenly vanished, like a meteor of the night, and left thee alone upon thy gloomy path? Will not Orange, at the head of thy friends, contrive some daring scheme? Will not the people assemble, and with gathering might attempt the rescue of their faithful friend?

Ye walls, which thus gird me round, separate me not from the well-intentioned zeal of so many kindly souls. And may the courage with which my glance was wont to inspire them now return again from their hearts to mine. Yes! they assemble in thousands! they come! they stand beside me! their pious wish rises urgently to heaven, and implores a miracle; and if no angel stoops for my deliverance, I see them grasp eagerly their lance and sword. The gates are forced, the bolts are riven, the walls fall beneath their conquering hands, and Egmont advances, joyously, to hail the freedom of the rising morn. How many well-known faces receive me with loud acclaim! O Clara! wert thou a man I should see thee here the very first, and thank thee for that which it is galling to owe even to a king — liberty.

Scene III. *Clara's House.*

Clara (*enters from her chamber with a lamp and a glass of water; she places the glass upon the table and steps to the window*). Brackenburg, is it you? What noise was that?

No one yet? No one! I will set the lamp in the window, that he may see that I am still awake, that I still watch for him. He promised me tidings. Tidings? horrible certainty! — Egmont condemned! — what tribunal has the right to summon him? — And they dare to condemn him! — Does the king condemn him, or the duke? And the regent withdraws herself! Orange hesitates, and all his friends? — Is this the world, of whose fickleness and treachery I have heard so much, and as yet experienced nothing? Is this the world? — Who could be so base as to bear malice against one so dear? Could villainy itself be audacious enough to overwhelm with sudden destruction the object of a nation's homage? Yet so it is — it is — O Egmont, I held thee safe before God and man, safe as in my arms! What was I to thee? Thou hast called me thine, my whole being was devoted to thee. What am I now? In vain I stretch out my hand to the toils that environ thee. Thou helpless and I free! — Here is the key that unlocks my chamber door. My going out and my coming in depend upon my own caprice; yet, alas, to aid thee I am powerless! — Oh, bind me that I may not despair; hurl me into the deepest dungeon, that I may dash my head against the damp walls, groan for freedom, and dream how I would rescue him if fetters did not hold me bound. — Now I am free, and in freedom lies the anguish of impotence. — Conscious of my own existence, yet unable to stir a limb in his behalf, alas! even this insignificant portion of thy being, thy Clara, is, like thee, a captive, and, separated from thee, consumes her expiring energies in the agonies of death. — I hear a stealthy step, — a cough — Brackenburg, — 'tis he! — Kind, unhappy man, thy destiny remains ever the same; thy love opens to thee the door at night, alas! to what a doleful meeting. (*Enter* BRACKENBURG.) Thou comest so pale, so terrified! Brackenburg! What is it?

BRACKENBURG. I have sought thee through perils and circuitous paths. The principal streets are occupied with troops; — through lanes and by-ways have I stolen to thee!

CLARA. Tell me, how is it?

BRACKENBURG (*seating himself*). O Clara, let me weep. I loved him not. He was the rich man who lured to better pasture the poor man's solitary lamb. I have never cursed him, God has created me with a true and tender heart. My life was consumed in anguish, and each day I hoped would end my misery.

CLARA. Let that be forgotten, Brackenburg! Forget thyself. Speak to me of him! Is it true? Is he condemned?

BRACKENBURG. He is! I know it.

CLARA. And still lives?

BRACKENBURG. Yes, he still lives.

CLARA. How canst thou be sure of that? Tyranny murders the hero in the night! His blood flows concealed from every eye. The people, stunned and bewildered, lie buried in sleep, dream of deliverance, dream of the fulfilment of their impotent wishes, while, indignant at our supineness, his spirit abandons the world. He is no more! Deceive me not; deceive not thyself!

BRACKENBURG. No, — he lives! and the Spaniards, alas, are preparing for the people, on whom they are about to trample, a terrible spectacle, in order to crush forever, by a violent blow, each heart that yet pants for freedom.

CLARA. Proceed! Calmly pronounce my death-warrant also! Near and more near I approach that blessed land, and already from those realms of peace I feel the breath of consolation. Say on.

BRACKENBURG. From casual words, dropped here and there by the guards, I learned that secretly in the market-place they were preparing some terrible spectacle. Through by-ways and familiar lanes I stole to my cousin's house, and from a back window looked out upon the market-place. Torches waved to and fro, in the hands of a wide circle of Spanish soldiers. I sharpened my unaccustomed sight, and out of the darkness there arose before me a scaffold, black, spacious and lofty! The sight filled me with horror. Several persons were employed in covering with black cloth such portions of the woodwork as yet remained white and visible. The steps were covered last, also with black; — I saw it all. They seemed preparing for the celebration of some horrible sacrifice. A white crucifix, that shone like silver through the night, was raised on one side. As I gazed, the terrible conviction strengthened in my mind. Scattered torches still gleamed here and there; gradually they flickered and went out. Suddenly the hideous birth of night returned into its mother's womb.

CLARA. Hush, Brackenburg! Be still! Let this veil rest upon my soul. The spectres are vanished; and thou, gentle night, lend thy mantle to the inwardly fermenting earth, she will no longer endure the loathsome burden, shuddering, she rends open her yawning chasms, and with a crash swallows the murderous scaffold. And that God, whom in their rage they have insulted, sends down His angel from on high; at the hallowed touch of the messenger bolts and bars fly back; he pours around our friend a mild radiance, and leads him gently through the night to liberty. My path leads also through the darkness to meet him.

BRACKENBURG (*detaining her*). My child, whither wouldst thou go? What wouldst thou do?

CLARA. Softly, my friend, lest some one should awake! Lest we should awake ourselves! Knowest thou this phial, Brackenburg? I took it from thee once in jest, when thou, as was thy wont, didst threaten, in thy impatience, to end thy days. And now my friend ——

BRACKENBURG. In the name of all the saints!

CLARA. Thou canst not hinder me. Death is my portion! Grudge me not the quiet and easy death which thou hadst prepared for thyself. Give me thine hand! At the moment when I unclose that dismal portal through which there is no return, I may tell thee, with this pressure of the hand, how sincerely I have loved, how deeply I have pitied thee. My brother died young; I chose thee to fill his place; thy heart rebelled, thou didst torment thyself and me, demanding, with ever-increasing fervor, that which fate had not destined for thee. Forgive me and farewell! Let me call thee brother. 'Tis a name that embraces many names. Receive, with a true heart, the last fair token of the departing spirit — take this kiss. Death unites all, Brackenburg — us too it will unite!

BRACKENBURG. Let me then die with thee! Share it! oh, share it! There is enough to extinguish two lives!

CLARA. Hold! Thou must live, thou canst live. Support my mother, who, without thee, would be a prey to want. Be to her what I can no longer be, live together, and weep for me. Weep for our country, and for him who could alone have upheld it. The present generation must still endure this bitter woe; vengeance itself could not obliterate it. Poor souls, live on, through this gap in time, which is time no longer. To-day the world suddenly stands still, its course is arrested, and my pulse will beat but for a few minutes longer. Farewell.

BRACKENBURG. Oh, live with us, as we live only for thy sake! In taking thine own life thou wilt take ours also;

still live and suffer. We will stand by thee; nothing shall sever us from thy side, and love, with ever-watchful solicitude, shall prepare for thee the sweetest consolation in its loving arms. Be ours! Ours! I dare not say, mine.

CLARA. Hush, Brackenburg! Thou feelest not what chord thou touchest. Where hope appears to thee I see only despair.

BRACKENBURG. Share hope with the living! Pause on the brink of the precipice, cast one glance into the gulf below, and then look back on us.

CLARA. I have conquered; call me not back to the struggle.

BRACKENBURG. Thou art stunned; enveloped in night, thou seekest the abyss. Every light is not yet extinguished, yet many days! ——

CLARA. Alas! Alas! Cruelly thou dost rend the veil from before mine eyes. Yes, the day will dawn! Despite its misty shroud it needs must dawn. Timidly the burgher gazes from his window, night leaves behind an ebon speck; he looks, and the scaffold looms fearfully in the morning light. With re-awakened anguish the desecrated image of the Saviour lifts to the Father its imploring eyes. The sun veils his beams, he will not mark the hero's death-hour. Slowly the fingers go their round — one hour strikes after another — hold! Now is the time. The thought of the morning scares me into the grave. (*She goes to the window as if to look out, and drinks secretly.*)

BRACKENBURG. Clara! Clara!

CLARA (*goes to the table and drinks water*). Here is the remainder. I invite thee not to follow me. Do as thou wilt: farewell. Extinguish this lamp silently and without delay; I am going to rest. Steal quietly away, close the door after thee. Be still! Wake not my mother! Go, save thyself, if thou wouldst not be taken for my murderer.

[*Exit.*

BRACKENBURG. She leaves me for the last time as she has ever done. What human soul could conceive how cruelly she lacerates the heart that loves her. She leaves me to myself, leaves me to choose between life and death, and both are alike hateful to me. To die alone! Weep, ye tender souls! Fate has no sadder doom than mine. She shares with me the death-potion, yet sends me from her side! She draws me after her, yet thrusts me back into life! Oh, Egmont, how enviable a lot falls to thee! She goes before thee! The crown of victory from her hand is thine, she brings all heaven to meet thee!—And shall I follow? Again to stand aloof? To carry the inextinguishable jealousy even to yon distant realms? Earth is no longer a tarrying place for me, and hell and heaven both offer equal torture. Now welcome to the wretched the dread hand of annihilation! [*Exit.*

(*The scene remains some time unchanged. Music sounds, indicating* CLARA's *death; the lamp, which* BRACKENBURG *had forgotten to extinguish, flares up once or twice, and then suddenly expires. The scene changes to*

SCENE IV. *A Prison.*

EGMONT *is discovered sleeping on a couch. A rustling of keys is heard; the door opens; servants enter with torches;* FERDINAND *and* SILVA *follow, accompanied by soldiers;* EGMONT *starts from his sleep.*

EGMONT. Who are ye that thus rudely banish slumber from my eyes? What mean these vague and insolent glances? Why this fearful procession? With what dream of horror come ye to delude my half awakened soul?

SILVA. The duke sends us to announce your sentence.

EGMONT. Do you also bring the headsman who is to execute it?

SILVA. Listen, and you will know the doom that awaits you.

EGMONT. It is in keeping with the rest of your infamous proceedings. Hatched in night and in night achieved, so would this audacious act of injustice shroud itself from observation!—Step boldly forth, thou who dost bear the sword concealed beneath thy mantle; here is my head, the freest ever severed by tyranny from the trunk.

SILVA. You err! The righteous judges who have condemned you will not conceal their sentence from the light of day.

EGMONT. Then does their audacity exceed all imagination and belief.

SILVA (*takes the sentence from an attendant, unfolds it, and reads*). "In the king's name, and invested by his majesty with authority to judge all his subjects of whatever rank, not excepting the knights of the Golden Fleece, we declare——"

Egmont.   Can the king transfer that authority?

Silva.   "We declare, after a strict and legal investigation, thee, Henry, Count Egmont, Prince of Gaure, guilty of high treason, and pronounce thy sentence: — That at early dawn thou be led from this prison to the market-place, and that there, in sight of the people, and as a warning to all traitors, thou with the sword be brought from life to death.   Given at Brussels."   (*Date and year so indistinctly read as to be imperfectly heard by the audience.*) "Ferdinand, Duke of Alva, President of the Tribunal of Twelve."   Thou knowest now thy doom.   Brief time remains for the impending stroke, to arrange thy affairs, and to take leave of thy friends.   [*Exit* Silva *with followers.* Ferdinand *remains with two torch-bearers.   The stage is dimly lighted.*

Egmont (*stands for a time as if buried in thought, and allows* Silva *to retire without looking round.   He imagines himself alone, and, on raising his eyes, beholds* Alva's *son*).   Thou tarriest here?   Wouldst thou by thy presence augment my amazement, my horror?   Wouldst thou carry to thy father the welcome tidings that in unmanly fashion I despair.   Go.   Tell him that he deceives neither the world nor me.   At first it will be whispered cautiously behind his back, then spoken more and more loudly, and when at some future day the ambitious man descends from his proud eminence, a thousand voices will proclaim — that 'twas not the welfare of the state, not the honor of the king, not the tranquillity of the provinces, that brought him hither.   For his own selfish ends he, the warrior, has counselled war, that in war the value of his services might be enhanced.   He has excited this monstrous insurrection that his presence might be deemed necessary in order to quell it.   And I fall a victim to his mean hatred, his contemptible envy.   Yes, I know it, dying and mortally wounded I may utter it; long has the proud man envied me, long has he meditated and planned my ruin.

Even then, when still young, we played at dice together, and the heaps of gold, one after the other, passed rapidly from his side to mine; he would look on with affected composure, while inwardly consumed with rage, more at my success than at his own loss.   Well do I remember the fiery glance, the treacherous pallor that overspread his features, when, at a public festival, we shot for a wager before assembled thousands.   He challenged me, and both nations stood by; Spaniards and Netherlanders wagered on either side; I was the victor; his ball missed, mine hit the mark, and the air was rent by acclamations from my friends. His shot now hits me. Tell him that I know this, that I know him, that the world despises every trophy that a paltry spirit erects for itself by base and surreptitious arts. And thou! If it be possible for a son to swerve from the manners of his father, practise shame betimes, while thou art compelled to feel shame for him whom thou wouldst fain revere with thy whole heart.

FERDINAND. I listen without interrupting thee! Thy reproaches fall like blows upon a helmet. I feel the shock, but I am armed. They strike, they wound me not; I am sensible only to the anguish that lacerates my heart. Alas! Alas! Have I lived to witness such a scene? Am I sent hither to behold a spectacle like this?

EGMONT. Dost thou break out into lamentations? What moves, what agitates thee thus? Is it a late remorse at having lent thyself to this infamous conspiracy? Thou art so young, thy exterior is so prepossessing. Thy demeanor towards me was so friendly, so unreserved! So long as I beheld thee, I was reconciled with thy father; and crafty, ay, more crafty than he, thou hast lured me into the toils. Thou art the wretch! The monster! Whoso confides in him does so at his own peril; but who could apprehend danger in trusting thee? Go! Go! rob me not of the few moments that are left to me! Go, that I may collect my thoughts, forget the world, and first of all thee!

FERDINAND. What can I say? I stand and gaze on thee, yet see thee not; I am scarcely conscious of my own existence. Shall I seek to excuse myself? Shall I assure thee that it was not till the last moment that I was made aware of my father's intentions? That I acted as a constrained, a passive instrument of his will? What signifies now the opinion thou mayest entertain of me? Thou art lost; and I, miserable wretch, stand here only to assure thee of it, only to lament thy doom.

EGMONT. What strange voice, what unexpected consolation comes thus to cheer my passage to the grave? Thou, the son of my first, of almost my only enemy, thou dost pity me, thou art not associated with my murderers? Speak! In what light must I regard thee?

FERDINAND. Cruel father! Yes, I recognize thy nature in this command. Thou didst know my heart, my disposi-

tion, which thou hast so often censured as the inheritance
of a tender-hearted mother. To mould me into thine own
likeness thou hast sent me hither. Thou dost compel me
to behold this man on the verge of the yawning grave, in
the grasp of an arbitrary doom, that I may experience the
profoundest anguish; that thus, rendered callous to every
fate, I may henceforth meet every event with a heart unmoved.

EGMONT. I am amazed! Be calm! Act, speak like a
man.

FERDINAND. Oh, that I were a woman! That they
might say — what moves, what agitates thee? Tell me of a
greater, a more monstrous crime, make me the spectator of
a more direful deed; I will thank thee, I will say: this was
nothing.

EGMONT. Thou dost forget thyself. Consider where
thou art!

FERDINAND. Let this passion rage, let me give vent to
my anguish! I will not seem composed when my whole
inner being is convulsed. Thee must I behold here?
Thee? It is horrible! Thou understandest me not! How
shouldst thou understand me? Egmont! Egmont!

(Falling on his neck.)

EGMONT. Explain this mystery.

FERDINAND. It is no mystery.

EGMONT. Why art thou moved so deeply by the fate of
a stranger?

FERDINAND. Not a stranger! Thou art no stranger to
me. Thy name it was that, even from my boyhood, shone
before me like a star in heaven! How often have I made
inquiries concerning thee, and listened to the story of thy
deeds. The youth is the hope of the boy, the man of the
youth. Thus didst thou walk before me, ever before me;
I saw thee without envy, and followed after, step by step;
at length I hoped to see thee — I saw thee, and my heart
flew to thy embrace. I had destined thee for myself, and
when I beheld thee, I made choice of thee anew. I hoped
now to know thee, to live with thee, to be thy friend, —
thy — 'tis over now and I see thee here!

EGMONT. My friend, if it can be any comfort to thee,
be assured that the very moment we met my heart was
drawn towards thee. Now listen! Let us exchange a few
quiet words. Tell me: is it the stern, the settled purpose
of thy father to take my life?

FERDINAND.   It is.

EGMONT.   This sentence is not a mere empty scare-crow,
designed to terrify me, to punish me through fear and
intimidation, to humiliate me, that he may then raise me
again by the royal favor?

FERDINAND.   Alas, no!   At first I flattered myself with
this delusive hope; and even then my heart was filled with
grief and anguish to behold thee thus.   Thy doom is real!
is certain!   No, I cannot command myself.   Who will
counsel, who will aid me, to meet the inevitable?

EGMONT.   Hearken then to me!   If thy heart is impelled
so powerfully in my favor, if thou dost abhor the tyranny
that holds me fettered, then deliver me!   The moments are
precious.   Thou art the son of the all-powerful, and thou hast
power thyself.   Let us fly!   I know the roads; the means
of effecting our escape cannot be unknown to thee.   These
walls, a few short miles, alone separate me from my friends.
Loose these fetters, conduct me to them; be ours.   The
king, on some future day, will doubtless thank my deliverer.
Now he is taken by surprise, or perchance he is ignorant of
the whole proceeding.   Thy father ventures on this daring
step, and majesty, though horror-struck at the deed, must
needs sanction the irrevocable.   Thou dost deliberate?
Oh, contrive for me the way to freedom!   Speak; nourish
hope in a living soul.

FERDINAND.   Cease!   Oh, cease!   Every word deepens
my despair.   There is here no outlet, no counsel, no escape. — 'Tis this thought that tortures me, that seizes my
heart, and rends it as with talons.   I have myself spread
the net.   I know its firm, inextricable knots;   I know that
every avenue is barred alike to courage and to stratagem.
I feel that I, too, like thyself, like all the rest, am fettered.
Think'st thou that I should give way to lamentation if any
means of safety remained untried?   I have thrown myself
at his feet, remonstrated, implored.   He has sent me hither,
in order to blast in this fatal moment every remnant of joy
and happiness that yet survived within my heart.

EGMONT.   And is there no deliverance?

FERDINAND.   None!

EGMONT (*stamping his foot*).   No deliverance! — Sweet
life!   Sweet pleasant habitude of existence and of activity!
from thee must I part!   Not in the tumult of battle, amid
the din of arms, the excitement of the fray, dost thou send
me a hasty farewell; thine is no hurried leave; thou dost

not abridge the moment of separation. Once more let me clasp thy hand, gaze once more into thine eyes, feel with keen emotion, thy beauty and thy worth, then resolutely tear myself away, and say;—depart!

FERDINAND. Must I stand by and look passively on; unable to save thee or to give thee aid! What voice avails for lamentation! What heart but must break under the pressure of such anguish?

EGMONT. Be calm!

FERDINAND. Thou canst be calm, thou canst renounce, led on by necessity, thou canst advance to the direful struggle with the courage of a hero. What can I do? What ought I to do? Thou dost conquer thyself and us; thou art the victor; I survive both myself and thee. I have lost my light at the banquet, my banner on the field. The future lies before me dark, desolate, perplexed.

EGMONT. Young friend, whom by a strange fatality, at the same moment I both win and lose, who dost feel for me, who dost suffer for me the agonies of death, — look on me;—thou wilt not lose me. If my life was a mirror in which thou didst love to contemplate thyself so be also my death. Men are not together only when in each other's presence;—the distant, the departed, also live for us. I shall live for thee, and for myself I have lived long enough. I have enjoyed each day; each day I have performed, with prompt activity, the duties enjoined by my conscience Now my life ends, as it might have ended, long, long ago, on the sands of Gravelines. I shall cease to live; but I have lived. My friend, follow in my steps, lead a cheerful and a joyous life, and dread not the approach of death.

FERDINAND. Thou shouldst have saved thyself for us, thou couldst have saved thyself. Thou art the cause of thine own destruction. Often have I listened when able men discoursed concerning thee; foes and friends, they would dispute long as to thy worth; but on one point they were agreed, none ventured to deny, every one confessed, that thou wert treading a dangerous path. How often have I longed to warn thee! Hadst thou then no friends?

EGMONT. I was warned.

FERDINAND. And when I found all these allegations, point for point, in the indictment, together with thy answers, containing much that might serve to palliate thy conduct, but no evidence weighty enough fully to exculpate thee——

EGMONT. No more of this. Man imagines that he directs his life, that he governs his actions, when in fact his existence is irresistibly controlled by his destiny. Let us not dwell upon this subject; these reflections I can dismiss with ease — not so my apprehensions for these provinces; yet they too will be cared for. Could my blood flow for many, bring peace to my people, how freely should it flow! Alas! This may not be. Yet it ill becomes a man idly to speculate when the power to act is no longer his. If thou canst restrain or guide the fatal power of thy father, do so. Alas, who can? — Farewell!

FERDINAND. I cannot leave thee.

EGMONT. Let me urgently recommend my followers to thy care! I have worthy men in my service; let them not be dispersed, let them not become destitute! How fares it with Richard, my secretary?

FERDINAND. He is gone before thee. They have beheaded him as thy accomplice in high treason.

EGMONT. Poor soul! — Yet one word, and then farewell, I can no more. However powerfully the spirit may be stirred, nature at length irresistibly asserts her rights; and like a child, who, enveloped in a serpent's folds, enjoys refreshing slumber, so the weary one lays himself down to rest before the gates of death, and sleeps soundly, as though a toilsome journey yet lay before him. — One word more, — I know a maiden; thou wilt not despise her because she was mine. Since I can recommend her to thy care, I shall die in peace. Thy soul is noble! in such a man a woman is sure to find a protector. Lives my old Adolphus? Is he free?

FERDINAND. The active old man, who always attended thee on horseback?

EGMONT. The same.

FERDINAND. He lives, he is free.

EGMONT. He knows her dwelling; let him guide thy steps thither, and reward him to his dying day for having shown thee the way to this jewel. — Farewell!

FERDINAND. I cannot leave thee.

EGMONT (*urging him towards the door.*) Farewell!

FERDINAND. Oh, let me linger yet a moment!

EGMONT. No leave-taking, my friend.

(*He accompanies* FERDINAND *to the door, and then tears himself away;* FERDINAND, *overwhelmed with grief, hastily retires.*)

Egmont. Hostile man! Thou didst not think thou would render me this service through thy son. He has been the means of relieving my mind from the pressure of care and sorrow, from fear and every anxious feeling. Gently, yet urgently, nature claims her final tribute. 'Tis past!—'Tis resolved! And the reflections which, in the suspense of last night, kept me wakeful on my couch, now lull my senses to repose with invincible certainty. (*He seats himself upon the couch; music.*) Sweet sleep! Like the purest happiness, thou comest most willingly, uninvited, unsought. Thou dost loosen the knots of earnest thoughts, dost mingle all images of joy and of sorrow; unimpeded the circle of inner harmony flows on, and, wrapped in fond delusion, we sink away and cease to be.

(He sleeps; music accompanies his slumber. Behind his couch the wall appears to open and discovers a brilliant apparition. Freedom in a celestial garb, surrounded by a glory, reposes on a cloud. Her features are those of Clara, *and she inclines towards the sleeping hero. Her countenance betokens compassion, she seems to lament his fate. Quickly she recovers herself, and with an encouraging gesture exhibits the symbols of freedom, the bundle of arrows, with the staff and cap. She encourages him to be of good cheer, and while she signifies to him that his death will secure the freedom of the provinces, she hails him as a conqueror, and extends to him a laurel crown. As the wreath approaches his head,* Egmont *moves like one asleep, and reclines with his face towards her. She holds the wreath suspended over his head;—martial music is heard in the distance; at the first sound the vision disappears. The music grows louder and louder.* Egmont *awakes. The prison is dimly illuminated by the dawn. — His first impulse is to lift his hand to his head; he stands up, and gazes round, his hand still upraised.)*

The crown is vanished! Beautiful vision, the light of day has frighted thee! Yes, they revealed themselves to my sight uniting in one radiant form the two sweetest joys of my heart. Divine Liberty borrowed the mien of my beloved one; the lovely maiden arrayed herself in the celestial garb of my friend. In a solemn moment they appeared united, with aspect more earnest than tender. With blood-stained feet the vision approached; the waving folds of her robe also were tinged with blood. It was my blood, and the blood of many brave hearts. No! It shall not be shed in vain! Forward! Brave people! The goddess of liberty leads you on! And as the sea breaks through and destroys the barriers that would oppose its fury, so do ye overwhelm the bulwark of tyranny, and with her impetuous flood sweep it away from the land which it usurps. (*Drums.*)

Hark! Hark! How often has this sound summoned my joyous steps to the field of battle and of victory! How bravely did I tread, with my gallant comrades, the dangerous path of fame! And now from this dungeon I shall go forth to meet a glorious death; I die for freedom, for the cause of which I have lived and fought, and for which I now offer myself up a sorrowing sacrifice. (*The background is occupied by Spanish soldiers with halberts.*)

Yes, lead them on! Close your ranks; ye terrify me not. I am accustomed to stand amid the serried ranks of war, and environed by the threatening forms of death; to feel, with double zest, the energy of life. (*Drums.*)

The foe closes round on every side! Swords are flashing; courage, friends! Behind are your parents, your wives, your children! (*Pointing to the guard.*)

And these are impelled by the word of their leader, not by their own free will. Protect your homes! And to save those who are most dear to you, be ready to follow my example, and to fall with joy.

(*Drums. As he advances through the guards towards the door in the background the curtain falls. The music joins in, and the scene closes with a symphony of victory.*)

THE WAYWARD LOVER:

A PASTORAL DRAMA IN VERSE AND IN ONE ACT.

TRANSLATED BY EDGAR A. BOWRING, C.B.

This little drama was written in the years 1767 and 1768, whilst Goethe, at the age of eighteen, was still a student at Leipsic. It commemorates his attachment to Katarina Schönkopf, the circumstances of which are illustrated by the characters of Eridon and Amina.

DRAMATIS PERSONÆ.

Egle.	Eridon.
Amina.	Lamon.

THE WAYWARD LOVER.

Scene I.

AMINA *and* EGLE *are sitting on one side of the theatre making garlands.* LAMON *enters, bringing a basket of flowers.*

LAMON (*putting down the basket*).

I've brought more flowers.

EGLE.

Oh, thanks!

LAMON.

        How fair they are!   Just see!

This pink is thine.

EGLE.

The rose? ——

LAMON.

        Dear child, that's not for thee!
Amina shall to-day receive this floweret fair;
I think a rose looks best contrasted with black hair.

EGLE.

And this thou callest polite, obliging in a lover?

LAMON.

For one who loves, thou'rt slow my nature to discover.
I'm perfectly aware thou lovest only me,
And my true heart in turn will ever beat for thee;
Thou knowest it. Yet thou seekest still stronger chains
       than these?
Is it so wrong to think that other maids can please?
I let thee say; that youth is handsome, this one charming,
Or full of wit, and I see nothing there alarming,
But say so too.

681

EGLE.

Ne'er lose thy temper, nor will I.
Both make the same mistake. To words of flattery
Oft listen I well pleased ; soft words dost thou address,
When I'm not there to hear, to many a shepherdess.
The heart should never deem a little jesting hard ;
'Gainst fickleness a mind that's cheerful is a guard.
I'm subject less than thou to jealousy's dominion.

(*To* AMINA.)

Thou smilest at us ?   Say, dear friend, what's thy opinion ?

AMINA.

I've none.

EGLE.

And yet thou knowest I'm happy whilst thou'rt sad.

AMINA.

How so ?

EGLE.

How so ! Instead of being, like us, glad,
And making all Love's sulks before your laughter fly,
Thy pain begins whene'er thy lover meets thine eye.
I never knew a more unpleasant, selfish creature.
Thou think'st he loves thee. No, I better know his nature ;
He sees that thou obeyest. The tyrant loves thee solely
Because thou art a maid who will obey him wholly.

AMINA.

He oft obeys me, too.

·EGLE.

To be still more thy master.
Thou watchest all his looks, for fear of some disaster ;
The power that in our looks Dame Nature has installed,
Whereby mankind are cowed, and charmingly enthralled,
Hast thou to him transferred, and thou art happy now
If he looks only pleased. With deeply wrinkled brow,
Contracted eyebrows, eyes all wild and dark as night,
And tightly fastened lips, a very charming sight
Appears he every day, till kisses, tears, harangues,
Disperse each wintry cloud that o'er his forehead hangs.

AMINA.

Thou knowest him not enough, thou never wert his lover ;
It is not selfishness that clouds his forehead over.

A whimsical chagrin upon his bosom preys,
And spoils for both of us the finest summer days:
And yet I'm well content that when my voice he hears,
And all my coaxing words, each whim soon disappears.

EGLE.

A mighty bliss, indeed, which one full well might spare!
But name one single joy that he allowed thee e'er.
How throbbed thy breast, whene'er a dance appeared in
     view!
Thy lover flies the dance, and takes thee with him, too.
No wonder he can't bear thy presence at a feast;
He hates the very glass touched by thee in the least.
As rivals deems he e'en the birds that chance to please thee;
How could he happy be, to see another seize thee,
And press thee to his heart, and whisper words of love,
As in the whirling dance before his eyes ye move?

AMINA.

Pray be not so unfair, without the least objection
He let me join this feast, with thee as my protection.

EGLE.

Thou'lt learn the truth soon.

AMINA.

How?

EGLE.

Now, wherefore comes he not?

AMINA.

He little loves the dance.

EGLE.

Tis nothing but a plot.
If thou returnest well pleased, he'll ask thee in a trice:—
"You had a happy day?"—"Yes."—"That is very nice.
"You played?"—"At forfeits."—"Ah! was Damon also
     there?
"You danced?"—"Yes, round the tree."—"I fain had
     seen the pair.
"He danced right well? And what reward received the
     youth?"

AMINA (smiling.

Yes.

EGLE.

Smilest thou?

AMINA.

Yes, my friend, that is his tone, in truth. —
More flowers!

LAMON.

The best are these.

AMINA.

It is with joy I see
How he the world doth grudge the slightest look from me;
I in this envy see how deep my lover's love,
And this proud consciousness doth all my pangs remove.

EGLE.

I pity thee, poor child.   No hope for thee remains,
Since thou thy misery lovest; thou dost but shake thy chains;
And makest thyself believe 'tis music.

AMINA.

For this bow
One ribbon still I need.

EGLE (*to* LAMON).
A little time ago
Thou stolest one from me, at that last feast in May.

LAMON.

I'll fetch it.

EGLE.

Make good haste; return without delay.

Scene II.

Egle, Amina.

AMINA.

He sets but little store on what his love presented.

EGLE.

With his demeanor I myself am not contented.
For playful signs of love too little careth he,
Which please a feeling heart, however small they be.
And yet believe me, friend, the torment is far less
To be too little loved, than worshipped to excess.

Fidelity I prize; 'tis that alone can give
With certainty true calm, to last us whilst we live.

AMINA.

Ah, friend! indeed a heart thus tender is a prize.
'Tis true he grieves me oft, yet pities he my sighs.
If from his lips a sound of blame or wrath is heard,
I've nothing more to do than speak a kindly word,
And straightway he is changed, his anger disappears,
He even weeps with me, when he observes my tears,
Falls humbly at my feet, and begs me to forgive.

EGLE.

And thou forgivest him?

AMINA.
Yes.

EGLE.
What a way to live!
The lover who offends to go on pardoning ever!
Take pains to win his love, and be rewarded never!

AMINA.

What cannot e'er be changed ——

EGLE.
Not changed? 'Twould easy be
To alter him.

AMINA.
How so?

EGLE.
I'll teach the way to thee.
The source of all thy griefs, the discontent oppressive
Of Eridon ——

AMINA.
Is what?

EGLE.
Thy tenderness excessive.

AMINA.

I thought my plan would love reciprocal engender.

EGLE.

Thou'rt wrong; be harsh and cold, and thou wilt find him
tender.

Just try this course for once, make him some pain endure:
A man prefers to strive, he cares not to be sure.
If Eridon should come to spend with thee an hour,
He knows it but too well, thou'rt wholly in his power.
No rival is at hand, with whom to disagree,
He knows thou lovest him far more than he loves thee.
His bliss is far too great, he well deserves our laughter;
As he no pangs e'er feels, he needs must pangs run after.
He sees that in the world thou lovest him alone,
He doubts, because by thee no doubts are ever shown.
So treat him that he'll think thou carest little for him;
He'll storm, indeed, but that will very soon pass o'er him.
One look from thee will then please more than now a kiss;
Make him afraid, and he will then soon know true bliss.

AMINA.

Yes, that is very well; but then I'm quite unable
To carry out thy plan.

EGLE.

Thy courage is unstable.
Go, thou art far too weak.   Look there!

AMINA.

My Eridon!

EGLE.

I thought so.   Ah, my poor child! he comes, and thou anon
Dost shake with joy: that ne'er will do.   To make him change,
Thou must, when he appears, a calmer mien arrange;
That heaving of thy breast! Thy face, too, all aglow!
And then——

AMINA.

O let me be, Amina loves not so.

SCENE III.

ERIDON *advances slowly, with his arms crossed.* AMINA
arises and runs to meet him. EGLE *continues sitting over
her work.*

AMINA (*taking him by the hand*).

My own dear Eridon!

ERIDON (*kissing her hand*).
My darling!

EGLE (*aside*).
Ah, how pleasant?

AMINA.
What flowers! Explain my friend, who gave thee such a
present?

ERIDON.
Who? My own loved one.

AMINA.
What! my gift of yesterday,
As fresh as they were then?

ERIDON.
Whate'er thou givest, say,
Is it not dear to me? But those I gave thee?

AMINA.
Oh,
I in this festal wreath have placed them.

ERIDON.
Be it so!
Love in each young man's heart, and envy in each maid
Wilt thou excite.

EGLE.
Rejoice to find thy love repaid
By such a maiden's love, for which so many vie.

ERIDON.
I cannot happy be to hear so many sigh.

EGLE.
Thou shouldst be; few men's lot with thine could e'er compare.

ERIDON (*to* AMINA).
Now speak about the fête; will Damon, too, be there?

EGLE (*interrupting*).
That he would present be, I heard him.say by chance.

ERIDON (*to* AMINA).

My child, and who will be thy partner in the dance?
(*As* AMINA *does not answer he turns to* EGLE.)
Take care to choose for her the one she holds most dear.

AMINA.

That cannot be, my friend, since thou wilt not be near!

EGLE.

Now, hear me, Eridon, I cannot bear it more,
Strange pleasure is it thus to plague Amina sore.
Forsake her if thou thinkest that she's no longer true,
But if thou thinkest she loves, this course no more pursue.

ERIDON.

I never plague her.

EGLE.

     No? How strange are all thy measures!
From jealousy to cast a gloom upon her pleasures,
To doubt, although the fact is known to thee full clearly,
If she ——

ERIDON.

Wilt thou be bail that she doth love me dearly?

AMINA.

I love thee not?

ERIDON.

     What proof hast thou at thy command?
Who let bold Damon steal a nosegay from her hand?
Who took that ribbon fair which youthful Thirsis brought?

AMINA.

My Eridon! ——

ERIDON.

     All this was not a dream, methought.
And what was their reward? Thou kisses canst bestow!

AMINA.

Canst thou not, dearest, too?

EGLE.

     Oh, peace, he'll nothing know!
Whate'er there was to say thou said'st it o'er and o'er,
He listens for a time, and then complains once more.

And what's the use? If thou his charges shouldst disclaim
He'll go away in peace, and next time do the same.

ERIDON.

With justice, too, perchance.

AMINA.

What! I unfaithful? oh,
Amina false, my friend? Dost thou believe it?

ERIDON.

No!
I cannot, will not.

AMINA.

Say, in all my life did I
E'er give occasion?

ERIDON.

Thou dost oft a cause supply.

AMINA.

When was I faithless?

ERIDON.

Ne'er! Hence all these cares of mine:
Through levity thou err'st, and never by design.
As trifles thou dost hold the things I weighty deem;
The things that vex me most to thee as nothing seem.

EGLE.

Well! If she deems them naught where is the mischief,
        pray?

ERIDON.

She often asked the same; it vexes me, I say.

EGLE.

What then? Amina ne'er forgets her own position.

ERIDON.

Too much to deem her true, too little for suspicion.

EGLE.

More than a woman's heart e'er loved she loveth thee.

ERIDON.

And dances, pleasures, games, she loves as much as me.

EGLE.

Who cannot this endure should only love our mothers!

AMINA.

Peace, Egle!   Eridon, my joy thy language smothers.
Our friends will tell thee how I think of thee all day,
E'en when we're far from thee, and full of mirth and play;
How oft I with chagrin, that spoils my pleasure, cry,
"I wonder where he is!" because thou art not nigh.
If thou believest me not, O come to-day with me,
And settle for thyself if I'm untrue to thee.
I'll dance with thee alone, I'll never leave thy side,
This arm shall cling to thine, this hand in thine abide.
If my behavior then the least mistrust should wake——

ERIDON.

To keep oneself in check, no proof of love can make.

EGLE.

Behold her falling tears! they're flowing in thy honor;
Ne'er thought I that thy heart so basely looked upon her.
The boundless discontent, incessant and diseased,
Which ever asks for more, the more it is appeased, —
The pride which will not let within thy sight appear
The guileless joys of youth her bosom holds so dear, —
Within thy hateful heart alternately they reign,
Thou heedest not her love, thou heedest not her pain.
She's dear to me, and thou no more shalt treat her ill;
To fly thee will be hard; to love thee, harder still.

AMINA (*aside*).

Ah, wherefore must my heart with love be flowing o'er!

ERIDON

(*standing still for a moment, and then timidly approachiug
Amina and taking her hand*).

Amina, dearest child!   Canst thou forgive once more?

AMINA.

Have I not granted oft forgiveness full, complete?

ERIDON.

Thou noble, best of hearts, let me before thy feet—

AMINA.

Arise, my Eridon!

EGLE.

Thy many thanks withhold;
What one too warmly feels, will soon again grow cold.

ERIDON.

And all this warmth of heart with which I honor her —

EGLE.

A greater bliss would be, if somewhat less it were.
More calmly would ye live, and all her pain and thine —

ERIDON.

Forgive me once again, more wisdom shall be mine.

AMINA.

Dear Eridon, now go, a nosegay pick for me;
If gathered by thy hand, how charming it will be!

ERIDON.

Thou hast a rose there now!

AMINA.

Her Lamon gave me this.
It suits me well.

ERIDON (*touchily*).

Indeed —

AMINA.

O take it not amiss,
And thou shalt have it, dear.

ERIDON (*embracing her, and kissing her hand*).

I'll bring thee flowers with speed.
[*Exit.*

SCENE IV.

AMINA, EGLE. *Presently* LAMON.

EGLE.

O poor, good-hearted child, this plan will ne'er succeed!
The more that it is fed, more hungry grows his pride.
Take heed, 'twill rob thee else of all thou lovest beside.

AMINA.

One care alone I have, lest he should not be true.

EGLE.

How charming! One can see thy love is very new.
'Tis always so at first; when once one's heart is given,
One thinks of nothing else but love from morn till even.
If we, then, at this time a touching novel read,
How greatly this one loved, and that one, true indeed,
That hero soft of heart, so bold when dangers hover,
So mighty in the fight, because he was a lover, —
Our head 'gins whirling round, we deem it our own story.
We fain would wretched be, or covered o'er with glory.
A youthful heart soon takes impressions from a novel;
A loving heart still less inclines on earth to grovel;
And so we long time love, until we find that we,
Instead of being true, were fools to a degree.

AMINA.

Yet that is not my case.

EGLE.

A patient oft will tell

The doctor in a rage that he is sound and well.
Do we believe him? No. Despite his opposition,
His medicine he must take. And that is thy condition.

AMINA.

'Tis true of children, yes; but 'tis not true of me;
Am I a child?

EGLE.

Thou lovest!

AMINA.

Thou, too!

EGLE.

Yes, love as we!

First moderate the storm which hurries thee along!
One can be very calm, although one's love is strong,

LAMON.

Here is the ribbon!

AMINA.

Thanks!

EGLE.

Thou art a laggard wooer!

LAMON.

I was upon the hill when Chloris called me to her,
And made me deck her hat with flowers ere she dismissed
    me.

EGLE.

And what was thy reward?

LAMON.

        Mine? None; she only kissed me.
Whatever one may do, no maiden can afford
To give a greater prize than kisses in reward.

AMINA (*showing* EGLE *the wreath with the loop*).
Is all now right?

EGLE.

Yes, ·come!

(*She hangs the wreath on* AMINA, *so that the loop comes on
  the right shoulder. In the meantime she talks to* LAMON.)
                To-day right merry be!

LAMON.

Right noisy be to-day. We feel not half the glee
When we demurely meet, discussing in full quorum
Our loved one's whims, or else the duties of decorum.

EGLE.

Thou'rt very right.

LAMON.

O, yes!

EGLE.

        Amina! Sit thou here!
(AMINA *sits down.* EGLE *puts flowers in her hair, while she
         continues.*)
Come, give me back the kiss that Chloris gave thee, dear!

LAMON (*kissing her*).
Most gladly. Here it is.

AMINA.

        How very strange ye are!

EGLE.

Were Eridon the same, thou wouldst be happier far.

AMINA.

He ne'er, instead of me, would kiss another maid.

LAMON.

Where is the rose?

EGLE.

When he attempted to upbraid,
She gave it him for peace.

AMINA.

I wish to be polite.

LAMON.

If thou dost pardon him, he'll pardon thee.   Quite right!
Yes, each the other plagues in turn, I clearly see.

EGLE.

(*As a sign that she is ready with the decoration for the head*).   There!

LAMON.

Good!

AMINA.

I wish the flowers were ready now for me
That Eridon should bring.

EGLE.

Do thou await him here.
I'll go and deck myself.   Come also, Lamon, dear!
We'll leave thee here alone, but soon be back again.

Scene V.

AMINA.   (*Presently* ERIDON.)

What enviable bliss!   O, what a tender swain!
How wish I that it but depended upon me
My Eridon content, myself made blest, to see!
Did I not to his hands such influence o'er me give,
Far happier he would be, and I in peace should live.
If to o'ercome this power I seeming coldness try,
At my indifference he'll into fury fly.
I know his wrath, and dread to feel it; thou, my heart,
Wouldst very badly play so difficult a part.

Yet, if thou wouldst succeed as fully as thy friend,
And 'stead of serving him, his will to thine wouldst bend,
To-day's the very time;   I never must allow
The chance to pass . . . He comes!   My heart, take cour-
    age now!

ERIDON (*giving her flowers*).
They're not so very good, my child! pray, pardon me,
I gathered them in haste.

AMINA.
Enough, they are from thee.

ERIDON.
They're not so blooming quite, as those fair roses were
That Damon stole from thee.

AMINA (*placing them in her bosom*).
    I'll keep them safely there.
There where thou art enshrined, these flowers should also
    blow.

ERIDON.
If there alone they're safe ——

AMINA.
Hast thou suspicions? ——

ERIDON.
    No!
I've none, my child; 'tis fear alone I feel to-day.
The best of hearts forgets, 'midst merry sport and play,
When happy in the dance, and at the noisy fête,
What duty may enjoin, and wisdom may dictate.
Thou may'st perhaps think of me, when in this joyous vein,
Yet thou dost not attempt the freedom to restrain
Which youths allow themselves to practise, bit by bit,
If maidens but in jest a liberty permit.
Their idle pride presumes to treat as love ere long
A pleasant playful mien.

AMINA.
    Enough, if they are wrong.
'Tis true that loving sighs pursue me by the score;
Yet thou dost hold my heart, and say, what wouldst thou
    more?

Poor fellows! upon me thou mightest let them look;
They think that wonder ——

ERIDON.

       No, such thoughts I will not brook.
'Tis that that vexes me. Well know I thou art mine;
Yet one of them perchance the same thing may opine,
And gaze upon thine eyes, and think to give a kiss,
And triumph in the thought that he has spoiled my bliss.

AMINA.

Destroy his triumph, then! Beloved one, with me go;
Let them the preference see which thou ——

ERIDON.

          I thank thee, no!
That sacrifice to claim would show a cruel will;
Thou, child, wouldst be ashamed of one who danced so ill;
I know whom in the dance as partner thou approvest;
The one who dances best, and not the one thou lovest.

AMINA.

That is the truth.

ERIDON (with restrained irony).

      Ah, yes, I often have regretted
The gifts of Damaris, so light of foot, and petted!
How well he dances!

AMINA.

Yes, none like him in the dance.

ERIDON.

And each maid ——

AMINA.

Prizes him ——

ERIDON.

Adores him for't!

AMINA.

Perchance.

ERIDON.

Perchance? The devil! Yes!

AMINA.

What mean those strange grimaces?

ERIDON.

Thou askest? Thou'lt drive me mad. Thy conduct a dis-
    grace is!

AMINA.

Mine? Art not thou the cause of my and thy great woe?
Oh, cruel Eridon! How canst thou treat me so?

ERIDON.

I must; I love thee well. 'Tis love that makes me vex
    thee.
Loved I not thee so much I never should perplex thee.
My feeling, tender heart with ecstasy beats high,
When thy hand presses mine, when on me smiles thine eye.
I thank the gods who give such bliss without alloy,
Yet only I demand that none shall share my joy.

AMINA.

Of what dost thou complain! No others share it now.

ERIDON.

Yet thou endurest them? No hatred feelest thou?

AMINA.

I hate them? Why should I?

ERIDON.

                    Because they dare to love thee.

AMINA.

A pretty ground!

ERIDON.

                    I see thou lettest their sighing move thee;
Their feelings thou must spare; and lessened is thy pleasure;
Unless thou ——

AMINA.

                    Eridon's injustice knows no measure!
Does love require that we humanity should shun?
A heart that truly loves, can hate no other one.
This tender feeling ne'er with such base thoughts can dwell,
Never at least with me.

ERIDON.

                    Thou vindicatest well
The gentle sex's proud and high prerogative,
If twenty blockheads kneel, the twenty to deceive!

To-day's a day when pride may specially enfold thee.
To-day thou'lt many see, who as a goddess hold thee;
Full many a youthful heart will throb for thee right hard,
Remember me, when swarms of fools around thee run;
I am the greatest! Go!

AMINA (*aside*).

Fly, weak heart, he has won.
Ye gods, lives he for naught but to destroy my peace?
Must my distress still last, and never, never cease?

(*To* ERIDON.)

The gentle bonds of love thou turnest to a yoke:
A tyrant thou to me, yet I my love invoke!
With tenderness to all thy wrath have I replied,
I ever yield to thee, yet thou'rt not satisfied.
No sacrifice I've spared. Contented ne'er art thou.
My pleasure of to-day thou claimest? Thou hast it now!
(*She takes the wreaths out of her hair and from her shoulder,
throws them away and continues in a restrained calm voice.*)
Now say, dear Eridon? Thou lovest me better so,
Than for the feast arrayed? Thine anger now forego.
Thou wilt not look at me? Remains thy heart still hard-
ened?

ERIDON (*falling down before her*).

Amina, thee I love! Be my vile conduct pardoned !
Go to the feast.

AMINA.

My friend, with thee I'd sooner stay;
A loving song will serve to while the time away.

ERIDON.

Dear child, now go !

AMINA.

Go thou, and quickly fetch thy flute.

ERIDON.

Thou will'st it ?

SCENE VI.

AMINA.

He seems sad, yet feels rejoicings mute.
In vain wilt thou on him thy tenderness bestow.
He feels my sacrifice?   He little heeds it; no,
He deems it but his due.   What wouldst thou, my poor
    heart?
Thou murmurest in my breast.   Deserved I all this smart?
Yes, thou deservest it well!   Thou seest he never ceases
To torture thee, and yet thy love for him increases.
I will not bear it more.   Hush!   Ha, I hear the din
Of music there.   My heart doth throb, my foot joins in.
I'll go!   My troubled breast my misery proclaims!
How wretched do I feel!   My heart with burning flames
Consumes.   Off, to the feast!   He will not let me move!
Unhappy maiden!   See this is the bliss of love!
(*She throws herself on a bank, and weeps; as the others
    enter, she dries her eyes and rises.*)
Alas, they now approach!   How can I face their jeers!

Scene VII.

Amina, Egle, Lamon.

EGLE.

Make haste!   The march begins!   Amina!   What!   In
    tears?

LAMON (*picking up the wreaths*).
The garlands?

EGLE.
What means this?   Who tore them off?   Confess!

AMINA.
Myself.

EGLE.
Wilt thou not go?

AMINA.
If he will let me, yes.

EGLE.

If who will let thee?   Say, why talk in this mysterious
And unaccustomed tone?   Be not so shy and serious!
Is't Eridon?

AMINA.

Yes, he!

EGLE.

I thought that it was so.
Thou fool! and will thy wrongs ne'er make thee wiser grow?
Thou hast a promise made that thou with him wilt stay,
And pass in tears and sighs such a delightful day?
He's flattered, child, when thou for all his whims thus
    carest.

    (*After a pause, whilst she makes signs to* LAMON.)
Yet thou far better lookest when thou the garland wearest.
Come, put it on! and hang the other o'er thee thus!
Thou'rt charming now.

    (AMINA *stands with downcast eyes, and lets* EGLE *have her
    way.* EGLE *gives a sign to* LAMON.)
                But, ah! 'tis fully time for us
To join the march.

LAMON.

Quite right!   My dearest child, adieu!

AMINA (*sorrowfully*).

Farewell!

EGLE (*departing*).

Amina! now, wilt thou join us, too?
    (AMINA *looks at her sadly, and is silent.*)

LAMON (*taking* EGLE *by the hand to lead her off*).

O leave her to herself!   With spite I'm fit to die;
The charming dance she'll spoil with her perversity!
The dance both right and left, she knows it all by heart;
I fully thought that she would take her proper part.
She'll stop at home now!   Come, I've nothing more to say.

EGLE.

Thou dost forego the dance!   I pity thee to-day.
He dances well!   Good-bye!
(EGLE *seeks to kiss* AMINA.   AMINA *falls on her neck, and
    weeps.*)

AMINA.

Complete is my dismay.

EGLE.

Thou weepest.

AMINA.

My saddened heart in grief despairing sinks!
I tain would . . . Eridon, I hate thee now, methinks!

EGLE.

He merits it. But no! A lover who e'er hated?
Love him thou shouldst, nor let thyself be subjugated.
I long have told thee this. Come!

LAMON.

Join the dance with me!

AMINA.

And Eridon?

EGLE.

Now go! I'll stay! He'll yield, thou'lt see,
And join thee. Say, would this afford thee any pleasure?

AMINA.

Immense!

LAMON.

Now come! Dost hear the shawm's soft, dulcet measure?
The charming melody?
(*He takes* AMINA *by the hand, and sings and dances.*)

EGLE (*sings*).

If ever a lover with jealousy vile
Annoys thee, complains of a nod or a smile,
Accuses of falsehood or other invention,
Then sing thou, and dance thou, and pay no attention.
(LAMON *carries* AMINA *off with him to the dance.*)

AMINA (*as she goes*).

Fail not in thy persuasion!

Scene VIII.

Egle, *and presently* Eridon, *with a flute and songs.*

EGLE

'Tis well! We soon shall see! I long have sought occasion
This shepherd to convert, and make his ways more courtly.
To-day's my wish fulfilled; I'll teach thee manners shortly!
I'll show thee who thou art; and at the least suggestion —
He comes! List, Eridon!

ERIDON.
Where is she?

EGLE.

> What a question!

With Lamon yonder, where thou hearest the cornets blow.

ERIDON (*throwing his flute on the ground and tearing the songs*).

Vile infidelity!

EGLE.
Art mad?

ERIDON.

> I should be so.*

The hypocrite first tears the garland from her brow
With smiling face, and says: I will not dance, dear, now!
Did I insist on that? And . . . O!
(*He stamps with his foot, and throws the torn songs away.*)

EGLE (*in a composed voice*).

> Let me inquire

What right hast thou to make her from the dance retire?
Thou wishest that a heart, which with thy love is filled,
Should know no other joys than those by thee instilled?
Dost think all impulses for pleasure are suppressed,
As soon as thoughts of love pervade a maiden's breast?
Enough, if she to thee her dearest hours will give,
On thee, when absent, think, with thee would ever live.
'Tis folly, then, my friend, in grief to make her dwell;
So let her love the dance, and games, and thee, as well.

---

* This line in the original contains the only false Alexandrine in the play. — E. A. B.

ERIDON (*dropping his arms and looking up*).
Ah!

EGLE.

Tell me, dost thou deem that any love is shown
By keeping her with thee?   'Tis slavery alone.
Thou comest: at the fête no other she may see;
Thou goest: and forthwith she needs must go with thee;
She lingers: straightway thou dost give her looks unkind;
She follows thee, but oft her heart is left behind.

ERIDON.

Perhaps always!

EGLE.

People hear, when bitter words are said,
There where no freedom is, all joys will soon be dead.
Thus are we made.   A child a few words may have sung;
You bid him sing away.   He starts and holds his tongue.
If thou her freedom leavest, her love thou'st forfeit ne'er;
If thou behavest too ill, she'll hate thee; so beware!

ERIDON.

She'll hate me?

EGLE.

Rightly too.   Then seize a day like this,
And for thyself procure love's tenderness and bliss!
None but a tender heart, by its own glow impelled,
Can constant be, by love incessantly upheld.
Confess now, canst thou tell if any bird is true,
When kept within a cage?

ERIDON.
No!

EGLE.

If, with freedom new
It flies o'er gardens, fields, and yet to thee returns?

ERIDON.

Quite right, I understand!

EGLE.

What rapture in thee burns,
To see the little thing, which loves thee tenderly,
Its freedom know, and yet the preference give to thee!

And if thy maiden e'er, excited by the dance,
From any fête comes back, and seeks thee, while each
    glance
Betrays that all her joys imperfect bliss supply,
While thou, her lover, thou, her own one, art not by;
If she will then declare one kiss of thine to be
More than a thousand fêtes: who would not envy thee?

IDON (moved).

O Egle!

EGLE.

    Tremble lest the gods should take amiss
That one so blest as thou so little knows his bliss!
Up! Be contented, friend! Or they'll the tears that flow
From that poor maid, avenge.

ERIDON.

        Could I accustomed grow,
To see how in the dance her hands so many press, —
While this one ogles her, she looks at that one! Yes,
When I on this reflect, my heart feels like to break!

EGLE.

What nonsense! What a fuss for trifles thou dost make!
There's nothing in a kiss!

ERIDON.

      A kiss is naught, say'st thou?

EGLE.

Methinks that in his heart there is some feeling now,
If thus he talks. But say, wilt thou forgive her, friend?
For when thou art displeased, her sorrow knows no end.

ERIDON.

Ah, friend!

EGLE (flatteringly).

    This will not do! Thou also art a lover.
Farewell! (She takes him by the hand).
    Thou'rt all aglow!

ERIDON.

    My blood is boiling over ——

EGLE.

With anger still? Enough! Thy pardon now has she.
I'll hasten to her straight. She'll trembling ask for thee;

I'll tell her: he is kind; composure this will give her,
Her heart will softer beat, she'll love thee more than ever.
(She looks at him sentimentally.)
She'll surely seek thee out when ended is the feast,
And by the search itself her love will be increased.
(EGLE affects still more tenderness, and leans upon his
      shoulder. He takes her hand and kisses it.)
She'll find thee presently! O what a moment this!
Press her against thy breast and feel thy perfect bliss!
A maid, when dancing, looks more fair, her cheeks are
      glowing.
Her mouth is wreathed with smiles, her loosened locks are
      flowing
Over her heaving breast, more tender charms enhance
The beauties of her form, when whirling in the dance;
Her throbbing pulses glow, and as her body sways,
Each nerve appears to thrill and greater life displays.
(She pretends to feel a tender rapture, and sinks upon his
      breast, whilst he places his arm around her waist.)
The bliss of seeing this what rapture can excel?
Thou'lt go not to the fête, and therefore canst not tell.

ERIDON.

Dear friend, upon thy breast I feel it all too well!
(He falls upon EGLE's neck and kisses her, while she offers
      no resistance. She then steps back a few paces, and
      asks in an indifferent tone.)
Lovest thou Amina?

ERIDON.
As myself!

EGLE.
Yet darest thou
To kiss me? Thou shalt pay the penalty, I vow!
Thou faithless man!

ERIDON.
But what dost thou suppose that I ——

EGLE.

Yes, I suppose it all. My friend, right tenderly
Thou kissedst me, 'tis true. Therewith I'm well content.
Was my kiss good? No doubt: thy hot lips prove assent.
And ask for more. Poor child! Amina, wert thou here!

ERIDON.

I would she were!

EGLE.

How vain!   She'd wretched be, poor dear!

ERIDON.

Ay she would scold me well.   Thou must betray me not.
I've kissed thee, but that kiss will not hurt her a jot;
And if Amina give me kisses most enchanting,
May I not feel that thine in rapture are not wanting?

EGLE.

Best ask herself.

SCENE IX.

AMINA, EGLE, ERIDON.

ERIDON.

Woe's me!

AMINA.

I long to see him so!
My own dear Eridon!   'Twas Egle made me go.
Alas, I broke my word; my friend, I'll go not now.

ERIDON (aside).

Wretch that I am!

AMINA.

Thou'rt wroth? thy face avertest thou?

ERIDON (aside).

What can I say?

AMINA.

Alas!   Is all this anger due
For such a little fault?   Thou'rt in the right, 'tis true,
And yet ——

EGLE.

O let him go!   He gave me such a kiss!
And likes it still.

AMINA.

Kissed thee?

EGLE.

Right tenderly!

AMINA.

Ah, this

Too much is for my heart!   Thy love is thus unsteady ?
Unhappy I !   My friend deserteth me already !
Who kisses other maids, his own will shortly fly.
Ah ! since I thee have loved, like this ne'er acted I ;
To try to reach my lips, no youth has been so daring ;
E'en when I forfeits played my kisses have been sparing.
My heart as much as thine is plagued by jealousy,
Yet I'll forgive thee all, if thou wilt turn to me.
And yet, poor heart, in vain art thou so well protected !
No love for me he feels, since he thy wiles suspected.
The mighty advocate for thee in vain doth plead.

ERIDON.

What loving tenderness !   How vast my shame, indeed !

AMINA.

My friend, oh, how couldst thou seduce away my lover ?

EGLE.

Be comforted, good child !   Thy woes will soon be over.
Well know I Eridon, and know that he is true.

AMINA.

And has—

EGLE.

Ay, thou art right, and he has kissed me, too.
I know how it occurred ; his fault thou mayest condone.
How deeply he repents !

ERIDON (falling down before AMINA).

Amina!   O my own! .
Oh, blame her ! she appeared so pretty when I kissed
Her mouth was very close, and I could not resist.
Yet, if thou knowest me well, thou pardon must impart ;
A little joy like that will not despoil my heart.

EGLE.

Amina, kiss him, since he answers so discreetly !
Despite those little joys, ye love each other sweetly.

To ERIDON.

My friend, thou on thyself must judgment pass this time;
Although she loves the dance, thou see'st that is no crime.

(*Mocking him.*)

If in the dance a youth her hand may chance to press, —
While this one ogles her, she looks at that one, — yes,
Of even this, thou knowest, thou oughtest not to complain.
I trust that thou wilt ne'er Amina plague again.
Methinks thou'lt with us go.

AMINA.

Come, join the fête.

ERIDON.

I will;

A kiss has been my cure.

EGLE (*to* AMINA).

Thou'lt take that kiss not ill.
Should jealousy again his bosom seek to kindle,
Remind him of that kiss, and 'twill to nothing dwindle. —
And, O ye jealous ones, if maidens plague you e'er,
Recall *your own* false tricks, and blame them, if ye dare.

www.ingramcontent.com/pod-product-compliance
Lightning Source LLC
Chambersburg PA
CBHW020511110726
47899CB00004B/1075